The Dover Anthology of American Literature Volume II

From 1865 to 1922

DOVER THRIFT EDITIONS

Edited by
Bob Blaisdell

Dover Publications
Garden City, New York

DOVER THRIFT EDITIONS

GENERAL EDITOR: MARY CAROLYN WALDREP
EDITOR OF THIS VOLUME: SUSAN L. RATTINER

Copyright

Bibliographical Note

The Dover Anthology of American Literature, Volume II: From 1865 to 1922, first published by Dover Publications in 2014, is a new anthology reprinted from standard sources. For the sake of authenticity, inconsistencies in spelling and punctuation have been retained in the texts unless otherwise indicated.

Library of Congress Cataloging-in-Publication Data

The Dover Anthology of American Literature, Volume II : From 1865 to 1922 / edited by Bob Blaisdell.
pages cm. — (Dover Thrift Editions)
Summary: "At the end of the Civil War, another long and arduous struggle began as the nation attempted to reunite. Literature offered a path toward solidarity, and this concise anthology surveys the writings of major American authors from the war's end to the dawn of the Jazz Age. Featured works include those of Emily Dickinson, Wallace Stevens, William Carlos Williams, Robert Frost, Langston Hughes, and other poets. Mark Twain is prominently represented among the storytellers, along with Ambrose Bierce, Stephen Crane, and F. Scott Fitzgerald. Three short novels appear in their entirety: *Daisy Miller* by Henry James, *The Call of the Wild* by Jack London, and *Ethan Frome* by Edith Wharton. Speeches by Sitting Bull and Theodore Roosevelt, memoirs by Booker T. Washington and Helen Keller, and many other selections recapture a vibrant era in American literature. Informative introductory notes and suggestions for further reading supplement the authoritative texts."— Provided by publisher.
Includes bibliographical references.
Volume I: ISBN-13: 978-0-486-78076-4 (paperback)—ISBN-10: 0-486-78076-7
Volume II: ISBN-13: 978-0-486-78077-1 (paperback)—ISBN-10: 0-486-78077-5
1. American literature. I. Blaisdell, Robert, editor of compilation.
PS507.D68 2014
810.8—dc23

2014010332

Manufactured in the United States of America
78077509 2023
www.doverpublications.com

Contents

PAGE

T. S. Eliot

Wallace Stevens

William Carlos Williams

NOTE

THIS SECOND VOLUME of the anthology begins with the end of the Civil War (1861–1865), a catastrophe that devastated and necessarily recast the nation. One of the ways in which the states became united again was through literature. With universal education the rule, America became super-literate; reading was the great technology. Readers hungered for printed words, so books, magazines, and newspapers proliferated. The unofficially crowned prince and princess of American literature, Mark Twain and Emily Dickinson, helped change what the nation and the world thought of as peculiarly *American* writing. That is, it was colloquial, quick, irreverent. There was nothing and no one like Dickinson or Twain anywhere else.

Notwithstanding Walt Whitman, Emily Dickinson is certainly the highlight of nineteenth-century American poetry; she sang of herself all the way to the other side of the spectrum from Whitman's "Song of Myself." It sometimes seems his colossal ego needed the weight of all mankind to balance himself. Whitman's formula for success was the opposite of Dickinson's quiet self-scrutinizing reserve, and so it's appropriate we start with her poetry and with her letters that tentatively reached out to a Civil War hero (Thomas W. Higginson, an outstanding writer himself, who helped bring Dickinson's work to light after her death in 1886). The first of a number of selections by Mark Twain begins with his comic recollections of how he started his writing career in a newspaper office in Nevada mining-country. The last selection of Twain's work is a speech; public speaking was a comic sideline he carried on all over the world.

One story of the development of American literature is that it discovered itself by going overseas to Europe; Twain himself was hugely popular in England and he trotted the globe lecturing, learning, and looking for material. Henry James, on the other hand, is America's novelist of its European expatriate communities. But America didn't discover as much about itself from those Americans writing home from Europe as it did from European immigrants. The tremendous influx of immigrants continually enlivened the language and complicated and deepened the nation's psychology. Immigrants then and now reminded America of what it was, is and ought to be. We also see in fiction and in selections from memoirs (e.g. Rose Cohen's) the rapid effects of America on individuals and cultures. Admittedly, all of the contributors but one, the great Sioux chief Sitting Bull, are immigrants or descendants of immigrants. Sitting Bull tells us in eloquent speeches how Native Americans saw their lands disappear as European Americans swept across the country and the U.S. government claimed natives' territory or broke treaties.

By the end of the nineteenth century, literature by African American authors found multiple audiences; their writing helped unite black Americans in literary and educational communities. Fiction by Charles W. Chesnutt and Paul Laurence Dunbar appeared in major magazines while nonfiction by social reformers, among them the controversial Booker T. Washington, challenged white Americans to reconsider thoughtless prejudices and legal inequalities.

Though Emily Dickinson was shy about publication of her work, many other women authors of her time weren't. We present several masterful short stories by, among others, Mary E. Wilkins Freeman, Charlotte Perkins Gilman, Kate Chopin and Willa Cather. Gertrude Stein, arguably the most influential experimental American writer of the twentieth century, contributes an amusing and characteristically intriguing "dialogue."

Memoirs and autobiographies were among the popular American genres, as they are today, and we have included excerpts from a few, most notably Helen Keller's and Ulysses S. Grant's. Blind and deaf, Keller tells of learning how to speak, read, and write; her story was and is amazing and inspiring. The former President and Civil War general Grant's remarkable plainspoken memoirs were only written under duress at the end of his life, but were immediately, immensely, deservedly popular.

Students and readers unfamiliar with American literature should remind themselves that much of the best of our writing *reads* colloquially, in the lively common language of speech. Ever since Benjamin Franklin's first-person skits and sketches in the early eighteenth century, American literature (continuing into the twenty-first century in the work, for example, of the extraordinary Junot Díaz) has thrived on the voice of natural conversation. So if the American dialects in the work by Twain, Chesnutt, or Chopin, among others, seem challenging, read it *aloud!* You will *hear* the sense lift up off the page.

We have included three short novels, among the most captivating in American literature after Herman Melville's, namely *Daisy Miller* by Henry James, *The Call of the Wild* by Jack London, and *Ethan Frome* by Edith Wharton.

We have ordered the selections chronologically, after a fashion. That is, the first publication by a particular writer determines his or her works' chronological appearance; we bunch the other selected works (if any) by that author in chronological order after the first one. This somewhat loose arrangement allows us to watch the procession of works and writers as they make their entrances on the literary scene. We witness Langston Hughes, one of the most important writers of the twentieth century, get his start in 1921, as a nineteen-year-old, with the acclaimed "The Negro Speaks of Rivers." The chronological arrangement also lets us be struck by the unprecedented and never again equaled florescence of American poetry in the 1910s: in that decade, Ezra Pound, William Carlos Williams, Robert Frost, Wallace Stevens, T. S. Eliot, H.D., and Carl Sandburg wrote so many great poems that we're reminded or freshly persuaded that there really are golden ages in the arts.

We conclude this volume with the dazzling F. Scott Fitzgerald, whose life and career seemed to have mimicked the arc of many of his fictional works. Famous, though slight, Fitzgerald's "The Curious Case of Benjamin Button" reverses time in somewhat the manner in which we look over our shoulders at American literature. We can start in the old days of Emily Dickinson and Mark Twain and then read our way back to the present. The editor acknowledges that there are works unrepresented here that, after all, *should* have been; he also acknowledges that there are no doubt choices of works we *have* included that will bewilder some readers. The best solution to this frustration? Keep reading beyond these covers.

For their help with this compilation, I wish to thank two friends, the poet John Wilson, for selecting the poems by William

Carlos Williams and Ezra Pound, and the critic Kia Penso, for her guidance in selecting Wallace Stevens's poems. Finally, let me thank Dover editor Susan L. Rattiner for her help in organizing, correcting and focusing this volume and senior editor John Grafton for proposing and spearheading *The Dover Anthology of American Literature*.

—BOB BLAISDELL
New York City
February 2014

EMILY DICKINSON

As radically original and private a poet as Walt Whitman was radically original and public, Emily Dickinson (1830–1886) grew up in Amherst, Massachusetts, and attended college at Mount Holyoke for a year. When she was thirty-one years old, she initiated a correspondence with the writer and activist Thomas Wentworth Higginson. We present seven of Dickinson's letters after an assemblage of twenty-two of her nearly 1,800 poems (only ten poems of hers were published in her lifetime). Our selection of poems spans probably two decades. The best source of dates of original composition (usually only approximate) is The Complete Poems of Emily Dickinson, *edited by Thomas H. Johnson, Little, Brown and Company, Boston, n.d. (c. 1960). The dates provided here are based on Johnson's research. Dickinson did not as a rule title her poems, though Higginson and Mabel Loomis Todd, in preparing them for publication, added topical or thematic titles to some. We have bracketed those titles or quoted the first line as a title guide.*

[Escape] (c. 1859)

I never hear the word "escape"
Without a quicker blood,
A sudden expectation,
A flying attitude.

I never hear of prisons broad
By soldiers battered down,
But I tug childish at my bars,—
Only to fail again!

SOURCE: *Poems by Emily Dickinson: Edited by Two of Her Friends, Mabel Loomis Todd and T. W. Higginson.* Second Series. Boston: Roberts Brothers, 1892.

[Compensation] (c. 1859)

For each ecstatic instant
We must an anguish pay
In keen and quivering ratio
To the ecstasy.

For each beloved hour
Sharp pittances of years,
Bitter contested farthings
And coffers heaped with tears.

SOURCE: *Poems by Emily Dickinson: Edited by Two of Her Friends, Mabel Loomis Todd and T. W. Higginson*. Second Series. Boston: Roberts Brothers, 1892.

"A wounded deer leaps highest" (c. 1860)

A wounded deer leaps highest,
I've heard the hunter tell;
'T is but the ecstasy of death,
And then the brake is still.

The smitten rock that gushes,
The trampled steel that springs:
A cheek is always redder
Just where the hectic stings!

Mirth is the mail of anguish,
In which it caution arm,
Lest anybody spy the blood
And "You're hurt" exclaim!

SOURCE: *Poems by Emily Dickinson: Edited by Two of Her Friends, Mabel Loomis Todd and T. W. Higginson*. Second Series. Boston: Roberts Brothers, 1892.

"Heaven is what I cannot reach!" (c. 1861)

Heaven is what I cannot reach!
The apple on the tree,
Provided it do hopeless hang,
That "heaven" is, to me.

The color on the cruising cloud,
The interdicted ground
Behind the hill, the house behind,—
There Paradise is found!

Source: *Poems by Emily Dickinson: Edited by Two of Her Friends, Mabel Loomis Todd and T. W. Higginson.* Third Series. Boston: Roberts Brothers, 1896.

[Hope] (c. 1861)

Hope is the thing with feathers
That perches in the soul,
And sings the tune without the words,
And never stops at all,

And sweetest in the gale is heard;
And sore must be the storm
That could abash the little bird
That kept so many warm.

I've heard it in the chillest land,
And on the strangest sea;
Yet, never, in extremity,
It asked a crumb of me.

Source: *Poems by Emily Dickinson: Edited by Two of Her Friends, Mabel Loomis Todd and T. W. Higginson.* Second Series. Boston: Roberts Brothers, 1892.

"There's a certain slant of light" (c. 1861)

There's a certain slant of light,
On winter afternoons,
That oppresses, like the weight
Of cathedral tunes.

Heavenly hurt it gives us;
We can find no scar,
But internal difference
Where the meanings are.

None may teach it anything,
'T is the seal, despair,—
An imperial affliction
Sent us of the air.

When it comes, the landscape listens,
Shadows hold their breath;
When it goes, 't is like the distance
On the look of death.

SOURCE: *Poems by Emily Dickinson: Edited by Two of Her Friends, Mabel Loomis Todd and T. W. Higginson*. Second Series. Boston: Roberts Brothers, 1892.

"I'm nobody! Who are you?" (c. 1861)

I'm nobody! Who are you?
Are you nobody, too?
Then there's a pair of us—don't tell!
They'd banish us, you know.

How dreary to be somebody!
How public, like a frog
To tell your name the livelong day
To an admiring bog!

SOURCE: *Poems by Emily Dickinson: Edited by Two of Her Friends, Mabel Loomis Todd and T. W. Higginson*. Second Series. Boston: Roberts Brothers, 1892.

"The nearest dream recedes, unrealized" (c. 1861)

The nearest dream recedes, unrealized.
  The heaven we chase
  Like the June bee
  Before the school-boy
  Invites the race;
  Stoops to an easy clover—
Dips—evades—teases—deploys;
  Then to the royal clouds
  Lifts his light pinnace
  Heedless of the boy
Staring, bewildered, at the mocking sky.

  Homesick for steadfast honey,
  Ah! the bee flies not
That brews that rare variety.

Source: *Poems by Emily Dickinson: Edited by Two of Her Friends, Mabel Loomis Todd and T. W. Higginson*. Second Series. Boston: Roberts Brothers, 1892.

[The Master] (c. 1862)

He fumbles at your spirit
  As players at the keys
Before they drop full music on;
  He stuns you by degrees,

Prepares your brittle substance
  For the ethereal blow,
By fainter hammers, further heard,
  Then nearer, then so slow

Your breath has time to straighten,
  Your brain to bubble cool,—
Deals one imperial thunderbolt
  That scalps your naked soul.

Source: *Poems by Emily Dickinson: Edited by Two of Her Friends, Mabel Loomis Todd and T. W. Higginson*. Third Series. Boston: Roberts Brothers, 1896.

[In the Garden] (c. 1862)

A bird came down the walk:
He did not know I saw;
He bit an angle-worm in halves
And ate the fellow, raw.

And then he drank a dew
From a convenient grass,
And then hopped sidewise to the wall
To let a beetle pass.

He glanced with rapid eyes
That hurried all abroad,—
They looked like frightened beads, I thought;
He stirred his velvet head

Like one in danger; cautious,
I offered him a crumb,
And he unrolled his feathers
And rowed him softer home

Than oars divide the ocean,
Too silver for a seam,
Or butterflies, off banks of noon,
Leap, plashless, as they swim.

SOURCE: *Poems by Emily Dickinson: Edited by Two of Her Friends, Mabel Loomis Todd and T. W. Higginson.* Second Series. Boston: Roberts Brothers, 1892.

[Retrospect] (c. 1862)

'T was just this time last year I died.
I know I heard the corn,
When I was carried by the farms,—
It had the tassels on.

I thought how yellow it would look
When Richard went to mill;
And then I wanted to get out,
But something held my will.

I thought just how red apples wedged
The stubble's joints between;
And carts went stooping round the fields
To take the pumpkins in.

I wondered which would miss me least,
And when Thanksgiving came,
If father 'd multiply the plates
To make an even sum.

And if my stocking hung too high,
Would it blur the Christmas glee,
That not a Santa Claus could reach
The altitude of me?

But this sort grieved myself, and so
I thought how it would be
When just this time, some perfect year,
Themselves should come to me.

SOURCE: *Poems by Emily Dickinson: Edited by Two of Her Friends, Mabel Loomis Todd and T. W. Higginson.* Third Series. Boston: Roberts Brothers, 1896.

"I died for beauty, but was scarce" (c. 1862)

I died for beauty, but was scarce
Adjusted in the tomb,
When one who died for truth was lain
In an adjoining room.

He questioned softly why I failed?
"For beauty," I replied.
"And I for truth,—the two are one;
We brethren are," he said.

And so, as kinsmen met a night,
We talked between the rooms,
Until the moss had reached our lips,
And covered up our names.

SOURCE: *Poems by Emily Dickinson: Edited by Two of Her Friends, Mabel Loomis Todd and T. W. Higginson.* Second Series. Boston: Roberts Brothers, 1892.

[Dying] (c. 1862)

I heard a fly buzz when I died;
The stillness round my form
Was like the stillness in the air
Between the heaves of storm.

The eyes beside had wrung them dry,
And breaths were gathering sure
For that last onset, when the king
Be witnessed in his power.

I willed my keepsakes, signed away
What portion of me I
Could make assignable,—and then
There interposed a fly,

With blue, uncertain, stumbling buzz,
Between the light and me;
And then the windows failed, and then
I could not see to see.

SOURCE: *Poems by Emily Dickinson: Edited by Two of Her Friends, Mabel Loomis Todd and T. W. Higginson.* Third Series. Boston: Roberts Brothers, 1896.

"It was not death, for I stood up" (c. 1862)

It was not death, for I stood up,
And all the dead lie down;
It was not night, for all the bells
Put out their tongues, for noon.

It was not frost, for on my flesh
I felt siroccos crawl,—
Nor fire, for just my marble feet
Could keep a chancel cool.

And yet it tasted like them all;
The figures I have seen
Set orderly, for burial,
Reminded me of mine,

As if my life were shaven
And fitted to a frame,
And could not breathe without a key;
And 't was like midnight, some,

When everything that ticked has stopped,
And space stares, all around,
Or grisly frosts, first autumn morns,
Repeal the beating ground.

But most like chaos,—stopless, cool,—
Without a chance or spar,
Or even a report of land
To justify despair.

Source: *Poems by Emily Dickinson: Edited by Two of Her Friends, Mabel Loomis Todd and T. W. Higginson*. Second Series. Boston: Roberts Brothers, 1892.

[The Railway Train] (c. 1862)

I like to see it lap the miles,
And lick the valleys up,
And stop to feed itself at tanks;
And then, prodigious, step

Around a pile of mountains,
And, supercilious, peer
In shanties by the sides of roads;
And then a quarry pare

To fit its sides, and crawl between,
Complaining all the while
In horrid, hooting stanza;
Then chase itself down hill

And neigh like Boanerges;
Then, punctual as a star,
Stop—docile and omnipotent—
At its own stable door.

SOURCE: *Poems by Emily Dickinson: Edited by Two of Her Friends, Mabel Loomis Todd and T. W. Higginson.* Second Series. Boston: Roberts Brothers, 1892.

[The Mystery of Pain] (c. 1862)

Pain has an element of blank;
It cannot recollect
When it began, or if there were
A day when it was not.

It has no future but itself,
Its infinite realms contain
Its past, enlightened to perceive
New periods of pain.

SOURCE: *Poems by Emily Dickinson: Edited by Two of Her Friends, Mabel Loomis Todd and T. W. Higginson.* Second Series. Boston: Roberts Brothers, 1892.

[A Thunder-storm] (c. 1864)

The wind begun to rock the grass
With threatening tunes and low,—
He flung a menace at the earth,
A menace at the sky.

The leaves unhooked themselves from trees
And started all abroad;
The dust did scoop itself like hands
And throw away the road.

The wagons quickened on the streets,
The thunder hurried slow;
The lightning showed a yellow beak,
And then a livid claw.

The birds put up the bars to nests,
The cattle fled to barns;
There came one drop of giant rain,
And then, as if the hands

That held the dams had parted hold,
The waters wrecked the sky,
But overlooked my father's house,
Just quartering a tree.

SOURCE: *Poems by Emily Dickinson: Edited by Two of Her Friends, Mabel Loomis Todd and T. W. Higginson*. Second Series. Boston: Roberts Brothers, 1892.

[The Lost Thought] (c. 1864)

I felt a cleaving in my mind
  As if my brain had split;
I tried to match it, seam by seam,
  But could not make them fit.

The thought behind I strove to join
Unto the thought before,
But sequence ravelled out of reach
Like balls upon a floor.

SOURCE: *Poems by Emily Dickinson: Edited by Two of Her Friends, Mabel Loomis Todd and T. W. Higginson.* Third Series. Boston: Roberts Brothers, 1896.

[The Snake] (c. 1865)

A narrow fellow in the grass
Occasionally rides;
You may have met him,—did you not,
His notice sudden is.

The grass divides as with a comb,
A spotted shaft is seen;
And then it closes at your feet
And opens further on.

He likes a boggy acre,
A floor too cool for corn.
Yet when a child, and barefoot,
I more than once, at morn,

Have passed, I thought, a whip-lash
Unbraiding in the sun,—
When, stooping to secure it,
It wrinkled, and was gone.

Several of nature's people
I know, and they know me;
I feel for them a transport
Of cordiality;

But never met this fellow,
Attended or alone,
Without a tighter breathing,
And zero at the bone.

SOURCE: *Poems by Emily Dickinson: Edited by Two of Her Friends, Mabel Loomis Todd and T. W. Higginson*. Second Series. Boston: Roberts Brothers, 1892.

"Nature rarer uses yellow" (c. 1865)

Nature rarer uses yellow
  Than another hue;
Saves she all of that for sunsets,—
  Prodigal of blue,

Spending scarlet like a woman,
  Yellow she affords
Only scantly and selectly,
  Like a lover's words.

SOURCE: *Poems by Emily Dickinson: Edited by Two of Her Friends, Mabel Loomis Todd and T. W. Higginson*. Second Series. Boston: Roberts Brothers, 1892.

[A Book] (c. 1873)

There is no frigate like a book
  To take us lands away,
Nor any coursers like a page
  Of prancing poetry.
This traverse may the poorest take
  Without oppress of toll;
How frugal is the chariot
  That bears a human soul!

SOURCE: *Poems by Emily Dickinson: Edited by Two of Her Friends, Mabel Loomis Todd and T. W. Higginson*. Third Series. Boston: Roberts Brothers, 1896.

[The Humming-Bird] (c. 1879)

A route of evanescence
With a revolving wheel;
A resonance of emerald,
A rush of cochineal;
And every blossom on the bush
Adjusts its tumbled head,—
The mail from Tunis, probably,
An easy morning's ride.

SOURCE: *Poems by Emily Dickinson: Edited by Two of Her Friends, Mabel Loomis Todd and T. W. Higginson.* Second Series. Boston: Roberts Brothers, 1892.

Letters to Thomas Wentworth Higginson (1862–1869)

Having been writing her verses in private, Dickinson looked for a mentor. When she read a compelling article about the craft of writing in The Atlantic Monthly *magazine, "Letter to a Young Contributor," she wrote to the author, Thomas Wentworth Higginson, who, as she had guessed, was a sympathetic soul. The Civil War was underway, however, and Higginson soon volunteered to command a "colored" troop (about which he wrote the fascinating memoir* Army Life in a Black Regiment*). After Dickinson's death, Higginson and Mabel Loomis Todd edited three volumes of their friend's poetry, which excited great interest, and a volume of her letters. With the publication of the letters, Higginson described the history of his correspondence and relationship with Dickinson. Higginson notes: "These were my earliest letters from Emily Dickinson, in their order. From this time and up to her death (May 15, 1886) we corresponded at varying intervals, she always persistently keeping up this attitude of 'Scholar,' and assuming on my part a preceptorship which it is almost needless to say did not exist. Always glad to hear her 'recite,' as she called it, I soon abandoned all attempt to guide in the slightest degree this extraordinary nature, and simply accepted her confidences, giving as much as I could of what might interest her in return."*

[April 15, 1862]

Mr. Higginson,

Are you too deeply occupied to say if my verse is alive?

The mind is so near itself it cannot see distinctly, and I have none to ask.

Should you think it breathed, and had you the leisure to tell me, I should feel quick gratitude.

If I make the mistake, that you dared to tell me would give me sincerer honor toward you.

I inclose my name, asking you, if you please, sir, to tell me what is true?

That you will not betray me it is needless to ask, since honor is its own pawn.

[April 26, 1862]

Mr. Higginson,

Your kindness claimed earlier gratitude, but I was ill, and write to-day from my pillow.

Thank you for the surgery; it was not so painful as I supposed. I bring you others, as you ask, though they might not differ. While my thought is undressed, I can make the distinction; but when I put them in the gown, they look alike and numb.

You asked how old I was? I made no verse, but one or two, until this winter, sir.

. . .

I had a terror since September, I could tell to none; and so I sing, as the boy does of the burying ground, because I am afraid.

You inquire my books. For poets, I have Keats, and Mr. and Mrs. Browning. For prose, Mr. Ruskin, Sir Thomas Browne, and the Revelations. I went to school, but in your manner of the phrase had no education. When a little girl, I had a friend who taught me Immortality; but venturing too near, himself, he never returned. Soon after my tutor died, and for several years my lexicon was my only companion. Then I found one more, but he was not contented I be his scholar, so he left the land.

You ask of my companions. Hills, sir, and the sundown, and a dog large as myself, that my father bought me. They are better than beings because they know, but do not tell; and the noise in the pool at noon excels my piano.

I have a brother and sister; my mother does not care for thought, and father, too busy with his briefs to notice what we do. He buys me many books, but begs me not to read them, because he fears they joggle the mind. They are religious, except me, and address an eclipse, every morning, whom they call their "Father."

But I fear my story fatigues you. I would like to learn. Could you tell me how to grow, or is it unconveyed, like melody or witchcraft?

You speak of Mr. Whitman. I never read his book, but was told that it was disgraceful.

I read Miss Prescott's Circumstance, but it followed me in the dark, so I avoided her.

Two editors of journals came to my father's house this winter, and asked me for my mind, and when I asked them "why" they said I was penurious, and they would use it for the world.

I could not weigh myself, myself. My size felt small to me. I read your chapters in the Atlantic, and experienced honor for you. I was sure you would not reject a confiding question.

Is this, sir, what you asked me to tell you?

Your friend,
E. DICKINSON.

[June 7, 1862]

Dear Friend,

Your letter gave no drunkenness, because I tasted rum before. Domingo comes but once; yet I have had few pleasures so deep as your opinion, and if I tried to thank you, my tears would block my tongue.

My dying tutor told me that he would like to live till I had been a poet, but Death was much of mob as I could master, then. And when, far afterward, a sudden light on orchards, or a new fashion in the wind troubled my attention, I felt a palsy, here, the verses just relieve.

Your second letter surprised me, and for a moment, swung. I had not supposed it. Your first gave no dishonor, because the true are not ashamed. I thanked you for your justice, but could not drop the bells whose jingling cooled my tramp. Perhaps the balm seemed better, because you bled me first. I smile when you suggest that I delay "to publish," that being foreign to my thought as firmament to fin.

If fame belonged to me, I could not escape her; if she did not, the longest day would pass me on the chase, and the approbation of my dog would forsake me then. My barefoot rank is better.

You think my gait "spasmodic." I am in danger, sir. You think me "uncontrolled." I have no tribunal.

Would you have time to be the "friend" you should think I need? I have a little shape: it would not crowd your desk, nor make much racket as the mouse that dents your galleries.

If I might bring you what I do—not so frequent to trouble you—and ask you if I told it clear, 't would be control to me. The sailor cannot see the North, but knows the needle can. The "hand you stretch me in the dark" I put mine in, and turn away. I have no Saxon now:—

As if I asked a common alms,
And in my wondering hand
A stranger pressed a kingdom,
And I, bewildered, stand;
As if I asked the Orient
Had it for me a morn,
And it should lift its purple dikes
And shatter me with dawn!

But, will you be my preceptor, Mr Higginson?
Your friend,
E. DICKINSON.

[July 1862]

Could you believe me without? I had no portrait, now, but am small, like the wren; and my hair is bold, like the chestnut bur; and my eyes, like the sherry in the glass, that the guest leaves. Would this do just as well?

It often alarms father. He says death might occur, and he has moulds of all the rest, but has no mould of me; but I noticed the quick wore off those things in a few days, and forestall the dishonor. You will think no caprice of me.

You said "Dark." I know the butterfly, and the lizard, and the orchis. Are not those *your* countrymen?

I am happy to be your scholar, and will deserve the kindness I cannot repay.

If you truly consent, I recite now. Will you tell me my fault, frankly as to yourself, for I had rather wince than die. Men do not call the surgeon to commend the bone, but to set it, sir, and fracture within is more critical. And for this, preceptor, I shall bring you obedience, the blossom from my garden, and every gratitude I know.

Perhaps you smile at me. I could not stop for that. My business is circumference. An ignorance, not of customs, but if caught with the dawn, or the sunset see me, myself the only kangaroo among the beauty, sir, if you please, it afflicts me, and I thought that instruction would take it away.

Because you have much business, beside the growth of me, you will appoint, yourself, how often I shall come, without your inconvenience.

And if at any time you regret you received me, or I prove a different fabric to that you supposed, you must banish me.

When I state myself, as the representative of the verse, it does not mean me, but a supposed person.

You are true about the "perfection." To-day makes Yesterday mean.

You spoke of Pippa Passes. I never heard anybody speak of Pippa Passes before. You see my posture is benighted.

To thank you baffles me. Are you perfectly powerful? Had I a pleasure you had not, I could delight to bring it.

YOUR SCHOLAR.

[August 1862]

Dear Friend,

Are these more orderly? I thank you for the truth.

I had no monarch in my life, and cannot rule myself; and when I try to organize, my little force explodes and leaves me bare and charred.

I think you called me "wayward." Will you help me improve?

I suppose the pride that stops the breath, in the core of woods, is not of ourself.

You say I confess the little mistake, and omit the large. Because I can see orthography; but the ignorance out of sight is my preceptor's charge.

Of "shunning men and women," they talk of hallowed things, aloud, and embarrass my dog. He and I don't object to them, if they'll exist their side. I think Carlo [her dog] would please you. He is dumb, and brave. I think you would like the chestnut tree I met in my walk. It hit my notice suddenly, and I thought the skies were in blossom.

Then there's a noiseless noise in the orchard that I let persons hear.

You told me in one letter you could not come to see me "now," and I made no answer; not because I had none, but did not think myself the price that you should come so far.

I do not ask so large a pleasure, lest you might deny me.

You say, "Beyond your knowledge." You would not jest with me, because I believe you; but, preceptor, you cannot mean it?

All men say "What" to me, but I thought it a fashion.

When much in the woods, as a little girl, I was told that the snake would bite me, that I might pick a poisonous flower, or goblins kidnap me; but I went along and met no one but angels, who were far shyer of me than I could be of them, so I have n't that confidence in fraud which many exercise.

I shall observe your precept, though I don't understand it, always.

I marked a line in one verse, because I met it after I made it, and never consciously touch a paint mixed by another person.

I do not let go it, because it is mine. Have you the portrait of Mrs. Browning?

Persons sent me three. If you had none, will you have mine?
YOUR SCHOLAR.

[February 1863]

Dear Friend,

I did not deem that planetary forces annulled, but suffered an exchange of territory, or world.

I should have liked to see you before you became improbable. War feels to me an oblique place. Should there be other summers, would you perhaps come?

I found you were gone, by accident, as I find systems are, or seasons of the year, and obtain no cause, but suppose it a treason of progress that dissolves as it goes. Carlo still remained, and I told him

Best gains must have the losses' test,
To constitute them gains.

My shaggy ally assented.

Perhaps death gave me awe for friends, striking sharp and early, for I held them since in a brittle love, of more alarm than peace. I trust you may pass the limit of war; and though not reared to prayer, when service is had in church for our arms, I include yourself. . . . I was thinking to-day, as I noticed, that the "Supernatural" was only the Natural disclosed.

Not "Revelation" 't is that waits,
But our unfurnished eyes.

But I fear I detain you. Should you, before this reaches you, experience immortality, who will inform me of the exchange? Could you, with honor, avoid death, I entreat you, sir. It would bereave
YOUR GNOME.
I trust the "Procession of Flowers" was not a premonition.

[June 1869]

Dear Friend,

A letter always feels to me like immortality because it is the mind alone without corporeal friend. Indebted in our talk to attitude and accent, there seems a spectral power in thought that walks alone. I would like to thank you for your great kindness, but never try to lift the words which I cannot hold.

Should you come to Amherst, I might then succeed, though gratitude is the timid wealth of those who have nothing. I am sure that you speak the truth, because the noble do, but your letters always surprise me.

My life has been too simple and stern to embarrass any. "Seen of Angels," scarcely my responsibility.

It is difficult not to be fictitious in so fair a place, but tests' severe repairs are permitted all.

When a little girl I remember hearing that remarkable passage and preferring the "Power," not knowing at the time that "Kingdom" and "Glory" were included.

You noticed my dwelling alone. To an emigrant, country is idle except it be his own. You speak kindly of seeing me; could it please your convenience to come so far as Amherst, I should be very glad, but I do not cross my father's ground to any house or town.

Of our greatest acts we are ignorant. You were not aware that you saved my life. To thank you in person has been since then one of my few requests. . . . You will excuse each that I say, because no one taught me.

SOURCE: Thomas Wentworth Higginson. "Emily Dickinson's Letters," *The Atlantic Monthly* (October 1891).

MARK TWAIN

Mark Twain (1835–1910), the pen name of Samuel Clemens, is American literature's most prominent and important author. For more than forty years he was popular and great, writing almost invariably humorously and always in a conversational, unmistakably American voice. He started as a journalist and never lost his easy immediacy, even when, at the end of his life, he was reeling from the deaths of two of his children and his wife.

Roughing It (1872)

We readers and editors have become accustomed to divvying up prose literature into the categories of fiction or nonfiction. This makes Roughing It *hard to describe: it is certainly a travel book as well as a memoir, but what to call the marvelous tall tales that hilariously emerge here and there? Chapter 42 contains an account of his start in newspaper work in Virginia City, Nevada. In Chapter 53 he remembers, from those days in Nevada, an endless tale.*

Chapter 42

What to do next?

It was a momentous question. I had gone out into the world to shift for myself, at the age of thirteen (for my father had endorsed for friends; and although he left us a sumptuous legacy of pride in his fine Virginian stock and its national distinction, I presently found that I could not live on that alone without occasional bread to wash it down with). I had gained a livelihood in various vocations, but had not dazzled anybody with my successes; still the list was before me, and the amplest liberty in the matter of choosing, provided I wanted to work—which I did not, after being so wealthy. I had once been a grocery clerk, for one day, but had consumed so much sugar in that time that I was relieved from further duty by the proprietor; said he wanted me outside, so that he could have my custom. I had studied law an entire week, and then given it up because it was so prosy and tiresome. I had engaged briefly in the study of blacksmithing, but wasted so much time trying to fix the bellows so that it would blow itself, that the master turned me adrift in disgrace, and told me I would come to no good. I had been a bookseller's clerk for awhile, but the customers bothered me so much I could not read with any comfort, and so the proprietor gave me a furlough and forgot to put a limit to it. I had clerked in a drug store part of a summer, but my prescriptions were unlucky, and we appeared to sell more stomach pumps than soda water. So I had to go. I had made of myself a tolerable printer, under the impression that I would be another Franklin some day, but somehow had missed the connection thus far. There was no berth open in the Esmeralda *Union,* and besides I had always been such a slow compositor that I looked with envy upon the achievements of apprentices of two years' standing; and when I took a "take," foremen were in the habit of suggesting that it would be wanted "some time during the year." I was a good average St. Louis and New Orleans pilot and by no means ashamed of my abilities in that line; wages were two hundred and fifty dollars a month and no board to pay, and I did long to stand behind a wheel again and never roam any more—but I had been making such an ass of myself lately in grandiloquent letters home about my blind lead and my European excursion that I did what many and many a poor disappointed miner had done before; said "It is all over with me now, and I will never go back home to be pitied—and snubbed." I had been a private secretary, a silver miner and a silver mill operative, and amounted to less than nothing in each, and now—

What to do next?

I yielded to Higbie's appeals and consented to try the mining once more. We climbed far up on the mountain side and went to work on a little rubbishy claim of ours that had a shaft on it eight feet deep. Higbie descended into it and worked bravely with his pick till he had loosened up a deal of rock and dirt and then I went down with a long-handled shovel (the most awkward invention yet contrived by man) to throw it out. You must brace the shovel forward with the side of your knee till it is full, and then, with a skillful toss, throw it backward over your left shoulder. I made the toss, and landed the mess just on the edge of the shaft and it all came back on my head and down the back of my neck. I never said a word, but climbed out and walked home. I inwardly resolved that I would starve before I would make a target of myself and shoot rubbish at it with a long-handled shovel. I sat down, in the cabin, and gave myself up to solid misery—so to speak. Now in pleasanter days I had amused myself with writing letters to the chief paper of the Territory, the Virginia *Daily Territorial Enterprise,* and had always been surprised when they appeared in print. My good opinion of the editors had steadily declined; for it seemed to me that they might have found something better to fill up with than my literature. I had found a letter in the post office as I came home from the hillside, and finally I opened it. Eureka! (I never did know what Eureka meant, but it seems to be as proper a word to heave in as any when no other that sounds pretty offers.) It was a deliberate offer to me of Twenty-Five Dollars a week to come up to Virginia and be city editor of the *Enterprise.*

I would have challenged the publisher in the "blind lead" days—I wanted to fall down and worship him, now. Twenty-five Dollars a week—it looked like bloated luxury—a fortune, a sinful and lavish waste of money. But my transports cooled when I thought of my inexperience and consequent unfitness for the position—and straightway, on top of this, my long array of failures rose up before me. Yet if I refused this place I must presently become dependent upon somebody for my bread, a thing necessarily distasteful to a man who had never experienced such a humiliation since he was thirteen years old. Not much to be proud of, since it is so common—but then it was all I had to *be* proud of. So I was scared into being a city editor. I would have declined, otherwise. Necessity is the mother of "taking chances." I do not doubt that if, at that time, I had been offered a salary to translate the Talmud from the original Hebrew, I would have accepted—albeit with diffidence and some misgivings—and thrown as much variety into it as I could for the money.

I went up to Virginia and entered upon my new vocation. I was a rusty-looking city editor, I am free to confess—coatless, slouch hat, blue woolen shirt, pantaloons stuffed into boot-tops, whiskered half down to the waist, and the universal navy revolver slung to my belt. But I secured a more Christian costume and discarded the revolver. I had never had occasion to kill anybody, nor ever felt a desire to do so, but had worn the thing in deference to popular sentiment, and in order that I might not, by its absence, be offensively conspicuous, and a subject of remark. But the other editors, and all the printers, carried revolvers. I asked the chief editor and proprietor (Mr. Goodman, I will call him, since it describes him as well as any name could do) for some instructions with regard to my duties, and he told me to go all over town and ask all sorts of people all sorts of questions, make notes of the information gained, and write them out for publication. And he added:

"Never say 'We learn' so-and-so, or 'It is reported,' or 'It is rumored,' or 'We understand' so-and-so, but go to headquarters and get the absolute facts, and then speak out and say 'It *is* so-and-so.' Otherwise, people will not put confidence in your news. Unassailable certainty is the thing that gives a newspaper the firmest and most valuable reputation."

It was the whole thing in a nutshell; and to this day when I find a reporter commencing his article with "We understand," I gather a suspicion that he has not taken as much pains to inform himself as he ought to have done. I moralize well, but I did not always practice well when I was a city editor; I let fancy get the upper hand of fact too often when there was a dearth of news. I can never forget my first day's experience as a reporter. I wandered about town questioning everybody, boring everybody, and finding out that nobody knew anything. At the end of five hours my notebook was still barren. I spoke to Mr. Goodman. He said:

"Dan used to make a good thing out of the hay wagons in a dry time when there were no fires or inquests. Are there no hay wagons in from the Truckee? If there are, you might speak of the renewed activity and all that sort of thing, in the hay business, you know. It isn't sensational or exciting, but it fills up and looks business-like."

I canvassed the city again and found one wretched old hay truck dragging in from the country. But I made affluent use of it. I multiplied it by sixteen, brought it into town from sixteen different directions, made sixteen separate items out of it, and got up such another sweat about hay as Virginia City had never seen in the world before.

This was encouraging. Two nonpareil columns had to be filled, and I was getting along. Presently, when things began to look dismal again, a desperado killed a man in a saloon and joy returned once more. I never was so glad over any mere trifle before in my life. I said to the murderer:

"Sir, you are a stranger to me, but you have done me a kindness this day which I can never forget. If whole years of gratitude can be to you any slight compensation, they shall be yours. I was in trouble and you have relieved me nobly and at a time when all seemed dark and drear. Count me your friend from this time forth, for I am not a man to forget a favor."

If I did not really say that to him I at least felt a sort of itching desire to do it. I wrote up the murder with a hungry attention to details, and when it was finished experienced but one regret—namely, that they had not hanged my benefactor on the spot, so that I could work him up too.

Next I discovered some emigrant wagons going into camp on the plaza and found that they had lately come through the hostile Indian country and had fared rather roughly. I made the best of the item that the circumstances permitted, and felt that if I were not confined within rigid limits by the presence of the reporters of the other papers I could add particulars that would make the article much more interesting. However, I found one wagon that was going on to California, and made some judicious inquiries of the proprietor. When I learned, through his short and surly answers to my cross-questioning, that he was certainly going on and would not be in the city next day to make trouble, I got ahead of the other papers, for I took down his list of names and added his party to the killed and wounded. Having more scope here, I put this wagon through an Indian fight that to this day has no parallel in history.

My two columns were filled. When I read them over in the morning I felt that I had found my legitimate occupation at last. I reasoned within myself that news, and stirring news, too, was what a paper needed, and I felt that I was peculiarly endowed with the ability to furnish it. Mr. Goodman said that I was as good a reporter as Dan. I desired no higher commendation. With encouragement like that, I felt that I could take my pen and murder all the immigrants on the plains if need be and the interests of the paper demanded it.

Chapter 53

Every now and then, in these days, the boys used to tell me I ought to get one Jim Blaine to tell me the stirring story of his grandfather's old ram—but they always added that I must not mention the matter unless Jim was drunk at the time—just comfortably and sociably drunk. They kept this up until my curiosity was on the rack to hear the story. I got to haunting Blaine; but it was of no use, the boys always found fault with his condition; he was often moderately but never satisfactorily drunk. I never watched a man's condition with such absorbing interest, such anxious solicitude; I never so pined to see a man uncompromisingly drunk before. At last, one evening I hurried to his cabin, for I learned that this time his situation was such that even the most fastidious could find no fault with it—he was tranquilly, serenely, symmetrically drunk—not a hiccup to mar his voice, not a cloud upon his brain thick enough to obscure his memory. As I entered, he was sitting upon an empty powder-keg, with a clay pipe in one hand and the other raised to command silence. His face was round, red, and very serious; his throat was bare and his hair tumbled; in general appearance and costume he was a stalwart miner of the period. On the pine table stood a candle, and its dim light revealed "the boys" sitting here and there on bunks, candle-boxes, powder-kegs, etc. They said:

"Sh—! Don't speak—he's going to commence."

The Story of the Old Ram

I found a seat at once, and Blaine said:

"I don't reckon them times will ever come again. There never was a more bullier old ram than what he was. Grandfather fetched him from Illinois—got him of a man by the name of Yates—Bill Yates—maybe you might have heard of him; his father was a deacon—Baptist—and he was a rustler, too; a man had to get up rather early to get the start of old Thankful Yates; it was him that put the Greens up to jining teams with my grandfather when he moved west. Seth Green was prob'ly the pick of the flock; he married a Wilkerson—Sarah Wilkerson—good cretur, she was—one of the likeliest heifers that was ever raised in old Stoddard, everybody said that knowed her. She could heft a bar'l of flour as easy as I can flirt a flapjack. And spin? Don't mention it! Independent? Humph! When Sile Hawkins come a browsing around her, she let him know that for all his tin he couldn't trot in harness alongside of *her*. You see, Sile Hawkins was—no, it warn't Sile Hawkins, after all—it was a galoot by the name of Filkins—I disremember his first name; but he *was* a stump—come into pra'r meeting drunk, one night, hooraying for Nixon, becuz he thought it was a primary; and old deacon Ferguson up and scooted him through the window and he lit on old Miss Jefferson's head, poor old filly. She was a good soul—had a glass eye and used to lend it to old Miss Wagner, that hadn't any, to receive company in; it warn't big enough, and when Miss Wagner warn't noticing, it would get twisted around in the socket, and look up, maybe, or out to one side, and every which way, while t' other one was looking as straight ahead as a spyglass. Grown people didn't mind it, but it most always made the children cry, it was so sort of scary. She tried packing it in raw cotton, but it wouldn't work, somehow—the cotton would get loose and stick out and look so kind of awful that the children couldn't stand it no way. She was always dropping it out, and turning up her old deadlight on the company empty, and making them oncomfortable, becuz *she* never could tell when it hopped out, being blind on that side, yon see. So somebody would have to hunch her and say, 'Your game eye has fetched loose, Miss Wagner dear'—and then all of them would have to sit and wait till she jammed it in again—wrong side before, as a general thing, and green as a bird's egg, being a bashful cretur and easy sot back before company. But being wrong side before warn't much difference, anyway, becuz her own eye was sky-blue and the glass one was yaller on the front side, so whichever way she turned it it didn't match nohow. Old Miss Wagner was considerable on the borrow, she was. When she had a quilting, or Dorcas S'iety at her house she gen'ally borrowed Miss Higgins's wooden leg to stump around on; it was considerable shorter than her other pin, but much *she* minded that. She said she couldn't abide crutches when she had company, becuz they were so slow; said when she had company and things had to be done, she wanted to get up and hump herself. She was as bald as a jug, and so she used to borrow Miss Jacops's wig—Miss Jacops was the coffin-peddler's wife—a ratty old buzzard, he was, that used to go roosting around where people was sick, waiting for 'em; and there that old rip would sit all day, in the shade, on a coffin that he judged would fit the can'idate; and if it was a slow customer and kind of uncertain, he'd fetch his rations and a blanket along and sleep in the coffin nights. He was anchored out that way, in frosty weather, for about three weeks, once, before old Robbins's place, waiting for him; and after that, for as much as two years, Jacops was not on speaking terms with the old man, on account of his disapp'inting him. He got one of his feet froze, and lost money, too, becuz old Robbins took a favorable turn and got well. The next time Robbins got sick, Jacops tried to make up with him, and varnished up the same old coffin and fetched it along; but old Robbins was too many for him; he had him in, and 'peared to be powerful weak; he bought the coffin for ten dollars and Jacops was to pay it back and twenty-five more besides if Robbins didn't like the coffin after he'd tried it. And then Robbins died, and at the funeral he bursted off the lid and riz up in his shroud and told the parson to let up on the performances, becuz he could *not* stand such a coffin as that. You see he had been in a trance once before, when he was young, and he took the chances on another, cal'lating that if he made the trip it was money in his pocket, and if he missed fire he couldn't lose a cent. And, by George, he sued Jacops for the rhino and got judgment; and he set up the coffin in his back parlor and said he 'lowed to take his time, now. It was always an aggravation to Jacops, the way that miserable old thing acted. He moved back to Indiany pretty soon—went to Wellsville—Wellsville was the place the Hogadorns was from. Mighty fine family. Old Maryland stock. Old Squire Hogadorn could carry around more mixed licker, and cuss better than most any man I ever see. His second wife was the widder Billings—she that was Becky Martin; her dam was deacon Dunlap's first wife. Her oldest child, Maria, married a missionary and died in grace—et up by the savages. They et *him,* too, poor feller—biled him. It warn't the custom, so they say, but they explained to friends of his'n that went down there to bring away his things, that they'd tried missionaries every other way and never could get any good out of 'em—and so it annoyed all his relations to find out that that man's life was fooled away just out of a dern'd experiment, so to speak. But mind you, there ain't anything ever reely lost; everything that people can't understand and don't see the reason of does good if you only hold on and give it a fair shake; Prov'dence don't fire no blank ca'tridges, boys. That there missionary's substance, unbeknowns to himself, actu'ly converted every last one of them heathens that took a chance at the barbacue. Nothing ever fetched them but that. Don't tell *me* it was an accident that he was biled. There ain't no such a thing as an accident. When my uncle Lem was leaning up agin a scaffolding once, sick, or drunk, or suthin, an Irishman with a hod full of bricks fell on him out of the third story and broke the old man's back in two places. People said it was an accident. Much accident there was about that. He didn't know what he was there for, but he was there for a good object. If he hadn't been there the Irishman would have been killed. Nobody can ever make me believe anything different from that. Uncle Lem's dog was there. Why didn't the Irishman fall on the dog? Becuz the dog would a seen him a coming and stood from under. That's the reason the dog warn't appinted. A dog can't be depended on to carry out a special providence. Mark my words it was a put-up thing. Accidents don't happen, boys. Uncle Lem's dog—I wish you could a seen that dog. He was a reglar shepherd—or ruther he was part bull and part shepherd—splendid animal; belonged to Parson Hagar before Uncle Lem got him. Parson Hagar belonged to the Western Reserve Hagars; prime family; his mother was a Watson; one of his sisters married a Wheeler; they settled in Morgan County, and he got nipped by the machinery in a carpet factory and went through in less than a quarter of a minute; his widder bought the piece of carpet that had his remains wove in, and people come a hundred mile to 'tend the funeral. There was fourteen yards in the piece. She wouldn't let them roll him up, but planted him just so—full length. The church was middling small where they preached the funeral, and they had to let one end of the coffin stick out of the window. They didn't bury him—they planted one end, and let him stand up, same as a monument. And they nailed a sign on it and put—put on—put on it—sacred to—the m-e-m-o-r-y—of fourteen y-a-r-d-s—of three-ply car---pet—containing all that was—m-o-r-t-a-l—of—of—W-i-l-l-i-a-m—W-h-e—"

Jim Blaine had been growing gradually drowsy and drowsier—his head nodded, once, twice, three times—dropped peacefully upon his breast, and he fell tranquilly asleep. The tears were running down the boys' cheeks—they were suffocating with suppressed laughter—and had been from the start, though I had never noticed it. I perceived that I was "sold." I learned then that Jim Blaine's peculiarity was that whenever he reached a certain stage of intoxication, no human power could keep him from setting out, with impressive unction, to tell about a wonderful adventure which he had once had with his grandfather's old ram—and the mention of the ram in the first sentence was as far as any man had ever heard him get, concerning it. He always maundered off, interminably, from one thing to another, till his whisky got the best of him and he fell asleep. What the thing was that happened to him and his grandfather's old ram is a dark mystery to this day, for nobody has ever yet found out.

SOURCE: Mark Twain. *Roughing It.* Hartford: American Publishing Company, 1872.

The Adventures of Tom Sawyer (1876)

Twain set out to write a novel reminiscent of his own childhood growing up in a small town on the Mississippi River. Though he wrote The Adventures of Tom Sawyer *for adults, it became the most popular American children's novel of the century. We excerpt here only one of the many famous scenes. The character Tom Sawyer reappeared in* Adventures of Huckleberry Finn *and other works.*

Chapter 2: The Glorious Whitewasher

Saturday morning was come, and all the summer world was bright and fresh, and brimming with life. There was a song in every heart; and if the heart was young the music issued at the lips. There was cheer in every face and a spring in every step. The locust trees were in bloom and the fragrance of the blossoms filled the air. Cardiff Hill, beyond the village and above it, was green with vegetation, and it lay just far enough away to seem a Delectable Land, dreamy, reposeful, and inviting.

Tom appeared on the sidewalk with a bucket of whitewash and a long-handled brush. He surveyed the fence, and all gladness left him and a deep melancholy settled down upon his spirit. Thirty yards of board fence nine feet high. Life to him seemed hollow, and existence but a burden. Sighing he dipped his brush and passed it along the topmost plank; repeated the operation; did it again; compared the insignificant whitewashed streak with the far-reaching continent of unwhitewashed fence, and sat down on a tree-box discouraged. Jim came skipping out at the gate with a tin pail, and singing "Buffalo Gals." Bringing water from the town pump had always been hateful work in Tom's eyes, before, but now it did not strike him so. He remembered that there was company at the pump. White, mulatto, and Negro boys and girls were always there waiting their turns, resting, trading playthings, quarreling, fighting, skylarking. And he remembered that although the pump was only a hundred and fifty yards off, Jim never got back with a bucket of water under an hour—and even then somebody generally had to go after him. Tom said:

"Say, Jim, I'll fetch the water if you'll whitewash some."

Jim shook his head and said: "Can't, Mars Tom. Ole missis, she tole me I got to go an' git dis water an' not stop foolin' roun' wid anybody. She say she spec' Mars Tom gwine to ax me to whitewash, an' so she tole me go 'long an' 'tend to my own business—she 'lowed *she'd* 'tend to de whitewashin'."

"Oh, never you mind what she said, Jim. That's the way she always talks. Gimme the bucket—I won't be gone only a minute. *She* won't ever know."

"Oh, I dasn't, Mars Tom. Ole missis she'd take an' tar de head off'n me. 'Deed she would."

"*She!* She never licks anybody—whacks 'em over the head with her thimble—and who cares for that, I'd like to know. She talks awful, but talk don't hurt—anyways it don't if she don't cry. Jim, I'll give you a marvel. I'll give you a white alley!"

Jim began to waver.

"White alley, Jim! And it's a bully taw."

"My! Dat's a mighty gay marvel, *I* tell you! But Mars Tom, I's powerful 'fraid ole missis—"

"And besides, if you will I'll show you my sore toe."

Jim was only human—this attraction was too much for him. He put down his pail, took the white alley, and bent over the toe with absorbing interest while the bandage was being unwound. In another moment he was flying down the street with his pail and a tingling rear, Tom was whitewashing with vigor, and Aunt Polly was retiring from the field with a slipper in her hand and triumph in her eye.

But Tom's energy did not last. He began to think of the fun he had planned for this day, and his sorrows multiplied. Soon the free boys would come tripping along on all sorts of delicious expeditions, and they would make a world of fun of him for having to work—the very thought of it burnt him like fire. He got out his worldly wealth and examined it—bits of toys, marbles, and trash; enough to buy an exchange of *work*, maybe, but not half enough to buy so much as half an hour of pure freedom. So he returned his straitened means to his pocket, and gave up the idea of trying to buy the boys. At this dark and hopeless moment an inspiration burst upon him! Nothing less than a great, magnificent inspiration.

He took up his brush and went tranquilly to work. Ben Rogers hove in sight presently—the very boy, of all boys, whose ridicule he had been dreading. Ben's gait was the hop-skip-and-jump—proof enough that his heart was light and his anticipations high. He was eating an apple, and giving a long, melodious whoop, at intervals, followed by a deep-toned ding-dong-dong, ding-dong-dong, for he was personating a steamboat. As he drew near, he slackened speed, took the middle of the street, leaned far over to starboard and rounded to ponderously and with laborious pomp and circumstance—for he was personating the *Big Missouri*, and considered himself to be drawing nine feet of water. He was boat and captain and engine bells combined, so he had to imagine himself standing on his own hurricane deck giving the orders and executing them:

"Stop her, sir! Ting-a-ling-ling!" The headway ran almost out and he drew up slowly toward the sidewalk.

"Ship up to back! Ting-a-ling-ling!" His arms straightened and stiffened down his sides.

"Set her back on the stabboard! Ting-a-ling-ling! Chow! Ch-chow-wow! Chow!" His right hand, meantime, describing stately circles—for it was representing a forty-foot wheel.

"Let her go back on the labboard! Ting-a-ling-ling! Chow-ch-chow-chow!" The left hand began to describe circles.

"Stop the stabboard! Ting-a-ling-ling! Stop the labbord! Come ahead on the stabboard! Stop her! Let your outside turn over slow! Ting-a-ling-ling! Chow-ow-ow! Get out that head-line! *Lively* now! Come—out with your spring line—what're you about there! Take a turn round that stump with the bight of it! Stand by that stage, now—let her go! Done with the engines, sir! Ting-a-ling-ling! *Sh't! sh't! sh't!*" (trying the gauge cocks).

Tom went on whitewashing—paid no attention to the steamboat. Ben stared a moment and then said:

"Hi-*yi! You're* up a stump, ain't you!"

No answer. Tom surveyed his last touch with the eye of an artist; then he gave his brush another gentle sweep and surveyed the result, as before. Ben ranged up alongside of him. Tom's mouth watered for the apple, but he stuck to his work. Ben said:

"Hello, old chap, you got to work, hey?"

Tom wheeled suddenly and said:

"Why it's you, Ben! I warn't noticing."

"Say—*I*'m going in a-swimming, *I* am. Don't you wish you could? But of course you'd druther *work*—wouldn't you? Course you would!"

Tom contemplated the boy a bit, and said:

"What do you call work?"

"Why ain't *that* work?"

Tom resumed his whitewashing, and answered carelessly:

"Well, maybe it is, and maybe it ain't. All I know is, it suits Tom Sawyer."

"Oh come, now, you don't mean to let on that you *like* it?"

The brush continued to move.

"Like it? Well, I don't see why I oughtn't to like it. Does a boy get a chance to whitewash a fence every day?"

That put the thing in a new light. Ben stopped nibbling his apple. Tom swept his brush daintily back and forth—stepped back to note the effect—added a touch here and there—criticized the effect again—Ben watching every move and getting more and more interested, more and more absorbed. Presently he said:

"Say, Tom, let *me* whitewash a little."

Tom considered, was about to consent; but he altered his mind:

"No—no—I reckon it wouldn't hardly do, Ben. You see, Aunt Polly's awful particular about this fence—right here on the street, you know—but if it was the back fence I wouldn't mind and *she* wouldn't. Yes, she's awful particular about this fence; it's got to be done very careful; I reckon there ain't one boy in a thousand, maybe two thousand, that can do it the way it's got to be done."

"No—is that so? Oh come, now—lemme just try. Only just a little—I'd let *you*, if you was me, Tom."

"Ben, I'd like to, honest injun; but Aunt Polly—well, Jim wanted to do it, but she wouldn't let him; Sid wanted to do it, and she wouldn't let Sid. Now don't you see how I'm fixed? If you was to tackle this fence and anything was to happen to it—"

"Oh, shucks, I'll be just as careful. Now lemme try. Say—I'll give you the core of my apple."

"Well, here—No, Ben, now don't. I'm afeard—"

"I'll give you *all* of it!"

Tom gave up the brush with reluctance in his face, but alacrity in his heart. And while the late steamer *Big Missouri* worked and sweated in the sun, the retired artist sat on a barrel in the shade close by, dangled his legs, munched his apple, and planned the slaughter of more innocents. There was no lack of material; boys happened along every little while; they came to jeer, but remained to whitewash. By the time Ben was fagged out, Tom had traded the next chance to Billy Fisher for a kite, in good repair; and when *he* played out, Johnny Miller bought in for a dead rat and a string to swing it with—and so on, and so on, hour after hour. And when the middle of the afternoon came, from being a poor poverty-stricken boy in the morning, Tom was literally rolling in wealth. He had, besides the things before mentioned, twelve marbles, part of a Jew's-harp, a piece of blue bottle glass to look through, a spool cannon, a key that wouldn't unlock anything, a fragment of chalk, a glass stopper of a decanter, a tin soldier, a couple of tadpoles, six fire-crackers, a kitten with only one eye, a brass door-knob, a dog collar—but no dog—the handle of a knife, four pieces of orange peel, and a dilapidated old window sash.

He had had a nice, good, idle time all the while, plenty of company—and the fence had three coats of whitewash on it! If he hadn't run out of whitewash, he would have bankrupted every boy in the village.

Tom said to himself that it was not such a hollow world, after all. He had discovered a great law of human action, without knowing it—namely, that in order to make a man or a boy covet a thing, it is only necessary to make the thing difficult to attain. If he had been a great and wise philosopher, like the writer of this book, he would now have comprehended that Work consists of whatever a body is *obliged* to do, and that Play consists of whatever a body is not obliged to do. And this would help him to understand why constructing artificial flowers or performing on a treadmill is work, while rolling tenpins or climbing Mont Blanc is only amusement. There are wealthy gentlemen in England who drive four-horse passenger coaches twenty or thirty miles on a daily line, in the summer, because the privilege costs them considerable money; but if they were offered wages for the service, that would turn it into work and then they would resign.

The boy mused awhile over the substantial change which had taken place in his worldly circumstances, and then wended toward headquarters to report.

SOURCE: Mark Twain. *The Adventures of Tom Sawyer.* Hartford: The American Publishing Company, 1876.

Adventures of Huckleberry Finn (1885)

Whether Adventures of Huckleberry Finn *is the most important or most controversial or best loved of American novels, it is extraordinary. It is about so many topics, among them friendship, freedom, slavery and conscience. As a sequel to* The Adventures of Tom Sawyer, Adventures of Huckleberry Finn *contradicts the adage about sequels always being less good than the originals. The comic and rollicking* Huck Finn *has a depth and heft that Twain did not attempt in* Tom Sawyer. *Published in 1885, it has been banned over the years (into the present) by particular libraries and schools for any number of reasons, all of them thickheaded. We quote Twain's "Explanatory" note to the 1885 edition: "In this book a number of dialects are used, to wit: the Missouri negro dialect; the extremest form of the backwoods Southwestern dialect; the ordinary 'Pike County' dialect; and four modified varieties of this last. The shadings have not been done in a haphazard fashion, or by guesswork; but painstakingly, and with the trustworthy guidance and support of personal familiarity with these several forms of speech. I make this explanation for the reason that without it many readers would suppose that all these characters were trying to talk alike and not succeeding." He announced the scene as "the Mississippi Valley . . . forty to fifty years ago." The novel's plot is simple: Huckleberry narrates how he helped Jim, a slave, escape the South. On the other hand, the adventures—of which there are many—are complicated. We present a few.*

Chapter 1

You don't know about me, without you have read a book by the name of *The Adventures of Tom Sawyer;* but that ain't no matter. That book was made by Mr. Mark Twain, and he told the truth, mainly. There was things which he stretched, but mainly he told the truth. That is nothing. I never seen anybody but lied, one time or another, without it was Aunt Polly, or the widow, or maybe Mary. Aunt Polly—Tom's Aunt Polly, she is—and Mary, and the Widow Douglas, is all told about in that book—which is mostly a true book; with some stretchers, as I said before.

Now the way that the book winds up, is this: Tom and me found the money that the robbers hid in the cave, and it made us rich. We got six thousand dollars apiece—all gold. It was an awful sight of money when it was piled up. Well, Judge Thatcher, he took it and put it out at interest, and it fetched us a dollar a day apiece, all the year round—more than a body could tell what to do with. The Widow Douglas, she took me for her son, and allowed she would sivilize me; but it was rough living in the house all the time, considering how dismal regular and decent the widow was in all her ways; and so when I couldn't stand it no longer, I lit out. I got into my old rags, and my sugar-hogshead again, and was free and satisfied. But Tom Sawyer, he hunted me up and said he was going to start a band of robbers, and I might join if I would go back to the widow and be respectable. So I went back.

The widow she cried over me, and called me a poor lost lamb, and she called me a lot of other names, too, but she never meant no harm by it. She put me in them new clothes again, and I couldn't do nothing but sweat and sweat, and feel all cramped up. Well, then, the old thing commenced again. The widow rung a bell for supper, and you had to come to time. When you got to the table you couldn't go right to eating, but you had to wait for the widow to tuck down her head and grumble a little over the victuals, though there warn't really anything the matter with them. That is, nothing only everything was cooked by itself. In a barrel of odds and ends it is different; things get mixed up, and the juice kind of swaps around, and the things go better.

After supper she got out her book and learned me about Moses and the Bulrushers; and I was in a sweat to find out all about him; but by-and-by she let it out that Moses had been dead a considerable long time; so then I didn't care no more about him; because I don't take no stock in dead people.

Pretty soon I wanted to smoke, and asked the widow to let me. But she wouldn't. She said it was a mean practice and wasn't clean, and I must try to not do it any more. That is just the way with some people. They get down on a thing when they don't know nothing about it. Here she was a bothering about Moses, which was no kin to her, and no use to anybody, being gone, you see, yet finding a power of fault with me for doing a thing that had some good in it. And she took snuff too; of course that was all right, because she done it herself.

Her sister, Miss Watson, a tolerable slim old maid, with goggles on, had just come to live with her, and took a set at me now, with a spelling-book. She worked me middling hard for about an hour, and then the widow made her ease up. I couldn't stood it much longer. Then for an hour it was deadly dull, and I was fidgety. Miss Watson would say, "Don't put your feet up there, Huckleberry;" and "Don't scrunch up like that, Huckleberry—set up straight;" and pretty soon she would say, "Don't gap and stretch like that,

Huckleberry—why don't you try to behave?" Then she told me all about the bad place, and I said I wished I was there. She got mad, then, but I didn't mean no harm. All I wanted was to go somewheres; all I wanted was a change, I warn't particular. She said it was wicked to say what I said; said she wouldn't say it for the whole world; *she* was going to live so as to go to the good place. Well, I couldn't see no advantage in going where she was going, so I made up my mind I wouldn't try for it. But I never said so, because it would only make trouble, and wouldn't do no good.

Now she had got a start, and she went on and told me all about the good place. She said all a body would have to do there was to go around all day long with a harp and sing, forever and ever. So I didn't think much of it. But I never said so. I asked her if she reckoned Tom Sawyer would go there, and, she said, not by a considerable sight. I was glad about that, because I wanted him and me to be together.

Miss Watson she kept pecking at me, and it got tiresome and lonesome. By-and-by they fetched the niggers in and had prayers, and then everybody was off to bed. I went up to my room with a piece of candle and put it on the table. Then I set down in a chair by the window and tried to think of something cheerful, but it warn't no use. I felt so lonesome I most wished I was dead. The stars was shining, and the leaves rustled in the woods ever so mournful; and I heard an owl, away off, who-whooing about somebody that was dead, and a whippowill and a dog crying about somebody that was going to die; and the wind was trying to whisper something to me and I couldn't make out what it was, and so it made the cold shivers run over me. Then away out in the woods I heard that kind of a sound that a ghost makes when it wants to tell about something that's on its mind and can't make itself understood, and so can't rest easy in its grave and has to go about that way every night grieving. I got so down-hearted and scared, I did wish I had some company. Pretty soon a spider went crawling up my shoulder, and I flipped it off and it lit in the candle; and before I could budge it was all shriveled up. I didn't need anybody to tell me that that was an awful bad sign and would fetch me some bad luck, so I was scared and most shook the clothes off of me. I got up and turned around in my tracks three times and crossed my breast every time; and then I tied up a little lock of my hair with a thread to keep witches away. But I hadn't no confidence. You do that when you've lost a horse-shoe that you've found, instead of nailing it up over the door, but I hadn't ever heard anybody say it was any way to keep off bad luck when you'd killed a spider.

I set down again, a shaking all over, and got out my pipe for a smoke; for the house was all as still as death, now, and so the widow wouldn't know. Well, after a long time I heard the clock away off in the town go boom—boom—boom—twelve licks; and all still again—stiller than ever. Pretty soon I heard a twig snap, down in the dark amongst the trees—something was a stirring. I set still and listened. Directly I could just barely hear a *"me-yow! me-yow!"* down there. That was good! Says I, *"me-yow! me-yow!"* as soft as I could, and then I put out the light and scrambled out of the window onto the shed. Then I slipped down to the ground and crawled in amongst the trees, and sure enough there was Tom Sawyer waiting for me.

Chapter 4

Well, three or four months run along, and it was well into the winter, now. I had been to school most all the time, and could spell, and read, and write just a little, and could say the multiplication table up to six times seven is thirty-five, and I don't reckon I could ever get any further than that if I was to live forever. I don't take no stock in mathematics, anyway.

At first I hated the school, but by-and-by I got so I could stand it. Whenever I got uncommon tired I played hookey, and the hiding I got next day done me good and cheered me up. So the longer I went to school the easier it got to be. I was getting sort of used to the widow's ways, too, and they warn't so raspy on me. Living in a house, and sleeping in a bed, pulled on me pretty tight, mostly, but before the cold weather I used to slide out and sleep in the woods, sometimes, and so that was a rest to me. I liked the old ways best, but I was getting so I liked the new ones, too, a little bit. The widow said I was coming along slow but sure, and doing very satisfactory. She said she warn't ashamed of me.

One morning I happened to turn over the salt-cellar at breakfast. I reached for some of it as quick as I could, to throw over my left shoulder and keep off the bad luck, but Miss Watson was in ahead of me, and crossed me off. She says, "Take your hands away, Huckleberry, what a mess you are always making." The widow put in a good word for me, but that warn't going to keep off the bad luck, I knowed that well enough. I started out, after breakfast, feeling worried and shaky, and wondering where it was going to fall on me, and what it was going to be. There is ways to keep off some kinds of bad luck, but this wasn't one of them kind; so I never tried to do anything, but just poked along low-spirited and on the watch-out.

I went down the front garden and clumb over the stile, where you go through the high board fence. There was an inch of new snow on the ground, and I seen somebody's tracks. They had come up from the quarry and stood around the stile a while, and then went on around the garden fence. It was funny they hadn't come in, after standing around so. I couldn't make it out. It was very curious, somehow. I was going to follow around, but I stooped down to look at the tracks first. I didn't notice anything at first, but next I did. There was a cross in the left boot-heel made with big nails, to keep off the devil.

I was up in a second and shinning down the hill. I looked over my shoulder every now and then, but I didn't see nobody. I was at Judge Thatcher's as quick as I could get there. He said:

"Why, my boy, you are all out of breath. Did you come for your interest?"

"No, sir," I says; "is there some for me?"

"Oh, yes, a half-yearly is in, last night. Over a hundred and fifty dollars. Quite a fortune for you. You better let me invest it along with your six thousand, because if you take it you'll spend it."

"No sir," I says, "I don't want to spend it. I don't want it at all—nor the six thousand, nuther. I want you to take it; I want to give it to you—the six thousand and all."

He looked surprised. He couldn't seem to make it out. He says:

"Why, what can you mean, my boy?"

I says, "Don't you ask me no questions about it, please. You'll take it—won't you?"

He says:

"Well, I'm puzzled. Is something the matter?"

"Please take it," says I, "and don't ask me nothing—then I won't have to tell no lies."

He studied a while, and then he says:

"Oho-o! I think I see. You want to *sell* all your property to me—not give it. That's the correct idea."

Then he wrote something on a paper and read it over, and says:

"There—you see it says 'for a consideration.' That means I have bought it of you and paid you for it. Here's a dollar for you. Now, you sign it."

So I signed it, and left.

Miss Watson's nigger, Jim, had a hair-ball as big as your fist, which had been took out of the fourth stomach of an ox, and he used to do magic with it. He said there was a spirit inside of it, and it knowed everything. So I went to him that night and told him pap was here again, for I found his tracks in the snow. What I wanted to know, was, what he was going to do, and was he going to stay? Jim got out his hair-ball, and said something over it, and then he held it up and dropped it on the floor. It fell pretty solid, and only rolled about an inch. Jim tried it again, and then another time, and it acted just the same. Jim got down on his knees and put his ear against it and listened. But it warn't no use; he said it wouldn't talk. He said sometimes it wouldn't talk without money. I told him I had an old slick counterfeit quarter that warn't no good because the brass showed through the silver a little, and it wouldn't pass nohow, even if the brass didn't show, because it was so slick it felt greasy, and so that would tell on it every time. (I reckoned I wouldn't say nothing about the dollar I got from the judge.) I said it was pretty bad money, but maybe the hair-ball would take it, because maybe it wouldn't know the difference. Jim smelt it, and bit it, and rubbed it, and said he would manage so the hair-ball would think it was good. He said he would split open a raw Irish potato and stick the quarter in between and keep it there all night, and next morning you couldn't see no brass, and it wouldn't feel greasy no more, and so anybody in town would take it in a minute, let alone a hair-ball. Well, I knowed a potato would do that, before, but I had forgot it.

Jim put the quarter under the hair-ball and got down and listened again. This time he said the hair-ball was all right. He said it would tell my whole fortune if I wanted it to. I says, go on. So the hair-ball talked to Jim, and Jim told it to me. He says:

"Yo' ole father doan' know, yit, what he's a-gwyne to do. Sometimes he spec he'll go 'way, en den agin he spec he'll stay. De bes' way is to res' easy en let de ole man take his own way. Dey's two angels hoverin' roun' 'bout him. One uv 'em is white en shiny, en 'tother one is black. De white one gits him to go right a little while, den de black one sail in en bust it all up. A body can't tell, yit, which one gwyne to fetch him at de las'. But you is all right. You gwyne to have considable trouble in yo' life, en considable joy. Sometimes you gwyne to git hurt, en sometimes you gwyne to git sick; but every time you's gwyne to git well agin. Dey's two gals flyin' 'bout you in yo' life. One uv 'em's light en 'tother one is dark. One is rich en 'tother is po'. You's gwyne to marry de po' one fust en de rich one by-en-by. You wants to keep 'way fum de water as much as you kin, en don't run no resk, 'kase it's down in de bills dat you's gwyne to git hung."

When I lit my candle and went up to my room that night, there set pap—his own self!

Chapter 5

I had shut the door to. Then I turned around, and there he was. I used to be scared of him all the time, he tanned me so much. I reckoned I was scared now, too; but in a minute I see I was mistaken. That is, after the first jolt, as you may say, when my breath sort of hitched—he being so unexpected; but right away after, I see I warn't scared of him worth bothering about.

He was most fifty, and he looked it. His hair was long and tangled and greasy, and hung down, and you could see his eyes shining through like he was behind vines. It was all black, no gray; so was his long, mixed-up whiskers. There warn't no color in his face, where his face showed; it was white; not like another man's white, but a white to make a body sick, a white to make a body's flesh crawl—a tree-toad white, a fish-belly white. As for his clothes—just rags, that was all. He had one ankle resting on 'tother knee; the boot on that foot was busted, and two of his toes stuck through, and he worked them now and then. His hat was laying on the floor; an old black slouch with the top caved in, like a lid.

I stood a-looking at him; he set there a-looking at me, with his chair tilted back a little. I set the candle down. I noticed the window was up; so he had clumb in by the shed. He kept a-looking me all over. By-and-by he says:

"Starchy clothes—very. You think you're a good deal of a big-bug, *don't* you?"

"Maybe I am, maybe I ain't," I says.

"Don't you give me none o' your lip," says he. "You've put on considerable many frills since I been away. I'll take you down a peg before I get done with you. You're educated, too, they say; can read and write. You think you're better'n your father, now, don't you, because he can't? *I'll* take it out of you. Who told you you might meddle with such hifalut'n foolishness, hey?—who told you you could?"

"The widow. She told me."

"The widow, hey?—and who told the widow she could put in her shovel about a thing that ain't none of her business?"

"Nobody never told her."

"Well, I'll learn her how to meddle. And looky here—you drop that school, you hear? I'll learn people to bring up a boy to put on airs over his own father and let on to be better'n what *he* is. You lemme catch you fooling around that school again, you hear? Your mother couldn't read, and she couldn't write, nuther, before she died. None of the family couldn't; before *they* died. *I* can't; and here you're a-swelling yourself up like this. I ain't the man to stand it—you hear? Say—lemme hear you read."

I took up a book and begun something about General Washington and the wars. When I'd read about a half a minute, he fetched the book a whack with his hand and knocked it across the house. He says:

"It's so. You can do it. I had my doubts when you told me. Now looky here; you stop that putting on frills. I won't have it. I'll lay for you, my smarty; and if I catch you about that school I'll tan you good. First you know you'll get religion, too. I never see such a son."

He took up a little blue and yaller picture of some cows and a boy, and says:

"What's this?"

"It's something they give me for learning my lessons good."

He tore it up, and says—

"I'll give you something better—I'll give you a cowhide."

He set there a-mumbling and a-growling a minute, and then he says—

"*Ain't* you a sweet-scented dandy, though? A bed; and bedclothes; and a look'n-glass; and a piece of carpet on the floor—and your own father got to sleep with the hogs in the tanyard. I never see such a son. I bet I'll take some o' these frills out o' you before I'm done with you. Why there ain't no end to your airs—they say you're rich. Hey?—how's that?"

"They lie—that's how."

"Looky here—mind how you talk to me; I'm a-standing about all I can stand, now—so don't gimme no sass. I've been in town two days, and I hain't heard nothing but about you bein' rich. I heard about it away down the river, too. That's why I come. You git me that money tomorrow—I want it."

"I hain't got no money."

"It's a lie. Judge Thatcher's got it. You git it. I want it."

"I hain't got no money, I tell you. You ask Judge Thatcher; he'll tell you the same."

"All right. I'll ask him; and I'll make him pungle, too, or I'll know the reason why. Say—how much you got in your pocket? I want it."

"I hain't got only a dollar, and I want that to—"

"It don't make no difference what you want it for—you just shell it out."

He took it and bit it to see if it was good, and then he said he was going down town to get some whisky; said he hadn't had a drink all day. When he had got out on the shed, he put his head in again, and cussed me for putting on frills and trying to be better than him; and when I reckoned he was gone, he come back and put his head in again, and told me to mind about that school, because he was going to lay for me and lick me if I didn't drop that.

Next day he was drunk, and he went to Judge Thatcher's and bullyragged him and tried to make him give up the money; but he couldn't, and then he swore he'd make the law force him.

The judge and the widow went to law to get the court to take me away from him and let one of them be my guardian; but it was a new judge that had just come, and he didn't know the old man; so he said courts mustn't interfere and separate families if they could help it; said he'd druther not take a child away from its father. So Judge Thatcher and the widow had to quit on the business.

That pleased the old man till he couldn't rest. He said he'd cowhide me till I was black and blue if I didn't raise some money for him. I borrowed three dollars from Judge Thatcher, and pap took it and got drunk and went a-blowing around and cussing and whooping and carrying on; and he kept it up all over town, with a tin pan, till most midnight; then they jailed him, and next day they had him before court, and jailed him again for a week. But he said *he* was satisfied; said he was boss of his son, and he'd make it warm for *him*.

When he got out the new judge said he was going to make a man of him. So he took him to his own house, and dressed him up clean and nice, and had him to breakfast and dinner and supper with the family, and was just old pie to him, so to speak. And after supper he talked to him about temperance and such things till the old man cried, and said he'd been a fool, and fooled away his life; but now he was going to turn over a new leaf and be a man nobody wouldn't be ashamed of, and he hoped the judge would help him and not look down on him. The judge said he could hug him for them words; so *he* cried, and his wife she cried again; pap said he'd been a man that had always been misunderstood before, and the judge said he believed it. The old man said that what a man wanted that was down, was sympathy; and the judge said it was so; so they cried again. And when it was bedtime, the old man rose up and held out his hand, and says:

"Look at it gentlemen, and ladies all; take ahold of it; shake it. There's a hand that was the hand of a hog; but it ain't so no more; it's the hand of a man that's started in on a new life, and 'll die before he'll go back. You mark them words—don't forget I said them. It's a clean hand now; shake it—don't be afeard."

So they shook it, one after the other, all around, and cried. The judge's wife she kissed it. Then the old man he signed a pledge—made his mark. The judge said it was the holiest time on record, or something like that. Then they tucked the old man into a beautiful room, which was the spare room, and in the night sometime he got powerful thirsty and clumb out onto the porch-roof and slid down a stanchion and traded his new coat for a jug of forty-rod, and clumb back again and had a good old time; and towards daylight he crawled out again, drunk as a fiddler, and rolled off the porch and broke his left arm in two places and was most froze to death when somebody found him after sun-up. And when they come to look at that spare room, they had to take soundings before they could navigate it.

The judge he felt kind of sore. He said he reckoned a body could reform the old man with a shot-gun, maybe, but he didn't know no other way.

Chapter 6

Well, pretty soon the old man was up and around again, and then he went for Judge Thatcher in the courts to make him give up that money, and he went for me, too, for not stopping school. He catched me a couple of times and thrashed me, but I went to school just the same, and dodged him or out-run him most of the time. I didn't want to go to school much, before, but I reckoned I'd go now to spite pap. That law trial was a slow business; appeared like they warn't ever going to get started on it; so every now and then I'd borrow two or three dollars off of the judge for him, to keep from getting a cowhiding. Every time he got money he got drunk; and every time he got drunk he raised Cain around town; and every time he raised Cain he got jailed. He was just suited—this kind of thing was right in his line.

He got to hanging around the widow's too much, and so she told him at last, that if he didn't quit using around there she would make trouble for him. Well, *wasn't* he mad? He said he would show who was Huck Finn's boss. So he watched out for me one day in the spring, and catched me, and took me up the river about three mile, in a skiff, and crossed over to the Illinois shore where it was woody and there warn't no houses but an old log hut in a place where the timber was so thick you couldn't find it if you didn't know where it was.

He kept me with him all the time, and I never got a chance to run off. We lived in that old cabin, and he always locked the door and put the key under his head, nights. He had a gun which he had stole, I reckon, and we fished and hunted, and that was what we lived on. Every little while he locked me in and went down to the store, three miles, to the ferry, and traded fish and game for whisky and fetched it home and got drunk and had a good time, and licked me. The widow she found out where I was by-and-by, and she sent a man over to try to get hold of me, but pap drove him off with the gun, and it warn't long after that till I was used to being where I was, and liked it, all but the cowhide part.

It was kind of lazy and jolly, laying off comfortable all day, smoking and fishing, and no books nor study. Two months or more run along, and my clothes got to be all rags and dirt, and I didn't see how I'd ever got to like it so well at the widow's, where you had to wash, and eat on a plate, and comb up, and go to bed and get up regular, and be forever bothering over a book and have old Miss Watson pecking at you all the time. I didn't want to go back no more. I had stopped cussing, because the widow didn't like it; but now I took to it again because pap hadn't no objections. It was pretty good times up in the woods there, take it all around.

But by-and-by pap got too handy with his hick'ry, and I couldn't stand it. I was all over welts. He got to going away so much, too, and locking me in. Once he locked me in and was gone three days. It was dreadful lonesome. I judged he had got drowned and I wasn't ever going to get out any more. I was scared. I made up my mind I would fix up some way to leave there. I had tried to get out of that cabin many a time, but I couldn't find no way. There warn't a window to it big enough for a dog to get through. I couldn't get up the chimbly, it was too narrow. The door was thick, solid oak slabs. Pap was pretty careful not to leave a knife or anything in the cabin when he was away; I reckon I had hunted the place over as much as a hundred times; well, I was 'most all the time at it, because it was about the only way to put in the time. But this time I found something at last; I found an old rusty wood-saw without any handle; it was laid in between a rafter and the clapboards of the roof. I greased it up and went to work. There was an old horse-blanket nailed against the logs at the far end of the cabin behind the table, to keep the wind from blowing through the chinks and putting the candle out. I got under the table and raised the blanket and went to work to saw a section of the big bottom log out, big enough to let me through. Well, it was a good long job, but I was getting towards the end of it when I heard pap's gun in the woods. I got rid of the signs of my work, and dropped the blanket and hid my saw, and pretty soon pap come in.

Pap warn't in a good humor—so he was his natural self. He said he was down to town, and everything was going wrong. His lawyer said he reckoned he would win his lawsuit and get the money, if they ever got started on the trial; but then there was ways to put it off a long time, and Judge Thatcher knowed how to do it. And he said people allowed there'd be another trial to get me away from him and give me to the widow for my guardian, and they guessed it would win, this time. This shook me up considerable, because I didn't want to go back to the widow's any more and be so cramped up and sivilized, as they called it. Then the old man got to cussing, and cussed everything and everybody he could think of, and then cussed them all over again to make sure he hadn't skipped any, and after that he polished off with a kind of a general cuss all round, including a considerable parcel of people which he didn't know the names of, and so called them what's-his-name, when he got to them, and went right along with his cussing.

He said he would like to see the widow get me. He said he would watch out, and if they tried to come any such game on him he knowed of a place six or seven mile off, to stow me in, where they might hunt till they dropped and they couldn't find me. That made me pretty uneasy again, but only for a minute; I reckoned I wouldn't stay on hand till he got that chance.

The old man made me go to the skiff and fetch the things he had got. There was a fifty-pound sack of corn meal, and a side of bacon, ammunition, and a four-gallon jug of whisky, and an old book and two newspapers for wadding, besides some tow. I toted up a load, and went back and set down on the bow of the skiff to rest. I thought it all over, and I reckoned I would walk off with the gun and some lines, and take to the woods when I run away. I guessed I wouldn't stay in one place, but just tramp right across the country, mostly night times, and hunt and fish to keep alive, and so get so far away that the old man nor the widow couldn't ever find me any more. I judged I would saw out and leave that night if pap got drunk enough, and I reckoned he would. I got so full of it I didn't notice how long I was staying, till the old man hollered and asked me whether I was asleep or drownded.

I got the things all up to the cabin, and then it was about dark. While I was cooking supper the old man took a swig or two and got sort of warmed up, and went to ripping again. He had been drunk over in town, and laid in the gutter all night, and he was a sight to look at. A body would a thought he was Adam, he was just all mud. Whenever his liquor begun to work, he most always went for the govment. This time he says:

"Call this a govment! why, just look at it and see what it's like. Here's the law a-standing ready to take a man's son away from him—a man's own son, which he has had all the trouble and all the anxiety and all the expense of raising. Yes, just as that man has got that son raised at last, and ready to go to work and begin to do suthin' for *him* and give him a rest, the law up and goes for him. And they call *that* govment! That ain't all, nuther. The law backs that old Judge Thatcher up and helps him to keep me out o' my property. Here's what the law does. The law takes a man worth six thousand dollars and upards, and jams him into an old trap of a cabin like this, and lets him go round in clothes that ain't fitten for a hog. They call that govment! A man can't get his rights in a govment like this. Sometimes I've a mighty notion to just leave the country for good and all. Yes, and I *told* 'em so; I told old Thatcher so to his face. Lots of 'em heard me, and can tell what I said. Says I, for two cents I'd leave the blamed country and never come anear it agin. Them's the very words. I says, look at my hat—if you call it a hat—but the lid raises up and the rest of it goes down till it's below my chin, and then it ain't rightly a hat at all, but more like my head was shoved up through a jint o' stove-pipe. Look at it, says I—such a hat for me to wear—one of the wealthiest men in this town, if I could git my rights.

"Oh, yes, this is a wonderful govment, wonderful. Why, looky here. There was a free nigger there, from Ohio; a mulatter, most as white as a white man. He had the whitest shirt on you ever see, too, and the shiniest hat; and there ain't a man in that town that's got as fine clothes as what he had; and he had a gold watch and chain, and a silver-headed cane—the awfulest old gray-headed nabob in the State. And what do you think? They said he was a p'fessor in a college, and could talk all kinds of languages, and knowed everything. And that ain't the wust. They said he could *vote,* when he was at home. Well, that let me out. Thinks I, what is the country a-coming to? It was 'lection day, and I was just about to go and vote, myself, if I warn't too drunk to get there; but when they told me there was a State in this country where they'd let that nigger vote, I drawed out. I says I'll never vote agin. Them's the very words I said; they all heard me; and the country may rot for all me—I'll never vote agin as long as I live. And to see the cool way of that nigger—why, he wouldn't a give me the road if I hadn't shoved him out o' the way. I says to the people, why ain't this nigger put up at auction and sold?—that's what I want to know. And what do you reckon they said? Why, they said he couldn't be sold till he'd been in the State six months, and he hadn't been there that long yet. There, now—that's a specimen. They call that a govment that can't sell a free nigger till he's been in the State six months. Here's a govment that calls itself a govment, and lets on to be a govment, and thinks it is a govment, and yet's got to set stock-still for six whole months before it can take a-hold of a prowling, thieving, infernal, white-shirted free nigger, and—"

Pap was agoing on so, he never noticed where his old limber legs was taking him to, so he went head over heels over the tub of salt pork, and barked both shins, and the rest of his speech was all the hottest kind of language—mostly hove at the nigger and the govment, though he give the tub some, too, all along, here and there. He hopped around the cabin considerable, first on one leg and then on the other, holding first one shin and then the other one, and at last he let out with his left foot all of a sudden and fetched the tub a rattling kick. But it warn't good judgment, because that was the boot that had a couple of his toes leaking out of the front end of it; so now he raised a howl that fairly made a body's hair raise, and down he went in the dirt, and rolled there, and held his toes; and the cussing he done then laid over anything he had ever done previous. He said so his own self, afterwards. He had heard old Sowberry Hagan in his best days, and he said it laid over him, too; but I reckon that was sort of piling it on, maybe.

After supper pap took the jug, and said he had enough whisky there for two drunks and one delirium tremens. That was always his word. I judged he would be blind drunk in about an hour, and then I would steal the key, or saw myself out, one or 'tother. He drank and drank, and tumbled down on his blankets by-and-by; but luck didn't run my way. He didn't go sound asleep, but was uneasy. He groaned, and moaned, and thrashed around this way and that, for a long time. At last I got so sleepy I couldn't keep my eyes open, all I could do, and so before I knowed what I was about I was sound asleep, and the candle burning.

I don't know how long I was asleep, but all of a sudden there was an awful scream and I was up. There was pap, looking wild and skipping around every which way and yelling about snakes. He said they was crawling up his legs; and then he would give a jump and scream, and say one had bit him on the cheek—but I couldn't see no snakes. He started and run round and round the cabin, hollering "take him off! take him off! he's biting me on the neck!" I never see a man look so wild in the eyes. Pretty soon he was all fagged out, and fell down panting; then he rolled over and over, wonderful fast, kicking things every which way, and striking and grabbing at the air with his hands, and screaming, and saying there was devils ahold of him. He wore out, by-and-by, and laid still a while, moaning. Then he laid stiller, and didn't make a sound. I could hear the owls and the wolves, away off in the woods, and it seemed terrible still. He was laying over by the corner. By-and-by he raised up, part way, and listened, with his head to one side. He says, very low:

"Tramp—tramp—tramp; that's the dead; tramp—tramp—tramp; they're coming after me; but I won't go. Oh, they're here! don't touch me—don't! hands off—they're cold; let go—Oh, let a poor devil alone!"

Then he went down on all fours and crawled off begging them to let him alone, and he rolled himself up in his blanket and wallowed in under the old pine table, still a-begging; and then he went to crying. I could hear him through the blanket.

By-and-by he rolled out and jumped up on his feet looking wild, and he see me and went for me. He chased me round and round the place, with a clasp-knife, calling me the Angel of Death and saying he would kill me and then I couldn't come for him no more. I begged, and told him I was only Huck; but he laughed *such* a screechy laugh, and roared and cussed, and kept on chasing me up. Once when I turned short and dodged under his arm he made a grab and got me by the jacket between my shoulders, and I thought I was gone; but I slid out of the jacket quick as lightning, and saved myself. Pretty soon he was all tired out, and dropped down with his back against the door, and said he would rest a minute and then kill me. He put his knife under him, and said he would sleep and get strong, and then he would see who was who.

So he dozed off, pretty soon. By-and-by I got the old split-bottom chair and clumb up, as easy as I could, not to make any noise, and got down the gun. I slipped the ramrod down it to make sure it was loaded, then I laid it across the turnip barrel, pointing towards pap, and set down behind it to wait for him to stir. And how slow and still the time did drag along.

Chapter 7

"Git up! what you 'bout!"

I opened my eyes and looked around, trying to make out where I was. It was after sun-up, and I had been sound asleep. Pap was standing over me looking sour—and sick, too. He says—

"What you doin' with this gun?"

I judged he didn't know nothing about what he had been doing, so I says:

"Somebody tried to get in, so I was laying for him."

"Why didn't you roust me out?"

"Well I tried to, but I couldn't; I couldn't budge you."

"Well, all right. Don't stand there palavering all day, but out with you and see if there's a fish on the lines for breakfast. I'll be along in a minute."

He unlocked the door and I cleared out, up the riverbank. I noticed some pieces of limbs and such things floating down, and a sprinkling of bark; so I knowed the river had begun to rise. I reckoned I would have great times, now, if I was over at the town. The June rise used to be always luck for me; because as soon as that rise begins, here comes cordwood floating down, and pieces of log rafts—sometimes a dozen logs together; so all you have to do is to catch them and sell them to the woodyards and the sawmill.

I went along up the bank with one eye out for pap and 'tother one out for what the rise might fetch along. Well, all at once here comes a canoe; just a beauty, too, about thirteen or fourteen foot long, riding high like a duck. I shot headfirst off of the bank, like a frog, clothes and all on, and struck out for the canoe. I just expected there'd be somebody laying down in it, because people often done that to fool folks, and when a chap had pulled a skiff out most to it they'd raise up and laugh at him. But it warn't so this time. It was a drift-canoe, sure enough, and I clumb in and paddled her ashore. Thinks I, the old man will be glad when he sees this—she's worth ten dollars. But when I got to shore pap wasn't in sight yet, and as I was running her into a little creek like a gully, all hung over with vines and willows, I struck another idea: I judged I'd hide her good, and then, 'stead of taking to the woods when I run off, I'd go down the river about fifty mile and camp in one place for good, and not have such a rough time tramping on foot.

It was pretty close to the shanty, and I thought I heard the old man coming all the time; but I got her hid; and then I out and looked around a bunch of willows, and there was the old man down the path a piece just drawing a bead on a bird with his gun. So he hadn't seen anything.

When he got along, I was hard at it taking up a "trot" line. He abused me a little for being so slow but I told him, I fell in the river and that was what made me so long. I knowed he would see I was wet, and then he would be asking questions. We got five cat-fish off of the lines and went home.

While we laid off, after breakfast, to sleep up, both of us being about wore out, I got to thinking that if I could fix up some way to keep pap and the widow from trying to follow me, it would be a certainer thing than trusting to luck to get far enough off before they missed me; you see, all kinds of things might happen. Well, I didn't see no way for a while, but by-and-by pap raised up a minute, to drink another barrel of water, and he says:

"Another time a man comes a-prowling round here, you roust me out, you hear? That man warn't here for no good. I'd a shot him. Next time, you roust me out, you hear?"

Then he dropped down and went to sleep again—but what he had been saying give me the very idea I wanted. I says to myself, I can fix it now so nobody won't think of following me.

About twelve o'clock we turned out and went along up the bank. The river was coming up pretty fast, and lots of drift-wood going by on the rise. By-and-by, along comes part of a log raft—nine logs fast together. We went out with the skiff and towed it ashore. Then we had dinner. Anybody but pap would a waited and seen the day through, so as to catch more stuff; but that warn't pap's style. Nine logs was enough for one time; he must shove right over to town and sell. So he locked me in and took the skiff and started off towing the raft about half-past three. I judged he wouldn't come back that night. I waited till I reckoned he had got a good start, then I out with my saw and went to work on that log again. Before he was 'tother side of the river I was out of the hole; him and his raft was just a speck on the water away off yonder.

I took the sack of corn meal and took it to where the canoe was hid, and shoved the vines and branches apart and put it in; then I done the same with the side of bacon; then the whisky jug. I took all the coffee and sugar there was, and all the ammunition; I took the wadding; I took the bucket and gourd, I took a dipper and a tin cup, and my old saw and two blankets, and the skillet and the coffee-pot. I took fish-lines and matches and other things—everything that was worth a cent. I cleaned out the place. I wanted an axe, but there wasn't any, only the one out at the woodpile, and I knowed why I was going to leave that. I fetched out the gun, and now I was done.

I had wore the ground a good deal, crawling out of the hole and dragging out so many things. So I fixed that as good as I could from the outside by scattering dust on the place, which covered up the smoothness and the sawdust. Then I fixed the piece of log back into its place, and put two rocks under it and one against it to hold it there—for it was bent up at that place, and didn't quite touch ground. If you stood four or five foot away and didn't know it was sawed, you wouldn't ever notice it; and besides, this was the back of the cabin and it warn't likely anybody would go fooling around there.

It was all grass clear to the canoe; so I hadn't left a track. I followed around to see. I stood on the bank and looked out over the river. All safe. So I took the gun and went up a piece into the woods, and was hunting around for some birds, when I see a wild pig; hogs soon went wild in them bottoms after they had got away from the prairie farms. I shot this fellow and took him into camp.

I took the axe and smashed in the door—I beat it and hacked it considerable, a-doing it. I fetched the pig in and took him back nearly to the table and hacked into his throat with the ax, and laid him down on the ground to bleed—I say ground because it *was* ground—hard packed, and no boards. Well, next I took an old sack and put a lot of big rocks in it,—all I could drag—and I started it from the pig and dragged it to the door and through the woods down to the river and dumped it in, and down it sunk, out of sight. You could easy see that something had been dragged over the ground. I did wish Tom Sawyer was there, I knowed he would take an interest in this kind of business, and throw in the fancy touches. Nobody could spread himself like Tom Sawyer in such a thing as that.

Well, last I pulled out some of my hair, and blooded the ax good, and stuck it on the back side, and slung the axe in the corner. Then I took up the pig and held him to my breast with my jacket (so he couldn't drip) till I got a good piece below the house and then dumped him into the river. Now I thought of something else. So I went and got the bag of meal and my old saw out of the canoe and fetched them to the house. I took the bag to where it used to stand, and ripped a hole in the bottom of it with the saw, for there warn't no knives and forks on the place—pap done everything with his clasp-knife, about the cooking. Then I carried the sack about a hundred yards across the grass and through the willows east of the house, to a shallow lake that was five mile wide and full of rushes—and ducks too, you might say, in the season. There was a slough or a creek leading out of it on the other side, that went miles away, I don't know where, but it didn't go to the river. The meal sifted out and made a little track all the way to the lake. I dropped pap's whetstone there too, so as to look like it had been done by accident. Then I tied up the rip in the meal sack with a string, so it wouldn't leak no more, and took it and my saw to the canoe again.

It was about dark, now; so I dropped the canoe down the river under some willows that hung over the bank, and waited for the moon to rise. I made fast to a willow; then I took a bite to eat, and by-and-by laid down in the canoe to smoke a pipe and lay out a plan. I says to myself, they'll follow the track of that sackful of rocks to the shore and then drag the river for me. And they'll follow that meal track to the lake and go browsing down the creek that leads out of it to find the robbers that killed me and took the things. They won't ever hunt the river for anything but my dead carcass. They'll soon get tired of that, and won't bother no more about me. All right; I can stop anywhere I want to. Jackson's Island is good enough for me; I know that island pretty well, and nobody ever comes there. And then I can paddle over to town, nights, and slink around and pick up things I want. Jackson's Island's the place.

I was pretty tired, and the first thing I knowed, I was asleep. When I woke up I didn't know where I was, for a minute. I set up and looked around, a little scared. Then I remembered. The river looked miles and miles across. The moon was so bright I could a counted the drift logs that went a slipping along, black and still, hundreds of yards out from shore. Everything was dead quiet, and it looked late, and *smelt* late. You know what I mean—I don't know the words to put it in.

I took a good gap and a stretch, and was just going to unhitch and start, when I heard a sound away over the water. I listened. Pretty soon I made it out. It was that dull kind of a regular sound that comes from oars working in rowlocks when it's a still night. I peeped out through the willow branches, and there it was—a skiff, away across the water. I couldn't tell how many was in it. It kept a-coming, and when it was abreast of me I see there warn't but one man in it. Thinks I, maybe it's pap, though I warn't expecting him. He dropped below me, with the current, and by-and-by he came a-swinging up shore in the easy water, and he went by so close I could a reached out the gun and touched him. Well, it *was* pap, sure enough—and sober, too, by the way he laid to his oars.

I didn't lose no time. The next minute I was a-spinning down stream soft but quick in the shade of the bank. I made two mile and a half, and then struck out a quarter of a mile or more towards the middle of the river, because pretty soon I would be passing the ferry landing and people might see me and hail me. I got out amongst the drift-wood and then laid down in the bottom of the canoe and let her float. I laid there and had a good rest and a smoke out of my pipe, looking away into the sky, not a cloud in it. The sky looks ever so deep when you lay down on your back in the moonshine; I never knowed it before. And how far a body can hear on the water such nights! I heard people talking at the ferry landing. I heard what they said, too, every word of it. One man said it was getting towards the long days and the short nights, now. 'Tother one said *this* warn't one of the short ones, he reckoned—and then they laughed, and he said it over again and they laughed again; then they waked up another fellow and told him, and laughed, but he didn't laugh; he ripped out something brisk and said let him alone. The first fellow said he 'lowed to tell it to his old woman—she would think it was pretty good; but he said that warn't nothing to some things he had said in his time. I heard one man say it was nearly three o'clock, and he hoped daylight wouldn't wait more than about a week longer. After that, the talk got further and further away, and I couldn't make out the words any more, but I could hear the mumble; and now and then a laugh, too, but it seemed a long ways off.

I was away below the ferry now. I rose up and there was Jackson's Island, about two mile and a half down stream, heavy-timbered and standing up out of the middle of the river, big and dark and solid, like a steamboat without any lights. There warn't any signs of the bar at the head—it was all under water now.

It didn't take me long to get there. I shot past the head at a ripping rate, the current was so swift, and then I got into the dead water and landed on the side towards the Illinois shore. I run the canoe into a deep dent in the bank that I knowed about; I had to part the willow branches to get in; and when I made fast nobody could a seen the canoe from the outside.

I went up and set down on a log at the head of the island and looked out on the big river and the black drift-wood, and away over to the town, three mile away, where there was three or four lights twinkling. A monstrous big lumber raft was about a mile up stream, coming along down, with a lantern in the middle of it. I watched it come creeping down, and when it was most abreast of where I stood I heard a man say, "Stern oars, there! heave her head to stabboard!" I heard that just as plain as if the man was by my side.

There was a little gray in the sky now; so I stepped into the woods and laid down for a nap before breakfast.

[In the intervening chapters, on the island Huckleberry finds Jim, who is running away after hearing he was going to be sold in New Orleans. When Jim is tracked down to the island, he and Huck set out on the Mississippi River.]

Chapter 12

It must a been close onto one o'clock when we got below the island at last, and the raft did seem to go mighty slow. If a boat was to come along, we was going to take to the canoe and break for the Illinois shore; and it was well a boat didn't come, for we hadn't ever thought to put the gun into the canoe, or a fishing-line or anything to eat. We was in ruther too much of a sweat to think of so many things. It warn't good judgment to put *everything* on the raft.

If the men went to the island, I just expect they found the camp fire I built, and watched it all night for Jim to come. Anyways, they stayed away from us, and if my building the fire never fooled them it warn't no fault of mine. I played it as low-down on them as I could.

When the first streak of day began to show, we tied up to a tow-head in a big bend on the Illinois side, and hacked off cottonwood branches with the hatchet and covered up the raft with them so she looked like there had been a cave-in in the bank there. A tow-head is a sand-bar that has cotton-woods on it as thick as harrow-teeth.

We had mountains on the Missouri shore and heavy timber on the Illinois side, and the channel was down the Missouri shore at that place, so we warn't afraid of anybody running across us. We laid there all day and watched the rafts and steamboats spin down the Missouri shore, and up-bound steamboats fight the big river in the middle. I told Jim all about the time I had jabbering with that woman; and Jim said she was a smart one, and if she was to start after us herself *she* wouldn't set down and watch a camp fire—no, sir, she'd fetch a dog. Well, then, I said, why couldn't she tell her husband to fetch a dog? Jim said he bet she did think of it by the time the men was ready to start, and he believed they must a gone up town to get a dog and so they lost all that time, or else we wouldn't be here on a tow-head sixteen or seventeen mile below the village—no, indeedy, we would be in that same old town again. So I said I didn't care what was the reason they didn't get us, as long as they didn't.

When it was beginning to come on dark, we poked our heads out of the cottonwood thicket and looked up, and down, and across; nothing in sight; so Jim took up some of the top planks of the raft and built a snug wigwam to get under in blazing weather and rainy, and to keep the things dry. Jim made a floor for the wigwam, and raised it a foot or more above the level of the raft, so now the blankets and all the traps was out of the reach of steamboat waves. Right in the middle of the wigwam we made a layer of dirt about five or six inches deep with a frame around it for to hold it to its place; this was to build a fire on in sloppy weather or chilly; the wigwam would keep it from being seen. We made an extra steering oar, too, because one of the others might get broke, on a snag or something. We fixed up a short forked stick to hang the old lantern on; because we must always light the lantern whenever we see a steamboat coming down stream, to keep from getting run over; but we wouldn't have to light it for up-stream boats unless we see we was in what they call a "crossing"; for the river was pretty high yet, very low banks being still a little under water; so up-bound boats didn't always run the channel, but hunted easy water.

This second night we run between seven and eight hours, with a current that was making over four mile an hour. We catched fish, and talked, and we took a swim now and then to keep off sleepiness. It was kind of solemn, drifting down the big still river, laying on our backs looking up at the stars, and we didn't ever feel like talking loud, and it warn't often that we laughed, only a little kind of a low chuckle. We had mighty good weather, as a general thing, and nothing ever happened to us at all, that night, nor the next, nor the next.

Every night we passed towns, some of them away up on black hillsides, nothing but just a shiny bed of lights, not a house could you see. The fifth night we passed St. Louis, and it was like the whole world lit up. In St. Petersburg they used to say there was twenty or thirty thousand people in St. Louis, but I never believed it till I see that wonderful spread of lights at two o'clock that still night. There warn't a sound there; everybody was asleep.

Every night, now, I used to slip ashore, towards ten o'clock, at some little village, and buy ten or fifteen cents' worth of meal or bacon or other stuff to eat; and sometimes I lifted a chicken that warn't roosting comfortable, and took him along. Pap always said, take a chicken when you get a chance, because if you don't want him yourself you can easy find somebody that does, and a good deed ain't ever forgot. I never see pap when he didn't want the chicken himself, but that is what he used to say, anyway.

Mornings, before daylight, I slipped into corn fields and borrowed a watermelon, or a mushmelon, or a punkin, or some new corn, or things of that kind. Pap always said it warn't no harm to borrow things, if you was meaning to pay them back, sometime; but the widow said it warn't anything but a soft name for stealing, and no decent body would do it. Jim said he reckoned the widow was partly right and pap was partly right; so the best way would be for us to pick out two or three things from the list and say we wouldn't borrow them anymore—then he reckoned it wouldn't be no harm to borrow the others. So we talked it over all one night, drifting along down the river, trying to make up our minds whether to drop the watermelons, or the cantelopes, or the mushmelons, or what. But towards daylight we got it all settled satisfactory, and concluded to drop crabapples and p'simmons. We warn't feeling just right, before that, but it was all comfortable now. I was glad the way it come out, too, because crabapples ain't ever good, and the p'simmons wouldn't be ripe for two or three months yet.

We shot a water-fowl now and then, that got up too early in the morning or didn't go to bed early enough in the evening. Take it all around, we lived pretty high.

The fifth night below St. Louis we had a big storm after midnight, with a power of thunder and lightning, and the rain poured down in a solid sheet. We stayed in the wigwam and let the raft take care of itself. When the lightning glared out we could see a big straight river ahead, and high rocky bluffs on both sides. By-and-by says I, "Hel-*lo*, Jim, looky yonder!" It was a steamboat that had killed herself on a rock. We was drifting straight down for her. The lightning showed her very distinct. She was leaning over, with part of her upper deck above water, and you could see every little chimbly-guy clean and clear, and a chair by the big bell, with an old slouch hat hanging on the back of it, when the flashes come.

Well, it being away in the night, and stormy, and all so mysterious-like, I felt just the way any other boy would a felt when I see that wreck laying there so mournful and lonesome in the middle of the river. I wanted to get aboard of her and slink around a little, and see what there was there. So I says:

"Le's land on her, Jim."

But Jim was dead against it, at first. He says:

"I doan' want to go fool'n 'long er no wrack. We's doin' blame' well, en we better let blame' well alone, as de good book says. Like as not dey's a watchman on dat wrack."

"Watchman your grandmother," I says; "there ain't nothing to watch but the texas and the pilot-house; and do you reckon anybody's going to resk his life for a texas and a pilot-house such a night as this, when it's likely to break up and wash off down the river any minute?" Jim couldn't say nothing to that, so he didn't try. "And besides," I says, "we might borrow something worth having, out of the captain's stateroom. Seegars, *I* bet you—and cost five cents apiece, solid cash. Steamboat captains is always rich, and get sixty dollars a month, and *they* don't care a cent what a thing costs, you know, long as they want it. Stick a candle in your pocket; I can't rest, Jim, till we give her a rummaging. Do you reckon Tom Sawyer would ever go by this thing? Not for pie, he wouldn't. He'd call it an adventure—that's what he'd call it; and he'd land on that wreck if it was his last act. And wouldn't he throw style into it?—wouldn't he spread himself, nor nothing? Why, you'd think it was Christopher C'lumbus discovering Kingdom-Come. I wish Tom Sawyer *was* here."

Jim he grumbled a little, but give in. He said we mustn't talk any more than we could help, and then talk mighty low. The lightning showed us the wreck again, just in time, and we fetched the stabboard derrick, and made fast there.

The deck was high out, here. We went sneaking down the slope of it to labboard, in the dark, towards the texas, feeling our way slow with our feet, and spreading our hands out to fend off the guys, for it was so dark we couldn't see no sign of them. Pretty soon we struck the forward end of the skylight, and clumb onto it; and the next step fetched us in front of the captain's door, which was open, and by Jimminy, away down through the texas-hall we see a light! and all in the same second we seem to hear low voices in yonder!

Jim whispered and said he was feeling powerful sick, and told me to come along. I says, all right; and was going to start for the raft; but just then I heard a voice wail out and say:

"Oh, please don't, boys; I swear I won't ever tell!"

Another voice said, pretty loud:

"It's a lie, Jim Turner. You've acted this way before. You always want more'n your share of the truck, and you've always got it, too, because you've swore 't if you didn't you'd tell. But this time you've said it jest one time too many. You're the meanest, treacherousest hound in this country."

By this time Jim was gone for the raft. I was just a-biling with curiosity; and I says to myself, Tom Sawyer wouldn't back out now, and so I won't either; I'm agoing to see what's going on here. So I dropped on my hands and knees, in the little passage, and crept aft in the dark, till there warn't but about one stateroom betwixt me and the cross-hall of the texas. Then, in there I see a man stretched on the floor and tied hand and foot, and two men standing over him, and one of them had a dim lantern in his hand, and the other one had a pistol. This one kept pointing the pistol at the man's head on the floor and saying—

"I'd *like* to! And I orter, too, a mean skunk!"

The man on the floor would shrivel up, and say: "Oh, please don't, Bill—I hain't ever goin' to tell."

And every time he said that the man with the lantern would laugh, and say:

"'Deed you *ain't!* You never said no truer thing 'n that, you bet you." And once he said: "Hear him beg! and yit if we hadn't got the best of him and tied him, he'd a killed us both. And what *for?* Jist for noth'n. Jist because we stood on our *rights*—that's what for. But I lay you ain't agoin' to threaten nobody any more, Jim Turner. Put *up* that pistol, Bill."

Bill says:

"I don't want to, Jake Packard. I'm for killin' him—and didn't he kill old Hatfield jist the same way—and don't he deserve it?"

"But I don't *want* him killed, and I've got my reasons for it."

"Bless yo' heart for them words, Jake Packard! I'll never forgit you, long's I live!" says the man on the floor, sort of blubbering.

Packard didn't take no notice of that, but hung up his lantern on a nail, and started towards where I was, there in the dark, and motioned Bill to come. I crawfished as fast as I could, about two yards, but the boat slanted so that I couldn't make very good time; so to keep from getting run over and catched I crawled into a stateroom on the upper side. The men come a-pawing along in the dark, and when Packard got to my stateroom, he says:

"Here—come in here."

And in he come, and Bill after him. But before they got in, I was up in the upper berth, cornered, and sorry I come. Then they stood there, with their hands on the ledge of the berth, and talked. I couldn't see them, but I could tell where they was, by the whisky they'd been having. I was glad I didn't drink whisky; but it wouldn't made much difference, anyway, because most of the time they couldn't a treed me because I didn't breathe. I was too scared. And besides, a body *couldn't* breathe, and hear such talk. They talked low and earnest. Bill wanted to kill Turner. He says:

"He's said he'll tell, and he will. If we was to give both our shares to him *now,* it wouldn't make no difference after the row, and the way we've served him. Shore's you're born, he'll turn State's evidence; now you hear *me.* I'm for putting him out of his troubles."

"So'm I," says Packard, very quiet.

"Blame it, I'd sorter begun to think you wasn't. Well, then, that's all right. Le's go and do it."

"Hold on a minute; I hain't had my say yit. You listen to me. Shooting's good, but there's quieter ways if the thing's *got* to be done. But what *I* say, is this: it ain't good sense to go court'n around after a halter, if you can git at what you're up to in some way that's jist as good and at the same time don't bring you into no resks. Ain't that so?"

"You bet it is. But how you goin' to manage it this time?"

"Well, my idea is this: we'll rustle around and gether up whatever pickins we've overlooked in the staterooms, and shove for shore and hide the truck. Then we'll wait. Now I say it ain't agoin' to be more 'n two hours befo' this wrack breaks up and washes off down the river. See? He'll be drownded, and won't have nobody to blame for it but his own self. I reckon that's a considerable sight better'n killin' of him. I'm unfavorable to killin' a man as long as you can git around it; it ain't good sense, it ain't good morals. Ain't I right?"

"Yes—I reck'n you are. But s'pose she *don't* break up and wash off?"

"Well, we can wait the two hours, anyway, and see, can't we?"

"All right, then; come along."

So they started, and I lit out, all in a cold sweat, and scrambled forward. It was dark as pitch there; but I said in a kind of a coarse whisper, "Jim!" and he answered up, right at my elbow, with a sort of a moan, and I says:

"Quick, Jim, it ain't no time for fooling around and moaning; there's a gang of murderers in yonder, and if we don't hunt up their boat and set her drifting down the river so these fellows can't get away from the wreck, there's one of 'em going to be in a bad fix. But if we find their boat we can put *all* of 'em in a bad fix—for the Sheriff 'll get 'em. Quick—hurry! I'll hunt the labboard side, you hunt the stabboard. You start at the raft, and—"

"Oh, my lordy, lordy! *Raf'?* Dey ain' no raf' no mo', she done broke loose en gone!—'en here we is!"

Chapter 13

Well, I catched my breath and most fainted. Shut up on a wreck with such a gang as that! But it warn't no time to be sentimentering. We'd *got* to find that boat, now—had to have it for ourselves. So we went a-quaking and shaking down the stabboard side, and slow work it was, too—seemed a week before we got to the stern. No sign of a boat. Jim said he didn't believe he could go any further—so scared he hadn't hardly any strength left, he said. But I said come on, if we get left on this wreck, we are in a fix, sure. So on we prowled, again. We struck for the stern of the texas, and found it, and then scrabbled along forwards on the skylight, hanging on from shutter to shutter, for the edge of the skylight was in the water. When we got pretty close to the cross-hall door, there was the skiff, sure enough! I could just barely see her. I felt ever so thankful. In another second I would a been aboard of her; but just then the door opened. One of the men stuck his head out, only about a couple of foot from me, and I thought I was gone; but he jerked it in again, and says:

"Heave that blame lantern out o' sight, Bill!"

He flung a bag of something into the boat, and then got in himself, and set down. It was Packard. Then Bill *he* come out and got in. Packard says, in a low voice:

"All ready—shove off!"

I couldn't hardly hang onto the shutters, I was so weak. But Bill says:

"Hold on—'d you go through him?"

"No. Didn't you?"

"No. So he's got his share o' the cash, yet."

"Well, then, come along—no use to take truck and leave money."

"Say—won't he suspicion what we're up to?"

"Maybe he won't. But we got to have it anyway. Come along."

So they got out and went in.

The door slammed to, because it was on the careened side; and in a half second I was in the boat, and Jim come atumbling after me. I out with my knife and cut the rope, and away we went!

We didn't touch an oar, and we didn' speak nor whisper, nor hardly even breathe. We went gliding swift along, dead silent, past the tip of the paddle-box, and past the stern; then in a second or two more we was a hundred yards below the wreck, and the darkness soaked her up, every last sign of her, and we was safe, and knowed it.

When we was three or four hundred yards down stream, we see the lantern show like a little spark at the texas door, for a second, and we knowed by that that the rascals had missed their boat, and was beginning to understand that they was in just as much trouble, now, as Jim Turner was.

Then Jim manned the oars, and we took out after our raft. Now was the first time that I begun to worry about the men—I reckon I hadn't had time to before. I begun to think how dreadful it was, even for murderers, to be in such a fix. I says to myself, there ain't no telling but I might come to be a murderer myself, yet, and then how would *I* like it? So says I to Jim:

"The first light we see, we'll land a hundred yards below it or above it, in a place where it's a good hiding-place for you and the skiff, and then I'll go and fix up some kind of a yarn, and get somebody to go for that gang and get them out of their scrape, so they can be hung when their time comes."

But that idea was a failure; for pretty soon it begun to storm again, and this time worse than ever. The rain poured down, and never a light showed; everybody in bed, I reckon. We boomed along down the river, watching for lights and watching for our raft. After a long time the rain let up, but the clouds staid, and the lightning kept whimpering, and by-and-by a flash showed us a black thing ahead, floating, and we made for it.

It was the raft, and mighty glad was we to get aboard of it again. We seen a light now, away down to the right, on shore. So I said I would go for it. The skiff was half full of plunder which that gang had stole, there on the wreck. We hustled it onto the raft in a pile, and I told Jim to float along down, and show a light when he judged he had gone about two mile, and keep it burning till I come; then I manned my oars and shoved for the light. As I got down towards it, three or four more showed—up on a hillside. It was a village. I closed in above the shore-light, and laid on my oars and floated. As I went by, I see it was a lantern hanging on the jackstaff of a double-hull ferry-boat. I skimmed around for the watchman, a-wondering whereabouts he slept; and by-and-by I found him roosting on the bitts, forward, with his head down between his knees. I give his shoulder two or three little shoves, and begun to cry.

He stirred up, in a kind of a startlish way; but when he see it was only me, he took a good gap and stretch, and then he says:

"Hello, what's up? Don't cry, bub. What's the trouble?"

I says:

"Pap, and mam, and sis, and—"

Then I broke down. He says:

"Oh, dang it, now, *don't* take on so; we all has to have our troubles and this'n'll come out all right. What's the matter with 'em?"

"They're—they're—are you the watchman of the boat?"

"Yes," he says, kind of pretty-well-satisfied like. "I'm the captain and the owner, and the mate, and the pilot, and watchman, and head deck-hand; and sometimes I'm the freight and passengers. I ain't as rich as old Jim Hornback, and I can't be so blame' generous and good to Tom, Dick and Harry as what he is, and slam around money the way he does; but I've told him a many a time 't I wouldn't trade places with him; for, says I, a sailor's life's the life for me, and I'm derned if *I'd* live two mile out o' town, where there ain't nothing ever goin' on, not for all his spondulicks and as much more on top of it. Says I—"

I broke in and says:

"They're in an awful peck of trouble, and—"

"*Who* is?"

"Why, pap, and mam, and sis, and Miss Hooker; and if you'd take your ferry-boat and go up there—"

"Up where? Where are they?"

"On the wreck."

"What wreck?"

"Why, there ain't but one."

"What, you don't mean the *Walter Scott?*"

"Yes."

"Good land! what are they doin' *there,* for gracious sakes?"

"Well, they didn't go there a-purpose."

"I bet they didn't! Why, great goodness, there ain't no chance for 'em if they don't git off mighty quick! Why, how in the nation did they ever git into such a scrape?"

"Easy enough. Miss Hooker was a-visiting, up there to the town—"

"Yes, Booth's Landing—go on."

"She was a-visiting, there at Booth's Landing, and just in the edge of the evening she started over with her nigger woman in the horse-ferry, to stay all night at her friend's house, Miss What-you-may-call-her, I disremember her name, and they lost their steering-oar, and swung around and went a-floating down, stern-first, about two mile, and saddle-baggsed on the wreck, and the ferry man and the nigger woman and the horses was all lost, but Miss Hooker she made a grab and got aboard the wreck. Well, about an hour after dark, we come along down in our trading-scow, and it was so dark we didn't notice the wreck till we was right on it; and so *we* saddle-baggsed; but all of us was saved but Bill Whipple—and oh, he *was* the best cretur!—I most wish't it had been me, I do."

"My George! It's the beatenest thing I ever struck. And *then* what did you all do?"

"Well, we hollered and took on, but it's so wide there, we couldn't make nobody hear. So pap said somebody got to get ashore and get help somehow. I was the only one that could swim, so I made a dash for it, and Miss Hooker she said if I didn't strike help sooner, come here and hunt up her uncle, and he'd fix the thing. I made the land about a mile below, and been fooling along ever since, trying to get people to do something, but they said, 'What, in such a night and such a current? there ain't no sense in it; go for the steam-ferry.' Now if you'll go, and—"

"By Jackson, I'd *like* to, and, blame it, I don't know but I will; but who in the dingnation's agoin' to *pay* for it? Do you reckon your pap—"

"Why *that's* all right. Miss Hooker she told me, *particular,* that her uncle Hornback—"

"Great guns! is *he* her uncle? Looky here, you break for that light over yonder-way, and turn out west when you git there, and about a quarter of a mile out you'll come to the tavern; tell 'em to dart you out to Jim Hornback's and he'll foot the bill. And don't you fool around any, because he'll want to know the news. Tell him I'll have his niece all safe before he can get to town. Hump yourself, now; I'm agoing up around the corner here, to roust out my engineer."

I struck for the light, but as soon as he turned the corner I went back and got into my skiff and bailed her out and then pulled up shore in the easy water about six hundred yards, and tucked myself in among some woodboats; for I couldn't rest easy till I could see the ferry-boat start. But take it all around, I was feeling ruther comfortable on accounts of taking all this trouble for that gang, for not many would a done it. I wished the widow knowed about it. I judged she would be proud of me for helping these rapscallions, because rapscallions and dead beats is the kind the widow and good people takes the most interest in.

Well, before long, here comes the wreck, dim and dusky, sliding along down! A kind of cold shiver went through me, and then I struck out for her. She was very deep, and I see in a minute there warn't much chance for anybody being alive in her. I pulled all around her and hollered a little, but there wasn't any answer; all dead still. I felt a little bit heavy-hearted about the gang, but not much, for I reckoned if they could stand it, I could.

Then here comes the ferry-boat; so I shoved for the middle of the river on a long down-stream slant; and when I judged I was out of eye-reach, I laid on my oars, and looked back and see her go and smell around the wreck for Miss Hooker's remainders, because the captain would know her uncle Hornback would want them; and then pretty soon the ferryboat give it up and went for shore, and I laid into my work and went a-booming down the river.

It did seem a powerful long time before Jim's light showed up; and when it did show, it looked like it was a thousand mile off. By the time I got there the sky was beginning to get a little gray in the east; so we struck for an island, and hid the raft, and sunk the skiff, and turned in and slept like dead people.

[After further adventures on the Mississippi, Jim and Huck are burdened by two con-men traveling with them on their raft. In the final scene of the chapter (the novel continues another 20 chapters) Jim tells Huck of a regrettable memory.]

Chapter 23

Well, all day him and the king was hard at it, rigging up a stage, and a curtain, and a row of candles for footlights; and that night the house was jam full of men in no time. When the place couldn't hold no more, the duke he quit tending door and went around the back way and come onto the stage and stood up before the curtain, and made a little speech, and praised up this tragedy, and said it was the most thrillingest one that ever was; and so he went on a-bragging about the tragedy and about Edmund Kean the Elder, which was to play the main principal part in it; and at last when he'd got everybody's expectations up high enough, he rolled up the curtain, and the next minute the king come a-prancing out on all fours, naked; and he was painted all over, ring-streaked-and-striped, all sorts of colors, as splendid as a rainbow. And—but never mind the rest of his outfit, it was just wild, but it was awful funny. The people most killed themselves laughing; and when the king got done capering, and capered off behind the scenes, they roared and clapped and stormed and haw-hawed till he come back and done it over again; and after that, they made him do it another time. Well, it would a made a cow laugh to see the shines that old idiot cut.

Then the duke he lets the curtain down, and bows to the people, and says the great tragedy will be performed only two nights more, on accounts of pressing London engagements, where the seats is all sold aready for it in Drury Lane; and then he makes them another bow, and says if he has succeeded in pleasing them and instructing them, he will be deeply obleeged if they will mention it to their friends and get them to come and see it.

Twenty people sings out:

"What, is it over? Is that *all?*"

The duke says yes. Then there was a fine time. Everybody sings out "sold," and rose up mad, and was agoing for that stage and them tragedians. But a big fine-looking man jumps up on a bench, and shouts:

"Hold on! Just a word, gentlemen." They stopped to listen. "We are sold—mighty badly sold. But we don't want to be the laughing-stock of this whole town, I reckon, and never hear the last of this thing as long as we live. *No.* What we want, is to go out of here quiet, and talk this show up, and sell the *rest* of the town! Then we'll all be in the same boat. Ain't that sensible?" ("You bet it is!—the jedge is right!" everybody sings out.) "All right, then—not a word about any sell. Go along home, and advise everybody to come and see the tragedy."

Next day you couldn't hear nothing around that town but how splendid that show was. House was jammed again, that night, and we sold this crowd the same way. When me and the king and the duke got home to the raft, we all had a supper; and by-and-by, about midnight, they made Jim and me back her out and float her down the middle of the river and fetch her in and hide her about two mile below town.

The third night the house was crammed again—and they warn't newcomers, this time, but people that was at the show the other two nights. I stood by the duke at the door, and I see that every man that went in had his pockets bulging, or something muffled up under his coat—and I see it warn't no perfumery neither, not by a long sight. I smelt sickly eggs by the barrel, and rotten cabbages, and such things; and if I know the signs of a dead cat being around, and I bet I do, there was sixty-four of them went in. I shoved in there for a minute, but it was too various for me, I couldn't stand it. Well, when the place couldn't hold no more people, the duke he give a fellow a quarter and told him to tend door for him a minute, and then he started around for the stage door, I after him; but the minute we turned the corner and was in the dark, he says:

"Walk fast, now, till you get away from the houses, and then shin for the raft like the dickens was after you!"

I done it, and he done the same. We struck the raft at the same time, and in less than two seconds we was gliding down stream, all dark and still, and edging towards the middle of the river, nobody saying a word. I reckoned the poor king was in for a gaudy time of it with the audience, but nothing of the sort; pretty soon he crawls out from under the wigwam, and says:

"Well, how'd the old thing pan out this time, Duke?"

He hadn't been up town at all.

We never showed a light till we was about ten mile below that village. Then we lit up and had a supper, and the king and the duke fairly laughed their bones loose over the way they'd served them people. The duke says:

"Greenhorns, flatheads! *I* knew the first house would keep mum and let the rest of the town get roped in; and I knew they'd lay for us the third night, and consider it was *their* turn now. Well, it *is* their turn, and I'd give something to know how much they'd take for it. I *would* just like to know how they're putting in their opportunity. They can turn it into a picnic, if they want to—they brought plenty provisions."

Them rapscallions took in four hundred and sixty-five dollars in that three nights. I never see money hauled in by the wagon-load like that, before.

By-and-by, when they was asleep and snoring, Jim says:

"Don't it 'sprise you, de way dem kings carries on, Huck?"

"No," I says, "it don't."

"Why don't it, Huck?"

"Well, it don't, because it's in the breed. I reckon they're all alike."

"But, Huck, dese kings o' ourn is regular rapscallions; dat's jist what dey is; dey's reglar rapscallions."

"Well, that's what I'm a-saying; all kings is mostly rapscallions, as fur as I can make out."

"Is dat so?"

"You read about them once—you'll see. Look at Henry the Eight; this'n 's a Sunday-School Superintendent to *him*. And look at Charles Second, and Louis Fourteen, and Louis Fifteen, and James Second, and Edward Second, and Richard Third, and forty more; besides all them Saxon heptarchies that used to rip around so in old times and raise Cain. My, you ought to seen old Henry the Eight when he was in bloom. He *was* a blossom. He used to marry a new wife every day, and chop off her head next morning. And he would do it just as indifferent as if he was ordering up eggs. 'Fetch up Nell Gwynn,' he says. They fetch her up. Next morning, 'Chop off her head!' And they chop it off. 'Fetch up Jane Shore,' he says; and up she comes. Next morning, 'Chop off her head'—and they chop it off. 'Ring up Fair Rosamun.' Fair Rosamun answers the bell. Next morning, 'Chop off her head.' And he made every one of them tell him a tale every night; and he kept that up till he had hogged a thousand and one tales that way, and then he put them all in a book, and called it Domesday Book—which was a good name and stated the case. You don't know kings, Jim, but I know them; and this old rip of ourn is one of the cleanest I've struck in history. Well, Henry he takes a notion he wants to get up some trouble with this country. How does he go at it—give notice?—give the country a show? No. All of a sudden he heaves all the tea in Boston Harbor overboard, and whacks out a declaration of independence, and dares them to come on. That was *his* style—he never give anybody a chance. He had suspicions of his father, the Duke of Wellington. Well, what did he do?—ask him to show up? No—drownded him in a butt of mamsey, like a cat. Spose people left money laying around where he was—what did he do? He collared it. Spose he contracted to do a thing; and you paid him, and didn't set down there and see that he done it—what did he do? He always done the other thing. Spose he opened his mouth—what then? If he didn't shut it up powerful quick, he'd lose a lie, every time. That's the kind of a bug Henry was; and if we'd a had him along 'stead of our kings, he'd a fooled that town a heap worse than ourn done. I don't say that ourn is lambs, because they ain't, when you come right down to the cold facts; but they ain't nothing to *that* old ram, anyway. All I say is, kings is kings, and you got to make allowances. Take them all around, they're a mighty ornery lot. It's the way they're raised."

"But dis one do *smell* so like de nation, Huck."

"Well, they all do, Jim. *We* can't help the way a king smells; history don't tell no way."

"Now de duke, he's a tolerble likely man, in some ways."

"Yes, a duke's different. But not very different. This one's a middling, hard lot, for a duke. When he's drunk, there ain't no near-sighted man could tell him from a king."

"Well, anyways, I doan' hanker for no mo' un um, Huck. Dese is all I kin stan'."

"It's the way I feel, too, Jim. But we've got them on our hands, and we got to remember what they are, and make allowances. Sometimes I wish we could hear of a country that's out of kings."

What was the use to tell Jim these warn't real kings and dukes? It wouldn't a done no good; and besides, it was just as I said; you couldn't tell them from the real kind.

I went to sleep, and Jim didn't call me when it was my turn. He often done that. When I waked up, just at day-break, he was sitting there with his head down betwixt his knees, moaning and mourning to himself. I didn't take notice, nor let on. I knowed what it was about. He was thinking about his wife and his children, away up yonder, and he was low and homesick; because he hadn't ever been away from home before in his life; and I do believe he cared just as much for his people as white folks does for their'n. It don't seem natural, but I reckon it's so. He was often moaning and mourning that way, nights, when he judged I was asleep, and saying, "Po' little 'Lizabeth! po' little Johnny! it's mighty hard; I spec' I ain't ever gwyne to see you no mo', no mo'!" He was a mighty good nigger, Jim was.

But this time I somehow got to talking to him about his wife and young ones; and by-and-by he says:

"What makes me feel so bad dis time, 'uz bekase I hear sumpn over yonder on de bank like a whack, er a slam, while ago, en it mine me er de time I treat my little 'Lizabeth so ornery. She warn't on'y 'bout fo' year ole, en she tuck de sk'yarlet-fever, en had a powful rough spell; but she got well, en one day she was a-stannin' aroun', en I says to her, I says:

" 'Shet de do'.'

"She never done it; jis' stood dah, kiner smilin' up at me. It make me mad; en I says agin, mighty loud, I says:

" 'Doan' you hear me? Shet de do'!'

"She jis stood de same way, kiner smilin' up. I was a-bilin'! I says:

" 'I lay I *make* you mine!' "

"En wid dat I fetch' her a slap side de head dat sont her a-sprawlin'. Den I went into de yuther room, en 'uz gone 'bout ten minutes; en when I come back, dah was dat do' a-stannin' open *yit,* en dat chile stannin' mos' right in it, a-lookin' down and mournin', en de tears runnin' down. My, but I *wuz* mad, I was agwyne for de chile, but jis' den—it was a do' dat open innerds—jis' den, 'long come de wind en slam it to, behine de chile, ker-*blam!*—en my lan', de chile never move'! My breff mos' hop outer me; en I feel so—so—I doan' know *how* I feel. I crope out, all a-tremblin', en crope aroun' en open de do' easy en slow, en poke my head in behine de chile, sof' en still, en all uv a sudden I says *pow!* jis' as loud as I could yell. *She never budge!* Oh, Huck, I bust out a-cryin' en grab her up in my arms, en say, 'Oh, de po' little thing! de Lord God Amighty fogive po' ole Jim, kaze he never gwyne to fogive hisself as long's he live!' Oh, she was plumb deef en dumb, Huck, plumb deef en dumb—en I'd ben a-treat'n her so!"

SOURCE: Mark Twain. *Adventures of Huckleberry Finn.* New York: Charles L. Webster and Company, 1885.

To the Whitefriars (1899)

Twain was not only one of the most popular writers in the English language, he was a popular and entertaining speaker. Here he gives a speech, about making speeches, at the Whitefriars men's club in London on June 16, 1899.

Mr. Chairman and Brethren of the Vow—in whatever the vow is; for although I have been a member of this club for five-and-twenty years, I don't know any more about what that vow is than Mr. Austin seems to. But whatever the vow is, I don't care what it is. I have made a thousand vows.

There is no pleasure comparable to making a vow in the presence of one who appreciates that vow, in the presence of men who honor and appreciate you for making the vow, and men who admire you for making the vow.

There is only one pleasure higher than that, and that is to get outside and break the vow. A vow is always a pledge of some kind or other for the protection of your own morals and principles or somebody else's, and generally, by the irony of fate, it is for the protection of your own morals.

Hence we have pledges that make us eschew tobacco or wine, and while you are taking the pledge there is a holy influence about that makes you feel you are reformed, and that you can never be so happy again in this world until—you get outside and take a drink.

I had forgotten that I was a member of this club—it is so long ago. But now I remember that I was here five-and-twenty years ago, and that I was then at a dinner of the Whitefriars Club, and it was in those old days when you had just made two great finds. All London was talking about nothing else than that they had found Livingstone, and that the lost Sir Roger Tichborne had been found—and they were trying him for it.

And at the dinner, Chairman—(I do not know who he was)—failed to come to time. The gentleman who had been appointed to pay me the customary compliments and to introduce me forgot the compliments, and did not know what they were.

And George Augustus Sala came in at the last moment, just when I was about to go without compliments altogether. And that man was a gifted man. They just called on him instantaneously, while he was going to sit down, to introduce the stranger, and Sala made one of those marvelous speeches which he was capable of making. I think no man talked so fast as Sala did. One did not need wine while he was making a speech. The rapidity of his utterance made a man drunk in a minute. An incomparable speech was that, an impromptu speech, and an impromptu speech is a seldom thing, and he did it so well.

He went into the whole history of the United States, and made it entirely new to me. He filled it with episodes and incidents that Washington never heard of, and he did it so convincingly that although I knew none of it had happened, from that day to this I do not know any history but Sala's.

I do not know anything so sad as a dinner where you are going to get up and say something by-and-by, and you do not know what it is. You sit and wonder and wonder what the gentleman is going to say who is going to introduce you. You know that if he says something severe, that if he will deride you, or traduce you, or do anything of that kind, he will furnish you with a text, because anybody can get up and talk against that.

Anybody can get up and straighten out his character. But when a gentleman gets up and merely tells the truth about you, what can you do?

Mr. Austin has done well. He has supplied so many texts that I will have to drop out a lot of them, and that is about as difficult as when you do not have any text at all. Now, he made a beautiful and smooth speech without any difficulty at all, and I could have done that if I had gone on with the schooling with which I began. I see here a gentleman on my left who was my master in the art of oratory more than twenty-five years ago.

When I look upon the inspiring face of Mr. Depew, it carries me a long way back. An old and valued friend of mine is he, and I saw his career as it came along, and it has reached pretty well up to now, when he, by another miscarriage of justice, is a United States Senator. But those were delightful days when I was taking lessons in oratory.

My other master—the Ambassador—is not here yet. Under those two gentlemen I learned to make after-dinner speeches, and it was charming.

You know the New England dinner is the great occasion on the other side of the water. It is held every year to celebrate the landing of the Pilgrims. Those Pilgrims were a lot of people who were not needed in England, and you know they had great rivalry, and they were persuaded to go elsewhere, and they chartered a ship called *Mayflower* and set sail, and I have heard it said that they pumped the Atlantic Ocean through that ship sixteen times.

They fell in over there with the Dutch from Rotterdam, Amsterdam, and a lot of other places with profane names, and it is from that gang that Mr. Depew is descended.

On the other hand, Mr. [Joseph] Choate is descended from those Puritans who landed on a bitter night in December. Every year those people used to meet at a great banquet in New York, and those masters of mind in oratory had to make speeches. It was Doctor Depew's business to get up there and apologize for the Dutch, and Mr. Choate had to get up later and explain the crimes of the Puritans, and grand, beautiful times we used to have.

It is curious that after that long lapse of time I meet the Whitefriars again, some looking as young and fresh as in the old days, others showing a certain amount of wear and tear, and here, after all this time, I find one of the masters of oratory and the others named in the list.

And here we three meet again as exiles on one pretext or another, and you will notice that while we are absent there is a pleasing tranquility in America—a building up of public confidence. We are doing the best we can for our country. I think we have spent our lives in serving our country, and we never serve it to greater advantage than when we get out of it.

But impromptu speaking—that is what I was trying to learn. That is a difficult thing. I used to do it in this way. I used to begin about a week ahead, and write out my impromptu speech and get it by heart. Then I brought it to the New England dinner printed on a piece of paper in my pocket, so that I could pass it to the reporters all cut and dried, and in order to do an impromptu speech as it should be done you have to indicate the places for pauses and hesitations. I put them all in it. And then you want the applause in the right places.

When I got to the place where it should come in, if it did not come in I did not care, but I had it marked in the paper. And these masters of mind used to wonder why it was my speech came out in the morning in the first person, while theirs went through the butchery of synopsis.

I do that kind of speech (I mean an offhand speech), and do it well, and make no mistake in such a way to deceive the audience completely and make that audience believe it is an impromptu speech—that is art.

I was frightened out of it at last by an experience of Doctor Hayes. He was a sort of Nansen of that day. He had been to the North Pole, and it made him celebrated. He had even seen the polar bear climb the pole.

He had made one of those magnificent voyages such as Nansen made, and in those days when a man did anything which greatly distinguished him for the moment he had to come on to the lecture platform and tell all about it.

Doctor Hayes was a great, magnificent creature like Nansen, superbly built. He was to appear in Boston. He wrote his lecture out, and it was his purpose to read it from manuscript; but in an evil hour he concluded that it would be a good thing to preface it with something rather handsome, poetical, and beautiful that he could get off by heart and deliver as if it were the thought of the moment.

He had not had my experience, and could not do that. He came on the platform, held his manuscript down, and began with a beautiful piece of oratory. He spoke something like this: "When a lonely human being, a pigmy in the midst of the architecture of nature, stands solitary on those icy waters and looks abroad to the horizon and sees mighty castles and temples of eternal ice raising up their pinnacles tipped by the pencil of the departing sun—"

Here a man came across the platform and touched him on the shoulder, and said: "One minute." And then to the audience:

"Is Mrs. John Smith in the house? Her husband has slipped on the ice and broken his leg."

And you could see the Mrs. John Smiths get up everywhere and drift out of the house, and it made great gaps everywhere. Then Doctor Hayes began again: "When a lonely man, a pigmy in the architecture—"

The janitor came in again and shouted: "It is not Mrs. John Smith! It is Mrs. John Jones!"

Then all the Mrs. Joneses got up and left. Once more the speaker started, and was in the midst of the sentence when he was interrupted again, and the result was that the lecture was not delivered. But the lecturer interviewed the janitor afterward in a private room, and of the fragments of the janitor they took "twelve basketsful."

Now, I don't want to sit down just in this way. I have been talking with so much levity that I have said no serious thing, and you are really no better or wiser, although Robert Buchanan has suggested that I am a person who deals in wisdom. I have said nothing which would make you better than when you came here.

I should be sorry to sit down without having said one serious word which you can carry home and relate to your children and the old people who are not able to get away.

And this is just a little maxim which has saved me from many a difficulty and many a disaster, and in times of tribulation and uncertainty has come to my rescue, as it shall to yours if you observe it as I do day and night.

I always use it in an emergency, and you can take it home as a legacy from me, and it is: "When in doubt, tell the truth."

SOURCE: Mark Twain. *Mark Twain's Speeches.* With an introduction by William Dean Howells. New York: Harper and Brothers Publishers, 1910.

SITTING BULL, TATANKA YOTANKA

A chief and wise-man of the Sioux, Sitting Bull (c. 1830–1890) was their greatest leader and a sharp-witted and poetic speaker. At an Indian council in 1875 at the Powder River, Sitting Bull described his mistrust of the American people.

Behold, My Friends, the Spring Is Come (1875)

BEHOLD, MY FRIENDS, the spring is come; the earth has gladly received the embraces of the sun, and we shall soon see the results of their love! Every seed is awakened, and all animal life. It is through this mysterious power that we too have our being, and we therefore yield to our neighbors, even to our animal neighbors, the same right as ourselves to inhabit this vast land.

Yet hear me, friends! we have now to deal with another people, small and feeble when our forefathers first met with them, but now great and overbearing. Strangely enough, they have a mind to till the soil, and the love of possessions is a disease in them. These people have made many rules that the rich may break, but the poor may not! They have a religion in which the poor worship, but the rich will not! They even take tithes of the poor and weak to support the rich and those who rule. They claim this mother of ours, the Earth, for their own use, and fence their neighbors away from her, and deface her with their buildings and their refuse. They compel her to produce out of season, and when sterile she is made to take medicine in order to produce again. All this is sacrilege.

This nation is like a spring freshet; it overruns its banks and destroys all who are in its path. We cannot dwell side by side. Only seven years ago we made a treaty by which we were assured that the buffalo country should be left to us forever. Now they threaten to take that from us also. My brothers, shall we submit? or shall we say to them: "First kill me, before you can take possession of my fatherland!"

SOURCE: Charles A. Eastman (Ohiyesa). *Indian Heroes and Great Chieftains*. Boston: Little, Brown, 1918.

This Land Belongs to Us (c. 1882)

When the chief, after his surrender to the U.S. Army, was a prisoner of war at Fort Randall in 1881–1883, a journalist visited Sitting Bull among his braves, two wives, and several children.

(The chief put his thumbs together, as though he were comparing them . . . and began.)

I HAVE LIVED a long time, and I have seen a great deal, and I have always had a reason for everything I have done. Every act of my life has had an object in view, and no man can say that I have neglected facts or failed to think.

I am one of the last chiefs of the independent Sioux nation, and the place I hold among my people was held by my ancestors before me. If I had no place in the world, I would not be here, and the fact of my existence entitles me to exercise any influence I possess. I am satisfied that I was brought into this life for a purpose; otherwise, why am I here?

This land belongs to us, for the Great Spirit gave it to us when he put us here. We were free to come and go, and to live in our own way. But white men, who belong to another land, have come upon us, and are forcing us to live according to their ideas. That is an injustice; we have never dreamed of making white men live as we live.

White men like to dig in the ground for their food. My people prefer to hunt the buffalo as their fathers did. White men like to stay in one place. My people want to move their tepees here and there to the different hunting grounds. The life of white men is slavery. They are prisoners in towns or farms. The life my people want is a life of freedom. I have seen nothing that a white man has, houses or railways or clothing or food, that is as good as the right to move in the open country, and live in our own fashion. Why has our blood been shed by your soldiers?

(Sitting Bull drew a square on the ground with his thumb nail. The Indians craned their necks to see what he was doing.)

There! Your soldiers made a mark like that in our country, and said that we must live there. They fed us well, and sent their doctors to heal our sick. They said that we should live without having to work. But they told us that we must go only so far in this direction, and only so far in that direction. They gave us meat, but they took away our liberty. The white men had many things that we wanted, but we could see that they did not have the one thing we liked best,—freedom. I would rather live in a tepee and go without meat when game is scarce than give up my privileges as a free Indian, even though I could have all that white men have. We marched across the lines of our reservation, and the soldiers followed us. They attacked our village, and we killed them all. What would you do if your home was attacked? You would stand up like a brave man and defend it. That is our story. I have spoken.

SOURCE: James Creelman. *On the Great Highway: The Wanderings and Adventures of a Special Correspondent*. Boston: Lothrop Publishing Company, 1901.

BRET HARTE

For a time, Bret Harte (1836–1902) was almost as popular a writer as Mark Twain. Born and raised in New York State, he gained his literary reputation in California, where he wrote "Western" poetry and many comic stories. This humorous and touching story takes place, however, in New England, the eastern shore of his short-story collection Drift from Two Shores.

My Friend, the Tramp (1878)

I HAD BEEN sauntering over the clover downs of a certain noted New England seaport. It was a Sabbath morning, so singularly reposeful and gracious, so replete with the significance of the seventh day of rest, that even the Sabbath bells ringing a mile away over the salt marshes had little that was monitory, mandatory, or even supplicatory in their drowsy voices. Rather they seemed to call from their cloudy towers, like some renegade muezzin: "Sleep is better than prayer; sleep on, O sons of the Puritans! Slumber still, O deacons and vestrymen! Let, oh let those feet that are swift to wickedness curl up beneath thee! those palms that are itching for the shekels of the ungodly lie clasped beneath thy pillow! Sleep is better than prayer."

And, indeed, though it was high morning, sleep was still in the air. Wrought upon at last by the combined influences of sea and sky and atmosphere, I succumbed, and lay down on one of the boulders of a little stony slope that gave upon the sea. The great Atlantic lay before me, not yet quite awake, but slowly heaving the rhythmical expiration of slumber. There was no sail visible in the misty horizon. There was nothing to do but to lie and stare at the unwinking ether.

Suddenly I became aware of the strong fumes of tobacco. Turning my head, I saw a pale blue smoke curling up from behind an adjacent boulder. Rising, and climbing over the intermediate granite, I came upon a little hollow, in which, comfortably extended on the mosses and lichens, lay a powerfully built man. He was very ragged; he was very dirty; there was a strong suggestion about him of his having too much hair, too much nail, too much perspiration; too much of those superfluous excrescences and exudations that society and civilization strive to keep under. But it was noticeable that he had not much of anything else. It was The Tramp.

With that swift severity with which we always visit rebuke upon the person who happens to present any one of our vices offensively before us, in his own person, I was deeply indignant at his laziness. Perhaps I showed it in my manner, for he rose to a half-sitting attitude, returned my stare apologetically, and made a movement toward knocking the fire from his pipe against the granite.

"Shure, sur, and if I'd belaved that I was trispassin' on yer honor's grounds, it's meself that would hev laid down on the say shore and takin' the salt waves for me blankits. But it's sivinteen miles I've walked this blessed noight, with nothin' to sustain me, and hevin' a mortal wakeness to fight wid in me bowels, by reason of starvation, and only a bit o' baccy that the Widdy Maloney giv' me at the cross roads, to kape me up entoirley. But it was the dark day I left me home in Milwaukee to walk to Boston; and if ye'll oblige a lone man who has left a wife and six children in Milwaukee, wid the loan of twenty-five cints, furninst the time he gits worruk, God'll be good to ye."

It instantly flashed through my mind that the man before me had the previous night partaken of the kitchen hospitality of my little cottage, two miles away. That he presented himself in the guise of a distressed fisherman, mulcted of his wages by an inhuman captain; that he had a wife lying sick of consumption in the next village, and two children, one of whom was a cripple, wandering in the streets of Boston. I remembered that this tremendous indictment against Fortune touched the family, and that the distressed fisherman was provided with clothes, food, and some small change. The food and small change had disappeared, but the garments for the consumptive wife, where were they? He had been using them for a pillow.

I instantly pointed out this fact, and charged him with the deception. To my surprise, he took it quietly, and even a little complacently.

"Bedad, yer roight; ye see, sur" (confidentially), "ye see, sur, until I get worruk—and it's worruk I'm lukin' for—I have to desave now and thin to shute the locality. Ah, God save us! but on the say-coast thay'r that har-rud upon thim that don't belong to the say."

I ventured to suggest that a strong, healthy man like him might have found work somewhere between Milwaukee and Boston.

"Ah, but ye see I got free passage on a freight train, and didn't sthop. It was in the Aist that I expected to find worruk."

"Have you any trade?"

"Trade, is it? I'm a brickmaker, God knows, and many's the lift I've had at makin' bricks in Milwaukee. Shure, I've as aisy a hand at it as any man. Maybe yer honor might know of a kill hereabout?"

Now to my certain knowledge, there was not a brick kiln within fifty miles of that spot, and of all unlikely places to find one would have been this sandy peninsula, given up to the summer residences of a few wealthy people. Yet I could not help admiring the assumption of the scamp, who knew this fact as well as myself. But I said, "I can give you work for a day or two;" and, bidding him gather up his sick wife's apparel, led the way across the downs to my cottage. At first I think the offer took him by surprise, and gave him some consternation, but he presently recovered his spirits, and almost instantly his speech. "Ah, worruk, is it? God be praised! it's meself that's ready and willin'. Though maybe me hand is spoilt wid brickmakin'."

I assured him that the work I would give him would require no delicate manipulation, and so we fared on over the sleepy downs. But I could not help noticing that, although an invalid, I was a much better pedestrian than my companion, frequently leaving him behind, and that even as a "tramp," he was etymologically an impostor. He had a way of lingering beside the fences we had to climb over, as if to continue more confidentially the history of his misfortunes and troubles, which he was delivering to me during our homeward walk, and I noticed that he could seldom resist the invitation of a mossy boulder or a tussock of salt grass. "Ye see, sur," he would say, suddenly sitting down, "it's along uv me misfortunes beginnin' in Milwaukee that—" and it was not until I was out of hearing that he would languidly gather his traps again and saunter after me. When I reached my own garden gate he leaned for a moment over it, with both of his powerful arms extended downward, and said, "Ah, but it's a blessin' that Sunday comes to give rest fur the wake and the weary, and them as walks sivinteen miles to get it." Of course I took the hint. There was evidently no work to be had from my friend, the Tramp, that day. Yet his countenance brightened as he saw the limited extent of my domain, and observed that the garden, so called, was only a flower-bed about twenty-five by ten. As he had doubtless before this been utilized, to the extent of his capacity, in digging, he had probably expected that kind of work; and I daresay I discomfited him by pointing him to an almost leveled stone wall, about twenty feet long, with the remark that his work would be the rebuilding of that stone wall, with stone brought from the neighboring slopes. In a few moments he was comfortably provided for in the kitchen, where the cook, a woman of his own nativity, apparently, "chaffed" him with a raillery that was to me quite unintelligible. Yet I noticed that when, at sunset, he accompanied Bridget to the spring for water, ostentatiously flourishing the empty bucket in his hand, when they returned in the gloaming Bridget was carrying the water, and my friend, the Tramp, was some paces behind her, cheerfully "colloguing," and picking blackberries.

At seven the next morning he started in cheerfully to work. At nine, A.M., he had placed three large stones on the first course in position, an hour having been spent in looking for a pick and hammer, and in the incidental "chaffing" with Bridget. At ten o'clock I went to overlook his work; it was a rash action, as it caused him to respectfully doff his hat, discontinue his labors, and lean back against the fence in cheerful and easy conversation. "Are you fond uv blackberries, Captain?" I told him that the children were in the habit of getting them from the meadow beyond, hoping to estop the suggestion I knew was coming. "Ah, but, Captain, it's meself that with wanderin' and havin' nothin' to pass me lips but the berries I'd pick from the hedges,—it's meself knows where to find thim. Sure, it's yer childer, and foine boys they are, Captain, that's besaching me to go wid 'em to the place, known'st only to meself." It is unnecessary to say that he triumphed. After the manner of vagabonds of all degrees, he had enlisted the women and children on his side—and my friend, the Tramp, had his own way. He departed at eleven and returned at four, P.M., with a tin dinner-pail half filled. On interrogating the boys it appeared that they had had a "bully time," but on cross-examination it came out that *they* had picked the berries. From four to six, three more stones were laid, and the arduous labors of the day were over. As I stood looking at the first course of six stones, my friend, the Tramp, stretched his strong arms out to their fullest extent and said: "Ay, but it's worruk that's good for me; give me worruk, and it's all I'll be askin' fur."

I ventured to suggest that he had not yet accomplished much.

"Wait till to-morror. Ah, but ye'll see thin. It's me hand that's yet onaisy wid brick-makin' and sthrange to the shtones. An ye'll wait till to-morror?"

Unfortunately I did not wait. An engagement took me away at an early hour, and when I rode up to my cottage at noon my eyes were greeted with the astonishing spectacle of my two boys hard at work laying the courses of the stone wall, assisted by Bridget and Norah, who were dragging stones from the hillsides, while comfortably stretched on the top of the wall lay my friend, the Tramp, quietly overseeing the operation with lazy and humorous comment. For an instant I was foolishly indignant, but he soon brought me to my senses. "Shure, sur, it's only larnin' the boys the habits uv industhry I was—and may they niver know, be the same token, what it is to worruk fur the bread betune their lips. Shure it's but makin' 'em think it play I was. As fur the colleens beyint in the kitchen, sure isn't it betther they was helping your honor here than colloguing with themselves inside?"

Nevertheless, I thought it expedient to forbid henceforth any interruption of servants or children with my friend's "worruk." Perhaps it was the result of this embargo that the next morning early the Tramp wanted to see me.

"And it's sorry I am to say it to ye, sur," he began, "but it's the handlin' of this stun that's desthroyin' me touch at the brick-makin', and it's better I should lave ye and find worruk at me own thrade. For it's worruk I am nadin'. It isn't meself, Captain, to ate the bread of oidleness here. And so good-by to ye, and if it's fifty cints ye can be givin' me ontil I'll find a kill—it's God that'll repay ye."

He got the money. But he got also conditionally a note from me to my next neighbor, a wealthy retired physician, possessed of a large domain, a man eminently practical and businesslike in his management of it. He employed many laborers on the sterile waste he called his "farm," and it occurred to me that if there really was any work in my friend, the Tramp, which my own indolence and preoccupation had failed to bring out, he was the man to do it.

I met him a week after. It was with some embarrassment that I inquired after my friend, the Tramp. "Oh, yes," he said, reflectively, "let's see: he came Monday and left me Thursday. He was, I think, a stout, strong man, a well-meaning, good-humored fellow, but afflicted with a most singular variety of diseases. The first day I put him at work in the stables he developed chills and fever caught in the swamps of Louisiana—"

"Excuse me," I said hurriedly, "you mean in Milwaukee!"

"I know what I'm talking about," returned the Doctor, testily; "he told me his whole wretched story—his escape from the Confederate service, the attack upon him by armed negroes, his concealment in the bayous and swamps—"

"Go on, Doctor," I said, feebly; "you were speaking of his work."

"Yes. Well, his system was full of malaria; the first day I had him wrapped up in blankets, and dosed with quinine. The next day he was taken with all the symptoms of cholera morbus, and I had to keep him up on brandy and capsicum. Rheumatism set in on the following day, and incapacitated him for work, and I concluded I had better give him a note to the director of the City Hospital than keep him here. As a pathological study he was good; but as I was looking for a man to help about the stable, I couldn't afford to keep him in both capacities."

As I never could really tell when the Doctor was in joke or in earnest, I dropped the subject. And so my friend, the Tramp, gradually faded from my memory, not however without leaving behind him in the barn where he had slept a lingering flavor of whisky, onions, and fluffiness. But in two weeks this had gone, and the "Shebang" (as my friends irreverently termed my habitation) knew him no more. Yet it was pleasant to think of him as having at last found a job at brick-making, or having returned to his family at Milwaukee, or making his Louisiana home once more happy with his presence, or again tempting the fish-producing main—this time with a noble and equitable captain.

It was a lovely August morning when I rode across the sandy peninsula to visit a certain noted family, whereof all the sons were valiant and the daughters beautiful. The front of the house was deserted, but on the rear veranda I heard the rustle of gowns, and above it arose what seemed to be the voice of Ulysses, reciting his wanderings. There was no mistaking that voice, it was my friend, the Tramp!

From what I could hastily gather from his speech, he had walked from St. John, N. B., to rejoin a distressed wife in New York, who was, however, living with opulent but objectionable relatives. "An' shure, miss, I wouldn't be askin' ye the loan of a cint if I could get worruk at me trade of carpet-wavin'—and may be ye know of some manufacthory where they wave carpets beyant here. Ah, miss, and if ye don't give me a cint, it's enough for the loikes of me to know that me troubles has brought the tears in the most beautiful oiyes in the wurruld, and God bless ye for it, miss!"

Now I knew that the Most Beautiful Eyes in the World belonged to one of the most sympathetic and tenderest hearts in the world, and I felt that common justice demanded my interference between it and one of the biggest scamps in the world. So, without waiting to be announced by the servant, I opened the door, and joined the group on the veranda.

If I expected to touch the conscience of my friend, the Tramp, by a dramatic entrance, I failed utterly; for no sooner did he see me, than he instantly gave vent to a howl of delight, and, falling on his knees before me, grasped my hand, and turned oratorically to the ladies.

"Oh, but it's himself—himself that has come as a witness to me carrakther! Oh, but it's himself that lifted me four wakes ago, when I was lyin' with a mortal wakeness on the say-coast, and tuk me to his house. Oh, but it's himself that shupported me over the faldes, and whin the chills and faver came on me and I shivered wid the cold, it was himself, God bless him, as sthripped the coat off his back, and giv it me, sayin', 'Take it, Dinnis, it's shtarved with the cowld say air ye'll be entoirely.' Ah, but look at him—will ye, miss! Look at his swate, modist face—a blushin' like your own, miss. Ah! look at him, will ye? He'll be denyin' of it in a minit—may the blessin' uv God folly him. Look at him, miss! Ah, but it's a swate pair ye'd make! (the rascal knew I was a married man.) Ah, miss, if you could see him wroightin' day and night with such an illigant hand of his own—(he had evidently believed from the gossip of my servants that I was a professor of chirography)—if ye could see him, miss, as I have, ye'd be proud of him."

He stopped out of breath. I was so completely astounded I could say nothing: the tremendous indictment I had framed to utter as I opened the door vanished completely. And as the Most Beautiful Eyes in the Wurruld turned gratefully to mine—well—

I still retained enough principle to ask the ladies to withdraw, while I would take upon myself the duty of examining into the case of my friend, the Tramp, and giving him such relief as was required. (I did not know until afterward, however, that the rascal had already despoiled their scant purses of three dollars and fifty cents.) When the door was closed upon them I turned upon him.

"You infernal rascal!"

"Ah, Captain, and would ye be refusin' *me* a carrakther and me givin' *ye* such a one as Oi did! God save us! but if ye'd hav' seen the luk that the purty one give ye. Well, before the chills and faver bruk me spirits entirely, when I was a young man, and makin' me tin dollars a week brick-makin', it's meself that wud hav' given—"

"I consider," I broke in, "that a dollar is a fair price for your story, and as I shall have to take it all back and expose you before the next twenty-four hours pass, I think you had better hasten to Milwaukee, New York, or Louisiana."

I handed him the dollar. "Mind, I don't want to see your face again."

"Ye wun't, Captain."

And I did not.

But it so chanced that later in the season, when the migratory inhabitants had flown to their hot-air registers in Boston and Providence, I breakfasted with one who had lingered. It was a certain Boston lawyer,—replete with principle, honesty, self-discipline, statistics, aesthetics, and a perfect consciousness of possessing all these virtues, and a full recognition of their market values. I think he tolerated me as a kind of foreigner, gently but firmly waiving all argument on any topic, frequently distrusting my facts, generally my deductions, and always my ideas. In conversation he always appeared to descend only half way down a long moral and intellectual staircase, and always delivered his conclusions over the balusters.

I had been speaking of my friend, the Tramp. "There is but one way of treating that class of impostors; it is simply to recognize the fact that the law calls him a 'vagrant,' and makes his trade a misdemeanor. Any sentiment on the other side renders you *particeps criminis.* I don't know but an action would lie against you for encouraging tramps. Now, I have an efficacious way of dealing with these gentry." He rose and took a double-barreled fowling-piece from the chimney. "When a tramp appears on my property,

I warn him off. If he persists, I fire on him—as I would on any criminal trespasser."

"Fire on him?" I echoed in alarm.

"Yes—*but with powder only!* Of course *he* does n't know that. But he does n't come back."

It struck me for the first time that possibly many other of my friend's arguments might be only blank cartridges, and used to frighten off other trespassing intellects.

"Of course, if the tramp still persisted, I would be justified in using shot. Last evening I had a visit from one. He was coming over the wall. My shot gun was efficacious; you should have seen him run!"

It was useless to argue with so positive a mind, and I dropped the subject. After breakfast I strolled over the downs, my friend promising to join me as soon as he arranged some household business.

It was a lovely, peaceful morning, not unlike the day when I first met my friend, the Tramp. The hush of a great benediction lay on land and sea. A few white sails twinkled afar, but sleepily; one or two large ships were creeping in lazily, like my friend, the Tramp. A voice behind me startled me.

My host had rejoined me. His face, however, looked a little troubled.

"I just now learned something of importance," he began. "It appears that with all my precautions that Tramp has visited my kitchen, and the servants have entertained him. Yesterday morning, it appears, while I was absent, he had the audacity to borrow my gun to go duck-shooting. At the end of two or three hours he returned with two ducks and—the gun."

"That was, at least, honest."

"Yes—but! That fool of a girl says that, as he handed back the gun, he told her it was all right, and that he had loaded it up again to save the master trouble."

I think I showed my concern in my face, for he added, hastily: "It was only duck-shot; a few wouldn't hurt him!"

Nevertheless, we both walked on in silence for a moment.

"I thought the gun kicked a little," he said at last, musingly; "but the idea of—Hallo! what's this?"

He stopped before the hollow where I had first seen my Tramp. It was deserted, but on the mosses there were spots of blood and fragments of an old gown, blood-stained, as if used for bandages. I looked at it closely: it was the gown intended for the consumptive wife of my friend, the Tramp.

But my host was already nervously tracking the blood-stains that on rock, moss, and boulder were steadily leading toward the sea. When I overtook him at last on the shore, he was standing before a flat rock, on which lay a bundle I recognized, tied up in a handkerchief, and a crooked grape-vine stick.

"He may have come here to wash his wounds—salt is a styptic," said my host, who had recovered his correct precision of statement.

I said nothing, but looked toward the sea. Whatever secret lay hid in its breast, it kept it fast. Whatever its calm eyes had seen that summer night, it gave no reflection now. It lay there passive, imperturbable, and reticent. But my friend, the Tramp, was gone!

Source: Bret Harte. *Drift from Two Shores*. Boston: Houghton, Osgood and Company, 1878.

HENRY JAMES

Henry James (1843–1916) would win greater fame and regard as the author of A Portrait of a Lady *and other novels, but in this, his first successful book, he displays a lighter, airier, quicker touch, as he describes the protagonist Frederick Winterbourne's infatuation with the visiting American debutante Daisy Miller. The story is set in a resort in Switzerland and in Rome.*

Daisy Miller: A Study in Two Parts (1878)

Part I[1]

At the little town of Vevay, in Switzerland, there is a particularly comfortable hotel. There are, indeed, many hotels for the entertainment of tourists is the business of the place, which, as many travellers will remember, is seated upon the edge of a remarkably blue lake—a lake that it behooves every tourist to visit. The shore of the lake presents an unbroken array of establishments of this order, of every category, from the "grand hotel" of the newest fashion, with a chalk-white front, a hundred balconies, and a dozen flags flying from its roof, to the little Swiss *pension* of an elder day, with its name inscribed in German-looking lettering upon a pink or yellow wall, and an awkward summer-house in the angle of the garden. One of the hotels at Vevay, however, is famous, even classical, being distinguished from many of its upstart neighbors by an air both of luxury and of maturity. In this region, in the month of June, American travellers are extremely numerous; it may be said, indeed, that Vevay assumes at this period some of the characteristics of an American watering-place. There are sights

1. The first part was titled "Les Trois Couronnes" [The Three Crowns] in the original 1878 *Cornhill Magazine* publication.

and sounds which evoke a vision, an echo, of Newport and Saratoga. There is a flitting hither and thither of "stylish" young girls, a rustling of muslin flounces, a rattle of dance music in the morning hours, a sound of high-pitched voices at all times. You receive an impression of these things at the excellent inn of the "Trois Couronnes," and are transported in fancy to the Ocean House or to Congress Hall. But at the "Trois Couronnes," it must be added, there are other features that are much at variance with these suggestions: neat German waiters, who look like secretaries of legation; Russian princesses sitting in the garden; little Polish boys walking about, held by the hand, with their governors; a view of the sunny crest of the Dent du Midi and the picturesque towers of the Castle of Chillon.

I hardly know whether it was the analogies or the differences that were uppermost in the mind of a young American, who, two or three years ago, sat in the garden of the "Trois Couronnes," looking about him, rather idly, at some of the graceful objects I have mentioned. It was a beautiful summer morning, and in whatever fashion the young American looked at things, they must have seemed to him charming. He had come from Geneva the day before by the little steamer, to see his aunt, who was staying at the hotel—Geneva having been for a long time his place of residence. But his aunt had a headache—his aunt had almost always a headache—and now she was shut up in her room, smelling camphor, so that he was at liberty to wander about. He was some seven-and-twenty years of age; when his friends spoke of him, they usually said that he was at Geneva "studying." When his enemies spoke of him, they said—but, after all, he had no enemies; he was an extremely amiable fellow, and universally liked. What I should say is, simply, that when certain persons spoke of him they affirmed that the reason of his spending so much time at Geneva was that he was extremely devoted to a lady who lived there—a foreign lady—a person older than himself. Very few Americans—indeed, I think none—had ever seen this lady, about whom there were some singular stories. But Winterbourne had an old attachment for the little metropolis of Calvinism; he had been put to school there as a boy, and he had afterward gone to college there—circumstances which had led to his forming a great many youthful friendships. Many of these he had kept, and they were a source of great satisfaction to him.

After knocking at his aunt's door, and learning that she was indisposed, he had taken a walk about the town, and then he had come in to his breakfast. He had now finished his breakfast; but he was drinking a small cup of coffee, which had been served to him on a little table in the garden by one of the waiters who looked like an *attaché*. At last he finished his coffee and lit a cigarette. Presently a small boy came walking along the path—an urchin of nine or ten. The child, who was diminutive for his years, had an aged expression of countenance, a pale complexion, and sharp little features. He was dressed in knickerbockers, with red stockings, which displayed his poor little spindle-shanks; he also wore a brilliant red cravat. He carried in his hand a long alpenstock, the sharp point of which he thrust into everything that he approached—the flower-beds, the garden-benches, the trains of the ladies' dresses. In front of Winterbourne he paused, looking at him with a pair of bright, penetrating little eyes.

"Will you give me a lump of sugar?" he asked, in a sharp, hard little voice—a voice immature, and yet, somehow, not young.

Winterbourne glanced at the small table near him, on which his coffee-service rested, and saw that several morsels of sugar remained. "Yes, you may take one," he answered; "but I don't think sugar is good for little boys."

This little boy stepped forward and carefully selected three of the coveted fragments, two of which he buried in the pocket of his knickerbockers, depositing the other as promptly in another place. He poked his alpenstock, lance-fashion, into Winterbourne's bench, and tried to crack the lump of sugar with his teeth.

"Oh, blazes; it's har-r-d!" he exclaimed, pronouncing the adjective in a peculiar manner.

Winterbourne had immediately perceived that he might have the honor of claiming him as a fellow-countryman. "Take care you don't hurt your teeth," he said, paternally.

"I haven't got any teeth to hurt. They have all come out. I have only got seven teeth. My mother counted them last night, and one came out right afterward. She said she'd slap me if any more came out. I can't help it. It's this old Europe. It's the climate that makes them come out. In America they didn't come out. It's these hotels."

Winterbourne was much amused. "If you eat three lumps of sugar, your mother will certainly slap you," he said.

"She's got to give me some candy, then," rejoined his young interlocutor. "I can't get any candy here—any American candy. American candy's the best candy."

"And are American little boys the best little boys?" asked Winterbourne.

"I don't know. I'm an American boy," said the child.

"I see you are one of the best!" laughed Winterbourne.

"Are you an American man?" pursued this vivacious infant. And then, on Winterbourne's affirmative reply—"American men are the best," he declared.

His companion thanked him for the compliment; and the child, who had now got astride of his alpenstock, stood looking about him, while he attacked a second lump of sugar. Winterbourne wondered if he himself had been like this in his infancy, for he had been brought to Europe at about this age.

"Here comes my sister!" cried the child, in a moment. "She's an American girl."

Winterbourne looked along the path and saw a beautiful young lady advancing. "American girls are the best girls," he said, cheerfully, to his young companion.

"My sister ain't the best!" the child declared. "She's always blowing at me."

"I imagine that is your fault, not hers," said Winterbourne. The young lady meanwhile had drawn near. She was dressed in white muslin, with a hundred frills and flounces, and knots of pale-colored ribbon. She was bare-headed; but she balanced in her hand a large parasol, with a deep border of embroidery; and she was strikingly, admirably pretty. "How pretty they are!" thought Winterbourne, straightening himself in his seat, as if he were prepared to rise.

The young lady paused in front of his bench, near the parapet of the garden, which overlooked the lake. The little boy had now converted his alpenstock into a vaulting-pole, by the aid of which he was springing about in the gravel, and kicking it up not a little.

"Randolph," said the young lady, "what *are* you doing?"

"I'm going up the Alps," replied Randolph. "This is the way!" And he gave another little jump, scattering the pebbles about Winterbourne's ears.

"That's the way they come down," said Winterbourne.

"He's an American man!" cried Randolph, in his little hard voice.

The young lady gave no heed to this announcement, but looked straight at her brother. "Well, I guess you had better be quiet," she simply observed.

It seemed to Winterbourne that he had been in a manner presented. He got up and stepped slowly toward the young girl, throwing away his cigarette. "This little boy and I have made acquaintance," he said, with great civility. In Geneva, as he had been perfectly aware, a young man was not at liberty to speak to a young unmarried lady except under certain rarely occurring conditions; but here at Vevay, what conditions could be better than these?—a pretty American girl coming and standing in front of you in a garden. This pretty American girl, however, on hearing Winterbourne's observation, simply glanced at him; she then turned her head and looked over the parapet, at the lake and the opposite mountains. He wondered whether he had gone too far; but he decided that he must advance farther, rather than retreat. While he was thinking of something else to say, the young lady turned to the little boy again.

"I should like to know where you got that pole," she said.

"I bought it," responded Randolph.

"You don't mean to say you're going to take it to Italy?"

"Yes, I am going to take it to Italy," the child declared.

The young girl glanced over the front of her dress, and smoothed out a knot or two of ribbon. Then she rested her eyes upon the prospect again. "Well, I guess you had better leave it somewhere," she said, after a moment.

"Are you going to Italy?" Winterbourne inquired, in a tone of great respect.

The young lady glanced at him again. "Yes, sir," she replied. And she said nothing more.

"Are you—a—going over the Simplon?" Winterbourne pursued, a little embarrassed.

"I don't know," she said. "I suppose it's some mountain. Randolph, what mountain are we going over?"

"Going where?" the child demanded.

"To Italy," Winterbourne explained.

"I don't know," said Randolph. "I don't want to go to Italy. I want to go to America."

"Oh, Italy is a beautiful place!" rejoined the young man.

"Can you get candy there?" Randolph loudly inquired.

"I hope not," said his sister. "I guess you have had enough candy, and mother thinks so too."

"I haven't had any for ever so long—for a hundred weeks!" cried the boy, still jumping about.

The young lady inspected her flounces and smoothed her ribbons again; and Winterbourne presently risked an observation upon the beauty of the view. He was ceasing to be embarrassed, for he had begun to perceive that she was not in the least embarrassed herself. There had not been the slightest alteration in her charming complexion; she was evidently neither offended nor flattered. If she looked another way when he spoke to her, and seemed not particularly to hear him, this was simply her habit, her manner. Yet, as he talked a little more, and pointed out some of the objects of interest in the view, with which she appeared quite unacquainted, she gradually gave him more of the benefit of her glance; and then he saw that this glance was perfectly direct and unshrinking. It was not, however, what would have been called an immodest glance, for the young girl's eyes were singularly honest and fresh. They were wonderfully pretty eyes; and, indeed, Winterbourne had not seen for a long time anything prettier than his fair countrywoman's various features—her complexion, her nose, her ears, her teeth. He had a great relish for feminine beauty; he was addicted to observing and analyzing it; and as regards this young lady's face he made several observations. It was not at all insipid, but it was not exactly expressive; and though it was eminently delicate, Winterbourne mentally accused it—very forgivingly—of a want of finish. He thought it very possible that Master Randolph's sister was a coquette; he was sure she had a spirit of her own; but in her bright, sweet, superficial little visage there was no mockery, no irony. Before long it became obvious that she was much disposed toward conversation. She told him that they were going to Rome for the winter—she and her mother and Randolph. She asked him if he was a "real American"; she shouldn't have taken him for one; he seemed more like a German—this was said after a little hesitation—especially when he spoke. Winterbourne, laughing, answered that he had met Germans who spoke like Americans; but that he had not, so far as he remembered, met an American who spoke like a German. Then he asked her if she should not be more comfortable in sitting upon the bench which he had just quitted. She answered that she liked standing up and walking about; but she presently sat down. She told him she was from New York State—"if you know where that is." Winterbourne learned more about her by catching hold of her small, slippery brother and making him stand a few minutes by his side.

"Tell me your name, my boy," he said.

"Randolph C. Miller," said the boy, sharply. "And I'll tell you her name;" and he leveled his alpenstock at his sister.

"You had better wait till you are asked!" said this young lady, calmly.

"I should like very much to know your name," said Winterbourne.

"Her name is Daisy Miller!" cried the child. "But that isn't her real name; that isn't her name on her cards."

"It's a pity you haven't got one of my cards!" said Miss Miller.

"Her real name is Annie P. Miller," the boy went on.

"Ask him *his* name," said his sister, indicating Winterbourne.

But on this point Randolph seemed perfectly indifferent; he continued to supply information with regard to his own family. "My father's name is Ezra B. Miller," he announced. "My father ain't in Europe; my father's in a better place than Europe."

Winterbourne imagined for a moment that this was the manner in which the child had been taught to intimate that Mr. Miller had been removed to the sphere of celestial reward. But Randolph immediately added, "My father's in Schenectady. He's got a big business. My father's rich, you bet!"

"Well!" ejaculated Miss Miller, lowering her parasol and looking at the embroidered border. Winterbourne presently released the child, who departed, dragging his alpenstock along the path. "He doesn't like Europe," said the young girl. "He wants to go back."

"To Schenectady, you mean?"

"Yes; he wants to go right home. He hasn't got any boys here. There is one boy here, but he always goes round with a teacher; they won't let him play."

"And your brother hasn't any teacher?" Winterbourne inquired.

"Mother thought of getting him one, to travel round with us. There was a lady told her of a very good teacher; an American lady—perhaps you know her—Mrs. Sanders. I think she came from Boston. She told her of this teacher, and we thought of getting him to travel round with us. But Randolph said he didn't want a teacher traveling round with us. He said he wouldn't have lessons when he was in the cars. And we *are* in the cars about half the time. There was an English lady we met in the cars—I think her name was Miss Featherstone; perhaps you know her. She wanted to know why I didn't give Randolph lessons—give him 'instruction,' she called it. I guess he could give me more instruction than I could give him. He's very smart."

"Yes," said Winterbourne; "he seems very smart."

"Mother's going to get a teacher for him as soon as we get to Italy. Can you get good teachers in Italy?"

"Very good, I should think," said Winterbourne.

"Or else she's going to find some school. He ought to learn some more. He's only nine. He's going to college." And in this way Miss Miller continued to converse upon the affairs of her family, and upon other topics. She sat there with her extremely pretty hands, ornamented with very brilliant rings, folded in her lap, and with her pretty eyes now resting upon those of Winterbourne, now wandering over the garden, the people who passed by, and the beautiful view. She talked to Winterbourne as if she had known him a long time. He found it very pleasant. It was many years since he had heard a young girl talk so much. It might have been said of this unknown young lady, who had come and sat down beside him upon a bench, that she chattered. She was very quiet; she sat in a charming, tranquil attitude; but her lips and her eyes were constantly moving. She had a soft, slender, agreeable voice, and her tone was decidedly sociable. She gave Winterbourne a history of her movements and intentions, and those of her mother and brother, in Europe, and enumerated, in particular, the various hotels at which they had stopped. "That English lady in the cars," she said—"Miss Featherstone—asked me if we didn't all live in hotels in America. I told her I had never been in so many hotels in my life as since I came to Europe. I have never seen so many—it's nothing but hotels." But Miss Miller did not make this remark with a querulous accent; she appeared to be in the best humor with everything. She declared that the hotels were very good, when once you got used to their ways, and that Europe was perfectly sweet. She was not disappointed—not a bit. Perhaps it was because she had heard so much about it before. She had ever so many intimate friends that had been there ever so many times. And then she had had ever so many dresses and things from Paris. Whenever she put on a Paris dress she felt as if she were in Europe.

"It was a kind of a wishing-cap," said Winterbourne.

"Yes," said Miss Miller, without examining this analogy; "it always made me wish I was here. But I needn't have done that for dresses. I am sure they send all the pretty ones to America; you see the most frightful things here. The only thing I don't like," she proceeded, "is the society. There isn't any society; or, if there is, I don't know where it keeps itself. Do you? I suppose there is some society somewhere, but I haven't seen anything of it. I'm very fond of society, and I have always had a great deal of it. I don't mean only in Schenectady, but in New York. I used to go to New York every winter. In New York I had lots of society. Last winter I had seventeen dinners given me; and three of them were by gentlemen," added Daisy Miller. "I have more friends in New York than in Schenectady—more gentleman friends; and more young lady friends too," she resumed in a moment. She paused again for an instant; she was looking at Winterbourne with all her prettiness in her lively eyes and in her light, slightly monotonous smile. "I have always had," she said, "a great deal of gentlemen's society."

Poor Winterbourne was amused, perplexed, and decidedly charmed. He had never yet heard a young girl express herself in just this fashion; never, at least, save in cases where to say such things seemed a kind of demonstrative evidence of a certain laxity of deportment. And yet was he to accuse Miss Daisy Miller of actual or potential *inconduite*, as they said at Geneva? He felt that he had lived at Geneva so long that he had lost a good deal; he had become dishabituated to the American tone. Never, indeed, since he had grown old enough to appreciate things, had he encountered a young American girl of so pronounced a type as this. Certainly she was very charming, but how deucedly sociable! Was she simply a pretty girl from New York State? were they all like that, the pretty girls who had a good deal of gentlemen's society? Or was she also a designing, an audacious, an unscrupulous young person? Winterbourne had lost his instinct in this matter, and his reason could not help him. Miss Daisy Miller looked extremely innocent. Some people had told him that, after all, American girls were exceedingly innocent; and others had told him that, after all, they were not. He was inclined to think Miss Daisy Miller was a flirt—a pretty American flirt. He had never, as yet, had any relations with young ladies of this category. He had known, here in Europe, two or three women—persons older than Miss Daisy Miller, and provided, for respectability's sake, with husbands—

who were great coquettes—dangerous, terrible women, with whom one's relations were liable to take a serious turn. But this young girl was not a coquette in that sense; she was very unsophisticated; she was only a pretty American flirt. Winterbourne was almost grateful for having found the formula that applied to Miss Daisy Miller. He leaned back in his seat; he remarked to himself that she had the most charming nose he had ever seen; he wondered what were the regular conditions and limitations of one's intercourse with a pretty American flirt. It presently became apparent that he was on the way to learn.

"Have you been to that old castle?" asked the young girl, pointing with her parasol to the far-gleaming walls of the Château de Chillon.

"Yes, formerly, more than once," said Winterbourne. "You too, I suppose, have seen it?"

"No; we haven't been there. I want to go there dreadfully. Of course I mean to go there. I wouldn't go away from here without having seen that old castle."

"It's a very pretty excursion," said Winterbourne, "and very easy to make. You can drive, you know, or you can go by the little steamer."

"You can go in the cars," said Miss Miller.

"Yes; you can go in the cars," Winterbourne assented.

"Our courier says they take you right up to the castle," the young girl continued. "We were going last week; but my mother gave out. She suffers dreadfully from dyspepsia. She said she couldn't go. Randolph wouldn't go either; he says he doesn't think much of old castles. But I guess we'll go this week, if we can get Randolph."

"Your brother is not interested in ancient monuments?" Winterbourne inquired, smiling.

"He says he don't care much about old castles. He's only nine. He wants to stay at the hotel. Mother's afraid to leave him alone, and the courier won't stay with him; so we haven't been to many places. But it will be too bad if we don't go up there." And Miss Miller pointed again at the Château de Chillon.

"I should think it might be arranged," said Winterbourne. "Couldn't you get some one to stay for the afternoon with Randolph?"

Miss Miller looked at him a moment, and then, very placidly, "I wish *you* would stay with him!" she said.

Winterbourne hesitated a moment. "I should much rather go to Chillon with you."

"With me?" asked the young girl, with the same placidity.

She didn't rise, blushing, as a young girl at Geneva would have done; and yet Winterbourne, conscious that he had been very bold, thought it possible she was offended. "With your mother," he answered, very respectfully.

But it seemed that both his audacity and his respect were lost upon Miss Daisy Miller. "I guess my mother won't go, after all," she said. "She don't like to ride round in the afternoon. But did you really mean what you said just now—that you would like to go up there?"

"Most earnestly," Winterbourne declared.

"Then we may arrange it. If mother will stay with Randolph, I guess Eugenio will."

"Eugenio?" the young man inquired.

"Eugenio's our courier. He doesn't like to stay with Randolph; he's the most fastidious man I ever saw. But he's a splendid courier. I guess he'll stay at home with Randolph if mother does, and then we can go to the castle."

Winterbourne reflected for an instant as lucidly as possible—"we" could only mean Miss Daisy Miller and himself. This programme seemed almost too agreeable for credence; he felt as if he ought to kiss the young lady's hand. Possibly he would have done so, and quite spoiled the project; but at this moment another person, presumably Eugenio, appeared. A tall, handsome man, with superb whiskers, wearing a velvet morning-coat and a brilliant watch-chain, approached Miss Miller, looking sharply at her companion. "Oh, Eugenio!" said Miss Miller, with the friendliest accent.

Eugenio had looked at Winterbourne from head to foot; he now bowed gravely to the young lady. "I have the honor to inform mademoiselle that luncheon is upon the table."

Miss Miller slowly rose. "See here, Eugenio!" she said; "I'm going to that old castle, anyway."

"To the Château de Chillon, mademoiselle?" the courier inquired. "Mademoiselle has made arrangements?" he added, in a tone which struck Winterbourne as very impertinent.

Eugenio's tone apparently threw, even to Miss Miller's own apprehension, a slightly ironical light upon the young girl's situation. She turned to Winterbourne, blushing a little—a very little. "You won't back out?" she said.

"I shall not be happy till we go!" he protested.

"And you are staying in this hotel?" she went on. "And you are really an American?"

The courier stood looking at Winterbourne offensively. The young man, at least, thought his manner of looking an offence to Miss Miller; it conveyed an imputation that she "picked up" acquaintances. "I shall have the honor of presenting to you a person who will tell you all about me," he said, smiling, and referring to his aunt.

"Oh, well, we'll go some day," said Miss Miller. And she gave him a smile and turned away. She put up her parasol and walked back to the inn beside Eugenio. Winterbourne stood looking after her; and as she moved away, drawing her muslin furbelows over the gravel, said to himself that she had the *tournure* of a princess.

He had, however, engaged to do more than proved feasible, in promising to present his aunt, Mrs. Costello, to Miss Daisy Miller. As soon as the former lady had got better of her headache he waited upon her in her apartment; and, after the proper inquiries in regard to her health, he asked her if she had observed in the hotel an American family—a mamma, a daughter, and a little boy.

"And a courier?" said Mrs. Costello. "Oh yes, I have observed them. Seen them—heard them—and kept out of their way." Mrs. Costello was a widow with a fortune; a person of much distinction, who frequently intimated that, if she were not so dreadfully liable to sick-headaches, she would probably have left a deeper impress upon her time. She had a long, pale face, a high nose, and a great deal of very striking white hair, which she wore in large puffs and *rouleaux* over the top of her head. She had two sons married in New York, and another who was now in Europe. This young man was amusing himself at Hambourg; and, though he was on his travels, was rarely perceived to visit any particular city at the moment selected by his mother for her own appearance there. Her nephew, who had come up to Vevay expressly to see her, was therefore more attentive than those who, as she said, were nearer to her. He had imbibed at Geneva the idea that one must always be attentive to one's aunt. Mrs. Costello had not seen him for many years, and she was greatly pleased with him, manifesting her approbation by initiating him into many of the secrets of that social sway which, as she gave him to understand, she exerted in the American capital. She admitted that she was very exclusive; but, if he were acquainted with New York, he would see that one had to be. And her picture of the minutely hierarchical constitution of the society of that city, which she presented to him in many different lights, was, to Winterbourne's imagination, almost oppressively striking.

He immediately perceived, from her tone, that Miss Daisy Miller's place in the social scale was low. "I am afraid you don't approve of them," he said.

"They are very common," Mrs. Costello declared. "They are the sort of Americans that one does one's duty by not—not accepting."

"Ah, you don't accept them?" said the young man.

"I can't, my dear Frederick. I would if I could, but I can't."

"The young girl is very pretty," said Winterbourne, in a moment.

"Of course she's pretty. But she is very common."

"I see what you mean, of course," said Winterbourne, after another pause.

"She has that charming look that they all have," his aunt resumed. "I can't think where they pick it up; and she dresses in perfection—no, you don't know how well she dresses. I can't think where they get their taste."

"But, my dear aunt, she is not, after all, a Camanche savage."

"She is a young lady," said Mrs. Costello, "who has an intimacy with her mamma's courier."

"An intimacy with the courier?" the young man demanded.

"Oh, the mother is just as bad! They treat the courier like a familiar friend—like a gentleman. I shouldn't wonder if he dines with them. Very likely they have never seen a man with such good manners, such fine clothes, so like a gentleman. He probably corresponds to the young lady's idea of a count. He sits with them in the garden in the evening. I think he smokes."

Winterbourne listened with interest to these disclosures; they helped him to make up his mind about Miss Daisy. Evidently she was rather wild. "Well," he said, "I am not a courier, and yet she was very charming to me."

"You had better have said at first," said Mrs. Costello, with dignity, "that you had made her acquaintance."

"We simply met in the garden, and we talked a bit."

"*Tout bonnement!* And pray what did you say?"

"I said I should take the liberty of introducing her to my admirable aunt."

"I am much obliged to you."

"It was to guarantee my respectability," said Winterbourne.

"And pray who is to guarantee hers?"

"Ah, you are cruel!" said the young man. "She's a very nice young girl."

"You don't say that as if you believed it," Mrs. Costello observed.

"She is completely uncultivated," Winterbourne went on. "But she is wonderfully pretty, and, in short, she is very nice. To prove that I believe it, I am going to take her to the Château de Chillon."

"You two are going off there together? I should say it proved just the contrary. How long had you known her, may I ask, when this interesting project was formed? You haven't been twenty-four hours in the house."

"I had known her half an hour!" said Winterbourne, smiling.

"Dear me!" cried Mrs. Costello. "What a dreadful girl!"

Her nephew was silent for some moments. "You really think, then," he began, earnestly, and with a desire for trustworthy information—"you really think that—" But he paused again.

"Think what, sir?" said his aunt.

"That she is the sort of young lady who expects a man, sooner or later, to carry her off?"

"I haven't the least idea what such young ladies expect a man to do. But I really think that you had better not meddle with little American girls that are uncultivated, as you call them. You have lived too long out of the country. You will be sure to make some great mistake. You are too innocent."

"My dear aunt, I am not so innocent," said Winterbourne, smiling and curling his mustache.

"You are guilty too, then!"

Winterbourne continued to curl his mustache, meditatively. "You won't let the poor girl know you then?" he asked at last.

"Is it literally true that she is going to the Château de Chillon with you?"

"I think that she fully intends it."

"Then, my dear Frederick," said Mrs. Costello, "I must decline the honor of her acquaintance. I am an old woman, but I am not too old, thank Heaven, to be shocked!"

"But don't they all do these things—the young girls in America?" Winterbourne inquired.

Mrs. Costello stared a moment. "I should like to see my granddaughters do them!" she declared, grimly.

This seemed to throw some light upon the matter, for Winterbourne remembered to have heard that his pretty cousins in New York were "tremendous flirts." If, therefore, Miss Daisy Miller exceeded the liberal margin allowed to these young ladies, it was probable that anything might be expected of her. Winterbourne was impatient to see her again, and he was vexed with himself that, by instinct, he should not appreciate her justly.

Though he was impatient to see her, he hardly knew what he should say to her about his aunt's refusal to become acquainted with her; but he discovered, promptly enough, that with Miss Daisy Miller there was no great need of walking on tiptoe. He found her that evening in the garden, wandering about in the warm starlight like an indolent sylph, and swinging to and fro the largest fan he had ever beheld. It was ten o'clock. He had dined with his aunt, had been sitting with her since dinner, and had just taken leave of her till the morrow. Miss Daisy Miller seemed very glad to see him; she declared it was the longest evening she had ever passed.

"Have you been all alone?" he asked.

"I have been walking round with mother. But mother gets tired walking round," she answered.

"Has she gone to bed?"

"No; she doesn't like to go to bed," said the young girl. "She doesn't sleep—not three hours. She says she doesn't know how she lives. She's dreadfully nervous. I guess she sleeps more than she thinks. She's gone somewhere after Randolph; she wants to try to get him to go to bed. He doesn't like to go to bed."

"Let us hope she will persuade him," observed Winterbourne.

"She will talk to him all she can; but he doesn't like her to talk to him," said Miss Daisy, opening her fan. "She's going to try to get Eugenio to talk to him. But he isn't afraid of Eugenio. Eugenio's a splendid courier, but he can't make much impression on Randolph! I don't believe he'll go to bed before eleven." It appeared that Randolph's vigil was in fact triumphantly prolonged, for Winterbourne strolled about with the young girl for some time without meeting her mother. "I have been looking round for that lady you want to introduce me to," his companion resumed. "She's your aunt." Then, on Winterbourne's admitting the fact, and expressing some curiosity as to how she had learned it, she said she had heard all about Mrs. Costello from the chamber-maid. She was very quiet, and very *comme il faut;* she wore white puffs; she spoke to no one, and she never dined at the *table d'hôte*. Every two days she had a headache. "I think that's a lovely description, headache and all!" said Miss Daisy, chattering along in her thin, gay voice. "I want to know her ever so much. I know just what *your* aunt would be; I know I should like her. She would be very exclusive. I like a lady to be exclusive; I'm dying to be exclusive myself. Well, we *are* exclusive, mother and I. We don't speak to every one—or they don't speak to us. I suppose it's about the same thing. Anyway, I shall be ever so glad to know your aunt."

Winterbourne was embarrassed. "She would be most happy," he said; "but I am afraid those headaches will interfere."

The young girl looked at him through the dusk. "But I suppose she doesn't have a headache every day," she said, sympathetically.

Winterbourne was silent a moment. "She tells me she does," he answered at last, not knowing what to say.

Miss Daisy Miller stopped, and stood looking at him. Her prettiness was still visible in the darkness; she was opening and closing her enormous fan. "She doesn't want to know me!" she said, suddenly. "Why don't you say so? You needn't be afraid. I'm not afraid!" And she gave a little laugh.

Winterbourne fancied there was a tremor in her voice; he was touched, shocked, mortified by it. "My dear young lady," he protested, "she knows no one. It's her wretched health."

The young girl walked on a few steps, laughing still. "You needn't be afraid," she repeated. "Why should she want to know me?" Then she paused again; she was close to the parapet of the garden, and in front of her was the starlit lake. There was a vague sheen upon its surface, and in the distance were dimly-seen mountain forms. Daisy Miller looked out upon the mysterious prospect, and then she gave another little laugh. "Gracious! she *is* exclusive!" she said. Winterbourne wondered whether she was seriously wounded, and for a moment almost wished that her sense of injury might be such as to make it becoming in him to attempt to reassure and comfort her. He had a pleasant sense that she would be very approachable for consolatory purposes. He felt then, for the instant, quite ready to sacrifice his aunt, conversationally; to admit that she was a proud, rude woman, and to declare that they needn't mind her. But before he had time to commit himself to this perilous mixture of gallantry and impiety, the young lady, resuming her walk, gave an exclamation in quite another tone.

"Well, here's mother! I guess she hasn't got Randolph to go to bed." The figure of a lady appeared, at a distance, very indistinct in the darkness, and advancing with a slow and wavering movement. Suddenly it seemed to pause.

"Are you sure it is your mother? Can you distinguish her in this thick dusk?" Winterbourne asked.

"Well!" cried Miss Daisy Miller, with a laugh; "I guess I know my own mother. And when she has got on my shawl, too! She is always wearing my things."

The lady in question, ceasing to advance, hovered vaguely about the spot at which she had checked her steps.

"I am afraid your mother doesn't see you," said Winterbourne. "Or perhaps," he added, thinking, with Miss Miller, the joke permissible—"perhaps she feels guilty about your shawl."

"Oh, it's a fearful old thing!" the young girl replied, serenely. "I told her she could wear it. She won't come here, because she sees you."

"Ah, then," said Winterbourne, "I had better leave you."

"Oh no; come on!" urged Miss Daisy Miller.

"I'm afraid your mother doesn't approve of my walking with you."

Miss Miller gave him a serious glance. "It isn't for me; it's for you—that is, it's for *her*. Well, I don't know who it's for! But mother doesn't like any of my gentlemen friends. She's right down timid. She always makes a fuss if I introduce a gentleman. But I *do* introduce them—almost always. If I didn't introduce my gentlemen friends to mother," the young girl added, in her little soft, flat monotone, "I shouldn't think it was natural."

"To introduce me," said Winterbourne, "you must know my name." And he proceeded to pronounce it.

"Oh, dear, I can't say all that!" said his companion, with a laugh. But by this time they had come up to Mrs. Miller, who, as they drew near, walked to the parapet of the garden and leaned upon it, looking intently at the lake, and turning her back to them. "Mother!" said the young girl, in a tone of decision. Upon this the elder lady turned round. "Mr. Winterbourne," said Miss Daisy Miller, introducing the young man very frankly and prettily. "Common," she was, as Mrs. Costello had pronounced her; yet it was a wonder to Winterbourne that, with her commonness, she had a singularly delicate grace.

Her mother was a small, spare, light person, with a wandering eye, a very exiguous nose, and a large forehead, decorated with a certain amount of thin, much-frizzled hair. Like her daughter, Mrs. Miller was dressed with extreme elegance; she had enormous diamonds in her ears. So far as Winterbourne could observe, she gave him no greeting—she certainly was not looking at him. Daisy was near her, pulling her shawl straight. "What are you doing, poking round here?" this young lady inquired, but by no means with that harshness of accent which her choice of words may imply.

"I don't know," said her mother, turning toward the lake again.

"I shouldn't think you'd want that shawl!" Daisy exclaimed.

"Well, I do!" her mother answered, with a little laugh.

"Did you get Randolph to go to bed?" asked the young girl.

"No; I couldn't induce him," said Mrs. Miller, very gently. "He wants to talk to the waiter. He likes to talk to that waiter."

"I was telling Mr. Winterbourne," the young girl went on; and to the young man's ear her tone might have indicated that she had been uttering his name all her life.

"Oh yes!" said Winterbourne; "I have the pleasure of knowing your son."

Randolph's mamma was silent; she turned her attention to the lake. But at last she spoke. "Well, I don't see how he lives!"

"Anyhow, it isn't so bad as it was at Dover," said Daisy Miller.

"And what occurred at Dover?" Winterbourne asked.

"He wouldn't go to bed at all. I guess he sat up all night in the public parlor. He wasn't in bed at twelve o'clock: I know that."

"It was half-past twelve," declared Mrs. Miller, with mild emphasis.

"Does he sleep much during the day?" Winterbourne demanded.

"I guess he doesn't sleep much," Daisy rejoined.

"I wish he would!" said her mother. "It seems as if he couldn't."

"I think he's real tiresome," Daisy pursued.

Then, for some moments, there was silence. "Well, Daisy Miller," said the elder lady, presently, "I shouldn't think you'd want to talk against your own brother!"

"Well, he *is* tiresome, mother," said Daisy, quite without the asperity of a retort.

"He's only nine," urged Mrs. Miller.

"Well, he wouldn't go to that castle," said the young girl. "I'm going there with Mr. Winterbourne."

To this announcement, very placidly made, Daisy's mamma offered no response. Winterbourne took for granted that she deeply disapproved of the projected excursion; but he said to himself that she was a simple, easily-managed person, and that a few deferential protestations would take the edge from her displeasure. "Yes," he began; "your daughter has kindly allowed me the honor of being her guide."

Mrs. Miller's wandering eyes attached themselves, with a sort of appealing air, to Daisy, who, however, strolled a few steps farther, gently humming to herself. "I presume you will go in the cars," said her mother.

"Yes, or in the boat," said Winterbourne.

"Well, of course, I don't know," Mrs. Miller rejoined. "I have never been to that castle."

"It is a pity you shouldn't go," said Winterbourne, beginning to feel reassured as to her opposition. And yet he was quite prepared to find that, as a matter of course, she meant to accompany her daughter.

"We've been thinking ever so much about going," she pursued; "but it seems as if we couldn't. Of course Daisy—she wants to go round. But there's a lady here—I don't know her name—she says she shouldn't think we'd want to go to see castles *here*; she should think we'd want to wait till we got to Italy. It seems as if there would be so many there," continued Mrs. Miller, with an air of increasing confidence. "Of course we only want to see the principal ones. We visited several in England," she presently added.

"Ah yes! in England there are beautiful castles," said Winterbourne. "But Chillon, here, is very well worth seeing."

"Well, if Daisy feels up to it—" said Mrs. Miller, in a tone impregnated with a sense of the magnitude of the enterprise. "It seems as if there was nothing she wouldn't undertake."

"Oh, I think she'll enjoy it!" Winterbourne declared. And he desired more and more to make it a certainty that he was to have the privilege of a *tête-à-tête* with the young lady, who was still strolling along in front of them, softly vocalizing. "You are not disposed, madam," he inquired, "to undertake it yourself?"

Daisy's mother looked at him an instant askance, and then walked forward in silence. Then—"I guess she had better go alone," she said simply. Winterbourne observed to himself that this was a very different type of maternity from that of the vigilant matrons who massed themselves in the forefront of social intercourse in the dark old city at the other end of the lake. But his meditations were interrupted by hearing his name very distinctly pronounced by Mrs. Miller's unprotected daughter.

"Mr. Winterbourne!" murmured Daisy.

"Mademoiselle!" said the young man.

"Don't you want to take me out in a boat?"

"At present?" he asked.

"Of course!" said Daisy.

"Well, Annie Miller!" exclaimed her mother.

"I beg you, madam, to let her go," said Winterbourne, ardently; for he had never yet enjoyed the sensation of guiding through the summer starlight a skiff freighted with a fresh and beautiful young girl.

"I shouldn't think she'd want to," said her mother. "I should think she'd rather go in-doors."

"I'm sure Mr. Winterbourne wants to take me," Daisy declared. "He's so awfully devoted!"

"I will row you over to Chillon in the starlight."

"I don't believe it!" said Daisy.

"Well!" ejaculated the elder lady again.

"You haven't spoken to me for half an hour," her daughter went on.

"I have been having some very pleasant conversation with your mother," said Winterbourne.

"Well, I want you to take me out in a boat!" Daisy repeated. They had all stopped, and she had turned round and was looking at Winterbourne. Her face wore a charming smile, her pretty eyes were gleaming, she was swinging her great fan about. No; it's impossible to be prettier than that, thought Winterbourne.

"There are half a dozen boats moored at that landing-place," he said, pointing to certain steps which descended from the garden to the lake. "If you will do me the honor to accept my arm, we will go and select one of them."

Daisy stood there smiling; she threw back her head and gave a little, light laugh. "I like a gentleman to be formal!" she declared.

"I assure you it's a formal offer."

"I was bound I would make you say something," Daisy went on.

"You see, it's not very difficult," said Winterbourne. "But I am afraid you are chaffing me."

"I think not, sir," remarked Mrs. Miller, very gently.

"Do, then, let me give you a row," he said to the young girl.

"It's quite lovely, the way you say that!" cried Daisy.

"It will be still more lovely to do it."

"Yes, it would be lovely!" said Daisy. But she made no movement to accompany him; she only stood there laughing.

"I should think you had better find out what time it is," interposed her mother.

"It is eleven o'clock, madam," said a voice, with a foreign accent, out of the neighboring darkness; and Winterbourne, turning, perceived the florid personage who was in attendance upon the two ladies. He had apparently just approached.

"Oh, Eugenio," said Daisy, "I am going out in a boat!"

Eugenio bowed. "At eleven o'clock, mademoiselle?"

"I am going with Mr. Winterbourne—this very minute."

"Do tell her she can't," said Mrs. Miller to the courier.

"I think you had better not go out in a boat, mademoiselle," Eugenio declared.

Winterbourne wished to Heaven this pretty girl were not so familiar with her courier; but he said nothing.

"I suppose you don't think it's proper!" Daisy exclaimed. "Eugenio doesn't think anything's proper."

"I am at your service," said Winterbourne.

"Does mademoiselle propose to go alone?" asked Eugenio of Mrs. Miller.

"Oh no; with this gentleman!" answered Daisy's mamma.

The courier looked for a moment at Winterbourne—the latter thought he was smiling—and then, solemnly, with a bow, "As mademoiselle pleases!" he said.

"Oh, I hoped you would make a fuss!" said Daisy. "I don't care to go now."

"I myself shall make a fuss if you don't go," said Winterbourne.

"That's all I want—a little fuss!" And the young girl began to laugh again.

"Mr. Randolph has gone to bed!" the courier announced, frigidly.

"Oh, Daisy; now we can go!" said Mrs. Miller.

Daisy turned away from Winterbourne, looking at him, smiling, and fanning herself. "Good-night," she said; "I hope you are disappointed, or disgusted, or something!"

He looked at her, taking the hand she offered him. "I am puzzled," he answered.

"Well, I hope it won't keep you awake!" she said, very smartly; and, under the escort of the privileged Eugenio, the two ladies passed toward the house.

Winterbourne stood looking after them; he was indeed puzzled. He lingered beside the lake for a quarter of an hour, turning over the mystery of the young girl's sudden familiarities and caprices. But the only very definite conclusion he came to was that he should enjoy deucedly "going off" with her somewhere.

Two days afterward he went off with her to the Castle of Chillon. He waited for her in the large hall of the hotel, where the couriers, the servants, the foreign tourists, were lounging about and staring. It was not the place he should have chosen, but she had appointed it. She came tripping down-stairs, buttoning her long gloves, squeezing her folded parasol against her pretty figure, dressed in the perfection of a soberly elegant traveling costume. Winterbourne was a man of imagination and, as our ancestors used to say, sensibility; as he looked at her dress and, on the great staircase, her little rapid, confiding step, he felt as if there were something romantic going forward. He could have believed he was going to elope with her. He passed out with her among all the idle people that were assembled there; they were all looking at her very hard; she had begun to chatter as soon as she joined him. Winterbourne's preference had been that they should be conveyed to Chillon in a carriage; but she expressed a lively wish to go in the little steamer; she declared that she had a passion for steamboats. There was always such a lovely breeze upon the water, and you saw such lots of people. The sail was not long, but Winterbourne's companion found time to say a great many things. To the young man himself their little excursion was so much of an escapade—an adventure—that, even allowing for her habitual sense of freedom, he had some expectation of seeing her regard it in the same way. But it must be confessed that, in this particular, he was disappointed. Daisy Miller was extremely animated, she was in charming spirits; but she was apparently not at all excited; she was not fluttered; she avoided neither his eyes nor those of anyone else; she blushed neither when she looked at him nor when she felt that people were looking at her. People continued to look at her a great deal, and Winterbourne took much satisfaction in his pretty companion's distinguished air. He had been a little afraid that she would talk loud, laugh overmuch, and even, perhaps, desire to move about the boat a good deal. But he quite forgot his fears; he sat smiling, with his eyes upon her face, while, without moving from her place, she delivered herself of a great number of original reflections. It was the most charming garrulity he had ever heard. He had assented to the idea that she was "common"; but was she so, after all, or was he simply getting used to her commonness? Her conversation was chiefly of what metaphysicians term the objective cast, but every now and then it took a subjective turn.

"What on *earth* are you so grave about?" she suddenly demanded, fixing her agreeable eyes upon Winterbourne's.

"Am I grave?" he asked. "I had an idea I was grinning from ear to ear."

"You look as if you were taking me to a funeral. If that's a grin, your ears are very near together."

"Should you like me to dance a hornpipe on the deck?"

"Pray do, and I'll carry round your hat. It will pay the expenses of our journey."

"I never was better pleased in my life," murmured Winterbourne.

She looked at him a moment, and then burst into a little laugh. "I like to make you say those things! You're a queer mixture!"

In the castle, after they had landed, the subjective element decidedly prevailed. Daisy tripped about the vaulted chambers, rustled her skirts in the corkscrew staircases, flirted back with a pretty little cry and a shudder from the edge of the *oubliettes*, and turned a singularly well-shaped ear to everything that Winterbourne told her about the place. But he saw that she cared very little for feudal antiquities, and that the dusky traditions of Chillon made but a slight impression upon her. They had the good fortune to have been able to walk about without other companionship than that of the custodian; and Winterbourne arranged with this functionary that they should not be hurried—that they should linger and pause wherever they chose. The custodian interpreted the bargain generously—Winterbourne, on his side, had been generous—and ended by leaving them quite to themselves. Miss Miller's observations were not remarkable for logical consistency; for anything she wanted to say she was sure to find a pretext. She found a great many pretexts in the rugged embrasures of Chillon for asking Winterbourne sudden questions about himself—his family, his previous history, his tastes, his habits, his intentions—and for supplying information upon corresponding points in her own personality. Of her own tastes, habits, and intentions Miss Miller was prepared to give the most definite, and indeed the most favorable account.

"Well, I hope you know enough!" she said to her companion, after he had told her the history of the unhappy Bonivard. "I never saw a man that knew so much!" The history of Bonivard had evidently, as they say, gone into one ear and out of the other. But Daisy went on to say that she wished Winterbourne would travel with them and "go round" with them; they might know something, in that case. "Don't you want to come and teach Randolph?" she asked. Winterbourne said that nothing could possibly please him so much, but that he had unfortunately other occupations. "Other occupations? I don't believe it!" said Miss Daisy. "What do you mean? You are not in business." The young man admitted that he was not in business; but he had engagements which, even within a day or two, would force him to go back to Geneva. "Oh, bother!" she said: "I don't believe it!" and she began to talk about something else. But a few moments later, when he was pointing out to her the pretty design of an antique fireplace, she broke out irrelevantly, "You don't mean to say you are going back to Geneva?"

"It is a melancholy fact that I shall have to return to Geneva to-morrow."

"Well, Mr. Winterbourne," said Daisy, "I think you're horrid!"

"Oh, don't say such dreadful things!" said Winterbourne—"just at the last!"

"The last!" cried the young girl; "I call it the first. I have half a mind to leave you here and go straight back to the hotel alone." And for the next ten minutes she did nothing but call him horrid. Poor Winterbourne was fairly bewildered; no young lady had as yet done him the honor to be so agitated by the announcement of his movements. His companion, after this, ceased to pay any attention to the curiosities of Chillon or the beauties of the lake; she opened fire upon the mysterious charmer in Geneva whom she appeared to have instantly taken it for granted that he was hurrying back to see. How did Miss Daisy Miller know that there was a charmer in Geneva? Winterbourne, who denied the existence of such a person, was quite unable to discover; and he was divided between amazement at the rapidity of her induction and amusement at the frankness of her *persiflage*. She seemed to him, in all this, an extraordinary mixture of innocence and crudity. "Does she never allow you more than three days at a time?" asked Daisy, ironically. "Doesn't she give you a vacation in summer? There's no one so hard worked but they can get leave to go off somewhere at this season. I suppose, if you stay another day, she'll come after you in the boat. Do wait over till Friday, and I will go down to the landing to see her arrive!" Winterbourne began to think he had been wrong to feel disappointed in the temper in which the young lady had embarked. If he had missed the personal accent, the personal accent was now making its appearance. It sounded very distinctly, at last, in her telling him she would stop "teasing" him if he would promise her solemnly to come down to Rome in the winter.

"That's not a difficult promise to make," said Winterbourne. "My aunt has taken an apartment in Rome for the winter, and has already asked me to come and see her."

"I don't want you to come for your aunt," said Daisy; "I want you to come for me." And this was the only allusion that the young man was ever to hear her make to his invidious kinswoman. He declared that, at any rate, he would certainly come. After this Daisy stopped teasing. Winterbourne took a carriage, and they drove back to Vevay in the dusk; the young girl was very quiet.

In the evening Winterbourne mentioned to Mrs. Costello that he had spent the afternoon at Chillon with Miss Daisy Miller.

"The Americans—of the courier?" asked this lady.

"Ah, happily," said Winterbourne, "the courier stayed at home."

"She went with you all alone?"

"All alone."

Mrs. Costello sniffed a little at her smelling-bottle. "And that," she exclaimed, "is the young person whom you wanted me to know!"

Part II[2]

Winterbourne, who had returned to Geneva the day after his excursion to Chillon, went to Rome toward the end of January. His aunt had been established there for several weeks, and he had received a couple of letters from her. "Those people you were so devoted to last summer at Vevay have turned up here, courier and

2. The second part was titled "Rome" in the original 1878 *Cornhill Magazine* publication.

all," she wrote. "They seem to have made several acquaintances, but the courier continues to be the most *intime.* The young lady, however, is also very intimate with some third-rate Italians, with whom she rackets about in a way that makes much talk. Bring me that pretty novel of Cherbuliez's—'Paule Méré'—and don't come later than the 23d."

In the natural course of events, Winterbourne, on arriving in Rome, would presently have ascertained Mrs. Miller's address at the American banker's, and have gone to pay his compliments to Miss Daisy. "After what happened at Vevay, I think I may certainly call upon them," he said to Mrs. Costello.

"If, after what happens—at Vevay and everywhere—you desire to keep up the acquaintance, you are very welcome. Of course a man may know every one. Men are welcome to the privilege!"

"Pray what is it that happens—here, for instance?" Winterbourne demanded.

"The girl goes about alone with her foreigners. As to what happens further, you must apply elsewhere for information. She has picked up half a dozen of the regular Roman fortune-hunters, and she takes them about to people's houses. When she comes to a party she brings with her a gentleman with a good deal of manner and a wonderful mustache."

"And where is the mother?"

"I haven't the least idea. They are very dreadful people."

Winterbourne meditated a moment. "They are very ignorant—very innocent only. Depend upon it they are not bad."

"They are hopelessly vulgar," said Mrs. Costello. "Whether or no being hopelessly vulgar is being 'bad' is a question for the metaphysicians. They are bad enough to dislike, at any rate; and for this short life that is quite enough."

The news that Daisy Miller was surrounded by half a dozen wonderful mustaches checked Winterbourne's impulse to go straightway to see her. He had, perhaps, not definitely flattered himself that he had made an ineffaceable impression upon her heart, but he was annoyed at hearing of a state of affairs so little in harmony with an image that had lately flitted in and out of his own meditations; the image of a very pretty girl looking out of an old Roman window and asking herself urgently when Mr. Winterbourne would arrive. If, however, he determined to wait a little before reminding Miss Miller of his claims to her consideration, he went very soon to call upon two or three other friends.

One of these friends was an American lady who had spent several winters at Geneva, where she had placed her children at school. She was a very accomplished woman, and she lived in the Via Gregoriana. Winterbourne found her in a little crimson drawing-room on a third floor; the room was filled with southern sunshine. He had not been there ten minutes when the servant came in, announcing "Madame Mila!" This announcement was presently followed by the entrance of little Randolph Miller, who stopped in the middle of the room and stood staring at Winterbourne. An instant later his pretty sister crossed the threshold; and then, after a considerable interval, Mrs. Miller slowly advanced.

"I know you!" said Randolph.

"I'm sure you know a great many things," exclaimed Winterbourne, taking him by the hand. "How is your education coming on?"

Daisy was exchanging greetings very prettily with her hostess; but when she heard Winterbourne's voice she quickly turned her head. "Well, I declare!" she said.

"I told you I should come, you know," Winterbourne rejoined, smiling.

"Well, I didn't believe it," said Miss Daisy.

"I am much obliged to you," laughed the young man.

"You might have come to see me!" said Daisy.

"I arrived only yesterday."

"I don't believe that!" the young girl declared.

Winterbourne turned with a protesting smile to her mother; but this lady evaded his glance, and, seating herself, fixed her eyes upon her son. "We've got a bigger place than this," said Randolph. "It's all gold on the walls."

Mrs. Miller turned uneasily in her chair. "I told you if I were to bring you, you would say something!" she murmured.

"I told *you*!" Randolph exclaimed. "I tell *you*, sir!" he added, jocosely, giving Winterbourne a thump on the knee. "It *is* bigger, too!"

Daisy had entered upon a lively conversation with her hostess; Winterbourne judged it becoming to address a few words to her mother. "I hope you have been well since we parted at Vevay," he said.

Mrs. Miller now certainly looked at him—at his chin. "Not very well, sir," she answered.

"She's got the dyspepsia," said Randolph. "I've got it too. Father's got it. I've got it most!"

This announcement, instead of embarrassing Mrs. Miller, seemed to relieve her. "I suffer from the liver," she said. "I think it's this climate; it's less bracing than Schenectady, especially in the winter season. I don't know whether you know we reside at Schenectady. I was saying to Daisy that I certainly hadn't found any one like Dr. Davis, and I didn't believe I should. Oh, at Schenectady he stands first; they think everything of him. He has so much to do, and yet there was nothing he wouldn't do for me. He said he never saw anything like my dyspepsia, but he was bound to cure it. I'm sure there was nothing he wouldn't try. He was just going to try something new when we came off. Mr. Miller wanted Daisy to see Europe for herself. But I wrote to Mr. Miller that it seems as if I couldn't get on without Dr. Davis. At Schenectady he stands at the very top; and there's a great deal of sickness there, too. It affects my sleep."

Winterbourne had a good deal of pathological gossip with Dr. Davis's patient, during which Daisy chattered unremittingly to her own companion. The young man asked Mrs. Miller how she was pleased with Rome. "Well, I must say I am disappointed," she answered. "We had heard so much about it; I suppose we had heard too much. But we couldn't help that. We had been led to expect something different."

"Ah, wait a little, and you will become very fond of it," said Winterbourne.

"I hate it worse and worse every day!" cried Randolph.

"You are like the infant Hannibal," said Winterbourne.

"No, I ain't!" Randolph declared at a venture.

"You are not much like an infant," said his mother. "But we have seen places," she resumed, "that I should put a long way before Rome." And in reply to Winterbourne's interrogation, "There's Zürich," she concluded, "I think Zürich is lovely; and we hadn't heard half so much about it."

"The best place we've seen is the City of Richmond!" said Randolph.

"He means the ship," his mother explained. "We crossed in that ship. Randolph had a good time on the *City of Richmond*."

"It's the best place I've seen," the child repeated. "Only it was turned the wrong way."

"Well, we've got to turn the right way some time," said Mrs. Miller, with a little laugh. Winterbourne expressed the hope that her daughter at least found some gratification in Rome, and she declared that Daisy was quite carried away. "It's on account of the society—the society's splendid. She goes round everywhere; she has made a great number of acquaintances. Of course she goes round more than I do. I must say they have been very sociable; they have taken her right in. And then she knows a great many gentlemen. Oh, she thinks there's nothing like Rome. Of course, it's a great deal pleasanter for a young lady if she knows plenty of gentlemen."

By this time Daisy had turned her attention again to Winterbourne. "I've been telling Mrs. Walker how mean you were!" the young girl announced.

"And what is the evidence you have offered?" asked Winterbourne, rather annoyed at Miss Miller's want of appreciation of the zeal of an admirer who on his way down to Rome had stopped neither at Bologna nor at Florence, simply because of a certain sentimental impatience. He remembered that a cynical compatriot had once told him that American women—the pretty ones, and this gave a largeness to the axiom—were at once the most exacting in the world and the least endowed with a sense of indebtedness.

"Why, you were awfully mean at Vevay," said Daisy. "You wouldn't do anything. You wouldn't stay there when I asked you."

"My dearest young lady," cried Winterbourne, with eloquence, "have I come all the way to Rome to encounter your reproaches?"

"Just hear him say that!" said Daisy to her hostess, giving a twist to a bow on this lady's dress. "Did you ever hear anything so quaint?"

"So quaint, my dear?" murmured Mrs. Walker, in the tone of a partisan of Winterbourne.

"Well, I don't know," said Daisy, fingering Mrs. Walker's ribbons. "Mrs. Walker, I want to tell you something."

"Mother-r," interposed Randolph, with his rough ends to his words, "I tell you you've got to go. Eugenio'll raise—something!"

"I'm not afraid of Eugenio," said Daisy, with a toss of her head. "Look here, Mrs. Walker," she went on, "you know I'm coming to your party."

"I am delighted to hear it."

"I've got a lovely dress!"

"I am very sure of that."

"But I want to ask a favor—permission to bring a friend."

"I shall be happy to see any of your friends," said Mrs. Walker, turning with a smile to Mrs. Miller.

"Oh, they are not my friends," answered Daisy's mamma, smiling shyly, in her own fashion. "I never spoke to them."

"It's an intimate friend of mine—Mr. Giovanelli," said Daisy, without a tremor in her clear little voice or a shadow on her brilliant little face.

Mrs. Walker was silent a moment; she gave a rapid glance at Winterbourne. "I shall be glad to see Mr. Giovanelli," she then said.

"He's an Italian," Daisy pursued, with the prettiest serenity. "He's a great friend of mine; he's the handsomest man in the world—except Mr. Winterbourne! He knows plenty of Italians, but he wants to know some Americans. He thinks ever so much of Americans. He's tremendously clever. He's perfectly lovely!"

It was settled that this brilliant personage should be brought to Mrs. Walker's party, and then Mrs. Miller prepared to take her leave. "I guess we'll go back to the hotel," she said.

"You may go back to the hotel, mother, but I'm going to take a walk," said Daisy.

"She's going to walk with Mr. Giovanelli," Randolph proclaimed.

"I am going to the Pincio," said Daisy, smiling.

"Alone, my dear—at this hour?" Mrs. Walker asked. The afternoon was drawing to a close—it was the hour for the throng of carriages and of contemplative pedestrians. "I don't think it's safe, my dear," said Mrs. Walker.

"Neither do I," subjoined Mrs. Miller. "You'll get the fever, as sure as you live. Remember what Dr. Davis told you!"

"Give her some medicine before she goes," said Randolph.

The company had risen to its feet; Daisy, still showing her pretty teeth, bent over and kissed her hostess. "Mrs. Walker, you are too perfect," she said. "I'm not going alone; I am going to meet a friend."

"Your friend won't keep you from getting the fever," Mrs. Miller observed.

"Is it Mr. Giovanelli?" asked the hostess.

Winterbourne was watching the young girl; at this question his attention quickened. She stood there smiling and smoothing her bonnet ribbons; she glanced at Winterbourne. Then, while she glanced and smiled, she answered, without a shade of hesitation, "Mr. Giovanelli—the beautiful Giovanelli."

"My dear young friend," said Mrs. Walker, taking her hand, pleadingly, "don't walk off to the Pincio at this hour to meet a beautiful Italian."

"Well, he speaks English," said Mrs. Miller.

"Gracious me!" Daisy exclaimed, "I don't want to do anything improper. There's an easy way to settle it." She continued to glance at Winterbourne. "The Pincio is only a hundred yards distant; and if Mr. Winterbourne were as polite as he pretends, he would offer to walk with me!"

Winterbourne's politeness hastened to affirm itself, and the young girl gave him gracious leave to accompany her. They passed down-stairs before her mother, and at the door Winterbourne perceived Mrs. Miller's carriage drawn up, with the ornamental courier whose acquaintance he had made at Vevay seated within. "Good-bye, Eugenio!" cried Daisy; "I'm going to take a walk." The distance from the Via Gregoriana to the beautiful garden at the other end of the Pincian Hill is, in fact, rapidly traversed. As the day was splendid, however, and the concourse of vehicles, walkers, and loungers numerous, the young Americans found their progress much delayed. This fact was highly agreeable to Winterbourne, in spite of his consciousness of his singular situation. The slow-moving, idly gazing Roman crowd bestowed much attention upon the extremely pretty young foreign lady who was passing through it upon his arm; and he wondered what on earth had been in Daisy's mind when she proposed to expose herself, unattended, to its appreciation. His own mission, to her sense, apparently, was to consign her to the hands of Mr. Giovanelli; but Winterbourne, at once annoyed and gratified, resolved that he would do no such thing.

"Why haven't you been to see me?" asked Daisy. "You can't get out of that."

"I have had the honor of telling you that I have only just stepped out of the train."

"You must have stayed in the train a good while after it stopped!" cried the young girl, with her little laugh. "I suppose you were asleep. You have had time to go to see Mrs. Walker."

"I knew Mrs. Walker—" Winterbourne began to explain.

"I know where you knew her. You knew her at Geneva. She told me so. Well, you knew me at Vevay. That's just as good. So you ought to have come." She asked him no other question than this; she began to prattle about her own affairs. "We've got splendid rooms at the hotel; Eugenio says they're the best rooms in Rome. We are going to stay all winter, if we don't die of the fever; and I guess we'll stay then. It's a great deal nicer than I thought; I thought it would be fearfully quiet; I was sure it would be awfully poky. I was sure we should be going round all the time with one of those dreadful old men that explain about the pictures and things. But we only had about a week of that, and now I'm enjoying myself. I know ever so many people, and they are all so charming. The society's extremely select. There are all kinds—English, and Germans, and Italians. I think I like the English best. I like their style of conversation. But there are some lovely Americans. I never saw anything so hospitable. There's something or other every day. There's not much dancing; but I must say I never thought dancing was everything. I was always fond of conversation. I guess I shall have plenty at Mrs. Walker's, her rooms are so small." When they had passed the gate of the Pincian Gardens, Miss Miller began to wonder where Mr. Giovanelli might be. "We had better go straight to that place in front," she said, "where you look at the view."

"I certainly shall not help you to find him," Winterbourne declared.

"Then I shall find him without you," said Miss Daisy.

"You certainly won't leave me!" cried Winterbourne.

She burst into her little laugh. "Are you afraid you'll get lost—or run over? But there's Giovanelli, leaning against that tree. He's staring at the women in the carriages: did you ever see anything so cool?"

Winterbourne perceived at some distance a little man standing with folded arms nursing his cane. He had a handsome face, an artfully poised hat, a glass in one eye, and a nosegay in his buttonhole. Winterbourne looked at him a moment, and then said, "Do you mean to speak to that man?"

"Do I mean to speak to him? Why, you don't suppose I mean to communicate by signs?"

"Pray understand, then," said Winterbourne, "that I intend to remain with you."

Daisy stopped and looked at him, without a sign of troubled consciousness in her face; with nothing but the presence of her charming eyes and her happy dimples. "Well, she's a cool one!" thought the young man.

"I don't like the way you say that," said Daisy. "It's too imperious."

"I beg your pardon if I say it wrong. The main point is to give you an idea of my meaning."

The young girl looked at him more gravely, but with eyes that were prettier than ever. "I have never allowed a gentleman to dictate to me, or to interfere with anything I do."

"I think you have made a mistake," said Winterbourne. "You should sometimes listen to a gentleman—the right one."

Daisy began to laugh again. "I do nothing but listen to gentlemen!" she exclaimed. "Tell me if Mr. Giovanelli is the right one?"

The gentleman with the nosegay in his bosom had now perceived our two friends, and was approaching the young girl with obsequious rapidity. He bowed to Winterbourne as well as to the latter's companion; he had a brilliant smile, an intelligent eye; Winterbourne thought him not a bad-looking fellow. But he nevertheless said to Daisy, "No, he's not the right one."

Daisy evidently had a natural talent for performing introductions; she mentioned the name of each of her companions to the other. She strolled alone with one of them on each side of her; Mr. Giovanelli, who spoke English very cleverly—Winterbourne afterward learned that he had practised the idiom upon a great many American heiresses—addressed her a great deal of very polite nonsense; he was extremely urbane, and the young American, who said nothing, reflected upon that profundity of Italian cleverness which enables people to appear more gracious in proportion as they are more acutely disappointed. Giovanelli, of course, had counted upon something more intimate; he had not bargained for a party of three. But he kept his temper in a manner which suggested far-stretching intentions. Winterbourne flattered himself that he had taken his measure. "He is not a gentleman," said the young American; "he is only a clever imitation of one. He is a music-master, or a penny-a-liner, or a third-rate artist. D—n his good looks!" Mr. Giovanelli had certainly a very pretty face; but Winterbourne felt a superior indignation at his own lovely fellow-countrywoman's not knowing the difference between a spurious gentleman and a real one. Giovanelli chattered and jested, and made himself wonderfully agreeable. It was true that, if he was an imitation, the imitation was brilliant. "Nevertheless," Winterbourne said to himself, "a nice girl ought to know!" And then he came back to the question whether this was, in fact, a nice girl. Would a nice girl, even allowing for her being a little American flirt, make a rendezvous with a presumably low-lived foreigner? The rendezvous in this case, indeed, had been in broad daylight, and in the most crowded corner of Rome; but was it not impossible to regard the choice of these circumstances as a proof of extreme cynicism? Singular though it may seem, Winterbourne was vexed that the young girl, in joining her *amoroso*, should not appear more impatient of his own company, and he was vexed because of his inclination. It was impossible to regard her as a perfectly well-conducted young lady; she was wanting in a certain indispensable delicacy. It would therefore simplify matters greatly to be able to treat her as the object of one of those sentiments which are called by romancers "lawless passions." That she should seem to wish to get rid of him would help him to think more lightly of her, and to be able to think more lightly of her would make her much less perplexing. But Daisy, on this occasion, continued to present herself as an inscrutable combination of audacity and innocence.

She had been walking some quarter of an hour, attended by her two cavaliers, and responding in a tone of very childish gayety, as it seemed to Winterbourne, to the pretty speeches of Mr. Giovanelli, when a carriage that had detached itself from the revolving train drew up beside the path. At the same moment Winterbourne perceived that his friend Mrs. Walker—the lady whose house he had lately left—was seated in the vehicle, and was beckoning to him. Leaving Miss Miller's side, he hastened to obey her summons. Mrs. Walker was flushed; she wore an excited air. "It is really too dreadful," she said. "That girl must not do this sort of thing. She must not walk here with you two men. Fifty people have noticed her."

Winterbourne raised his eyebrows. "I think it's a pity to make too much fuss about it."

"It's a pity to let the girl ruin herself!"

"She is very innocent," said Winterbourne.

"She's very crazy!" cried Mrs. Walker. "Did you ever see anything so imbecile as her mother? After you had all left me just now, I could not sit still for thinking of it. It seemed too pitiful, not even to attempt to save her. I ordered the carriage and put on my bonnet, and came here as quickly as possible. Thank Heaven I have found you!"

"What do you propose to do with us?" asked Winterbourne, smiling.

"To ask her to get in, to drive her about here for half an hour, so that the world may see she is not running absolutely wild, and then to take her safely home."

"I don't think it's a very happy thought," said Winterbourne; "but you can try."

Mrs. Walker tried. The young man went in pursuit of Miss Miller, who had simply nodded and smiled at his interlocutor in the carriage, and had gone her way with her companion. Daisy, on learning that Mrs. Walker wished to speak to her, retraced her steps with a perfect good grace and with Mr. Giovanelli at her side. She declared that she was delighted to have a chance to present this gentleman to Mrs. Walker. She immediately achieved the introduction, and declared that she had never in her life seen anything so lovely as Mrs. Walker's carriage-rug.

"I am glad you admire it," said this lady, smiling sweetly. "Will you get in and let me put it over you?"

"Oh no, thank you," said Daisy. "I shall admire it much more as I see you driving round with it."

"Do get in and drive with me!" said Mrs. Walker.

"That would be charming, but it's so enchanting just as I am!" and Daisy gave a brilliant glance at the gentlemen on either side of her.

"It may be enchanting, dear child, but it is not the custom here," urged Mrs. Walker, leaning forward in her victoria, with her hands devoutly clasped.

"Well, it ought to be, then!" said Daisy. "If I didn't walk I should expire."

"You should walk with your mother, dear," cried the lady from Geneva, losing patience.

"With my mother dear!" exclaimed the young girl. Winterbourne saw that she scented interference. "My mother never walked ten steps in her life. And then, you know," she added, with a laugh, "I am more than five years old."

"You are old enough to be more reasonable. You are old enough, dear Miss Miller, to be talked about."

Daisy looked at Mrs. Walker, smiling intensely. "Talked about? What do you mean?"

"Come into my carriage, and I will tell you."

Daisy turned her quickened glance again from one of the gentlemen beside her to the other. Mr. Giovanelli was bowing to and fro, rubbing down his gloves and laughing very agreeably; Winterbourne thought it a most unpleasant scene. "I don't think I want to know what you mean," said Daisy, presently. "I don't think I should like it."

Winterbourne wished that Mrs. Walker would tuck in her carriage-rug and drive away; but this lady did not enjoy being defied, as she afterward told him. "Should you prefer being thought a very reckless girl?" she demanded.

"Gracious!" exclaimed Daisy. She looked again at Mr. Giovanelli, then she turned to Winterbourne. There was a little pink flush in her cheek; she was tremendously pretty. "Does Mr. Winterbourne think," she asked, slowly, smiling, throwing back her head and glancing at him from head to foot, "that, to save my reputation, I ought to get into the carriage?"

Winterbourne colored; for an instant he hesitated greatly. It seemed so strange to hear her speak that way of her "reputation." But he himself, in fact, must speak in accordance with gallantry. The finest gallantry, here, was simply to tell her the truth; and the truth, for Winterbourne, as the few indications I have been able to give have made him known to the reader, was that Daisy Miller should take Mrs. Walker's advice. He looked at her exquisite prettiness, and then he said, very gently, "I think you should get into the carriage."

Daisy gave a violent laugh. "I never heard anything so stiff! If this is improper, Mrs. Walker," she pursued, "then I am all improper, and you must give me up. Good-bye; I hope you'll have a lovely ride!" and, with Mr. Giovanelli, who made a triumphantly obsequious salute, she turned away.

Mrs. Walker sat looking after her, and there were tears in Mrs. Walker's eyes. "Get in here, sir," she said to Winterbourne, indicating the place beside her. The young man answered that he felt bound to accompany Miss Miller; whereupon Mrs. Walker declared that if he refused her this favor she would never speak to him again. She was evidently in earnest. Winterbourne overtook Daisy and her companion, and, offering the young girl his hand, told her that Mrs. Walker had made an imperious claim upon his society. He expected that in answer she would say something rather free, something to commit herself still further to that "recklessness" from which Mrs. Walker had so charitably endeavored to dissuade her. But she only shook his hand, hardly looking at him; while Mr. Giovanelli bade him farewell with a too emphatic flourish of the hat.

Winterbourne was not in the best possible humor as he took his seat in Mrs. Walker's victoria. "That was not clever of you," he said, candidly, while the vehicle mingled again with the throng of carriages.

"In such a case," his companion answered, "I don't wish to be clever; I wish to be *earnest*!"

"Well, your earnestness has only offended her and put her off."

"It has happened very well," said Mrs. Walker. "If she is so perfectly determined to compromise herself, the sooner one knows it the better; one can act accordingly."

"I suspect she meant no harm," Winterbourne rejoined.

"So I thought a month ago. But she has been going too far."

"What has she been doing?"

"Everything that is not done here. Flirting with any man she could pick up; sitting in corners with mysterious Italians; dancing all the evening with the same partners; receiving visits at eleven o'clock at night. Her mother goes away when visitors come."

"But her brother," said Winterbourne, laughing, "sits up till midnight."

"He must be edified by what he sees. I'm told that at their hotel every one is talking about her, and that a smile goes round among all the servants when a gentleman comes and asks for Miss Miller."

"The servants be hanged!" said Winterbourne, angrily. "The poor girl's only fault," he presently added, "is that she is very uncultivated."

"She is naturally indelicate," Mrs. Walker declared. "Take that example this morning. How long had you known her at Vevay?"

"A couple of days."

"Fancy, then, her making it a personal matter that you should have left the place!"

Winterbourne was silent for some moments; then he said, "I suspect, Mrs. Walker, that you and I have lived too long at Geneva!" And he added a request that she should inform him with what particular design she had made him enter her carriage.

"I wished to beg you to cease your relations with Miss Miller—not to flirt with her—to give her no further opportunity to expose herself—to let her alone, in short."

"I'm afraid I can't do that," said Winterbourne. "I like her extremely."

"All the more reason that you shouldn't help her to make a scandal."

"There shall be nothing scandalous in my attentions to her."

"There certainly will be in the way she takes them. But I have said what I had on my conscience," Mrs. Walker pursued. "If you wish to rejoin the young lady I will put you down. Here, by-the-way, you have a chance."

The carriage was traversing that part of the Pincian Garden that overhangs the wall of Rome and overlooks the beautiful Villa Borghese. It is bordered by a large parapet, near which there are several seats. One of the seats at a distance was occupied by a gentleman and a lady, toward whom Mrs. Walker gave a toss of her head. At the same moment these persons rose and walked toward the parapet. Winterbourne had asked the coachman to stop; he now descended from the carriage. His companion looked at him a moment in silence; then, while he raised his hat, she drove majestically away. Winterbourne stood there; he had turned his eyes toward Daisy and her cavalier. They evidently saw no one; they were too deeply occupied with each other. When they reached the low garden-wall, they stood a moment looking off at the great flat-topped pine-clusters of the Villa Borghese; then Giovanelli seated himself, familiarly, upon the broad ledge of the wall. The western sun in the opposite sky sent out a brilliant shaft through a couple of cloud-bars, whereupon Daisy's companion took her parasol out of her hands and opened it. She came a little nearer, and he held the parasol over her; then, still holding it, he let it rest upon her shoulder, so that both of their heads were hidden from Winterbourne. This young man lingered a moment, then he began to walk. But he walked—not toward the couple with the parasol; toward the residence of his aunt, Mrs. Costello.

He flattered himself on the following day that there was no smiling among the servants when he, at least, asked for Mrs. Miller at her hotel. This lady and her daughter, however, were not at home; and on the next day after, repeating his visit, Winterbourne again had the misfortune not to find them. Mrs. Walker's party took place on the evening of the third day, and, in spite of the frigidity of his last interview with the hostess, Winterbourne was among the guests. Mrs. Walker was one of those American ladies who, while residing abroad, make a point, in their own phrase, of studying European society; and she had on this occasion collected several specimens of her diversely-born fellow-mortals to serve, as it were, as text-books. When Winterbourne arrived, Daisy Miller was not there, but in a few moments he saw her mother come in alone, very shyly and ruefully. Mrs. Miller's hair above her exposed-looking temples was more frizzled than ever. As she approached Mrs. Walker, Winterbourne also drew near.

"You see, I've come all alone," said poor Mrs. Miller. "I'm so frightened; I don't know what to do. It's the first time I've ever been to a party alone, especially in this country. I wanted to bring Randolph or Eugenio, or some one, but Daisy just pushed me off by myself. I ain't used to going round alone."

"And does not your daughter intend to favor us with her society?" demanded Mrs. Walker, impressively.

"Well, Daisy's all dressed," said Mrs. Miller, with that accent of the dispassionate, if not of the philosophic, historian with which she always recorded the current incidents of her daughter's career. "She got dressed on purpose before dinner. But she's got a friend of hers there; that gentleman—the Italian—that she wanted to bring. They've got going at the piano; it seems as if they couldn't leave off. Mr. Giovanelli sings splendidly. But I guess they'll come before very long," concluded Mrs. Miller, hopefully.

"I'm sorry she should come in that way," said Mrs. Walker.

"Well, I told her that there was no use in her getting dressed before dinner if she was going to wait three hours," responded Daisy's mamma. "I didn't see the use of her putting on such a dress as that to sit round with Mr. Giovanelli."

"This is most horrible!" said Mrs. Walker, turning away and addressing herself to Winterbourne. "*Elle s'affiche.* It's her revenge for my having ventured to remonstrate with her. When she comes, I shall not speak to her."

Daisy came after eleven o'clock; but she was not, on such an occasion, a young lady to wait to be spoken to. She rustled forward in radiant loveliness, smiling and chattering, carrying a large bouquet, and attended by Mr. Giovanelli. Every one stopped talking, and turned and looked at her. She came straight to Mrs. Walker. "I'm afraid you thought I never was coming, so I sent mother off to tell you. I wanted to make Mr. Giovanelli practise some things before he came; you know he sings beautifully, and I want you to ask him to sing. This is Mr. Giovanelli; you know I introduced him to you; he's got the most lovely voice, and he knows the most charming set of songs. I made him go over them this evening on purpose; we had the greatest time at the hotel." Of all this Daisy delivered herself with the sweetest, brightest audibleness, looking now at her hostess and now round the room, while she gave a series of little pats, round her shoulders, to the edges of her dress. "Is there any one I know?" she asked.

"I think every one knows you!" said Mrs. Walker, pregnantly, and she gave a very cursory greeting to Mr. Giovanelli. This gentleman bore himself gallantly. He smiled and bowed, and showed his white teeth; he curled his mustaches and rolled his eyes, and performed all the proper functions of a handsome Italian at an evening party. He sang very prettily half a dozen songs, though Mrs. Walker afterward declared that she had been quite unable to find out who asked him. It was apparently not Daisy who had given him his orders. Daisy sat at a distance from the piano; and though she had publicly, as it were, professed a high admiration for his singing, talked, not inaudibly, while it was going on.

"It's a pity these rooms are so small; we can't dance," she said to Winterbourne, as if she had seen him five minutes before.

"I am not sorry we can't dance," Winterbourne answered; "I don't dance."

"Of course you don't dance; you're too stiff," said Miss Daisy. "I hope you enjoyed your drive with Mrs. Walker!"

"No, I didn't enjoy it; I preferred walking with you."

"We paired off: that was much better," said Daisy. "But did you ever hear anything so cool as Mrs. Walker's wanting me to get into her carriage and drop poor Mr. Giovanelli, and under the pretext that it was proper? People have different ideas! It would have been most unkind; he had been talking about that walk for ten days."

"He should not have talked about it at all," said Winterbourne; "he would never have proposed to a young lady of this country to walk about the streets with him."

"About the streets?" cried Daisy, with her pretty stare. "Where, then, would he have proposed to her to walk? The Pincio is not the streets, either; and I, thank goodness, am not a young lady of this country. The young ladies of this country have a dreadfully poky time of it, so far as I can learn; I don't see why I should change my habits for *them*."

"I am afraid your habits are those of a flirt," said Winterbourne, gravely.

"Of course they are," she cried, giving him her little smiling stare again. "I'm a fearful, frightful flirt! Did you ever hear of a nice girl that was not? But I suppose you will tell me now that I am not a nice girl."

"You're a very nice girl; but I wish you would flirt with me, and me only," said Winterbourne.

"Ah! thank you—thank you very much; you are the last man I should think of flirting with. As I have had the pleasure of informing you, you are too stiff."

"You say that too often," said Winterbourne.

Daisy gave a delighted laugh. "If I could have the sweet hope of making you angry, I should say it again."

"Don't do that; when I am angry I'm stiffer than ever. But if you won't flirt with me, do cease, at least, to flirt with your friend at the piano; they don't understand that sort of thing here."

"I thought they understood nothing else!" exclaimed Daisy.

"Not in young unmarried women."

"It seems to me much more proper in young unmarried women than in old married ones," Daisy declared.

"Well," said Winterbourne, "when you deal with natives you must go by the custom of the place. Flirting is a purely American custom; it doesn't exist here. So when you show yourself in public with Mr. Giovanelli, and without your mother—"

"Gracious! poor mother!" interposed Daisy.

"Though you may be flirting, Mr. Giovanelli is not; he means something else."

"He isn't preaching, at any rate," said Daisy, with vivacity. "And if you want very much to know, we are neither of us flirting; we are too good friends for that: we are very intimate friends."

"Ah!" rejoined Winterbourne, "if you are in love with each other, it is another affair."

She had allowed him up to this point to talk so frankly that he had no expectation of shocking her by this ejaculation; but she immediately got up, blushing visibly, and leaving him to exclaim mentally that little American flirts were the queerest creatures in the world. "Mr. Giovanelli, at least," she said, giving her interlocutor a single glance, "never says such very disagreeable things to me."

Winterbourne was bewildered; he stood staring. Mr. Giovanelli had finished singing. He left the piano and came over to Daisy.

"Won't you come into the other room and have some tea?" he asked, bending before her with his ornamental smile.

Daisy turned to Winterbourne, beginning to smile again. He was still more perplexed, for this inconsequent smile made nothing clear, though it seemed to prove, indeed, that she had a sweetness and softness that reverted instinctively to the pardon of offences. "It has never occurred to Mr. Winterbourne to offer me any tea," she said, with her little tormenting manner.

"I have offered you advice," Winterbourne rejoined.

"I prefer weak tea!" cried Daisy, and she went off with the brilliant Giovanelli. She sat with him in the adjoining room, in the embrasure of the window, for the rest of the evening. There was an interesting performance at the piano, but neither of these young people gave heed to it. When Daisy came to take leave of Mrs. Walker, this lady conscientiously repaired the weakness of which she had been guilty at the moment of the young girl's arrival. She turned her back straight upon Miss Miller, and left her to depart with what grace she might. Winterbourne was standing near the door; he saw it all. Daisy turned very pale, and looked at her mother; but Mrs. Miller was humbly unconscious of any violation of the usual social forms. She appeared, indeed, to have felt an incongruous impulse to draw attention to her own striking observance of them. "Good-night, Mrs. Walker," she said; "we've had a beautiful evening. You see, if I let Daisy come to parties without me, I don't want her to go away without me." Daisy turned away, looking with a pale, grave face at the circle near the door; Winterbourne saw that, for the first moment, she was too much shocked and puzzled even for indignation. He on his side was greatly touched.

"That was very cruel," he said to Mrs. Walker.

"She never enters my drawing-room again!" replied his hostess.

Since Winterbourne was not to meet her in Mrs. Walker's drawing-room, he went as often as possible to Mrs. Miller's hotel. The ladies were rarely at home; but when he found them, the devoted Giovanelli was always present. Very often the brilliant little Roman was in the drawing-room with Daisy alone, Mrs. Miller being apparently constantly of the opinion that discretion is the better part of surveillance. Winterbourne noted, at first with surprise, that Daisy on these occasions was never embarrassed or annoyed by his own entrance; but he very presently began to feel that she had no more surprises for him; the unexpected in her behavior was the only thing to expect. She showed no displeasure at her *tête-à-tête* with Giovanelli being interrupted; she could chatter as freshly and freely with two gentlemen as with one; there was always, in her conversation, the same odd mixture of audacity and puerility. Winterbourne remarked to himself that if she was seriously interested in Giovanelli, it was very singular that she should not take more trouble to preserve the sanctity of their interviews; and he liked her the more for her innocent-looking indifference and her apparently inexhaustible good-humor. He could hardly have said why, but she seemed to him a girl who would never be jealous. At the risk of exciting a somewhat derisive smile on the reader's part, I may affirm that with regard to the women who had hitherto interested him, it very often seemed to Winterbourne among the possibilities that, given certain contingencies, he should be afraid—literally afraid—of these ladies; he had a pleasant sense that he should never be afraid of Daisy Miller. It must be added that this sentiment was not altogether flattering to Daisy; it was part of his conviction, or rather of his apprehension, that she would prove a very light young person.

But she was evidently very much interested in Giovanelli. She looked at him whenever he spoke; she was perpetually telling him to do this and to do that; she was constantly "chaffing" and abusing him. She appeared completely to have forgotten that Winterbourne had said anything to displease her at Mrs. Walker's little party. One Sunday afternoon, having gone to St. Peter's with his aunt, Winterbourne perceived Daisy strolling about the great church in company with the inevitable Giovanelli. Presently he pointed out the young girl and her cavalier to Mrs. Costello. This lady looked at them a moment through her eye-glass, and then she said:

"That's what makes you so pensive in these days, eh?"

"I had not the least idea I was pensive," said the young man.

"You are very much preoccupied; you are thinking of something."

"And what is it," he asked, "that you accuse me of thinking of?"

"Of that young lady's—Miss Baker's, Miss Chandler's—what's her name?—Miss Miller's intrigue with that little barber's block."

"Do you call it an intrigue," Winterbourne asked—"an affair that goes on with such peculiar publicity?"

"That's their folly," said Mrs. Costello; "it's not their merit."

"No," rejoined Winterbourne, with something of that pensiveness to which his aunt had alluded. "I don't believe that there is anything to be called an intrigue."

"I have heard a dozen people speak of it; they say she is quite carried away by him."

"They are certainly very intimate," said Winterbourne.

Mrs. Costello inspected the young couple again with her optical instrument. "He is very handsome. One easily sees how it is. She thinks him the most elegant man in the world, the finest gentleman. She has never seen anything like him; he is better, even, than the courier. It was the courier probably who introduced him; and if he succeeds in marrying the young lady, the courier will come in for a magnificent commission."

"I don't believe she thinks of marrying him," said Winterbourne, "and I don't believe he hopes to marry her."

"You may be very sure she thinks of nothing. She goes on from day to day, from hour to hour, as they did in the Golden Age. I can imagine nothing more vulgar. And at the same time," added Mrs. Costello, "depend upon it that she may tell you any moment that she is 'engaged.'"

"I think that is more than Giovanelli expects," said Winterbourne.

"Who is Giovanelli?"

"The little Italian. I have asked questions about him, and learned something. He is apparently a perfectly respectable little man. I believe he is, in a small way, a *cavaliere avvocato*. But he doesn't move in what are called the first circles. I think it is really not absolutely impossible that the courier introduced him. He is evidently immensely charmed with Miss Miller. If she thinks him the finest gentleman in the world, he, on his side, has never found himself in personal contact with such splendor, such opulence, such expensiveness, as this young lady's. And then she must seem to him wonderfully pretty and interesting. I rather doubt that he dreams of marrying her. That must appear to him too impossible a piece of luck. He has nothing but his handsome face to offer, and there is a substantial Mr. Miller in that mysterious land of dollars. Giovanelli knows that he hasn't a title to offer. If he were only a count or a *marchese!* He must wonder at his luck, at the way they have taken him up."

"He accounts for it by his handsome face, and thinks Miss Miller a young lady *qui se passe ses fantaisies!*"[3] said Mrs. Costello.

"It is very true," Winterbourne pursued, "that Daisy and her mamma have not yet risen to that stage of—what shall I call it?—of culture at which the idea of catching a count or a marchese begins. I believe that they are intellectually incapable of that conception."

"Ah! but the *avvocato* can't believe it," said Mrs. Costello.

Of the observation excited by Daisy's "intrigue," Winterbourne gathered that day at St. Peter's sufficient evidence. A dozen of the American colonists in Rome came to talk with Mrs. Costello, who sat on a little portable stool at the base of one of the great pilasters. The vesper service was going forward in splendid chants and organ-tones in the adjacent choir, and meanwhile, between Mrs. Costello and her friends, there was a great deal said about poor little Miss Miller's going really "too far." Winterbourne was not pleased with what he heard; but when, coming out upon the great steps of the church, he saw Daisy, who had emerged before him, get into an open cab with her accomplice and roll away through the cynical streets of Rome, he could not deny to himself that she was going very far indeed. He felt very sorry for her—not exactly that he believed that she had completely lost her head, but because it was painful to hear so much that was pretty, and undefended, and natural, assigned to a vulgar place among the categories of disorder. He made an attempt after this to give a hint to Mrs. Miller. He met one day in the Corso a friend, a tourist like himself, who had just come out of the Doria Palace, where he had been walking through the beautiful gallery. His friend talked for a moment about the superb portrait of Innocent X. by Velasquez which hangs in one of the cabinets of the palace, and then said, "And in the same cabinet, by-the-way, I had the pleasure of contemplating a picture of a different kind—that pretty American girl whom you pointed out to me last week." In answer to Winterbourne's inquiries, his friend narrated that the pretty American girl—prettier than ever—was seated with a companion in the secluded nook in which the great papal portrait was enshrined.

"Who was her companion?" asked Winterbourne.

3. *qui se passe ses fantaisies:* French for "who indulges herself."

"A little Italian with a bouquet in his button-hole. The girl is delightfully pretty, but I thought I understood from you the other day that she was a young lady *du meilleur monde*."

"So she is!" answered Winterbourne; and having assured himself that his informant had seen Daisy and her companion but five minutes before, he jumped into a cab and went to call on Mrs. Miller. She was at home; but she apologized to him for receiving him in Daisy's absence.

"She's gone out somewhere with Mr. Giovanelli," said Mrs. Miller. "She's always going round with Mr. Giovanelli."

"I have noticed that they are very intimate," Winterbourne observed.

"Oh, it seems as if they couldn't live without each other!" said Mrs. Miller. "Well, he's a real gentleman, anyhow. I keep telling Daisy she's engaged!"

"And what does Daisy say?"

"Oh, she says she isn't engaged. But she might as well be!" this impartial parent resumed; "she goes on as if she was. But I've made Mr. Giovanelli promise to tell me, if *she* doesn't. I should want to write to Mr. Miller about it—shouldn't you?"

Winterbourne replied that he certainly should; and the state of mind of Daisy's mamma struck him as so unprecedented in the annals of parental vigilance that he gave up as utterly irrelevant the attempt to place her upon her guard.

After this Daisy was never at home, and Winterbourne ceased to meet her at the houses of their common acquaintance, because, as he perceived, these shrewd people had quite made up their minds that she was going too far. They ceased to invite her; and they intimated that they desired to express to observant Europeans the great truth that, though Miss Daisy Miller was a young American lady, her behavior was not representative—was regarded by her compatriots as abnormal. Winterbourne wondered how she felt about all the cold shoulders that were turned toward her, and sometimes it annoyed him to suspect that she did not feel at all. He said to himself that she was too light and childish, too uncultivated and unreasoning, too provincial, to have reflected upon her ostracism, or even to have perceived it. Then at other moments he believed that she carried about in her elegant and irresponsible little organism a defiant, passionate, perfectly observant consciousness of the impression she produced. He asked himself whether Daisy's defiance came from the consciousness of innocence, or from her being, essentially, a young person of the reckless class. It must be admitted that holding one's self to a belief in Daisy's "innocence" came to seem to Winterbourne more and more a matter of fine-spun gallantry. As I have already had occasion to relate, he was angry at finding himself reduced to chopping logic about this young lady; he was vexed at his want of instinctive certitude as to how far her eccentricities were generic, national, and how far they were personal. From either view of them he had somehow missed her, and now it was too late. She was "carried away" by Mr. Giovanelli.

A few days after his brief interview with her mother, he encountered her in that beautiful abode of flowering desolation known as the Palace of the Cæsars. The early Roman spring had filled the air with bloom and perfume, and the rugged surface of the Palatine was muffled with tender verdure. Daisy was strolling along the top of one of those great mounds of ruin that are embanked with mossy marble and paved with monumental inscriptions. It seemed to him that Rome had never been so lovely as just then. He stood looking off at the enchanting harmony of line and color that remotely encircles the city, inhaling the softly humid odors, and feeling the freshness of the year and the antiquity of the place reaffirm themselves in mysterious interfusion. It seemed to him also that Daisy had never looked so pretty; but this had been an observation of his whenever he met her. Giovanelli was at her side, and Giovanelli, too, wore an aspect of even unwonted brilliancy.

"Well," said Daisy, "I should think you would be lonesome!"

"Lonesome?" asked Winterbourne.

"You are always going round by yourself. Can't you get any one to walk with you?"

"I am not so fortunate," said Winterbourne, "as your companion."

Giovanelli, from the first, had treated Winterbourne with distinguished politeness. He listened with a deferential air to his remarks; he laughed punctiliously at his pleasantries; he seemed disposed to testify to his belief that Winterbourne was a superior young man. He carried himself in no degree like a jealous wooer; he had obviously a great deal of tact; he had no objection to your expecting a little humility of him. It even seemed to Winterbourne at times that Giovanelli would find a certain mental relief in being able to have a private understanding with him—to say to him, as an intelligent man, that, bless you, *he* knew how extraordinary was this young lady, and didn't flatter himself with delusive—or at least *too* delusive—hopes of matrimony and dollars. On this occasion he strolled away from his companion to pluck a sprig of almond-blossom, which he carefully arranged in his button-hole.

"I know why you say that," said Daisy, watching Giovanelli. "Because you think I go round too much with *him*." And she nodded at her attendant.

"Every one thinks so—if you care to know," said Winterbourne.

"Of course I care to know!" Daisy exclaimed, seriously. "But I don't believe it. They are only pretending to be shocked. They don't really care a straw what I do. Besides, I don't go round so much."

"I think you will find they do care. They will show it disagreeably."

Daisy looked at him a moment. "How disagreeably?"

"Haven't you noticed anything?" Winterbourne asked.

"I have noticed you. But I noticed you were as stiff as an umbrella the first time I saw you."

"You will find I am not so stiff as several others," said Winterbourne, smiling.

"How shall I find it?"

"By going to see the others."

"What will they do to me?"

"They will give you the cold shoulder. Do you know what that means?"

Daisy was looking at him intently; she began to color. "Do you mean as Mrs. Walker did the other night?"

"Exactly!" said Winterbourne.

She looked away at Giovanelli, who was decorating himself with his almond blossom. Then looking back at Winterbourne, "I shouldn't think you would let people be so unkind!" she said.

"How can I help it?" he asked.

"I should think you would say something."

"I do say something;" and he paused a moment. "I say that your mother tells me that she believes you are engaged."

"Well, she does," said Daisy, very simply.

Winterbourne began to laugh. "And does Randolph believe it?" he asked.

"I guess Randolph doesn't believe anything," said Daisy. Randolph's scepticism excited Winterbourne to further hilarity, and he observed that Giovanelli was coming back to them. Daisy, observing it too, addressed herself again to her countryman. "Since you have mentioned it," she said, "I *am* engaged." . . . Winterbourne looked at her; he had stopped laughing. "You don't believe!" she added.

He was silent a moment; and then, "Yes, I believe it," he said.

"Oh no, you don't!" she answered. "Well, then—I am not!"

The young girl and her cicerone were on their way to the gate of the enclosure, so that Winterbourne, who had but lately entered, presently took leave of them. A week afterward he went to dine at a beautiful villa on the Cælian Hill, and, on arriving, dismissed his hired vehicle. The evening was charming, and he promised himself the satisfaction of walking home beneath the Arch of Constantine and past the vaguely-lighted monuments of the Forum. There was a waning moon in the sky, and her radiance was not brilliant, but she was veiled in a thin cloud-curtain which seemed to diffuse and equalize it. When, on his return from the villa (it was eleven o'clock), Winterbourne approached the dusky circle of the Colosseum, it recurred to him, as a lover of the picturesque, that the interior, in the pale moonshine, would be well worth a glance. He turned aside and walked to one of the empty arches, near which, as he observed, an open carriage—one of the little Roman street-cabs—was stationed. Then he passed in, among the cavernous shadows of the great structure, and emerged upon the clear and silent arena. The place had never seemed to him more impressive. One-half of the gigantic circus was in deep shade, the other was sleeping in the luminous dusk. As he stood there he began to murmur Byron's famous lines, out of "Manfred;" but before he had finished his quotation he remembered that if nocturnal meditations in the Colosseum are recommended by the poets, they are deprecated by the doctors. The historic atmosphere was there, certainly; but the historic atmosphere, scientifically considered, was no better than a villainous miasma. Winterbourne walked to the middle of the arena, to take a more general glance, intending thereafter to make a hasty retreat. The great cross in the centre was covered with shadow; it was only as he drew near it that he made it out distinctly. Then he saw that two persons were stationed upon the low steps which formed its base. One of these was a woman, seated; her companion was standing in front of her.

Presently the sound of the woman's voice came to him distinctly in the warm night air. "Well, he looks at us as one of the old lions or tigers may have looked at the Christian martyrs!" These were the words he heard, in the familiar accent of Miss Daisy Miller.

"Let us hope he is not very hungry," responded the ingenious Giovanelli. "He will have to take me first; you will serve for dessert!"

Winterbourne stopped, with a sort of horror, and, it must be added, with a sort of relief. It was as if a sudden illumination had been flashed upon the ambiguity of Daisy's behavior, and the riddle had become easy to read. She was a young lady whom a gentleman need no longer be at pains to respect. He stood there, looking at her—looking at her companion, and not reflecting that though he saw them vaguely, he himself must have been more brightly visible. He felt angry with himself that he had bothered so much about the right way of regarding Miss Daisy Miller. Then, as he was going to advance again, he checked himself; not from the fear that he was doing her injustice, but from a sense of the danger of appearing unbecomingly exhilarated by this sudden revulsion from cautious criticism. He turned away toward the entrance of the place, but, as he did so, he heard Daisy speak again.

"Why, it was Mr. Winterbourne! He saw me, and he cuts me!"

What a clever little reprobate she was, and how smartly she played at injured innocence! But he wouldn't cut her. Winterbourne came forward again, and went toward the great cross. Daisy had got up; Giovanelli lifted his hat. Winterbourne had now begun to think simply of the craziness, from a sanitary point of view, of a delicate young girl lounging away the evening in this nest of malaria. What if she *were* a clever little reprobate? that was no reason for her dying of the *perniciosa*. "How long have you been here?" he asked, almost brutally.

Daisy, lovely in the flattering moonlight, looked at him a moment. Then—"All the evening," she answered, gently. . . . "I never saw anything so pretty."

"I am afraid," said Winterbourne, "that you will not think Roman fever very pretty. This is the way people catch it. I wonder," he added, turning to Giovanelli, "that you, a native Roman, should countenance such a terrible indiscretion."

"Ah," said the handsome native, "for myself I am not afraid."

"Neither am I—for you! I am speaking for this young lady."

Giovanelli lifted his well-shaped eyebrows and showed his brilliant teeth. But he took Winterbourne's rebuke with docility.

"I told the Signorina it was a grave indiscretion; but when was the Signorina ever prudent?"

"I never was sick, and I don't mean to be!" the Signorina declared. "I don't look like much, but I'm healthy! I was bound to see the Colosseum by moonlight; I shouldn't have wanted to go home without that; and we have had the most beautiful time, haven't we, Mr. Giovanelli? If there has been any danger, Eugenio can give me some pills. He has got some splendid pills."

"I should advise you," said Winterbourne, "to drive home as fast as possible and take one!"

"What you say is very wise," Giovanelli rejoined. "I will go and make sure the carriage is at hand." And he went forward rapidly.

Daisy followed with Winterbourne. He kept looking at her; she seemed not in the least embarrassed. Winterbourne said nothing; Daisy chattered about the beauty of the place. "Well, I *have* seen the Colosseum by moonlight!" she exclaimed. "That's one good thing." Then, noticing Winterbourne's silence, she asked him why he didn't speak. He made no answer; he only began to laugh. They passed under one of the dark archways; Giovanelli was in front with the carriage. Here Daisy stopped a moment, looking at the young American. "*Did* you believe I was engaged, the other day?" she asked.

"It doesn't matter what I believed the other day," said Winterbourne, still laughing.

"Well, what do you believe now?"

"I believe that it makes very little difference whether you are engaged or not!"

He felt the young girl's pretty eyes fixed upon him through the thick gloom of the archway; she was apparently going to answer. But Giovanelli hurried her forward. "Quick! quick!" he said; "if we get in by midnight we are quite safe."

Daisy took her seat in the carriage, and the fortunate Italian placed himself beside her. "Don't forget Eugenio's pills!" said Winterbourne, as he lifted his hat.

"I don't care," said Daisy in a little strange tone, "whether I have Roman fever or not!" Upon this the cab-driver cracked his whip, and they rolled away over the desultory patches of the antique pavement.

Winterbourne, to do him justice, as it were, mentioned to no one that he had encountered Miss Miller, at midnight, in the Colosseum with a gentleman; but nevertheless, a couple of days later, the fact of her having been there under these circumstances was known to every member of the little American circle, and commented accordingly. Winterbourne reflected that they had of course known it at the hotel, and that, after Daisy's return, there had been an exchange of remarks between the porter and the cab-driver. But the young man was conscious, at the same moment, that it had ceased to be a matter of serious regret to him that the little American flirt should be "talked about" by low-minded menials. These people, a day or two later, had serious information to give: the little American flirt was alarmingly ill. Winterbourne, when the rumor came to him, immediately went to the hotel for more news. He found that two or three charitable friends had preceded him, and that they were being entertained in Mrs. Miller's salon by Randolph.

"It's going round at night," said Randolph—"that's what made her sick. She's always going round at night. I shouldn't think she'd want to, it's so plaguy dark. You can't see anything here at night, except when there's a moon. In America there's always a moon!" Mrs. Miller was invisible; she was now, at least, giving her daughter the advantage of her society. It was evident that Daisy was dangerously ill.

Winterbourne went often to ask for news of her, and once he saw Mrs. Miller, who, though deeply alarmed, was, rather to his surprise, perfectly composed, and, as it appeared, a most efficient and judicious nurse. She talked a good deal about Dr. Davis, but Winterbourne paid her the compliment of saying to himself that she was not, after all, such a monstrous goose. "Daisy spoke of you the other day," she said to him. "Half the time she doesn't know what she's saying, but that time I think she did. She gave me a message, she told me to tell you. She told me to tell you that she never was engaged to that handsome Italian. I am sure I am very glad; Mr. Giovanelli hasn't been near us since she was taken ill. I thought he was so much of a gentleman; but I don't call that very polite! A lady told me that he was afraid I was angry with him for taking Daisy round at night. Well, so I am; but I suppose he knows I'm a lady. I would scorn to scold him. Anyway, she says she's not engaged. I don't know why she wanted you to know; but she said to me three times, 'Mind you tell Mr. Winterbourne.' And then she told me to ask if you remembered the time you went to that castle in Switzerland. But I said I wouldn't give any such messages as that. Only, if she is not engaged, I'm sure I'm glad to know it."

But, as Winterbourne had said, it mattered very little. A week after this the poor girl died; it had been a terrible case of the fever. Daisy's grave was in the little Protestant cemetery, in an angle of the wall of imperial Rome, beneath the cypresses and the thick spring-flowers. Winterbourne stood there beside it, with a number of other mourners; a number larger than the scandal excited by the young lady's career would have led you to expect. Near him stood Giovanelli, who came nearer still before Winterbourne turned away. Giovanelli was very pale: on this occasion he had no flower in his button-hole; he seemed to wish to say something. At last he said, "She was the most beautiful young lady I ever saw, and the most amiable;" and then he added in a moment, "and she was the most innocent."

Winterbourne looked at him, and presently repeated his words, "And the most innocent?"

"The most innocent!"

Winterbourne felt sore and angry. "Why the devil," he asked, "did you take her to that fatal place?"

Mr. Giovanelli's urbanity was apparently imperturbable. He looked on the ground a moment, and then he said, "For myself I had no fear; and she wanted to go."

"That was no reason!" Winterbourne declared.

The subtle Roman again dropped his eyes. "If she had lived, I should have got nothing. She would never have married me, I am sure."

"She would never have married you?"

"For a moment I hoped so. But no. I am sure."

Winterbourne listened to him: he stood staring at the raw protuberance among the April daisies. When he turned away again, Mr. Giovanelli, with his light, slow step, had retired.

Winterbourne almost immediately left Rome; but the following summer he again met his aunt, Mrs. Costello, at Vevay. Mrs. Costello was fond of Vevay. In the interval Winterbourne had often thought of Daisy Miller and her mystifying manners. One day he spoke of her to his aunt—said it was on his conscience that he had done her injustice.

"I am sure I don't know," said Mrs. Costello. "How did your injustice affect her?"

"She sent me a message before her death which I didn't understand at the time; but I have understood it since. She would have appreciated one's esteem."

"Is that a modest way," asked Mrs. Costello, "of saying that she would have reciprocated one's affection?"

Winterbourne offered no answer to this question; but he presently said, "You were right in that remark that you made last summer. I was booked to make a mistake. I have lived too long in foreign parts."

Nevertheless, he went back to live at Geneva, whence there continue to come the most contradictory accounts of his motives of sojourn: a report that he is "studying" hard—an intimation that he is much interested in a very clever foreign lady.

SOURCE: Henry James, Jr. *Daisy Miller: A Study*. New York: Harper & Brothers, 1878.

ULYSSES S. GRANT

As the great general and former president Ulysses S. Grant (1822–1885) neared the end of his life, Grant's friend Mark Twain encouraged him to finish writing his memoirs. No president ever wrote memoirs so well or as straightforwardly. This chapter describes his life immediately after his military service in the Mexican War in 1854 and leads up to "the coming crisis," the Civil War, where Grant, to the surprise of many, eventually led the Union Army to its victory over the armies of the seceded states that made up the Confederacy.

Chapter 16 from *Personal Memoirs of U. S. Grant* (1885)

MY FAMILY, ALL this while, was at the East. It consisted now of a wife and two children [Frederick Dent and Ulysses, Jr.]. I saw no chance of supporting them on the Pacific coast out of my pay as an army officer. I concluded, therefore, to resign, and in March applied for a leave of absence until the end of the July following, tendering my resignation to take effect at the end of that time. I left the Pacific coast very much attached to it, and with the full expectation of making it my future home. That expectation and that hope remained uppermost in my mind until the Lieutenant-Generalcy bill was introduced into Congress in the winter of 1863–4. The passage of that bill, and my promotion, blasted my last hope of ever becoming a citizen of the further West.

In the late summer of 1854 I rejoined my family, to find in it a son whom I had never seen, born while I was on the Isthmus of Panama. I was now to commence, at the age of thirty-two, a new struggle for our support. My wife had a farm near St. Louis, to which we went, but I had no means to stock it. A house had to be built also. I worked very hard, never losing a day because of bad weather, and accomplished the object in a moderate way. If nothing else could be done I would load a cord of wood on a wagon and take it to the city for sale. I managed to keep along very well until 1858, when I was attacked by fever and ague. I had suffered very severely and for a long time from this disease, while a boy in Ohio. It lasted now over a year, and, while it did not keep me in the house, it did interfere greatly with the amount of work I was able to perform. In the fall of 1858 I sold out my stock, crops and farming utensils at auction, and gave up farming.

In the winter I established a partnership with Harry Boggs, a cousin of Mrs. Grant, in the real estate agency business. I spent that winter at St. Louis myself, but did not take my family into town until the spring. Our business might have become prosperous if I had been able to wait for it to grow. As it was, there was no more than one person could attend to, and not enough to support two families. While a citizen of Saint Louis and engaged in the real estate agency business, I was a candidate for the office of county engineer, an office of respectability and emolument which would have been very acceptable to me at that time. The incumbent was appointed by the county court, which consisted of five members. My opponent had the advantage of birth over me (he was a citizen by adoption) and carried off the prize. I now withdrew from the co-partnership with Boggs, and, in May, 1860, removed to Galena, Illinois, and took a clerkship in my father's store.

While a citizen of Missouri, my first opportunity for casting a vote at a Presidential election occurred. I had been in the army from before attaining my majority and had thought but little about politics, although I was a Whig by education and a great admirer of Mr. Clay. But the Whig party had ceased to exist before I had an opportunity of exercising the privilege of casting a ballot; the Know-Nothing party had taken its place, but was on the wane; and the Republican party was in a chaotic state and had not yet received a name. It had no existence in the Slave States except at points on the borders next to Free States. In St. Louis City and County, what afterwards became the Republican party was known as the Free-Soil Democracy, led by the Honorable Frank P. Blair. Most of my neighbors had known me as an officer of the army with Whig proclivities. They had been on the same side, and, on the death of their party, many had become Know-Nothings, or members of the American party. There was a lodge near my new home, and I was invited to join it. I accepted the invitation; was initiated; attended a meeting just one week later, and never went to another afterwards.

I have no apologies to make for having been one week a member of the American party; for I still think native-born citizens of the United States should have as much protection, as many privileges in their native country, as those who voluntarily select it for a home. But all secret, oath-bound political parties are dangerous to any nation, no matter how pure or how patriotic the motives and principles which first bring them together. No political party can or ought to exist when one of its cornerstones is opposition to freedom of thought and to the right to worship God "according to the dictate of one's own conscience," or according to the creed of any religious denomination whatever. Nevertheless, if a sect sets up its laws as binding above the State laws, wherever the two come in conflict this claim must be resisted and suppressed at whatever cost.

Up to the Mexican war there were a few out and out abolitionists, men who carried their hostility to slavery into all elections, from those for a justice of the peace up to the Presidency of the United States. They were noisy but not numerous. But the great majority of people at the North, where slavery did not exist, were opposed to the institution, and looked upon its existence in any part of the country as unfortunate. They did not hold the States where slavery existed responsible for it; and believed that protection should be given to the right of property in slaves until some satisfactory way could be reached to be rid of the institution. Opposition to slavery was not a creed of either political party. In some sections more anti-slavery men belonged to the Democratic party, and in others to the Whigs. But with the inauguration of the Mexican war, in fact with the annexation of Texas, "the inevitable conflict" commenced.

As the time for the Presidential election of 1856—the first at which I had the opportunity of voting—approached, party feeling began to run high. The Republican party was regarded in the South and the border States not only as opposed to the extension of slavery, but as favoring the compulsory abolition of the institution without compensation to the owners. The most horrible visions seemed to present themselves to the minds of people who, one would suppose, ought to have known better. Many educated and, otherwise, sensible persons appeared to believe that emancipation meant social equality. Treason to the Government was openly advocated and was not rebuked. It was evident to my mind that the election of a Republican President in 1856 meant the secession of all the Slave States, and rebellion. Under these circumstances I preferred the success of a candidate whose election would prevent or postpone secession, to seeing the country plunged into a war the end of which no man could foretell. With a Democrat elected by the unanimous vote of the Slave States, there could be no pretext for secession for four years. I very much hoped that the passions of the people would subside in that time, and the catastrophe be averted altogether; if it was not, I believed the country would be better prepared to receive the shock and to resist it. I therefore voted for James Buchanan for President. Four years later the Republican party was successful in electing its candidate to the Presidency. The civilized world has learned the consequence. Four millions of human beings held as chattels have been liberated; the ballot has been given to them; the free schools of the country have been opened to their children. The nation still lives, and the people are just as free to avoid social intimacy with the blacks as ever they were, or as they are with white people.

While living in Galena I was nominally only a clerk supporting myself and family on a stipulated salary. In reality my position was different. My father had never lived in Galena himself, but had established my two brothers there [Simpson and Orville], the one next younger than myself in charge of the business, assisted by the youngest. When I went there it was my father's intention to give up all connection with the business himself, and to establish his three sons in it: but the brother who had really built up the business was sinking with consumption [Simpson], and it was not thought best to make any change while he was in this condition. He lived until September, 1861, when he succumbed to that insidious disease which always flatters its victims into the belief that they are growing better up to the close of life. A more honorable man never transacted business. In September, 1861, I was engaged in an employment which required all my attention elsewhere.

During the eleven months that I lived in Galena prior to the first call for volunteers, I had been strictly attentive to my business, and had made but few acquaintances other than customers and people engaged in the same line with myself. When the election took place in November, 1860, I had not been a resident of Illinois long enough to gain citizenship and could not, therefore, vote. I was really glad of this at the time, for my pledges would have compelled me to vote for Stephen A. Douglas, who had no possible chance of election. The contest was really between Mr. [John C.] Breckinridge and Mr. Lincoln; between minority rule and rule by the majority. I wanted, as between these candidates, to see Mr. Lincoln elected. Excitement ran high during the canvas, and torch-light processions enlivened the scene in the generally quiet streets of Galena many nights during the campaign. I did not parade with either party, but occasionally met with the "wide awakes"—Republicans—in their rooms, and superintended their drill. It was evident, from the time of the Chicago nomination to the close of the canvass, that the election of the Republican candidate would be the signal for some of the Southern States to secede. I still had hopes that the four years which had elapsed since the first nomination of a Presidential candidate by a party distinctly opposed to slavery extension, had given time for the extreme pro-slavery sentiment to cool down; for the Southerners to think well before they took the awful leap which they had so vehemently threatened. But I was mistaken.

The Republican candidate was elected, and solid substantial people of the North-west, and I presume the same order of people throughout the entire North, felt very serious, but determined, after this event. It was very much discussed whether the South would carry out its threat to secede and set up a separate government, the corner-stone of which should be, protection to the "Divine" institution of slavery. For there were people who believed in the "divinity" of human slavery, as there are now people who believe Mormonism and Polygamy to be ordained by the Most High. We forgive them for entertaining such notions, but forbid their practice. It was generally believed that there would be a flurry; that some of the extreme Southern States would go so far as to pass ordinances of secession. But the common impression was that this step was so plainly suicidal for the South, that the movement would not spread over much of the territory and would not last long.

Doubtless the founders of our government, the majority of them at least, regarded the confederation of the colonies as an experiment. Each colony considered itself a separate government; that the confederation was for mutual protection against a foreign foe, and the prevention of strife and war among themselves. If there had been a desire on the part of any single State to withdraw from the compact at any time while the number of States was limited to the original thirteen, I do not suppose there would have been any to contest the right, no matter how much the determination might have been regretted. The problem changed on the ratification of the Constitution by all the colonies; it changed still more when amendments were added; and if the right of any one State to withdraw continued to exist at all after the ratification of the Constitution, it certainly ceased on the formation of new States, at least so far as the new States themselves were concerned. It was never possessed at all by Florida or the States west of the Mississippi, all of which were purchased by the treasury of the entire nation. Texas and the territory brought into the Union in consequence of annexation, were purchased with both blood and treasure; and Texas, with a domain greater than that of any European state except Russia, was permitted to retain as state property all the public lands within its borders. It would have been ingratitude and injustice of the most flagrant sort for this State to withdraw from the Union after all that had been spent and done to introduce her; yet, if separation had actually occurred, Texas must necessarily have gone with the South, both on account of her institutions and her geographical position. Secession was illogical as well as impracticable; it was revolution.

Now, the right of revolution is an inherent one. When people are oppressed by their government, it is a natural right they enjoy to relieve themselves of the oppression, if they are strong enough, either by withdrawal from it, or by overthrowing it and substituting a government more acceptable. But any people or part of a people who resort to this remedy, stake their lives, their property, and every claim for protection given by citizenship—on the issue. Victory, or the conditions imposed by the conqueror—must be the result.

In the case of the war between the States it would have been the exact truth if the South had said,—"We do not want to live with you Northern people any longer; we know our institution of slavery is obnoxious to you, and, as you are growing numerically stronger than we, it may at some time in the future be endangered. So long as you permitted us to control the government, and with the aid of a few friends at the North to enact laws constituting your section a guard against the escape of our property, we were willing to live with you. You have been submissive to our rule heretofore; but it looks now as if you did not intend to continue so, and we will remain in the Union no longer." Instead of this the seceding States cried lustily,—"Let us alone; you have no constitutional power to interfere with us." Newspapers and people at the North reiterated the cry. Individuals might ignore the constitution; but the Nation itself must not only obey it, but must enforce the strictest construction of that instrument; the construction put upon it by the Southerners themselves. The fact is the constitution did not apply to any such contingency as the one existing from 1861 to 1865. Its framers never dreamed of such a contingency occurring. If they had foreseen it, the probabilities are they would have sanctioned the right of a State or States to withdraw rather than that there should be war between brothers.

The framers were wise in their generation and wanted to do the very best possible to secure their own liberty and independence, and that also of their descendants to the latest days. It is preposterous to suppose that the people of one generation can lay down the best and only rules of government for all who are to come after them, and under unforeseen contingencies. At the time of the framing of our constitution the only physical forces that had been subdued and made to serve man and do his labor, were the currents in the streams and in the air we breathe. Rude machinery, propelled by water power, had been invented; sails to propel ships upon the waters had been set to catch the passing breeze—but the application of steam to propel vessels against both wind and current, and machinery to do all manner of work had not been thought of. The instantaneous transmission of messages around the world by means of electricity would probably at that day have been attributed to witchcraft or a league with the Devil. Immaterial circumstances had changed as greatly as material ones. We could not and ought not to be rigidly bound by the rules laid down under circumstances so different for emergencies so utterly unanticipated. The fathers themselves would have been the first to declare that their prerogatives were not irrevocable. They would surely have resisted secession could they have lived to see the shape it assumed.

I travelled through the Northwest considerably during the winter of 1860-1. We had customers in all the little towns in south-west Wisconsin, south-east Minnesota and north-east Iowa. These generally knew I had been a captain in the regular army and had served through the Mexican war. Consequently wherever I stopped at night, some of the people would come to the public-house where I was, and sit till a late hour discussing the probabilities of the future. My own views at that time were like those officially expressed by Mr. [William H.] Seward at a later day, that "the war would be over in ninety days." I continued to entertain these views until after the battle of Shiloh. I believe now that there would have been no more battles at the West after the capture of Fort Donelson if all the troops in that region had been under a single commander who would have followed up that victory.

There is little doubt in my mind now that the prevailing sentiment of the South would have been opposed to secession in 1860 and 1861, if there had been a fair and calm expression of opinion, unbiased by threats, and if the ballot of one legal voter had counted for as much as that of any other. But there was no calm discussion of the question. Demagogues who were too old to enter the army if there should be a war, others who entertained so high an opinion of their own ability that they did not believe they could be spared from the direction of the affairs of state in such an event, declaimed vehemently and unceasingly against the North, against its aggressions upon the South; its interference with Southern rights, etc., etc. They denounced the Northerners as cowards, poltroons, Negro-worshippers; claimed that one Southern man was equal to five Northern men in battle; that if the South would stand up for its rights the North would back down. Mr. Jefferson Davis said in a speech, delivered at La Grange, Mississippi, before the secession of that State, that he would agree to drink all the blood spilled south of Mason and Dixon's line if there should be a war. The young men who would have the fighting to do in case of war, believed all these statements, both in regard to the aggressiveness of the North and its cowardice. They, too, cried out for a separation from such people. The great bulk of the legal voters of the South were men who owned no slaves; their homes were generally in the hills and poor country; their facilities for educating their children, even up to the point of reading and writing, were very limited; their interest in the contest was very meagre—what there was, if they had been capable of seeing it, was with the North; they too needed emancipation. Under the old regime they were looked down upon by those who controlled all the affairs in the interest of slave owners, as poor white trash who were allowed the ballot so long as they cast it according to direction.

I am aware that this last statement may be disputed and individual testimony perhaps adduced to show that in ante-bellum days the ballot was as untrammelled in the South as in any section of the country; but in the face of any such contradiction I reassert the statement. The shot-gun was not resorted to. Masked men did not ride over the country at night intimidating voters; but there was a firm feeling that a class existed in every State with a sort of divine right to control public affairs. If they could not get this control by one means they must by another. The end justified the means. The coercion, if mild, was complete.

There were two political parties, it is true, in all the States, both strong in numbers and respectability, but both equally loyal to the institution which stood paramount in Southern eyes to all other institutions in state or nation. The slave-owners were the minority, but governed both parties. Had politics ever divided the slave-holders and the non-slave-holders, the majority would have been obliged to yield, or internecine war would have been the consequence. I do not know that the Southern people were to blame for this condition of affairs. There was a time when slavery was not profitable, and the discussion of the merits of the institution was confined almost exclusively to the territory where it existed. The States of Virginia and Kentucky came near abolishing slavery by their own acts, one State defeating the measure by a tie vote and the other only lacking one. But when the institution became profitable, all talk of its abolition ceased where it existed; and naturally, as human nature is constituted, arguments were adduced in its support. The cotton-gin probably had much to do with the justification of slavery.

The winter of 1860-1 will be remembered by middle-aged people of today as one of great excitement. South Carolina promptly seceded after the result of the Presidential election was known. Other Southern States proposed to follow. In some of them the Union sentiment was so strong that it had to be suppressed by force. Maryland, Delaware, Kentucky and Missouri, all Slave States, failed to pass ordinances of secession; but they were all represented in the so-called congress of the so-called Confederate States. The Governor and Lieutenant-Governor of Missouri, in 1861, [Claiborne F.] Jackson and [Thomas C.] Reynolds, were both supporters of the rebellion and took refuge with the enemy. The governor soon died, and the lieutenant-governor assumed his office; issued proclamations as governor of the State; was recognized as such by the Confederate Government, and continued his pretensions until the collapse of the rebellion. The South claimed the sovereignty of States, but claimed the right to coerce into their confederation such States as they wanted, that is, all the

States where slavery existed. They did not seem to think this course inconsistent. The fact is, the Southern slave-owners believed that, in some way, the ownership of slaves conferred a sort of patent of nobility—a right to govern independent of the interest or wishes of those who did not hold such property. They convinced themselves, first, of the divine origin of the institution and, next, that that particular institution was not safe in the hands of any body of legislators but themselves.

Meanwhile the Administration of President Buchanan looked helplessly on and proclaimed that the general government had no power to interfere; that the Nation had no power to save its own life. Mr. Buchanan had in his cabinet two members at least, who were as earnest—to use a mild term—in the cause of secession as Mr. Davis or any Southern statesman. One of them, [John B.] Floyd, the Secretary of War, scattered the army so that much of it could be captured when hostilities should commence, and distributed the cannon and small arms from Northern arsenals throughout the South so as to be on hand when treason wanted them. The navy was scattered in like manner. The President did not prevent his cabinet preparing for war upon their government, either by destroying its resources or storing them in the South until a *de facto* government was established with Jefferson Davis as its President, and Montgomery, Alabama, as the Capital. The secessionists had then to leave the cabinet. In their own estimation they were aliens in the country which had given them birth. Loyal men were put into their places. Treason in the executive branch of the government was estopped. But the harm had already been done. The stable door was locked after the horse had been stolen.

During all of the trying winter of 1860–1, when the Southerners were so defiant that they would not allow within their borders the expression of a sentiment hostile to their views, it was a brave man indeed who could stand up and proclaim his loyalty to the Union. On the other hand men at the North—prominent men—proclaimed that the government had no power to coerce the South into submission to the laws of the land; that if the North undertook to raise armies to go south, these armies would have to march over the dead bodies of the speakers. A portion of the press of the North was constantly proclaiming similar views. When the time arrived for the President-elect to go to the capital of the Nation to be sworn into office, it was deemed unsafe for him to travel, not only as a President-elect, but as any private citizen should be allowed to do. Instead of going in a special car, receiving the good wishes of his constituents at all the stations along the road, he was obliged to stop on the way and to be smuggled into the capital. He disappeared from public view on his journey, and the next the country knew, his arrival was announced at the capital. There is little doubt that he would have been assassinated if he had attempted to travel openly throughout his journey.

SOURCE: Ulysses Simpson Grant. *Personal Memoirs of U. S. Grant.* 2 vols. New York: Charles L. Webster & Company, 1885–86.

AMBROSE BIERCE

Ambrose Bierce (1842–1914?) was a veteran of the Union Army and author of a number of writings about the Civil War. The first of these two stories has been anthologized as a ghost story for its effectiveness in depicting a young picket guard, under intense stress, suffering delusions.

A Tough Tussle (1888)

One night in the autumn of 1861 a man sat alone in the heart of a forest in Western Virginia. The region was then, and still is, one of the wildest on the continent—the Cheat Mountain country. There was no lack of people close at hand, however; within two miles of where the man sat was the now silent camp of a whole Federal brigade. Somewhere about—it might be still nearer—was a force of the enemy, the numbers unknown. It was this uncertainty as to its numbers and position that accounted for the man's presence in that lonely spot; he was a young officer of a Federal infantry regiment, and his business there was to guard his sleeping comrades in the camp against a surprise. He was in command of a detachment of men constituting a picket guard. These men he had stationed just at nightfall in an irregular line, determined by the nature of the ground, several hundred yards in front of where he now sat. The line ran through the forest, among the rocks and laurel thickets, the men fifteen or twenty paces apart, all in concealment and under injunction of strict silence and unremitting vigilance. In four hours, if nothing occurred, they would be relieved by a fresh detachment from the reserve now resting in care of its captain some distance away to the left and rear. Before stationing his men the young officer of whom we are speaking had pointed out to his two sergeants the spot at which he would be found in case it should be necessary to consult him, or if his presence at the front line should be required.

It was a quiet enough spot—the fork of an old wood road, on the two branches of which, prolonging themselves deviously forward in the dim moonlight, the sergeants were themselves stationed, a few paces in rear of the line. If driven sharply back by a sudden onset of the enemy—and pickets are not expected to make a stand after firing—the men would come into the converging roads, and, naturally following them to their point of intersection, could be rallied and "formed." In his small way the young lieutenant was something of a strategist; if Napoleon had planned as intelligently at Waterloo, he would have won the battle and been overthrown later.

Second Lieutenant Brainerd Byring was a brave and efficient officer, young and comparatively inexperienced as he was in the business of killing his fellow-men. He had enlisted in the very first days of the war as a private, with no military knowledge whatever, had been made first sergeant of his company on account of his education and engaging manner, and had been lucky enough to lose his captain by a Confederate bullet; in the resulting promotions he had got a commission. He had been in several engagements, such as they were—at Philippi, Rich Mountain, Carrick's Ford and Greenbrier—and had borne himself with such gallantry as not to attract attention of his superior officers. The exhilaration of battle was agreeable to him, but the sight of the dead, with their clay faces, blank eyes, and stiff bodies, which, when not unnaturally shrunken, were unnaturally swollen, had always intolerably affected him. He felt toward them a kind of reasonless antipathy which was something more than the physical and spiritual repugnance common to us all. Doubtless this feeling was due to his unusually acute sensibilities—his keen sense of the beautiful, which these hideous things outraged. Whatever may have been the cause, he could not look upon a dead body without a loathing which had in it an element of resentment. What others have respected as the dignity of death had to him no existence—was altogether unthinkable. Death was a thing to be hated. It was not picturesque, it had no tender and solemn side—a dismal thing, hideous in all its manifestations and suggestions. Lieutenant Byring was a braver man than anybody knew, for nobody knew his horror of that which he was ever ready to encounter.

Having posted his men, instructed his sergeants, and retired to his station, he seated himself on a log, and, with senses all alert, began his vigil. For greater ease he loosened his sword belt, and, taking his heavy revolver from his holster, laid it on the log beside him. He felt very comfortable, though he hardly gave the fact a thought, so intently did he listen for any sound from the front which might have a menacing significance—a shout, a shot, or the footfall of one of his sergeants coming to apprise him of something worth knowing. From the vast, invisible ocean of moonlight overhead fell, here and there, a slender, broken stream that seemed to plash against the intercepting branches and trickle to earth, forming small white pools among the clumps of laurel. But these leaks were few and served only to accentuate the blackness of his environment, which his imagination found it easy to people with all manner of unfamiliar shapes, menacing, uncanny, or merely grotesque.

He to whom the portentous conspiracy of night and solitude and silence in the heart of a great forest is not an unknown experience needs not to be told what another world it all is—how even the most commonplace and familiar objects take on another character. The trees group themselves differently; they draw closer together, as if in fear. The very silence has another quality than the silence of the day. And it is full of half-heard whispers, whispers that startle—ghosts of sounds long dead. There are living sounds, too, such as are never heard under other conditions: notes of strange night birds, the cries of small animals in sudden encounters with stealthy foes, or in their dreams, a rustling in the dead leaves—it may be the leap of a wood rat, it may be the footstep of a panther.

What caused the breaking of that twig?—what the low, alarmed twittering in that bushful of birds? There are sounds without a name, forms without substance, translations in space of objects which have not been seen to move, movements wherein nothing is observed to change its place. Ah, children of the sunlight and the gaslight, how little you know of the world in which you live!

Surrounded at a little distance by armed and watchful friends, Byring felt utterly alone. Yielding himself to the solemn and mysterious spirit of the time and place, he had forgotten the nature of his connection with the visible and audible aspects and phases of the night. The forest was boundless; men and the habitations of men did not exist. The universe was one primeval mystery of darkness, without form and void, himself the sole dumb questioner of its eternal secret. Absorbed in the thoughts born of this mood, he suffered the time to slip away unnoted. Meantime the infrequent patches of white light lying amongst the undergrowth had undergone changes of size, form, and place. In one of them near by, just at the roadside, his eye fell upon an object which he had not previously observed. It was almost before his face as he sat; he could have sworn that it had not before been there. It was partly covered in shadow, but he could see that it was a human figure. Instinctively he adjusted the clasp of his sword belt and laid hold of his pistol—again he was in a world of war, by occupation an assassin.

The figure did not move. Rising, pistol in hand, he approached. The figure lay upon its back, its upper part in shadow, but standing above it and looking down upon the face, he saw that it was a dead body. He shuddered and turned from it with a feeling of sickness and disgust, resumed his seat upon the log, and, forgetting military prudence, struck a match and lit a cigar. In the sudden blackness that followed the extinction of the flame he felt a sense of relief; he could no longer see the object of his aversion. Nevertheless, he kept his eyes set in that direction until it appeared again with growing distinctness. It seemed to have moved a trifle nearer.

"Damn the thing!" he muttered. "What does it want?"

It did not appear to be in need of anything but a soul.

Byring turned away his eyes and began humming a tune, but he broke off in the middle of a bar and looked at the dead man. Its presence annoyed him, though he could hardly have had a quieter neighbor. He was conscious, too, of a vague, indefinable feeling which was new to him. It was not fear but rather a sense of the supernatural—in which he did not at all believe.

"I have inherited it," he said to himself. "I suppose it will require a thousand years—perhaps ten thousand—for humanity to outgrow this feeling. Where and when did it originate? Away back, probably, in what is called the cradle of the human race—the plains of Central Asia. What we inherit as a superstition our barbarous ancestors must have held as a reasonable conviction. Doubtless they believed themselves justified by facts whose nature we cannot even conjecture in thinking a dead body a malign thing endowed with some strange power of mischief, with perhaps a will and a purpose to exert it. Possibly they had some awful form of religion of which that was one of the chief doctrines, sedulously taught by their priesthood, just as ours teach the immortality of the soul. As the Aryan moved westward to and through the Caucasus passes and spread over Europe, new conditions of life must have resulted in the formulation of new religions. The old belief in the malevolence of the dead body was lost from the creeds, and even perished from tradition, but it left its heritage of terror, which is transmitted from generation to generation—is as much a part of us as our blood and bones."

In following out his thought he had forgotten that which suggested it; but now his eye fell again upon the corpse. The shadow had now altogether uncovered it. He saw the sharp profile, the chin in the air, the whole face, ghastly white in the moonlight. The clothing was gray, the uniform of a Confederate soldier. The coat and waistcoat, unbuttoned, had fallen away on each side, exposing the white shirt. The chest seemed unnaturally prominent, but the abdomen had sunk in, leaving a sharp projection at the line of the lower ribs. The arms were extended, the left knee was thrust upward. The whole posture impressed Byring as having been studied with a view to the horrible.

"Bah!" he exclaimed; "he was an actor—he knows how to be dead."

He drew away his eyes, directing them resolutely along one of the roads leading to the front, and resumed his philosophizing where he had left off.

"It may be that our Central Asian ancestors had not the custom of burial. In that case it is easy to understand their fear of the dead, who really were a menace and an evil. They bred pestilences. Children were taught to avoid the places where they lay, and to run away if by inadvertence they came near a corpse. I think, indeed, I'd better go away from this chap."

He half rose to do so, then remembered that he told his men in front, and the officer in the rear who was to relieve him, that he could at any time be found at that spot. It was a matter of pride, too. If he abandoned his post, he feared they would think he feared the corpse. He was no coward, and he was not going to incur anybody's ridicule. So he again seated himself, and, to prove his courage, looked boldly at the body. The right arm—the one farthest from him—was now in shadow. He could barely see the hand which, he had before observed, lay at the root of a clump of laurel. There had been no change, a fact which gave him a certain comfort, he could not have said why. He did not at once remove his eyes; that which we do not wish to see has a strange fascination, sometimes irresistible. Of the woman who covers her face with her hands, and looks between the fingers, let it be said that the wits have dealt with her not altogether justly.

Byring suddenly became conscious of a pain in his right hand. He withdrew his eyes from his enemy and looked at it. He was grasping the hilt of his drawn sword so tightly that it hurt him. He observed, too, that he was leaning forward in a strained attitude—crouching like a gladiator ready to spring at the throat of an antagonist. His teeth were clenched, and he was breathing hard. This matter was soon set right, and as his muscles relaxed and he drew a long breath, he felt keenly enough the ludicrousness of the incident. It affected him to laughter. Heavens! what sound was that?—what mindless devil was uttering an unholy glee in mockery of human merriment? He sprang to his feet and looked about him, not recognizing his own laugh.

He could no longer conceal from himself the horrible fact of his cowardice; he was thoroughly frightened! He would have run from the spot, but his legs refused their office; they gave way beneath him, and he sat again upon the log, violently trembling. His face was wet, his whole body bathed in a chill perspiration. He could not even cry out. Distinctly he heard behind him a stealthy tread, as of some wild animal, and dared not look over his shoulder. Had the soulless living joined forces with the soulless dead?—was it an animal? Ah, if he could but be assured of that! But by no effort of will could he now unfix his gaze from the face of the dead man.

I repeat that Lieutenant Byring was a brave and intelligent man. But what would you have? Shall a man cope, single-handed, with so monstrous an alliance as that of night and solitude and silence and the dead?—while an incalculable host of his own ancestors shriek into the ear of his spirit their coward counsel, sing their doleful death songs in his heart and disarm his very blood of all its iron? The odds are too great—courage was not made for such rough use as that.

One sole conviction now had the man in possession: that the body had moved. It lay nearer to the edge of its plot of light—there could be no doubt of it. It had also moved its arms, for, look, they are both in the shadow! A breath of cold air struck Byring full in the face; the branches of trees above him stirred and moaned. A strongly-defined shadow passed across the face of the dead, left it luminous, passed back upon it and left it half obscured. The horrible thing was visibly moving. At that moment a single shot rang out upon the picket line—a lonelier and louder, though more distant, shot than ever had been heard by mortal ear! It broke the spell of that enchanted man; it slew the silence and the solitude, dispersed the hindering host from Central Asia, and released his modern manhood. With a cry like that of some great bird pouncing upon its prey, he sprang forward, hot-hearted for action!

Shot after shot now came from the front. There were shoutings and confusion, hoof beats and desultory cheers. Away to the rear, in the sleeping camp, was a singing of bugles and a grumble of drums. Pushing through the thickets on either side the roads came the Federal pickets, in full retreat, firing backward at random as they ran. A straggling group that had followed back one of the roads, as instructed, suddenly sprang away into the bushes as half a hundred horsemen thundered by them, striking wildly with their sabers as they passed. At headlong speed these mounted madmen shot past the spot where Byring had sat, and vanished round an angle of the road, shouting and firing their pistols. A moment later there was a roar of musketry, followed by dropping shots—they had encountered the reserve guard in line; and back they came in dire confusion, with here and there an empty saddle and many a maddened horse, bullet-stung, snorting and plunging with pain. It was all over—"an affair of outposts."

The line was re-established with fresh men, the roll called, the stragglers were reformed. The Federal commander, with a part of his staff, imperfectly clad, appeared upon the scene, asked a few questions, looked exceedingly wise, and retired. After standing at arms for an hour, the brigade in camp "swore a prayer or two" and went to bed.

Early the next morning a fatigue party, commanded by a captain and accompanied by a surgeon, searched the ground for dead and wounded. At the fork of the road, a little to one side, they found two bodies lying close together—that of a Federal officer and that of a Confederate private. The officer had died of a sword-thrust through the heart, but not, apparently, until he had inflicted upon his enemy no fewer than five dreadful wounds. The dead officer lay on his face in a pool of blood, the weapon still in his breast. They turned him on his back and the surgeon removed it.

"Gad!" said the captain—"it is Byring!"—adding, with a glance at the other, "They had a tough tussle."

The surgeon was examining the sword. It was that of a line officer of Federal infantry—exactly like the one worn by the captain. It was, in fact, Byring's own. The only other weapon discovered was an undischarged revolver in the dead officer's belt.

The surgeon laid down the sword and approached the other body. It was frightfully gashed and stabbed, but there was no blood. He took hold of the left foot and tried to straighten the leg. In the effort the body was displaced. The dead do not wish to be moved when comfortable—it protested with a faint, sickening odor. Where it had lain were a few maggots, manifesting an imbecile activity.

The surgeon looked at the captain. The captain looked at the surgeon.

SOURCE: Ambrose Bierce. *Tales of Soldiers and Civilians*. New York: Lovell, Coryell and Company, 1891.

An Occurrence at Owl Creek Bridge (1890)

This, the most anthologized short story about the Civil War, was not published until twenty-five years after that war's conclusion. It may remind some present-day readers of the fantastical tales of the Argentine Jorge Luis Borges.

1.

A man stood upon a railroad bridge in Northern Alabama, looking down into the swift waters twenty feet below. The man's hands were behind his back, the wrists bound with a cord. A rope loosely encircled his neck. It was attached to a stout cross-timber above his head, and the slack fell to the level of his knees. Some loose boards laid upon the sleepers supporting the metals of the railway supplied a footing for him, and his executioners—two private soldiers of the Federal army, directed by a sergeant, who in civil life may have been a deputy sheriff. At a short remove upon the same temporary platform was an officer in the uniform of his rank, armed. He was a captain. A sentinel at each end of the bridge stood with his rifle in the position known as "support," that is to say, vertical in front of the left shoulder, the hammer resting on the forearm thrown straight across the chest—a formal and unnatural position, enforcing an erect carriage of the body. It did not appear to be the duty of these two men to know what was occurring at the center of the bridge; they merely blockaded the two ends of the foot plank which traversed it.

Beyond one of the sentinels nobody was in sight; the railroad ran straight away into a forest for a hundred yards, then, curving, was lost to view. Doubtless there was an outpost further along. The other bank of the stream was open ground—a gentle acclivity crowned with a stockade of vertical tree trunks, loop-holed for rifles, with a single embrasure through which protruded the muzzle of a brass cannon commanding the bridge. Midway of the slope between bridge and fort were the spectators—a single company of infantry in line, at "parade rest," the butts of the rifles on the ground, the barrels inclining slightly backward against the right shoulder, the hands crossed upon the stock. A lieutenant stood at the right of the line, the point of his sword upon the ground, his left hand resting upon his right. Excepting the group of four at the center of the bridge not a man moved. The company faced the bridge, staring stonily, motionless. The sentinels, facing the banks of the stream, might have been statues to adorn the bridge. The captain stood with folded arms, silent, observing the work of his subordinates but making no sign. Death is a dignitary who, when he comes announced, is to be received with formal manifestations of respect, even by those most familiar with him. In the code of military etiquette silence and fixity are forms of deference.

The man who was engaged in being hanged was apparently about thirty-five years of age. He was a civilian, if one might judge from his dress, which was that of a planter. His features were good—a straight nose, firm mouth, broad forehead, from which his long, dark hair was combed straight back, falling behind his ears to the collar of his well-fitting frock coat. He wore a mustache and pointed beard but no whiskers; his eyes were large and dark gray and had a kindly expression which one would hardly have expected in one whose neck was in the hemp. Evidently this was no vulgar assassin. The liberal military code makes provision for hanging many kinds of people, and gentlemen are not excluded.

The preparations being complete, the two private soldiers stepped aside and each drew away the plank upon which he had been standing. The sergeant turned to the captain, saluted and placed himself immediately behind that officer, who in turn moved apart one pace. These movements left the condemned man and the sergeant standing on the two ends of the same plank, which spanned three of the cross-ties of the bridge. The end upon which the civilian stood almost, but not quite, reached a fourth. This plank had been held in place by the weight of the captain; it was now held by that of the sergeant. At a signal from the former, the latter would step aside, the plank would tilt and the condemned man go down between two ties. The arrangement commended itself to his judgment as simple and effective. His face had not been covered nor his eyes bandaged. He looked a moment at his "unsteadfast footing," then let his gaze wander to the swirling water of the stream racing madly beneath his feet. A piece of dancing driftwood caught his attention and his eyes followed it down the current. How slowly it appeared to move! What a sluggish stream!

He closed his eyes in order to fix his last thoughts upon his wife and children. The water, touched to gold by the early sun, the brooding mists under the banks at some distance down the stream, the fort, the soldiers, the piece of drift—all had distracted him. And now he became conscious of a new disturbance. Striking through the thought of his dear ones was a sound which he could neither ignore nor understand, a sharp, distinct, metallic percussion like the stroke of a blacksmith's hammer upon the anvil; it had the same ringing quality. He wondered what it was, and whether immeasurably distant or near by—it seemed both. Its recurrence was regular, but as slow as the tolling of a death knell. He awaited each stroke with impatience and—he knew not why—apprehension. The intervals of silence grew progressively longer; the delays became maddening. With their greater infrequency the sounds increased in strength and sharpness. They hurt his ear like the thrust of a knife; he feared he would shriek. What he heard was the ticking of his watch.

He unclosed his eyes and saw again the water below him. "If I could free my hands," he thought, "I might throw off the noose and spring into the stream. By diving I could evade the bullets, and, swimming vigorously, reach the bank, take to the woods, and get away home. My home, thank God, is as yet outside their lines; my wife and little ones are still beyond the invader's farthest advance."

As these thoughts, which have here to be set down in words, were flashed into the doomed man's brain rather than evolved from it, the captain nodded to the sergeant. The sergeant stepped aside.

2.

Peyton Farquhar was a well-to-do planter, of an old and highly-respected Alabama family. Being a slave owner, and, like other slave owners, a politician, he was naturally an original secessionist and ardently devoted to the Southern cause. Circumstances of an imperious nature which it is unnecessary to relate here, had prevented him from taking service with the gallant army which had fought the disastrous campaigns ending with the fall of Corinth, and he chafed under the inglorious restraint, longing for the release of his energies, the larger life of the soldier, the opportunity for distinction. That opportunity, he felt, would come, as it comes to all in war time. Meanwhile he did what he could. No service was too humble for him to perform in aid of the South, no adventure too perilous for him to undertake if consistent with the character of a civilian who was at heart a soldier, and who in good faith and without too much qualification assented to at least a part of the frankly villainous dictum that all is fair in love and war.

One evening while Farquhar and his wife were sitting on a rustic bench near the entrance to his grounds, a gray-clad soldier rode up to the gate and asked for a drink of water. Mrs. Farquhar was only too happy to serve him with her own white hands. While she was gone to fetch the water, her husband approached the dusty horseman and inquired eagerly for news from the front.

"The Yanks are repairing the railroads," said the man, "and are getting ready for another advance. They have reached the Owl Creek bridge, put it in order, and built a stockade on the other bank. The commandant has issued an order, which is posted everywhere, declaring that any civilian caught interfering with the railroad, its bridges, tunnels, or trains, will be summarily hanged. I saw the order."

"How far is it to the Owl Creek bridge?" Farquhar asked.

"About thirty miles?"

"Is there no force on this side the creek?"

"Only a picket post half a mile out, on the railroad, and a single sentinel at this end of the bridge."

"Suppose a man—a civilian and student of hanging—should elude the picket post and perhaps get the better of the sentinel," said Farquhar, smiling, "what could he accomplish?"

The soldier reflected. "I was there a month ago," he replied. "I observed that the flood of last winter had lodged a great quantity of driftwood against the wooden pier at this end of the bridge. It is now dry and would burn like tow."

The lady had now brought the water, which the soldier drank. He thanked her ceremoniously, bowed to her husband, and rode away. An hour later, after nightfall, he repassed the plantation, going northward in the direction from which he had come. He was a Federal scout.

3.

As Peyton Farquhar fell straight downward through the bridge, he lost consciousness and was as one already dead. From this state he was awakened—ages later, it seemed to him—by the pain of a sharp pressure upon his throat, followed by a sense of suffocation. Keen, poignant agonies seemed to shoot from his neck downward through every fiber of his body and limbs. These pains appeared to flash along well-defined lines of ramification and to beat with an inconceivably rapid periodicity. They seemed like streams of pulsating fire heating him to an intolerable temperature. As to his head, he was conscious of nothing but a feeling of fullness—of congestion. These sensations were unaccompanied by thought. The intellectual part of his nature was already effaced; he had power only to feel, and feeling was torment. He was conscious of motion. Encompassed in a luminous cloud, of which he was now merely the fiery heart, without material substance, he swung through unthinkable arcs of oscillation, like a vast pendulum. Then all at once, with terrible suddenness, the light about him shot upward with the noise of a loud plash; a frightful roaring was in his ears, and all was cold and dark. The power of thought was restored; he knew that the rope had broken and he had fallen into the stream. There was no additional strangulation; the noose about his neck was already suffocating him and kept the water from his lungs. To die of hanging at the bottom of a river!—the idea seemed to him ludicrous. He opened his eyes in the blackness and saw above him a gleam of light, but how distant, how inaccessible! He was still sinking, for the light became fainter and fainter until it was a mere glimmer. Then it began to grow and brighten, and he knew that he was rising toward the surface—knew it with reluctance, for he was now very comfortable. "To be hanged and drowned," he thought, "that is not so bad; but I do not wish to be shot. No; I will not be shot; that is not fair."

He was not conscious of an effort, but a sharp pain in his wrists apprised him that he was trying to free his hands. He gave the struggle his attention, as an idler might observe the feat of a juggler, without interest in the outcome. What splendid effort!—what magnificent, what superhuman strength! Ah, that was a fine endeavor! Bravo! The cord fell away; his arms parted and floated upward, the hands dimly seen on each side in the growing light. He watched them with a new interest as first one and then the other pounced upon the noose at his neck. They tore it away and thrust it fiercely aside, its undulations resembling those of a water snake. "Put it back, put it back!" He thought he shouted these words to his hands, for the undoing of the noose had been succeeded by the direst pang which he had yet experienced. His neck ached horribly; his brain was on fire; his heart, which had been fluttering faintly, gave a great leap, trying to force itself out at his mouth. His whole body was racked and wrenched with an insupportable anguish! But his disobedient hands gave no heed to the command. They beat the water vigorously with quick, downward strokes, forcing him to the surface. He felt his head emerge; his eyes were blinded by the sunlight; his chest expanded convulsively, and with a supreme and crowning agony his lungs engulfed a great draught of air, which instantly he expelled in a shriek!

He was now in full possession of his physical senses. They were, indeed, preternaturally keen and alert. Something in the awful disturbance of his organic system had so exalted and refined them that they made record of things never before perceived. He felt the ripples upon his face and heard their separate sounds as they struck. He looked at the forest on the bank of the stream, saw the individual trees, the leaves and the veining of each leaf—saw the very insects upon them, the locusts, the brilliant-bodied flies, the gray spiders stretching their webs from twig to twig. He noted the prismatic colors in all the dewdrops upon a million blades of grass. The humming of the gnats that danced above the eddies of the stream, the beating of the dragon flies' wings, the strokes of the water spiders' legs, like oars which had lifted their boat—all these made audible music. A fish slid along beneath his eyes and he heard the rush of its body parting the water.

He had come to the surface facing down the stream; in a moment the visible world seemed to wheel slowly round, himself the pivotal point, and he saw the bridge, the fort, the soldiers upon the bridge, the captain, the sergeant, the two privates, his executioners. They were in silhouette against the blue sky. They shouted and gesticulated, pointing at him; the captain had drawn his pistol, but did not fire; the others were unarmed. Their movements were grotesque and horrible, their forms gigantic.

Suddenly he heard a sharp report and something struck the water smartly within a few inches of his head, spattering his face with spray. He heard a second report, and saw one of the sentinels with his rifle at his shoulder, a light cloud of blue smoke rising from the muzzle. The man in the water saw the eye of the man on the bridge gazing into his own through the sights of the rifle. He observed that it was a gray eye, and remembered having read that gray eyes were keenest and that all famous marksmen had them. Nevertheless, this one had missed.

A counter swirl had caught Farquhar and turned him half round; he was again looking into the forest on the bank opposite the fort. The sound of a clear, high voice in a monotonous singsong now rang out behind him and came across the water with a distinctness that pierced and subdued all other sounds, even the beating of the ripples in his ears. Although no soldier, he had frequented camps enough to know the dread significance of that deliberate, drawling, aspirated chant; the lieutenant on shore was taking a part in the morning's work. How coldly and pitilessly—with what an even, calm intonation, presaging and enforcing tranquillity in the men—with what accurately-measured intervals fell those cruel words:

"Attention, company. . . . Shoulder arms. . . . Ready. . . . Aim. . . . Fire."

Farquhar dived—dived as deeply as he could. The water roared in his ears like the voice of Niagara, yet he heard the dulled thunder of the volley, and, rising again toward the surface, met shining bits of metal, singularly flattened, oscillating slowly downward. Some of them touched him on the face and hands, then fell away, continuing their descent. One lodged between his collar and neck; it was uncomfortably warm, and he snatched it out.

As he rose to the surface, gasping for breath, he saw that he had been a long time under water; he was perceptibly farther down stream—nearer to safety. The soldiers had almost finished reloading; the metal ramrods flashed all at once in the sunshine as they were drawn from the barrels, turned in the air, and thrust into their sockets. The two sentinels fired again, independently and ineffectually.

The hunted man saw all this over his shoulder; he was now swimming vigorously with the current. His brain was as energetic as his arms and legs; he thought with the rapidity of lightning.

"The officer," he reasoned, "will not make that martinet's error a second time. It is as easy to dodge a volley as a single shot. He has probably already given the command to fire at will. God help me, I cannot dodge them all!"

An appalling plash within two yards of him, followed by a loud rushing sound, *diminuendo*, which seemed to travel back through the air to the fort and died in an explosion which stirred the very river to its deeps! A rising sheet of water, which curved over him, fell down upon him, blinded him, strangled him! The cannon had taken a hand in the game. As he shook his head free from the commotion of the smitten water, he heard the deflected shot humming through the air ahead, and in an instant it was cracking and smashing the branches in the forest beyond.

"They will not do that again," he thought; "the next time they will use a charge of grape. I must keep my eye upon the gun; the smoke will apprise me—the report arrives too late; it lags behind the missile. It is a good gun."

Suddenly he felt himself whirled round and round—spinning like a top. The water, the banks, the forest, the now distant bridge, fort and men—all were commingled and blurred. Objects were represented by their colors only; circular horizontal streaks of color—that was all he saw. He had been caught in a vortex and was being whirled on with a velocity of advance and gyration which made him giddy and sick. In a few moments he was flung upon the gravel at the foot of the left bank of the stream—the southern bank—and behind a projecting point which concealed him from his enemies. The sudden arrest of his motion, the abrasion of one of his hands on the gravel, restored him and he wept with delight. He dug his fingers into the sand, threw it over himself in handfuls and audibly blessed it. It looked like gold, like diamonds, rubies, emeralds; he could think of nothing beautiful which it did not resemble. The trees upon the bank were giant garden plants; he noted a definite order in their arrangement, inhaled the fragrance of their blooms. A strange, roseate light shone through the spaces among their trunks, and the wind made in their branches the music of æolian harps. He had no wish to perfect his escape, was content to remain in that enchanting spot until retaken.

A whizz and rattle of grapeshot among the branches high above his head roused him from his dream. The baffled cannoneer had fired him a random farewell. He sprang to his feet, rushed up the sloping bank, and plunged into the forest.

All that day he traveled, laying his course by the rounding sun. The forest seemed interminable; nowhere did he discover a break in it, not even a woodman's road. He had not known that he lived in so wild a region. There was something uncanny in the revelation.

By nightfall he was fatigued, footsore, famishing. The thought of his wife and children urged him on. At last he found a road which led him in what he knew to be the right direction. It was as wide and straight as a city street, yet it seemed untraveled. No fields bordered it, no dwelling anywhere. Not so much as the barking of a dog suggested human habitation. The black bodies of the great trees formed a straight wall on both sides, terminating on the horizon in a point, like a diagram in a lesson in perspective. Overhead, as he looked up through this rift in the wood, shone great golden stars looking unfamiliar and grouped in strange constellations. He was sure they were arranged in some order which had a secret and malign significance. The wood on either side was full of singular noises, among which—once, twice, and again—he distinctly heard whispers in an unknown tongue.

His neck was in pain, and, lifting his hand to it, he found it horribly swollen. He knew that it had a circle of black where the rope had bruised it. His eyes felt congested; he could no longer close them. His tongue was swollen with thirst; he relieved its fever by thrusting it forward from between his teeth into the cool air. How softly the turf had carpeted the untraveled avenue! He could no longer feel the roadway beneath his feet!

Doubtless, despite his suffering, he fell asleep while walking, for now he sees another scene—perhaps he has merely recovered from a delirium. He stands at the gate of his own home. All is as he left it, and all bright and beautiful in the morning sunshine. He must have traveled the entire night. As he pushes open the gate and passes up the wide white walk, he sees a flutter of female garments; his wife, looking fresh and cool and sweet, steps down from the veranda to meet him. At the bottom of the steps she stands waiting, with a smile of ineffable joy, an attitude of matchless grace and dignity. Ah, how beautiful she is! He springs forward with extended arms. As he is about to clasp her, he feels a stunning blow upon the back of the neck; a blinding white light blazes all about him, with a sound like the shock of a cannon—then all is darkness and silence!

Peyton Farquhar was dead; his body, with a broken neck, swung gently from side to side beneath the timbers of the Owl Creek bridge.

SOURCE: Ambrose Bierce. *Tales of Soldiers and Civilians.* New York: Lovell, Coryell and Company, 1891.

MARY E. WILKINS FREEMAN

Mary E. Wilkins Freeman (1852–1930) was a popular author for several decades. In this tight-knit drama of domestic relations, Freeman presents the extraordinary Sarah Penn, who informs an interfering minister, "There ain't no use talkin', Mr. Hersey. . . . I've thought it all over an' over, an' I believe I'm doin' what's right. I've made it the subject of prayer, an' it's betwixt me an' the Lord an' Adoniram. There ain't no call for nobody else to worry about it."

The Revolt of "Mother" (1891)

"FATHER!"

"What is it?"

"What are them men diggin' over there in the field for?"

There was a sudden dropping and enlarging of the lower part of the old man's face, as if some heavy weight had settled therein; he shut his mouth tight, and went on harnessing the great bay mare. He hustled the collar on to her neck with a jerk.

"Father!"

The old man slapped the saddle upon the mare's back.

"Look here, father, I want to know what them men are diggin' over in the field for, an' I'm goin' to know."

"I wish you'd go into the house, mother, an' 'tend to your own affairs," the old man said then. He ran his words together, and his speech was almost as inarticulate as a growl.

But the woman understood; it was her most native tongue. "I ain't goin' into the house till you tell me what them men are doin' over there in the field," said she.

Then she stood waiting. She was a small woman, short and straight-waisted like a child in her brown cotton gown. Her forehead was mild and benevolent between the smooth curves of gray hair; there were meek downward lines about her nose and mouth; but her eyes, fixed upon the old man, looked as if the meekness had been the result of her own will, never of the will of another.

They were in the barn, standing before the wide-open doors. The spring air, full of the smell of growing grass and unseen blossoms, came in their faces. The deep yard in front was littered with farm-wagons and piles of wood; on the edges, close to the fence and the house, the grass was a vivid green, and there were some dandelions.

The old man glanced doggedly at his wife as he tightened the last buckles on the harness. She looked as immovable to him as one of the rocks in his pasture-land, bound to the earth with generations of blackberry vines. He slapped the reins over the horse, and started forth from the barn.

"*Father!*" said she.

The old man pulled up. "What is it?"

"I want to know what them men are diggin' over there in that field for."

"They're diggin' a cellar, I s'pose, if you've got to know."

"A cellar for what?"

"A barn."

"A barn? You ain't goin' to build a barn over there where we was goin' to have a house, father?"

The old man said not another word. He hurried the horse into the farm wagon, and clattered out of the yard, jouncing as sturdily on his seat as a boy.

The woman stood a moment looking after him, then she went out of the barn across a corner of the yard to the house. The house, standing at right angles with the great barn and a long reach of sheds and out-buildings, was infinitesimal compared with them. It was scarcely as commodious for people as the little boxes under the barn eaves were for doves.

A pretty girl's face, pink and delicate as a flower, was looking out of one of the house windows. She was watching three men who were digging over in the field which bounded the yard near the road line. She turned quietly when the woman entered.

"What are they digging for, mother?" said she. "Did he tell you?"

"They're diggin' for—a cellar for a new barn."

"Oh, mother, he ain't going to build another barn?"

"That's what he says."

A boy stood before the kitchen glass combing his hair. He combed slowly and painstakingly, arranging his brown hair in a smooth hillock over his forehead. He did not seem to pay any attention to the conversation.

"Sammy, did you know father was going to build a new barn?" asked the girl.

The boy combed assiduously.

"Sammy!"

He turned, and showed a face like his father's under his smooth crest of hair. "Yes, I s'pose I did," he said, reluctantly.

"How long have you known it?" asked his mother.

"'Bout three months, I guess."

"Why didn't you tell of it?"

"Didn't think 'twould do no good."

"I don't see what father wants another barn for," said the girl, in her sweet, slow voice. She turned again to the window, and stared out at the digging men in the field. Her tender, sweet face was full of a gentle distress. Her forehead was as bald and innocent as a baby's, with the light hair strained back from it in a row of curl-papers. She was quite large, but her soft curves did not look as if they covered muscles.

Her mother looked sternly at the boy. "Is he goin' to buy more cows?" said she.

The boy did not reply; he was tying his shoes.

"Sammy, I want you to tell me if he's goin' to buy more cows."

"I s'pose he is."

"How many?"

"Four, I guess."

His mother said nothing more. She went into the pantry and there was a clatter of dishes. The boy got his cap from a nail behind the door, took an old arithmetic from the shelf, and started for school. He was lightly built, but clumsy. He went out of the yard with a curious spring in the hips, that made his loose home-made jacket tilt up in the rear.

The girl went to the sink, and began to wash the dishes that were piled up there. Her mother came promptly out of the pantry, and shoved her aside. "You wipe 'em," said she; "I'll wash. There's a good many this mornin'."

The mother plunged her hands vigorously into the water, the girl wiped the plates slowly and dreamily. "Mother," said she, "don't you think it's too bad father's going to build that new barn, much as we need a decent house to live in?"

Her mother scrubbed a dish fiercely. "You ain't found out yet we're women-folks, Nanny Penn," said she. "You ain't seen enough of men-folks yet to. One of these days you'll find it out, an' then you'll know that we know only what men-folks think we do, so far as any use of it goes, an' how we'd ought to reckon men-folks in with Providence an' not complain of what they do any more than we do of the weather."

"I don't care; I don't believe George is anything like that, anyhow," said Nanny. Her delicate face flushed pink, her lips pouted softly, as if she were going to cry.

"You wait an' see. I guess George Eastman ain't no better than other men. You hadn't ought to judge father, though. He can't help it, 'cause he don't look at things jest the way we do. An' we've been pretty comfortable here, after all. The roof don't leak—ain't never but once—that's one thing. Father's kept it shingled right up."

"I do wish we had a parlor."

"I guess it won't hurt George Eastman any to come to see you in a nice clean kitchen. I guess a good many girls don't have as good a place as this. Nobody's ever heard me complain."

"I ain't complained either, mother."

"Well, I don't think you'd better, a good father an' a good home as you've got. S'pose your father made you go out an' work for your livin'? Lots of girls have to that ain't no stronger an' better able to than you be."

Sarah Penn washed the frying-pan with a conclusive air. She scrubbed the outside of it as faithfully as the inside. She was a masterly keeper of her box of a house. Her one living-room never seemed to have in it any of the dust which the friction of life with inanimate matter produces. She swept, and there seemed to be no dirt to go before the broom; she cleaned, and one could see no difference. She was like an artist so perfect that he has apparently no art. To-day she got out a mixing bowl and a board, and rolled some pies, and there was no more flour upon her than upon her daughter who was doing finer work. Nanny was to be married in the fall, and she was sewing on some white cambric and embroidery. She sewed industriously while her mother cooked, her soft milk-white hands and wrists showed whiter than her delicate work.

"We must have the stove moved out in the shed before long," said Mrs. Penn. "Talk about not havin' things, it's been a real blessin' to be able to put a stove up in that shed in hot weather. Father did one good thing when he fixed that stove-pipe out there."

Sarah Penn's face as she rolled her pies had that expression of meek vigor which might have characterized one of the New Testament saints. She was making mince-pies. Her husband, Adoniram Penn, liked them better than any other kind. She baked twice a week. Adoniram often liked a piece of pie between meals. She hurried this morning. It had been later than usual when she began, and she wanted to have a pie baked for dinner. However deep a resentment she might be forced to hold against her husband, she would never fail in sedulous attention to his wants.

Nobility of character manifests itself at loop-holes when it is not provided with large doors. Sarah Penn's showed itself to-day in flaky dishes of pastry. So she made the pies faithfully, while across the table she could see, when she glanced up from her work, the sight that rankled in her patient and steadfast soul—the digging of the cellar of the new barn in the place where Adoniram forty years ago had promised her their new house should stand.

The pies were done for dinner. Adoniram and Sammy were home a few minutes after twelve o'clock. The dinner was eaten with serious haste. There was never much conversation at the table in the Penn family. Adoniram asked a blessing, and they ate promptly, then rose up and went about their work.

Sammy went back to school, taking soft sly lopes out of the yard like a rabbit. He wanted a game of marbles before school, and feared his father would give him some chores to do. Adoniram hastened to the door and called after him, but he was out of sight.

"I don't see what you let him go for, mother," said he. "I wanted him to help me unload that wood."

Adoniram went to work out in the yard unloading wood from the wagon. Sarah put away the dinner dishes, while Nanny took down her curl-papers and changed her dress. She was going down to the store to buy some more embroidery and thread.

When Nanny was gone, Mrs. Penn went to the door. "Father!" she called.

"Well, what is it?"

"I want to see you jest a minute, father."

"I can't leave this wood nohow. I've got to git it unloaded an' go for a load of gravel afore two o'clock. Sammy had ought to helped me. You hadn't ought to let him go to school so early."

"I want to see you jest a minute."

"I tell ye I can't, nohow, mother."

"Father, you come here." Sarah Penn stood in the door like a queen; she held her head as if it bore a crown; there was that patience which makes authority royal in her voice. Adoniram went.

Mrs. Penn led the way into the kitchen, and pointed to a chair. "Sit down, father," said she; "I've got somethin' I want to say to you."

He sat down heavily; his face was quite stolid, but he looked at her with restive eyes. "Well, what is it, mother?"

"I want to know what you're buildin' that new barn for, father?"

"I ain't got nothin' to say about it."

"It can't be you think you need another barn?"

"I tell ye I ain't got nothin' to say about it, mother; an' I ain't goin' to say nothin'."

"Be you goin' to buy more cows?"

Adoniram did not reply; he shut his mouth tight.

"I know you be, as well as I want to. Now, father, look here"—Sarah Penn had not sat down; she stood before her husband in the humble fashion of a Scripture woman—"I'm goin' to talk real plain to you: I never have sence I married you, but I'm goin' to now. I ain't never complained, an' I ain't goin' to complain now, but I'm goin' to talk plain. You see this room here, father; you look at it well. You see there ain't no carpet on the floor, an' you see the paper is all dirty, an' droppin' off the walls. We ain't had no new paper on it for ten year, an' then I put it on myself an' it didn't cost but ninepence a roll. You see this room, father; it's all the one I've had to work in an' eat in an' sit in sence we was married. There ain't another woman in the whole town whose husband ain't got half the means you have but what's got better. It's all the room Nanny's got to have her company in; an' there ain't one of her mates but what's got better, an' their fathers not so able as hers is. It's all the room she'll have to be married in. What would you have thought, father, if we had had our weddin' in a room no better than this? I was married in my mother's parlor, with a carpet on the floor, an' stuffed furniture, an' a mahogany card-table. An' this is all the room my daughter will have to be married in. Look here, father!"

Sarah Penn went across the room as though it were a tragic stage. She flung open a door and disclosed a tiny bedroom, only large enough for a bed and bureau, with a path between. "There, father," said she—"there's all the room I've had to sleep in forty year. All my children were born there—the two that died, an' the two that's livin'. I was sick with a fever there."

She stepped to another door and opened it. It led into the small, ill-lighted pantry. "Here," said she, "is all the buttery I've got—every place I've got for my dishes, to set away my victuals in, an' to keep my milk-pans in. Father, I've been takin' care of the milk of six cows in this place, an' now you're goin' to build a new barn, an' keep more cows, an' give me more to do in it."

She threw open another door. A narrow crooked flight of stairs wound upward from it. "There, father," said she; "I want you to look at the stairs that go up to them two unfinished chambers that are all the places our son an' daughter have had to sleep in all their lives. There ain't a prettier girl in town nor a more ladylike one than Nanny, an' that's the place she has to sleep in. It ain't so good as your horse's stall; it ain't so warm an' tight."

Sarah Penn went back and stood before her husband. "Now, father," said she, "I want to know if you think you're doin' right an' accordin' to what you profess. Here, when we was married, forty year ago, you promised me faithful that we should have a new house built in that lot over in the field before the year was out. You said you had money enough, an' you wouldn't ask me to live in no such place as this. It is forty year now, an' you've been makin' more money, an' I've been savin' of it for you ever since, an' you ain't built no house yet. You've built sheds an' cow-houses an' one new barn, an' now you're goin' to build another. Father, I want to know if you think it's right. You're lodgin' your dumb beasts better than you are your own flesh an' blood. I want to know if you think it's right."

"I ain't got nothin' to say."

"You can't say nothin' without ownin' it ain't right, father. An' there's another thing—I ain't complained; I've got along forty year, an' I s'pose I should forty more, if it wa'n't for that—if we don't have another house. Nanny she can't live with us after she's married. She'll have to go somewheres else to live away from us, an' it don't seem as if I could have it so, noways, father. She wa'n't ever strong. She's got considerable color, but there wa'n't ever any backbone to her. I've always took the heft of everything off her, an' she ain't fit to keep house an' do everything herself. She'll be all worn out inside of a year. Think of her doin' all the washin' an' ironin' an' bakin' with them soft white hands an' arms, an' sweepin'! I can't have it so, noways, father."

Mrs. Penn's face was burning; her mild eyes gleamed. She had pleaded her little cause like a Webster; she had ranged from severity to pathos; but her opponent employed that obstinate silence which makes eloquence futile with mocking echoes. Adoniram arose clumsily.

"Father, ain't you got nothin' to say?" said Mrs. Penn.

"I've got to go off after that load of gravel. I can't stan' here talkin' all day."

"Father, won't you think it over, an' have a house built there instead of a barn?"

"I ain't got nothin' to say."

Adoniram shuffled out. Mrs. Penn went into her bedroom. When she came out, her eyes were red. She had a roll of unbleached cotton cloth. She spread it out on the kitchen table, and began cutting out some shirts for her husband. The men over in the field had a team to help them this afternoon; she could hear their halloos. She had a scanty pattern for the shirts; she had to plan and piece the sleeves.

Nanny came home with her embroidery, and sat down with her needle-work. She had taken down her curl-papers, and there was a soft roll of fair hair like an aureole over her forehead; her face was as delicately fine and clear as porcelain. Suddenly she looked up, and the tender red flamed all over her face and neck. "Mother," said she.

"What say?"

"I've been thinking—I don't see how we're goin' to have any—wedding in this room. I'd be ashamed to have his folks come if we didn't have anybody else."

"Mebbe we can have some new paper before then; I can put it on. I guess you won't have no call to be ashamed of your belongin's."

"We might have the wedding in the new barn," said Nanny, with gentle pettishness. "Why, mother, what makes you look so?"

Mrs. Penn had started, and was staring at her with a curious expression. She turned again to her work, and spread out a pattern carefully on the cloth. "Nothin'," said she.

Presently Adoniram clattered out of the yard in his two-wheeled dump cart, standing as proudly upright as a Roman charioteer. Mrs. Penn opened the door and stood there a minute looking out; the halloos of the men sounded louder.

It seemed to her all through the spring months that she heard nothing but the halloos and the noises of saws and hammers. The new barn grew fast. It was a fine edifice for this little village. Men came on pleasant Sundays, in their meeting suits and clean shirt bosoms, and stood around it admiringly. Mrs. Penn did not speak of it, and Adoniram did not mention it to her, although sometimes, upon a return from inspecting it, he bore himself with injured dignity.

"It's a strange thing how your mother feels about the new barn," he said, confidentially, to Sammy one day.

Sammy only grunted after an odd fashion for a boy: he had learned it from his father.

The barn was all completed ready for use by the third week in July. Adoniram had planned to move his stock in on Wednesday; on Tuesday he received a letter which changed his plans. He came in with it early in the morning. "Sammy's been to the post-office," said he, "an' I've got a letter from Hiram." Hiram was Mrs. Penn's brother, who lived in Vermont.

"Well," said Mrs. Penn, "what does he say about the folks?"

"I guess they're all right. He says he thinks if I come up country right off there's a chance to buy jest the kind of a horse I want." He stared reflectively out of the window at the new barn.

Mrs. Penn was making pies. She went on clapping the rolling-pin into the crust, although she was very pale, and her heart beat loudly.

"I dun' know but what I'd better go," said Adoniram. "I hate to go off jest now, right in the midst of hayin', but the ten-acre lot's cut, an' I guess Rufus an' the others can git along without me three or four days. I can't get a horse round here to suit me, nohow, an' I've got to have another for all that wood-haulin' in the fall. I told Hiram to watch out, an' if he got wind of a good horse to let me know. I guess I'd better go."

"I'll get out your clean shirt an' collar," said Mrs. Penn calmly.

She laid out Adoniram's Sunday suit and his clean clothes on the bed in the little bedroom. She got his shaving-water and razor ready. At last she buttoned on his collar and fastened his black cravat.

Adoniram never wore his collar and cravat except on extra occasions. He held his head high, with a rasped dignity. When he was all ready, with his coat and hat brushed, and a lunch of pie and cheese in a paper bag, he hesitated on the threshold of the door. He looked at his wife, and his manner was defiantly apologetic. "*If* them cows come to-day, Sammy can drive 'em into the new barn," said he; "an' when they bring the hay up, they can pitch it in there."

"Well," replied Mrs. Penn.

Adoniram set his shaven face ahead and started. When he had cleared the door-step, he turned and looked back with a kind of nervous solemnity. "I shall be back by Saturday if nothin' happens," said he.

"Do be careful, father," returned his wife.

She stood in the door with Nanny at her elbow and watched him out of sight. Her eyes had a strange, doubtful expression in them; her peaceful forehead was contracted. She went in, and about her baking again. Nanny sat sewing. Her wedding-day was drawing nearer, and she was getting pale and thin with her steady sewing. Her mother kept glancing at her.

"Have you got that pain in your side this mornin'?" she asked.

"A little."

Mrs. Penn's face, as she worked, changed, her perplexed forehead smoothed, her eyes were steady, her lips firmly set. She formed a maxim for herself, although incoherently with her unlettered thoughts. "Unsolicited opportunities are the guide-posts of the Lord to the new roads of life," she repeated in effect, and she made up her mind to her course of action.

"S'posin' I *had* wrote to Hiram," she muttered once, when she was in the pantry—"s'posin' I had wrote, an' asked him if he knew of any horse? But I didn't, an' father's goin' wa'n't none of my doin'. It looks like a providence." Her voice rang out quite loud at the last.

"What you talkin' about, mother?" called Nanny.

"Nothin'."

Mrs. Penn hurried her baking; at eleven o'clock it was all done. The load of hay from the west field came slowly down the cart track, and drew up at the new barn. Mrs. Penn ran out. "Stop!" she screamed—"stop!"

The men stopped and looked; Sammy upreared from the top of the load, and stared at his mother.

"Stop!" she cried out again. "Don't you put the hay in that barn; put it in the old one."

"Why, he said to put it in here," returned one of the haymakers, wonderingly. He was a young man, a neighbor's son, whom Adoniram hired by the year to help on the farm.

"Don't you put the hay in the new barn; there's room enough in the old one, ain't there?" said Mrs. Penn.

"Room enough," returned the hired man, in his thick, rustic tones. "Didn't need the new barn, nohow, far as room's concerned. Well, I s'pose he changed his mind." He took hold of the horses' bridles.

Mrs. Penn went back to the house. Soon the kitchen windows were darkened, and a fragrance like warm honey came into the room.

Nanny laid down her work. "I thought father wanted them to put the hay into the new barn?" she said, wonderingly.

"It's all right," replied her mother.

Sammy slid down from the load of hay, and came in to see if dinner was ready.

"I ain't goin' to get a regular dinner to-day, as long as father's gone," said his mother. "I've let the fire go out. You can have some bread an' milk an' pie. I thought we could get along." She set out some bowls of milk, some bread, and a pie on the kitchen table. "You'd better eat your dinner now," said she. "You might jest as well get through with it. I want you to help me afterward."

Nanny and Sammy stared at each other. There was something strange in their mother's manner. Mrs. Penn did not eat anything herself. She went into the pantry, and they heard her moving dishes while they ate. Presently she came out with a pile of plates. She got the clothes-basket out of the shed, and packed them in it. Nanny and Sammy watched. She brought out cups and saucers, and put them in with the plates.

"What you goin' to do, mother?" inquired Nanny, in a timid voice. A sense of something unusual made her tremble, as if it were a ghost. Sammy rolled his eyes over his pie.

"You'll see what I'm goin' to do," replied Mrs. Penn. "If you're through, Nanny, I want you to go up-stairs an' pack up your things; an' I want you, Sammy, to help me take down the bed in the bedroom."

"Oh, mother, what for?" gasped Nanny.

"You'll see."

During the next few hours a feat was performed by this simple, pious New England mother which was equal in its way to Wolfe's storming of the Heights of Abraham. It took no more genius and audacity of bravery for Wolfe to cheer his wondering soldiers up those steep precipices, under the sleeping eyes of the enemy, than for Sarah Penn, at the head of her children, to move all their little household goods into the new barn while her husband was away.

Nanny and Sammy followed their mother's instructions without a murmur; indeed, they were overawed. There is a certain uncanny and superhuman quality about all such purely original undertakings as their mother's was to them. Nanny went back and forth with her light loads, and Sammy tugged with sober energy.

At five o'clock in the afternoon the little house in which the Penns had lived for forty years had emptied itself into the new barn.

Every builder builds somewhat for unknown purposes, and is in a measure a prophet. The architect of Adoniram Penn's barn, while he designed it for the comfort of four-footed animals, had planned better than he knew for the comfort of humans. Sarah Penn saw at a glance its possibilities. Those great box-stalls, with quilts hung before them, would make better bedrooms than the one she had occupied for forty years, and there was a tight carriage-room. The harness-room, with its chimney and shelves, would make a kitchen of her dreams. The great middle space would make a parlor, by-and-by, fit for a palace. Up-stairs there was as much room as down. With partitions and windows, what a house would there be! Sarah looked at the row of stanchions before the allotted space for cows, and reflected that she would have her front entry there.

At six o'clock the stove was up in the harness-room, the kettle was boiling, and the table set for tea. It looked almost as home-like as the abandoned house across the yard had ever done. The young hired man milked, and Sarah directed him calmly to bring the milk to the new barn. He came gaping, dropping little blots of foam from the brimming pails on the grass. Before the next morning he had spread the story of Adoniram Penn's wife moving into the new barn all over the little village. Men assembled in the store and talked it over, women with shawls over their heads scuttled into each other's houses before their work was done. Any deviation from the ordinary course of life in this quiet town was enough to stop all progress in it. Everybody paused to look at the staid, independent figure on the side track. There was a difference of opinion with regard to her. Some held her to be insane; some, of a lawless and rebellious spirit.

Friday the minister went to see her. It was in the forenoon, and she was at the barn door shelling pease for dinner. She looked up and returned his salutation with dignity, then she went on with her work. She did not invite him in. The saintly expression of her face remained fixed, but there was an angry flush over it.

The minister stood awkwardly before her, and talked. She handled the pease as if they were bullets. At last she looked up, and her eyes showed the spirit that her meek front had covered for a lifetime.

"There ain't no use talkin', Mr. Hersey," said she. "I've thought it all over an' over, an' I believe I'm doin' what's right. I've made it the subject of prayer, an' it's betwixt me an' the Lord an' Adoniram. There ain't no call for nobody else to worry about it."

"Well, of course, if you have brought it to the Lord in prayer, and feel satisfied that you are doing right, Mrs. Penn," said the minister, helplessly. His thin gray-bearded face was pathetic. He was a sickly man; his youthful confidence had cooled; he had to scourge himself up to some of his pastoral duties as relentlessly as a Catholic ascetic, and then he was prostrated by the smart.

"I think it's right jest as much as I think it was right for our forefathers to come over from the old country 'cause they didn't have what belonged to 'em," said Mrs. Penn. She arose. The barn threshold might have been Plymouth Rock from her bearing. "I don't doubt you mean well, Mr. Hersey," said she, "but there are things people hadn't ought to interfere with. I've been a member of the church for over forty year. I've got my own mind an' my own feet, an' I'm goin' to think my own thoughts an' go my own ways, an' nobody but the Lord is goin' to dictate to me unless I've a mind to have him. Won't you come in an' set down? How is Mis' Hersey?"

"She is well, I thank you," replied the minister. He added some more perplexed apologetic remarks; then he retreated.

He could expound the intricacies of every character study in the Scriptures, he was competent to grasp the Pilgrim Fathers and all historical innovators, but Sarah Penn was beyond him. He could deal with primal cases, but parallel ones worsted him. But, after all, although it was aside from his province, he wondered more how Adoniram Penn would deal with his wife than how the Lord would. Everybody shared the wonder. When Adoniram's four new cows arrived, Sarah ordered three to be put in the old barn, the other in the house shed where the cooking-stove had stood. That added to the excitement. It was whispered that all four cows were domiciled in the house.

Toward sunset on Saturday, when Adoniram was expected home, there was a knot of men in the road near the new barn. The hired man had milked, but he still hung around the premises. Sarah Penn had supper all ready. There were brown-bread and baked beans and a custard pie; it was the supper that Adoniram loved on a Saturday night. She had on a clean calico, and she bore herself imperturbably. Nanny and Sammy kept close at her heels. Their eyes were large, and Nanny was full of nervous tremors. Still there was to them more pleasant excitement than anything else. An inborn confidence in their mother over their father asserted itself.

Sammy looked out of the harness-room window. "There he is," he announced, in an awed whisper. He and Nanny peeped around the casing. Mrs. Penn kept on about her work. The children watched Adoniram leave the new horse standing in the drive while he went to the house door. It was fastened. Then he went around to the shed. That door was seldom locked, even when the family was away. The thought how her father would be confronted by the cow flashed upon Nanny. There was a hysterical sob in her throat. Adoniram emerged from the shed and stood looking about in a dazed fashion. His lips moved; he was saying something, but they could not hear what it was. The hired man was peeping around a corner of the old barn, but nobody saw him.

Adoniram took the new horse by the bridle and led him across the yard to the new barn. Nanny and Sammy slunk close to their mother. The barn doors rolled back, and there stood Adoniram, with the long mild face of the great Canadian farm horse looking over his shoulder.

Nanny kept behind her mother, but Sammy stepped suddenly forward, and stood in front of her.

Adoniram stared at the group. "What on airth you all down here for?" said he. "What's the matter over to the house?"

"We've come here to live, father," said Sammy. His shrill voice quavered out bravely.

"What"—Adoniram sniffed—"what is it smells like cookin'?" said he. He stepped forward and looked in the open door of the harness-room. Then he turned to his wife. His old bristling face was pale and frightened. "What on airth does this mean, mother?" he gasped.

"You come in here, father," said Sarah. She led the way into the harness-room and shut the door. "Now, father," said she, "you needn't be scared. I ain't crazy. There ain't nothin' to be upset over. But we've come here to live, an' we're goin' to live here. We've got jest as good a right here as new horses an' cows. The house wa'n't fit for us to live in any longer, an' I made up my mind I wa'n't goin' to stay there. I've done my duty by you forty year, an' I'm goin' to do it now; but I'm goin' to live here. You've got to put in some windows and partitions; an' you'll have to buy some furniture."

"Why, mother!" the old man gasped.

"You'd better take your coat off an' get washed—there's the wash-basin—an' then we'll have supper."

"Why, mother!"

Sammy went past the window, leading the new horse to the old barn. The old man saw him, and shook his head speechlessly. He tried to take off his coat, but his arms seemed to lack the power. His wife helped him. She poured some water into the tin basin, and put in a piece of soap. She got the comb and brush, and smoothed his thin gray hair after he had washed. Then she put the beans, hot bread, and tea on the table. Sammy came in, and the family drew up. Adoniram sat looking dazedly at his plate, and they waited.

"Ain't you goin' to ask a blessin', father?" said Sarah.

And the old man bent his head and mumbled.

All through the meal he stopped eating at intervals, and stared furtively at his wife; but he ate well. The home food tasted good to him, and his old frame was too sturdily healthy to be affected by his mind. But after supper he went out, and sat down on the step of the smaller door at the right of the barn, through which he had meant his Jerseys to pass in stately file, but which Sarah designed for her front house-door, and he leaned his head on his hands.

After the supper dishes were cleared away and the milk-pans washed, Sarah went out to him. The twilight was deepening. There was a clear green glow in the sky. Before them stretched the smooth level of field; in the distance was a cluster of hay-stacks like the huts of a village; the air was very cool and calm and sweet. The landscape might have been an ideal one of peace.

Sarah bent over and touched her husband on one of his thin, sinewy shoulders. "Father!"

The old man's shoulders heaved: he was weeping.

"Why, don't do so, father," said Sarah.

"I'll—put up the—partitions, an'—everything you—want, mother."

Sarah put her apron up to her face; she was overcome by her own triumph.

Adoniram was like a fortress whose walls had no active resistance, and went down the instant the right besieging tools were used. "Why, mother," he said, hoarsely, "I hadn't no idee you was so set on't as all this comes to."

Source: Mary E. Wilkins Freeman. *A New England Nun and Other Stories*. New York: Harper and Brothers, 1891.

CHARLOTTE PERKINS GILMAN

Charlotte Perkins Gilman (1860–1935) was a prolific author and an important women's rights advocate. "The Yellow Wallpaper," the disturbing account of a woman going mad, has taken its place as one of the standard works of American short fiction.

The Yellow Wallpaper (1892)

It is very seldom that mere ordinary people like John and myself secure ancestral halls for the summer.

A colonial mansion, a hereditary estate, I would say a haunted house, and reach the height of romantic felicity—but that would be asking too much of fate!

Still I will proudly declare that there is something queer about it.

Else, why should it be let so cheaply? And why have stood so long untenanted?

John laughs at me, of course, but one expects that in marriage.

John is practical in the extreme. He has no patience with faith, an intense horror of superstition, and he scoffs openly at any talk of things not to be felt and seen and put down in figures.

John is a physician, and *perhaps*—(I would not say it to a living soul, of course, but this is dead paper and a great relief to my mind—) *perhaps* that is one reason I do not get well faster.

You see, he does not believe I am sick!

And what can one do?

If a physician of high standing, and one's own husband, assures friends and relatives that there is really nothing the matter with one but temporary nervous depression—a slight hysterical tendency—what is one to do?

My brother is also a physician, and also of high standing, and he says the same thing.

So I take phosphates or phosphites—whichever it is, and tonics, and journeys, and air, and exercise, and am absolutely forbidden to "work" until I am well again.

Personally, I disagree with their ideas.

Personally, I believe that congenial work, with excitement and change, would do me good.

But what is one to do?

I did write for a while in spite of them; but it *does* exhaust me a good deal—having to be so sly about it, or else meet with heavy opposition.

I sometimes fancy that in my condition if I had less opposition and more society and stimulus—but John says the very worst thing I can do is to think about my condition, and I confess it always makes me feel bad.

So I will let it alone and talk about the house.

The most beautiful place! It is quite alone, standing well back from the road, quite three miles from the village. It makes me think of English places that you read about, for there are hedges and walls and gates that lock, and lots of separate little houses for the gardeners and people.

There is a *delicious* garden! I never saw such a garden—large and shady, full of box-bordered paths, and lined with long grape-covered arbors with seats under them.

There were greenhouses, too, but they are all broken now.

There was some legal trouble, I believe, something about the heirs and co-heirs; anyhow, the place has been empty for years.

That spoils my ghostliness, I am afraid, but I don't care—there is something strange about the house—I can feel it.

I even said so to John one moonlight evening, but he said what I felt was a *draught*, and shut the window.

I get unreasonably angry with John sometimes. I'm sure I never used to be so sensitive. I think it is due to this nervous condition.

But John says if I feel so, I shall neglect proper self-control; so I take pains to control myself—before him, at least, and that makes me very tired.

I don't like our room a bit. I wanted one downstairs that opened on the piazza and had roses all over the window, and such pretty old-fashioned chintz hangings! but John would not hear of it.

He said there was only one window and not room for two beds, and no near room for him if he took another.

He is very careful and loving, and hardly lets me stir without special direction.

I have a schedule prescription for each hour in the day; he takes all care from me, and so I feel basely ungrateful not to value it more.

He said we came here solely on my account, that I was to have perfect rest and all the air I could get. "Your exercise depends on your strength, my dear," said he, "and your food somewhat on your appetite; but air you can absorb all the time." So we took the nursery at the top of the house.

It is a big, airy room, the whole floor nearly, with windows that look all ways, and air and sunshine galore. It was nursery first and then playroom and gymnasium, I should judge; for the windows are barred for little children, and there are rings and things in the walls.

The paint and paper look as if a boys' school had used it. It is stripped off—the paper—in great patches all around the head of my bed, about as far as I can reach, and in a great place on the other side of the room low down. I never saw a worse paper in my life.

One of those sprawling flamboyant patterns committing every artistic sin.

It is dull enough to confuse the eye in following, pronounced enough to constantly irritate and provoke study, and when you follow the lame uncertain curves for a little distance they suddenly commit suicide—plunge off at outrageous angles, destroy themselves in unheard of contradictions.

The color is repellent, almost revolting; a smouldering unclean yellow, strangely faded by the slow-turning sunlight.

It is a dull yet lurid orange in some places, a sickly sulphur tint in others.

No wonder the children hated it! I should hate it myself if I had to live in this room long.

There comes John, and I must put this away,—he hates to have me write a word.

We have been here two weeks, and I haven't felt like writing before, since that first day.

I am sitting by the window now, up in this atrocious nursery, and there is nothing to hinder my writing as much as I please, save lack of strength.

John is away all day, and even some nights when his cases are serious.

I am glad my case is not serious!

But these nervous troubles are dreadfully depressing.

John does not know how much I really suffer. He knows there is no *reason* to suffer, and that satisfies him.

Of course it is only nervousness. It does weigh on me so not to do my duty in any way!

I meant to be such a help to John, such a real rest and comfort, and here I am a comparative burden already!

Nobody would believe what an effort it is to do what little I am able,—to dress and entertain, and order things.

It is fortunate Mary is so good with the baby. Such a dear baby!

And yet I *cannot* be with him, it makes me so nervous.

I suppose John never was nervous in his life. He laughs at me so about this wallpaper!

At first he meant to repaper the room, but afterwards he said that I was letting it get the better of me, and that nothing was worse for a nervous patient than to give way to such fancies.

He said that after the wallpaper was changed it would be the heavy bedstead, and then the barred windows, and then that gate at the head of the stairs, and so on.

"You know the place is doing you good," he said, "and really, dear, I don't care to renovate the house just for a three months' rental."

"Then do let us go downstairs," I said, "there are such pretty rooms there."

Then he took me in his arms and called me a blessed little goose, and said he would go down cellar, if I wished, and have it whitewashed into the bargain.

But he is right enough about the beds and windows and things.

It is an airy and comfortable room as any one need wish, and, of course, I would not be so silly as to make him uncomfortable just for a whim.

I'm really getting quite fond of the big room, all but that horrid paper.

Out of one window I can see the garden, those mysterious deep-shaded arbors, the riotous old-fashioned flowers, and bushes and gnarly trees.

Out of another I get a lovely view of the bay and a little private wharf belonging to the estate. There is a beautiful shaded lane that runs down there from the house. I always fancy I see people walking in these numerous paths and arbors, but John has cautioned me not to give way to fancy in the least. He says that with my imaginative power and habit of story-making, a nervous weakness like mine is sure to lead to all manner of excited fancies, and that I ought to use my will and good sense to check the tendency. So I try.

I think sometimes that if I were only well enough to write a little it would relieve the press of ideas and rest me.

But I find I get pretty tired when I try.

It is so discouraging not to have any advice and companionship about my work. When I get really well, John says we will ask Cousin Henry and Julia down for a long visit; but he says he would as soon put fireworks in my pillow-case as to let me have those stimulating people about now.

I wish I could get well faster.

But I must not think about that. This paper looks to me as if it *knew* what a vicious influence it had!

There is a recurrent spot where the pattern lolls like a broken neck and two bulbous eyes stare at you upside down.

I get positively angry with the impertinence of it and the everlastingness. Up and down and sideways they crawl, and those absurd, unblinking eyes are everywhere. There is one place where two breadths didn't match, and the eyes go all up and down the line, one a little higher than the other.

I never saw so much expression in an inanimate thing before, and we all know how much expression they have! I used to lie awake as a child and get more entertainment and terror out of blank walls and plain furniture than most children could find in a toy-store.

I remember what a kindly wink the knobs of our big, old bureau used to have, and there was one chair that always seemed like a strong friend.

I used to feel that if any of the other things looked too fierce I could always hop into that chair and be safe.

The furniture in this room is no worse than inharmonious, however, for we had to bring it all from downstairs. I suppose when this was used as a playroom they had to take the nursery things out, and no wonder! I never saw such ravages as the children have made here.

The wallpaper, as I said before, is torn off in spots, and it sticketh closer than a brother—they must have had perseverance as well as hatred.

Then the floor is scratched and gouged and splintered, the plaster itself is dug out here and there, and this great heavy bed which is all we found in the room, looks as if it had been through the wars.

But I don't mind it a bit—only the paper.

There comes John's sister. Such a dear girl as she is, and so careful of me! I must not let her find me writing.

She is a perfect and enthusiastic housekeeper, and hopes for no better profession. I verily believe she thinks it is the writing which made me sick!

But I can write when she is out, and see her a long way off from these windows.

There is one that commands the road, a lovely shaded winding road, and one that just looks off over the country. A lovely country, too, full of great elms and velvet meadows.

This wallpaper has a kind of subpattern in a different shade, a particularly irritating one, for you can only see it in certain lights, and not clearly then.

But in the places where it isn't faded and where the sun is just so—I can see a strange, provoking, formless sort of figure, that seems to skulk about behind that silly and conspicuous front design.

There's sister on the stairs!

Well, the Fourth of July is over! The people are gone and I am tired out. John thought it might do me good to see a little company, so we just had mother and Nellie and the children down for a week.

Of course I didn't do a thing. Jennie sees to everything now.

But it tired me all the same.

John says if I don't pick up faster he shall send me to Weir Mitchell in the fall.

But I don't want to go there at all. I had a friend who was in his hands once, and she says he is just like John and my brother, only more so!

Besides, it is such an undertaking to go so far.

I don't feel as if it was worth while to turn my hand over for anything, and I'm getting dreadfully fretful and querulous.

I cry at nothing, and cry most of the time.

Of course I don't when John is here, or anybody else, but when I am alone.

And I am alone a good deal just now. John is kept in town very often by serious cases, and Jennie is good and lets me alone when I want her to.

So I walk a little in the garden or down that lovely lane, sit on the porch under the roses, and lie down up here a good deal.

I'm getting really fond of the room in spite of the wallpaper. Perhaps *because* of the wallpaper.

It dwells in my mind so!

I lie here on this great immovable bed,—it is nailed down, I believe—and follow that pattern about by the hour. It is as good as gymnastics, I assure you. I start, we'll say, at the bottom, down in the corner over there where it has not been touched, and I determine for the thousandth time that I *will* follow that pointless pattern to some sort of a conclusion.

I know a little of the principle of design, and I know this thing was not arranged on any laws of radiation, or alternation, or repetition, or symmetry, or anything else that I ever heard of.

It is repeated, of course, by the breadths, but not otherwise.

Looked at in one way each breadth stands alone, the bloated curves and flourishes—a kind of "debased Romanesque" with *delirium tremens*—go waddling up and down in isolated columns of fatuity.

But, on the other hand, they connect diagonally, and the sprawling outlines run off in great slanting waves of optic horror, like a lot of wallowing seaweeds in full chase.

The whole thing goes horizontally, too, at least it seems so, and I exhaust myself in trying to distinguish the order of its going in that direction.

They have used a horizontal breadth for a frieze, and that adds wonderfully to the confusion.

There is one end of the room where it is almost intact, and there, when the crosslights fade and the low sun shines directly upon it, I can almost fancy radiation after all,—the interminable grotesque seem to form around a common centre and rush off in headlong plunges of equal distraction.

It makes me tired to follow it. I will take a nap I guess.

I don't know why I should write this.

I don't want to.

I don't feel able.

And I know John would think it absurd. But I *must* say what I feel and think in some way—it is such a relief!

But the effort is getting to be greater than the relief.

Half the time now I am awfully lazy, and lie down ever so much.

John says I mustn't lose my strength, and has me take cod liver oil and lots of tonics and things, to say nothing of ale and wine and rare meat.

Dear John! He loves me very dearly, and hates to have me sick. I tried to have a real earnest reasonable talk with him the other day, and tell him how I wish he would let me go and make a visit to Cousin Henry and Julia.

But he said I wasn't able to go, nor able to stand it after I got there; and I did not make out a very good case for myself, for I was crying before I had finished.

It is getting to be a great effort for me to think straight. Just this nervous weakness I suppose.

And dear John gathered me up in his arms, and just carried me upstairs and laid me on the bed, and sat by me and read to me till it tired my head.

He said I was his darling and his comfort and all he had, and that I must take care of myself for his sake, and keep well.

He says no one but myself can help me out of it, that I must use my will and self-control and not let any silly fancies run away with me.

There's one comfort, the baby is well and happy, and does not have to occupy this nursery with the horrid wallpaper.

If we had not used it, that blessed child would have! What a fortunate escape! Why, I wouldn't have a child of mine, an impressionable little thing, live in such a room for worlds.

I never thought of it before, but it is lucky that John kept me here after all, I can stand it so much easier than a baby, you see.

Of course I never mention it to them any more—I am too wise,—but I keep watch of it all the same.

There are things in that paper that nobody knows but me, or ever will.

Behind that outside pattern the dim shapes get clearer every day.

It is always the same shape, only very numerous.

And it is like a woman stooping down and creeping about behind that pattern. I don't like it a bit. I wonder—I begin to think—I wish John would take me away from here!

* * *

It is so hard to talk with John about my case, because he is so wise, and because he loves me so.

But I tried it last night.

It was moonlight. The moon shines in all around just as the sun does.

I hate to see it sometimes, it creeps so slowly, and always comes in by one window or another.

John was asleep and I hated to waken him, so I kept still and watched the moonlight on that undulating wallpaper till I felt creepy.

The faint figure behind seemed to shake the pattern, just as if she wanted to get out.

I got up softly and went to feel and see if the paper *did* move, and when I came back John was awake.

"What is it, little girl?" he said. "Don't go walking about like that—you'll get cold."

I thought it was a good time to talk, so I told him that I really was not gaining here, and that I wished he would take me away.

"Why darling!" said he, "our lease will be up in three weeks, and I can't see how to leave before.

"The repairs are not done at home, and I cannot possibly leave town just now. Of course if you were in any danger, I could and would, but you really are better, dear, whether you can see it or not. I am a doctor, dear, and I know. You are gaining flesh and color, your appetite is better, I feel really much easier about you."

"I don't weigh a bit more," said I, "nor as much; and my appetite may be better in the evening when you are here, but it is worse in the morning when you are away!"

"Bless her little heart!" said he with a big hug, "she shall be as sick as she pleases! But now let's improve the shining hours by going to sleep, and talk about it in the morning!"

"And you won't go away?" I asked gloomily.

"Why, how can I, dear? It is only three weeks more and then we will take a nice little trip of a few days while Jennie is getting the house ready. Really dear you are better!"

"Better in body perhaps—" I began, and stopped short, for he sat up straight and looked at me with such a stern, reproachful look that I could not say another word.

"My darling," said he, "I beg of you, for my sake and for our child's sake, as well as for your own, that you will never for one instant let that idea enter your mind! There is nothing so dangerous, so fascinating, to a temperament like yours. It is a false and foolish fancy. Can you not trust me as a physician when I tell you so?"

So of course I said no more on that score, and we went to sleep before long. He thought I was asleep first, but I wasn't, and lay there for hours trying to decide whether that front pattern and the back pattern really did move together or separately.

On a pattern like this, by daylight, there is a lack of sequence, a defiance of law, that is a constant irritant to a normal mind.

The color is hideous enough, and unreliable enough, and infuriating enough, but the pattern is torturing.

You think you have mastered it, but just as you get well underway in following, it turns a back-somersault and there you are. It slaps you in the face, knocks you down, and tramples upon you. It is like a bad dream.

The outside pattern is a florid arabesque, reminding one of a fungus. If you can imagine a toadstool in joints, an interminable string of toadstools, budding and sprouting in endless convolutions—why, that is something like it.

That is, sometimes!

There is one marked peculiarity about this paper, a thing nobody seems to notice but myself, and that is that it changes as the light changes.

When the sun shoots in through the east window—I always watch for that first long, straight ray—it changes so quickly that I never can quite believe it.

That is why I watch it always.

By moonlight—the moon shines in all night when there is a moon—I wouldn't know it was the same paper.

At night in any kind of light, in twilight, candlelight, lamplight, and worst of all by moonlight, it becomes bars! The outside pattern I mean, and the woman behind it is as plain as can be.

I didn't realize for a long time what the thing was that showed behind, that dim sub-pattern, but now I am quite sure it is a woman.

By daylight she is subdued, quiet. I fancy it is the pattern that keeps her so still. It is so puzzling. It keeps me quiet by the hour.

I lie down ever so much now. John says it is good for me, and to sleep all I can.

Indeed he started the habit by making me lie down for an hour after each meal.

It is a very bad habit I am convinced, for you see I don't sleep.

And that cultivates deceit, for I don't tell them I'm awake—O no!

The fact is I am getting a little afraid of John.

He seems very queer sometimes, and even Jennie has an inexplicable look.

It strikes me occasionally, just as a scientific hypothesis,—that perhaps it is the paper!

I have watched John when he did not know I was looking, and come into the room suddenly on the most innocent excuses, and I've caught him several times *looking at the paper!* And Jennie too. I caught Jennie with her hand on it once.

She didn't know I was in the room, and when I asked her in a quiet, a very quiet voice, with the most restrained manner possible, what she was doing with the paper—she turned around as if she had been caught stealing, and looked quite angry—asked me why I should frighten her so!

Then she said that the paper stained everything it touched, that she had found yellow smooches on all my clothes and John's, and she wished we would be more careful!

Did not that sound innocent? But I know she was studying that pattern, and I am determined that nobody shall find it out but myself!

Life is very much more exciting now than it used to be. You see I have something more to expect, to look forward to, to watch. I really do eat better, and am more quiet than I was.

John is so pleased to see me improve! He laughed a little the other day, and said I seemed to be flourishing in spite of my wallpaper.

I turned it off with a laugh. I had no intention of telling him it was *because* of the wallpaper—he would make fun of me. He might even want to take me away.

I don't want to leave now until I have found it out. There is a week more, and I think that will be enough.

* * *

I'm feeling ever so much better! I don't sleep much at night, for it is so interesting to watch developments; but I sleep a good deal in the daytime.

In the daytime it is tiresome and perplexing.

There are always new shoots on the fungus, and new shades of yellow all over it. I cannot keep count of them, though I have tried conscientiously.

It is the strangest yellow, that wallpaper! It makes me think of all the yellow things I ever saw—not beautiful ones like buttercups, but old foul, bad yellow things.

But there is something else about that paper—the smell! I noticed it the moment we came into the room, but with so much air and sun it was not bad. Now we have had a week of fog and rain, and whether the windows are open or not, the smell is here.

It creeps all over the house.

I find it hovering in the dining-room, skulking in the parlor, hiding in the hall, lying in wait for me on the stairs.

It gets into my hair.

Even when I go to ride, if I turn my head suddenly and surprise it—there is that smell!

Such a peculiar odor, too! I have spent hours in trying to analyze it, to find what it smelled like.

It is not bad—at first, and very gentle, but quite the subtlest, most enduring odor I ever met.

In this damp weather it is awful, I wake up in the night and find it hanging over me.

It used to disturb me at first. I thought seriously of burning the house—to reach the smell.

But now I am used to it. The only thing I can think of that it is like is the *color* of the paper! A yellow smell.

There is a very funny mark on this wall, low down, near the mop-board. A streak that runs round the room. It goes behind every piece of furniture, except the bed, a long, straight, even *smooch*, as if it had been rubbed over and over.

I wonder how it was done and who did it, and what they did it for. Round and round and round—round and round and round—it makes me dizzy!

★ ★ ★

I really have discovered something at last.

Through watching so much at night, when it changes so, I have finally found out.

The front pattern *does* move—and no wonder! The woman behind shakes it!

Sometimes I think there are a great many women behind, and sometimes only one, and she crawls around fast, and her crawling shakes it all over.

Then in the very bright spots she keeps still, and in the very shady spots she just takes hold of the bars and shakes them hard.

And she is all the time trying to climb through. But nobody could climb through that pattern—it strangles so; I think that is why it has so many heads.

They get through, and then the pattern strangles them off and turns them upside down, and makes their eyes white!

If those heads were covered or taken off it would not be half so bad.

I think that woman gets out in the daytime!

And I'll tell you why—privately—I've seen her!

I can see her out of every one of my windows!

It is the same woman, I know, for she is always creeping, and most women do not creep by daylight.

I see her in that long shaded lane, creeping up and down. I see her in those dark grape arbors, creeping all around the garden.

I see her on that long road under the trees, creeping along, and when a carriage comes she hides under the blackberry vines.

I don't blame her a bit. It must be very humiliating to be caught creeping by daylight!

I always lock the door when I creep by daylight. I can't do it at night, for I know John would suspect something at once.

And John is so queer now, that I don't want to irritate him. I wish he would take another room! Besides, I don't want anybody to get that woman out at night but myself.

I often wonder if I could see her out of all the windows at once.

But, turn as fast as I can, I can only see out of one at one time.

And though I always see her, she *may* be able to creep faster than I can turn!

I have watched her sometimes away off in the open country, creeping as fast as a cloud shadow in a high wind.

If only that top pattern could be gotten off from the under one! I mean to try it, little by little.

I have found out another funny thing, but I shan't tell it this time! It does not do to trust people too much.

There are only two more days to get this paper off, and I believe John is beginning to notice. I don't like the look in his eyes.

And I heard him ask Jennie a lot of professional questions about me. She had a very good report to give.

She said I slept a good deal in the daytime.

John knows I don't sleep very well at night, for all I'm so quiet!

He asked me all sorts of questions, too, and pretended to be very loving and kind.

As if I couldn't see through him!

Still, I don't wonder he acts so, sleeping under this paper for three months.

It only interests me, but I feel sure John and Jennie are secretly affected by it.

Hurrah! This is the last day, but it is enough. John is to stay in town overnight, and won't be out until this evening.

Jennie wanted to sleep with me—the sly thing! but I told her I should undoubtedly rest better for a night all alone.

That was clever, for really I wasn't alone a bit! As soon as it was moonlight and that poor thing began to crawl and shake the pattern, I got up and ran to help her.

I pulled and she shook, I shook and she pulled, and before morning we had peeled off yards of that paper.

A strip about as high as my head and half around the room.

And then when the sun came and that awful pattern began to laugh at me, I declared I would finish it to-day!

We go away to-morrow, and they are moving all my furniture down again to leave things as they were before.

Jennie looked at the wall in amazement, but I told her merrily that I did it out of pure spite at the vicious thing.

She laughed and said she wouldn't mind doing it herself, but I must not get tired.

How she betrayed herself that time!

But I am here, and no person touches this paper but me,—not *alive*!

She tried to get me out of the room—it was too patent! But I said it was so quiet and empty and clean now that I believed I would lie down again and sleep all I could; and not to wake me even for dinner—I would call when I woke.

So now she is gone, and the servants are gone, and the things are gone, and there is nothing left but that great bedstead nailed down, with the canvas mattress we found on it.

We shall sleep downstairs to-night, and take the boat home to-morrow.

I quite enjoy the room, now it is bare again.

How those children did tear about here!

This bedstead is fairly gnawed!

But I must get to work.

I have locked the door and thrown the key down into the front path.

I don't want to go out, and I don't want to have anybody come in, till John comes.

I want to astonish him.

I've got a rope up here that even Jennie did not find. If that woman does get out, and tries to get away, I can tie her!

But I forgot I could not reach far without anything to stand on!

This bed will *not* move!

I tried to lift and push it until I was lame, and then I got so angry I bit off a little piece of one corner—but it hurt my teeth.

Then I peeled off all the paper I could reach standing on the floor. It sticks horribly and the pattern just enjoys it! All those strangled heads and bulbous eyes and waddling fungus growths just shriek with derision!

I am getting angry enough to do something desperate. To jump out of the window would be admirable exercise, but the bars are too strong even to try.

Besides I wouldn't do it. Of course not. I know well enough that a step like that is improper and might be misconstrued.

I don't like to *look* out of the windows even—there are so many of those creeping women, and they creep so fast.

I wonder if they all come out of that wallpaper as I did?

But I am securely fastened now by my well-hidden rope—you don't get *me* out in the road there!

I suppose I shall have to get back behind the pattern when it comes night, and that is hard!

It is so pleasant to be out in this great room and creep around as I please!

I don't want to go outside. I won't, even if Jennie asks me to.

For outside you have to creep on the ground, and everything is green instead of yellow.

But here I can creep smoothly on the floor, and my shoulder just fits in that long smooch around the wall, so I cannot lose my way.

Why there's John at the door!

It is no use, young man, you can't open it!

How he does call and pound!

Now he's crying for an axe.

It would be a shame to break down that beautiful door!

"John dear!" said I in the gentlest voice, "the key is down by the front steps, under a plantain leaf!"

That silenced him for a few moments.

Then he said—very quietly indeed, "Open the door, my darling!"

"I can't," said I. "The key is down by the front door under a plantain leaf!"

And then I said it again, several times, very gently and slowly, and said it so often that he had to go and see, and he got it of course, and came in. He stopped short by the door.

"What is the matter?" he cried. "For God's sake, what are you doing!"

I kept on creeping just the same, but I looked at him over my shoulder.

"I've got out at last," said I, "in spite of you and Jane. And I've pulled off most of the paper, so you can't put me back!"

Now why should that man have fainted? But he did, and right across my path by the wall, so that I had to creep over him every time!

SOURCE: Charlotte Perkins Gilman. *"The Yellow Wallpaper,"* first published in *The New England Magazine,* January 1892.

Just as experimental as "The Yellow Wallpaper" but perhaps more surprising and impressive is this later story by Gilman.

If I Were a Man (1914)

"If I were a man, . . ." that was what pretty little Mollie Mathewson always said when Gerald would not do what she wanted him to—which was seldom.

That was what she said this bright morning, with a stamp of her little high-heeled slipper, just because he had made a fuss about that bill, the long one with the "account rendered," which she had forgotten to give him the first time and been afraid to the second—and now he had taken it from the postman himself.

Mollie was "true to type." She was a beautiful instance of what is reverentially called "a true woman." Little, of course—no true woman may be big. Pretty, of course—no true woman could possibly be plain. Whimsical, capricious, charming, changeable, devoted to pretty clothes and always "wearing them well," as the esoteric phrase has it. (This does not refer to the clothes—they do not wear well in the least—but to some special grace of putting them on and carrying them about, granted to but few, it appears.)

She was also a loving wife and a devoted mother possessed of "the social gift" and the love of "society" that goes with it, and, with all these was fond and proud of her home and managed it as capably as—well, as most women do.

If ever there was a true woman it was Mollie Mathewson, yet she was wishing heart and soul she was a man.

And all of a sudden she was!

She was Gerald, walking down the path so erect and square-shouldered, in a hurry for his morning train, as usual, and, it must be confessed, in something of a temper.

Her own words were ringing in her ears—not only the "last word," but several that had gone before, and she was holding her lips tight shut, not to say something she would be sorry for. But instead of acquiescence in the position taken by that angry little figure on the veranda, what she felt was a sort of superior pride, a sympathy as with weakness, a feeling that "I must be gentle with her," in spite of the temper.

A man! Really a man—with only enough subconscious memory of herself remaining to make her recognize the differences.

At first there was a funny sense of size and weight and extra thickness, the feet and hands seemed strangely large, and her long, straight, free legs swung forward at a gait that made her feel as if on stilts.

This presently passed, and in its place, growing all day, wherever she went, came a new and delightful feeling of being *the right size*.

Everything fitted now. Her back snugly against the seat-back, her feet comfortably on the floor. Her feet? . . . His feet! She studied them carefully. Never before, since her early school days, had she felt such freedom and comfort as to feet—they were firm and solid on the ground when she walked; quick, springy, safe—as when, moved by an unrecognizable impulse, she had run after, caught, and swung aboard the car.

Another impulse fished in a convenient pocket for change—instantly, automatically, bringing forth a nickel for the conductor and a penny for the newsboy.

These pockets came as a revelation. Of course she had known they were there, had counted them, made fun of them, mended them, even envied them; but she never had dreamed of how it *felt* to have pockets.

Behind her newspaper she let her consciousness, that odd mingled consciousness, rove from pocket to pocket, realizing the armored assurance of having all those things at hand, instantly get-at-able, ready to meet emergencies. The cigar case gave her a warm feeling of comfort—it was full; the firmly held fountain pen, safe unless she stood on her head; the keys, pencils, letters, documents, notebook, checkbook, bill folder—all at once, with a deep rushing sense of power and pride, she felt what she had never felt before in all her life—the possession of money, of her own earned money—hers to give or to withhold, not to beg for, tease for, wheedle for—hers.

That bill—why, if it had come to her—to him, that is—he would have paid it as a matter of course, and never mentioned it—to her.

Then, being he, sitting there so easily and firmly with his money in his pockets, she wakened to his life-long consciousness about money. Boyhood—its desires and dreams, ambitions. Young manhood—working tremendously for the wherewithal to make a home—for her. The present years with all their net of cares and hopes and dangers; the present moment, when he needed every cent for special plans of great importance, and this bill, long overdue and demanding payment, meant an amount of inconvenience wholly unnecessary if it had been given him when it first came; also, the man's keen dislike of that "account rendered."

"Women have no business sense!" she found herself saying. "And all that money just for hats—idiotic, useless, ugly things!"

With that she began to see the hats of the women in the car as she had never seen hats before. The men's seemed normal, dignified, becoming, with enough variety for personal taste, and with distinction in style and in age, such as she had never noticed before. But the women's—

With the eyes of a man and the brain of a man; with the memory of a whole lifetime of free action wherein the hat, close-fitting on cropped hair, had been no handicap; she now perceived the hats of women.

The massed fluffed hair was at once attractive and foolish, and on that hair, at every angle, in all colors, tipped, twisted, tortured into every crooked shape, made of any substance chance might offer, perched these formless objects. Then, on their formlessness the trimmings—these squirts of stiff feathers, these violent outstanding bows of glistening ribbon, these swaying, projecting masses of plumage which tormented the faces of bystanders.

Never in all her life had she imagined that this idolized millinery could look, to those who paid for it, like the decorations of an insane monkey.

And yet, when there came into the car a little woman, as foolish as any, but pretty and sweet-looking, up rose Gerald Mathewson and gave her his seat. And, later, when there came in a handsome red-cheeked girl, whose hat was wilder, more violent in color and eccentric in shape than any other—when she stood nearby and her soft curling plumes swept his cheek once and again—he felt a sense of sudden pleasure at the intimate tickling touch—and she, deep down within, felt such a wave of shame as might well drown a thousand hats forever.

When he took his train, his seat in the smoking car, she had a new surprise. All about him were the other men, commuters too, and many of them friends of his.

To her, they would have been distinguished as "Mary Wade's husband," "the man Belle Grant is engaged to," "that rich Mr. Shopworth," or "that pleasant Mr. Beale." And they would all have lifted their hats to her, bowed, made polite conversation if near enough—especially Mr. Beale.

Now came the feeling of open-eyed acquaintance, of knowing men—as they were. The mere amount of this knowledge was a surprise to her—the whole background of talk from boyhood up, the gossip of barber-shop and club, the conversation of morning and evening hours on trains, the knowledge of political affiliation, of business standing and prospects, of character—in a light she had never known before.

They came and talked to Gerald, one and another. He seemed quite popular. And as they talked, with this new memory and new understanding, an understanding which seemed to include all these men's minds, there poured in on the submerged consciousness beneath a new, a startling knowledge—what men really think of women.

Good, average, American men were there; married men for the most part, and happy—as happiness goes in general. In the minds of each and all there seemed to be a two-story department, quite apart from the rest of their ideas, a separate place where they kept their thoughts and feelings about women.

In the upper half were the tenderest emotions, the most exquisite ideals, the sweetest memories, all lovely sentiments as to "home" and "mother," all delicate admiring adjectives, a sort of sanctuary, where a veiled statue, blindly adored, shared place with beloved yet commonplace experiences.

In the lower half—here that buried consciousness woke to keen distress—they kept quite another assortment of ideas. Here, even in this clean-minded husband of hers, was the memory of stories told at men's dinners, of worse ones overheard in street or car, of base traditions, coarse epithets, gross experiences—known, though not shared.

And all these in the department "woman," while in the rest of the mind—here was new knowledge indeed.

The world opened before her. Not the world she had been reared in—where Home had covered all the map, almost, and the rest had been "foreign," or "unexplored country," but the world as it was—man's world, as made, lived in, and seen, by men.

It was dizzying. To see the houses that fled so fast across the car window, in terms of builders' bills, or of some technical insight into materials and methods; to see a passing village with lamentable knowledge of who "owned it" and of how its Boss was rapidly aspiring in state power, or of how that kind of paving was a failure;

to see shops, not as mere exhibitions of desirable objects, but as business ventures, many mere sinking ships, some promising a profitable voyage—this new world bewildered her.

She—as Gerald—had already forgotten about that bill, over which she—as Mollie—was still crying at home. Gerald was "talking business" with this man, "talking politics" with that, and now sympathizing with the carefully withheld troubles of a neighbor.

Mollie had always sympathized with the neighbor's wife before.

She began to struggle violently with this large dominant masculine consciousness. She remembered with sudden clearness things she had read, lectures she had heard, and resented with increasing intensity this serene masculine preoccupation with the male point of view.

Mr. Miles, the little fussy man who lived on the other side of the street, was talking now. He had a large complacent wife; Mollie had never liked her much, but had always thought him rather nice—he was so punctilious in small courtesies.

And here he was talking to Gerald—such talk!

"Had to come in here," he said. "Gave my seat to a dame who was bound to have it. There's nothing they won't get when they make up their minds to it—eh?"

"No fear!" said the big man in the next seat. "They haven't much mind to make up, you know—and if they do, they'll change it."

"The real danger," began the Rev. Alfred Smythe, the new Episcopal clergyman, a thin, nervous, tall man with a face several centuries behind the times, "is that they will overstep the limits of their God-appointed sphere."

"Their natural limits ought to hold 'em, I think," said cheerful Dr. Jones. "You can't get around physiology, I tell you."

"I've never seen any limits, myself, not to what they want, anyhow," said Mr. Miles. "Merely a rich husband and a fine house and no end of bonnets and dresses, and the latest thing in motors, and a few diamonds—and so on. Keeps us pretty busy."

There was a tired gray man across the aisle. He had a very nice wife, always beautifully dressed, and three unmarried daughters, also beautifully dressed—Mollie knew them. She knew he worked hard, too, and she looked at him now a little anxiously.

But he smiled cheerfully.

"Do you good, Miles," he said. "What else would a man work for? A good woman is about the best thing on earth."

"And a bad one's the worst, that's sure," responded Miles.

"She's a pretty weak sister, viewed professionally," Dr. Jones averred with solemnity, and the Rev. Alfred Smythe added, "She brought evil into the world."

Gerald Mathewson sat up straight. Something was stirring in him which he did not recognize—yet could not resist.

"Seems to me we all talk like Noah," he suggested drily. "Or the ancient Hindu scriptures. Women have their limitations, but so do we, God knows. Haven't we known girls in school and college just as smart as we were?"

"They cannot play our games," coldly replied the clergyman.

Gerald measured his meager proportions with a practiced eye.

"I never was particularly good at football myself," he modestly admitted, "but I've known women who could outlast a man in all-round endurance. Besides—life isn't spent in athletics!"

This was sadly true. They all looked down the aisle where a heavy ill-dressed man with a bad complexion sat alone. He had held the top of the columns once, with headlines and photographs. Now he earned less than any of them.

"It's time we woke up," pursued Gerald, still inwardly urged to unfamiliar speech. "Women are pretty much *people*, seems to me. I know they dress like fools—but who's to blame for that? We invent all those idiotic hats of theirs, and design their crazy fashions, and, what's more, if a woman is courageous enough to wear common-sense clothes—and shoes—which of us wants to dance with her?

"Yes, we blame them for grafting on us, but are we willing to let our wives work? We are not. It hurts our pride, that's all. We are always criticizing them for making mercenary marriages, but what do we call a girl who marries a chump with no money? Just a poor fool, that's all. And they know it.

"As for Mother Eve—I wasn't there and can't deny the story, but I will say this. If she brought evil into the world, we men have had the lion's share of keeping it going ever since—how about that?"

They drew into the city, and all day long in his business, Gerald was vaguely conscious of new views, strange feelings, and the submerged Mollie learned and learned.

SOURCE: Charlotte Perkins Gilman. "If I Were a Man," originally published: *Physical Culture* magazine, July 1914.

PAUL LAURENCE DUNBAR

Paul Laurence Dunbar (1872–1906) grew up in Dayton, Ohio. His parents had been born into slavery and moved North after the Civil War, in which his father had served as a soldier in the Union Army. The only African-American in his high school, Dunbar was a wonder, publishing poetry and newspaper articles in his teens. In his twenties, he placed some of his celebrated, neatly crafted stories in national magazines, later collected in The Heart of Happy Hollow.

Sympathy (1896)

I know what the caged bird feels, alas!
When the sun is bright on the upland slopes;
When the wind stirs soft through the springing grass,
And the river flows like a stream of glass;
When the first bird sings and the first bud opes,
And the faint perfume from its chalice steals—
I know what the caged bird feels!

I know why the caged bird beats his wing
Till its blood is red on the cruel bars;
For he must fly back to his perch and cling
When he fain would be on the bough a-swing;
And a pain still throbs in the old, old scars
And they pulse again with a keener sting—
I know why he beats his wing!

I know why the caged bird sings, ah me,
When his wing is bruised and his bosom sore,—
When he beats his bars and he would be free;
It is not a carol of joy or glee,

But a prayer that he sends from his heart's deep core,
But a plea, that upward to Heaven he flings—
I know why the caged bird sings!

SOURCE: Paul Laurence Dunbar. *Lyrics of the Hearthside*. New York: Dodd, Mead and Company, 1913.

We Wear the Mask (1896)

We wear the mask that grins and lies,
It hides our cheeks and shades our eyes,—
This debt we pay to human guile;
With torn and bleeding hearts we smile,
And mouth with myriad subtleties.

Why should the world be over-wise,
In counting all our tears and sighs?
Nay, let them only see us, while
We wear the mask.

We smile, but, O great Christ, our cries
To thee from tortured souls arise.
We sing, but oh the clay is vile
Beneath our feet, and long the mile;
But let the world dream otherwise,
We wear the mask!

SOURCE: Paul Laurence Dunbar. *Lyrics of Lowly Life*. New York: Young People's Ministry Movement of the United States and Canada. 1896.

The Scapegoat (1904)

1.

The law is usually supposed to be a stern mistress, not to be lightly wooed, and yielding only to the most ardent pursuit. But even law, like love, sits more easily on some natures than on others.

This was the case with Mr. Robinson Asbury. Mr. Asbury had started life as a bootblack in the growing town of Cadgers. From this he had risen one step and become porter and messenger in a barbershop. This rise fired his ambition, and he was not content until he had learned to use the shears and the razor and had a chair of his own. From this, in a man of Robinson's temperament, it was only a step to a shop of his own, and he placed it where it would do the most good.

Fully one-half of the population of Cadgers was composed of Negroes, and with their usual tendency to colonize, a tendency encouraged, and in fact compelled, by circumstances, they had gathered into one part of the town. Here in alleys, and streets as dirty and hardly wider, they thronged like ants.

It was in this place that Mr. Asbury set up his shop, and he won the hearts of his prospective customers by putting up the significant sign, "Equal Rights Barber-Shop." This legend was quite unnecessary, because there was only one race about, to patronize the place. But it was a delicate sop to the people's vanity, and it served its purpose.

Asbury came to be known as a clever fellow, and his business grew. The shop really became a sort of club, and, on Saturday nights especially, was the gathering-place of the men of the whole Negro quarter. He kept the illustrated and race journals there, and those who cared neither to talk nor listen to someone else might see pictured the doings of high society in very short skirts or read in the Negro papers how Miss Boston had entertained Miss Blueford to tea on such and such an afternoon. Also, he kept the policy returns, which was wise, if not moral.

It was his wisdom rather more than his morality that made the party managers after a while cast their glances toward him as a man who might be useful to their interests. It would be well to have a man—a shrewd, powerful man—down in that part of the town who could carry his people's vote in his vest pocket, and who at any time its delivery might be needed, could hand it over without hesitation. Asbury seemed that man, and they settled upon him. They gave him money, and they gave him power and patronage. He took it all silently and he carried out his bargain faithfully. His hands and his lips alike closed tightly when there was anything within them. It was not long before he found himself the big Negro of the district and, of necessity, of the town. The time came when, at a critical moment, the managers saw that they had not reckoned without their host in choosing this barber of the black district as the leader of his people.

Now, so much success must have satisfied any other man. But in many ways Mr. Asbury was unique. For a long time he himself had done very little shaving—except of notes, to keep his hand in. His time had been otherwise employed. In the evening hours he had been wooing the coquettish Dame Law, and, wonderful to say, she had yielded easily to his advances.

It was against the advice of his friends that he asked for admission to the bar. They felt that he could do more good in the place where he was.

"You see, Robinson," said old Judge Davis, "it's just like this: If you're not admitted, it'll hurt you with the people; if you are admitted, you'll move uptown to an office and get out of touch with them."

Asbury smiled an inscrutable smile. Then he whispered something into the judge's ear that made the old man wrinkle from his neck up with appreciative smiles.

"Asbury," he said, "you are—you are—well, you ought to be white, that's all. When we find a black man like you we send him to State's prison. If you were white, you'd go to the Senate."

The Negro laughed confidently.

He was admitted to the bar soon after, whether by merit or by connivance is not to be told.

"Now he will move uptown," said the black community. "Well, that's the way with a colored man when he gets a start."

But they did not know Robinson Asbury yet. He was a man of surprises, and they were destined to disappointment. He did not move uptown. He built an office in a small open space next his shop, and there hung out his shingle.

"I will never desert the people who have done so much to elevate me," said Mr. Asbury. "I will live among them and I will die among them."

This was a strong card for the barber-lawyer. The people seized upon the statement as expressing a nobility of an altogether unique brand.

They held a mass meeting and indorsed him. They made resolutions that extolled him, and the Negro band came around and serenaded him, playing various things in varied time.

All this was very sweet to Mr. Asbury, and the party managers chuckled with satisfaction and said, "That Asbury, that Asbury!"

Now there is a fable extant of a man who tried to please everybody, and his failure is a matter of record. Robinson Asbury was not more successful. But be it said that his ill success was due to no fault or shortcoming of his.

For a long time his growing power had been looked upon with disfavor by the colored law firm of Bingo & Latchett. Both Mr. Bingo and Mr. Latchett themselves aspired to be Negro leaders in Cadgers, and they were delivering Emancipation Day orations and riding at the head of processions when Mr. Asbury was blacking boots. Is it any wonder, then, that they viewed with alarm his sudden rise? They kept their counsel, however, and treated with him, for it was best. They allowed him his scope without open revolt until the day upon which he hung out his shingle. This was the last straw. They could stand no more. Asbury had stolen their other chances from them, and now he was poaching upon the last of their preserves. So Mr. Bingo and Mr. Latchett put their heads together to plan the downfall of their common enemy.

The plot was deep and embraced the formation of an opposing faction made up of the best Negroes of the town. It would have looked too much like what it was for the gentlemen to show themselves in the matter, and so they took into their confidence Mr. Isaac Morton, the principal of the colored school, and it was under his ostensible leadership that the new faction finally came into being.

Mr. Morton was really an innocent young man, and he had ideals which should never have been exposed to the air. When the wily confederates came to him with their plan he believed that his worth had been recognized, and at last he was to be what Nature destined him for—a leader.

The better class of Negroes—by that is meant those who were particularly envious of Asbury's success—flocked to the new man's standard. But whether the race be white or black, political virtue is always in a minority, so Asbury could afford to smile at the force arrayed against him.

The new faction met together and resolved. They resolved, among other things, that Mr. Asbury was an enemy to his race and a menace to civilization. They decided that he should be abolished; but, as they couldn't get out an injunction against him, and as he had the whole undignified but still voting black belt behind him, he went serenely on his way.

"They're after you hot and heavy, Asbury," said one of his friends to him.

"Oh, yes," was the reply, "they're after me, but after a while I'll get so far away that they'll be running in front."

"It's all the best people, they say."

"Yes. Well, it's good to be one of the best people, but your vote only counts one just the same."

The time came, however, when Mr. Asbury's theory was put to the test. The Cadgerites celebrated the first of January as Emancipation Day. On this day there was a large procession, with speechmaking in the afternoon and fireworks at night. It was the custom to concede the leadership of the coloured people of the town to the man who managed to lead the procession. For two years past this honour had fallen, of course, to Robinson Asbury, and there had been no disposition on the part of anybody to try conclusions with him.

Mr. Morton's faction changed all this. When Asbury went to work to solicit contributions for the celebration, he suddenly became aware that he had a fight upon his hands. All the better-class Negroes were staying out of it. The next thing he knew was that plans were on foot for a rival demonstration.

"Oh," he said to himself, "that's it, is it? Well, if they want a fight they can have it."

He had a talk with the party managers, and he had another with Judge Davis.

"All I want is a little lift, judge," he said, "and I'll make 'em think the sky has turned loose and is vomiting niggers."

The judge believed that he could do it. So did the party managers. Asbury got his lift. Emancipation Day came.

There were two parades. At least, there was one parade and the shadow of another. Asbury's, however, was not the shadow. There was a great deal of substance about it—substance made up of many people, many banners, and numerous bands. He did not have the best people. Indeed, among his cohorts there were a good many of the pronounced rag-tag and bobtail. But he had noise and numbers. In such cases, nothing more is needed. The success of Asbury's side of the affair did everything to confirm his friends in their good opinion of him.

When he found himself defeated, Mr. Silas Bingo saw that it would be policy to placate his rival's just anger against him. He called upon him at his office the day after the celebration.

"Well, Asbury," he said, "you beat us, didn't you?"

"It wasn't a question of beating," said the other calmly. "It was only an inquiry as to who were the people—the few or the many."

"Well, it was well done, and you've shown that you are a manager. I confess that I haven't always thought that you were doing the wisest thing in living down here and catering to this class of people when you might, with your ability, to be much more to the better class."

"What do they base their claims of being better on?"

"Oh, there ain't any use discussing that. We can't get along without you, we see that. So I, for one, have decided to work with you for harmony."

"Harmony. Yes, that's what we want."

"If I can do anything to help you at any time, why you have only to command me."

"I am glad to find such a friend in you. Be sure, if I ever need you, Bingo, I'll call on you."

"And I'll be ready to serve you."

Asbury smiled when his visitor was gone. He smiled, and knitted his brow. "I wonder what Bingo's got up his sleeve," he said. "He'll bear watching."

It may have been pride at his triumph, it may have been gratitude at his helpers, but Asbury went into the ensuing campaign with reckless enthusiasm. He did the most daring things for the party's sake. Bingo, true to his promise, was ever at his side ready to serve him. Finally, association and immunity made danger less fearsome; the rival no longer appeared a menace.

With the generosity born of obstacles overcome, Asbury determined to forgive Bingo and give him a chance. He let him in on a deal, and from that time they worked amicably together until the election came and passed.

It was a close election and many things had had to be done, but there were men there ready and waiting to do them. They were successful, and then the first cry of the defeated party was, as usual, "Fraud! Fraud!" The cry was taken up by the jealous, the disgruntled, and the virtuous.

Someone remembered how two years ago the registration books had been stolen. It was known upon good authority that money had been freely used. Men held up their hands in horror at the suggestion that the Negro vote had been juggled with, as if that were a new thing. From their pulpits ministers denounced the machine and bade their hearers rise and throw off the yoke of a corrupt municipal government. One of those sudden fevers of reform had taken possession of the town and threatened to destroy the successful party.

They began to look around them. They must purify themselves. They must give the people some tangible evidence of their own yearnings after purity. They looked around them for a sacrifice to lay upon the altar of municipal reform. Their eyes fell upon Mr. Bingo. No, he was not big enough. His blood was too scant to wash away the political stains. Then they looked into each other's eyes and turned their gaze away to let it fall upon Mr. Asbury. They really hated to do it. But there must be a scapegoat. The god from the Machine commanded them to slay him.

Robinson Asbury was charged with many crimes—with all that he had committed and some that he had not. When Mr. Bingo saw what was afoot he threw himself heart and soul into the work of his old rival's enemies. He was of incalculable use to them.

Judge Davis refused to have anything to do with the matter. But in spite of his disapproval it went on. Asbury was indicted and tried. The evidence was all against him, and no one gave more damaging testimony than his friend, Mr. Bingo. The judge's charge was favourable to the defendant, but the current of popular opinion could not be entirely stemmed. The jury brought in a verdict of guilty.

"Before I am sentenced, judge, I have a statement to make to the court. It will take less than ten minutes."

"Go on, Robinson," said the judge kindly.

Asbury started, in a monotonous tone, a recital that brought the prosecuting attorney to his feet in a minute. The judge waved him down, and sat transfixed by a sort of fascinated horror as the convicted man went on. The before-mentioned attorney drew a knife and started for the prisoner's dock. With difficulty he was restrained. A dozen faces in the court-room were red and pale by turns.

"He ought to be killed," whispered Mr. Bingo audibly.

Robinson Asbury looked at him and smiled, and then he told a few things of him. He gave the ins and outs of some of the misdemeanors of which he stood accused. He showed who were the men behind the throne. And still, pale and transfixed, Judge Davis waited for his own sentence.

Never were ten minutes so well taken up. It was a tale of rottenness and corruption in high places told simply and with the stamp of truth upon it.

He did not mention the judge's name. But he had torn the mask from the face of every other man who had been concerned in his downfall. They had shorn him of his strength, but they had forgotten that he was yet able to bring the roof and pillars tumbling about their heads.

The judge's voice shook as he pronounced sentence upon his old ally—a year in State's prison.

Some people said it was too light, but the judge knew what it was to wait for the sentence of doom, and he was grateful and sympathetic.

When the sheriff led Asbury away the judge hastened to have a short talk with him.

"I'm sorry, Robinson," he said, "and I want to tell you that you were no more guilty than the rest of us. But why did you spare me?"

"Because I knew you were my friend," answered the convict.

"I tried to be, but you were the first man that I've ever known since I've been in politics who ever gave me any decent return for friendship."

"I reckon you're about right, judge."

In politics, party reform usually lies in making a scapegoat of someone who is only as criminal as the rest, but a little weaker. Asbury's friends and enemies had succeeded in making him bear the burden of all the party's crimes, but their reform was hardly a success, and their protestations of a change of heart were received with doubt. Already there were those who began to pity the victim and to say that he had been hardly dealt with.

Mr. Bingo was not of these; but he found, strange to say, that his opposition to the idea went but a little way, and that even with Asbury out of his path he was a smaller man than he was before. Fate was strong against him. His poor, prosperous humanity could not enter the lists against a martyr. Robinson Asbury was now a martyr.

2.

A year is not a long time. It was short enough to prevent people from forgetting Robinson, and yet long enough for their pity to grow strong as they remembered. Indeed, he was not gone a year. Good behavior cut two months off the time of his sentence, and by the time people had come around to the notion that he was really the greatest and smartest man in Cadgers he was at home again.

He came back with no flourish of trumpets, but quietly, humbly. He went back again into the heart of the black district. His business had deteriorated during his absence, but he put new blood and new life into it. He did not go to work in the shop himself, but, taking down the shingle that had swung idly before his office door during his imprisonment, he opened the little room as a news- and cigar-stand.

Here anxious, pitying custom came to him and he prospered again. He was very quiet. Uptown hardly knew that he was again in Cadgers, and it knew nothing whatever of his doings.

"I wonder why Asbury is so quiet," they said to one another. "It isn't like him to be quiet." And they felt vaguely uneasy about him.

So many people had begun to say, "Well, he was a mighty good fellow after all."

Mr. Bingo expressed the opinion that Asbury was quiet because he was crushed, but others expressed doubt as to this. There are calms and calms, some after and some before the storm. Which was this?

They waited a while, and, as no storm came, concluded that this must be the after-quiet. Bingo, reassured, volunteered to go and seek confirmation of this conclusion.

He went, and Asbury received him with an indifferent, not to say, impolite, demeanor.

"Well, we're glad to see you back, Asbury," said Bingo patronizingly. He had variously demonstrated his inability to lead during his rival's absence and was proud of it. "What are you going to do?"

"I'm going to work."

"That's right. I reckon you'll stay out of politics."

"What could I do even if I went in?"

"Nothing now, of course; but I didn't know—"

He did not see the gleam in Asbury's half shut eyes. He only marked his humility, and he went back swelling with the news.

"Completely crushed—all the run taken out of him," was his report.

The black district believed this, too, and a sullen, smoldering anger took possession of them. Here was a good man ruined. Some of the people whom he had helped in his former days—some of the rude, coarse people of the low quarter who were still sufficiently unenlightened to be grateful—talked among themselves and offered to get up a demonstration for him. But he denied them. No, he wanted nothing of the kind. It would only bring him into unfavorable notice. All he wanted was that they would always be his friends and would stick by him.

They would to the death.

There were again two factions in Cadgers. The schoolmaster could not forget how once on a time he had been made a tool of by Mr. Bingo. So he revolted against his rule and set himself up as the leader of an opposing clique. The fight had been long and strong, but had ended with odds slightly in Bingo's favor.

But Mr. Morton did not despair. As the first of January and Emancipation Day approached, he arrayed his hosts, and the fight for supremacy became fiercer than ever. The schoolteacher brought the school-children in for chorus singing, secured an able orator, and the best essayist in town. With all this, he was formidable.

Mr. Bingo knew that he had the fight of his life on his hands, and he entered with fear as well as zest. He, too, found an orator, but he was not sure that he was as good as Morton's. There was no doubt but that his essayist was not. He secured a band, but still he felt unsatisfied. He had hardly done enough, and for the schoolmaster to beat him now meant his political destruction.

It was in this state of mind that he was surprised to receive a visit from Mr. Asbury.

"I reckon you're surprised to see me here," said Asbury, smiling.

"I am pleased, I know." Bingo was astute.

"Well, I just dropped in on business."

"To be sure, to be sure, Asbury. What can I do for you?"

"It's more what I can do for you that I came to talk about," was the reply.

"I don't believe I understand you."

"Well, it's plain enough. They say that the schoolteacher is giving you a pretty hard fight."

"Oh, not so hard."

"No man can be too sure of winning, though. Mr. Morton once did me a mean turn when he started the faction against me."

Bingo's heart gave a great leap, and then stopped for the fraction of a second.

"You were in it, of course," pursued Asbury, "but I can look over your part in it in order to get even with the man who started it."

It was true, then, thought Bingo gladly. He did not know. He wanted revenge for his wrongs and upon the wrong man. How well the schemer had covered his tracks! Asbury should have his revenge and Morton would be the sufferer.

"Of course, Asbury, you know what I did I did innocently."

"Oh, yes, in politics we are all lambs and the wolves are only to be found in the other party. We'll pass that, though. What I want to say is that I can help you to make your celebration an overwhelming success. I still have some influence down in my district."

"Certainly, and very justly, too. Why, I should be delighted with your aid. I could give you a prominent place in the procession."

"I don't want it; I don't want to appear in this at all. All I want is revenge. You can have all the credit, but let me down my enemy."

Bingo was perfectly willing, and, with their heads close together, they had a long and close consultation. When Asbury was gone, Mr. Bingo lay back in his chair and laughed. "I'm a slick duck," he said.

From that hour Mr. Bingo's cause began to take on the appearance of something very like a boom. More bands were hired. The interior of the State was called upon and a more eloquent orator secured. The crowd hastened to array itself on the growing side.

With surprised eyes, the schoolmaster beheld the wonder of it, but he kept to his own purpose with dogged insistence, even when he saw that he could not turn aside the overwhelming defeat that threatened him. But in spite of his obstinacy, his hours were dark and bitter. Asbury worked like a mole, all underground, but he was indefatigable. Two days before the celebration time everything was perfected for the biggest demonstration that Cadgers had ever known. All the next day and night he was busy among his allies.

On the morning of the great day, Mr. Bingo, wonderfully caparisoned, rode down to the hall where the parade was to form. He was early. No one had yet come. In an hour a score of men all told had collected. Another hour passed, and no more had come. Then there smote upon his ear the sound of music. They were coming at last. Bringing his sword to his shoulder, he rode forward to the middle of the street. Ah, there they were. But—but—could he believe his eyes? They were going in another direction, and at their head rode—Morton! He gnashed his teeth in fury. He had been led into a trap and betrayed. The procession passing had been his—all his. He heard them cheering, and then, oh! climax of infidelity, he saw his own orator go past in a carriage, bowing and smiling to the crowd.

There was no doubting who had done this thing. The hand of Asbury was apparent in it. He must have known the truth all along, thought Bingo. His allies left him one by one for the other hall, and he rode home in a humiliation deeper than he had ever known before.

Asbury did not appear at the celebration. He was at his little news-stand all day.

In a day or two the defeated aspirant had further cause to curse his false friend. He found that not only had the people defected from him, but that the thing had been so adroitly managed that he appeared to be in fault, and three-fourths of those who knew him were angry at some supposed grievance. His cup of bitterness was full when his partner, a quietly ambitious man, suggested that they dissolve their relations.

His ruin was complete.

The lawyer was not alone in seeing Asbury's hand in his downfall. The party managers saw it too, and they met together to discuss the dangerous factor which, while it appeared to slumber, was so terribly awake. They decided that he must be appeased, and they visited him.

He was still busy at his news-stand. They talked to him adroitly, while he sorted papers and kept an impassive face. When they were all done, he looked up for a moment and replied, "You know, gentlemen, as an ex-convict I am not in politics."

Some of them had the grace to flush.

"But you can use your influence," they said.

"I am not in politics," was his only reply.

And the spring elections were coming on. Well, they worked hard, and he showed no sign. He treated with neither one party nor the other. "Perhaps," thought the managers, "he is out of politics," and they grew more confident.

It was nearing eleven o'clock on the morning of election when a cloud no bigger than a man's hand appeared upon the horizon. It came from the direction of the black district. It grew, and the managers of the party in power looked at it, fascinated by an ominous dread. Finally it began to rain Negro voters, and as one man they voted against their former candidates. Their organization was perfect. They simply came, voted, and left, but they overwhelmed everything. Not one of the party that had damned Robinson Asbury was left in power save old Judge Davis. His majority was overwhelming.

The generalship that had engineered the thing was perfect. There were loud threats against the news-dealer. But no one bothered him except a reporter. The reporter called to see just how it was done. He found Asbury very busy sorting papers. To the newspaper-man's questions he had only this reply, "I am not in politics, sir."

But Cadgers had learned its lesson.

SOURCE: Paul Laurence Dunbar. *The Heart of Happy Hollow*. New York: Dodd, Mead and Company, 1904.

NAVAJO, PIMA, INUIT

NATIVE AMERICAN SONGS AND CHANTS

As Brian Swann notes in his introduction to the volume from which these verses, recorded by ethnologists, appeared: "Native American literature is all of a piece, from traditional songs and ceremonies that continue to this day . . . to the many poets who are now at the forefront of contemporary American literature."[1]

Song from the Mountain Chant (Navajo) (1896)

the voice that makes the land lovely
again and again in sounds
among the dark clouds
the thunder's voice
the voice above
The voice that makes the land lovely

The voice that makes the land lovely
the voice below
the voice of the grasshopper
among the little plants
again and again it sounds
the voice that makes the land lovely

SOURCE: Washington Matthews. "Songs of the Navajo." *Land of Sunshine*, Volume 5. 1896.

---

1. Brian Swann, editor. *Native American Songs and Poems: An Anthology*. Mineola, New York: Dover Publications, 1996.

Quail Song (Pima) (1903)

The gray quails bunched tight together.
Above, Coyote trotted by.
He stopped. He looked.

The blue quails ran and huddled together.
Coyote looked at them,
sideways.

SOURCE: Frank Russell. "The Pima Indians." *Eleventh Annual Report of the Bureau of American Ethnology, 1889–1890.* Washington, D.C.: Government Printing Office. 1903.

Dance Song (Inuit) (1913–1918)

The animals are beautiful.
There is no song about it
since words are hard to find—
Seals on the ice down there—
When I found a few words
I fastened them to the music—
they left for their breathing holes—
The animals are beautiful.
There is no song about it
since words are hard to find—
Antlered caribou on the land over there—
When I found a few words
I fastened them to the music—
when it crossed the tundra over there—
The animals are beautiful.
There is no song about it
since words are hard to find—
Bearded seals on the ice down here—
When I found a few words
I fastened them to the music
when they left for their breathing holes.

SOURCE: Helen H. Roberts and Diamond Jenness. "Songs of the Copper Eskimos." *Report of the Canadian Arctic Expedition.* Volume 14. 1913–1918.

STEPHEN CRANE

The author of The Red Badge of Courage *was born six years after the end of the Civil War, about which cataclysm he wrote that famous novel and this story (among many other stories). Stephen Crane died of tuberculosis in 1900. The alternate title of this story could have been "Brotherly Love."*

The Little Regiment (1896)

1.

The fog made the clothes of the men of the column in the roadway seem of a luminous quality. It imparted to the heavy infantry overcoats a new color, a kind of blue which was so pale that a regiment might have been merely a long, low shadow in the mist. However, a muttering, one part grumble, three parts joke, hovered in the air above the thick ranks, and blended in an undertoned roar, which was the voice of the column.

The town on the southern shore of the little river loomed spectrally, a faint etching upon the gray cloud-masses which were shifting with oily languor. A long row of guns upon the northern bank had been pitiless in their hatred, but a little battered belfry could be dimly seen still pointing with invincible resolution toward the heavens.

The enclouded air vibrated with noises made by hidden colossal things. The infantry tramplings, the heavy rumbling of the artillery, made the earth speak of gigantic preparation. Guns on distant heights thundered from time to time with sudden, nervous roar, as if unable to endure in silence a knowledge of hostile troops massing, other guns going to position. These sounds, near and remote, defined an immense battleground, described the tremendous width of the stage of the prospective drama. The voices of the guns, slightly casual, unexcited in their challenges and warnings, could not destroy the unutterable eloquence of the word in the air, a meaning of impending struggle which made the breath halt at the lips.

The column in the roadway was ankle-deep in mud. The men swore piously at the rain which drizzled upon them, compelling them to stand always very erect in fear of the drops that would sweep in under their coat-collars. The fog was as cold as wet clothes. The men stuffed their hands deep in their pockets, and huddled their muskets in their arms. The machinery of orders had rooted these soldiers deeply into the mud precisely as almighty nature roots mullein stalks.

They listened and speculated when a tumult of fighting came from the dim town across the river. When the noise lulled for a time they resumed their descriptions of the mud and graphically exaggerated the number of hours they had been kept waiting. The general commanding their division rode along the ranks, and they cheered admiringly, affectionately, crying out to him gleeful prophecies of the coming battle. Each man scanned him with a peculiarly keen personal interest, and afterward spoke of him with unquestioning devotion and confidence, narrating anecdotes which were mainly untrue.

When the jokers lifted the shrill voices which invariably belonged to them, flinging witticisms at their comrades, a loud laugh would sweep from rank to rank, and soldiers who had not heard would lean forward and demand repetition. When were borne past them some wounded men with gray and blood-smeared faces, and eyes that rolled in that helpless beseeching for assistance from the sky which comes with supreme pain, the soldiers in the mud watched intently, and from time to time asked of the bearers an account of the affair. Frequently they bragged of their corps, their division, their brigade, their regiment. Anon they referred to the mud and the cold drizzle. Upon this threshold of a wild scene of death they, in short, defied the proportion of events with that splendor of heedlessness which belongs only to veterans.

"Like a lot of wooden soldiers," swore Billie Dempster, moving his feet in the thick mass, and casting a vindictive glance indefinitely; "standing in the mud for a hundred years."

"Oh, shut up!" murmured his brother Dan. The manner of his words implied that this fraternal voice near him was an indescribable bore.

"Why should I shut up?" demanded Billie.

"Because you're a fool," cried Dan, taking no time to debate it; "the biggest fool in the regiment."

There was but one man between them, and he was habituated. These insults from brother to brother had swept across his chest, flown past his face, many times during two long campaigns. Upon this occasion he simply grinned first at one, then at the other.

The way of these brothers was not an unknown topic in regimental gossip. They had enlisted simultaneously, with each sneering loudly at the other for doing it. They left their little town, and went forward with the flag, exchanging protestations of undying suspicion. In the camp life they so openly despised each other that, when entertaining quarrels were lacking, their companions often contrived situations calculated to bring forth display of this fraternal dislike.

Both were large-limbed, strong young men, and often fought with friends in camp unless one was near to interfere with the other. This latter happened rather frequently, because Dan, preposterously willing for any manner of combat, had a very great horror of seeing Billie in a fight; and Billie, almost odiously ready himself, simply refused to see Dan stripped to his shirt and with his fists aloft. This sat queerly upon them, and made them the objects of plots.

When Dan jumped through a ring of eager soldiers and dragged forth his raving brother by the arm, a thing often predicted would almost come to pass. When Billie performed the same office for Dan, the prediction would again miss fulfillment by an inch. But indeed they never fought together, although they were perpetually upon the verge.

They expressed longing for such conflict. As a matter of truth, they had at one time made full arrangement for it, but even with the encouragement and interest of half of the regiment they somehow failed to achieve collision.

If Dan became a victim of police duty, no jeering was so destructive to the feelings as Billie's comment. If Billie got a call to appear at the headquarters, none would so genially prophesy his complete undoing as Dan. Small misfortunes to one were, in truth, invariably greeted with hilarity by the other, who seemed to see in them great re-enforcement of his opinion.

As soldiers, they expressed each for each a scorn intense and blasting. After a certain battle, Billie was promoted to corporal.

When Dan was told of it, he seemed smitten dumb with astonishment and patriotic indignation. He stared in silence, while the dark blood rushed to Billie's forehead, and he shifted his weight from foot to foot. Dan at last found his tongue, and said: "Well, I'm durned!" If he had heard that an army mule had been appointed to the post of corps commander, his tone could not have had more derision in it. Afterward, he adopted a fervid insubordination, an almost religious reluctance to obey the new corporal's orders, which came near to developing the desired strife.

It is here finally to be recorded also that Dan, most ferociously profane in speech, very rarely swore in the presence of his brother; and that Billie, whose oaths came from his lips with the grace of falling pebbles, was seldom known to express himself in this manner when near his brother Dan.

At last the afternoon contained a suggestion of evening. Metallic cries rang suddenly from end to end of the column. They inspired at once a quick, business-like adjustment. The long thing stirred in the mud. The men had hushed, and were looking across the river. A moment later the shadowy mass of pale blue figures was moving steadily toward the stream. There could be heard from the town a clash of swift fighting and cheering. The noise of the shooting coming through the heavy air had its sharpness taken from it, and sounded in thuds.

There was a halt upon the bank above the pontoons. When the column went winding down the incline, and streamed out upon the bridge, the fog had faded to a great degree, and in the clearer dusk the guns on a distant ridge were enabled to perceive the crossing. The long whirling outcries of the shells came into the air above the men. An occasional solid shot struck the surface of the river, and dashed into view a sudden vertical jet. The distance was subtly illuminated by the lightning from the deep-booming guns. One by one the batteries on the northern shore aroused, the innumerable guns bellowing in angry oration at the distant ridge. The rolling thunder crashed and reverberated as a wild surf sounds on a still night, and to this music the column marched across the pontoons.

The waters of the grim river curled away in a smile from the ends of the great boats, and slid swiftly beneath the planking. The dark, riddled walls of the town upreared before the troops, and from a region hidden by these hammered and tumbled houses came incessantly the yells and firings of a prolonged and close skirmish.

When Dan had called his brother a fool, his voice had been so decisive, so brightly assured, that many men had laughed, considering it to be great humor under the circumstances. The incident happened to rankle deep in Billie. It was not any strange thing that his brother had called him a fool. In fact, he often called him a fool with exactly the same amount of cheerful and prompt conviction, and before large audiences, too. Billie wondered in his own mind why he took such profound offence in this case; but, at any rate, as he slid down the bank and on to the bridge with his regiment, he was searching his knowledge for something that would pierce Dan's blithesome spirit. But he could contrive nothing at this time, and his impotency made the glance which he was once able to give his brother still more malignant.

The guns far and near were roaring a fearful and grand introduction for this column which was marching upon the stage of death. Billie felt it, but only in a numb way. His heart was cased in that curious dissonant metal which covers a man's emotions at such times. The terrible voices from the hills told him that in this wide conflict his life was an insignificant fact, and that his death would be an insignificant fact. They portended the whirlwind to which he would be as necessary as a butterfly's waved wing. The solemnity, the sadness of it came near enough to make him wonder why he was neither solemn nor sad. When his mind vaguely adjusted events according to their importance to him, it appeared that the uppermost thing was the fact that upon the eve of battle, and before many comrades, his brother had called him a fool.

Dan was in a particularly happy mood. "Hurray! Look at 'em shoot," he said, when the long witches' croon of the shells came into the air. It enraged Billie when he felt the little thorn in him, and saw at the same time that his brother had completely forgotten it.

The column went from the bridge into more mud. At this southern end there was a chaos of hoarse directions and commands. Darkness was coming upon the earth, and regiments were being hurried up the slippery bank. As Billie floundered in the black mud, amid the swearing, sliding crowd, he suddenly resolved that, in the absence of other means of hurting Dan, he would avoid looking at him, refrain from speaking to him, pay absolutely no heed to his existence; and this done skillfully would, he imagined, soon reduce his brother to a poignant sensitiveness.

At the top of the bank the column again halted and rearranged itself, as a man after a climb rearranges his clothing. Presently the great steel-backed brigade, an infinitely graceful thing in the rhythm and ease of its veteran movement, swung up a little narrow, slanting street.

Evening had come so swiftly that the fighting on the remote borders of the town was indicated by thin flashes of flame. Some building was on fire, and its reflection upon the clouds was an oval of delicate pink.

2.

All demeanor of rural serenity had been wrenched violently from the little town by the guns and by the waves of men which had surged through it. The hand of war laid upon this village had in an instant changed it to a thing of remnants. It resembled the place of a monstrous shaking of the earth itself. The windows, now mere unsightly holes, made the tumbled and blackened dwellings seem skeletons. Doors lay splintered to fragments. Chimneys had flung their bricks everywhere. The artillery fire had not neglected the rows of gentle shade-trees which had lined the streets. Branches and heavy trunks cluttered the mud in driftwood tangles, while a few shattered forms had contrived to remain dejectedly, mournfully upright. They expressed an innocence, a helplessness, which perforce created a pity for their happening into this cauldron of battle. Furthermore, there was under foot a vast collection of odd things reminiscent of the charge, the fight, the retreat. There were boxes and barrels filled with earth, behind which riflemen had lain snugly, and in these little trenches were the dead in blue with the dead in gray, the poses eloquent of the struggles for possession of the town until the history of the whole conflict was written plainly in the streets.

And yet the spirit of this little city, its quaint individuality, poised in the air above the ruins, defying the guns, the sweeping volleys; holding in contempt those avaricious blazes which had attacked many dwellings. The hard earthen sidewalks proclaimed the games that had been played there during long lazy days, in the careful shadows of the trees. "General Merchandise," in faint letters upon a long board, had to be read with a slanted glance, for the sign dangled by one end; but the porch of the old store was a palpable legend of wide-hatted men, smoking.

This subtle essence, this soul of the life that had been, brushed like invisible wings the thoughts of the men in the swift columns that came up from the river.

In the darkness a loud and endless humming arose from the great blue crowds bivouacked in the streets. From time to time a sharp spatter of firing from far picket lines entered this bass chorus. The smell from the smouldering ruins floated on the cold night breeze.

Dan, seated ruefully upon the doorstep of a shot-pierced house, was proclaiming the campaign badly managed. Orders had been issued forbidding camp-fires.

Suddenly he ceased his oration, and scanning the group of his comrades, said: "Where's Billie? Do you know?"

"Gone on picket."

"Get out! Has he?" said Dan. "No business to go on picket. Why don't some of them other corporals take their turn?"

A bearded private was smoking his pipe of confiscated tobacco, seated comfortably upon a horse-hair trunk which he had dragged from the house. He observed: "*Was* his turn."

"No such thing," cried Dan. He and the man on the horse-hair trunk held discussion in which Dan stoutly maintained that if his brother had been sent on picket it was an injustice. He ceased his argument when another soldier, upon whose arms could faintly be seen the two stripes of a corporal, entered the circle. "Humph," said Dan, "where you been?"

The corporal made no answer. Presently Dan said: "Billie, where you been?"

His brother did not seem to hear these inquiries. He glanced at the house which towered above them, and remarked casually to the man on the horse-hair trunk: "Funny, ain't it? After the pelting this town got, you'd think there wouldn't be one brick left on another."

"Oh," said Dan, glowering at his brother's back. "Getting mighty smart, ain't you?"

The absence of camp-fires allowed the evening to make apparent its quality of faint silver light in which the blue clothes of the throng became black, and the faces became white expanses, void of expression. There was considerable excitement a short distance from the group around the doorstep. A soldier had chanced upon a hoop-skirt, and arrayed in it he was performing a dance amid the applause of his companions. Billie and a greater part of the men immediately poured over there to witness the exhibition.

"What's the matter with Billie?" demanded Dan of the man upon the horse-hair trunk.

"How do I know?" rejoined the other in mild resentment. He arose and walked away. When he returned he said briefly, in a weather-wise tone, that it would rain during the night.

Dan took a seat upon one end of the horse-hair trunk. He was facing the crowd around the dancer, which in its hilarity swung this way and that way. At times he imagined that he could recognize his brother's face.

He and the man on the other end of the trunk thoughtfully talked of the army's position. To their minds, infantry and artillery were in a most precarious jumble in the streets of the town; but they did not grow nervous over it, for they were used to having the army appear in a precarious jumble to their minds. They had learned to accept such puzzling situations as a consequence of their position in the ranks, and were now usually in possession of a simple but perfectly immovable faith that somebody understood the jumble. Even if they had been convinced that the army was a headless monster, they would merely have nodded with the veteran's singular cynicism. It was none of their business as soldiers. Their duty was to grab sleep and food when occasion permitted, and cheerfully fight wherever their feet were planted until more orders came. This was a task sufficiently absorbing.

They spoke of other corps, and this talk being confidential, their voices dropped to tones of awe. "The Ninth"—"The First"—"The Fifth"—"The Sixth"—"The Third"—the simple numerals rang with eloquence, each having a meaning which was to float through many years as no intangible arithmetical mist, but as pregnant with individuality as the names of cities.

Of their own corps they spoke with a deep veneration, an idolatry, a supreme confidence which apparently would not blanch to see it match against everything.

It was as if their respect for other corps was due partly to a wonder that organizations not blessed with their own famous numeral could take such an interest in war. They could prove that their division was the best in the corps, and that their brigade was the best in the division. And their regiment—it was plain that no fortune of life was equal to the chance which caused a man to be born, so to speak, into this command, the keystone of the defending arch.

At times Dan covered with insults the character of a vague, unnamed general to whose petulance and busy-body spirit he ascribed the order which made hot coffee impossible.

Dan said that victory was certain in the coming battle. The other man seemed rather dubious. He remarked upon the fortified line of hills, which had impressed him even from the other side of the river. "Shucks," said Dan. "Why, we—" He pictured a splendid overflowing of these hills by the sea of men in blue. During the period of this conversation Dan's glance searched the merry throng about the dancer. Above the babble of voices in the street a far-away thunder could sometimes be heard—evidently from the very edge of the horizon—the boom-boom of restless guns.

3.

Ultimately the night deepened to the tone of black velvet. The outlines of the fireless camp were like the faint drawings upon ancient tapestry. The glint of a rifle, the shine of a button, might have been of threads of silver and gold sewn upon the fabric of the night. There was little presented to the vision, but to a sense more subtle there was discernible in the atmosphere something like a pulse; a mystic beating which would have told a stranger of the presence of a giant thing—the slumbering mass of regiments and batteries.

With fires forbidden, the floor of a dry old kitchen was thought to be a good exchange for the cold earth of December, even if a shell had exploded in it and knocked it so out of shape that when a man lay curled in his blanket his last waking thought was likely to be of the wall that bellied out above him as if strongly anxious to topple upon the score of soldiers.

Billie looked at the bricks ever about to descend in a shower upon his face, listened to the industrious pickets plying their rifles on the border of the town, imagined some measure of the din of the coming battle, thought of Dan and Dan's chagrin, and rolling over in his blanket went to sleep with satisfaction.

At an unknown hour he was aroused by the creaking of boards. Lifting himself upon his elbow, he saw a sergeant prowling among the sleeping forms. The sergeant carried a candle in an old brass candle-stick. He would have resembled some old farmer on an unusual midnight tour if it were not for the significance of his gleaming buttons and striped sleeves.

Billie blinked stupidly at the light until his mind returned from the journeys of slumber. The sergeant stooped among the unconscious soldiers, holding the candle close, and peering into each face.

"Hello, Haines," said Billie. "Relief?"

"Hello, Billie," said the sergeant. "Special duty."

"Dan got to go?"

"Jameson, Hunter, McCormack, D. Dempster. Yes. Where is he?"

"Over there by the winder," said Billie, gesturing. "What is it for, Haines?"

"You don't think I know, do you?" demanded the sergeant. He began to pipe sharply but cheerily at men upon the floor. "Come, Mac, get up here. Here's a special for you. Wake up, Jameson. Come along, Dannie, me boy."

Each man at once took this call to duty as a personal affront. They pulled themselves out of their blankets, rubbed their eyes, and swore at whoever was responsible. "Them's orders," cried the sergeant. "Come! Get out of here." An undetailed head with dishevelled hair thrust out from a blanket, and a sleepy voice said: "Shut up, Haines, and go home."

When the detail clanked out of the kitchen, all but one of the remaining men seemed to be again asleep. Billie, leaning on his elbow, was gazing into darkness. When the footsteps died to silence, he curled himself into his blanket.

At the first cool lavender lights of daybreak he aroused again, and scanned his recumbent companions. Seeing a wakeful one he asked: "Is Dan back yet?"

The man said: "Hain't seen 'im."

Billie put both hands behind his head, and scowled into the air. "Can't see the use of these cussed details in the nighttime," he muttered in his most unreasonable tones. "Darn nuisances. Why can't they—" He grumbled at length and graphically.

When Dan entered with the squad, however, Billie was convincingly asleep.

4.

The regiment trotted in double time along the street, and the colonel seemed to quarrel over the right of way with many artillery officers. Batteries were waiting in the mud, and the men of them, exasperated by the bustle of this ambitious infantry, shook their fists from saddle and caisson, exchanging all manner of taunts and jests. The slanted guns continued to look reflectively at the ground.

On the outskirts of the crumbled town a fringe of blue figures were firing into the fog. The regiment swung out into skirmish lines, and the fringe of blue figures departed, turning their backs and going joyfully around the flank.

The bullets began a low moan off toward a ridge which loomed faintly in the heavy mist. When the swift crescendo had reached its climax, the missiles zipped just overhead, as if piercing an invisible curtain. A battery on the hill was crashing with such tumult that it was as if the guns had quarrelled and had fallen pell-mell and snarling upon each other. The shells howled on their journey toward the town. From short range distance there came a spatter of musketry, sweeping along an invisible line and making faint sheets of orange light.

Some in the new skirmish lines were beginning to fire at various shadows discerned in the vapor, forms of men suddenly revealed by some humor of the laggard masses of clouds. The crackle of musketry began to dominate the purring of the hostile bullets. Dan, in the front rank, held his rifle poised, and looked into the fog keenly, coldly, with the air of a sportsman. His nerves were so steady that it was as if they had been drawn from his body, leaving him merely a muscular machine; but his numb heart was somehow beating to the pealing march of the fight.

The waving skirmish line went backward and forward, ran this way and that way. Men got lost in the fog, and men were found again. Once they got too close to the formidable ridge, and the thing burst out as if repulsing a general attack. Once another blue regiment was apprehended on the very edge of firing into them. Once a friendly battery began an elaborate and scientific process of extermination. Always as busy as brokers, the men slid here and there over the plain, fighting their foes, escaping from their friends, leaving a history of many movements in the wet yellow turf, cursing the atmosphere, blazing away every time they could identify the enemy.

In one mystic changing of the fog, as if the fingers of spirits were drawing aside these draperies, a small group of the gray skirmishers, silent, statuesque, were suddenly disclosed to Dan and those about him. So vivid and near were they that there was something uncanny in the revelation.

There might have been a second of mutual staring. Then each rifle in each group was at the shoulder. As Dan's glance flashed along the barrel of his weapon, the figure of a man suddenly loomed as if the musket had been a telescope. The short black beard, the slouch hat, the pose of the man as he sighted to shoot, made a quick picture in Dan's mind. The same moment, it would seem, he pulled his own trigger, and the man, smitten, lurched forward, while his exploding rifle made a slanting crimson streak in the air, and the slouch hat fell before the body. The billows of the fog, governed by singular impulses, rolled between.

"You got that feller sure enough," said a comrade to Dan. Dan looked at him absent-mindedly.

5.

When the next morning calmly displayed another fog, the men of the regiment exchanged eloquent comments; but they did not abuse it at length, because the streets of the town now contained enough galloping aides to make three troops of cavalry, and they knew that they had come to the verge of the great fight.

Dan conversed with the man who had once possessed a horsehair trunk; but they did not mention the line of hills which had furnished them in more careless moments with an agreeable topic. They avoided it now as condemned men do the subject of death, and yet the thought of it stayed in their eyes as they looked at each other and talked gravely of other things.

The expectant regiment heaved a long sigh of relief when the sharp call: "Fall in," repeated indefinitely, arose in the streets. It was inevitable that a bloody battle was to be fought, and they wanted to get it off their minds. They were, however, doomed again to spend a long period planted firmly in the mud. They craned their necks, and wondered where some of the other regiments were going.

At last the mists rolled carelessly away. Nature made at this time all provisions to enable foes to see each other, and immediately the roar of guns resounded from every hill. The endless cracking of the skirmishers swelled to rolling crashes of musketry. Shells screamed with panther-like noises at the houses. Dan looked at the man of the horse-hair trunk, and the man said: "Well, here she comes!"

The tenor voices of younger officers and the deep and hoarse voices of the older ones rang in the streets. These cries pricked like spurs. The masses of men vibrated from the suddenness with which they were plunged into the situation of troops about to fight. That the orders were long-expected did not concern the emotion.

Simultaneous movement was imparted to all these thick bodies of men and horses that lay in the town. Regiment after regiment swung rapidly into the streets that faced the sinister ridge.

This exodus was theatrical. The little sober-hued village had been like the cloak which disguises the king of drama. It was now put aside, and an army, splendid thing of steel and blue, stood forth in the sunlight.

Even the soldiers in the heavy columns drew deep breaths at the sight, more majestic than they had dreamed. The heights of the enemy's position were crowded with men who resembled people come to witness some mighty pageant. But as the column moved steadily to their positions, the guns, matter-of-fact warriors, doubled their number, and shells burst with red thrilling tumult on the crowded plain. One came into the ranks of the regiment, and after the smoke and the wrath of it had faded, leaving motionless figures, everyone stormed according to the limits of his vocabulary, for veterans detest being killed when they are not busy.

The regiment sometimes looked sideways at its brigade companions composed of men who had never been in battle; but no frozen blood could withstand the heat of the splendor of this army before the eyes on the plain, these lines so long that the flanks were little streaks, this mass of men of one intention. The recruits carried themselves heedlessly. At the rear was an idle battery, and three artillery men in a foolish row on a caisson nudged each other and grinned at the recruits. "You'll catch it pretty soon," they called out. They were impersonally gleeful, as if they themselves were not also likely to catch it pretty soon. But with this picture of an army in their hearts, the new men perhaps felt the devotion which the drops may feel for the wave; they were of its power and glory;

they smiled jauntily at the foolish row of gunners, and told them to go to blazes.

The column trotted across some little bridges, and spread quickly into lines of battle. Before them was a bit of plain, and back of the plain was the ridge. There was no time left for considerations. The men were staring at the plain, mightily wondering how it would feel to be out there, when a brigade in advance yelled and charged. The hill was all gray smoke and fire-points.

That fierce elation in the terrors of war, catching a man's heart and making it burn with such ardor that he becomes capable of dying, flashed in the faces of the men like colored lights, and made them resemble leashed animals, eager, ferocious, daunting at nothing. The line was really in its first leap before the wild, hoarse crying of the orders.

The greed for close quarters which is the emotion of a bayonet charge, came then into the minds of the men and developed until it was a madness. The field, with its faded grass of a Southern winter, seemed to this fury miles in width.

High, slow-moving masses of smoke, with an odor of burning cotton, engulfed the line until the men might have been swimmers. Before them the ridge, the shore of this gray sea, was outlined, crossed, and re-crossed by sheets of flame. The howl of the battle arose to the noise of innumerable wind demons.

The line, galloping, scrambling, plunging like a herd of wounded horses, went over a field that was sown with corpses, the records of other charges.

Directly in front of the black-faced, whooping Dan, carousing in this onward sweep like a new kind of fiend, a wounded man appeared, raising his shattered body, and staring at this rush of men down upon him. It seemed to occur to him that he was to be trampled; he made a desperate, piteous effort to escape; then finally huddled in a waiting heap. Dan and the soldier near him widened the interval between them without looking down, without appearing to heed the wounded man. This little clump of blue seemed to reel past them as boulders reel past a train.

Bursting through a smoke-wave, the scampering, unformed bunches came upon the wreck of the brigade that had preceded them, a floundering mass stopped afar from the hill by the swirling volleys.

It was as if a necromancer had suddenly shown them a picture of the fate which awaited them; but the line with muscular spasm hurled itself over this wreckage and onward, until men were stumbling amid the relics of other assaults, the point where the fire from the ridge consumed.

The men, panting, perspiring, with crazed faces, tried to push against it; but it was as if they had come to a wall. The wave halted, shuddered in an agony from the quick struggle of its two desires, then toppled, and broke into a fragmentary thing which has no name.

Veterans could now at last be distinguished from recruits. The new regiments were instantly gone, lost, scattered, as if they never had been. But the sweeping failure of the charge, the battle, could not make the veterans forget their business. With a last throe, the band of maniacs drew itself up and blazed a volley at the hill, insignificant to those iron intrenchments, but nevertheless expressing that singular final despair which enables men to coolly defy the walls of a city of death.

After this episode the men renamed their command. They called it the Little Regiment.

6.

"I seen Dan shoot a feller yesterday. Yes sir. I'm sure it was him that done it. And maybe he thinks about that feller now, and wonders if *he* tumbled down just about the same way. Them things come up in a man's mind."

Bivouac fires upon the sidewalks, in the streets, in the yards, threw high their wavering reflections, which examined, like slim, red fingers, the dingy, scarred walls and the piles of tumbled brick. The droning of voices again arose from great blue crowds.

The odor of frying bacon, the fragrance from countless little coffee-pails floated among the ruins. The rifles, stacked in the shadows, emitted flashes of steely light. Wherever a flag lay horizontally from one stack to another was the bed of an eagle which had led men into the mystic smoke.

The men about a particular fire were engaged in holding in check their jovial spirits. They moved whispering around the blaze, although they looked at it with a certain fine contentment, like laborers after a day's hard work.

There was one who sat apart. They did not address him save in tones suddenly changed. They did not regard him directly, but always in little sidelong glances.

At last a soldier from a distant fire came into this circle of light. He studied for a time the man who sat apart. Then he hesitatingly stepped closer, and said: "Got any news, Dan?"

"No," said Dan.

The new-comer shifted his feet. He looked at the fire, at the sky, at the other men, at Dan. His face expressed a curious despair; his tongue was plainly in rebellion. Finally, however, he contrived to say: "Well, there's some chance yet, Dan. Lots of the wounded are still lying out there, you know. There's some chance yet."

"Yes," said Dan.

The soldier shifted his feet again, and looked miserably into the air. After another struggle he said: "Well, there's some chance yet, Dan." He moved hastily away.

One of the men of the squad, perhaps encouraged by this example, now approached the still figure. "No news yet, hey?" he said, after coughing behind his hand.

"No," said Dan.

"Well," said the man, "I've been thinking of how he was fretting about you the night you went on special duty. You recollect? Well, sir, I was surprised. He couldn't say enough about it. I swan, I don't believe he slep' a wink after you left, but just lay awake cussing special duty and worrying. I was surprised. But there he lay cussing. He—"

Dan made a curious sound, as if a stone had wedged in his throat. He said: "Shut up, will you?"

Afterward the men would not allow this moody contemplation of the fire to be interrupted.

"Oh, let him alone, can't you?"

"Come away from there, Casey!"

"Say, can't you leave him be?"

They moved with reverence about the immovable figure, with its countenance of mask-like invulnerability.

7.

After the red round eye of the sun had stared long at the little plain and its burden, darkness, a sable mercy, came heavily upon it, and the wan hands of the dead were no longer seen in strange frozen gestures.

The heights in front of the plain shone with tiny camp-fires, and from the town in the rear, small shimmerings ascended from the blazes of the bivouac. The plain was a black expanse upon which, from time to time, dots of light, lanterns, floated slowly here and there. These fields were long steeped in grim mystery.

Suddenly, upon one dark spot, there was a resurrection. A strange thing had been groaning there, prostrate. Then it suddenly dragged itself to a sitting posture, and became a man.

The man stared stupidly for a moment at the lights on the hill, then turned and contemplated the faint coloring over the town. For some moments he remained thus, staring with dull eyes, his face unemotional, wooden.

Finally he looked around him at the corpses dimly to be seen. No change flashed into his face upon viewing these men. They seemed to suggest merely that his information concerning himself was not too complete. He ran his fingers over his arms and chest, bearing always the air of an idiot upon a bench at an almshouse door.

Finding no wound in his arms nor in his chest, he raised his hand to his head, and the fingers came away with some dark liquid upon them. Holding these fingers close to his eyes, he scanned them in the same stupid fashion, while his body gently swayed.

The soldier rolled his eyes again toward the town. When he arose, his clothing peeled from the frozen ground like wet paper. Hearing the sound of it, he seemed to see reason for deliberation. He paused and looked at the ground, then at his trousers, then at the ground.

Finally he went slowly off toward the faint reflection, holding his hands palm outward before him, and walking in the manner of a blind man.

8.

The immovable Dan again sat unaddressed in the midst of comrades, who did not joke aloud. The dampness of the usual morning fog seemed to make the little camp-fires furious.

Suddenly a cry arose in the streets, a shout of amazement and delight. The men making breakfast at the fire looked up quickly. They broke forth in clamorous exclamation: "Well! Of all things! Dan! Dan! Look who's coming! Oh, Dan!"

Dan the silent raised his eyes and saw a man, with a bandage of the size of a helmet about his head, receiving a furious demonstration from the company. He was shaking hands, and explaining, and haranguing to a high degree.

Dan started. His face of bronze flushed to his temples. He seemed about to leap from the ground, but then suddenly he sank back, and resumed his impassive gazing.

The men were in a flurry. They looked from one to the other. "Dan! Look! See who's coming!" some cried again. "Dan! Look!"

He scowled at last, and moved his shoulders sullenly. "Well, don't I know it?"

But they could not be convinced that his eyes were in service. "Dan! Why can't you look? See who's coming!"

He made a gesture then of irritation and rage. "Curse it! Don't I know it?"

The man with a bandage of the size of a helmet moved forward, always shaking hands and explaining. At times his glance wandered to Dan, who sat with his eyes riveted.

After a series of shiftings, it occurred naturally that the man with the bandage was very near to the man who saw the flames. He paused, and there was a little silence. Finally he said: "Hello, Dan."

"Hello, Billie."

SOURCE: Stephen Crane. *The Little Regiment and Other Episodes of the American Civil War.* New York: D. Appleton and Company, 1896. [First published: *McClure's Magazine*, June 1896.]

KATE CHOPIN

Born in 1851, Kate Chopin, a mother of six, took up writing after the death of her husband. The primary subjects in her first two books of short stories were the people of New Orleans and Louisiana, where she had lived for several years. She died in 1904. "A Pair of Silk Stockings" is perhaps the most famous short story in literature about shopping. "Azélie" is about a poor Cajun girl who also shops, no less recklessly; she may seem kin to some of the Mississippi heroines William Faulkner would create in the 1930s and '40s.

A Pair of Silk Stockings (1897)

LITTLE MRS. SOMMERS one day found herself the unexpected possessor of fifteen dollars. It seemed to her a very large amount of money, and the way in which it stuffed and bulged her worn old *porte-monnaie* gave her a feeling of importance such as she had not enjoyed for years.

The question of investment was one that occupied her greatly. For a day or two she walked about apparently in a dreamy state, but really absorbed in speculation and calculation. She did not wish to act hastily, to do anything she might afterward regret. But it was during the still hours of the night when she lay awake revolving plans in her mind that she seemed to see her way clearly toward a proper and judicious use of the money.

A dollar or two should be added to the price usually paid for Janie's shoes, which would insure their lasting an appreciable time longer than they usually did. She would buy so and so many yards of percale for new shirt waists for the boys and Janie and Mag. She had intended to make the old ones do by skilful patching. Mag should have another gown. She had seen some beautiful patterns, veritable bargains in the shop windows. And still there would be left enough for new stockings—two pairs apiece—and what darning that would save for a while! She would get caps for the boys and sailor-hats for the girls. The vision of her little brood looking fresh and dainty and new for once in their lives excited her and made her restless and wakeful with anticipation.

The neighbors sometimes talked of certain "better days" that little Mrs. Sommers had known before she had ever thought of being Mrs. Sommers. She herself indulged in no such morbid retrospection. She had no time—no second of time to devote to the past. The needs of the present absorbed her every faculty. A vision of the future like some dim, gaunt monster sometimes appalled her, but luckily to-morrow never comes.

Mrs. Sommers was one who knew the value of bargains; who could stand for hours making her way inch by inch toward the desired object that was selling below cost. She could elbow her way if need be; she had learned to clutch a piece of goods and hold it and stick to it with persistence and determination till her turn came to be served, no matter when it came.

But that day she was a little faint and tired. She had swallowed a light luncheon—no! when she came to think of it, between getting the children fed and the place righted, and preparing herself for the shopping bout, she had actually forgotten to eat any luncheon at all!

She sat herself upon a revolving stool before a counter that was comparatively deserted, trying to gather strength and courage to charge through an eager multitude that was besieging breast-works of shirting and figured lawn. An all-gone limp feeling had come over her and she rested her hand aimlessly upon the counter. She wore no gloves. By degrees she grew aware that her hand had encountered something very soothing, very pleasant to touch. She looked down to see that her hand lay upon a pile of silk stockings. A placard near by announced that they had been reduced in price from two dollars and fifty cents to one dollar and ninety-eight cents; and a young girl who stood behind the counter asked her if she wished to examine their line of silk hosiery. She smiled, just as if she had been asked to inspect a tiara of diamonds with the ultimate view of purchasing it. But she went on feeling the soft, sheeny luxurious things—with both hands now, holding them up to see them glisten, and to feel them glide serpent-like through her fingers.

Two hectic blotches came suddenly into her pale cheeks. She looked up at the girl.

"Do you think there are any eights-and-a-half among these?"

There were any number of eights-and-a-half. In fact, there were more of that size than any other. Here was a light-blue pair; there were some lavender, some all black and various shades of tan and gray. Mrs. Sommers selected a black pair and looked at them very long and closely. She pretended to be examining their texture, which the clerk assured her was excellent.

"A dollar and ninety-eight cents," she mused aloud. "Well, I'll take this pair." She handed the girl a five-dollar bill and waited for her change and for her parcel. What a very small parcel it was! It seemed lost in the depths of her shabby old shopping-bag.

Mrs. Sommers after that did not move in the direction of the bargain counter. She took the elevator, which carried her to an upper floor into the region of the ladies' waiting-rooms. Here, in a retired corner, she exchanged her cotton stockings for the new silk ones which she had just bought. She was not going through any acute mental process or reasoning with herself, nor was she striving to explain to her satisfaction the motive of her action. She was not thinking at all. She seemed for the time to be taking a rest from that laborious and fatiguing function and to have abandoned herself to some mechanical impulse that directed her actions and freed her of responsibility.

How good was the touch of the raw silk to her flesh! She felt like lying back in the cushioned chair and reveling for a while in the luxury of it. She did for a little while. Then she replaced her shoes, rolled the cotton stockings together and thrust them into her bag. After doing this she crossed straight over to the shoe department and took her seat to be fitted.

She was fastidious. The clerk could not make her out; he could not reconcile her shoes with her stockings, and she was not too easily pleased. She held back her skirts and turned her feet one way and her head another way as she glanced down at the polished, pointed-tipped boots. Her foot and ankle looked very pretty. She could not realize that they belonged to her and were a part of herself. She wanted an excellent and stylish fit, she told the young fellow who served her, and she did not mind the difference of a dollar or two more in the price so long as she got what she desired.

It was a long time since Mrs. Sommers had been fitted with gloves. On rare occasions when she had bought a pair they were always "bargains," so cheap that it would have been preposterous and unreasonable to have expected them to be fitted to the hand.

Now she rested her elbow on the cushion of the glove counter, and a pretty, pleasant young creature, delicate and deft of touch, drew a long-wristed "kid" over Mrs. Sommers' hand. She smoothed it down over the wrist and buttoned it neatly, and both lost themselves for a second or two in admiring contemplation of the little symmetrical gloved hand. But there were other places where money might be spent.

There were books and magazines piled up in the window of a stall a few paces down the street. Mrs. Sommers bought two high-priced magazines such as she had been accustomed to read in the days when she had been accustomed to other pleasant things. She carried them without wrapping. As well as she could she lifted her skirts at the crossings. Her stockings and boots and well fitting gloves had worked marvels in her bearing—had given her a feeling of assurance, a sense of belonging to the well-dressed multitude.

She was very hungry. Another time she would have stilled the cravings for food until reaching her own home, where she would have brewed herself a cup of tea and taken a snack of anything that was available. But the impulse that was guiding her would not suffer her to entertain any such thought.

There was a restaurant at the corner. She had never entered its doors; from the outside she had sometimes caught glimpses of spotless damask and shining crystal, and soft-stepping waiters serving people of fashion.

When she entered her appearance created no surprise, no consternation, as she had half feared it might. She seated herself at a small table alone, and an attentive waiter at once approached to take her order. She did not want a profusion; she craved a nice and tasty bite—a half dozen blue-points,[1] a plump chop with cress, a something sweet—a *crème-frappée*, for instance; a glass of Rhine wine, and after all a small cup of black coffee.

While waiting to be served she removed her gloves very leisurely and laid them beside her. Then she picked up a magazine and glanced through it, cutting the pages with a blunt edge of her

1. *blue-points:* a type of oyster from Blue Point, Long Island.

knife. It was all very agreeable. The damask was even more spotless than it had seemed through the window, and the crystal more sparkling. There were quiet ladies and gentlemen, who did not notice her, lunching at the small tables like her own. A soft, pleasing strain of music could be heard, and a gentle breeze was blowing through the window. She tasted a bite, and she read a word or two, and she sipped the amber wine and wiggled her toes in the silk stockings. The price of it made no difference. She counted the money out to the waiter and left an extra coin on his tray, whereupon he bowed before her as before a princess of royal blood.

There was still money in her purse, and her next temptation presented itself in the shape of a matinée poster.

It was a little later when she entered the theatre, the play had begun and the house seemed to her to be packed. But there were vacant seats here and there, and into one of them she was ushered, between brilliantly dressed women who had gone there to kill time and eat candy and display their gaudy attire. There were many others who were there solely for the play and acting. It is safe to say there was no one present who bore quite the attitude which Mrs. Sommers did to her surroundings. She gathered in the whole—stage and players and people in one wide impression, and absorbed it and enjoyed it. She laughed at the comedy and wept—she and the gaudy woman next to her wept over the tragedy. And they talked a little together over it. And the gaudy woman wiped her eyes and sniffled on a tiny square of filmy, perfumed lace and passed little Mrs. Sommers her box of candy.

The play was over, the music ceased, the crowd filed out. It was like a dream ended. People scattered in all directions. Mrs. Sommers went to the corner and waited for the cable car.

A man with keen eyes, who sat opposite to her, seemed to like the study of her small, pale face. It puzzled him to decipher what he saw there. In truth, he saw nothing—unless he were wizard enough to detect a poignant wish, a powerful longing that the cable car would never stop anywhere, but go on and on with her forever.

SOURCE: *Vogue* (September 16, 1897).

Azélie (1897)

Azélie crossed the yard with slow, hesitating steps. She wore a pink sunbonnet and a faded calico dress that had been made the summer before, and was now too small for her in every way. She carried a large tin pail on her arm. When within a few yards of the house she stopped under a chinaberry-tree, quite still, except for the occasional slow turning of her head from side to side.

Mr. Mathurin, from his elevation upon the upper gallery, laughed when he saw her; for he knew she would stay there, motionless, till some one noticed and questioned her.

The planter was just home from the city, and was therefore in an excellent humor, as he always was, on getting back to what he called *le grand air,* the space and stillness of the country, and the scent of the fields. He was in shirt-sleeves, walking around the gallery that encircled the big square white house. Beneath was a brick-paved portico upon which the lower rooms opened. At wide intervals were large whitewashed pillars that supported the upper gallery.

In one corner of the lower house was the store, which was in no sense a store for the general public, but maintained only to supply the needs of Mr. Mathurin's "hands."

"Eh bien! what do you want, Azélie?" the planter finally called out to the girl in French. She advanced a few paces, and, pushing back her sunbonnet, looked up at him with a gentle, inoffensive face—"to which you would give the good God without confession," he once described it.

"Bon jou', M'si' Mathurin," she replied; and continued in English: "I come git a li'le piece o' meat. We plumb out o' meat home."

"Well, well, the meat is n' going to walk to you, my chile: it has n' got feet. Go fine Mr. 'Polyte. He's yonda mending his buggy unda the shed." She turned away with an alert little step, and went in search of Mr. 'Polyte.

"That's you again!" the young man exclaimed, with a pretended air of annoyance, when he saw her. He straightened himself, and looked down at her and her pail with a comprehending glance. The sweat was standing in shining beads on his brown, good-looking face. He was in his shirt-sleeves, and the legs of his trousers were thrust into the tops of his fine, high-heeled boots. He wore his straw hat very much on one side, and had an air that was altogether *fanfaron*.[1] He reached to a back pocket for the store key, which was as large as the pistol that he sometimes carried in the same place. She followed him across the thick, tufted grass of the yard with quick, short steps that strove to keep pace with his longer, swinging ones.

When he had unlocked and opened the heavy door of the store, there escaped from the close room the strong, pungent odor of the varied wares and provisions massed within. Azélie seemed to like the odor, and, lifting her head, snuffed the air as people sometimes do upon entering a conservatory filled with fragrant flowers.

A broad ray of light streamed in through the open door, illumining the dingy interior. The double wooden shutters of the windows were all closed, and secured on the inside by iron hooks.

"Well, w'at you want, Azélie?" asked 'Polyte, going behind the counter with an air of hurry and importance. "I ain't got time to fool. Make has'e; say w'at you want."

Her reply was precisely the same that she had made to Mr. Mathurin.

"I come git a li'le piece o' meat. We plumb out o' meat home."

He seemed exasperated.

"Bonté! w'at you all do with meat yonda? You don't reflec' you about to eat up yo' crop befo' it's good out o' the groun', you all. I like to know w'y yo' pa don't go he'p with the killin' once aw'ile, an' git some fresh meat fo' a change."

She answered in an unshaded, unmodulated voice that was penetrating, like a child's: "Popa he do go he'p wid the killin'; but he say he can't work 'less he got salt meat. He got plenty to feed—him. He's got to hire he'p wid his crop, an' he's boun' to feed 'em; they won't year no diffe'nt. An' he's got gra'ma to feed, an' Sauterelle, an' me—"

"An' all the lazy-bone 'Cadians in the country that know w'ere they goin' to fine the coffee-pot always in the corna of the fire," grumbled 'Polyte.

With an iron hook he lifted a small piece of salt meat from the pork barrel, weighed it, and placed it in her pail. Then she wanted a little coffee. He gave it to her reluctantly. He was still more loath to let her have sugar; and when she asked for lard, he refused flatly.

She had taken off her sunbonnet, and was fanning herself with it, as she leaned with her elbows upon the counter, and let her eyes

1. *fanfaron*: French for "swaggering."

travel lingeringly along the well-lined shelves. 'Polyte stood staring into her face with a sense of aggravation that her presence, her manner, always stirred up in him.

The face was colorless but for the red, curved line of the lips. Her eyes were dark, wide, innocent, questioning eyes, and her black hair was plastered smooth back from the forehead and temples. There was no trace of any intention of coquetry in her manner. He resented this as a token of indifference toward his sex, and thought it inexcusable.

"Well, Azélie, if it's anything you don't see, ask fo' it," he suggested, with what he flattered himself was humor. But there was no responsive humor in Azélie's composition. She seriously drew a small flask from her pocket.

"Popa say, if you want to let him have a li'le dram, 'count o' his pains that's 'bout to cripple him."

"Yo' pa knows as well as I do we don't sell w'isky. Mr. Mathurin don't carry no license."

"I know. He say if you want to give 'im a li'le dram, he's willin' to do some work fo' you."

"No! Once fo' all, no!" And 'Polyte reached for the day-book, in which to enter the articles he had given to her.

But Azélie's needs were not yet satisfied. She wanted tobacco; he would not give it to her. A spool of thread; he rolled one up, together with two sticks of peppermint candy, and placed it in her pail. When she asked for a bottle of coal-oil, he grudgingly consented, but assured her it would be useless to cudgel her brain further, for he would positively let her have nothing more. He disappeared toward the coal-oil tank, which was hidden from view behind the piled-up boxes on the counter. When she heard him searching for an empty quart bottle, and making a clatter with the tin funnels, she herself withdrew from the counter against which she had been leaning.

After they quitted the store, 'Polyte, with a perplexed expression upon his face, leaned for a moment against one of the whitewashed pillars, watching the girl cross the yard. She had folded her sunbonnet into a pad, which she placed beneath the heavy pail that she balanced upon her head. She walked upright, with a slow, careful tread. Two of the yard dogs that had stood a moment before upon the threshold of the store door, quivering and wagging their tails, were following her now, with a little business-like trot. 'Polyte called them back.

The cabin which the girl occupied with her father, her grandmother, and her little brother Sauterelle, was removed some distance from the plantation house, and only its pointed roof could be discerned like a speck far away across the field of cotton, which was all in bloom. Her figure soon disappeared from view, and 'Polyte emerged from the shelter of the gallery, and started again toward his interrupted task. He turned to say to the planter, who was keeping up his measured tramp above:

"Mr. Mathurin, ain't it 'mos' time to stop givin' credit to Arsène Pauché. Look like that crop o' his ain't goin' to start to pay his account. I don't see, me, anyway, how you come to take that triflin' Li'le river gang on the place."

"I know it was a mistake, 'Polyte, but que voulez-vous?"[2] the planter returned, with a good-natured shrug. "Now they are yere, we can't let them starve, my frien'. Push them to work all you can. Hole back all supplies that are not necessary, an' nex' year we will let some one else enjoy the privilege of feeding them," he ended, with a laugh.

"I wish they was all back on Li'le river," 'Polyte muttered under his breath as he turned and walked slowly away.

Directly back of the store was the young man's sleeping-room. He had made himself quite comfortable there in his corner. He had screened his windows and doors; planted Madeira vines, which now formed a thick green curtain between the two pillars that faced his room; and had swung a hammock out there, in which he liked well to repose himself after the fatigues of the day.

He lay long in the hammock that evening, thinking over the day's happenings and the morrow's work, half dozing, half dreaming, and wholly possessed by the charm of the night, the warm, sweeping air that blew through the long corridor, and the almost unbroken stillness that enveloped him.

At times his random thoughts formed themselves into an almost inaudible speech: "I wish she would go 'way f'om yere."

One of the dogs came and thrust his cool, moist muzzle against 'Polyte's cheek. He caressed the fellow's shaggy head. "I don't know w'at's the matta with her," he sighed; "I don' b'lieve she's got good sense."

It was a long time afterward that he murmured again: "I wish to God she'd go 'way f'om yere!"

2. *que voulez-vous?*: French for "what do you want?"

The edge of the moon crept up—a keen, curved blade of light above the dark line of the cotton-field. 'Polyte roused himself when he saw it. "I didn' know it was so late," he said to himself—or to his dog. He entered his room at once, and was soon in bed, sleeping soundly.

It was some hours later that 'Polyte was roused from his sleep by—he did not know what; his senses were too scattered and confused to determine at once. There was at first no sound; then so faint a one that he wondered how he could have heard it. A door of his room communicated with the store, but this door was never used, and was almost completely blocked by wares piled up on the other side. The faint noise that 'Polyte heard, and which came from within the store, was followed by a flare of light that he could discern through the chinks, and that lasted as long as a match might burn.

He was now fully aware that some one was in the store. How the intruder had entered he could not guess, for the key was under his pillow with his watch and his pistol.

As cautiously as he could he donned an extra garment, thrust his bare feet into slippers, and crept out into the portico, pistol in hand.

The shutters of one of the store windows were open. He stood close to it, and waited, which he considered surer and safer than to enter the dark and crowded confines of the store to engage in what might prove a bootless struggle with the intruder.

He had not long to wait. In a few moments some one darted through the open window as nimbly as a cat. 'Polyte staggered back as if a heavy blow had stunned him. His first thought and his first exclamation were: "My God! how close I come to killin' you!"

It was Azélie. She uttered no cry, but made one quick effort to run when she saw him. He seized her arm and held her with a brutal grip. He put the pistol back into his pocket. He was shaking like a man with the palsy. One by one he took from her the parcels she was carrying, and flung them back into the store. There were not many: some packages of tobacco, a cheap pipe, some fishing-tackle, and the flask which she had brought with her in the afternoon. This he threw into the yard. It was still empty, for she had not been able to find the "key" to the whisky-barrel.

"So—so, you a thief!" he muttered savagely under his breath.

"You hurtin' me, Mr. 'Polyte," she complained, squirming. He somewhat relaxed, but did not relinquish, his hold upon her.

"I ain't no thief," she blurted.

"You was stealin'," he contradicted her sharply.

"I wasn' stealin'. I was jus' takin' a few li'le things you all too mean to gi' me. You all treat my popa like he was a dog. It's on'y las' week Mr. Mathurin sen' 'way to the city to fetch a fine buckboa'd fo' Son Ambroise, an' he's on'y a nigga, après tout. An' my popa he want a picayune tobacca? It's 'No'—" She spoke loud in her monotonous, shrill voice. 'Polyte kept saying: "Hush, I tell you! Hush! Somebody'll year you. Hush! It's enough you broke in the sto'—how you got in the sto'?" he added, looking from her to the open window.

"It was w'en you was behine the boxes to the coal-oil tank—I unhook' it," she explained sullenly.

"An' you don' know I could sen' you to Baton Rouge fo' that?" He shook her as though trying to rouse her to a comprehension of her grievous fault.

"Jus' fo' a li'le picayune o' tobacca!" she whimpered.

He suddenly abandoned his hold upon her, and left her free. She mechanically rubbed the arm that he had grasped so violently.

Between the long row of pillars the moon was sending pale beams of light. In one of these they were standing.

"Azélie," he said, "go 'way f'om yere quick; some one might fine you yere. W'en you want something in the sto', fo' yo'se'f or fo' yo' pa—I don' care—ask me fo' it. But you—but you can't neva set yo' foot inside that sto' again. Go 'way f'om yere quick as you can, I tell you!"

She tried in no way to conciliate him. She turned and walked away over the same ground she had crossed before. One of the big dogs started to follow her. 'Polyte did not call him back this time. He knew no harm could come to her, going through those lonely fields, while the animal was at her side.

He went at once to his room for the store key that was beneath his pillow. He entered the store, and refastened the window. When he had made everything once more secure, he sat dejectedly down upon a bench that was in the portico. He sat for a long time motionless. Then, overcome by some powerful feeling that was at work within him, he buried his face in his hands and wept, his whole body shaken by the violence of his sobs.

After that night 'Polyte loved Azélie desperately. The very action which should have revolted him had seemed, on the contrary, to inflame him with love. He felt that love to be a degradation—something that he was almost ashamed to acknowledge to himself; and he knew that he was hopelessly unable to stifle it.

He watched now in a tremor for her coming. She came very often, for she remembered every word he had said; and she did not hesitate to ask him for those luxuries which she considered necessities to her "popa's" existence. She never attempted to enter the store, but always waited outside, of her own accord, laughing, and playing with the dogs. She seemed to have no shame or regret for what she had done, and plainly did not realize that it was a disgraceful act. 'Polyte often shuddered with disgust to discern in her a being so wholly devoid of moral sense.

He had always been an industrious, bustling fellow, never idle. Now there were hours and hours in which he did nothing but long for the sight of Azélie. Even when at work there was that gnawing want at his heart to see her, often so urgent that he would leave everything to wander down by her cabin with the hope of seeing her. It was even something if he could catch a glimpse of Sauterelle playing in the weeds, or of Arsène lazily dragging himself about, and smoking the pipe which rarely left his lips now that he was kept so well supplied with tobacco.

Once, down the bank of the bayou, when 'Polyte came upon Azélie unexpectedly, and was therefore unprepared to resist the shock of her sudden appearance, he seized her in his arms, and covered her face with kisses. She was not indignant; she was not flustered or agitated, as might have been a susceptible, coquettish girl; she was only astonished, and annoyed.

"Wat you doin', Mr. 'Polyte?" she cried, struggling. "Leave me 'lone, I say! Leave me go!"

"I love you, I love you, I love you!" he stammered helplessly over and over in her face.

"You mus' los' yo' head," she told him, red from the effort of the struggle, when he released her.

"You right, Azélie; I b'lieve I los' my head," and he climbed up the bank of the bayou as fast as he could.

After that his behavior was shameful, and he knew it, and he did not care. He invented pretexts that would enable him to touch her hand with his. He wanted to kiss her again, and told her she might come into the store as she used to do. There was no need for her to unhook a window now; he gave her whatever she asked for, charging it always to his own account on the books. She permitted his caresses without returning them, and yet that was all he seemed to live for now. He gave her a little gold ring.

He was looking eagerly forward to the close of the season, when Arsène would go back to Little River. He had arranged to ask Azélie to marry him. He would keep her with him when the others went away. He longed to rescue her from what he felt to be the demoralizing influences of her family and her surroundings. 'Polyte believed he would be able to awaken Azélie to finer, better impulses when he should have her apart to himself.

But when the time came to propose it, Azélie looked at him in amazement. "Ah, b'en, no. I ain't goin' to stay yere wid you, Mr. 'Polyte; I'm goin' yonda on Li'le river wid my popa."

This resolve frightened him, but he pretended not to believe it.

"You jokin', Azélie; you mus' care a li'le about me. It looked to me all along like you cared some about me."

"An' my popa, donc? Ah, b'en, no."

"You don' rememba how lonesome it is on Li'le river, Azélie," he pleaded. "W'enever I think 'bout Li'le river it always make me sad—like I think about a graveyard. To me it's like a person mus' die, one way or otha, w'en they go on Li'le river. Oh, I hate it! Stay with me, Azélie; don' go 'way from me."

She said little, one way or the other, after that, when she had fully understood his wishes, and her reserve led him to believe, since he hoped it, that he had prevailed with her and that she had determined to stay with him and be his wife.

It was a cool, crisp morning in December that they went away. In a ramshackle wagon, drawn by an ill-mated team, Arsène Pauché and his family left Mr. Mathurin's plantation for their old familiar haunts on Little River. The grandmother, looking like a witch, with a black shawl tied over her head, sat upon a roll of bedding in the bottom of the wagon. Sauterelle's bead-like eyes glittered with mischief as he peeped over the side. Azélie, with the pink sunbonnet completely hiding her round young face, sat beside her father, who drove.

'Polyte caught one glimpse of the group as they passed in the road. Turning, he hurried into his room, and locked himself in.

It soon became evident that 'Polyte's services were going to count for little. He himself was the first to realize this. One day he approached the planter, and said: "Mr. Mathurin, befo' we start anotha year togetha, I betta tell you I'm goin' to quit." 'Polyte stood upon the steps, and leaned back against the railing. The planter was a little above on the gallery.

"W'at in the name o' sense are you talking about, 'Polyte!" he exclaimed in astonishment.

"It's jus' that; I'm boun' to quit."

"You had a better offer?"

"No; I ain't had no offa."

"Then explain yo'se'f, my frien'—explain yo'se'f," requested Mr. Mathurin, with something of offended dignity. "If you leave me, w'ere are you going?"

'Polyte was beating his leg with his limp felt hat. "I reckon I jus' as well go yonda on Li'le river—w'ere Azélie," he said.

SOURCE: Kate Chopin. *A Night in Acadie.* Chicago: Way and Williams, 1897.

CHARLES W. CHESNUTT

Charles Waddell Chesnutt (1858–1932) was the first commercially successful African-American writer of fiction. Born in Cleveland, Ohio, he grew up in North Carolina, became a teacher, married, and moved to New York City before returning to live in Cleveland, where he studied law. "Uncle Wellington's Wives" is one of his fine and wry stories about the "Color Line," a line that had consequential legal and social repercussions. That is, as this miniature novella unfolds, Uncle Wellington, living in a small town in North Carolina where he grew up, in the decade after the Civil War, yearns for something else, beyond his comfortable home with his impatient, hard-working wife.

Uncle Wellington's Wives (1899)

1.

UNCLE WELLINGTON BRABOY was so deeply absorbed in thought as he walked slowly homeward from the weekly meeting of the Union League, that he let his pipe go out, a fact of which he remained oblivious until he had reached the little frame house in the suburbs of Patesville, where he lived with aunt Milly, his wife. On this particular occasion the club had been addressed by a visiting brother from the North, Professor Patterson, a tall, well-formed mulatto, who wore a perfectly fitting suit of broadcloth, a shiny silk hat, and linen of dazzling whiteness,—in short, a gentleman of such distinguished appearance that the doors and windows of the offices and stores on Front Street were filled with curious observers as he passed through that thoroughfare in the early part of the day. This polished stranger was a traveling organizer of Masonic lodges, but he also claimed to be a high officer in the Union League, and had been invited to lecture before the local chapter of that organization at Patesville.

The lecture had been largely attended, and uncle Wellington Braboy had occupied a seat just in front of the platform. The subject of the lecture was "The Mental, Moral, Physical, Political, Social, and Financial Improvement of the Negro Race in America," a theme much dwelt upon, with slight variations, by colored orators. For to this struggling people, then as now, the problem of their uncertain present and their doubtful future was the chief concern of life. The period was the hopeful one. The Federal Government retained some vestige of authority in the South, and the newly emancipated race cherished the delusion that under the Constitution, that enduring rock on which our liberties are founded, and under the equal laws it purported to guarantee, they would enter upon the era of freedom and opportunity which their Northern friends had inaugurated with such solemn sanctions. The speaker pictured in eloquent language the state of ideal equality and happiness enjoyed by colored people at the North: how they sent their children to school with the white children; how they sat by white people in the churches and theatres, ate with them in the public restaurants, and buried their dead in the same cemeteries. The professor waxed eloquent with the development of his theme, and, as a finishing touch to an alluring picture, assured the excited audience that the intermarriage of the races was common, and that he himself had espoused a white woman.

Uncle Wellington Braboy was a deeply interested listener. He had heard something of these facts before, but his information had always come in such vague and questionable shape that he had paid little attention to it. He knew that the Yankees had freed the slaves, and that runaway negroes had always gone to the North to seek liberty; any such equality, however, as the visiting brother had depicted, was more than uncle Wellington had ever conceived as actually existing anywhere in the world. At first he felt inclined to doubt the truth of the speaker's statements; but the cut of his clothes, the eloquence of his language, and the flowing length of his whiskers, were so far superior to anything uncle Wellington had ever met among the colored people of his native State, that he felt irresistibly impelled to the conviction that nothing less than the advantages claimed for the North by the visiting brother could have produced such an exquisite flower of civilization. Any lingering doubts uncle Wellington may have felt were entirely dispelled by the courtly bow and cordial grasp of the hand with which the visiting brother acknowledged the congratulations showered upon him by the audience at the close of his address.

The more uncle Wellington's mind dwelt upon the professor's speech, the more attractive seemed the picture of Northern life presented. Uncle Wellington possessed in large measure the imaginative faculty so freely bestowed by nature upon the race from which the darker half of his blood was drawn. He had indulged in occasional day-dreams of an ideal state of social equality, but his wildest flights of fancy had never located it nearer than heaven, and he had felt some misgivings about its practical working even there. Its desirability he had never doubted, and the speech of the evening before had given a local habitation and a name to the forms his imagination had bodied forth. Giving full rein to his fancy, he saw in the North a land flowing with milk and honey,—a land peopled by noble men and beautiful women, among whom colored men and women moved with the ease and grace of acknowledged right. Then he placed himself in the foreground of the picture. What a fine figure he would have made in the world if he had been born at the free North! He imagined himself dressed like the professor, and passing the contribution-box in a white church; and most pleasant of his dreams, and the hardest to realize as possible, was that of the gracious white lady he might have called wife. Uncle Wellington was a mulatto, and his features were those of his white father, though tinged with the hue of his mother's race; and as he lifted the kerosene lamp at evening, and took a long look at his image in the little mirror over the mantelpiece, he said to himself that he was a very good-looking man, and could have adorned a much higher sphere in life than that in which the accident of birth had placed him. He fell asleep and dreamed that he lived in a two-story brick house, with a spacious flower garden in front, the whole inclosed by a high iron fence; that he kept a carriage and servants, and never did a stroke of work. This was the highest style of living in Patesville, and he could conceive of nothing finer.

Uncle Wellington slept later than usual the next morning, and the sunlight was pouring in at the open window of the bedroom, when his dreams were interrupted by the voice of his wife, in tones meant to be harsh, but which no ordinary degree of passion could rob of their native unctuousness.

"Git up f'm dere, you lazy, good-fuh-nuffin' nigger! Is you gwine ter sleep all de mawnin'? I 's ti'ed er dis yer runnin' 'roun' all night an' den sleepin' all day. You won't git dat tater patch hoed ovuh ter-day 'less'n you git up f'm dere an' git at it."

Uncle Wellington rolled over, yawned cavernously, stretched himself, and with a muttered protest got out of bed and put on his clothes. Aunt Milly had prepared a smoking breakfast of hominy and fried bacon, the odor of which was very grateful to his nostrils.

"Is breakfus' done ready?" he inquired, tentatively, as he came into the kitchen and glanced at the table.

"No, it ain't ready, an' 't ain't gwine ter be ready 'tel you tote dat wood an' water in," replied aunt Milly severely, as she poured two teacups of boiling water on two tablespoonfuls of ground coffee.

Uncle Wellington went down to the spring and got a pail of water, after which he brought in some oak logs for the fireplace and some lightwood for kindling. Then he drew a chair towards the table and started to sit down.

"Wonduh what 's de matter wid you dis mawnin' anyhow," remarked aunt Milly. "You must 'a' be'n up ter some devilment las' night, fer yo' recommemb'ance is so po' dat you fus' fergit ter git up, an' den fergit ter wash yo' face an' hands fo' you set down ter de table. I don' 'low nobody ter eat at my table dat a-way."

"I don' see no use 'n washin' 'em so much," replied Wellington wearily. "Dey gits dirty ag'in right off, an' den you got ter wash 'em ovuh ag'in; it 's jes' pilin' up wuk what don' fetch in nuffin'. De dirt don' show nohow, 'n' I don' see no advantage in bein' black, ef you got to keep on washin' yo' face 'n' han's jes' lack w'ite folks." He nevertheless performed his ablutions in a perfunctory way, and resumed his seat at the breakfast-table.

"Ole 'oman," he asked, after the edge of his appetite had been taken off, "how would you lack ter live at de Norf?"

"I dunno nuffin' 'bout de Norf," replied aunt Milly. "It 's hard 'nuff ter git erlong heah, whar we knows all erbout it."

"De brother what 'dressed de meetin' las' night say dat de wages at de Norf is twicet ez big ez dey is heah."

"You could make a sight mo' wages heah ef you 'd 'ten' ter yo' wuk better," replied aunt Milly.

Uncle Wellington ignored this personality, and continued, "An' he say de cullud folks got all de privileges er de w'ite folks,—dat dey chillen goes ter school tergedder, dat dey sets on same seats in chu'ch, an' sarves on jury, 'n' rides on de kyars an' steamboats wid de w'ite folks, an' eats at de fus' table."

"Dat 'u'd suit you," chuckled aunt Milly, "an' you 'd stay dere fer de secon' table, too. How dis man know 'bout all dis yer foolis'ness?" she asked incredulously.

"He come f'm de Norf," said uncle Wellington, "an' he 'speunced it all hisse'f."

"Well, he can't make me b'lieve it," she rejoined, with a shake of her head.

"An' you would n' lack ter go up dere an' 'joy all dese privileges?" asked uncle Wellington, with some degree of earnestness.

The old woman laughed until her sides shook. "Who gwine ter take me up dere?" she inquired.

"You got de money yo'se'f."

"I ain' got no money fer ter was'e," she replied shortly, becoming serious at once; and with that the subject was dropped.

Uncle Wellington pulled a hoe from under the house, and took his way wearily to the potato patch. He did not feel like working, but aunt Milly was the undisputed head of the establishment, and he did not dare to openly neglect his work.

In fact, he regarded work at any time as a disagreeable necessity to be avoided as much as possible. His wife was cast in a different mould. Externally she would have impressed the casual observer as a neat, well-preserved, and good-looking black woman, of middle age, every curve of whose ample figure—and her figure was all curves—was suggestive of repose. So far from being indolent, or even deliberate in her movements, she was the most active and energetic woman in the town. She went through the physical exercises of a prayer-meeting with astonishing vigor. It was exhilarating to see her wash a shirt, and a study to watch her do it up. A quick jerk shook out the dampened garment; one pass of her ample palm spread it over the ironing-board, and a few well-directed strokes with the iron accomplished what would have occupied the ordinary laundress for half an hour.

To this uncommon, and in uncle Wellington's opinion unnecessary and unnatural activity, his own habits were a steady protest. If aunt Milly had been willing to support him in idleness, he would have acquiesced without a murmur in her habits of industry. This she would not do, and, moreover, insisted on his working at least half the time. If she had invested the proceeds of her labor in rich food and fine clothing, he might have endured it better; but to her passion for work was added a most detestable thrift. She absolutely refused to pay for Wellington's clothes, and required him to furnish a certain proportion of the family supplies. Her savings were carefully put by, and with them she had bought and paid for the modest cottage which she and her husband occupied. Under her careful hand it was always neat and clean; in summer the little yard was gay with bright-colored flowers, and woe to the heedless pickaninny who should stray into her yard and pluck a rose or a verbena! In a stout oaken chest under her bed she kept a capacious stocking, into which flowed a steady stream of fractional currency. She carried the key to this chest in her pocket, a proceeding regarded by uncle Wellington with no little disfavor. He was of the opinion—an opinion he would not have dared to assert in her presence—that his wife's earnings were his own property; and he looked upon this stocking as a drunkard's wife might regard the saloon which absorbed her husband's wages.

Uncle Wellington hurried over the potato patch on the morning of the conversation above recorded, and as soon as he saw aunt Milly go away with a basket of clothes on her head, returned to the house, put on his coat, and went uptown.

He directed his steps to a small frame building fronting on the main street of the village, at a point where the street was intersected by one of the several creeks meandering through the town, cooling the air, providing numerous swimming-holes for the amphibious small boy, and furnishing water-power for grist-mills and saw-mills. The rear of the building rested on long brick pillars, built up from the bottom of the steep bank of the creek, while the front was level with the street. This was the office of Mr. Matthew Wright, the sole representative of the colored race at the bar of Chinquapin County. Mr. Wright came of an "old issue" free colored family, in which, though the negro blood was present in an attenuated strain, a line of free ancestry could be traced beyond the Revolutionary War. He had enjoyed exceptional opportunities, and enjoyed the distinction of being the first, and for a long time the only colored lawyer in North Carolina. His services were frequently called into requisition by impecunious people of his own race; when they had money they went to white lawyers, who, they shrewdly conjectured, would have more influence with judge or jury than a colored lawyer, however able.

Uncle Wellington found Mr. Wright in his office. Having inquired after the health of the lawyer's family and all his relations in detail, uncle Wellington asked for a professional opinion.

"Mistah Wright, ef a man's wife got money, whose money is dat befo' de law—his'n er her'n?"

The lawyer put on his professional air, and replied:—

"Under the common law, which in default of special legislative enactment is the law of North Carolina, the personal property of the wife belongs to her husband."

"But dat don' jes' tech de p'int, suh. I wuz axin' 'bout money."

"You see, uncle Wellington, your education has not rendered you familiar with legal phraseology. The term 'personal property' or 'estate' embraces, according to Blackstone, all property other than land, and therefore includes money. Any money a man's wife has is his, constructively, and will be recognized as his actually, as soon as he can secure possession of it."

"Dat is ter say, suh—my eddication don' quite 'low me ter understan' dat—dat is ter say—"

"That is to say, it's yours when you get it. It is n't yours so that the law will help you get it; but on the other hand, when you once lay your hands on it, it is yours so that the law won't take it away from you."

Uncle Wellington nodded to express his full comprehension of the law as expounded by Mr. Wright, but scratched his head in a way that expressed some disappointment. The law seemed to wobble. Instead of enabling him to stand up fearlessly and demand his own, it threw him back upon his own efforts; and the prospect of his being able to overpower or outwit aunt Milly by any ordinary means was very poor.

He did not leave the office, but hung around awhile as though there were something further he wished to speak about. Finally, after some discursive remarks about the crops and politics, he asked, in an offhand, disinterested manner, as though the thought had just occurred to him:—

"Mistah Wright, w'ile 's we 're talkin' 'bout law matters, what do it cos' ter git a defoce?"

"That depends upon circumstances. It is n't altogether a matter of expense. Have you and aunt Milly been having trouble?"

"Oh no, suh; I was jes' a-wond'rin'."

"You see," continued the lawyer, who was fond of talking, and had nothing else to do for the moment, "a divorce is not an easy thing to get in this State under any circumstances. It used to be the law that divorce could be granted only by special act of the legislature; and it is but recently that the subject has been relegated to the jurisdiction of the courts."

Uncle Wellington understood a part of this, but the answer had not been exactly to the point in his mind.

"S'pos'n', den, jes' fer de argyment, me an' my ole 'oman sh'd fall out en wanter separate, how could I git a defoce?"

"That would depend on what you quarreled about. It's pretty hard work to answer general questions in a particular way. If you merely wished to separate, it would n't be necessary to get a divorce; but if you should want to marry again, you would have to be divorced, or else you would be guilty of bigamy, and could be sent to the penitentiary. But, by the way, uncle Wellington, when were you married?"

"I got married 'fo' de wah, when I was livin' down on Rockfish Creek."

"When you were in slavery?"

"Yas, suh."

"Did you have your marriage registered after the surrender?"

"No, suh; never knowed nuffin' 'bout dat."

After the war, in North Carolina and other States, the freed people who had sustained to each other the relation of husband and wife as it existed among slaves, were required by law to register their consent to continue in the marriage relation. By this simple expedient their former marriages of convenience received the sanction of law, and their children the seal of legitimacy. In many cases, however, where the parties lived in districts remote from the larger towns, the ceremony was neglected, or never heard of by the freedmen.

"Well," said the lawyer, "if that is the case, and you and aunt Milly should disagree, it wouldn't be necessary for you to get a divorce, even if you should want to marry again. You were never legally married."

"So Milly ain't my lawful wife, den?"

"She may be your wife in one sense of the word, but not in such a sense as to render you liable to punishment for bigamy if you should marry another woman. But I hope you will never want to do anything of the kind, for you have a very good wife now."

Uncle Wellington went away thoughtfully, but with a feeling of unaccustomed lightness and freedom. He had not felt so free since the memorable day when he had first heard of the Emancipation Proclamation. On leaving the lawyer's office, he called at the workshop of one of his friends, Peter Williams, a shoemaker by trade, who had a brother living in Ohio.

"Is you hearn f'm Sam lately?" uncle Wellington inquired, after the conversation had drifted through the usual generalities.

"His mammy got er letter f'm 'im las' week; he 's livin' in de town er Groveland now."

"How 's he gittin' on?"

"He says he gittin' on monst'us well. He 'low ez how he make five dollars a day w'ite-washin', an' have all he kin do."

The shoemaker related various details of his brother's prosperity, and uncle Wellington returned home in a very thoughtful mood, revolving in his mind a plan of future action. This plan had been vaguely assuming form ever since the professor's lecture, and the events of the morning had brought out the detail in bold relief.

Two days after the conversation with the shoemaker, aunt Milly went, in the afternoon, to visit a sister of hers who lived several miles out in the country. During her absence, which lasted until nightfall, uncle Wellington went uptown and purchased a cheap oilcloth valise from a shrewd son of Israel, who had penetrated to this locality with a stock of notions and cheap clothing. Uncle Wellington had his purchase done up in brown paper, and took the parcel under his arm. Arrived at home he unwrapped the valise, and thrust into its capacious jaws his best suit of clothes, some underwear, and a few other small articles for personal use and adornment. Then he carried the valise out into the yard, and, first looking cautiously around to see if there was any one in sight, concealed it in a clump of bushes in a corner of the yard.

It may be inferred from this proceeding that uncle Wellington was preparing for a step of some consequence. In fact, he had fully made up his mind to go to the North; but he still lacked the most important requisite for traveling with comfort, namely, the money to pay his expenses. The idea of tramping the distance which separated him from the promised land of liberty and equality had never occurred to him. When a slave, he had several times been importuned by fellow servants to join them in the attempt to escape from bondage, but he had never wanted his freedom badly enough to walk a thousand miles for it; if he could have gone to Canada by stage-coach, or by rail, or on horseback, with stops for regular meals, he would probably have undertaken the trip. The funds he now needed for his journey were in aunt Milly's chest. He had thought a great deal about his right to this money. It was his wife's savings, and he had never dared to dispute, openly, her right to exercise exclusive control over what she earned; but the lawyer had assured him of his right to the money, of which he was already constructively in possession, and he had therefore determined to possess himself actually of the coveted stocking. It was impracticable for him to get the key of the chest. Aunt Milly kept it in her pocket by day and under her pillow at night. She was a light sleeper, and, if not awakened by the abstraction of the key, would certainly have been disturbed by the unlocking of the chest. But one alternative remained, and that was to break open the chest in her absence.

There was a revival in progress at the colored Methodist church. Aunt Milly was as energetic in her religion as in other respects, and had not missed a single one of the meetings. She returned at nightfall from her visit to the country and prepared a frugal supper. Uncle Wellington did not eat as heartily as usual. Aunt Milly perceived his want of appetite, and spoke of it. He explained it by saying that he did not feel very well.

"Is you gwine ter chu'ch ter-night?" inquired his wife.

"I reckon I 'll stay home an' go ter bed," he replied. "I ain't be'n feelin' well dis evenin', an' I 'spec' I better git a good night's res'."

"Well, you kin stay ef you mineter. Good preachin' 'u'd make you feel better, but ef you ain't gwine, don' fergit ter tote in some wood an' lighterd 'fo' you go ter bed. De moon is shinin' bright, an' you can't have no 'scuse 'bout not bein' able ter see."

Uncle Wellington followed her out to the gate, and watched her receding form until it disappeared in the distance. Then he re-entered the house with a quick step, and taking a hatchet from a corner of the room, drew the chest from under the bed. As he applied the hatchet to the fastenings, a thought struck him, and by the flickering light of the pine-knot blazing on the hearth, a look of hesitation might have been seen to take the place of the determined expression his face had worn up to that time. He had argued himself into the belief that his present action was lawful and justifiable. Though this conviction had not prevented him from trembling in every limb, as though he were committing a mere vulgar theft, it had still nerved him to the deed. Now even his moral courage began to weaken. The lawyer had told him that his wife's property was his own; in taking it he was therefore only exercising his lawful right. But at the point of breaking open the chest, it occurred to him that he was taking this money in order to get away from aunt Milly, and that he justified his desertion of her by the lawyer's opinion that she was not his lawful wife. If she was not his wife, then he had no right to take the money; if she was his wife, he had no right to desert her, and would certainly have no right to marry another woman. His scheme was about to go to shipwreck on this rock, when another idea occurred to him.

"De lawyer say dat in one sense er de word de ole 'oman is my wife, an' in anudder sense er de word she ain't my wife. Ef I goes ter de Norf an' marry a w'ite 'oman, I ain't commit no brigamy, 'caze in dat sense er de word she ain't my wife; but ef I takes dis money, I ain't stealin' it, 'caze in dat sense er de word she is my wife. Dat 'splains all de trouble away."

Having reached this ingenious conclusion, uncle Wellington applied the hatchet vigorously, soon loosened the fastenings of the chest, and with trembling hands extracted from its depths a capacious blue cotton stocking. He emptied the stocking on the table. His first impulse was to take the whole, but again there arose in his mind a doubt—a very obtrusive, unreasonable doubt, but a doubt, nevertheless—of the absolute rectitude of his conduct; and after a moment's hesitation he hurriedly counted the money—it was in bills of small denominations—and found it to be about two hundred and fifty dollars. He then divided it into two piles of one hundred and twenty-five dollars each. He put one pile into his pocket, returned the remainder to the stocking, and replaced it where he had found it. He then closed the chest and shoved it under the bed. After having arranged the fire so that it could safely be left burning, he took a last look around the room, and went out into the moonlight, locking the door behind him, and hanging the key on a nail in the wall, where his wife would be likely to look for it. He then secured his valise from behind the bushes, and left the yard. As he passed by the wood-pile, he said to himself:—

"Well, I declar' ef I ain't done fergot ter tote in dat lighterd; I reckon de ole 'oman 'll ha' ter fetch it in herse'f dis time."

He hastened through the quiet streets, avoiding the few people who were abroad at that hour, and soon reached the railroad station, from which a North-bound train left at nine o'clock. He went around to the dark side of the train, and climbed into a second-class car, where he shrank into the darkest corner and turned his face away from the dim light of the single dirty lamp. There were no passengers in the car except one or two sleepy negroes, who had got on at some other station, and a white man who had gone into the car to smoke, accompanied by a gigantic bloodhound.

Finally the train crept out of the station. From the window uncle Wellington looked out upon the familiar cabins and turpentine stills, the new barrel factory, the brickyard where he had once worked for some time; and as the train rattled through the outskirts of the town, he saw gleaming in the moonlight the white headstones of the colored cemetery where his only daughter had been buried several years before.

Presently the conductor came around. Uncle Wellington had not bought a ticket, and the conductor collected a cash fare. He was not acquainted with uncle Wellington, but had just had a drink at the saloon near the depot, and felt at peace with all mankind.

"Where are you going, uncle?" he inquired carelessly.

Uncle Wellington's face assumed the ashen hue which does duty for pallor in dusky countenances, and his knees began to tremble. Controlling his voice as well as he could, he replied that he was going up to Jonesboro, the terminus of the railroad, to work for a gentleman at that place. He felt immensely relieved when the conductor pocketed the fare, picked up his lantern, and moved away. It was very unphilosophical and very absurd that a man who was only doing right should feel like a thief, shrink from the sight of other people, and lie instinctively. Fine distinctions were not in uncle Wellington's line, but he was struck by the unreasonableness of his feelings, and still more by the discomfort they caused him. By and by, however, the motion of the train made him drowsy; his thoughts all ran together in confusion; and he fell asleep with his head on his valise, and one hand in his pocket, clasped tightly around the roll of money.

2.

The train from Pittsburgh drew into the Union Depot at Groveland, Ohio, one morning in the spring of 187–, with bell ringing and engine puffing; and from a smoking-car emerged the form of uncle Wellington Braboy, a little dusty and travel-stained, and with a sleepy look about his eyes. He mingled in the crowd, and, valise in hand, moved toward the main exit from the depot. There were several tracks to be crossed, and more than once a watchman snatched him out of the way of a baggage-truck, or a train backing into the depot. He at length reached the door, beyond which, and as near as the regulations would permit, stood a number of hackmen, vociferously soliciting patronage. One of them, a colored man, soon secured several passengers. As he closed the door after the last one he turned to uncle Wellington, who stood near him on the sidewalk, looking about irresolutely.

"Is you goin' uptown?" asked the hackman, as he prepared to mount the box.

"Yas, suh."

"I'll take you up fo' a quahtah, ef you want ter git up here an' ride on de box wid me."

Uncle Wellington accepted the offer and mounted the box. The hackman whipped up his horses, the carriage climbed the steep hill leading up to the town, and the passengers inside were soon deposited at their hotels.

"Whereabouts do you want to go?" asked the hackman of uncle Wellington, when the carriage was emptied of its last passengers.

"I want ter go ter Brer Sam Williams's," said Wellington.

"What's his street an' number?"

Uncle Wellington did not know the street and number, and the hackman had to explain to him the mystery of numbered houses, to which he was a total stranger.

"Where is he from?" asked the hackman, "and what is his business?"

"He is f'm Norf Ca'lina," replied uncle Wellington, "an' makes his livin' w'ite-washin'."

"I reckon I knows de man," said the hackman. "I 'spec' he 's changed his name. De man I knows is name' Johnson. He b'longs ter my chu'ch. I 'm gwine out dat way ter git a passenger fer de ten o'clock train, an' I 'll take you by dere."

They followed one of the least handsome streets of the city for more than a mile, turned into a cross street, and drew up before a small frame house, from the front of which a sign, painted in white upon a black background, announced to the reading public, in letters inclined to each other at various angles, that whitewashing and kalsomining were "dun" there. A knock at the door brought out a slatternly looking colored woman. She had evidently been disturbed at her toilet, for she held a comb in one hand, and the hair on one side of her head stood out loosely, while on the other side it was braided close to her head. She called her husband, who proved to be the Patesville shoemaker's brother. The hackman introduced the traveler, whose name he had learned on the way out, collected his quarter, and drove away.

Mr. Johnson, the shoemaker's brother, welcomed uncle Wellington to Groveland, and listened with eager delight to the news of the old town, from which he himself had run away many years before, and followed the North Star to Groveland. He had changed his name from "Williams" to "Johnson," on account of the Fugitive Slave Law, which, at the time of his escape from bondage, had rendered it advisable for runaway slaves to court obscurity. After the war he had retained the adopted name. Mrs. Johnson prepared breakfast for her guest, who ate it with an appetite sharpened by his journey. After breakfast he went to bed, and slept until late in the afternoon.

After supper Mr. Johnson took uncle Wellington to visit some of the neighbors who had come from North Carolina before the war. They all expressed much pleasure at meeting "Mr. Braboy," a title which at first sounded a little odd to uncle Wellington. At home he had been "Wellin'ton," "Brer Wellin'ton," or "uncle Wellin'ton;" it was a novel experience to be called "Mister," and he set it down, with secret satisfaction, as one of the first fruits of Northern liberty.

"Would you lack ter look 'roun' de town a little?" asked Mr. Johnson at breakfast next morning. "I ain' got no job dis mawnin', an' I kin show you some er de sights."

Uncle Wellington acquiesced in this arrangement, and they walked up to the corner to the street-car line. In a few moments a car passed. Mr. Johnson jumped on the moving car, and uncle Wellington followed his example, at the risk of life or limb, as it was his first experience of street cars.

There was only one vacant seat in the car and that was between two white women in the forward end. Mr. Johnson motioned to the seat, but Wellington shrank from walking between those two rows of white people, to say nothing of sitting between the two women, so he remained standing in the rear part of the car. A moment later, as the car rounded a short curve, he was pitched sidewise into the lap of a stout woman magnificently attired in a ruffled blue calico gown. The lady colored up, and uncle Wellington, as he struggled to his feet amid the laughter of the passengers, was absolutely helpless with embarrassment, until the conductor came up behind him and pushed him toward the vacant place.

"Sit down, will you," he said; and before uncle Wellington could collect himself, he was seated between the two white women. Everybody in the car seemed to be looking at him. But he came to the conclusion, after he had pulled himself together and reflected a few moments, that he would find this method of locomotion pleasanter when he got used to it, and then he could score one more glorious privilege gained by his change of residence.

They got off at the public square, in the heart of the city, where there were flowers and statues, and fountains playing. Mr. Johnson pointed out the court-house, the post-office, the jail, and other public buildings fronting on the square. They visited the market near by, and from an elevated point, looked down upon the extensive lumber yards and factories that were the chief sources of the city's prosperity. Beyond these they could see the fleet of ships that lined the coal and iron ore docks of the harbor. Mr. Johnson, who was quite a fluent talker, enlarged upon the wealth and prosperity of the city; and Wellington, who had never before been in a town of more than three thousand inhabitants, manifested sufficient interest and wonder to satisfy the most exacting *cicerone*. They called at the office of a colored lawyer and member of the legislature, formerly from North Carolina, who, scenting a new constituent and a possible client, greeted the stranger warmly, and in flowing speech pointed out the superior advantages of life at the North, citing himself as an illustration of the possibilities of life in a country really free. As they wended their way homeward to dinner uncle Wellington, with quickened pulse and rising hopes, felt that this was indeed the promised land, and that it must be flowing with milk and honey.

Uncle Wellington remained at the residence of Mr. Johnson for several weeks before making any effort to find employment. He spent this period in looking about the city. The most commonplace things possessed for him the charm of novelty, and he had come prepared to admire. Shortly after his arrival, he had offered to pay for his board, intimating at the same time that he had plenty of money. Mr. Johnson declined to accept anything from him for board, and expressed himself as being only too proud to have Mr. Braboy remain in the house on the footing of an honored guest, until he had settled himself. He lightened in some degree, however, the burden of obligation under which a prolonged stay on these terms would have placed his guest, by soliciting from the latter occasional small loans, until uncle Wellington's roll of money began to lose its plumpness, and with an empty pocket staring him in the face, he felt the necessity of finding something to do.

During his residence in the city he had met several times his first acquaintance, Mr. Peterson, the hackman, who from time to time inquired how he was getting along. On one of these occasions Wellington mentioned his willingness to accept employment. As good luck would have it, Mr. Peterson knew of a vacant situation. He had formerly been coachman for a wealthy gentleman residing on Oakwood Avenue, but had resigned the situation to go into business for himself. His place had been filled by an Irishman, who had just been discharged for drunkenness, and the gentleman that very day had sent word to Mr. Peterson, asking him if he could recommend a competent and trustworthy coachman.

"Does you know anything erbout hosses?" asked Mr. Peterson.

"Yas, indeed, I does," said Wellington. "I wuz raise' 'mongs' hosses."

"I tol' my ole boss I 'd look out fer a man, an' ef you reckon you kin fill de 'quirements er de situation, I 'll take yo' roun' dere ter-morrer mornin'. You wants ter put on yo' bes' clothes an' slick up, fer dey 're partic'lar people. Ef you git de place I'll expec' you ter pay me fer de time I lose in 'tendin' ter yo' business, fer time is money in dis country, an' folks don't do much fer nuthin'."

Next morning Wellington blacked his shoes carefully, put on a clean collar, and with the aid of Mrs. Johnson tied his cravat in a jaunty bow which gave him quite a sprightly air and a much younger look than his years warranted. Mr. Peterson called for him at eight o'clock. After traversing several cross streets they turned into Oakwood Avenue and walked along the finest part of it for about half a mile. The handsome houses of this famous avenue, the stately trees, the wide-spreading lawns, dotted with flower beds, fountains and statuary, made up a picture so far surpassing anything in Wellington's experience as to fill him with an almost oppressive sense of its beauty.

"Hit looks lack hebben," he said softly.

"It's a pootty fine street," rejoined his companion, with a judicial air, "but I don't like dem big lawns. It's too much trouble ter keep de grass down. One er dem lawns is big enough to pasture a couple er cows."

They went down a street running at right angles to the avenue, and turned into the rear of the corner lot. A large building of pressed brick, trimmed with stone, loomed up before them.

"Do de gemman lib in dis house?" asked Wellington, gazing with awe at the front of the building.

"No, dat 's de barn," said Mr. Peterson with good-natured contempt; and leading the way past a clump of shrubbery to the dwelling-house, he went up the back steps and rang the door-bell.

The ring was answered by a buxom Irishwoman, of a natural freshness of complexion deepened to a fiery red by the heat of a kitchen range. Wellington thought he had seen her before, but his mind had received so many new impressions lately that it was a minute or two before he recognized in her the lady whose lap he had involuntarily occupied for a moment on his first day in Groveland.

"Faith," she exclaimed as she admitted them, "an' it 's mighty glad I am to see ye ag'in, Misther Payterson! An' how hev ye be'n, Misther Payterson, sence I see ye lahst?"

"Middlin' well, Mis' Flannigan, middlin' well, 'ceptin' a tech er de rheumatiz. S'pose you be'n doin' well as usual?"

"Oh yis, as well as a dacent woman could do wid a drunken baste about the place like the lahst coachman. O Misther Payterson, it would make yer heart bleed to see the way the spalpeen cut up a-Saturday! But Misther Todd discharged 'im the same avenin', widout a characther, bad 'cess to 'im, an' we 've had no coachman sence at all, at all. An' it's sorry I am—"

The lady's flow of eloquence was interrupted at this point by the appearance of Mr. Todd himself, who had been informed of the men's arrival. He asked some questions in regard to Wellington's qualifications and former experience, and in view of his recent arrival in the city was willing to accept Mr. Peterson's recommendation instead of a reference. He said a few words about the nature of the work, and stated his willingness to pay Wellington the wages formerly allowed Mr. Peterson, thirty dollars a month and board and lodging.

This handsome offer was eagerly accepted, and it was agreed that Wellington's term of service should begin immediately. Mr. Peterson, being familiar with the work, and financially interested, conducted the new coachman through the stables and showed him what he would have to do. The silver-mounted harness, the variety of carriages, the names of which he learned for the first time, the arrangements for feeding and watering the horses,—these appointments of a rich man's stable impressed Wellington very much, and he wondered that so much luxury should be wasted on mere horses. The room assigned to him, in the second story of the barn, was a finer apartment than he had ever slept in; and the salary attached to the situation was greater than the combined monthly earnings of himself and aunt Milly in their Southern home. Surely, he thought, his lines had fallen in pleasant places.

Under the stimulus of new surroundings Wellington applied himself diligently to work, and, with the occasional advice of Mr. Peterson, soon mastered the details of his employment. He found the female servants, with whom he took his meals, very amiable ladies. The cook, Mrs. Katie Flannigan, was a widow. Her husband, a sailor, had been lost at sea. She was a woman of many words, and when she was not lamenting the late Flannigan's loss,—according to her story he had been a model of all the virtues,—she would turn the batteries of her tongue against the former coachman. This gentleman, as Wellington gathered from frequent remarks dropped by Mrs. Flannigan, had paid her attentions clearly susceptible of a serious construction. These attentions had not borne their legitimate fruit, and she was still a widow unconsoled,—hence Mrs. Flannigan's tears. The housemaid was a plump, good-natured German girl, with a pronounced German accent. The presence on washdays of a Bohemian laundress, of recent importation, added another to the variety of ways in which the English tongue was mutilated in Mr. Todd's kitchen. Association with the white women drew out all the native gallantry of the mulatto, and Wellington developed quite a helpful turn. His politeness, his willingness to lend a hand in kitchen or laundry, and the fact that he was the only male servant on the place, combined to make him a prime favorite in the servants' quarters.

It was the general opinion among Wellington's acquaintances that he was a single man. He had come to the city alone, had never been heard to speak of a wife, and to personal questions bearing upon the subject of matrimony had always returned evasive answers. Though he had never questioned the correctness of the lawyer's opinion in regard to his slave marriage, his conscience had never been entirely at ease since his departure from the South, and any positive denial of his married condition would have stuck in his throat. The inference naturally drawn from his reticence in regard to the past, coupled with his expressed intention of settling permanently in Groveland, was that he belonged in the ranks of the unmarried, and was therefore legitimate game for any widow or old maid who could bring him down. As such game is bagged easiest at short range, he received numerous invitations to tea-parties, where he feasted on unlimited chicken and pound cake. He used to compare these viands with the plain fare often served by aunt Milly, and the result of the comparison was another item to the credit of the North upon his mental ledger. Several of the colored ladies who smiled upon him were blessed with good looks, and uncle Wellington, naturally of a susceptible temperament, as people of lively imagination are apt to be, would probably have fallen a victim to the charms of some woman of his own race, had it not been for a strong counter-attraction in the person of Mrs. Flannigan. The attentions of the lately discharged coachman had lighted anew the smouldering fires of her widowed heart, and awakened longings which still remained unsatisfied. She was thirty-five years old, and felt the need of some one else to love. She was not a woman of lofty ideals; with her a man was a man—

"For a' that an' a' that;"

and, aside from the accident of color, uncle Wellington was as personable a man as any of her acquaintance. Some people might have objected to his complexion; but then, Mrs. Flannigan argued, he was at least half white; and, this being the case, there was no good reason why he should be regarded as black.

Uncle Wellington was not slow to perceive Mrs. Flannigan's charms of person, and appreciated to the full the skill that prepared the choice tidbits reserved for his plate at dinner. The prospect of securing a white wife had been one of the principal inducements offered by a life at the North; but the awe of white people in which he had been reared was still too strong to permit his taking any active steps toward the object of his secret desire, had not the lady herself come to his assistance with a little of the native coquetry of her race.

"Ah, Misther Braboy," she said one evening when they sat at the supper table alone,—it was the second girl's afternoon off, and she had not come home to supper,—"it must be an awful lonesome life ye 've been afther l'adin', as a single man, wid no one to cook fer ye, or look afther ye."

"It are a kind er lonesome life, Mis' Flannigan, an' dat's a fac'. But sence I had de privilege er eatin' yo' cookin' an' 'joyin' yo' society, I ain' felt a bit lonesome."

"Yer flatthrin' me, Misther Braboy. An' even if ye mane it"—

"I means eve'y word of it, Mis' Flannigan."

"An' even if ye mane it, Misther Braboy, the time is liable to come when things'll be different; for service is uncertain, Misther Braboy. An' then you'll wish you had some nice, clean woman, 'at knowed how to cook an' wash an' iron, ter look afther ye, an' make yer life comfortable."

Uncle Wellington sighed, and looked at her languishingly.

"It 'u'd all be well ernuff, Mis' Flannigan, ef I had n' met you; but I don' know whar I 's ter fin' a colored lady w'at 'll begin ter suit me after habbin' libbed in de same house wid you."

"Colored lady, indade! Why, Misther Braboy, ye don't nade ter demane yerself by marryin' a colored lady—not but they're as good as anybody else, so long as they behave themselves. There's many a white woman 'u'd be glad ter git as fine a lookin' man as ye are."

"Now *you're* flattrin' *me*, Mis' Flannigan," said Wellington. But he felt a sudden and substantial increase in courage when she had spoken, and it was with astonishing ease that he found himself saying:—

"Dey ain' but one lady, Mis' Flannigan, dat could injuce me ter want ter change de lonesomeness er my singleness fer de 'sponsibilities er matermony, an' I 'm feared she 'd say no ef I 'd ax her."

"Ye 'd better ax her, Misther Braboy, an' not be wastin' time a-wond'rin'. Do I know the lady?"

"You knows 'er better 'n anybody else, Mis' Flannigan. *You* is de only lady I 'd be satisfied ter marry after knowin' you. Ef you casts me off I 'll spen' de rest er my days in lonesomeness an' mis'ry."

Mrs. Flannigan affected much surprise and embarrassment at this bold declaration.

"Oh, Misther Braboy," she said, covering him with a coy glance, "an' it 's rale 'shamed I am to hev b'en talkin' ter ye ez I hev. It looks as though I 'd b'en doin' the coortin'. I did n't drame that I 'd b'en able ter draw yer affections to mesilf."

"I 's loved you ever sence I fell in yo' lap on de street car de fus' day I wuz in Groveland," he said, as he moved his chair up closer to hers.

One evening in the following week they went out after supper to the residence of Rev. Cæsar Williams, pastor of the colored Baptist church, and, after the usual preliminaries, were pronounced man and wife.

3.

According to all his preconceived notions, this marriage ought to have been the acme of uncle Wellington's felicity. But he soon found that it was not without its drawbacks. On the following morning Mr. Todd was informed of the marriage. He had no special objection to it, or interest in it, except that he was opposed on principle to having husband and wife in his employment at the same time. As a consequence, Mrs. Braboy, whose place could be more easily filled than that of her husband, received notice that her services would not be required after the end of the month. Her husband was retained in his place as coachman.

Upon the loss of her situation Mrs. Braboy decided to exercise the married woman's prerogative of letting her husband support her. She rented the upper floor of a small house in an Irish neighborhood. The newly wedded pair furnished their rooms on the installment plan and began housekeeping.

There was one little circumstance, however, that interfered slightly with their enjoyment of that perfect freedom from care which ought to characterize a honeymoon. The people who owned the house and occupied the lower floor had rented the upper part to Mrs. Braboy in person, it never occurring to them that her husband could be other than a white man. When it became known that he was colored, the landlord, Mr. Dennis O'Flaherty, felt that he had been imposed upon, and, at the end of the first month, served notice upon his tenants to leave the premises. When Mrs. Braboy, with characteristic impetuosity, inquired the meaning of this proceeding, she was informed by Mr. O'Flaherty that he did not care to live in the same house "wid naygurs." Mrs. Braboy resented the epithet with more warmth than dignity, and for a brief space of time the air was green with choice specimens of brogue, the altercation barely ceasing before it had reached the point of blows.

It was quite clear that the Braboys could not longer live comfortably in Mr. O'Flaherty's house, and they soon vacated the premises, first letting the rent get a couple of weeks in arrears as a punishment to the too fastidious landlord. They moved to a small house on Hackman Street, a favorite locality with colored people.

For a while, affairs ran smoothly in the new home. The colored people seemed, at first, well enough disposed toward Mrs. Braboy, and she made quite a large acquaintance among them. It was difficult, however, for Mrs. Braboy to divest herself of the consciousness that she was white, and therefore superior to her neighbors. Occasional words and acts by which she manifested this feeling were noticed and resented by her keen-eyed and sensitive colored neighbors. The result was a slight coolness between them. That her few white neighbors did not visit her, she naturally and no doubt correctly imputed to disapproval of her matrimonial relations.

Under these circumstances, Mrs. Braboy was left a good deal to her own company. Owing to lack of opportunity in early life, she was not a woman of many resources, either mental or moral. It is therefore not strange that, in order to relieve her loneliness, she should occasionally have recourse to a glass of beer, and, as the habit grew upon her, to still stronger stimulants. Uncle Wellington himself was no teetotaler, and did not interpose any objection so long as she kept her potations within reasonable limits, and was apparently none the worse for them; indeed, he sometimes joined her in a glass. On one of these occasions he drank a little too much, and, while driving the ladies of Mr. Todd's family to the opera, ran against a lamp-post and overturned the carriage, to the serious discomposure of the ladies' nerves, and at the cost of his situation.

A coachman discharged under such circumstances is not in the best position for procuring employment at his calling, and uncle Wellington, under the pressure of need, was obliged to seek some other means of livelihood. At the suggestion of his friend Mr. Johnson, he bought a whitewash brush, a peck of lime, a couple of pails, and a hand-cart, and began work as a whitewasher. His first efforts were very crude, and for a while he lost a customer in every person he worked for. He nevertheless managed to pick up a living during the spring and summer months, and to support his wife and himself in comparative comfort.

The approach of winter put an end to the whitewashing season, and left uncle Wellington dependent for support upon occasional jobs of unskilled labor. The income derived from these was very uncertain, and Mrs. Braboy was at length driven, by stress of circumstances, to the washtub, that last refuge of honest, able-bodied poverty, in all countries where the use of clothing is conventional.

The last state of uncle Wellington was now worse than the first. Under the soft firmness of aunt Milly's rule, he had not been required to do a great deal of work, prompt and cheerful obedience being chiefly what was expected of him. But matters were very different here. He had not only to bring in the coal and water, but to rub the clothes and turn the wringer, and to humiliate himself before the public by emptying the tubs and hanging out the wash in full view of the neighbors; and he had to deliver the clothes when laundered.

At times Wellington found himself wondering if his second marriage had been a wise one. Other circumstances combined to change in some degree his once rose-colored conception of life at the North. He had believed that all men were equal in this favored locality, but he discovered more degrees of inequality than he had ever perceived at the South. A colored man might be as good as a white man in theory, but neither of them was of any special consequence without money, or talent, or position. Uncle Wellington found a great many privileges open to him at the North, but he had not been educated to the point where he could appreciate them or take advantage of them; and the enjoyment of many of them was expensive, and, for that reason alone, as far beyond his reach as they had ever been. When he once began to admit even the possibility of a mistake on his part, these considerations presented themselves to his mind with increasing force. On occasions when Mrs. Braboy would require of him some unusual physical exertion, or when too frequent applications to the bottle had loosened her tongue, uncle Wellington's mind would revert, with a remorseful twinge of conscience, to the *dolce far niente* of his Southern home; a film would come over his eyes and brain, and, instead of the red-faced Irishwoman opposite him, he could see the black but comely disk of aunt Milly's countenance bending over the washtub; the elegant brogue of Mrs. Braboy would deliquesce into the soft dialect of North Carolina; and he would only be aroused from this blissful reverie by a wet shirt or a handful of suds thrown into his face, with which gentle reminder his wife would recall his attention to the duties of the moment.

There came a time, one day in spring, when there was no longer any question about it: uncle Wellington was desperately homesick.

Liberty, equality, privileges,—all were but as dust in the balance when weighed against his longing for old scenes and faces. It was the natural reaction in the mind of a middle-aged man who had tried to force the current of a sluggish existence into a new and radically different channel. An active, industrious man, making the change in early life, while there was time to spare for the waste of adaptation, might have found in the new place more favorable conditions than in the old. In Wellington age and temperament combined to prevent the success of the experiment; the spirit of enterprise and ambition into which he had been temporarily galvanized could no longer prevail against the inertia of old habits of life and thought.

One day when he had been sent to deliver clothes he performed his errand quickly, and boarding a passing street car, paid one of his very few five-cent pieces to ride down to the office of the Hon. Mr. Brown, the colored lawyer whom he had visited when he first came to the city, and who was well known to him by sight and reputation.

"Mr. Brown," he said, "I ain' gitt'n' 'long very well wid my ole 'oman."

"What's the trouble?" asked the lawyer, with business-like curtness, for he did not scent much of a fee.

"Well, de main trouble is she doan treat me right. An' den she gits drunk, an' wuss'n dat, she lays vi'lent han's on me. I kyars de marks er dat 'oman on my face now."

He showed the lawyer a long scratch on the neck.

"Why don't you defend yourself?"

"You don' know Mis' Braboy, suh; you don' know dat 'oman," he replied, with a shake of the head. "Some er dese yer w'ite women is monst'us strong in de wris'."

"Well, Mr. Braboy, it's what you might have expected when you turned your back on your own people and married a white woman. You weren't content with being a slave to the white folks once, but you must try it again. Some people never know when they've got enough. I don't see that there's any help for you; unless," he added suggestively, "you had a good deal of money."

"'Pears ter me I heared somebody say sence I be'n up heah, dat it wuz 'gin de law fer w'ite folks an' colored folks ter marry."

"That was once the law, though it has always been a dead letter in Groveland. In fact, it was the law when you got married, and until I introduced a bill in the legislature last fall to repeal it. But even that law did n't hit cases like yours. It was unlawful to make such a marriage, but it was a good marriage when once made."

"I don' jes' git dat th'oo my head," said Wellington, scratching that member as though to make a hole for the idea to enter.

"It's quite plain, Mr. Braboy. It's unlawful to kill a man, but when he 's killed he 's just as dead as though the law permitted it. I'm afraid you haven't much of a case, but if you 'll go to work and get twenty-five dollars together, I 'll see what I can do for you. We may be able to pull a case through on the ground of extreme cruelty. I might even start the case if you brought in ten dollars."

Wellington went away sorrowfully. The laws of Ohio were very little more satisfactory than those of North Carolina. And as for the ten dollars,—the lawyer might as well have told him to bring in the moon, or a deed for the Public Square. He felt very, very low as he hurried back home to supper, which he would have to go without if he were not on hand at the usual supper-time.

But just when his spirits were lowest, and his outlook for the future most hopeless, a measure of relief was at hand. He noticed, when he reached home, that Mrs. Braboy was a little preoccupied, and did not abuse him as vigorously as he expected after so long an absence. He also perceived the smell of strange tobacco in the house, of a better grade than he could afford to use. He thought perhaps some one had come in to see about the washing; but he was too glad of a respite from Mrs. Braboy's rhetoric to imperil it by indiscreet questions.

Next morning she gave him fifty cents.

"Braboy," she said, "ye 've be'n helpin' me nicely wid the washin', an' I 'm going ter give ye a holiday. Ye can take yer hook an' line an' go fishin' on the breakwater. I 'll fix ye a lunch, an' ye need n't come back till night. An' there's half a dollar; ye can buy yerself a pipe er terbacky. But be careful an' don't waste it," she added, for fear she was overdoing the thing.

Uncle Wellington was overjoyed at this change of front on the part of Mrs. Braboy; if she would make it permanent he did not see why they might not live together very comfortably.

The day passed pleasantly down on the breakwater. The weather was agreeable, and the fish bit freely. Towards evening Wellington started home with a bunch of fish that no angler need have been ashamed of. He looked forward to a good warm supper; for even if something should have happened during the day to alter his wife's mood for the worse, any ordinary variation would be more than balanced by the substantial addition of food to their larder. His mouth watered at the thought of the finny beauties sputtering in the frying-pan.

He noted, as he approached the house, that there was no smoke coming from the chimney. This only disturbed him in connection with the matter of supper. When he entered the gate he observed further that the window-shades had been taken down.

"'Spec' de ole 'oman's been house-cleanin'," he said to himself. "I wonder she did n' make me stay an' he'p 'er."

He went round to the rear of the house and tried the kitchen door. It was locked. This was somewhat of a surprise, and disturbed still further his expectations in regard to supper. When he had found the key and opened the door, the gravity of his next discovery drove away for the time being all thoughts of eating.

The kitchen was empty. Stove, table, chairs, wash-tubs, pots and pans, had vanished as if into thin air.

"Fo' de Lawd's sake!" he murmured in open-mouthed astonishment.

He passed into the other room,—they had only two,—which had served as bedroom and sitting-room. It was as bare as the first, except that in the middle of the floor were piled uncle Wellington's clothes. It was not a large pile, and on the top of it lay a folded piece of yellow wrapping-paper.

Wellington stood for a moment as if petrified. Then he rubbed his eyes and looked around him.

"W'at do dis mean?" he said. "Is I er-dreamin', er does I see w'at I 'pears ter see?" He glanced down at the bunch of fish which he still held. "Heah 's de fish; heah 's de house; heah I is; but whar 's de ole 'oman, an' whar 's de fu'niture? *I* can't figure out w'at dis yer all means."

He picked up the piece of paper and unfolded it. It was written on one side. Here was the obvious solution of the mystery,—that is, it would have been obvious if he could have read it; but he could not, and so his fancy continued to play upon the subject. Perhaps the house had been robbed, or the furniture taken back by the seller, for it had not been entirely paid for.

Finally he went across the street and called to a boy in a neighbor's yard.

"Does you read writin', Johnnie?"

"Yes, sir, I 'm in the seventh grade."

"Read dis yer paper fuh me."

The youngster took the note, and with much labor read the following:—

"Mr. Braboy:

"In lavin' ye so suddint I have ter say that my first husban' has turned up unixpected, having been saved onbeknownst ter me from a wathry grave an' all the money wasted I spint fer masses fer ter rist his sole an' I wish I had it back I feel it my dooty ter go an' live wid 'im again. I take the furnacher because I bought it yer close is yors I leave them and wishin' yer the best of luck I remane oncet yer wife but now agin

"Mrs. Katie Flannigan.

"N.B. I 'm lavin town terday so it won't be no use lookin' fer me."

On inquiry uncle Wellington learned from the boy that shortly after his departure in the morning a white man had appeared on the scene, followed a little later by a moving-van, into which the furniture had been loaded and carried away. Mrs. Braboy, clad in her best clothes, had locked the door, and gone away with the strange white man.

The news was soon noised about the street. Wellington swapped his fish for supper and a bed at a neighbor's, and during the evening learned from several sources that the strange white man had been at his house the afternoon of the day before. His neighbors intimated that they thought Mrs. Braboy's departure a good riddance of bad rubbish, and Wellington did not dispute the proposition.

Thus ended the second chapter of Wellington's matrimonial experiences. His wife's departure had been the one thing needful to convince him, beyond a doubt, that he had been a great fool. Remorse and homesickness forced him to the further conclusion that he had been knave as well as fool, and had treated aunt Milly shamefully. He was not altogether a bad old man, though very weak and erring, and his better nature now gained the ascendency. Of course his disappointment had a great deal to do with his remorse; most people do not perceive the hideousness of sin until they begin to reap its consequences. Instead of the beautiful Northern life he had dreamed of, he found himself stranded, penniless, in a strange land, among people whose sympathy he had forfeited, with no one to lean upon, and no refuge from the storms of life. His outlook was very dark, and there sprang up within him a wild longing to get back to North Carolina,—back to the little whitewashed cabin, shaded with china and mulberry trees; back to the wood-pile and the garden; back to the old cronies with whom he had swapped lies and tobacco for so many years. He longed to kiss the rod of aunt Milly's domination. He had purchased his liberty at too great a price.

The next day he disappeared from Groveland. He had announced his departure only to Mr. Johnson, who sent his love to his relations in Patesville.

It would be painful to record in detail the return journey of uncle Wellington—Mr. Braboy no longer—to his native town; how many weary miles he walked; how many times he risked his life on railroad tracks and between freight cars; how he depended for sustenance on the grudging hand of back-door charity. Nor would it be profitable or delicate to mention any slight deviations from the path of rectitude, as judged by conventional standards, to which he may occasionally have been driven by a too insistent hunger; or to refer in the remotest degree to a compulsory sojourn of thirty days in a city where he had no references, and could show no visible means of support. True charity will let these purely personal matters remain locked in the bosom of him who suffered them.

4.

Just fifteen months after the date when uncle Wellington had left North Carolina, a weather-beaten figure entered the town of Patesville after nightfall, following the railroad track from the north. Few would have recognized in the hungry-looking old brown tramp, clad in dusty rags and limping along with bare feet, the trim-looking middle-aged mulatto who so few months before had taken the train from Patesville for the distant North; so, if he had but known it, there was no necessity for him to avoid the main streets and sneak around by unfrequented paths to reach the old place on the other side of the town. He encountered nobody that he knew, and soon the familiar shape of the little cabin rose before him. It stood distinctly outlined against the sky, and the light streaming from the half-opened shutters showed it to be occupied. As he drew nearer, every familiar detail of the place appealed to his memory and to his affections, and his heart went out to the old home and the old wife. As he came nearer still, the odor of fried chicken floated out upon the air and set his mouth to watering, and awakened unspeakable longings in his half-starved stomach.

At this moment, however, a fearful thought struck him; suppose the old woman had taken legal advice and married again during his absence? Turn about would have been only fair play. He opened the gate softly, and with his heart in his mouth approached the window on tiptoe and looked in.

A cheerful fire was blazing on the hearth, in front of which sat the familiar form of aunt Milly—and another, at the sight of whom uncle Wellington's heart sank within him. He knew the other person very well; he had sat there more than once before uncle Wellington went away. It was the minister of the church to which his wife belonged. The preacher's former visits, however, had signified nothing more than pastoral courtesy, or appreciation of good eating. His presence now was of serious portent; for Wellington recalled, with acute alarm, that the elder's wife had died only a few weeks before his own departure for the North. What was the occasion of his presence this evening? Was it merely a pastoral call? or was he courting? or had aunt Milly taken legal advice and married the elder?

Wellington remembered a crack in the wall, at the back of the house, through which he could see and hear, and quietly stationed himself there.

"Dat chicken smells mighty good, Sis' Milly," the elder was saying; "I can't fer de life er me see why dat low-down husban' er yo'n could ever run away f'm a cook like you. It's one er de beatenis' things I ever heared. How he could lib wid you an' not 'preciate you *I* can't understan', no indeed I can't."

Aunt Milly sighed. "De trouble wid Wellin'ton wuz," she replied, "dat he did n' know when he wuz well off. He wuz alluz wishin' fer change, er studyin' 'bout somethin' new."

"Ez fer me," responded the elder earnestly, "I likes things what has be'n prove' an' tried an' has stood de tes', an' I can't 'magine how anybody could spec' ter fin' a better housekeeper er cook dan you is, Sis' Milly. I'm a gittin' mighty lonesome sence my wife died. De Good Book say it is not good fer man ter lib alone, en it 'pears ter me dat you an' me mought git erlong tergether monst'us well."

Wellington's heart stood still, while he listened with strained attention. Aunt Milly sighed.

"I ain't denyin', elder, but what I've be'n kinder lonesome myse'f fer quite a w'ile, an' I doan doubt dat w'at de Good Book say 'plies ter women as well as ter men."

"You kin be sho' it do," averred the elder, with professional authoritativeness; "yas 'm, you kin be cert'n sho'."

"But, of co'se," aunt Milly went on, "havin' los' my ole man de way I did, it has tuk me some time fer ter git my feelin's straighten' out like dey oughter be."

"I kin 'magine yo' feelin's, Sis' Milly," chimed in the elder sympathetically, "w'en you come home dat night an' foun' yo' chist broke open, an' yo' money gone dat you had wukked an' slaved fuh f'm mawnin' 'tel night, year in an' year out, an' w'en you foun' dat no-'count nigger gone wid his clo's an' you lef' all alone in de worl' ter scuffle 'long by yo'self."

"Yas, elder," responded aunt Milly, "I wa'n't used right. An' den w'en I heared 'bout his goin' ter de lawyer ter fin' out 'bout a defoce, an' w'en I heared w'at de lawyer said 'bout my not bein' his wife 'less he wanted me, it made me so mad, I made up my min' dat ef he ever put his foot on my do'sill ag'in, I 'd shet de do' in his face an' tell 'im ter go back whar he come f'm."

To Wellington, on the outside, the cabin had never seemed so comfortable, aunt Milly never so desirable, chicken never so appetizing, as at this moment when they seemed slipping away from his grasp forever.

"Yo' feelin's does you credit, Sis' Milly," said the elder, taking her hand, which for a moment she did not withdraw. "An' de way fer you ter close yo' do' tightes' ag'inst 'im is ter take me in his place. He ain' got no claim on you no mo'. He tuk his ch'ice 'cordin' ter w'at de lawyer tol' 'im, an' 'termine' dat he wa'n't yo' husban'. Ef he wa'n't yo' husban', he had no right ter take yo' money, an' ef he comes back here ag'in you kin hab 'im tuck up an' sent ter de penitenchy fer stealin' it."

Uncle Wellington's knees, already weak from fasting, trembled violently beneath him. The worst that he had feared was now likely to happen. His only hope of safety lay in flight, and yet the scene within so fascinated him that he could not move a step.

"It 'u'd serve him right," exclaimed aunt Milly indignantly, "ef he wuz sent ter de penitenchy fer life! Dey ain't nuthin' too mean ter be done ter 'im. What did I ever do dat he should use me like he did?"

The recital of her wrongs had wrought upon aunt Milly's feelings so that her voice broke, and she wiped her eyes with her apron.

The elder looked serenely confident, and moved his chair nearer hers in order the better to play the rôle of comforter. Wellington, on the outside, felt so mean that the darkness of the night was scarcely sufficient to hide him; it would be no more than right if the earth were to open and swallow him up.

"An' yet aftuh all, elder," said Milly with a sob, "though I knows you is a better man, an' would treat me right, I wuz so use' ter dat ole nigger, an' libbed wid 'im so long, dat ef he 'd open dat do' dis minute an' walk in, I 'm feared I 'd be foolish ernuff an' weak ernuff to forgive 'im an' take 'im back ag'in."

With a bound, uncle Wellington was away from the crack in the wall. As he ran round the house he passed the wood-pile and snatched up an armful of pieces. A moment later he threw open the door.

"Ole 'oman," he exclaimed, "here's dat wood you tol' me ter fetch in! Why, elder," he said to the preacher, who had started from his seat with surprise, "w'at's yo' hurry? Won't you stay an' hab some supper wid us?"

SOURCE: Charles W. Chesnutt. *The Wife of His Youth and Other Stories of the Color Line*. Boston and New York: Houghton, Mifflin and Company, 1899.

BOOKER T. WASHINGTON

Booker T. Washington (1856–1915), who gave himself the last name Washington as a schoolboy, was born a slave in Virginia. One of the most important figures in American history, he has been esteemed as an educator and denigrated as a political compromiser. His autobiography, in any case, is fascinating and informative. He here tells of his family's move to West Virginia, his work in a coal mine, and his passion for learning to read. Whatever the moral of his story, he writes, "I have great faith in the power and influence of facts."

From *Up from Slavery* (1901)

Chapter 2: Boyhood Days

After the coming of freedom there were two points upon which practically all the people on our place were agreed, and I find that this was generally true throughout the South: that they must change their names, and that they must leave the old plantation for at least a few days or weeks in order that they might really feel sure that they were free.

In some way a feeling got among the coloured people that it was far from proper for them to bear the surname of their former owners, and a great many of them took other surnames. This was one of the first signs of freedom. When they were slaves, a coloured person was simply called "John" or "Susan." There was seldom occasion for more than the use of the one name. If "John" or "Susan" belonged to a white man by the name of "Hatcher," sometimes he was called "John Hatcher," or as often "Hatcher's John." But there was a feeling that "John Hatcher" or "Hatcher's John" was not the proper title by which to denote a freeman; and so in many cases "John Hatcher" was changed to "John S. Lincoln" or "John S. Sherman," the initial "S" standing for no name, it being simply a part of what the coloured man proudly called his "entitles."

As I have stated, most of the coloured people left the old plantation for a short while at least, so as to be sure, it seemed, that they could leave and try their freedom on to see how it felt. After they had remained away for a time, many of the older slaves, especially, returned to their old homes and made some kind of contract with their former owners by which they remained on the estate.

My mother's husband, who was the stepfather of my brother John and myself, did not belong to the same owners as did my mother. In fact, he seldom came to our plantation. I remember seeing him there perhaps once a year, that being about Christmas time. In some way, during the war, by running away and following the Federal soldiers, it seems, he found his way into the new state of West Virginia. As soon as freedom was declared, he sent for my mother to come to the Kanawha Valley, in West Virginia. At that time a journey from Virginia over the mountains to West Virginia was rather a tedious and in some cases a painful undertaking. What little clothing and few household goods we had were placed in a cart, but the children walked the greater portion of the distance, which was several hundred miles.

I do not think any of us ever had been very far from the plantation, and the taking of a long journey into another state was quite an event. The parting from our former owners and the members of our own race on the plantation was a serious occasion. From the time of our parting till their death we kept up a correspondence with the older members of the family, and in later years we have kept in touch with those who were the younger members. We were several weeks making the trip, and most of the time we slept in the open air and did our cooking over a log fire out-of-doors. One night I recall that we camped near an abandoned log cabin, and my mother decided to build a fire in that for cooking, and afterward to make a "pallet" on the floor for our sleeping. Just as the fire had gotten well started a large black snake fully a yard and a half long dropped down the chimney and ran out on the floor. Of course we at once abandoned that cabin. Finally we reached our destination—a little town called Malden, which is about five miles from Charleston, the present capital of the state.

At that time salt-mining was the great industry in that part of West Virginia, and the little town of Malden was right in the midst of the salt-furnaces. My stepfather had already secured a job at a salt-furnace, and he had also secured a little cabin for us to live in. Our new house was no better than the one we had left on the old plantation in Virginia. In fact, in one respect it was worse. Notwithstanding the poor condition of our plantation cabin, we were at all times sure of pure air. Our new home was in the midst of a cluster of cabins crowded closely together, and as there were no sanitary regulations, the filth about the cabins was often intolerable. Some of our neighbours were coloured people, and some were the poorest and most ignorant and degraded white people. It was a motley mixture. Drinking, gambling, quarrels, fights, and shockingly immoral practices were frequent. All who lived in the little town were in one way or another connected with the salt business. Though I was a mere child, my stepfather put me and my brother at work in one of the furnaces. Often I began work as early as four o'clock in the morning.

The first thing I ever learned in the way of book knowledge was while working in this salt-furnace. Each salt-packer had his barrels marked with a certain number. The number allotted to my stepfather was "18." At the close of the day's work the boss of the packers would come around and put "18" on each of our barrels, and I soon learned to recognize that figure wherever I saw it, and after a while got to the point where I could make that figure, though I knew nothing about any other figures or letters.

From the time that I can remember having any thoughts about anything, I recall that I had an intense longing to learn to read. I determined, when quite a small child, that, if I accomplished nothing else in life, I would in some way get enough education to enable me to read common books and newspapers. Soon after we got settled in some manner in our new cabin in West Virginia, I induced my mother to get hold of a book for me. How or where she got it I do not know, but in some way she procured an old copy of Webster's "blue-back" spelling-book, which contained the alphabet, followed by such meaningless words as "ab," "ba," "ca," "da." I began at once to devour this book, and I think that it was the first one I ever had in my hands. I had learned from somebody that the way to begin to read was to learn the alphabet, so I tried in all the ways I could think of to learn it,—all of course without a teacher, for I could find no one to teach me. At that time there was not a single member of my race anywhere near us who could read, and I was too timid to approach any of the white people. In some way, within a few weeks, I mastered the greater portion of the alphabet. In all my efforts to learn to read my mother shared fully my ambition, and sympathized with me and aided me in every way that she could. Though she was totally ignorant, so far as mere book knowledge was concerned, she had high ambitions for her children, and a large fund of good, hard, common sense which seemed to enable her to meet and master every situation. If I have done anything in life worth attention, I feel sure that I inherited the disposition from my mother.

In the midst of my struggles and longing for an education, a young coloured boy who had learned to read in the state of Ohio came to Malden. As soon as the coloured people found out that he could read, a newspaper was secured, and at the close of nearly every day's work this young man would be surrounded by a group of men and women who were anxious to hear him read the news contained in the papers. How I used to envy this man! He seemed to me to be the one young man in all the world who ought to be satisfied with his attainments.

About this time the question of having some kind of a school opened for the coloured children in the village began to be discussed by members of the race. As it would be the first school for Negro children that had ever been opened in that part of Virginia, it was, of course, to be a great event, and the discussion excited the widest interest. The most perplexing question was where to find a teacher. The young man from Ohio who had learned to read the papers was considered, but his age was against him. In the midst of the discussion about a teacher, another young coloured man from Ohio, who had been a soldier, in some way found his way into town. It was soon learned that he possessed considerable education, and he was engaged by the coloured people to teach their first school. As yet no free schools had been started for coloured people in that section, hence each family agreed to pay a certain amount per month, with the understanding that the teacher was to "board 'round"—that is, spend a day with each family. This was not bad for the teacher, for each family tried to provide the very best on the day the teacher was to be its guest. I recall that I looked forward with an anxious appetite to the "teacher's day" at our little cabin.

This experience of a whole race beginning to go to school for the first time, presents one of the most interesting studies that has ever occurred in connection with the development of any race. Few people who were not right in the midst of the scenes can form any exact idea of the intense desire which the people of my race showed for an education. As I have stated, it was a whole race trying to go to school. Few were too young, and none too old, to make the attempt to learn. As fast as any kind of teachers could be secured, not only were day-schools filled, but night-schools as well. The great ambition of the older people was to try to learn to read the Bible before they died. With this end in view, men and women who were fifty or seventy-five years old would often be found in the night-school. Sunday-schools were formed soon after freedom, but the principal book studied in the Sunday-school was the spelling-book. Day-school, night-school, Sunday-school, were always crowded, and often many had to be turned away for want of room.

The opening of the school in the Kanawha Valley, however, brought to me one of the keenest disappointments that I ever experienced. I had been working in a salt-furnace for several months, and my stepfather had discovered that I had a financial value, and so, when the school opened, he decided that he could not spare me from my work. This decision seemed to cloud my every ambition. The disappointment was made all the more severe by reason of the fact that my place of work was where I could see the happy children passing to and from school, mornings and afternoons. Despite this disappointment, however, I determined that I would learn something, anyway. I applied myself with greater earnestness than ever to the mastering of what was in the "blue-back" speller.

My mother sympathized with me in my disappointment, and sought to comfort me in all the ways she could, and to help me find a way to learn. After a while I succeeded in making arrangements with the teacher to give me some lessons at night, after the day's work was done. These night lessons were so welcome that I think I learned more at night than the other children did during the day. My own experiences in the night-school gave me faith in the night-school idea, with which, in after years, I had to do both at Hampton and Tuskegee. But my boyish heart was still set upon going to the day-school, and I let no opportunity slip to push my case. Finally I won, and was permitted to go to the school in the day for a few months, with the understanding that I was to rise early in the morning and work in the furnace till nine o'clock, and return immediately after school closed in the afternoon for at least two more hours of work.

The schoolhouse was some distance from the furnace, and as I had to work till nine o'clock, and the school opened at nine, I found myself in a difficulty. School would always be begun before I reached it, and sometimes my class had recited. To get around this difficulty I yielded to a temptation for which most people, I suppose, will condemn me; but since it is a fact, I might as well state it. I have great faith in the power and influence of facts. It is seldom that anything is permanently gained by holding back a fact. There was a large clock in a little office in the furnace. This clock, of course, all the hundred or more workmen depended upon to regulate their hours of beginning and ending the day's work. I got the idea that the way for me to reach school on time was to move the clock hands from half-past eight up to the nine o'clock mark. This I found myself doing morning after morning, till the furnace "boss" discovered that something was wrong, and locked the clock in a case. I did not mean to inconvenience anybody. I simply meant to reach that schoolhouse in time.

When, however, I found myself at the school for the first time, I also found myself confronted with two other difficulties. In the first place, I found that all of the other children wore hats or caps on their heads, and I had neither hat nor cap. In fact, I do not remember that up to the time of going to school I had ever worn any kind of covering upon my head, nor do I recall that either I or anybody else had even thought anything about the need of covering for my head. But, of course, when I saw how all the other boys were dressed, I began to feel quite uncomfortable. As usual, I put the case before my mother, and she explained to me that she had no money with which to buy a "store hat," which was a rather new institution at that time among the members of my race and was considered quite the thing for young and old to own, but that she would find a way to help me out of the difficulty. She accordingly got two pieces of "homespun" (jeans) and sewed them together, and I was soon the proud possessor of my first cap.

The lesson that my mother taught me in this has always remained with me, and I have tried as best I could to teach it to others. I have always felt proud, whenever I think of the incident, that my mother had strength of character enough not to be led into the temptation of seeming to be that which she was not—of trying to impress my schoolmates and others with the fact that she was able to buy me a "store hat" when she was not. I have always felt proud that she refused to go into debt for that which she did not have the money to pay for. Since that time I have owned many kinds of caps and hats, but never one of which I have felt so proud of as the cap made of the two pieces of cloth sewed together by my mother. I have noted the fact, but without satisfaction, I need not add, that several of the boys who began their careers with "store hats" and who were my schoolmates and used to join in the sport that was made of me because I had only a "homespun" cap, have ended their careers in the penitentiary, while others are not able now to buy any kind of hat.

My second difficulty was with regard to my name, or rather *a* name. From the time when I could remember anything, I had been called simply "Booker." Before going to school it had never occurred to me that it was needful or appropriate to have an additional name. When I heard the school-roll called, I noticed that all of the children had at least two names, and some of them indulged in what seemed to me the extravagance of having three. I was in deep perplexity, because I knew that the teacher would demand of me at least two names, and I had only one. By the time the occasion came for the enrolling of my name, an idea occurred to me which I thought would make me equal to the situation; and so, when the teacher asked me what my full name was, I calmly told him "Booker Washington," as if I had been called by that name all my life; and by that name I have since been known. Later in my life I found that my mother had given me the name of "Booker Taliaferro" soon after I was born, but in some way that part of my name seemed to disappear and for a long while was forgotten, but as soon as I found out about it I revived it, and made my full name "Booker Taliaferro Washington." I think there are not many men in our country who have had the privilege of naming themselves in the way that I have.

More than once I have tried to picture myself in the position of a boy or man with an honoured and distinguished ancestry which I could trace back through a period of hundreds of years, and who had not only inherited a name, but fortune and a proud family homestead; and yet I have sometimes had the feeling that if I had inherited these, and had been a member of a more popular race, I should have been inclined to yield to the temptation of depending upon my ancestry and my colour to do that for me which I should do for myself. Years ago I resolved that because I had no ancestry myself I would leave a record of which my children would be proud, and which might encourage them to still higher effort.

The world should not pass judgment upon the Negro, and especially the Negro youth, too quickly or too harshly. The Negro boy has obstacles, discouragements, and temptations to battle with that are little known to those not situated as he is. When a white boy undertakes a task, it is taken for granted that he will succeed. On the other hand, people are usually surprised if the Negro boy does not fail. In a word, the Negro youth starts out with the presumption against him.

The influence of ancestry, however, is important in helping forward any individual or race, if too much reliance is not placed upon it. Those who constantly direct attention to the Negro youth's moral weaknesses, and compare his advancement with that of white youths, do not consider the influence of the memories which cling about the old family homesteads. I have no idea, as I have stated elsewhere, who my grandmother was. I have, or have had, uncles and aunts and cousins, but I have no knowledge as to where most of them are. My case will illustrate that of hundreds of thousands of black people in every part of our country. The very fact that the white boy is conscious that, if he fails in life, he will disgrace the whole family record, extending back through many generations, is of tremendous value in helping him to resist temptations. The fact that the individual has behind and surrounding him proud family history and connection serves as a stimulus to help him to overcome obstacles when striving for success.

The time that I was permitted to attend school during the day was short, and my attendance was irregular. It was not long before I had to stop attending day-school altogether, and devote all of my time again to work. I resorted to the night-school again. In fact, the greater part of the education I secured in my boyhood was gathered through the night-school after my day's work was done. I had difficulty often in securing a satisfactory teacher. Sometimes, after I had secured some one to teach me at night, I would find, much to my disappointment, that the teacher knew but little more than I did. Often I would have to walk several miles at night in order to recite my night-school lessons. There was never a time in my youth, no matter how dark and discouraging the days might be, when one resolve did not continually remain with me, and that was a determination to secure an education at any cost.

Soon after we moved to West Virginia, my mother adopted into our family, notwithstanding our poverty, an orphan boy, to whom afterward we gave the name of James B. Washington. He has ever since remained a member of the family.

After I had worked in the salt-furnace for some time, work was secured for me in a coal-mine which was operated mainly for the purpose of securing fuel for the salt-furnace. Work in the coal-mine I always dreaded. One reason for this was that any one who worked in a coal-mine was always unclean, at least while at work, and it was a very hard job to get one's skin clean after the day's work was over. Then it was fully a mile from the opening of the coal-mine to the face of the coal, and all, of course, was in the blackest darkness. I do not believe that one ever experiences anywhere else such darkness as he does in a coal-mine. The mine was divided into a large number of different "rooms" or departments, and, as I never was able to learn the location of all these "rooms," I many times found myself lost in the mine. To add to the horror of being lost, sometimes my light would go out, and then, if I did not happen to have a match, I would wander about in the darkness until by chance I found some one to give me a light. The work was not only hard, but it was dangerous. There was always the danger of being blown to pieces by a premature explosion of powder, or of being crushed by falling slate. Accidents from one or the other of these causes were frequently occurring, and this kept me in constant fear. Many children of the tenderest years were compelled then, as is now true, I fear, in most coal-mining districts, to spend a large part of their lives in these coal-mines, with little opportunity to get an education; and, what is worse, I have often noted that, as a rule, young boys who begin life in a coal-mine are often physically and mentally dwarfed. They soon lose ambition to do anything else than to continue as a coal-miner.

In those days, and later as a young man, I used to try to picture in my imagination the feelings and ambitions of a white boy with absolutely no limit placed upon his aspirations and activities. I used to envy the white boy who had no obstacles placed in the way of his becoming a Congressman, Governor, Bishop, or President by reason of the accident of his birth or race. I used to picture the way that I would act under such circumstances; how I would begin at the bottom and keep rising until I reached the highest round of success.

In later years, I confess that I do not envy the white boy as I once did. I have learned that success is to be measured not so much by the position that one has reached in life as by the obstacles which he has overcome while trying to succeed. Looked at from this standpoint, I almost reach the conclusion that often the Negro boy's birth and connection with an unpopular race is an advantage, so far as real life is concerned. With few exceptions, the Negro youth must work harder and must perform his tasks even better than a white youth in order to secure recognition. But out of the hard and unusual struggle through which he is compelled to pass, he gets a strength, a confidence, that one misses whose pathway is comparatively smooth by reason of birth and race.

From any point of view, I had rather be what I am, a member of the Negro race, than be able to claim membership with the most favoured of any other race. I have always been made sad when I have heard members of any race claiming rights and privileges, or certain badges of distinction, on the ground simply that they were members of this or that race, regardless of their own individual worth or attainments. I have been made to feel sad for such persons because I am conscious of the fact that mere connection with what is known as a superior race will not permanently carry an individual forward unless he has individual worth, and mere connection with what is regarded as an inferior race will not finally hold an individual back if he possesses intrinsic, individual merit. Every persecuted individual and race should get much consolation out of the great human law, which is universal and eternal, that merit, no matter under what skin found, is, in the long run, recognized and rewarded. This I have said here, not to call attention to myself as an individual, but to the race to which I am proud to belong.

SOURCE: Booker T. Washington. *Up from Slavery: An Autobiography*. New York: Doubleday, Page and Company, 1901.

HELEN KELLER

Helen Keller (1880–1968), who lost her sight and hearing as a toddler, soon became an inspiration to students and teachers everywhere. Anne Sullivan, her teacher, has written of her experiences teaching Keller, and here Keller writes of the extraordinary revelations of the world Sullivan helped her to make.

Chapters from *The Story of My Life* (1903)

Chapter 4

The most important day I remember in all my life is the one on which my teacher, Anne Mansfield Sullivan, came to me. I am filled with wonder when I consider the immeasurable contrasts between the two lives which it connects. It was the third of March, 1887, three months before I was seven years old.

On the afternoon of that eventful day, I stood on the porch, dumb, expectant. I guessed vaguely from my mother's signs and from the hurrying to and fro in the house that something unusual was about to happen, so I went to the door and waited on the steps. The afternoon sun penetrated the mass of honeysuckle that covered the porch, and fell on my upturned face. My fingers lingered almost unconsciously on the familiar leaves and blossoms which had just come forth to greet the sweet southern spring. I did not know what the future held of marvel or surprise for me. Anger and bitterness had preyed upon me continually for weeks and a deep languor had succeeded this passionate struggle.

Have you ever been at sea in a dense fog, when it seemed as if a tangible white darkness shut you in, and the great ship, tense and anxious, groped her way toward the shore with plummet and sounding-line, and you waited with beating heart for something to happen? I was like that ship before my education began, only I was without compass or sounding-line, and had no way of knowing how near the harbour was. "Light! give me light!" was the wordless cry of my soul, and the light of love shone on me in that very hour.

I felt approaching footsteps. I stretched out my hand as I supposed to my mother. Some one took it, and I was caught up and held close in the arms of her who had come to reveal all things to me, and, more than all things else, to love me.

The morning after my teacher came she led me into her room and gave me a doll. The little blind children at the Perkins Institution had sent it and Laura Bridgman had dressed it; but I did not know this until afterward. When I had played with it a little while, Miss Sullivan slowly spelled into my hand the word "d-o-l-l." I was at once interested in this finger play and tried to imitate it. When I finally succeeded in making the letters correctly I was flushed with childish pleasure and pride. Running downstairs to my mother I held up my hand and made the letters for doll. I did not know that I was spelling a word or even that words existed; I was simply making my fingers go in monkey-like imitation. In the days that followed I learned to spell in this uncomprehending way a great many words, among them *pin, hat, cup* and a few verbs like *sit, stand* and *walk*. But my teacher had been with me several weeks before I understood that everything has a name.

One day, while I was playing with my new doll, Miss Sullivan put my big rag doll into my lap also, spelled "d-o-l-l" and tried to make me understand that "d-o-l-l" applied to both. Earlier in the day we had had a tussle over the words "m-u-g" and "w-a-t-e-r." Miss Sullivan had tried to impress upon me that "m-u-g" is *mug* and that "w-a-t-e-r" is *water,* but I persisted in confounding the two. In despair she had dropped the subject for the time, only to renew it at the first opportunity. I became impatient at her repeated attempts and, seizing the new doll, I dashed it upon the floor. I was keenly delighted when I felt the fragments of the broken doll at my feet. Neither sorrow nor regret followed my passionate outburst. I had not loved the doll. In the still, dark world in which I lived there was no strong sentiment or tenderness. I felt my teacher sweep the fragments to one side of the hearth and I had a sense of satisfaction that the cause of my discomfort was removed. She brought me my hat, and I knew I was going out into the warm sunshine. This thought, if a wordless sensation may be called a thought, made me hop and skip with pleasure.

We walked down the path to the well-house, attracted by the fragrance of the honeysuckle with which it was covered. Some one was drawing water and my teacher placed my hand under the spout. As the cool stream gushed over one hand she spelled into the other the word *water,* first slowly, then rapidly. I stood still, my whole attention fixed upon the motions of her fingers. Suddenly I felt a misty consciousness as of something forgotten—a thrill of returning thought; and somehow the mystery of language was revealed to me. I knew then that "w-a-t-e-r" meant the wonderful cool something that was flowing over my hand. That living word awakened my soul, gave it light, hope, joy, set it free! There were barriers still, it is true, but barriers that could in time be swept away.

I left the well-house eager to learn. Everything had a name, and each name gave birth to a new thought. As we returned to the house every object which I touched seemed to quiver with life. That was because I saw everything with the strange, new sight that had come to me. On entering the door I remembered the doll I had broken. I felt my way to the hearth and picked up the pieces. I tried vainly to put them together. Then my eyes filled with tears; for I realized what I had done, and for the first time I felt repentance and sorrow.

I learned a great many new words that day. I do not remember what they all were; but I do know that *mother, father, sister, teacher* were among them—words that were to make the world blossom for me, "like Aaron's rod, with flowers." It would have been difficult to find a happier child than I was as I lay in my crib at the close of that eventful day and lived over the joys it had brought me, and for the first time longed for a new day to come.

Chapter 5

I recall many incidents of the summer of 1887 that followed my soul's sudden awakening. I did nothing but explore with my hands and learn the name of every object that I touched; and the more I handled things and learned their names and uses, the more joyous and confident grew my sense of kinship with the rest of the world.

When the time of daisies and buttercups came Miss Sullivan took me by the hand across the fields, where men were preparing the earth for the seed, to the banks of the Tennessee River, and there, sitting on the warm grass, I had my first lessons in the beneficence of nature. I learned how the sun and the rain make to grow out of the ground every tree that is pleasant to the sight and good for food, how birds build their nests and live and thrive from land to land, how the squirrel, the deer, the lion and every other creature finds food and shelter. As my knowledge of things grew I felt more and more the delight of the world I was in. Long before I learned to do a sum in arithmetic or describe the shape of the earth, Miss Sullivan had taught me to find beauty in the fragrant woods, in every blade of grass, and in the curves and dimples of my baby sister's hand. She linked my earliest thoughts with nature, and made me feel that "birds and flowers and I were happy peers."

But about this time I had an experience which taught me that nature is not always kind. One day my teacher and I were returning from a long ramble. The morning had been fine, but it was growing warm and sultry when at last we turned our faces homeward. Two or three times we stopped to rest under a tree by the wayside. Our last halt was under a wild cherry tree a short distance from the house. The shade was grateful, and the tree was so easy to climb that with my teacher's assistance I was able to scramble to a seat in the branches. It was so cool up in the tree that Miss Sullivan proposed that we have our luncheon there. I promised to keep still while she went to the house to fetch it.

Suddenly a change passed over the tree. All the sun's warmth left the air. I knew the sky was black, because all the heat, which meant light to me, had died out of the atmosphere. A strange odour came up from the earth. I knew it, it was the odour that always precedes a thunderstorm, and a nameless fear clutched at my heart. I felt absolutely alone, cut off from my friends and the firm earth. The immense, the unknown, enfolded me. I remained still and expectant; a chilling terror crept over me. I longed for my teacher's return; but above all things I wanted to get down from that tree.

There was a moment of sinister silence, then a multitudinous stirring of the leaves. A shiver ran through the tree, and the wind sent forth a blast that would have knocked me off had I not clung to the branch with might and main. The tree swayed and strained. The small twigs snapped and fell about me in showers. A wild impulse to jump seized me, but terror held me fast. I crouched down in the fork of the tree. The branches lashed about me. I felt the intermittent jarring that came now and then, as if something heavy had fallen and the shock had traveled up till it reached the limb I sat on. It worked my suspense up to the highest point, and just as I was thinking the tree and I should fall together, my teacher seized my hand and helped me down. I clung to her, trembling with joy to feel the earth under my feet once more. I had learned a new lesson—that nature "wages open war against her children, and under softest touch hides treacherous claws."

After this experience it was a long time before I climbed another tree. The mere thought filled me with terror. It was the sweet allurement of the mimosa tree in full bloom that finally overcame my fears. One beautiful spring morning when I was alone in the summer-house, reading, I became aware of a wonderful subtle fragrance in the air. I started up and instinctively stretched out my hands. It seemed as if the spirit of spring had passed through the summer-house. "What is it?" I asked, and the next minute I recognized the odour of the mimosa blossoms. I felt my way to the end of the garden, knowing that the mimosa tree was near the fence, at the turn of the path. Yes, there it was, all quivering in the warm sunshine, its blossom-laden branches almost touching the long grass. Was there ever anything so exquisitely beautiful in the world before! Its delicate blossoms shrank from the slightest earthly touch; it seemed as if a tree of paradise had been transplanted to earth. I made my way through a shower of petals to the great trunk and for one minute stood irresolute; then, putting my foot in the broad space between the forked branches, I pulled myself up into the tree. I had some difficulty in holding on, for the branches were very large and the bark hurt my hands. But I had a delicious sense that I was doing something unusual and wonderful, so I kept on climbing higher and higher, until I reached a little seat which somebody had built there so long ago that it had grown part of the tree itself. I sat there for a long, long time, feeling like a fairy on a rosy cloud. After that I spent many happy hours in my tree of paradise, thinking fair thoughts and dreaming bright dreams.

Chapter 6

I had now the key to all language, and I was eager to learn to use it. Children who hear acquire language without any particular effort; the words that fall from others' lips they catch on the wing, as it were, delightedly, while the little deaf child must trap them by a slow and often painful process. But whatever the process, the result is wonderful. Gradually from naming an object we advance step by step until we have traversed the vast distance between our first stammered syllable and the sweep of thought in a line of Shakespeare.

At first, when my teacher told me about a new thing I asked very few questions. My ideas were vague, and my vocabulary was inadequate; but as my knowledge of things grew, and I learned more and more words, my field of inquiry broadened, and I would return again and again to the same subject, eager for further information. Sometimes a new word revived an image that some earlier experience had engraved on my brain.

I remember the morning that I first asked the meaning of the word, "love." This was before I knew many words. I had found a few early violets in the garden and brought them to my teacher. She tried to kiss me; but at that time I did not like to have any one kiss me except my mother. Miss Sullivan put her arm gently round me and spelled into my hand, "I love Helen."

"What is love?" I asked.

She drew me closer to her and said, "It is here," pointing to my heart, whose beats I was conscious of for the first time. Her words puzzled me very much because I did not then understand anything unless I touched it.

I smelt the violets in her hand and asked, half in words, half in signs, a question which meant, "Is love the sweetness of flowers?"

"No," said my teacher.

Again I thought. The warm sun was shining on us.

"Is this not love?" I asked, pointing in the direction from which the heat came, "Is this not love?"

It seemed to me that there could be nothing more beautiful than the sun, whose warmth makes all things grow. But Miss Sullivan shook her head, and I was greatly puzzled and disappointed. I thought it strange that my teacher could not show me love.

A day or two afterward I was stringing beads of different sizes in symmetrical groups—two large beads, three small ones, and so on. I had made many mistakes, and Miss Sullivan had pointed them out again and again with gentle patience. Finally I noticed a very obvious error in the sequence and for an instant I concentrated my attention on the lesson and tried to think how I should have arranged the beads. Miss Sullivan touched my forehead and spelled with decided emphasis, "Think."

In a flash I knew that the word was the name of the process that was going on in my head. This was my first conscious perception of an abstract idea.

For a long time I was still—I was not thinking of the beads in my lap, but trying to find a meaning for "love" in the light of this new idea. The sun had been under a cloud all day, and there had been brief showers; but suddenly the sun broke forth in all its southern splendour.

Again I asked my teacher, "Is this not love?"

"Love is something like the clouds that were in the sky before the sun came out," she replied. Then in simpler words than these, which at that time I could not have understood, she explained: "You cannot touch the clouds, you know; but you feel the rain and know how glad the flowers and the thirsty earth are to have it after a hot day. You cannot touch love either; but you feel the sweetness that it pours into everything. Without love you would not be happy or want to play."

The beautiful truth burst upon my mind—I felt that there were invisible lines stretched between my spirit and the spirits of others.

From the beginning of my education Miss Sullivan made it a practice to speak to me as she would speak to any hearing child; the only difference was that she spelled the sentences into my hand instead of speaking them. If I did not know the words and idioms necessary to express my thoughts she supplied them, even suggesting conversation when I was unable to keep up my end of the dialogue.

This process was continued for several years; for the deaf child does not learn in a month, or even in two or three years, the numberless idioms and expressions used in the simplest daily intercourse. The little hearing child learns these from constant repetition and imitation. The conversation he hears in his home stimulates his mind and suggests topics and calls forth the spontaneous expression of his own thoughts. This natural exchange of ideas is denied to the deaf child. My teacher, realizing this, determined to supply the kinds of stimulus I lacked. This she did by repeating to me as far as possible, verbatim, what she heard, and by showing me how I could take part in the conversation. But it was a long time before I ventured to take the initiative, and still longer before I could find something appropriate to say at the right time.

The deaf and the blind find it very difficult to acquire the amenities of conversation. How much more this difficulty must be augmented in the case of those who are both deaf and blind! They cannot distinguish the tone of the voice or, without assistance, go up and down the gamut of tones that give significance to words; nor can they watch the expression of the speaker's face, and a look is often the very soul of what one says.

Chapter 7

The next important step in my education was learning to read.

As soon as I could spell a few words my teacher gave me slips of cardboard on which were printed words in raised letters. I quickly learned that each printed word stood for an object, an act, or a quality. I had a frame in which I could arrange the words in little sentences; but before I could ever put sentences in the frame I used to make them in objects. I found the slips of paper which represented, for example, "doll," "is," "on," "bed" and placed each name on its object; then I put my doll on the bed with the words *is, on, bed* arranged beside the doll, thus making a sentence of the words, and at the same time carrying out the idea of the sentence with the things themselves.

One day, Miss Sullivan tells me, I pinned the word *girl* on my pinafore and stood in the wardrobe. On the shelf I arranged the words, *is, in, wardrobe*. Nothing delighted me so much as this game. My teacher and I played it for hours at a time. Often everything in the room was arranged in object sentences.

From the printed slip it was but a step to the printed book. I took my "Reader for Beginners" and hunted for the words I knew; when I found them my joy was like that of a game of hide-and-seek. Thus I began to read. Of the time when I began to read connected stories I shall speak later.

For a long time I had no regular lessons. Even when I studied most earnestly it seemed more like play than work. Everything Miss Sullivan taught me she illustrated by a beautiful story or a poem. Whenever anything delighted or interested me she talked it over with me just as if she were a little girl herself. What many children think of with dread, as a painful plodding through grammar, hard sums and harder definitions, is to-day one of my most precious memories.

I cannot explain the peculiar sympathy Miss Sullivan had with my pleasures and desires. Perhaps it was the result of long association with the blind. Added to this she had a wonderful faculty for description. She went quickly over uninteresting details, and never nagged me with questions to see if I remembered the day-before-yesterday's lesson. She introduced dry technicalities of science little by little, making every subject so real that I could not help remembering what she taught.

We read and studied out of doors, preferring the sunlit woods to the house. All my early lessons have in them the breath of the woods—the fine, resinous odour of pine needles, blended with the perfume of wild grapes. Seated in the gracious shade of a wild tulip tree, I learned to think that everything has a lesson and a suggestion. "The loveliness of things taught me all their use." Indeed, everything that could hum, or buzz, or sing, or bloom, had a part in my education—noisy-throated frogs, katydids and crickets held in my hand until, forgetting their embarrassment, they trilled their reedy note, little downy chickens and wildflowers, the dogwood blossoms, meadow-violets and budding fruit trees. I felt the bursting cotton-bolls and fingered their soft fiber and fuzzy seeds; I felt the low soughing of the wind through the cornstalks, the silky rustling of the long leaves, and the indignant snort of my pony, as we caught him in the pasture and put the bit in his mouth—ah me! how well I remember the spicy, clovery smell of his breath!

Sometimes I rose at dawn and stole into the garden while the heavy dew lay on the grass and flowers. Few know what joy it is to feel the roses pressing softly into the hand, or the beautiful motion of the lilies as they sway in the morning breeze. Sometimes I caught an insect in the flower I was plucking, and I felt the faint noise of a pair of wings rubbed together in a sudden terror, as the little creature became aware of a pressure from without.

Another favourite haunt of mine was the orchard, where the fruit ripened early in July. The large, downy peaches would reach themselves into my hand, and as the joyous breezes flew about the trees the apples tumbled at my feet. Oh, the delight with which I gathered up the fruit in my pinafore, pressed my face against the smooth cheeks of the apples, still warm from the sun, and skipped back to the house!

Our favourite walk was to Keller's Landing, an old tumble-down lumber-wharf on the Tennessee River, used during the Civil War to land soldiers. There we spent many happy hours and played at learning geography. I built dams of pebbles, made islands and lakes, and dug river-beds, all for fun, and never dreamed that I was learning a lesson. I listened with increasing wonder to Miss Sullivan's descriptions of the great round world with its burning mountains, buried cities, moving rivers of ice, and many other things as strange. She made raised maps in clay, so that I could feel the mountain ridges and valleys, and follow with my fingers the devious course of rivers. I liked this, too; but the division of the earth into zones and poles confused and teased my mind. The illustrative strings and the orange stick representing the poles seemed so real that even to this day the mere mention of temperate zone suggests a series of twine circles; and I believe that if any one should set about it he could convince me that white bears actually climb the North Pole.

Arithmetic seems to have been the only study I did not like. From the first I was not interested in the science of numbers. Miss Sullivan tried to teach me to count by stringing beads in groups, and by arranging kindergarten straws I learned to add and subtract. I never had patience to arrange more than five or six groups at a time. When I had accomplished this my conscience was at rest for the day, and I went out quickly to find my playmates.

In this same leisurely manner I studied zoölogy and botany.

Once a gentleman, whose name I have forgotten, sent me a collection of fossils—tiny mollusk shells beautifully marked, and bits of sandstone with the print of birds' claws, and a lovely fern in bas-relief. These were the keys which unlocked the treasures of the antediluvian world for me. With trembling fingers I listened to Miss Sullivan's descriptions of the terrible beasts with uncouth, unpronounceable names, which once went tramping through the primeval forests, tearing down the branches of gigantic trees for food, and died in the dismal swamps of an unknown age. For a long time these strange creatures haunted my dreams, and this gloomy period formed a somber background to the joyous Now, filled with sunshine and roses and echoing with the gentle beat of my pony's hoof.

Another time a beautiful shell was given me, and with a child's surprise and delight I learned how a tiny mollusk had built the lustrous coil for his dwelling place, and how on still nights, when there is no breeze stirring the waves, the Nautilus sails on the blue waters of the Indian Ocean in his "ship of pearl." After I had learned a great many interesting things about the life and habits of the children of the sea—how in the midst of dashing waves the little polyps build the beautiful coral isles of the Pacific, and the foraminifera have made the chalkhills of many a land—my teacher read me "The Chambered Nautilus," and showed me that the shell-building process of the mollusks is symbolical of the development of the mind. Just as the wonder-working mantle of the Nautilus changes the material it absorbs from the water and makes it a part of itself, so the bits of knowledge one gathers undergo a similar change and become pearls of thought.

Again, it was the growth of a plant that furnished the text for a lesson. We bought a lily and set it in a sunny window. Very soon the green, pointed buds showed signs of opening. The slender, fingerlike leaves on the outside opened slowly, reluctant, I thought, to reveal the loveliness they hid; once having made a start, however, the opening process went on rapidly, but in order and systematically. There was always one bud larger and more beautiful than the rest, which pushed her outer covering back with more pomp, as if the beauty in soft, silky robes knew that she was the lily-queen by right divine, while her more timid sisters doffed their green hoods shyly, until the whole plant was one nodding bough of loveliness and fragrance.

Once there were eleven tadpoles in a glass globe set in a window full of plants. I remember the eagerness with which I made discoveries about them. It was great fun to plunge my hand into the bowl and feel the tadpoles frisk about, and to let them slip and slide between my fingers. One day a more ambitious fellow leaped beyond the edge of the bowl and fell on the floor, where I found him to all appearance more dead than alive. The only sign of life was a slight wriggling of his tail. But no sooner had he returned to his element than he darted to the bottom, swimming round and round in joyous activity. He had made his leap, he had seen the great world, and was content to stay in his pretty glass house under the big fuchsia tree until he attained the dignity of froghood. Then he went to live in the leafy pool at the end of the garden, where he made the summer nights musical with his quaint love-song.

Thus I learned from life itself. At the beginning I was only a little mass of possibilities. It was my teacher who unfolded and developed them. When she came, everything about me breathed of love and joy and was full of meaning. She has never since let pass an opportunity to point out the beauty that is in everything, nor has she ceased trying in thought and action and example to make my life sweet and useful.

It was my teacher's genius, her quick sympathy, her loving tact which made the first years of my education so beautiful. It was because she seized the right moment to impart knowledge that made it so pleasant and acceptable to me. She realized that a child's mind is like a shallow brook which ripples and dances merrily over the stony course of its education and reflects here a flower, there a bush, yonder a fleecy cloud; and she attempted to guide my mind on its way, knowing that like a brook it should be fed by mountain streams and hidden springs, until it broadened out into a deep river, capable of reflecting in its placid surface, billowy hills, the luminous shadows of trees and the blue heavens, as well as the sweet face of a little flower.

Any teacher can take a child to the classroom, but not every teacher can make him learn. He will not work joyously unless he feels that liberty is his, whether he is busy or at rest; he must feel the flush of victory and the heart-sinking of disappointment before he takes with a will the tasks distasteful to him and resolves to dance his way bravely through a dull routine of textbooks.

My teacher is so near to me that I scarcely think of myself apart from her. How much of my delight in all beautiful things is innate, and how much is due to her influence, I can never tell. I feel that her being is inseparable from my own, and that the footsteps of my life are in hers. All the best of me belongs to her—there is not a talent, or an inspiration or a joy in me that has not awakened by her loving touch.

SOURCE: Helen Keller. *The Story of My Life.* New York: Doubleday, Page and Company, 1903.

JACK LONDON

One of the most popular of American writers, Jack London (1876–1916) performs the trick of presenting a dramatic coming-of-age and self-realization novel through the perspective of a dog. Buck, the California-born son of a St. Bernard and a Scotch shepherd, is kidnapped during the Alaska gold rush of 1897.

The Call of the Wild (1903)

Chapter 1: Into the Primitive

"Old longings nomadic leap,
Chafing at custom's chain;
Again from its brumal sleep
Wakens the ferine strain."

BUCK DID NOT read the newspapers, or he would have known that trouble was brewing, not alone for himself, but for every tide-water dog, strong of muscle and with warm, long hair, from Puget Sound to San Diego. Because men, groping in the Arctic darkness, had found a yellow metal, and because steamship and transportation companies were booming the find, thousands of men were rushing into the Northland. These men wanted dogs, and the dogs they wanted were heavy dogs, with strong muscles by which to toil, and furry coats to protect them from the frost.

Buck lived at a big house in the sun-kissed Santa Clara Valley. Judge Miller's place, it was called. It stood back from the road, half hidden among the trees, through which glimpses could be caught of the wide cool veranda that ran around its four sides. The house was approached by gravelled driveways which wound about through wide-spreading lawns and under the interlacing boughs of tall poplars. At the rear things were on even a more spacious scale than at the front. There were great stables, where a dozen grooms and boys held forth, rows of vine-clad servants' cottages, an endless and orderly array of outhouses, long grape arbors, green pastures, orchards, and berry patches. Then there was the pumping plant for the artesian well, and the big cement tank where Judge Miller's boys took their morning plunge and kept cool in the hot afternoon.

And over this great demesne Buck ruled. Here he was born, and here he had lived the four years of his life. It was true, there were other dogs. There could not but be other dogs on so vast a place, but they did not count. They came and went, resided in the populous kennels, or lived obscurely in the recesses of the house after the fashion of Toots, the Japanese pug, or Ysabel, the Mexican hairless—strange creatures that rarely put nose out of doors or set foot to ground. On the other hand, there were the fox terriers, a score of them at least, who yelped fearful promises at Toots and Ysabel looking out of the windows at them and protected by a legion of housemaids armed with brooms and mops.

But Buck was neither house dog nor kennel dog. The whole realm was his. He plunged into the swimming tank or went hunting with the Judge's sons; he escorted Mollie and Alice, the Judge's daughters, on long twilight or early morning rambles; on wintry nights he lay at the Judge's feet before the roaring library fire; he carried the Judge's grandsons on his back, or rolled them in the grass, and guarded their footsteps through wild adventures down to the fountain in the stable yard, and even beyond, where the paddocks were, and the berry patches. Among the terriers he stalked imperiously, and Toots and Ysabel he utterly ignored, for he was king—king over all creeping, crawling, flying things of Judge Miller's place, humans included.

His father, Elmo, a huge St. Bernard, had been the Judge's inseparable companion, and Buck bid fair to follow in the way of his father. He was not so large—he weighed only one hundred and forty pounds—for his mother, Shep, had been a Scotch shepherd dog. Nevertheless, one hundred and forty pounds, to which was added the dignity that comes of good living and universal respect, enabled him to carry himself in right royal fashion. During the four years since his puppyhood he had lived the life of a sated aristocrat; he had a fine pride in himself, was ever a trifle egotistical, as country gentlemen sometimes become because of their insular situation. But he had saved himself by not becoming a mere pampered house dog. Hunting and kindred outdoor delights had kept down the fat and hardened his muscles; and to him, as to the cold-tubbing races, the love of water had been a tonic and a health preserver.

And this was the manner of dog Buck was in the fall of 1897, when the Klondike strike dragged men from all the world into the frozen North. But Buck did not read the newspapers, and he did not know that Manuel, one of the gardener's helpers, was an undesirable acquaintance. Manuel had one besetting sin. He loved to play Chinese lottery. Also, in his gambling, he had one besetting weakness—faith in a system; and this made his damnation certain. For to play a system requires money, while the wages of a gardener's helper do not lap over the needs of a wife and numerous progeny.

The Judge was at a meeting of the Raisin Growers' Association, and the boys were busy organizing an athletic club, on the memorable night of Manuel's treachery. No one saw him and Buck go off through the orchard on what Buck imagined was merely a stroll. And with the exception of a solitary man, no one saw them arrive at the little flag station known as College Park. This man talked with Manuel, and money chinked between them.

"You might wrap up the goods before you deliver 'm," the stranger said gruffly, and Manuel doubled a piece of stout rope around Buck's neck under the collar.

"Twist it, an' you'll choke 'm plentee," said Manuel, and the stranger grunted a ready affirmative.

Buck had accepted the rope with quiet dignity. To be sure, it was an unwonted performance: but he had learned to trust in men he knew, and to give them credit for a wisdom that outreached his own. But when the ends of the rope were placed in the stranger's hands, he growled menacingly. He had merely intimated his displeasure, in his pride believing that to intimate was to command. But to his surprise the rope tightened around his neck, shutting off his breath. In a quick rage he sprang at the man, who met him halfway, grappled him close by the throat, and with a deft twist threw him over on his back. Then the rope tightened mercilessly, while Buck struggled in a fury, his tongue lolling out of his mouth and his great chest panting futilely. Never in all his life had he been so vilely treated, and never in all his life had he been so angry. But his strength ebbed, his eyes glazed, and he knew nothing when the train was flagged and the two men threw him into the baggage car.

The next he knew, he was dimly aware that his tongue was hurting and that he was being jolted along in some kind of a conveyance. The hoarse shriek of a locomotive whistling a crossing told him where he was. He had travelled too often with the Judge not to know the sensation of riding in a baggage car. He opened his eyes, and into them came the unbridled anger of a kidnapped king. The man sprang for his throat, but Buck was too quick for him. His jaws closed on the hand, nor did they relax till his senses were choked out of him once more.

"Yep, has fits," the man said, hiding his mangled hand from the baggageman, who had been attracted by the sounds of struggle. "I'm takin' 'm up for the boss to 'Frisco. A crack dog-doctor there thinks that he can cure 'm."

Concerning that night's ride, the man spoke most eloquently for himself, in a little shed back of a saloon on the San Francisco water front.

"All I get is fifty for it," he grumbled, "an' I wouldn't do it over for a thousand, cold cash."

His hand was wrapped in a bloody handkerchief, and the right trouser leg was ripped from knee to ankle.

"How much did the other mug get?" the saloon-keeper demanded.

"A hundred," was the reply. "Wouldn't take a sou less, so help me."

"That makes a hundred and fifty," the saloon-keeper calculated; "and he's worth it, or I'm a squarehead."

The kidnapper undid the bloody wrappings and looked at his lacerated hand. "If I don't get the hydrophoby—"

"It'll be because you was born to hang," laughed the saloon-keeper. "Here lend me a hand before you pull your freight," he added.

Dazed, suffering intolerable pain from throat and tongue, with the life half throttled out of him, Buck attempted to face his tormentors. But he was thrown down and choked repeatedly, till they succeeded in filing the heavy brass collar from off his neck. Then the rope was removed, and he was flung into a cagelike crate.

There he lay for the remainder of the weary night, nursing his wrath and wounded pride. He could not understand what it all meant. What did they want with him, these strange men? Why were they keeping him pent up in this narrow crate? He did not know why, but he felt oppressed by the vague sense of impending calamity. Several times during the night he sprang to his feet when the shed door rattled open, expecting to see the Judge, or the boys at least. But each time it was the bulging face of the saloon-keeper that peered in at him by the sickly light of a tallow candle. And each time the joyful bark that trembled in Buck's throat was twisted into a savage growl.

But the saloon-keeper let him alone, and in the morning four men entered and picked up the crate. More tormentors, Buck decided, for they were evil-looking creatures, ragged and unkempt; and he stormed and raged at them through the bars. They only laughed and poked sticks at him, which he promptly assailed with his teeth till he realized that that was what they wanted. Whereupon he lay down sullenly and allowed the crate to be lifted into a wagon. Then he, and the crate in which he was imprisoned, began a passage through many hands. Clerks in the express office took charge of him; he was carted about in another wagon; a truck carried him, with an assortment of boxes and parcels, upon a ferry steamer; he was trucked off the steamer into a great railway depot, and finally he was deposited in an express car.

For two days and nights this express car was dragged along at the tail of shrieking locomotives; and for two days and nights Buck neither ate nor drank. In his anger he had met the first advances of the express messengers with growls, and they had retaliated by teasing him. When he flung himself against the bars, quivering and frothing, they laughed at him and taunted him. They growled and barked like detestable dogs, mewed, and flapped their arms and crowed. It was all very silly, he knew; but therefore the more outrage to his dignity, and his anger waxed and waxed. He did not mind the hunger so much, but the lack of water caused him severe suffering and fanned his wrath to fever-pitch. For that matter, high-strung and finely sensitive, the ill treatment had flung him into a fever, which was fed by the inflammation of his parched and swollen throat and tongue.

He was glad for one thing: the rope was off his neck. That had given them an unfair advantage; but now that it was off, he would show them. They would never get another rope around his neck. Upon that he was resolved. For two days and nights he neither ate nor drank, and during those two days and nights of torment, he accumulated a fund of wrath that boded ill for whoever first fell foul of him. His eyes turned blood-shot, and he was metamorphosed into a raging fiend. So changed was he that the Judge himself would not have recognized him; and the express messengers breathed with relief when they bundled him off the train at Seattle.

Four men gingerly carried the crate from the wagon into a small, high-walled back yard. A stout man, with a red sweater that sagged generously at the neck, came out and signed the book for the driver. That was the man, Buck divined, the next tormentor, and he hurled himself savagely against the bars. The man smiled grimly, and brought a hatchet and a club.

"You ain't going to take him out now?" the driver asked.

"Sure," the man replied, driving the hatchet into the crate for a pry.

There was an instantaneous scattering of the four men who had carried it in, and from safe perches on top the wall they prepared to watch the performance.

Buck rushed at the splintering wood, sinking his teeth into it, surging and wrestling with it. Wherever the hatchet fell on the outside, he was there on the inside, snarling and growling, as furiously anxious to get out as the man in the red sweater was calmly intent on getting him out.

"Now, you red-eyed devil," he said, when he had made an opening sufficient for the passage of Buck's body. At the same time he dropped the hatchet and shifted the club to his right hand.

And Buck was truly a red-eyed devil, as he drew himself together for the spring, hair bristling, mouth foaming, a mad glitter in his blood-shot eyes. Straight at the man he launched his one hundred and forty pounds of fury, surcharged with the pent passion of two days and nights. In mid-air, just as his jaws were about to close on the man, he received a shock that checked his body and brought his teeth together with an agonizing clip. He whirled over, fetching the ground on his back and side. He had never been struck by a club in his life, and did not understand. With a snarl that was part bark and more scream he was again on his feet and launched into the air. And again the shock came and he was brought crushingly to the ground. This time he was aware that it was the club, but his madness knew no caution. A dozen times he charged, and as often the club broke the charge and smashed him down.

After a particularly fierce blow, he crawled to his feet, too dazed to rush. He staggered limply about, the blood flowing from nose and mouth and ears, his beautiful coat sprayed and flecked with bloody slaver. Then the man advanced and deliberately dealt him a frightful blow on the nose. All the pain he had endured was as nothing compared with the exquisite agony of this. With a roar that was almost lionlike in its ferocity, he again hurled himself at the man. But the man, shifting the club from right to left, coolly caught him by the under jaw, at the same time wrenching downward and backward. Buck described a complete circle in the air, and half of another, then crashed to the ground on his head and chest.

For the last time he rushed. The man struck the shrewd blow he had purposely withheld for so long, and Buck crumpled up and went down, knocked utterly senseless.

"He's no slouch at dog-breakin', that's wot I say," one of the men on the wall cried enthusiastically.

"Druther break cayuses[1] any day, and twice on Sundays," was the reply of the driver, as he climbed on the wagon and started the horses.

Buck's senses came back to him, but not his strength. He lay where he had fallen, and from there he watched the man in the red sweater.

"'Answers to the name of Buck,'" the man soliloquized, quoting from the saloon-keeper's letter which had announced the consignment of the crate and contents. "Well, Buck, my boy," he went on in a genial voice, "we've had our little ruction, and the best thing we can do is to let it go at that. You've learned your place, and I know mine. Be a good dog and all 'll go well and the goose hang high. Be a bad dog, and I'll whale the stuffin' outa you. Understand?"

As he spoke he fearlessly patted the head he had so mercilessly pounded, and though Buck's hair involuntarily bristled at touch of the hand, he endured it without protest. When the man brought him water he drank eagerly, and later bolted a generous meal of raw meat, chuck by chunk, from the man's hand.

He was beaten (he knew that); but he was not broken. He saw, once for all, that he stood no chance against a man with a club. He had learned the lesson, and in all his after life he never forgot it. That club was a revelation. It was his introduction to the reign of

1. *cayuses*: wild horses

primitive law, and he met the introduction halfway. The facts of life took on a fiercer aspect; and while he faced that aspect uncowed, he faced it with all the latent cunning of his nature aroused. As the days went by, other dogs came, in crates and at the ends of ropes, some docilely, and some raging and roaring as he had come; and, one and all, he watched them pass under the dominion of the man in the red sweater. Again and again, as he looked at each brutal performance, the lesson was driven home to Buck: a man with a club was a law-giver, a master to be obeyed, though not necessarily conciliated. Of this last Buck was never guilty, though he did see beaten dogs that fawned upon the man, and wagged their tails, and licked his hand. Also he saw one dog, that would neither conciliate nor obey, finally killed in the struggle for mastery.

Now and again men came, strangers, who talked excitedly, wheedling, and in all kinds of fashions to the man in the red sweater. And at such times that money passed between them the strangers took one or more of the dogs away with them. Buck wondered where they went, for they never came back; but the fear of the future was strong upon him, and he was glad each time when he was not selected.

Yet his time came, in the end, in the form of a little weazened man who spat broken English and many strange and uncouth exclamations which Buck could not understand.

"Sacredam!" he cried, when his eyes lit upon Buck. "Dat one dam bully dog! Eh? How moch?"

"Three hundred, and a present at that," was the prompt reply of the man in the red sweater. "And seein' it's government money, you ain't got no kick coming, eh, Perrault?"

Perrault grinned. Considering that the price of dogs had been boomed skyward by the unwonted demand, it was not an unfair sum for so fine an animal. The Canadian Government would be no loser, nor would its despatches travel the slower. Perrault knew dogs, and when he looked at Buck he knew that he was one in a thousand—"One in ten t'ousand," he commented mentally.

Buck saw money pass between them, and was not surprised when Curly, a good-natured Newfoundland, and he were led away by the little weazened man. That was the last he saw of the man in the red sweater, and as Curly and he looked at receding Seattle from the deck of the *Narwhal*, it was the last he saw of the warm Southland. Curly and he were taken below by Perrault and turned over to a black-faced giant called François. Perrault was a French-Canadian, and swarthy; but François was a French-Canadian half-breed, and twice as swarthy. They were a new kind of men to Buck (of which he was destined to see many more), and while he developed no affection for them, he none the less grew honestly to respect them. He speedily learned that Perrault and François were fair men, calm and impartial in administering justice, and too wise in the way of dogs to be fooled by dogs.

In the 'tween-decks of the *Narwhal*, Buck and Curly joined two other dogs. One of them was a big, snow-white fellow from Spitzbergen who had been brought away by a whaling captain, and who had later accompanied a Geological Survey into the Barrens. He was friendly, in a treacherous sort of way, smiling into one's face the while he meditated some underhand trick, as, for instance, when he stole from Buck's food at the first meal. As Buck sprang to punish him, the lash of François's whip sang through the air, reaching the culprit first; and nothing remained to Buck but to recover the bone. That was fair of François, he decided, and the half-breed began his rise in Buck's estimation.

The other dog made no advances, nor received any; also, he did not attempt to steal from the newcomers. He was a gloomy, morose fellow, and he showed Curly plainly that all he desired was to be left alone, and further, that there would be trouble if he were not left alone. "Dave" he was called, and he ate and slept, or yawned between times, and took interest in nothing, not even when the *Narwhal* crossed Queen Charlotte Sound and rolled and pitched and bucked like a thing possessed. When Buck and Curly grew excited, half wild with fear, he raised his head as though annoyed, favored them with an incurious glance, yawned, and went to sleep again.

Day and night the ship throbbed to the tireless pulse of the propeller, and though one day was very like another, it was apparent to Buck that the weather was steadily growing colder. At last, one morning, the propeller was quiet, and the *Narwhal* was pervaded with an atmosphere of excitement. He felt it, as did the other dogs, and knew that a change was at hand. François leashed them and brought them on deck. At the first step upon the cold surface, Buck's feet sank into a white mushy something very like mud. He sprang back with a snort. More of this white stuff was falling through the air. He shook himself, but more of it fell upon him. He sniffed it curiously, then licked some up on his tongue. It bit like fire, and the next instant was gone. This puzzled him. He tried it again, with the same result. The onlookers laughed uproariously, and he felt ashamed, he knew not why, for it was his first snow.

Chapter 2: The Law of Club and Fang

Buck's first day on the Dyea beach was like a nightmare. Every hour was filled with shock and surprise. He had been suddenly jerked from the heart of civilization and flung into the heart of things primordial. No lazy, sun-kissed life was this, with nothing to do but loaf and be bored. Here was neither peace, nor rest, nor a moment's safety. All was confusion and action, and every moment life and limb were in peril. There was imperative need to be constantly alert; for these dogs and men were not town dogs and men. They were savages, all of them, who knew no law but the law of club and fang.

He had never seen dogs fight as these wolfish creatures fought, and his first experience taught him an unforgettable lesson. It is true, it was a vicarious experience, else he would not have lived to profit by it. Curly was the victim. They were camped near the log store, where she, in her friendly way, made advances to a husky dog the size of a full-grown wolf, though not half so large as she. There was no warning, only a leap in like a flash, a metallic clip of teeth, a leap out equally swift, and Curly's face was ripped open from eye to jaw.

It was the wolf manner of fighting, to strike and leap away; but there was more to it than this. Thirty or forty huskies ran to the spot and surrounded the combatants in an intent and silent circle. Buck did not comprehend that silent intentness, nor the eager way with which they were licking their chops. Curly rushed her antagonist, who struck again and leaped aside. He met her next rush with his chest, in a peculiar fashion that tumbled her off her feet. She never regained them. This was what the onlooking huskies had waited for. They closed in upon her, snarling and yelping, and she was buried, screaming with agony, beneath the bristling mass of bodies.

So sudden was it, and so unexpected, that Buck was taken aback. He saw Spitz run out his scarlet tongue in a way he had of laughing; and he saw François, swinging an axe, spring into the mess of dogs. Three men with clubs were helping him to scatter them. It did not take long. Two minutes from the time Curly went down, the last of her assailants were clubbed off. But she lay there limp and lifeless in the bloody, trampled snow, almost literally torn to pieces, the swart half-breed standing over her and cursing horribly. The scene often came back to Buck to trouble him in his sleep. So that was the way. No fair play. Once down, that was the end of you. Well, he would see to it that he never went down. Spitz ran out his tongue and laughed again, and from that moment Buck hated him with a bitter and deathless hatred.

Before he had recovered from the shock caused by the tragic passing of Curly, he received another shock. François fastened upon him an arrangement of straps and buckles. It was a harness, such as he had seen the grooms put on the horses at home. And as he had seen horses work, so he was set to work, hauling François on a sled to the forest that fringed the valley, and returning with a load of firewood. Though his dignity was sorely hurt by thus being made a draught animal, he was too wise to rebel. He buckled down with a will and did his best, though it was all new and strange. François was stern, demanding instant obedience, and by virtue of his whip receiving instant obedience; while Dave, who was an experienced wheeler, nipped Buck's hind quarters whenever he was in error. Spitz was the leader, likewise experienced, and while he could not always get at Buck, he growled sharp reproof now and again, or cunningly threw his weight in the traces to jerk Buck into the way he should go. Buck learned easily, and under the combined tuition of his two mates and François made remarkable progress. Ere they returned to camp he knew enough to stop at "ho," to go ahead at "mush," to swing wide on the bends, and to keep clear of the wheeler when the loaded sled shot downhill at their heels.

"T'ree vair' good dogs," François told Perrault. "Dat Buck, heem pool lak hell. I tich heem queek as anyt'ing."

By afternoon, Perrault, who was in a hurry to be on the trail with his despatches, returned with two more dogs. "Billee" and "Joe" he called them, two brothers, and true huskies both. Sons of the one mother though they were, they were different as day and night. Billee's one fault was his excessive good nature, while Joe was the very opposite, sour and introspective, with a perpetual snarl and a malignant eye. Buck received them in comradely fashion, Dave ignored them, while Spitz proceeded to thrash first one and then the other. Billee wagged his tail appeasingly, turned to run when he saw that appeasement was of no avail, and cried (still appeasingly) when Spitz's sharp teeth scored his flank. But no matter how Spitz circled, Joe whirled around on his heels to face him, mane bristling, ears laid back, lips writhing and snarling, jaws clipping together as fast as he could snap, and eyes diabolically gleaming—the incarnation of belligerent fear. So terrible was his appearance that Spitz was forced to forego disciplining him; but to cover his own discomfiture he turned upon the inoffensive and wailing Billee and drove him to the confines of the camp.

By evening Perrault secured another dog, an old husky, long and lean and gaunt, with a battle-scarred face and a single eye which flashed a warning of prowess that commanded respect. He was called Sol-leks, which means the Angry One. Like Dave, he asked nothing, gave nothing, expected nothing: and when he marched slowly and deliberately into their midst, even Spitz left him alone. He had one peculiarity which Buck was unlucky enough to discover. He did not like to be approached on his blind side. Of this offence Buck was unwittingly guilty, and the first knowledge he had of his indiscretion was when Sol-leks whirled upon him and slashed his shoulder to the bone for three inches up and down. Forever after Buck avoided his blind side, and to the last of their comradeship had no more trouble. His only apparent ambition, like Dave's, was to be left alone, though, as Buck was afterward to learn, each of them possessed one other and even more vital ambition.

That night Buck faced the great problem of sleeping. The tent, illumined by a candle, glowed warmly in the midst of the white plain; and when he, as a matter of course, entered it, both Perrault and François bombarded him with curses and cooking utensils, till he recovered from his consternation and fled ignominiously into the outer cold. A chill wind was blowing that nipped him sharply and bit with especial venom into his wounded shoulder. He lay down on the snow and attempted to sleep, but the frost soon drove him shivering to his feet. Miserable and disconsolate, he wandered about among the many tents, only to find that one place was as cold as another. Here and there savage dogs rushed upon him, but he bristled his neck-hair and snarled (for he was learning fast) and they let him go his way unmolested.

Finally an idea came to him. He would return and see how his own team mates were making out. To his astonishment, they had disappeared. Again he wandered about through the great camp, looking for them, and again he returned. Were they in the tent?

No, that could not be, else he would not have been driven out. Then where could they possibly be? With drooping tail and shivering body, very forlorn indeed, he aimlessly circled the tent. Suddenly the snow gave way beneath his fore legs and he sank down. Something wriggled under his feet. He sprang back, bristling and snarling, fearful of the unseen and unknown. But a friendly little yelp reassured him, and he went back to investigate. A whiff of warm air ascended to his nostrils, and there, curled up under the snow in a snug ball, lay Billee. He whined placatingly, squirmed and wriggled to show his good will and intentions, and even ventured, as a bribe for peace, to lick Buck's face with his warm wet tongue.

Another lesson. So that was the way they did it, eh? Buck confidently selected a spot, and with much fuss and wasted effort proceeded to dig a hole for himself. In a trice the heat from his body filled the confined space and he was asleep. The day had been long and arduous, and he slept soundly and comfortably, though he growled and barked and wrestled with bad dreams.

Nor did he open his eyes till roused by the noises of the waking camp. At first he did not know where he was. It had snowed during the night and he was completely buried. The snow walls pressed him on every side, and a great surge of fear swept through him—the fear of the wild thing for the trap. It was a token that he was harking back through his own life to the lives of his forebears, for he was a civilized dog, an unduly civilized dog and of his own experience knew no trap and so could not of himself fear it. The muscles of his whole body contracted spasmodically and instinctively, the hair on his neck and shoulders stood on end, and with a ferocious snarl he bounded straight up into the blinding day, the snow flying about him in a flashing cloud. Ere he landed on his feet, he saw the white camp spread out before him and knew where he was and remembered all that had passed from the time he went for a stroll with Manuel to the hole he had dug for himself the night before.

A shout from François hailed his appearance. "Wot I say?" the dog-driver cried to Perrault. "Dat Buck for sure learn queek as anyt'ing."

Perrault nodded gravely. As courier for the Canadian Government, bearing important despatches, he was anxious to secure the best dogs, and he was particularly gladdened by the possession of Buck.

Three more huskies were added to the team inside an hour, making a total of nine, and before another quarter of an hour had passed they were in harness and swinging up the trail toward the Dyea Cañon. Buck was glad to be gone, and though the work was hard he found he did not particularly despise it. He was surprised at the eagerness which animated the whole team and which was communicated to him; but still more surprising was the change wrought in Dave and Sol-leks. They were new dogs, utterly transformed by the harness. All passiveness and unconcern had dropped from them. They were alert and active, anxious that the work should go well, and fiercely irritable with whatever, by delay or confusion, retarded that work. The toil of the traces seemed the supreme expression of their being, and all that they lived for and the only thing in which they took delight.

Dave was wheeler or sled dog, pulling in front of him was Buck, then came Sol-leks; the rest of the team was strung out ahead, single file, to the leader, which position was filled by Spitz.

Buck had been purposely placed between Dave and Sol-leks so that he might receive instruction. Apt scholar that he was, they were equally apt teachers, never allowing him to linger long in error, and enforcing their teaching with their sharp teeth. Dave was fair and very wise. He never nipped Buck without cause, and he never failed to nip him when he stood in need of it. As François's whip backed him up, Buck found it to be cheaper to mend his ways than to retaliate. Once, during a brief halt, when he got tangled in the traces and delayed the start, both Dave and Sol-leks flew at him and administered a sound trouncing. The resulting tangle was even worse, but Buck took good care to keep the traces clear thereafter; and ere the day was done, so well had he mastered his work, his mates about ceased nagging him. François's whip snapped less frequently, and Perrault even honored Buck by lifting up his feet and carefully examining them.

It was a hard day's run, up the cañon, through Sheep Camp, past the Scales and the timber line, across glaciers and snowdrifts hundreds of feet deep, and over the great Chilkoot Divide, which stands between the salt water and the fresh and guards forbiddingly the sad and lonely North. They made good time down the chain of lakes which fills the craters of extinct volcanoes, and late that night pulled into the huge camp at the head of Lake Bennett, where thousands of goldseekers were building boats against the break-up of the ice in the spring. Buck made his hole in the snow and slept the sleep of the exhausted just, but all too early was routed out in the cold darkness and harnessed with his mates to the sled.

That day they made forty miles, the trail being packed; but the next day, and for many days to follow, they broke their own trail, worked harder, and made poorer time. As a rule, Perrault travelled ahead of the team, packing the snow with webbed shoes to make it easier for them. François, guiding the sled at the gee-pole, sometimes exchanged places with him but not often. Perrault was in a hurry, and he prided himself on his knowledge of ice, which knowledge was indispensable, for the fall ice was very thin, and where there was swift water, there was no ice at all.

Day after day, for days unending, Buck toiled in the traces. Always, they broke camp in the dark, and the first gray of dawn found them hitting the trail with fresh miles reeled off behind them. And always they pitched camp after dark, eating their bit of fish, and crawling to sleep into the snow. Buck was ravenous. The pound and a half of sundried salmon, which was his ration for each day, seemed to go nowhere. He never had enough, and suffered from perpetual hunger pangs. Yet the other dogs, because they weighed less and were born to the life, received a pound only of the fish and managed to keep in good condition.

He swiftly lost the fastidiousness which had characterized his old life. A dainty eater, he found that his mates, finishing first, robbed him of his unfinished ration. There was no defending it. While he was fighting off two or three, it was disappearing down the throats of the others. To remedy this, he ate as fast as they; and, so greatly did hunger compel him, he was not above taking what did not belong to him. He watched and learned. When he saw Pike, one of the new dogs, a clever malingerer and thief, slyly steal a slice of bacon when Perrault's back was turned, he duplicated the performance the following day, getting away with the whole chunk. A great uproar was raised, but he was unsuspected, while Dub, an awkward blunderer who was always getting caught, was punished for Buck's misdeed.

This first theft marked Buck as fit to survive in the hostile Northland environment. It marked his adaptability, his capacity to adjust himself to changing conditions, the lack of which would have meant swift and terrible death. It marked, further, the decay or going to pieces of his moral nature, a vain thing and a handicap in the ruthless struggle for existence. It was all well enough in the

Southland, under the law of love and fellowship, to respect private property and personal feelings; but in the Northland, under the law of club and fang, whoso took such things into account was a fool, and in so far as he observed them he would fail to prosper.

Not that Buck reasoned it out. He was fit, that was all, and unconsciously he accommodated himself to the new mode of life. All his days, no matter what the odds, he had never run from a fight. But the club of the man in the red sweater had beaten into him a more fundamental and primitive code. Civilized, he could have died for a moral consideration, say the defense of Judge Miller's riding whip; but the completeness of his decivilization was now evidenced by his ability to flee from the defense of a moral consideration and so save his hide. He did not steal for joy of it, but because of the clamor of his stomach. He did not rob openly, but stole secretly and cunningly, out of respect for club and fang. In short, the things he did were done because it was easier to do them than not to do them.

His development (or retrogression) was rapid. His muscles became hard as iron and he grew callous to all ordinary pain. He achieved an internal as well as external economy. He could eat anything, no matter how loathsome or indigestible; and, once eaten, the juices of his stomach extracted the last least particle of nutriment; and his blood carried it to the farthest reaches of his body, building it into the toughest and stoutest of tissues. Sight and scent became remarkably keen, while his hearing developed such acuteness that in his sleep he heard the faintest sound and knew whether it heralded peace or peril. He learned to bite the ice out with his teeth when it collected between his toes; and when he was thirsty and there was a thick scum of ice over the water hole, he would break it by rearing and striking it with stiff fore legs. His most conspicuous trait was an ability to scent the wind and forecast it a night in advance. No matter how breathless the air when he dug his nest by tree or bank, the wind that later blew inevitably found him to leeward, sheltered and snug.

And not only did he learn by experience, but instincts long dead became alive again. The domesticated generations fell from him. In vague ways he remembered back to the youth of the breed, to the time the wild dogs ranged in packs through the primeval forest, and killed their meat as they ran it down. It was no task for him to learn to fight with cut and slash and the quick wolf snap. In this manner had fought forgotten ancestors. They quickened the old life within him, and the old tricks which they had stamped into the heredity of the breed were his tricks. They came to him without effort or discovery, as though they had been his always. And when, on the still cold nights, he pointed his nose at a star and howled long and wolflike, it was his ancestors, dead and dust, pointing nose at star and howling down through the centuries and through him. And his cadences were their cadences, the cadences which voiced their woe and what to them was the meaning of the stillness, and the cold, and dark.

Thus, as token of what a puppet thing life is the ancient song surged through him and he came into his own again; and he came because men had found a yellow metal in the North, and because Manuel was a gardener's helper whose wages did not lap over the needs of his wife and divers small copies of himself.

Chapter 3: The Dominant Primordial Beast

The dominant primordial beast was strong in Buck, and under the fierce conditions of trail life it grew and grew. Yet it was a secret growth. His newborn cunning gave him poise and control. He was too busy adjusting himself to the new life to feel at ease, and not only did he not pick fights, but he avoided them whenever possible. A certain deliberateness characterized his attitude. He was not prone to rashness and precipitate action; and in the bitter hatred between him and Spitz he betrayed no impatience, shunned all offensive acts.

On the other hand, possibly because he divined in Buck a dangerous rival, Spitz never lost an opportunity of showing his teeth. He even went out of his way to bully Buck, striving constantly to start the fight which could end only in the death of one or the other. Early in the trip this might have taken place had it not been for an unwonted accident. At the end of this day they made a bleak and miserable camp on the shore of Lake Le Barge. Driving snow, a wind that cut like a white-hot knife, and darkness had forced them to grope for a camping place. They could hardly have fared worse. At their backs rose a perpendicular wall of rock, and Perrault and François were compelled to make their fire and spread their sleeping robes on the ice of the lake itself. The tent they had discarded at Dyea in order to travel light. A few sticks of driftwood furnished them with a fire that thawed down through the ice and left them to eat supper in the dark.

Close in under the sheltering rock Buck made his nest. So snug and warm was it, that he was loath to leave it when François distributed the fish which he had first thawed over the fire. But when Buck finished his ration and returned, he found his nest occupied. A warning snarl told him that the trespasser was Spitz. Till now Buck had avoided trouble with his enemy, but this was too much. The beast in him roared. He sprang upon Spitz with a fury which surprised them both, and Spitz particularly, for his whole experience with Buck had gone to teach him that his rival was an unusually timid dog, who managed to hold his own only because of his great weight and size.

François was surprised, too, when they shot out in a tangle from the disrupted nest and he divined the cause of the trouble. "A-a-ah!" he cried to Buck. "Gif it to heem, by Gar! Gif it to heem, the dirty t'eef!"

Spitz was equally willing. He was crying with sheer rage and eagerness as he circled back and forth for a chance to spring in. Buck was no less eager, and no less cautious, as he likewise circled back and forth for the advantage. But it was then that the unexpected happened, the thing which projected their struggle for supremacy far into the future, past many a weary mile of trail and toil.

An oath from Perrault, the resounding impact of a club upon a bony frame, and a shrill yelp of pain, heralded the breaking forth of pandemonium. The camp was suddenly discovered to be alive with skulking furry forms—starving huskies, four or five score of them, who had scented the camp from some Indian village. They had crept in while Buck and Spitz were fighting, and when the two men sprang among them with stout clubs they showed their teeth and fought back. They were crazed by the smell of the food. Perrault found one with head buried in the grub-box. His club landed heavily on the gaunt ribs, and the grub-box was capsized on the ground. On the instant a score of the famished brutes were scrambling for the bread and bacon. The clubs fell upon them unheeded. They yelped and howled under the rain of blows, but struggled none the less madly till the last crumb had been devoured.

In the meantime the astonished team-dogs had burst out of their nests only to be set upon by the fierce invaders. Never had Buck seen such dogs. It seemed as though their bones would burst through their skins. They were mere skeletons, draped loosely in draggled hides, with blazing eyes and slavered fangs. But the hunger-madness made them terrifying, irresistible. There was no opposing them. The team-dogs were swept back against the cliff at the first onset. Buck was beset by three huskies, and in a trice his head and shoulders were ripped and slashed. The din was frightful. Billee was crying as usual. Dave and Sol-leks, dripping blood from a score of wounds, were fighting bravely side by side. Joe was snapping like a demon. Once his teeth closed on the fore leg of a husky, and he crunched down through the bone. Pike, the malingerer, leaped upon the crippled animal, breaking its neck with a quick dash of teeth and a jerk. Buck got a frothing adversary by the throat, and was sprayed with blood when his teeth sank through the jugular. The warm taste of it in his mouth goaded him to greater fierceness. He flung himself upon another, and at the same time felt teeth sink into his own throat. It was Spitz treacherously attacking from the side.

Perrault and François, having cleaned out their part of the camp, hurried to save their sled-dogs. The wild wave of famished beasts rolled back before them, and Buck shook himself free. But it was only for a moment. The two men were compelled to run back to save the grub, upon which the huskies returned to the attack on the team. Billee, terrified into bravery, sprang through the savage circle and fled away over the ice. Pike and Dub followed on his heels, with the rest of the team behind. As Buck drew himself together to spring after them, out of the trail of his eye he saw Spitz rush upon him with the evident intention of overthrowing him. Once off his feet and under that mass of huskies, there was no hope for him. But he braced himself to the shock of Spitz's charge, then joined the flight out on the lake.

Later, the nine team-dogs gathered together and sought shelter in the forest. Though unpursued, they were in a sorry plight. There was not one who was not wounded in four or five places, while some were wounded grievously. Dub was badly injured in a hind leg; Dolly, the last husky added to the team at Dyea, had a badly torn throat; Joe had lost an eye; while Billee, the good-natured, with an ear chewed and rent to ribbons, cried and whimpered throughout the night. At daybreak they limped warily back to camp, to find the marauders gone and the two men in bad tempers. Fully half their grub supply was gone. The huskies had chewed through the sled lashings and canvas coverings. In fact, nothing, no matter how remotely eatable, had escaped them. They had eaten a pair of Perrault's moose-hide moccasins, chunks out of the leather traces, and even two feet of lash from the end of François's whip. He broke from a mournful contemplation of it to look over his wounded dogs.

"Ah, my frien's," he said softly, "mebbe it mek you mad dog, dose many bites. Mebbe all mad dog, sacredam! Wot you t'ink, eh, Perrault?"

The courier shook his head dubiously. With four hundred miles of trail still between him and Dawson, he could ill afford to have madness break out among his dogs. Two hours of cursing and exertion got the harnesses into shape, and the wound-stiffened team was under way, struggling painfully over the hardest part of the trail they had yet encountered, and for that matter, the hardest between them and Dawson.

The Thirty Mile River was wide open. Its wild water defied the frost, and it was in the eddies only and in the quiet places that the ice held at all. Six days of exhausting toil were required to cover those thirty terrible miles. And terrible they were, for every foot of them was accomplished at the risk of life to dog and man. A dozen times, Perrault, nosing the way, broke through the ice bridges, being saved by the long pole he carried, which he so held that it fell each time across the hole made by his body. But a cold snap was on, the thermometer registering fifty below zero, and each time he broke through he was compelled for very life to build a fire and dry his garments.

Nothing daunted him. It was because nothing daunted him that he had been chosen for government courier. He took all manner of risks, resolutely thrusting his little weazened face into the frost and struggling on from dim dawn to dark. He skirted the frowning shores on rim ice that bent and crackled under foot and on which they dared not halt. Once, the sled broke through, with Dave and Buck, and they were half-frozen and all but drowned by the time they were dragged out. The usual fire was necessary to save them. They were coated solidly with ice, and the two men kept them on the run around the fire, sweating and thawing, so close that they were singed by the flames.

At another time Spitz went through, dragging the whole team after him up to Buck, who strained backward with all his strength, his fore paws on the slippery edge and the ice quivering and snapping all around. But behind him was Dave, likewise straining backward, and behind the sled was François, pulling till his tendons cracked.

Again, the rim ice broke away before and behind, and there was no escape except up the cliff. Perrault scaled it by a miracle, while François prayed for just that miracle; and with every thong and sled-lashing and the last bit of harness rove into a long rope, the dogs were hoisted, one by one, to the cliff crest. François came up last, after the sled and load. Then came the search for a place to descend, which descent was ultimately made by the aid of the rope, and night found them back on the river with a quarter of a mile to the day's credit.

By the time they made the Houtalinqua and good ice, Buck was played out. The rest of the dogs were in like condition; but Perrault, to make up lost time, pushed them late and early. The first day they covered thirty-five miles to the Big Salmon; the next day thirty-five more to the Little Salmon; the third day forty miles, which brought them well up toward the Five Fingers.

Buck's feet were not so compact and hard as the feet of the huskies. His had softened during the many generations since the day his last wild ancestor was tamed by a cave-dweller or river man. All day long he limped in agony, and camp once made, lay down like a dead dog. Hungry as he was, he would not move to receive his ration of fish, which François had to bring to him. Also, the dog-driver rubbed Buck's feet for half an hour each night after supper, and sacrificed the tops of his own moccasins to make four moccasins for Buck. This was a great relief, and Buck caused even the weazened face of Perrault to twist itself into a grin one morning, when François forgot the moccasins and Buck lay on his back, his four feet waving appealingly in the air, and refused to budge without them. Later his feet grew hard to the trail, and the worn-out footgear was thrown away.

At the Pelly one morning, as they were harnessing up, Dolly, who had never been conspicuous for anything, went suddenly mad. She announced her condition by a long, heartbreaking wolf howl that sent every dog bristling with fear, then sprang straight for Buck. He had never seen a dog go mad, nor did he have any reason to fear madness; yet he knew that here was horror, and fled away from it in panic. Straight away he raced, with Dolly, panting and frothing, one leap behind; nor could she gain on him, so great was his terror, nor could he leave her, so great was her madness. He plunged through the wooded breast of the island, flew down to the lower end, crossed a back channel filled with rough ice to another island, gained a third island, curved back to the main river, and in desperation started to cross it. And all the time, though he did not look, he could hear her snarling just one leap behind. François called to him a quarter of a mile away and he doubled back, still one leap ahead, gasping painfully for air and putting all his faith in that François would save him. The dog-driver held the axe poised in his hand, and as Buck shot past him the axe crashed down upon mad Dolly's head.

Buck staggered over against the sled, exhausted, sobbing for breath, helpless. This was Spitz's opportunity. He sprang upon Buck, and twice his teeth sank into his unresisting foe and ripped and tore the flesh to the bone. Then François's lash descended, and Buck had the satisfaction of watching Spitz receive the worst whipping as yet administered to any of the team.

"One devil, dat Spitz," remarked Perrault. "Some dam day heem keel dat Buck."

"Dat Buck two devils," was François's rejoinder. "All de tam I watch dat Buck I know for sure. Lissen: some dam fine day heem get mad lak hell an' den heem chew dat Spitz all up an' spit heem out on de snow. Sure. I know."

From then on it was war between them. Spitz, as lead-dog and acknowledged master of the team, felt his supremacy threatened by this strange Southland dog. And strange Buck was to him, for of the many Southland dogs he had known, not one had shown up worthily in camp and on trail. They were all too soft, dying under the toil, the frost, and starvation. Buck was the exception. He alone endured and prospered, matching the husky in strength, savagery, and cunning. Then he was a masterful dog, and what made him dangerous was the fact that the club of the man in the red sweater had knocked all blind pluck and rashness out of his desire for mastery. He was preëminently cunning, and could bide his time with a patience that was nothing less than primitive.

It was inevitable that the clash for leadership should come. Buck wanted it. He wanted it because it was his nature, because he had been gripped tight by that nameless, incomprehensible pride of the trail and trace—that pride which holds dogs in the toil to the last gasp, which lures them to die joyfully in the harness, and breaks their hearts if they are cut out of the harness. This was the pride of Dave as wheel-dog, of Sol-leks as he pulled with all his strength; the pride that laid hold of them at break of camp, transforming them from sour and sullen brutes into straining, eager, ambitious creatures; the pride that spurred them on all day and dropped them at pitch of camp at night, letting them fall into gloomy unrest and uncontent. This was the pride that bore up Spitz and made him thrash the sled-dogs who blundered and shirked in the traces or hid away at harness-up time in the morning. Likewise it was this pride that made him fear Buck as a possible lead-dog. And this was Buck's pride, too.

He openly threatened the other's leadership. He came between him and the shirks he should have punished. And he did it deliberately. One night there was a heavy snowfall, and in the morning Pike, the malingerer, did not appear. He was securely hidden in his nest under a foot of snow. François called him and sought him in vain. Spitz was wild with wrath. He raged through the camp, smelling and digging in every likely place, snarling so frightfully that Pike heard and shivered in his hiding-place.

But when he was at last unearthed, and Spitz flew at him to punish him, Buck flew, with equal rage, in between. So unexpected was it, and so shrewdly managed, that Spitz was hurled backward and off his feet. Pike, who had been trembling abjectly, took heart at this open mutiny, and sprang upon his overthrown leader. Buck, to whom fair-play was a forgotten code, likewise sprang upon Spitz. But François, chuckling at the incident while unswerving in the administration of justice, brought his lash down upon Buck with all his might. This failed to drive Buck from his prostrate rival, and the butt of the whip was brought into play. Half-stunned by the blow, Buck was knocked backward and the lash laid upon him again and again, while Spitz soundly punished the many times offending Pike.

In the days that followed, as Dawson grew closer and closer, Buck still continued to interfere between Spitz and the culprits; but he did it craftily, when François was not around. With the covert mutiny of Buck, a general insubordination sprang up and increased. Dave and Sol-leks were unaffected, but the rest of the team went from bad to worse. Things no longer went right. There was continual bickering and jangling. Trouble was always afoot, and at the bottom of it was Buck. He kept François busy, for the dog-driver was in constant apprehension of the life-and-death struggle between the two which he knew must take place sooner or later; and on more than one night the sounds of quarrelling and strife among the other dogs turned him out of his sleeping robe, fearful that Buck and Spitz were at it.

But the opportunity did not present itself, and they pulled into Dawson one dreary afternoon with the great fight still to come. Here were many men, and countless dogs, and Buck found them all at work. It seemed the ordained order of things that dogs should work. All day they swung up and down the main street in long teams, and in the night their jingling bells still went by. They hauled cabin logs and firewood, freighted up to the mines, and did all manner of work that horses did in the Santa Clara Valley. Here and there Buck met Southland dogs, but in the main they were the wild wolf husky breed. Every night, regularly, at nine, at twelve, and three, they lifted a nocturnal song, a weird and eerie chant, in which it was Buck's delight to join.

With the aurora borealis flaming coldly overhead, or the stars leaping in the frost dance, and the land numb and frozen under its pall of snow, this song of the huskies might have been the defiance of life, only it was pitched in minor key, with long-drawn wailings and half-sobs, and was more the pleading of life, the articulate travail of existence. It was an old song, old as the breed itself—one of the first songs of the younger world in a day when songs were sad. It was invested with the woe of unnumbered generations, this plaint by which Buck was so strangely stirred. When he moaned and sobbed, it was with the pain of living that was of old the pain of his wild fathers, and the fear and mystery of the cold and dark that was to them fear and mystery. And that he should be stirred by it marked the completeness with which he harked back through the ages of fire and roof to the raw beginnings of life in the howling ages.

Seven days from the time they pulled into Dawson, they dropped down the steep bank by the Barracks to the Yukon Trail, and pulled for Dyea and Salt Water. Perrault was carrying despatches if anything more urgent than those he had brought in; also, the travel pride had gripped him, and he purposed to make the record trip of the year. Several things favored him in this. The week's rest had recuperated the dogs and put them in thorough trim. The trail they had broken into the country was packed hard by later journeyers. And further, the police had arranged in two or three places deposits of grub for dog and man, and he was travelling light.

They made Sixty Miles, which is a fifty-mile run, on the first day; and the second day saw them booming up the Yukon well on their way to Pelly. But such splendid running was achieved not without great trouble and vexation on the part of François. The insidious revolt led by Buck had destroyed the solidarity of the team. It no longer was as one dog leaping in the traces. The encouragement Buck gave the rebels led them into all kinds of petty misdemeanors. No more was Spitz a leader greatly to be feared. The old awe departed, and they grew equal to challenging his authority. Pike robbed him of half a fish one night, and gulped it down under the protection of Buck. Another night Dub and Joe fought Spitz and made him forego the punishment they deserved. And even Billee, the good-natured, was less good-natured, and whined not half so placatingly as in former days. Buck never came near Spitz without snarling and bristling menacingly. In fact, his conduct approached that of a bully, and he was given to swaggering up and down before Spitz's very nose.

The breaking down of discipline likewise affected the dogs in their relations with one another. They quarrelled and bickered more than ever among themselves, till at times the camp was a howling bedlam. Dave and Sol-leks alone were unaltered, though they were made irritable by the unending squabbling. François swore strange barbarous oaths, and stamped the snow in futile rage, and tore his hair. His lash was always singing among the dogs, but it was of small avail. Directly his back was turned they were at it again. He backed up Spitz with his whip, while Buck backed up the remainder of the team. François knew he was behind all the trouble, and Buck knew he knew; but Buck was too clever ever again to be caught red-handed. He worked faithfully in the harness, for the toil had become a delight to him; yet it was a greater delight slyly to precipitate a fight amongst his mates and tangle the traces.

At the mouth of the Tahkeena, one night after supper, Dub turned up a snowshoe rabbit, blundered it, and missed. In a second the whole team was in full cry. A hundred yards away was a camp of the Northwest Police, with fifty dogs, huskies all, who joined the chase. The rabbit sped down the river, turned off into a small creek, up the frozen bed of which it held steadily. It ran lightly on the surface of the snow, while the dogs ploughed through by main strength. Buck led the pack, sixty strong, around bend after bend, but he could not gain. He lay down low to the race, whining eagerly, his splendid body flashing forward, leap by leap, in the wan white moonlight. And leap by leap, like some pale frost wraith, the snowshoe rabbit flashed on ahead.

All that stirring of old instincts which at stated periods drives men out from the sounding cities to forest and plain to kill things by chemically propelled leaden pellets, the blood lust, the joy to kill—all this was Buck's, only it was infinitely more intimate. He was ranging at the head of the pack, running the wild thing down, the living meat, to kill with his own teeth and wash his muzzle to the eyes in warm blood.

There is an ecstasy that marks the summit of life, and beyond which life cannot rise. And such is the paradox of living, this ecstasy comes when one is most alive, and it comes as a complete forgetfulness that one is alive. This ecstasy, this forgetfulness of living, comes to the artist, caught up and out of himself in a sheet of flame; it comes to the soldier, war-mad on a stricken field and refusing quarter; and it came to Buck, leading the pack, sounding the old wolf-cry, straining after the food that was alive and that fled swiftly before him through the moonlight. He was sounding the deeps of his nature, and of the parts of his nature that were deeper than he, going back into the womb of Time. He was mastered by the sheer surging of life, the tidal wave of being, the perfect joy of each separate muscle, joint, and sinew and that it was everything that was not death, that it was aglow and rampant, expressing itself in movement, flying exultantly under the stars and over the face of dead matter that did not move.

But Spitz, cold and calculating even in his supreme moods, left the pack and cut across a narrow neck of land where the creek made a long bend around. Buck did not know of this, and as he rounded the bend, the frost wraith of a rabbit still flitting before him, he saw another and larger frost wraith leap from the overhanging bank into the immediate path of the rabbit. It was Spitz. The rabbit could not turn, and as the white teeth broke its back in mid air it shrieked as loudly as a stricken man may shriek. At sound of this, the cry of Life plunging down from Life's apex in the grip of Death, the full pack at Buck's heels raised a hell's chorus of delight.

Buck did not cry out. He did not check himself, but drove in upon Spitz, shoulder to shoulder, so hard that he missed the throat. They rolled over and over in the powdery snow. Spitz gained his feet almost as though he had not been overthrown, slashing Buck down the shoulder and leaping clear. Twice his teeth clipped together, like the steel jaws of a trap, as he backed away for better footing, with lean and lifting lips that writhed and snarled.

In a flash Buck knew it. The time had come. It was to the death. As they circled about, snarling, ears laid back, keenly watchful for the advantage, the scene came to Buck with a sense of familiarity. He seemed to remember it all—the white woods, and earth, and moonlight, and the thrill of battle. Over the whiteness and silence brooded a ghostly calm. There was not the faintest whisper of air—nothing moved, not a leaf quivered, the visible breaths of the dogs rising slowly and lingering in the frosty air. They had made short work of the snowshoe rabbit, these dogs that were ill-tamed wolves; and they were now drawn up in an expectant circle. They, too, were silent, their eyes only gleaming and their breaths drifting slowly upward. To Buck it was nothing new or strange, this scene of old time. It was as though it had always been, the wonted way of things.

Spitz was a practised fighter. From Spitzbergen through the Arctic, and across Canada and the Barrens, he had held his own with all manner of dogs and achieved to mastery over them. Bitter rage was his, but never blind rage. In passion to rend and destroy, he never forgot that his enemy was in like passion to rend and destroy. He never rushed till he was prepared to receive a rush; never attacked till he had first defended that attack.

In vain Buck strove to sink his teeth in the neck of the big white dog. Wherever his fangs struck for the softer flesh, they were countered by the fangs of Spitz. Fang clashed fang, and lips were cut and bleeding, but Buck could not penetrate his enemy's guard. Then he warmed up and enveloped Spitz in a whirlwind of rushes. Time and time again he tried for the snow-white throat, where life bubbled near to the surface, and each time and every time Spitz slashed him and got away. Then Buck took to rushing, as though for the throat, when, suddenly drawing back his head and curving in from the side, he would drive his shoulder at the shoulder of Spitz, as a ram by which to overthrow him. But instead, Buck's shoulder was slashed down each time as Spitz leaped lightly away.

Spitz was untouched, while Buck was streaming with blood and panting hard. The fight was growing desperate. And all the while the silent and wolfish circle waited to finish off whichever dog went down. As Buck grew winded, Spitz took to rushing, and he kept him staggering for footing. Once Buck went over, and the whole circle of sixty dogs started up; but he recovered himself, almost in mid air, and the circle sank down again and waited.

But Buck possessed a quality that made for greatness—imagination. He fought by instinct, but he could fight by head as well. He rushed, as though attempting the old shoulder trick, but at the last instant swept low to the snow and in. His teeth closed on Spitz's left fore leg. There was a crunch of breaking bone, and the white dog faced him on three legs. Thrice he tried to knock him over, then repeated the trick and broke the right fore leg. Despite the pain and helplessness, Spitz struggled madly to keep up. He saw the silent circle, with gleaming eyes, lolling tongues, and silvery breaths drifting upward, closing in upon him as he had seen similar circles close in upon beaten antagonists in the past. Only this time he was the one who was beaten.

There was no hope for him. Buck was inexorable. Mercy was a thing reserved for gentler climes. He manœvered for the final rush. The circle had tightened till he could feel the breaths of the huskies on his flanks. He could see them, beyond Spitz and to either side, half crouching for the spring, their eyes fixed upon him. A pause seemed to fall. Every animal was motionless as though turned to stone. Only Spitz quivered and bristled as he staggered back and forth, snarling with horrible menace, as though to frighten off impending death. Then Buck sprang in and out, but while he was in, shoulder had at last squarely met shoulder. The dark circle became a dot on the moon-flooded snow as Spitz disappeared from view. Buck stood and looked on, the successful champion, the dominant primordial beast who had made his kill and found it good.

Chapter 4: Who Has Won to Mastership

"Eh? Wot I say? I spik true w'en I say dat Buck two devils."

This was François's speech next morning when he discovered Spitz missing and Buck covered with wounds. He drew him to the fire and by its light pointed them out.

"Dat Spitz fight lak hell," said Perrault, as he surveyed the gaping rips and cuts.

"An' dat Buck fight lak two hells," was François's answer. "An' now we make good time. No more Spitz, no more trouble, sure."

While Perrault packed the camp outfit and loaded the sled, the dog-driver proceeded to harness the dogs. Buck trotted up to the place Spitz would have occupied as leader; but François, not noticing him, brought Sol-leks to the coveted position. In his judgment,

Sol-leks was the best lead-dog left. Buck sprang upon Sol-leks in a fury, driving him back and standing in his place.

"Eh? eh?" François cried, slapping his thighs gleefully. "Look at dat Buck. Heem keel dat Spitz, heem t'ink to take de job."

"Go 'way, Chook!" he cried, but Buck refused to budge.

He took Buck by the scruff of the neck, and though the dog growled threateningly, dragged him to one side and replaced Sol-leks. The old dog did not like it, and showed plainly that he was afraid of Buck. François was obdurate, but when he turned his back Buck again displaced Sol-leks, who was not at all unwilling to go.

François was angry. "Now, by Gar, I feex you!" he cried, coming back with a heavy club in his hand.

Buck remembered the man in the red sweater, and retreated slowly; nor did he attempt to charge in when Sol-leks was once more brought forward. But he circled just beyond the range of the club, snarling with bitterness and rage; and while he circled he watched the club so as to dodge it if thrown by François, for he was become wise in the way of clubs.

The driver went about his work, and he called to Buck when he was ready to put him in his old place in front of Dave. Buck retreated two or three steps. François followed him up, whereupon he again retreated. After some time of this, François threw down the club, thinking that Buck feared a thrashing. But Buck was in open revolt. He wanted, not to escape a clubbing, but to have the leadership. It was his by right. He had earned it, and he would not be content with less.

Perrault took a hand. Between them they ran him about for the better part of an hour. They threw clubs at him. He dodged. They cursed him, and his fathers and mothers before him, and all his seed to come after him down to the remotest generation, and every hair on his body and drop of blood in his veins; and he answered curse with snarl and kept out of their reach. He did not try to run away, but retreated around and around the camp, advertising plainly that when his desire was met, he would come in and be good.

François sat down and scratched his head. Perrault looked at his watch and swore. Time was flying, and they should have been on the trail an hour gone. François scratched his head again. He shook it and grinned sheepishly at the courier, who shrugged his shoulders in sign that they were beaten. Then François went up to where Sol-leks stood and called to Buck. Buck laughed, as dogs laugh, yet kept his distance. François unfastened Sol-leks's traces and put him back in his old place. The team stood harnessed to the sled in an unbroken line, ready for the trail. There was no place for Buck save at the front. Once more François called, and once more Buck laughed and kept away.

"T'row down de club," Perrault commanded.

François complied, whereupon Buck trotted in, laughing triumphantly, and swung around into position at the head of the team. His traces were fastened, the sled broken out, and with both men running they dashed out on to the river trail.

Highly as the dog-driver had forevalued Buck, with his two devils, he found, while the day was yet young, that he had undervalued. At a bound Buck took up the duties of leadership; and where judgment was required, and quick thinking and quick acting, he showed himself the superior even to Spitz, of whom François had never seen an equal.

But it was in giving the law and making his mates live up to it, that Buck excelled. Dave and Sol-leks did not mind the change in leadership. It was none of their business. Their business was to toil, and toil mightily, in the traces. So long as that was not interfered with, they did not care what happened. Billee, the good-natured, could lead for all they cared so long as he kept order. The rest of the team, however, had grown unruly during the last days of Spitz, and their surprise was great now that Buck proceeded to lick them into shape.

Pike, who pulled at Buck's heels, and who never put an ounce more of his weight against the breast band than he was compelled to do, was swiftly and repeatedly shaken for loafing, and ere the first day was done he was pulling more than ever before in his life. The first night in camp, Joe, the sour one, was punished roundly—a thing that Spitz had never succeeded in doing. Buck simply smothered him by virtue of superior weight, and cut him up till he ceased snapping and began to whine for mercy.

The general tone of the team picked up immediately. It recovered its old-time solidarity, and once more the dogs leaped as one dog in the traces. At the Rink Rapids two native huskies, Teek and Koona, were added; and the celerity with which Buck broke them in took away François's breath.

"Nevaire such a dog as dat Buck!" he cried. "No, nevaire! Heem worth one t'ousan' dollair, by Gar! Eh? Wot you say, Perrault?"

And Perrault nodded. He was ahead of the record then, and gaining day by day. The trail was in excellent condition, well packed and hard, and there was no new-fallen snow with which to contend. It was not too cold. The temperature dropped to fifty below zero and remained there the whole trip. The men rode and ran by turn, and the dogs were kept on the jump, with but infrequent stoppages.

The Thirty Mile River was comparatively coated with ice, and they covered in one day going out what had taken them ten days coming in. In one run they made a sixty-mile dash from the foot of Lake Le Barge to the White Horse Rapids. Across Marsh, Tagish, and Bennett (seventy miles of lakes), they flew so fast that the man whose turn it was to run towed behind the sled at the end of a rope. And on the last night of the second week they topped White Pass and dropped down the sea slope with the lights of Skagway and of the shipping at their feet.

It was a record run. Each day for fourteen days they had averaged forty miles. For three days Perrault and François threw chests up and down the main street of Skagway and were deluged with invitations to drink, while the team was the constant centre of a worshipful crowd of dog-busters and mushers. Then three or four Western bad men aspired to clean out the town, were riddled like timber boxes for their pains, and public interest turned to other idols. Next came official orders. François called Buck to him, threw his arms around him, wept over him. And that was the last of François and Perrault. Like other men, they passed out of Buck's life for good.

A Scotch half-breed took charge of him and his mates, and in company with a dozen other dog-teams he started back over the weary trail to Dawson. It was no light running now, nor record time, but heavy toil each day, with a heavy load behind; for this was the mail train, carrying word from the world to the men who sought gold under the shadow of the Pole.

Buck did not like it, but he bore up well to the work, taking pride in it after the manner of Dave and Sol-leks, and seeing that his mates, whether they prided in it or not, did their fair share. It was a monotonous life, operating with machine-like regularity. One day was very like another. At a certain time each morning the cooks turned out, fires were built, and breakfast was eaten. Then while some broke camp, others harnessed the dogs, and they were under way an hour or so before the darkness fell which gave warning of dawn. At night, camp was made. Some pitched the flies, others cut firewood and pine boughs for the beds, and still others carried water or ice for the cooks. Also, the dogs were fed. To them, this was the one feature of the day, though it was good to loaf around, after the fish was eaten, for an hour or so with the other dogs, of which there were fivescore and odd. There were fierce fighters among them, but three battles with the fiercest brought Buck to mastery, so that when he bristled and showed his teeth they got out of his way.

Best of all, perhaps, he loved to lie near the fire, hind legs crouched under him, fore legs stretched out in front, head raised, and eyes blinking dreamily at the flames. Sometimes he thought of Judge Miller's big house in the sun-kissed Santa Clara Valley, and of the cement swimming-tank, and Ysabel, the Mexican hairless, and Toots, the Japanese pug; but oftener he remembered the man in the red sweater, the death of Curly, the great fight with Spitz, and the good things he had eaten or would like to eat. He was not homesick. The Sunland was very dim and distant, and such memories had no power over him. Far more potent were the memories of his heredity that gave things he had never seen before a seeming familiarity; the instincts (which were but the memories of his ancestors become habits) which had lapsed in later days, and still later, in him, quickened and became alive again.

Sometimes as he crouched there, blinking dreamily at the flames, it seemed that the flames were of another fire, and that as he crouched by this other fire he saw another and different man from the half-breed cook before him. This other man was shorter of leg and longer of arm, with muscles that were stringy and knotty rather than rounded and swelling. The hair of this man was long and matted, and his head slanted back under it from the eyes. He uttered strange sounds, and seemed very much afraid of the darkness, into which he peered continually, clutching in his hand, which hung midway between knee and foot, a stick with a heavy stone made fast to the end. He was all but naked, a ragged and fire-scorched skin hanging part way down his back, but on his body there was much hair. In some places, across the chest and shoulders and down the outside of the arms and thighs, it was matted into almost a thick fur. He did not stand erect, but with trunk inclined forward from the hips, on legs that bent at the knees. About his body there was a peculiar springiness, or resiliency, almost catlike, and a quick alertness as of one who lived in perpetual fear of things seen and unseen.

At other times this hairy man squatted by the fire with head between his legs and slept. On such occasions his elbows were on his knees, his hands clasped above his head as though to shed rain by the hairy arms. And beyond that fire, in the circling darkness, Buck could see many gleaming coals, two by two, always two by two, which he knew to be the eyes of great beasts of prey. And he could hear the crashing of their bodies through the undergrowth, and the noises they made in the night. And dreaming there by the Yukon bank, with lazy eyes blinking at the fire, these sounds and sights of another world would make the hair to rise along his back and stand on end across his shoulders and up his neck, till he whimpered low and suppressedly, or growled softly, and the half-breed cook shouted at him, "Hey, you Buck, wake up!" Whereupon the other world would vanish and the real world come into his eyes, and he would get up and yawn and stretch as though he had been asleep.

It was a hard trip, with the mail behind them, and the heavy work wore them down. They were short of weight and in poor condition when they made Dawson, and should have had a ten days' or a week's rest at least. But in two days' time they dropped down the Yukon bank from the Barracks, loaded with letters for the outside. The dogs were tired, the drivers grumbling, and to make matters worse, it snowed every day. This meant a soft trail, greater friction on the runners, and heavier pulling for the dogs; yet the drivers were fair through it all, and did their best for the animals.

Each night the dogs were attended to first. They ate before the drivers ate, and no man sought his sleeping-robe till he had seen to the feet of the dogs he drove. Still, their strength went down. Since the beginning of the winter they had travelled eighteen hundred miles, dragging sleds the whole weary distance; and eighteen hundred miles will tell upon life of the toughest. Buck stood it, keeping his mates up to their work and maintaining discipline, though he too was very tired. Billee cried and whimpered regularly in his sleep each night. Joe was sourer than ever, and Sol-leks was unapproachable, blind side or other side.

But it was Dave who suffered most of all. Something had gone wrong with him. He became more morose and irritable, and when camp was pitched at once made his nest, where his driver fed him. Once out of the harness and down, he did not get on his feet again till harness-up time in the morning. Sometimes, in the traces, when jerked by a sudden stoppage of the sled, or by straining to start it, he would cry out with pain. The driver examined him, but could find nothing. All the drivers became interested in his case. They talked it over at mealtime, and over their last pipes before going to bed, and one night they held a consultation. He was brought from his nest to the fire and was pressed and prodded till he cried out many times. Something was wrong inside, but they could locate no broken bones, could not make it out.

By the time Cassiar Bar was reached, he was so weak that he was falling repeatedly in the traces. The Scotch half-breed called a halt and took him out of the team, making the next dog, Sol-leks, fast to the sled. His intention was to rest Dave, letting him run free behind the sled. Sick as he was, Dave resented being taken out, grunting and growling while the traces were unfastened, and whimpering broken-heartedly when he saw Sol-leks in the position he had held and served so long. For the pride of trace and trail was his, and sick unto death, he could not bear that another dog should do his work.

When the sled started, he floundered in the soft snow alongside the beaten trail, attacking Sol-leks with his teeth, rushing against him and trying to thrust him off into the soft snow on the other side, striving to leap inside his traces and get between him and the sled, and all the while whining and yelping and crying with grief and pain. The half-breed tried to drive him away with the whip; but he paid no heed to the stinging lash, and the man had not the heart to strike harder. Dave refused to run quietly on the trail behind the sled, where the going was easy, but continued to flounder alongside in the soft snow, where the going was most difficult, till exhausted. Then he fell, and lay where he fell, howling lugubriously as the long train of sleds churned by.

With the last remnant of his strength he managed to stagger along behind till the train made another stop, when he floundered past the sleds to his own, where he stood alongside Sol-leks. His driver lingered a moment to get a light for his pipe from the man behind. Then he returned and started his dogs. They swung out on the trail with remarkable lack of exertion, turned their heads uneasily, and stopped in surprise. The driver was surprised, too; the sled had not moved. He called his comrades to witness the sight. Dave had bitten through both of Sol-leks's traces, and was standing directly in front of the sled in his proper place.

He pleaded with his eyes to remain there. The driver was perplexed. His comrades talked of how a dog could break its heart through being denied the work that killed it, and recalled instances they had known, where dogs, too old for the toil, or injured, had died because they were cut out of the traces. Also, they held it a mercy, since Dave was to die anyway, that he should die in the traces, heart-easy and content. So he was harnessed in again, and proudly he pulled as of old, though more than once he cried out involuntarily from the bite of his inward hurt. Several times he fell down and was dragged in the traces, and once the sled ran upon him so that he limped thereafter on one of his hind legs.

But he held out till camp was reached, when his driver made a place for him by the fire. Morning found him too weak to travel. At harness-up time he tried to crawl to his driver. By convulsive efforts he got on his feet, staggered, and fell. Then he wormed his way forward slowly toward where the harnesses were being put on his mates. He would advance his fore legs and drag up his body with a sort of hitching movement, then he would advance his fore legs and hitch ahead again for a few more inches. His strength left him, and the last his mates saw of him he lay gasping in the snow and yearning toward them. But they could hear him mournfully howling till they passed out of sight behind a belt of river timber.

Here the train was halted. The Scotch half-breed slowly retraced his steps to the camp they had left. The men ceased talking. A revolver-shot rang out. The man came back hurriedly. The whips snapped, the bells tinkled merrily, the sleds churned along the trail; but Buck knew, and every dog knew, what had taken place behind the belt of river trees.

Chapter 5: The Toil of Trace and Trail

Thirty days from the time it left Dawson, the Salt Water Mail, with Buck and his mates at the fore, arrived at Skagway. They were in a wretched state, worn out and worn down. Buck's one hundred and forty pounds had dwindled to one hundred and fifteen. The rest of his mates, though lighter dogs, had relatively lost more weight than he. Pike, the malingerer, who, in his lifetime of deceit, had often successfully feigned a hurt leg, was now limping in earnest. Sol-leks was limping, and Dub was suffering from a wrenched shoulder blade.

They were all terribly footsore. No spring or rebound was left in them. Their feet fell heavily on the trail, jarring their bodies and doubling the fatigue of a day's travel. There was nothing the matter with them except that they were dead tired. It was not the dead-tiredness that comes through brief and excessive effort, from which recovery is a matter of hours; but it was the dead-tiredness that comes through the slow and prolonged strength drainage of months of toil. There was no power of recuperation left, no reserve strength to call upon. It had been all used, the last least bit of it. Every muscle, every fibre, every cell, was tired, dead tired. And there was reason for it. In less than five months they had travelled twenty-five hundred miles, during the last eighteen hundred of which they had had but five days' rest. When they arrived at Skagway they were apparently on their last legs. They could barely keep the traces taut, and on the down grades just managed to keep out of the way of the sled.

"Mush on, poor sore feets," the driver encouraged them as they tottered down the main street of Skagway. "Dis is de las'. Den we get one long res'. Eh? For sure. One bully long res'."

The drivers confidently expected a long stop-over. Themselves, they had covered twelve hundred miles with two days' rest, and in the nature of reason and common justice they deserved an interval of loafing. But so many were the men who had rushed into the Klondike, and so many were the sweethearts, wives, and kin that had not rushed in, that the congested mail was taking on Alpine proportions; also, there were official orders. Fresh batches of Hudson Bay dogs were to take the places of those worthless for the trail. The worthless ones were to be got rid of, and, since dogs count for little against dollars, they were to be sold.

Three days passed, by which time Buck and his mates found how really tired and weak they were. Then, on the morning of the fourth day, two men from the States came along and bought them, harness and all, for a song. The men addressed each other as "Hal" and "Charles." Charles was a middle-aged, lightish-colored man, with weak and watery eyes and a mustache that twisted fiercely and vigorously up, giving the lie to the limply drooping lip it concealed. Hal was a youngster of nineteen or twenty, with a big Colt's revolver and a hunting-knife strapped about him on a belt that fairly bristled with cartridges. This belt was the most salient thing about him. It advertised his callowness—a callowness sheer and unutterable. Both men were manifestly out of place, and why such as they should adventure the North is part of the mystery of things that passes understanding.

Buck heard the chaffering, saw the money pass between the man and the Government agent, and knew that the Scotch half-breed and the mail-train drivers were passing out of his life on the heels of Perrault and François and the others who had gone before. When driven with his mates to the new owners' camp, Buck saw a slipshod and slovenly affair, tent half stretched, dishes unwashed, everything in disorder; also, he saw a woman. "Mercedes" the men called her. She was Charles's wife and Hal's sister—a nice family party.

Buck watched them apprehensively as they proceeded to take down the tent and load the sled. There was a great deal of effort about their manner, but no businesslike method. The tent was rolled into an awkward bundle three times as large as it should have been. The tin dishes were packed away unwashed. Mercedes continually fluttered in the way of her men and kept up an unbroken chattering of remonstrance and advice. When they put a clothes-sack on the front of the sled, she suggested it should go on the back; and when they had it put on the back, and covered it over with a couple of other bundles, she discovered overlooked articles which could abide nowhere else but in that very sack, and they unloaded again.

Three men from a neighboring tent came out and looked on, grinning and winking at one another.

"You've got a right smart load as it is," said one of them; "and it's not me should tell you your business, but I wouldn't tote that tent along if I was you."

"Undreamed of!" cried Mercedes, throwing up her hands in dainty dismay. "However in the world could I manage without a tent?"

"It's springtime, and you won't get any more cold weather," the man replied.

She shook her head decidedly, and Charles and Hal put the last odds and ends on top the mountainous load.

"Think it'll ride?" one of the men asked.

"Why shouldn't it?" Charles demanded rather shortly.

"Oh, that's all right, that's all right," the man hastened meekly to say. "I was just a-wonderin', that is all. It seemed a mite top-heavy."

Charles turned his back and drew the lashings down as well as he could, which was not in the least well.

"An' of course the dogs can hike along all day with that contraption behind them," affirmed a second of the men.

"Certainly," said Hal, with freezing politeness, taking hold of the gee-pole with one hand and swinging his whip from the other. "Mush!" he shouted. "Mush on there!"

The dogs sprang against the breastbands, strained hard for a few moments, then relaxed. They were unable to move the sled.

"The lazy brutes, I'll show them," he cried, preparing to lash out at them with the whip.

But Mercedes interfered, crying, "Oh, Hal, you mustn't," as she caught hold of the whip and wrenched it from him. "The poor dears! Now you must promise you won't be harsh with them for the rest of the trip, or I won't go a step."

"Precious lot you know about dogs," her brother sneered; "and I wish you'd leave me alone. They're lazy, I tell you, and you've got to whip them to get anything out of them. That's their way. You ask anyone. Ask one of those men."

Mercedes looked at them imploringly, untold repugnance at sight of pain written in her pretty face.

"They're weak as water, if you want to know," came the reply from one of the men. "Plumb tuckered out, that's what's the matter. They need a rest."

"Rest be blanked," said Hal, with his beardless lips; and Mercedes said, "Oh!" in pain and sorrow at the oath.

But she was a clannish creature, and rushed at once to the defence of her brother. "Never mind that man," she said pointedly. "You're driving our dogs and you do what you think best with them."

Again Hal's whip fell upon the dogs. They threw themselves against the breastbands, dug their feet into the packed snow, got down low to it, and put forth all their strength. The sled held as though it were an anchor. After two efforts, they stood still, panting. The whip was whistling savagely, when once more Mercedes interfered. She dropped on her knees before Buck, with tears in her eyes, and put her arms around his neck.

"You poor, poor dears," she cried sympathetically, "why don't you pull hard?—then you wouldn't be whipped." Buck did not like her, but he was feeling too miserable to resist her, taking it as part of the day's miserable work.

One of the onlookers, who had been clenching his teeth to suppress hot speech, now spoke up:—

"It's not that I care a whoop what becomes of you, but for the dogs' sakes I just want to tell you, you can help them a mighty lot by breaking out that sled. The runners are froze fast. Throw your weight against the gee-pole, right and left, and break it out."

A third time the attempt was made, but this time, following the advice, Hal broke out the runners which had been frozen to the snow. The overloaded and unwieldy sled forged ahead, Buck and his mates struggling frantically under the rain of blows. A hundred yards ahead the path turned and sloped steeply into the main street. It would have required an experienced man to keep the top-heavy sled upright, and Hal was not such a man. As they swung on the turn the sled went over, spilling half its load through the loose lashings. The dogs never stopped. The lightened sled bounded on its side behind them. They were angry because of the ill treatment they had received and the unjust load. Buck was raging. He broke into a run, the team following his lead. Hal cried, "Whoa! whoa!" but they gave no heed. He tripped and was pulled off his feet. The capsized sled ground over him, and the dogs dashed on up the street, adding to the gayety of Skagway as they scattered the remainder of the outfit along its chief thoroughfare.

Kind-hearted citizens caught the dogs and gathered up the scattered belongings. Also, they gave advice. Half the load and twice the dogs, if they ever expected to reach Dawson, was what was said. Hal and his sister and brother-in-law listened unwillingly, pitched tent, and overhauled the outfit, canned goods were turned out that made men laugh, for canned goods on the Long Trail is a thing to dream about. "Blankets for a hotel," quoth one of the men who laughed and helped. "Half as many is too much; get rid of them. Throw away that tent, and all those dishes—who's going to wash them, anyway? Good Lord, do you think you're travelling on a Pullman?"

And so it went, the inexorable elimination of the superfluous. Mercedes cried when her clothes-bags were dumped on the ground and article after article was thrown out. She cried in general, and she cried in particular over each discarded thing. She clasped hands about knees, rocking back and forth brokenheartedly. She averred she would not go an inch, not for a dozen Charleses. She appealed to everybody and to everything, finally wiping her eyes and proceeding to cast out even articles of apparel that were imperative necessaries. And in her zeal, when she had finished with her own, she attacked the belongings of her men and went through them like a tornado.

This accomplished, the outfit, though cut in half, was still a formidable bulk. Charles and Hal went out in the evening and bought six Outside dogs. These added to the six of the original team, and Teek and Koona, the huskies obtained at the Rink Rapids on the record trip, brought the team up to fourteen. But the Outside dogs, though practically broken in since their landing, did not amount to much. Three were short-haired pointers, one was a Newfoundland, and the other two were mongrels of indeterminate breed. They did not seem to know anything, these newcomers. Buck and his comrades looked upon them with disgust, and though he speedily taught them their places and what not to do, he could not teach them what to do. They did not take kindly to trace and trail. With the exception of the two mongrels, they were bewildered and spirit-broken by the strange savage environment in which they found themselves and by ill treatment they had received. The two mongrels were without spirit at all; bones were the only things breakable about them.

With the newcomers hopeless and forlorn, and the old team worn out by twenty-five hundred miles of continuous trail, the outlook was anything but bright. The two men, however, were quite cheerful. And they were proud, too. They were doing the thing in style, with fourteen dogs. They had seen other sleds depart over the Pass for Dawson or come in from Dawson, but never had they seen a sled with so many as fourteen dogs. In the nature of Arctic travel there was a reason why fourteen dogs should not drag one sled, and that was that one sled could not carry the food for fourteen dogs. But Charles and Hal did not know this. They had worked the trip out with a pencil, so much to a dog, so many dogs, and so many days, Q. E. D. Mercedes looked over their shoulders and nodded comprehensively, it was all so very simple.

Late next morning Buck led the long team up the street. There was nothing lively about it, no snap or go in him and his fellows. They were starting dead weary. Four times he had covered the distance between Salt Water and Dawson, and the knowledge that, jaded and tired, he was facing the same trail once more, made him bitter. His heart was not in the work, nor was the heart of any dog. The Outsides were timid and frightened, the Insides without confidence in their masters.

Buck felt vaguely that there was no depending upon these two men and the woman. They did not know how to do anything, and as the days went by it became apparent that they could not learn. They were slack in all things, without order or discipline. It took them half the night to pitch a slovenly camp, and half the morning to break that camp and get the sled loaded in fashion so slovenly that for the rest of the day they were occupied in stopping and rearranging the load. Some days they did not make ten miles. On other days they were unable to get started at all. And on no day did they succeed in making more than half the distance used by the men as a basis in their dog-food computation.

It was inevitable that they should go short on dog-food. But they hastened it by overfeeding, bringing the day nearer when underfeeding would commence. The Outside dogs, whose digestions had not been trained by chronic famine to make the most of little, had voracious appetites. And when, in addition to this, the worn-out huskies pulled weakly, Hal decided that the orthodox ration was too small. He doubled it. And to cap it all, when Mercedes, with tears in her pretty eyes and a quaver in her throat, could not cajole him into giving the dogs still more, she stole from the fish-sacks and fed them slyly. But is was not food that Buck and the huskies needed, but rest. And though they were making poor time, the heavy load they dragged sapped their strength severely.

Then came the underfeeding. Hal awoke one day to the fact that his dog-food was half gone and the distance only quarter covered; further, that for love or money no additional dog-food was to be obtained. So he cut down even the orthodox ration and tried to increase the day's travel. His sister and brother-in-law seconded him; but they were frustrated by their heavy outfit and their own incompetence. It was a simple matter to give the dogs less food; but it was impossible to make the dogs travel faster, while their own inability to get under way earlier in the morning prevented them from travelling longer hours. Not only did they not know how to work dogs, but they did not know how to work themselves.

The first to go was Dub. Poor blundering thief that he was, always getting caught and punished, he had none the less been a faithful worker. His wrenched shoulder-blade, untreated and unrested, went from bad to worse, till finally Hal shot him with the big Colt's revolver. It is a saying of the country that an Outside dog starves to death on the ration of the husky, so the six Outside dogs under Buck could do no less than die on half the ration of the husky. The Newfoundland went first, followed by the three short-haired pointers, the two mongrels hanging more grittily on to life, but going in the end.

By this time all the amenities and gentleness of the Southland had fallen away from the three people. Shorn of its glamour and romance, Arctic travel became to them a reality too harsh for their manhood and womanhood. Mercedes ceased weeping over the dogs, being too occupied with weeping over herself and with quarrelling with her husband and brother. To quarrel was the one thing they were never too weary to do. Their irritability arose out of their misery, increased with it, doubled upon it, outdistanced it. The wonderful patience of the trail which comes to men who toil hard and suffer sore, and remain sweet of speech and kindly, did not come to these two men and the woman. They had no inkling of such a patience. They were stiff and in pain; their muscles ached, their bones ached, their very hearts ached; and because of this they became sharp of speech, and hard words were first on their lips in the morning and last at night.

Charles and Hal wrangled whenever Mercedes gave them a chance. It was the cherished belief of each that he did more than his share of the work, and neither forbore to speak this belief at every opportunity. Sometimes Mercedes sided with her husband, sometimes with her brother. The result was a beautiful and unending family quarrel. Starting from a dispute as to which should chop a few sticks for the fire (a dispute which concerned only Charles and Hal), presently would be lugged in the rest of the family, fathers, mothers, uncles, cousins, people thousands of miles away, and some of them dead. That Hal's views on art, or the sort of society plays his mother's brother wrote, should have anything to do with the chopping of a few sticks of firewood, passes comprehension; nevertheless the quarrel was as likely to tend in that direction as in the direction of Charles's political prejudices. And that Charles's sister's tale-bearing tongue should be relevant to the building of a Yukon fire, was apparent only to Mercedes, who disburdened herself of copious opinions upon that topic, and incidentally upon a few other traits unpleasantly peculiar to her husband's family. In the meantime the fire remained unbuilt, the camp half pitched, and the dogs unfed.

Mercedes nursed a special grievance—the grievance of sex. She was pretty and soft, and had been chivalrously treated all her days.

But the present treatment by her husband and brother was everything save chivalrous. It was her custom to be helpless. They complained. Upon which impeachment of what to her was her most essential sex prerogative, she made their lives unendurable. She no longer considered the dogs, and because she was sore and tired, she persisted in riding on the sled. She was pretty and soft, but she weighed one hundred and twenty pounds—a lusty last straw to the load dragged by the weak and starving animals. She rode for days, till they fell in the traces and the sled stood still. Charles and Hal begged her to get off and walk, pleaded with her, entreated, the while she wept and importuned Heaven with a recital of their brutality.

On one occasion they took her off the sled by main strength. They never did it again. She let her legs go limp like a spoiled child, and sat down on the trail. They went on their way, but she did not move. After they had travelled three miles they unloaded the sled, came back for her, and by main strength put her on the sled again.

In the excess of their own misery they were callous to the suffering of their animals. Hal's theory, which he practised on others, was that one must get hardened. He had started out preaching it to his sister and brother-in-law. Failing there, he hammered it into the dogs with a club. At the Five Fingers the dog-food gave out, and a toothless old squaw offered to trade them a few pounds of frozen horsehide for the Colt's revolver that kept the big hunting-knife company at Hal's hip. A poor substitute for food was this hide, just as it had been stripped from the starved horses of the cattlemen six months back. In its frozen state it was more like strips of galvanized iron, and when a dog wrestled it into his stomach it thawed into thin and innutritious leathery strings and into a mass of short hair, irritating and indigestible.

And through it all Buck staggered along at the head of the team as in a nightmare. He pulled when he could; when he could no longer pull, he fell down and remained down till blows from whip or club drove him to his feet again. All the stiffness and gloss had gone out of his beautiful furry coat. The hair hung down, limp and draggled, or matted with dried blood where Hal's club had bruised him. His muscles had wasted away to knotty strings, and the flesh pads had disappeared, so that each rib and every bone in his frame were outlined cleanly through the loose hide that was wrinkled in folds of emptiness. It was heart-breaking, only Buck's heart was unbreakable. The man in the red sweater had proved that.

As it was with Buck, so was it with his mates. They were perambulating skeletons. There were seven all together, including him. In their very great misery they had become insensible to the bite of the lash or the bruise of the club. The pain of the beating was dull and distant, just as the things their eyes saw and their ears heard seemed dull and distant. They were not half living, or quarter living. They were simply so many bags of bones in which sparks of life fluttered faintly. When a halt was made, they dropped down in the traces like dead dogs, and the spark dimmed and paled and seemed to go out. And when the club or whip fell upon them, the spark fluttered feebly up, and they tottered to their feet and staggered on.

There came a day when Billee, the good-natured, fell and could not rise. Hal had traded off his revolver, so he took the axe and knocked Billee on the head as he lay in the traces, then cut the carcass out of the harness and dragged it to one side. Buck saw, and his mates saw, and they knew that this thing was very close to them. In the next day Koona went, and but five of them remained: Joe, too far gone to be malignant; Pike, crippled and limping, only half conscious and not conscious enough longer to malinger; Solleks, the one-eyed, still faithful to the toil of trace and trail, and mournful in that he had so little strength with which to pull; Teek, who had not travelled so far that winter and who was now beaten more than the others because he was fresher; and Buck, still at the head of the team, but no longer enforcing discipline or striving to enforce it, blind with weakness half the time and keeping the trail by the loom of it and by the dim feel of his feet.

It was beautiful spring weather, but neither dogs nor humans were aware of it. Each day the sun rose earlier and set later. It was dawn by three in the morning, and twilight lingered till nine at night. The whole long day was a blaze of sunshine. The ghostly winter silence had given way to the great spring murmur of awakening life. This murmur arose from all the land, fraught with the joy of living. It came from the things that lived and moved again, things which had been as dead and which had not moved during the long months of frost. The sap was rising in the pines. The willows and aspens were bursting out in young buds. Shrubs and vines were putting on fresh garbs of green. Crickets sang in the nights, and in the days all manner of creeping, crawling things rustled forth into the sun. Partridges and woodpeckers were booming and knocking in the forest. Squirrels were chattering, birds singing, and overhead honked the wildfowl driving up from the South in cunning wedges that split the air.

From every hill slope came the trickle of running water, the music of unseen fountains. All things were thawing, bending, snapping. The Yukon was straining to break loose the ice that bound it down. It ate away from beneath; the sun ate from above. Air-holes formed, fissures sprang and spread apart, while thin sections of ice fell through bodily into the river. And amid all this bursting, rending, throbbing of awakening life, under the blazing sun and through the soft-sighing breezes, like wayfarers to death, staggered the two men, the woman, and the huskies.

With the dogs falling, Mercedes weeping and riding, Hal swearing innocuously, and Charles's eyes wistfully watering, they staggered into John Thornton's camp at the mouth of the White River. When they halted, the dogs dropped down as though they had all been struck dead. Mercedes dried her eyes and looked at John Thornton. Charles sat down on a log to rest. He sat down very slowly and painstakingly what of his great stiffness. Hal did the talking. John Thornton was whittling the last touches on an axe-handle he had made from a stick of birch. He whittled and listened, gave monosyllabic replies, and, when it was asked, terse advice. He knew the breed, and he gave his advice in the certainty that it would not be followed.

"They told us up above that the bottom was dropping out of the trail and that the best thing for us to do was to lay over," Hal said in response to Thornton's warning to take no more chances on the rotten ice. "They told us we couldn't make White River, and here we are." This last with a sneering ring of triumph in it.

"And they told you true," John Thornton answered. "The bottom's likely to drop out at any moment. Only fools, with the blind luck of fools, could have made it. I tell you straight, I wouldn't risk my carcass on that ice for all the gold in Alaska."

"That's because you're not a fool, I suppose," said Hal. "All the same, we'll go on to Dawson." He uncoiled his whip. "Get up there, Buck! Hi! Get up there! Mush on!"

Thornton went on whittling. It was idle, he knew, to get between a fool and his folly; while two or three fools more or less would not alter the scheme of things.

But the team did not get up at the command. It had long since passed into the stage where blows were required to rouse it. The whip flashed out, here and there, on its merciless errands. John Thornton compressed his lips. Sol-leks was the first to crawl to his feet. Teek followed. Joe came next, yelping with pain. Pike made painful efforts. Twice he fell over, when half up, and on the third attempt managed to rise. Buck made no effort. He lay quietly where he had fallen. The lash bit into him again and again, but he neither whined nor struggled. Several times Thornton started, as though to speak, but changed his mind. A moisture came into his eyes, and, as the whipping continued, he arose and walked irresolutely up and down.

This was the first time Buck had failed, in itself a sufficient reason to drive Hal into a rage. He exchanged the whip for the customary club. Buck refused to move under the rain of heavier blows which now fell upon him. Like his mates, he was barely able to get up, but, unlike them, he had made up his mind not to get up. He had a vague feeling of impending doom. This had been strong upon him when he pulled into the bank, and it had not departed from him. What of the thin and rotten ice he had felt under his feet all day, it seemed that he sensed disaster close at hand, out there ahead on the ice where his master was trying to drive him. He refused to stir. So greatly had he suffered, and so far gone was he, that the blows did not hurt much. And as they continued to fall upon him, the spark of life within flickered and went down. It was nearly out. He felt strangely numb. As though from a great distance, he was aware that he was being beaten. The last sensations of pain left him. He no longer felt anything, though very faintly he could hear the impact of the club upon his body. But it was no longer his body, it seemed so far away.

And then, suddenly, without warning, uttering a cry that was inarticulate and more like the cry of an animal, John Thornton sprang upon the man who wielded the club. Hal was hurled backward, as though struck by a falling tree. Mercedes screamed. Charles looked on wistfully, wiped his watery eyes, but did not get up because of his stiffness.

John Thornton stood over Buck, struggling to control himself, too convulsed with rage to speak.

"If you strike that dog again, I'll kill you," he at last managed to say in a choking voice.

"It's my dog," Hal replied, wiping the blood from his mouth as he came back. "Get out of my way, or I'll fix you. I'm going to Dawson."

Thornton stood between him and Buck, and evinced no intention of getting out of the way. Hal drew his long hunting-knife. Mercedes screamed, cried, laughed, and manifested the chaotic abandonment of hysteria. Thornton rapped Hal's knuckles with the axe-handle, knocking the knife to the ground. He rapped his knuckles again as he tried to pick it up. Then he stooped, picked it up himself, and with two strokes cut Buck's traces.

Hal had no fight left in him. Besides, his hands were full with his sister, or his arms, rather; while Buck was too near dead to be of further use in hauling the sled. A few minutes later they pulled out from the bank and down the river. Buck heard them go and raised his head to see. Pike was leading, Sol-leks was at the wheel, and between were Joe and Teek. They were limping and staggering. Mercedes was riding the loaded sled. Hal guided at the gee-pole, and Charles stumbled along in the rear.

As Buck watched them, Thornton knelt beside him and with rough, kindly hands searched for broken bones. By the time his search had disclosed nothing more than many bruises and a state of terrible starvation, the sled was a quarter of a mile away. Dog and man watched it crawling along over the ice. Suddenly, they saw its back end drop down, as into a rut, and the gee-pole, with Hal clinging to it, jerk into the air. Mercedes' scream came to their ears. They saw Charles turn and make one step to run back, and then a whole section of ice give way and dogs and humans disappear. A yawning hole was all that was to be seen. The bottom had dropped out of the trail.

John Thornton and Buck looked at each other.

"You poor devil," said John Thornton and Buck licked his hand.

Chapter 6: For the Love of a Man

When John Thornton froze his feet in the previous December, his partners had made him comfortable and left him to get well, going on themselves up the river to get out a raft of saw-logs for Dawson. He was still limping slightly at the time he rescued Buck, but with the continued warm weather even the slight limp left him. And here, lying by the river bank through the long spring days, watching the running water, listening lazily to the songs of birds and the hum of nature, Buck slowly won back his strength.

A rest comes very good after one has travelled three thousand miles, and it must be confessed that Buck waxed lazy as his wounds healed, his muscles swelled out, and the flesh came back to cover his bones. For that matter, they were all loafing,—Buck, John Thornton, and Skeet and Nig—waiting for the raft to come that was to carry them down to Dawson. Skeet was a little Irish setter who early made friends with Buck, who in a dying condition, was unable to resent her first advances. She had the doctor trait which some dogs possess, and as a mother cat washes her kittens, so she washed and cleansed Buck's wounds. Regularly, each morning after he had finished his breakfast, she performed her self-appointed task, till he came to look for her ministrations as much as he did for Thornton's. Nig, equally friendly though less demonstrative, was a huge black dog, half bloodhound and half deerhound, with eyes that laughed and a boundless good nature.

To Buck's surprise these dogs manifested no jealousy toward him. They seemed to share the kindliness and largeness of John Thornton. As Buck grew stronger they enticed him into all sorts of ridiculous games, in which Thornton himself could not forbear to join, and in this fashion Buck romped through his convalescence and into a new existence. Love, genuine passionate love, was his for the first time. This he had never experienced at Judge Miller's down in the sun-kissed Santa Clara Valley. With the Judge's sons, hunting and tramping, it had been a working partnership; with the Judge's grandsons, a sort of pompous guardianship; and with the Judge himself, a stately and dignified friendship. But love that was feverish and burning, that was adoration, that was madness, it had taken John Thornton to arouse.

This man had saved his life, which was something; but, further, he was the ideal master. Other men saw to the welfare of their dogs from a sense of duty and business expediency; he saw to the welfare of his as if they were his own children, because he could not help it. And he saw further. He never forgot a kindly greeting or a cheering word, and to sit down for a long talk with them ("gas" he called it) was as much his delight as theirs. He had a way of taking Buck's head roughly between his hands, and resting his own head upon Buck's, of shaking him back and forth, the while calling him ill names that to Buck were love names. Buck knew no greater joy than that rough embrace and the sound of murmured oaths, and at each jerk back and forth it seemed that his heart would be shaken out of his body so great was its ecstasy. And when, released, he sprang to his feet, his mouth laughing, his eyes eloquent, his throat vibrant with unuttered sound, and in that fashion remained without movement, John Thornton would reverently exclaim, "God! you can all but speak!"

Buck had a trick of love expression that was akin to hurt. He would often seize Thornton's hand in his mouth and close so fiercely that the flesh bore the impress of his teeth for some time afterward. And as Buck understood the oaths to be love words, so the man understood this feigned bite for a caress.

For the most part, however, Buck's love was expressed in adoration. While he went wild with happiness when Thornton touched him or spoke to him, he did not seek these tokens. Unlike Skeet, who was wont to shove her nose under Thornton's hand and nudge and nudge till petted, or Nig, who would stalk up and rest his great head on Thornton's knee, Buck was content to adore at a distance. He would lie by the hour, eager, alert, at Thornton's feet, looking up into his face, dwelling upon it, studying it, following with keenest interest each fleeting expression, every movement or change of feature. Or, as chance might have it, he would lie farther away, to the side or rear, watching the outlines of the man and the occasional movements of his body. And often, such was the communion in which they lived, the strength of Buck's gaze would draw John Thornton's head around, and he would return the gaze, without speech, his heart shining out of his eyes as Buck's heart shone out.

For a long time after his rescue, Buck did not like Thornton to get out of his sight. From the moment he left the tent to when he entered it again, Buck would follow at his heels. His transient masters since he had come into the Northland had bred in him a fear that no master could be permanent. He was afraid that Thornton would pass out of his life as Perrault and François and the Scotch half-breed had passed out. Even in the night, in his dreams, he was haunted by this fear. At such times he would shake off sleep and creep through the chill to the flap of the tent, where he would stand and listen to the sound of his master's breathing.

But in spite of this great love he bore John Thornton, which seemed to bespeak the soft civilizing influence, the strain of the primitive, which the Northland had aroused in him, remained alive and active. Faithfulness and devotion, things born of fire and roof, were his; yet he retained his wildness and wiliness. He was a thing of the wild, come in from the wild to sit by John Thornton's fire, rather than a dog of the soft Southland stamped with the marks of generations of civilization. Because of his very great love, he could not steal from this man, but from any other man, in any other camp, he did not hesitate an instant, while the cunning with which he stole enabled him to escape detection.

His face and body were scored by the teeth of many dogs, and he fought as fiercely as ever and more shrewdly. Skeet and Nig were too good-natured for quarrelling—besides, they belonged to John Thornton; but the strange dog, no matter what the breed or valor, swiftly acknowledged Buck's supremacy or found himself struggling for life with a terrible antagonist. And Buck was merciless. He had learned well the law of club and fang, and he never forewent an advantage or drew back from a foe he had started on the way to Death. He had lessoned from Spitz, and from the chief fighting dogs of the police and mail, and knew there was no middle course. He must master or be mastered; while to show mercy was a weakness. Mercy did not exist in the primordial life. It was misunderstood for fear, and such misunderstandings made for death. Kill or be killed, eat or be eaten, was the law; and this mandate, down out of the depths of Time, he obeyed.

He was older than the days he had seen and the breaths he had drawn. He linked the past with the present, and the eternity behind him throbbed through him in a mighty rhythm to which he swayed as the tides and seasons swayed. He sat by John Thornton's fire, a broad-breasted dog, white-fanged and long-furred; but behind him were the shades of all manner of dogs, half-wolves and wild wolves, urgent and prompting, tasting the savor of the meat he ate, thirsting for the water he drank, scenting the wind with him, listening with him and telling him the sounds made by the wild life in the forest, dictating his moods, directing his actions, lying down to sleep with him when he lay down, and dreaming with him and beyond him and becoming themselves the stuff of his dreams.

So peremptorily did these shades beckon him, that each day mankind and the claims of mankind slipped farther from him. Deep in the forest a call was sounding, and as often as he heard this call, mysteriously thrilling and luring, he felt compelled to turn his back upon the fire and the beaten earth around it, and to plunge into the forest, and on and on, he knew not where or why; nor did he wonder where or why, the call sounding imperiously, deep in the forest. But as often as he gained the soft unbroken earth and the green shade, the love for John Thornton drew him back to the fire again.

Thornton alone held him. The rest of mankind was as nothing. Chance travellers might praise or pet him; but he was cold under it all, and from a too demonstrative man he would get up and walk away. When Thornton's partners, Hans and Pete, arrived on the long-expected raft, Buck refused to notice them till he learned they were close to Thornton; after that he tolerated them in a passive sort of way, accepting favors from them as though he favored them by accepting. They were of the same large type as Thornton, living close to the earth, thinking simply and seeing clearly; and ere they swung the raft into the big eddy by the sawmill at Dawson, they understood Buck and his ways, and did not insist upon an intimacy such as obtained with Skeet and Nig.

For Thornton, however, his love seemed to grow and grow. He alone among men could put a pack upon Buck's back in the summer travelling. Nothing was too great for Buck to do, when Thornton commanded. One day (they had grub-staked themselves from the proceeds of the raft and left Dawson for the head-waters of the Tanana) the men and dogs were sitting on the crest of a cliff which fell away, straight down, to naked bedrock three hundred feet below. John Thornton was sitting near the edge, Buck at his shoulder. A thoughtless whim seized Thornton, and he drew the attention of Hans and Pete to the experiment he had in mind. "Jump, Buck!" he commanded, sweeping his arm out and over the chasm. The next instant he was grappling with Buck on the extreme edge, while Hans and Pete were dragging them back into safety.

"It's uncanny," Pete said, after it was over and they had caught their speech.

Thornton shook his head. "No, it is splendid, and it is terrible, too. Do you know, it sometimes makes me afraid."

"I'm not hankering to be the man that lays hands on you while he's around," Pete announced conclusively, nodding his head toward Buck.

"Py Jingo!" was Hans's contribution. "Not mineself either."

It was at Circle City, ere the year was out, that Pete's apprehensions were realized. "Black" Burton, a man evil-tempered and malicious, had been picking a quarrel with a tenderfoot at the bar, when Thornton stepped good-naturedly between. Buck, as was his custom, was lying in a corner, head on paws, watching his master's every action. Burton struck out, without warning, straight from the shoulder. Thornton was sent spinning, and saved himself from falling only by clutching the rail of the bar.

Those who were looking on heard what was neither bark nor yelp, but a something which is best described as a roar, and they saw Buck's body rise up in the air as he left the floor for Burton's throat. The man saved his life by instinctively throwing out his arm, but was hurled backward to the floor with Buck on top of him. Buck loosed his teeth from the flesh of the arm and drove in again for the throat. This time the man succeeded only in partly blocking, and his throat was torn open. Then the crowd was upon Buck, and he was driven off; but while a surgeon checked the bleeding, he prowled up and down, growling furiously, attempting to rush in, and being forced back by an array of hostile clubs. A "miners' meeting," called on the spot, decided that the dog had sufficient provocation, and Buck was discharged. But his reputation was made, and from that day his name spread through every camp in Alaska.

Later on, in the fall of the year, he saved John Thornton's life in quite another fashion. The three partners were lining a long and narrow poling-boat down a bad stretch of rapids on the Forty-Mile Creek. Hans and Pete moved along the bank, snubbing with a thin Manila rope from tree to tree, while Thornton remained in the boat, helping its descent by means of a pole, and shouting directions to the shore. Buck, on the bank, worried and anxious, kept abreast of the boat, his eyes never off his master.

At a particularly bad spot, where a ledge of barely submerged rocks jutted out into the river, Hans cast off the rope, and, while Thornton poled the boat out into the stream, ran down the bank with the end in his hand to snub the boat when it had cleared the ledge. This it did, and was flying down-stream in a current as swift as a mill-race, when Hans checked it with the rope and checked too suddenly. The boat flirted over and snubbed in to the bank bottom up, while Thornton, flung sheer out of it, was carried down-stream toward the worst part of the rapids, a stretch of wild water in which no swimmer could live.

Buck had sprung in on the instant; and at the end of three hundred yards, amid a mad swirl of water, he overhauled Thornton. When he felt him grasp his tail, Buck headed for the bank, swimming with all his splendid strength. But the progress shoreward was slow; the progress down-stream amazingly rapid. From below came the fatal roaring where the wild current went wilder and was rent in shreds and spray by the rocks which thrust through like the teeth of an enormous comb. The suck of the water as it took the beginning of the last steep pitch was frightful, and Thornton knew that the shore was impossible. He scraped furiously over a rock, bruised across a second, and struck a third with crushing force. He clutched its slippery top with both hands, releasing Buck, and above the roar of the churning water shouted: "Go, Buck! Go!"

Buck could not hold his own, and swept on down-stream, struggling desperately, but unable to win back. When he heard Thornton's command repeated, he partly reared out of the water, throwing his head high, as though for a last look, then turned obediently toward the bank. He swam powerfully and was dragged ashore by Pete and Hans at the very point where swimming ceased to be possible and destruction began.

They knew that the time a man could cling to a slippery rock in the face of that driving current was a matter of minutes, and they ran as fast as they could up the bank to a point far above where Thornton was hanging on. They attached the line with which they had been snubbing the boat to Buck's neck and shoulders, being careful that it should neither strangle him nor impede his swimming, and launched him into the stream. He struck out boldly, but not straight enough into the stream. He discovered the mistake too late, when Thornton was abreast of him and a bare half-dozen strokes away while he was being carried helplessly past.

Hans promptly snubbed with the rope, as though Buck were a boat. The rope thus tightening on him in the sweep of the current, he was jerked under the surface, and under the surface he remained till his body struck against the bank and he was hauled out. He was half drowned, and Hans and Pete threw themselves upon him, pounding the breath into him and the water out of him. He staggered to his feet and fell down. The faint sound of Thornton's voice came to them, and though they could not make out the words of it, they knew that he was in his extremity. His master's voice acted on Buck like an electric shock. He sprang to his feet and ran up the bank ahead of the men to the point of his previous departure.

Again the rope was attached and he was launched, and again he struck out, but this time straight into the stream. He had miscalculated once, but he would not be guilty of it a second time. Hans paid out the rope, permitting no slack, while Pete kept it clear of coils. Buck held on till he was on a line straight above Thornton; then he turned, and with the speed of an express train headed down upon him. Thornton saw him coming, and, as Buck struck him like a battering ram, with the whole force of the current behind him, he reached up and closed with both arms around the shaggy neck. Hans snubbed the rope around the tree, and Buck and Thornton were jerked under the water. Strangling, suffocating, sometimes one upper-most and sometimes the other, dragging over the jagged bottom, smashing against rocks and snags, they veered in to the bank.

Thornton came to, belly downward and being violently propelled back and forth across a drift log by Hans and Pete. His first glance was for Buck, over whose limp and apparently lifeless body Nig was setting up a howl, while Skeet was licking the wet face and closed eyes. Thornton was himself bruised and battered, and he went carefully over Buck's body, when he had been brought around, finding three broken ribs.

"That settles it," he announced. "We camp right here." And camp they did, till Buck's ribs knitted and he was able to travel.

That winter, at Dawson, Buck performed another exploit, not so heroic, perhaps, but one that puts his name many notches higher on the totem pole of Alaskan fame. This exploit was particularly gratifying to the three men; for they stood in need of the outfit which it furnished, and were enabled to make a long-desired trip into the virgin East, where miners had not yet appeared. It was brought about by a conversation in the Eldorado Saloon, in which men waxed boastful of their favorite dogs. Buck, because of his record, was the target for these men, and Thornton was driven stoutly to defend him. At the end of half an hour one man stated that his dog could start a sled with five hundred pounds and walk off with it; a second bragged six hundred for his dog; and a third, seven hundred.

"Pooh! Pooh!" said John Thornton. "Buck can start a thousand pounds."

"And break it out, and walk off with it for a hundred yards?" demanded Matthewson, a Bonanza king, he of the seven hundred vaunt.

"And break it out? and walk off with it for a hundred yards," John Thornton said coolly.

"Well," Matthewson said, slowly and deliberately, so that all could hear, "I've got a thousand dollars that says he can't. And there it is." So saying, he slammed a sack of gold dust of the size of a bologna sausage down upon the bar.

Nobody spoke. Thornton's bluff, if bluff it was, had been called. He could feel a flush of warm blood creeping up his face. His tongue had tricked him. He did not know whether Buck could start a thousand pounds. Half a ton! The enormousness of it appalled him. He had great faith in Buck's strength and had often thought him capable of starting such a load; but never, as now, had he faced the possibility of it, the eyes of a dozen men fixed upon him, silent and waiting. Further, he had no thousand dollars; nor had Hans and Pete.

"I've got a sled standing outside now, with twenty fifty-pound sacks of flour on it," Matthewson went on with brutal directness, "so don't let that hinder you."

Thornton did not reply. He did not know what to say. He glanced from face to face in the absent way of a man who has lost the power of thought and is seeking somewhere to find the thing that will start it going again. The face of Jim O'Brien, a Mastodon king and old-time comrade, caught his eyes. It was as a cue to him, seeming to rouse him to do what he would never have dreamed of doing.

"Can you lend me a thousand?" he asked, almost in a whisper.

"Sure," answered O'Brien, thumping down a plethoric sack by the side of Matthewson's. "Though it's little faith I'm having, John, that the beast can do the trick."

The Eldorado emptied its occupants into the street to see the test. The tables were deserted, and the dealers and gamekeepers came forth to see the outcome of the wager and to lay odds. Several hundred men, furred and mittened, banked around the sled within easy distance. Matthewson's sled, loaded with a thousand pounds of flour, had been standing for a couple of hours, and in the intense cold (it was sixty below zero) the runners had frozen fast to the hard-packed snow. Men offered odds of two to one that Buck could not budge the sled. A quibble arose concerning the phrase "break out." O'Brien contended it was Thornton's privilege to knock the runners loose, leaving Buck to "break it out" from a dead standstill. Matthewson insisted that the phrase included breaking the runners from the frozen grip of the snow. A majority of the men who had witnessed the making of the bet decided in his favor, whereat the odds went up to three to one against Buck. There were no takers. Not a man believed him capable of the feat. Thornton had been hurried into the wager, heavy with doubt; and now that he looked at the sled itself, the concrete fact, with the regular team of ten dogs curled up in the snow before it, the more impossible the task appeared. Matthewson waxed jubilant.

"Three to one!" he proclaimed. "I'll lay you another thousand at that figure, Thornton. What d'ye say?"

Thornton's doubt was strong in his face, but his fighting spirit was aroused—the fighting spirit that soars above odds, fails to recognize the impossible, and is deaf to all save the clamor for battle. He called Hans and Pete to him. Their sacks were slim, and with his own the three partners could rake together only two hundred dollars. In the ebb of their fortunes, this sum was their total capital; yet they laid it unhesitatingly against Matthewson's six hundred.

The team of ten dogs was unhitched, and Buck, with his own harness, was put into the sled. He had caught the contagion of the excitement, and he felt that in some way he must do a great thing for John Thornton. Murmurs of admiration at his splendid appearance went up. He was in perfect condition, without an ounce of superfluous flesh, and the one hundred and fifty pounds that he weighed were so many pounds of grit and virility. His furry coat shone with the sheen of silk. Down the neck and across the shoulders, his mane, in repose as it was, half bristled and seemed to lift with every movement, as though excess of vigor made each particular hair alive and active. The great breast and heavy fore legs were no more than in proportion with the rest of the body where the muscles showed in tight rolls underneath the skin. Men felt these muscles and proclaimed them hard as iron, and the odds went down to two to one.

"Gad, sir! Gad, sir!" stuttered a member of the latest dynasty, a king of the Skookum Benches. "I offer you eight hundred for him, sir, before the test, Sir; eight hundred just as he stands."

Thornton shook his head and stepped to Buck's side.

"You must stand off from him," Matthewson protested. "Free play and plenty of room."

The crowd fell silent; only could be heard the voices of the gamblers vainly offering two to one. Everybody acknowledged Buck a magnificent animal, but twenty fifty-pound sacks of flour bulked too large in their eyes for them to loosen their pouch-strings.

Thornton knelt down by Buck's side. He took his head in his two hands and rested cheek on cheek. He did not playfully shake him, as was his wont, or murmur soft love curses; but he whispered in his ear. "As you love me, Buck. As you love me," was what he whispered. Buck whined with suppressed eagerness.

The crowd was watching curiously. The affair was growing mysterious. It seemed like a conjuration. As Thornton got to his feet, Buck seized his mittened hand between his jaws, pressing in with his teeth and releasing slowly, half-reluctantly. It was the answer, in terms, not of speech, but of love. Thornton stepped well back.

"Now, Buck," he said.

Buck tightened the traces, then slacked them for a matter of several inches. It was the way he had learned.

"Gee!" Thornton's voice rang out, sharp in the tense silence.

Buck swung to the right, ending the movement in a plunge that took up the slack and with a sudden jerk arrested his one hundred and fifty pounds. The load quivered, and from under the runners arose a crisp crackling.

"Haw!" Thornton commanded.

Buck duplicated the manœuvre, this time to the left. The crackling turned into a snapping, the sled pivoting and the runners slipping and grating several inches to the side. The sled was broken out. Men were holding their breaths, intensely unconscious of the fact.

"Now, MUSH!"

Thornton's command cracked out like a pistol-shot. Buck threw himself forward, tightening the traces with a jarring lunge. His whole body was gathered compactly together in the tremendous effort, the muscles writhing and knotting like live things under the silky fur. His great chest was low to the ground, his head forward and down, while his feet were flying like mad, the claws scarring the hard-packed snow in parallel grooves. The sled swayed and trembled, half-started forward. One of his feet slipped, and one man groaned aloud. Then the sled lurched ahead in what appeared a rapid succession of jerks, though it never really came to a dead stop again . . . half an inch . . . an inch . . . two inches. . . . The jerks perceptibly diminished; as the sled gained momentum, he caught them up, till it was moving steadily along.

Men gasped and began to breathe again, unaware that for a moment they had ceased to breathe. Thornton was running behind, encouraging Buck with short, cheery words. The distance had been measured off, and as he neared the pile of firewood which marked the end of the hundred yards, a cheer began to grow and grow, which burst into a roar as he passed the firewood and halted at command. Every man was tearing himself loose, even Matthewson. Hats and mittens were flying in the air. Men were shaking hands, it did not matter with whom, and bubbling over in a general incoherent babel.

But Thornton fell on his knees beside Buck. Head was against head, and he was shaking him back and forth. Those who hurried up heard him cursing Buck, and he cursed him long and fervently, and softly and lovingly.

"Gad, sir! Gad, sir!" sputtered the Skookum Bench king. "I'll give you a thousand for him, sir, a thousand, sir—twelve hundred, sir."

Thornton rose to his feet. His eyes were wet. The tears were streaming frankly down his cheeks. "Sir," he said to the Skookum Bench king, "no, sir. You can go to hell, sir. It's the best I can do for you, sir."

Buck seized Thornton's hand in his teeth. Thornton shook him back and forth. As though animated by a common impulse, the onlookers drew back to a respectful distance, nor were they again indiscreet enough to interrupt.

Chapter 7: The Sounding of the Call

When Buck earned sixteen hundred dollars in five minutes for John Thornton, he made it possible for his master to pay off certain debts and to journey with his partners into the East after a fabled lost mine, the history of which was as old as the history of the country. Many men had sought it; few had found it; and more than a few there were who had never returned from the quest. This lost mine was steeped in tragedy and shrouded in mystery. No one knew of the first man. The oldest tradition stopped before it got back to him. From the beginning there had been an ancient and ramshackle cabin. Dying men had sworn to it, and to the mine the site of which it marked, clinching their testimony with nuggets that were unlike any known grade of gold in the Northland.

But no living man had looted this treasure house, and the dead were dead; wherefore John Thornton and Pete and Hans, with

Buck and half a dozen other dogs, faced into the East on an unknown trail to achieve where men and dogs as good as themselves had failed. They sledded seventy miles up the Yukon, swung to the left into the Stewart River, passed the Mayo and the McQuestion, and held on until the Stewart itself became a streamlet, threading the upstanding peaks which marked the backbone of the continent.

John Thornton asked little of man or nature. He was unafraid of the wild. With a handful of salt and a rifle he could plunge into the wilderness and fare wherever he pleased and as long as he pleased. Being in no haste, Indian fashion, he hunted his dinner in the course of the day's travel; and if he failed to find it, like the Indian, he kept on travelling, secure in the knowledge that sooner or later he would come to it. So, on this great journey into the East, straight meat was the bill of fare, ammunition and tools principally made up the load on the sled, and the time-card was drawn upon the limitless future.

To Buck it was boundless delight, this hunting, fishing, and indefinite wandering through strange places. For weeks at a time they would hold on steadily, day after day; and for weeks upon end they would camp, here and there, the dogs loafing and the men burning holes through frozen muck and gravel and washing countless pans of dirt by the heat of the fire. Sometimes they went hungry, sometimes they feasted riotously, all according to the abundance of game and the fortune of hunting. Summer arrived, and dogs and men, packs on their backs, rafted across blue mountain lakes, and descended or ascended unknown rivers in slender boats whipsawed from the standing forest.

The months came and went, and back and forth they twisted through the uncharted vastness, where no men were and yet where men had been if the Lost Cabin were true. They went across divides in summer blizzards, shivered under the midnight sun on naked mountains between the timber line and the eternal snows, dropped into summer valleys amid swarming gnats and flies, and in the shadows of glaciers picked strawberries and flowers as ripe and fair as any the Southland could boast. In the fall of the year they penetrated a weird lake country, sad and silent, where wildfowl had been, but where then there was no life nor sign of life—only the blowing of chill winds, the forming of ice in sheltered places, and the melancholy rippling of waves on lonely beaches.

And through another winter they wandered on the obliterated trails of men who had gone before. Once, they came upon a path blazed throughout the forest, an ancient path, and the Lost Cabin seemed very near. But the path began nowhere and ended nowhere, and it remained mystery, as the man who made it and the reason he made it remained mystery. Another time they chanced upon the time-graven wreckage of a hunting lodge, and amid the shreds of rotted blankets John Thornton found a long-barrelled flintlock. He knew it for a Hudson Bay Company gun of the young days in the Northwest, when such a gun was worth its height in beaver skins packed flat. And that was all—no hint as to the man who in an early day had reared the lodge and left the gun among the blankets.

Spring came on once more, and at the end of all their wandering they found, not the Lost Cabin, but a shallow placer in a broad valley where the gold showed like yellow butter across the bottom of the washing-pan. They sought no farther. Each day they worked earned them thousands of dollars in clean dust and nuggets, and they worked every day. The gold was sacked in moosehide bags, fifty pounds to the bag, and piled like so much fire-wood outside the spruce-bough lodge. Like giants they toiled, days flashing on the heels of days like dreams as they heaped the treasure up.

There was nothing for the dogs to do save the hauling in of meat now and again that Thornton killed, and Buck spent long hours musing by the fire. The vision of the short-legged hairy man came to him more frequently, now that there was little work to be done; and often, blinking by the fire, Buck wandered with him in that other world which he remembered.

The salient thing of this other world seemed fear. When he watched the hairy man sleeping by the fire, head between his knees and hands clasped above, Buck saw that he slept restlessly, with many starts and awakenings, at which times he would peer fearfully into the darkness and fling more wood upon the fire. Did they walk by the beach of a sea, where the hairy man gathered shell-fish and ate them as he gathered, it was with eyes that roved everywhere for hidden danger and with legs prepared to run like the wind at its first appearance. Through the forest they crept noiselessly, Buck at the hairy man's heels; and they were alert and vigilant, the pair of them, ears twitching and moving and nostrils quivering, for the man heard and smelled as keenly as Buck. The hairy man could spring up into the trees and travel ahead as fast as on the ground, swinging by the arms from limb to limb, sometimes a dozen feet apart, letting go and catching, never falling, never missing his grip. In fact, he seemed as much at home among the trees as on the ground; and Buck had memories of nights of vigil spent beneath trees wherein the hairy man roosted, holding on tightly as he slept.

And closely akin to the visions of the hairy man was the call still sounding in the depths of the forest. It filled him with a great unrest and strange desires. It caused him to feel a vague, sweet gladness, and he was aware of wild yearnings and stirrings for he knew not what. Sometimes he pursued the call into the forest, looking for it as though it were a tangible thing, barking softly or defiantly, as the mood might dictate. He would thrust his nose into the cool wood moss, or into the black soil where long grasses grew, and snort with joy at the fat earth smells; or he would crouch for hours, as if in concealment, behind fungus-covered trunks of fallen trees, wide-eyed and wide-eared to all that moved and sounded about him. It might be, lying thus, that he hoped to surprise this call he could not understand. But he did not know why he did these various things. He was impelled to do them, and did not reason about them at all.

Irresistible impulses seized him. He would be lying in camp, dozing lazily in the heat of the day, when suddenly his head would lift and his ears cock up, intent and listening, and he would spring to his feet and dash away, and on and on, for hours, through the forest aisles and across the open spaces where the niggerheads bunched. He loved to run down dry watercourses, and to creep and spy upon the bird life in the woods. For a day at a time he would lie in the underbrush where he could watch the partridges drumming and strutting up and down. But especially he loved to run in the dim twilight of the summer midnights, listening to the subdued and sleepy murmurs of the forest, reading signs and sounds as man may read a book, and seeking for the mysterious something that called—called, waking or sleeping, at all times, for him to come.

One night he sprang from sleep with a start, eager-eyed, nostrils quivering and scenting, his mane bristling in recurrent waves. From the forest came the call (or one note of it, for the call was many-noted), distinct and definite as never before—a long-drawn howl, like, yet unlike, any noise made by husky dog. And he knew it, in the old familiar way, as a sound heard before. He sprang through the sleeping camp and in swift silence dashed through the woods. As he drew closer to the cry he went more slowly, with caution in every movement, till he came to an open place among the trees, and looking out saw, erect on haunches, with nose pointed to the sky, a long, lean, timber wolf.

He had made no noise, yet it ceased from its howling and tried to sense his presence. Buck stalked into the open, half crouching, body gathered compactly together, tail straight and stiff, feet falling with unwonted care. Every movement advertised commingled threatening and overture of friendliness. It was the menacing truce that marks the meeting of wild beasts that prey. But the wolf fled at sight of him. He followed, with wild leapings, in a frenzy to overtake. He ran him into a blind channel, in the bed of the creek, where a timber jam barred the way. The wolf whirled about, pivoting on his hind legs after the fashion of Joe and of all cornered husky dogs, snarling and bristling, clipping his teeth together in a continuous and rapid succession of snaps.

Buck did not attack, but circled him about and hedged him in with friendly advances. The wolf was suspicious and afraid; for Buck made three of him in weight, while his head barely reached Buck's shoulder. Watching his chance, he darted away, and the chase was resumed. Time and again he was cornered and the thing repeated, though he was in poor condition or Buck could not so easily have overtaken him. He would run till Buck's head was even with his flank, when he would whirl around at bay, only to dash away again at the first opportunity.

But in the end Buck's pertinacity was rewarded; for the wolf, finding that no harm was intended, finally sniffed noses with him. Then they became friendly, and played about in the nervous, half-coy way with which fierce beasts belie their fierceness. After some time of this the wolf started off at an easy lope in a manner that plainly showed he was going somewhere. He made it clear to Buck that he was to come, and they ran side by side through the sombre twilight, straight up the creek bed, into the gorge from which it issued, and across the bleak divide where it took its rise.

On the opposite slope of the watershed they came down into a level country where were great stretches of forest and many streams, and through these great stretches they ran steadily, hour after hour, the sun rising higher and the day growing warmer. Buck was wildly glad. He knew he was at last answering the call, running by the side of his wood brother toward the place from where the call surely came. Old memories were coming upon him fast, and he was stirring to them as of old he stirred to the realities of which they were the shadows. He had done this thing before, somewhere in that other and dimly remembered world, and he was doing it again now, running free in the open, the unpacked earth underfoot, the wide sky overhead.

They stopped by a running stream to drink, and, stopping, Buck remembered John Thornton. He sat down. The wolf started on toward the place from where the call surely came, then returned to him, sniffing noses and making actions as though to encourage him. But Buck turned about and started slowly on the back track. For the better part of an hour the wild brother ran by his side, whining softly. Then he sat down, pointed his nose upward, and howled. It was a mournful howl, and as Buck held steadily on his way he heard it grow faint and fainter until it was lost in the distance.

John Thornton was eating dinner when Buck dashed into camp and sprang upon him, in a frenzy of affection, overturning him, scrambling upon him, licking his face, biting his hand—"playing the general tom-fool," as John Thornton characterized it, the while he shook Buck back and forth and cursed him lovingly.

For two days and nights Buck never left camp, never let Thornton out of his sight. He followed him about at his work, watched him while he ate, saw him into his blankets at night and out of them in the morning. But after two days the call in the forest began to sound more imperiously than ever. Buck's restlessness came back on him, and he was haunted by recollections of the wild brother, and of the smiling land beyond the divide and the run side by side through the wide forest stretches. Once again he took to wandering in the woods, but the wild brother came no more; and though he listened through long vigils, the mournful howl was never raised.

He began to sleep out at night, staying away from camp for days at a time; and once he crossed the divide at the head of the creek and went down into the land of timber and streams. There he wandered for a week, seeking vainly for fresh sign of the wild brother, killing his meat as he travelled and travelling with the long, easy lope that seems never to tire. He fished for salmon in a broad stream that emptied somewhere into the sea, and by this stream he killed a large black bear, blinded by the mosquitoes while likewise fishing, and raging through the forest helpless and terrible. Even so, it was a hard fight, and it aroused the last latent remnants of Buck's ferocity. And two days later, when he returned to his kill and found a dozen wolverenes quarrelling over the spoil, he scattered them like chaff; and those that fled left two behind who would quarrel no more.

The blood-longing became stronger than ever before. He was a killer, a thing that preyed, living on the things that lived, unaided, alone, by virtue of his own strength and prowess, surviving triumphantly in a hostile environment where only the strong survive. Because of all this he became possessed of a great pride in himself, which communicated itself like a contagion to his physical being. It advertised itself in all his movements, was apparent in the play of every muscle, spoke plainly as speech in the way he carried himself, and made his glorious furry coat if anything more glorious. But for the stray brown on his muzzle and above his eyes, and for the splash of white hair that ran midmost down his chest, he might well have been mistaken for a gigantic wolf, larger than the largest of the breed. From his St. Bernard father he had inherited size and weight, but it was his shepherd mother who had given shape to that size and weight. His muzzle was the long wolf muzzle, save that it was larger than the muzzle of any wolf; and his head, somewhat broader, was the wolf head on a massive scale.

His cunning was wolf cunning, and wild cunning; his intelligence, shepherd intelligence and St. Bernard intelligence; and all this, plus an experience gained in the fiercest of schools, made him as formidable a creature as any that roamed the wild. A carnivorous animal, living on a straight meat diet, he was in full flower, at the high tide of his life, overspilling with vigor and virility. When Thornton passed a caressing hand along his back, a snapping and crackling followed the hand, each hair discharging its pent magnetism at the contact. Every part, brain and body, nerve tissue and fibre, was keyed to the most exquisite pitch; and between all the parts there was a perfect equilibrium or adjustment. To sights and sounds and events which required action, he responded with lightning-like rapidity. Quickly as a husky dog could leap to defend from attack or to attack, he could leap twice as quickly. He saw the movement, or heard sound, and responded in less time than another dog required to compass the mere seeing or hearing. He perceived and determined and responded in the same instant. In point of fact the three actions of perceiving, determining, and responding were sequential; but so infinitesimal were the intervals of time between them that they appeared simultaneous. His muscles were surcharged with vitality, and snapped into play sharply, like steel springs. Life streamed through him in splendid flood, glad and rampant, until it seemed that it would burst him asunder in sheer ecstasy and put forth generously over the world.

"Never was there such a dog," said John Thornton one day, as the partners watched Buck marching out of camp.

"When he was made, the mold was broke," said Pete.

"Py Jingo! I t'ink so mineself," Hans affirmed.

They saw him marching out of camp, but they did not see the instant and terrible transformation which took place as soon as he was within the secrecy of the forest. He no longer marched. At once he became a thing of the wild, stealing along softly, cat-footed, a passing shadow that appeared and disappeared among the shadows. He knew how to take advantage of every cover, to crawl on his belly like a snake, and like a snake to leap and strike. He could take a ptarmigan from its nest, kill a rabbit as it slept, and snap in mid-air the little chipmunks fleeing a second too late for the trees. Fish, in open pools, were not too quick for him; nor were beaver, mending their dams, too wary. He killed to eat, not from wantonness; but he preferred to eat what he killed himself. So a lurking humor ran through his deeds, and it was his delight to steal upon the squirrels, and, when he all but had them, to let them go, chattering in mortal fear to the tree-tops.

As the fall of the year came on, the moose appeared in greater abundance, moving slowly down to meet the winter in the lower and less rigorous valleys. Buck had already dragged down a stray part-grown calf; but he wished strongly for larger and more formidable quarry, and he came upon it one day on the divide at the head of the creek. A band of twenty moose had crossed over from the land of streams and timber, and chief among them was a great bull. He was in a savage temper, and, standing over six feet from the ground, was as formidable an antagonist as ever Buck could desire. Back and forth the bull tossed his great palmated antlers, branching to fourteen points and embracing seven feet within the tips. His small eyes burned with a vicious and bitter light, while he roared with fury at sight of Buck.

From the bull's side, just forward of the flank, protruded a feathered arrow-end, which accounted for his savageness. Guided by that instinct which came from the old hunting days of the primordial world, Buck proceeded to cut the bull out from the herd. It was no slight task. He would bark and dance about in front of the bull, just out of reach of the great antlers and of the terrible splay hoofs which could have stamped his life out with a single blow. Unable to turn his back on the fanged danger and go on, the bull would be driven into paroxysms of rage. At such moments he charged Buck, who retreated craftily, luring him on by a simulated inability to escape. But when he was thus separated from his fellows, two or three of the younger bulls would charge back upon Buck and enable the wounded bull to rejoin the herd.

There is a patience of the wild—dogged, tireless, persistent as life itself—that holds motionless for endless hours the spider in its web, the snake in its coils, the panther in its ambuscade; this patience belongs peculiarly to life when it hunts its living food; and it belonged to Buck as he clung to the flank of the herd, retarding its march, irritating the young bulls, worrying the cows with their half-grown calves, and driving the wounded bull mad with helpless rage. For half a day this continued. Buck multiplied himself, attacking from all sides, enveloping the herd in a whirlwind of menace, cutting out his victim as fast as it could rejoin its mates, wearing out the patience of creatures preyed upon, which is a lesser patience than that of creatures preying.

As the day wore along and the sun dropped to its bed in the northwest (the darkness had come back and the fall nights were six hours long), the young bulls retraced their steps more and more reluctantly to the aid of their beset leader. The down-coming winter was harrying them on to the lower levels, and it seemed they could never shake off this tireless creature that held them back. Besides, it was not the life of the herd, or of the young bulls, that was threatened. The life of only one member was demanded, which was a remoter interest than their lives, and in the end they were content to pay the toll.

As twilight fell the old bull stood with lowered head, watching his mates—the cows he had known, the calves he had fathered, the bulls he had mastered—as they shambled on at a rapid pace through the fading light. He could not follow, for before his nose leaped the merciless fanged terror that would not let him go. Three hundred-weight more than half a ton he weighed; he had lived a long, strong life, full of fight and struggle, and at the end he faced death at the teeth of a creature whose head did not reach beyond his great knuckled knees.

From then on, night and day, Buck never left his prey, never gave it a moment's rest, never permitted it to browse the leaves of trees or the shoots of young birch and willow. Nor did he give the wounded bull opportunity to slake his burning thirst in the slender trickling streams they crossed. Often, in desperation, he burst into long stretches of flight. At such times Buck did not attempt to stay him, but loped easily at his heels, satisfied with the way the game was played, lying down when the moose stood still, attacking him fiercely when he strove to eat or drink.

The great head drooped more and more under its tree of horns, and the shambling trot grew weaker and weaker. He took to standing for long periods, with nose to the ground and dejected ears dropped limply; and Buck found more time in which to get water for himself and in which to rest. At such moments, panting with red lolling tongue and with eyes fixed upon the big bull, it appeared to Buck that a change was coming over the face of things. He could feel a new stir in the land. As the moose were coming into the land, other kinds of life were coming in. Forest and stream and air seemed palpitant with their presence. The news of it was borne in upon him, not by sight, or sound, or smell, but by some other and subtler sense. He heard nothing, saw nothing, yet knew that the land was somehow different; that through it strange things were afoot and ranging; and he resolved to investigate after he had finished the business in hand.

At last, at the end of the fourth day, he pulled the great moose down. For a day and a night he remained by the kill, eating and sleeping, turn and turn about. Then, rested, refreshed and strong, he turned his face toward camp and John Thornton. He broke into the long easy lope, and went on, hour after hour, never at loss for the tangled way, heading straight home through strange country with a certitude of direction that put man and his magnetic needle to shame.

As he held on he became more and more conscious of the new stir in the land. There was life abroad in it different from the life which had been there throughout the summer. No longer was this fact borne in upon him in some subtle, mysterious way. The birds talked of it, the squirrels chattered about it, the very breeze whispered of it. Several times he stopped and drew in the fresh morning air in great sniffs, reading a message which made him leap on with greater speed. He was oppressed with a sense of calamity happening, if it were not calamity already happened; and as he crossed the last watershed and dropped down into the valley toward camp, he proceeded with greater caution.

Three miles away he came upon a fresh trail that sent his neck hair rippling and bristling. It led straight toward camp and John Thornton. Buck hurried on, swiftly and stealthily, every nerve straining and tense, alert to the multitudinous details which told a story—all but the end. His nose gave him a varying description of the passage of the life on the heels of which he was travelling. He remarked the pregnant silence of the forest. The bird life had flitted. The squirrels were in hiding. One only he saw—a sleek gray fellow, flattened against a gray dead limb so that he seemed a part of it, a woody excrescence upon the wood itself.

As Buck slid along with the obscureness of a gliding shadow, his nose was jerked suddenly to the side as though a positive force had gripped and pulled it. He followed the new scent into a thicket and found Nig. He was lying on his side, dead where he had dragged himself, an arrow protruding, head and feathers, from either side of his body.

A hundred yards farther on, Buck came upon one of the sled-dogs Thornton had bought in Dawson. This dog was thrashing about in a death-struggle, directly on the trail, and Buck passed around him without stopping. From the camp came the faint sound of many voices, rising and falling in a sing-song chant. Bellying forward to the edge of the clearing, he found Hans, lying on his face, feathered with arrows like a porcupine. At the same instant Buck peered out where the spruce-bough lodge had been and saw what made his hair leap straight up on his neck and shoulders. A gust of overpowering rage swept over him. He did not know that he growled, but he growled aloud with a terrible ferocity. For the last time in his life he allowed passion to usurp cunning and reason, and it was because of his great love for John Thornton that he lost his head.

The Yeehats were dancing about the wreckage of the spruce-bough lodge when they heard a fearful roaring and saw rushing upon them an animal the like of which they had never seen before. It was Buck, a live hurricane of fury, hurling himself upon them in a frenzy to destroy. He sprang at the foremost man (it was the chief of the Yeehats), ripping the throat wide open till the rent jugular spouted a fountain of blood. He did not pause to worry the victim, but ripped in passing, with the next bound tearing wide the throat of a second man. There was no withstanding him. He plunged about in their very midst, tearing, rending, destroying, in constant and terrific motion which defied the arrows they discharged at him. In fact, so inconceivably rapid were his movements, and so closely were the Indians tangled together, that they shot one another with the arrows; and one young hunter, hurling a spear at Buck in mid-air, drove it through the chest of another hunter with such force that the point broke through the skin of the back and stood out beyond. Then a panic seized the Yeehats, and they fled in terror to the woods, proclaiming as they fled the advent of the Evil Spirit.

And truly Buck was the Fiend incarnate, raging at their heels and dragging them down like deer as they raced through the trees. It was a fateful day for the Yeehats. They scattered far and wide over the country, and it was not till a week later that the last of the survivors gathered together in a lower valley and counted their losses. As for Buck, wearying of the pursuit, he returned to the desolated camp. He found Pete where he had been killed in his blankets in the first moment of surprise. Thornton's desperate struggle was fresh-written on the earth, and Buck scented every detail of it down to the edge of a deep pool. By the edge, head and fore feet in the water, lay Skeet, faithful to the last. The pool itself, muddy and discolored from the sluice boxes, effectually hid what it contained, and it contained John Thornton; for Buck followed his trace into the water, from which no trace led away.

All day Buck brooded by the pool or roamed restlessly above the camp. Death, as a cessation of movement, as a passing out and away from the lives of the living, he knew, and he knew John Thornton was dead. It left a great void in him, somewhat akin to hunger, but a void which ached and ached, and which food could not fill. At times, when he paused to contemplate the carcasses of the Yeehats, he forgot the pain of it; and at such times he was aware of a great pride in himself—a pride greater than any he had yet experienced. He had killed man, the noblest game of all, and he had killed in the face of the law of club and fang. He sniffed the bodies curiously. They had died so easily. It was harder to kill a husky dog than them. They were no match at all, were it not for their arrows and spears and clubs. Thenceforward he would be unafraid of them except when they bore in their hands their arrows, spears, and clubs.

Night came on, and a full moon rose high over the trees into the sky, lighting the land till it lay bathed in ghostly day. And with the coming of the night, brooding and mourning by the pool, Buck came alive to a stirring of the new life in the forest other than that which the Yeehats had made. He stood up, listening and scenting. From far away drifted a faint, sharp yelp, followed by a chorus of similar sharp yelps. As the moments passed the yelps grew closer and louder. Again Buck knew them as things heard in that other world which persisted in his memory. He walked to the centre of the open space and listened. It was the call, the many-noted call, sounding more luringly and compelling than ever before. And as never before, he was ready to obey. John Thornton was dead. The last tie was broken. Man and the claims of man no longer bound him.

Hunting their living meat, as the Yeehats were hunting it, on the flanks of the migrating moose, the wolf pack had at last crossed over from the land of streams and timber and invaded Buck's valley. Into the clearing where the moonlight streamed, they poured in a silvery flood; and in the centre of the clearing stood Buck, motionless as a statue, waiting their coming. They were awed, so still and large he stood, and a moment's pause fell, till the boldest one leaped straight for him. Like a flash Buck struck, breaking the neck. Then he stood, without movement, as before, the stricken wolf rolling in agony behind him. Three others tried it in sharp succession; and one after the other they drew back, streaming blood from slashed throats or shoulders.

This was sufficient to fling the whole pack forward, pell-mell, crowded together, blocked and confused by its eagerness to pull down the prey. Buck's marvellous quickness and agility stood him in good stead. Pivoting on his hind legs, and snapping and gashing, he was everywhere at once, presenting a front which was apparently unbroken so swiftly did he whirl and guard from side to side. But to prevent them from getting behind him, he was forced back, down past the pool and into the creek bed, till he brought up against a high gravel bank. He worked along to a right angle in the bank which the men had made in the course of mining, and in this angle he came to bay, protected on three sides and with nothing to do but face the front.

And so well did he face it, that at the end of half an hour the wolves drew back discomfited. The tongues of all were out and lolling, the white fangs showing cruelly white in the moonlight.

Some were lying down with heads raised and ears pricked forward; others stood on their feet, watching him; and still others were lapping water from the pool. One wolf, long and lean and gray, advanced cautiously, in a friendly manner, and Buck recognized the wild brother with whom he had run for a night and a day. He was whining softly, and, as Buck whined, they touched noses.

Then an old wolf, gaunt and battle-scarred, came forward. Buck writhed his lips into the preliminary of a snarl, but sniffed noses with him. Whereupon the old wolf sat down, pointed nose at the moon, and broke out the long wolf howl. The others sat down and howled. And now the call came to Buck in unmistakable accents. He, too, sat down and howled. This over, he came out of his angle and the pack crowded around him, sniffing in half-friendly, half-savage manner. The leaders lifted the yelp of the pack and sprang away into the woods. The wolves swung in behind, yelping in chorus. And Buck ran with them, side by side with the wild brother, yelping as he ran.

And here may well end the story of Buck. The years were not many when the Yeehats noted a change in the breed of timber wolves; for some were seen with splashes of brown on head and muzzle, and with a rift of white centering down the chest. But more remarkable than this, the Yeehats tell of a Ghost Dog that runs at the head of the pack. They are afraid of this Ghost Dog, for it has cunning greater than they, stealing from their camps in fierce winters, robbing their traps, slaying their dogs, and defying their bravest hunters.

Nay, the tale grows worse. Hunters there are who fail to return to the camp, and hunters there have been whom their tribesmen found with throats slashed cruelly open and with wolf prints about them in the snow greater than the prints of any wolf. Each fall, when the Yeehats follow the movement of the moose, there is a certain valley which they never enter. And women there are who become sad when the word goes over the fire of how the Evil Spirit came to select that valley for an abiding-place.

In the summers there is one visitor, however, to that valley, of which the Yeehats do not know. It is a great, gloriously coated wolf, like, and yet unlike, all other wolves. He crosses alone from the smiling timber land and comes down into an open space among the trees. Here a yellow stream flows from rotted moose-hide sacks and sinks into the ground, with long grasses growing through it and vegetable mold overrunning it and hiding its yellow from the sun; and here he muses for a time, howling once, long and mournfully, ere he departs.

But he is not always alone. When the long winter nights come on and the wolves follow their meat into the lower valleys, he may be seen running at the head of the pack through the pale moonlight or glimmering borealis, leaping gigantic above his fellows, his great throat a-bellow as he sings a song of the younger world, which is the song of the pack.

SOURCE: Jack London. *The Call of the Wild.* New York: Macmillan Company, 1903. [First published: *The Saturday Evening Post,* June 20–July 18, 1903.]

THEODORE ROOSEVELT

As president of the United States (1901–1909), Theodore Roosevelt (1858–1919), a lifelong bird-lover and big-game hunter, created parkland in the United States the size of Western Europe. In the following speech, made at the Grand Canyon (Arizona Territory), in the midst of his awe and appreciation of the Grand Canyon, the rough-riding hero of San Juan Hill in the Spanish-American War of 1898 greets some of his former soldiers who hailed from the area. As noted in the speech, irrigation of the arid southwest was one of his other goals. No American president ever accomplished more for the environment. In 1908, Roosevelt put into law the designation of the Grand Canyon as a National Monument.

The Natural Wonder of the Grand Canyon (1903)

MR. GOVERNOR, AND you, my fellow citizens:

I am glad to be in Arizona to-day. From Arizona many gallant men came into the regiment which I had the honor to command. Arizona sent men who won glory on fought fields, and men to whom came a glorious and an honorable death fighting for the flag of their country. As long as I live it will be to me an inspiration to have served with Bucky O'Neill. I have met so many comrades whom I prize, for whom I feel respect and admiration and affection, that I shall not particularize among them except to say that there is none for whom I feel all of respect and admiration and affection more than for your Governor.

I have never been in Arizona before. It is one of the regions from which I expect most development through the wise action of the National Congress in passing the irrigation act. The first and biggest experiment now in view under that act is the one that we are trying in Arizona. I look forward to the effects of irrigation partly as applied by and through the government, still more as applied by individuals, and especially by associations of individuals, profiting by the example of the government, and possibly by help from it—I look forward to the effects of irrigation as being of greater consequence to all this region of country in the next fifty years than any other material movement whatsoever.

In the Grand Canyon, Arizona has a natural wonder which, so far as I know, is, in kind, absolutely unparalleled throughout the rest of the world. I want to ask you to do one thing in connection with it, in your own interest and in the interest of the country—to keep this great wonder of nature as it now is. I was delighted to learn of the wisdom of the Santa Fe railroad people in deciding not to build their hotel on the brink of the canyon. I hope you will not have a building of any kind, not a summer cottage, a hotel, or anything else, to mar the wonderful grandeur, the sublimity, the great loneliness and beauty of the canyon. Leave it as it is. You cannot improve on it. The ages have been at work on it, and man can only mar it. What you can do is to keep it for your children, your children's children and for all who come after you, as one of the great sights which every American, if he can travel at all, should see. We have gotten past the stage, my fellow-citizens, when we are to be pardoned if we treat any part of our country as something to be skinned for two or three years for the use of the present generation, whether it is the forest, the water, the scenery. Whatever it is, handle it so that your children's children will get the benefit of it. If you deal with irrigation, apply it under circumstances that will make it of benefit, not to the speculator who hopes to get profit out of it for two or three years, but handle it so that it will be of use to the home-maker, to the man who comes to live here, and to have his children stay after him. Keep the forests in the same way. Preserve the forests by use; preserve them for the ranchman and the stockman, for the people of the Territory, for the people of the region round about. Preserve them for that use, but use them so that they will not be squandered, that they will not be wasted, so that they will be of benefit to the Arizona of 1953 as well as the Arizona of 1903.

To the Indians here I want to say a word of welcome. In my regiment I had a good many Indians. They were good enough to fight and to die, and they are good enough to have me treat them exactly as square as any white man. There are many problems in connection with them. We must save them from corruption and from brutality; and I regret to say that at times we must save them from unregulated Eastern philanthropy. All I ask is a square deal for every man. Give him a fair chance. Do not let him wrong any one, and do not let him be wronged.

I believe in you. I am glad to see you. I wish you well with all my heart, and I know that your future will justify all the hopes we have.

SOURCE: *A Compilation of the Messages and Speeches of Theodore Roosevelt, 1901–1905.* Edited by Alfred Henry Lewis. Bureau of National Literature and Art, 1906.

O. HENRY

William Sydney Porter (1862–1910) served three years in prison for embezzlement from the bank where he worked in Texas. In 1901 he began a new career for himself in New York City as a short story writer, taking the pseudonym O. Henry. Within the decade, he became America's favorite author of clever entertaining tales.

The Cop and the Anthem (1906)

ON HIS BENCH in Madison Square Soapy moved uneasily. When wild geese honk high of nights, and when women without sealskin coats grow kind to their husbands, and when Soapy moves uneasily on his bench in the park, you may know that winter is near at hand.

A dead leaf fell in Soapy's lap. That was Jack Frost's card. Jack is kind to the regular denizens of Madison Square, and gives fair warning of his annual call. At the corners of four streets he hands his pasteboard to the North Wind, footman of the mansion of All Outdoors, so that the inhabitants thereof may make ready.

Soapy's mind became cognizant of the fact that the time had come for him to resolve himself into a singular Committee of Ways and Means to provide against the coming rigor. And therefore he moved uneasily on his bench.

The hibernatorial ambitions of Soapy were not of the highest. In them there were no considerations of Mediterranean cruises, of soporific Southern skies or drifting in the Vesuvian Bay. Three months on the Island was what his soul craved. Three months of assured board and bed and congenial company, safe from Boreas and bluecoats, seemed to Soapy the essence of things desirable.

For years the hospitable Blackwell's had been his winter quarters. Just as his more fortunate fellow New Yorkers had bought their tickets to Palm Beach and the Riviera each winter, so Soapy had made his humble arrangements for his annual hegira to the Island. And now the time was come. On the previous night three Sabbath newspapers, distributed beneath his coat, about his ankles and over his lap, had failed to repulse the cold as he slept on his bench near the spurting fountain in the ancient square. So the Island loomed big and timely in Soapy's mind. He scorned the provisions made in the name of charity for the city's dependents. In Soapy's opinion the Law was more benign than Philanthropy. There was an endless round of institutions, municipal and eleemosynary, on which he might set out and receive lodging and food accordant with the simple life. But to one of Soapy's proud spirit the gifts of charity are encumbered. If not in coin you must pay in humiliation of spirit for every benefit received at the hands of philanthropy. As Caesar had his Brutus, every bed of charity must have its toll of a bath, every loaf of bread its compensation of a private and personal inquisition. Wherefore it is better to be a guest of the law, which, though conducted by rules, does not meddle unduly with a gentleman's private affairs.

Soapy, having decided to go to the Island, at once set about accomplishing his desire. There were many easy ways of doing this. The pleasantest was to dine luxuriously at some expensive restaurant; and then, after declaring insolvency, be handed over quietly and without uproar to a policeman. An accommodating magistrate would do the rest.

Soapy left his bench and strolled out of the square and across the level sea of asphalt, where Broadway and Fifth Avenue flow together. Up Broadway he turned, and halted at a glittering café, where are gathered together nightly the choicest products of the grape, the silkworm, and the protoplasm.

Soapy had confidence in himself from the lowest button of his vest upward. He was shaven, and his coat was decent and his neat black, ready-tied four-in-hand had been presented to him by a lady missionary on Thanksgiving Day. If he could reach a table in the restaurant unsuspected success would be his. The portion of him that would show above the table would raise no doubt in the waiter's mind. A roasted mallard duck, thought Soapy, would be about the thing—with a bottle of Chablis, and then Camembert, a demi-tasse and a cigar. One dollar for the cigar would be enough. The total would not be so high as to call forth any supreme manifestation of revenge from the café management; and yet the meat would leave him filled and happy for the journey to his winter refuge.

But as Soapy set foot inside the restaurant door the head waiter's eye fell upon his frayed trousers and decadent shoes. Strong and ready hands turned him about and conveyed him in silence and haste to the sidewalk and averted the ignoble fate of the menaced mallard.

Soapy turned off Broadway. It seemed that his route to the coveted Island was not to be an epicurean one. Some other way of entering limbo must be thought of.

At a corner of Sixth Avenue electric lights and cunningly displayed wares behind plate-glass made a shop window conspicuous. Soapy took a cobblestone and dashed it through the glass. People came running around the corner, a policeman in the lead. Soapy stood still, with his hands in his pockets, and smiled at the sight of brass buttons.

"Where's the man that done that?" inquired the officer, excitedly.

"Don't you figure out that I might have had something to do with it?" said Soapy, not without sarcasm, but friendly, as one greets good fortune.

The policeman's mind refused to accept Soapy even as a clue. Men who smash windows do not remain to parley with the law's minions. They take to their heels. The policeman saw a man halfway down the block running to catch a car. With drawn club he joined in the pursuit. Soapy, with disgust in his heart, loafed along, twice unsuccessful.

On the opposite side of the street was a restaurant of no great pretensions. It catered to large appetites and modest purses. Its crockery and atmosphere were thick; its soup and napery thin. Into this place Soapy took his accusive shoes and telltale trousers without challenge. At a table he sat and consumed beefsteak, flapjacks, doughnuts and pie. And then to the waiter he betrayed the fact that the minutest coin and himself were strangers.

"Now, get busy and call a cop," said Soapy. "And don't keep a gentleman waiting."

"No cops for youse," said the waiter, with a voice like butter cakes and an eye like the cherry in a Manhattan cocktail. "Hey, Con!"

Neatly upon his left ear on the callous pavement two waiters pitched Soapy. He arose joint by joint, as a carpenter's rule opens, and beat the dust from his clothes. Arrest seemed but a rosy dream. The Island seemed very far away. A policeman who stood before a drug store two doors away laughed and walked down the street.

Five blocks Soapy travelled before his courage permitted him to woo capture again. This time the opportunity presented what he fatuously termed to himself a "cinch." A young woman of a modest and pleasing guise was standing before a show window gazing with sprightly interest at its display of shaving mugs and inkstands, and two yards from the window a large policeman of severe demeanor leaned against a water plug.

It was Soapy's design to assume the rôle of the despicable and execrated "masher." The refined and elegant appearance of his victim and the contiguity of the conscientious cop encouraged him to believe that he would soon feel the pleasant official clutch upon his arm that would insure his winter quarters on the right little, tight little isle.

Soapy straightened the lady missionary's ready-made tie, dragged his shrinking cuffs into the open, set his hat at a killing cant and sidled toward the young woman. He made eyes at her, was taken with sudden coughs and "hems," smiled, smirked and went brazenly through the impudent and contemptible litany of the "masher." With half an eye Soapy saw that the policeman was watching him fixedly. The young woman moved away a few steps, and again bestowed her absorbed attention upon the shaving mugs. Soapy followed, boldly stepping to her side, raised his hat and said:

"Ah there, Bedelia! Don't you want to come and play in my yard?"

The policeman was still looking. The persecuted young woman had but to beckon a finger and Soapy would be practically en route for his insular haven. Already he imagined he could feel the cozy warmth of the station-house. The young woman faced him and, stretching out a hand, caught Soapy's coat sleeve.

"Sure, Mike," she said joyfully, "if you'll blow me to a pail of suds. I'd have spoke to you sooner, but the cop was watching."

With the young woman playing the clinging ivy to his oak Soapy walked past the policeman overcome with gloom. He seemed doomed to liberty.

At the next corner he shook off his companion and ran. He halted in the district where by night are found the lightest streets, hearts, vows and librettos. Women in furs and men in greatcoats moved gaily in the wintry air. A sudden fear seized Soapy that some dreadful enchantment had rendered him immune to arrest. The thought brought a little of panic upon it, and when he came upon another policeman lounging grandly in front of a transplendent theatre he caught at the immediate straw of "disorderly conduct."

On the sidewalk Soapy began to yell drunken gibberish at the top of his harsh voice. He danced, howled, raved, and otherwise disturbed the welkin.

The policeman twirled his club, turned his back to Soapy and remarked to a citizen.

"'Tis one of them Yale lads celebratin' the goose egg they give to the Hartford College. Noisy; but no harm. We've instructions to lave them be."

Disconsolate, Soapy ceased his unavailing racket. Would never a policeman lay hands on him? In his fancy the Island seemed an unattainable Arcadia. He buttoned his thin coat against the chilling wind.

In a cigar store he saw a well-dressed man lighting a cigar at a swinging light. His silk umbrella he had set by the door on entering. Soapy stepped inside, secured the umbrella and sauntered off with it slowly. The man at the cigar light followed hastily.

"My umbrella," he said, sternly.

"Oh, is it?" sneered Soapy, adding insult to petit larceny. "Well, why don't you call a policeman? I took it. Your umbrella! Why don't you call a cop? There stands one on the corner."

The umbrella owner slowed his steps. Soapy did likewise, with a presentiment that luck would again run against him. The policeman looked at the two curiously.

"Of course," said the umbrella man—"that is—well, you know how these mistakes occur—I—if it's your umbrella I hope you'll excuse me—I picked it up this morning in a restaurant—If you recognize it as yours, why—I hope you'll—"

"Of course it's mine," said Soapy, viciously.

The ex-umbrella man retreated. The policeman hurried to assist a tall blonde in an opera cloak across the street in front of a street car that was approaching two blocks away.

Soapy walked eastward through a street damaged by improvements. He hurled the umbrella wrathfully into an excavation. He muttered against the men who wear helmets and carry clubs. Because he wanted to fall into their clutches, they seemed to regard him as a king who could do no wrong.

At length Soapy reached one of the avenues to the east where the glitter and turmoil was but faint. He set his face down this toward Madison Square, for the homing instinct survives even when the home is a park bench.

But on an unusually quiet corner Soapy came to a standstill. Here was an old church, quaint and rambling and gabled. Through one violet-stained window a soft light glowed, where, no doubt, the organist loitered over the keys, making sure of his mastery of the coming Sabbath anthem. For there drifted out to Soapy's ears sweet music that caught and held him transfixed against the convolutions of the iron fence.

The moon was above, lustrous and serene; vehicles and pedestrians were few; sparrows twittered sleepily in the eaves—for a little while the scene might have been a country churchyard. And the anthem that the organist played cemented Soapy to the iron fence, for he had known it well in the days when his life contained such things as mothers and roses and ambitions and friends and immaculate thoughts and collars.

The conjunction of Soapy's receptive state of mind and the influences about the old church wrought a sudden and wonderful change in his soul. He viewed with swift horror the pit into which he had tumbled, the degraded days, unworthy desires, dead hopes, wrecked faculties and base motives that made up his existence.

And also in a moment his heart responded thrillingly to this novel mood. An instantaneous and strong impulse moved him to battle with his desperate fate. He would pull himself out of the mire; he would make a man of himself again; he would conquer the evil that had taken possession of him. There was time; he was comparatively young yet: he would resurrect his old eager ambitions and pursue them without faltering. Those solemn but sweet organ notes had set up a revolution in him. Tomorrow he would go into the roaring downtown district and find work. A fur importer had once offered him a place as driver. He would find him to-morrow and ask for the position. He would be somebody in the world. He would—

Soapy felt a hand laid on his arm. He looked quickly around into the broad face of a policeman.

"What are you doin' here?" asked the officer.

"Nothin'," said Soapy.

"Then come along," said the policeman.

"Three months on the Island," said the Magistrate in the Police Court the next morning.

Source: O. Henry. *The Four Million*. New York: A. L. Burt Company, 1906.

The Ransom of Red Chief (1910)

IT LOOKED LIKE a good thing: but wait till I tell you. We were down South, in Alabama—Bill Driscoll and myself—when this kidnapping idea struck us. It was, as Bill afterward expressed it, "during a moment of temporary mental apparition"; but we didn't find that out till later.

There was a town down there, as flat as a flannel-cake, and called Summit, of course. It contained inhabitants of as undeleterious and self-satisfied a class of peasantry as ever clustered around a Maypole.

Bill and me had a joint capital of about six hundred dollars, and we needed just two thousand dollars more to pull off a fraudulent town-lot scheme in Western Illinois with. We talked it over on the front steps of the hotel. Philoprogenitiveness, says we, is strong in semi-rural communities; therefore, and for other reasons, a kidnapping project ought to do better there than in the radius of newspapers that send reporters out in plain clothes to stir up talk about such things. We knew that Summit couldn't get after us with anything stronger than constables and, maybe, some lackadaisical bloodhounds and a diatribe or two in the *Weekly Farmers' Budget*. So, it looked good.

We selected for our victim the only child of a prominent citizen named Ebenezer Dorset. The father was respectable and tight, a mortgage fancier and a stern, upright collection-plate passer and forecloser. The kid was a boy of ten, with bas-relief freckles, and hair the color of the cover of the magazine you buy at the news-stand when you want to catch a train. Bill and me figured that Ebenezer would melt down for a ransom of two thousand dollars to a cent. But wait till I tell you.

About two miles from Summit was a little mountain, covered with a dense cedar brake. On the rear elevation of this mountain was a cave. There we stored provisions.

One evening after sundown, we drove in a buggy past old Dorset's house. The kid was in the street, throwing rocks at a kitten on the opposite fence.

"Hey, little boy!" says Bill, "would you like to have a bag of candy and a nice ride?"

The boy catches Bill neatly in the eye with a piece of brick.

"That will cost the old man an extra five hundred dollars," says Bill, climbing over the wheel.

That boy put up a fight like a welter-weight cinnamon bear; but, at last, we got him down in the bottom of the buggy and drove away. We took him up to the cave, and I hitched the horse in the cedar brake. After dark I drove the buggy to the little village, three miles away, where we had hired it, and walked back to the mountain.

Bill was pasting court-plaster over the scratches and bruises on his features. There was a fire burning behind the big rock at the entrance of the cave, and the boy was watching a pot of boiling coffee, with two buzzard tail-feathers stuck in his red hair. He points a stick at me when I come up, and says:

"Ha! cursed paleface, do you dare to enter the camp of Red Chief, the terror of the plains?"

"He's all right now," says Bill, rolling up his trousers and examining some bruises on his shins. "We're playing Indian. We're making Buffalo Bill's show look like magic-lantern views of Palestine in the town hall. I'm Old Hank, the Trapper, Red Chief's captive, and I'm to be scalped at daybreak. By Geronimo! that kid can kick hard."

Yes, sir, that boy seemed to be having the time of his life. The fun of camping out in a cave had made him forget that he was a captive himself. He immediately christened me Snake-eye, the Spy, and announced that, when his braves returned from the war-path, I was to be broiled at the stake at the rising of the sun.

Then we had supper; and he filled his mouth full of bacon and bread and gravy, and began to talk. He made a during-dinner speech something like this:

"I like this fine. I never camped out before; but I had a pet 'possum once, and I was nine last birthday. I hate to go to school. Rats ate up sixteen of Jimmy Talbot's aunt's speckled hen's eggs. Are there any real Indians in these woods? I want some more gravy. Does the trees moving make the wind blow? We had five puppies. What makes your nose so red, Hank? My father has lots of money. Are the stars hot? I whipped Ed Walker twice, Saturday. I don't like girls. You dassent catch toads unless with a string. Do oxen make any noise? Why are oranges round? Have you got beds to sleep on in this cave? Amos Murray has got six toes. A parrot can talk, but a monkey or a fish can't. How many does it take to make twelve?"

Every few minutes he would remember that he was a pesky redskin, and pick up his stick rifle and tiptoe to the mouth of the cave to rubber for the scouts of the hated paleface. Now and then he would let out a war-whoop that made Old Hank the Trapper shiver. That boy had Bill terrorized from the start.

"Red Chief," says I to the kid, "would you like to go home?"

"Aw, what for?" says he. "I don't have any fun at home. I hate to go to school. I like to camp out. You won't take me back home again, Snake-eye, will you?"

"Not right away," says I. "We'll stay here in the cave awhile."

"All right!" says he. "That'll be fine. I never had such fun in all my life."

We went to bed about eleven o'clock. We spread down some wide blankets and quilts and put Red Chief between us. We weren't afraid he'd run away. He kept us awake for three hours, jumping up and reaching for his rifle and screeching: "Hist! pard," in mine and Bill's ears, as the fancied crackle of a twig or the rustle of a leaf revealed to his young imagination the stealthy approach of the outlaw band. At last, I fell into a troubled sleep, and dreamed that I had been kidnapped and chained to a tree by a ferocious pirate with red hair.

Just at daybreak, I was awakened by a series of awful screams from Bill. They weren't yells, or howls, or shouts, or whoops, or yawps, such as you'd expect from a manly set of vocal organs—they were simply indecent, terrifying, humiliating screams, such as women emit when they see ghosts or caterpillars. It's an awful thing to hear a strong, desperate, fat man scream incontinently in a cave at daybreak.

I jumped up to see what the matter was. Red Chief was sitting on Bill's chest, with one hand twined in Bill's hair. In the other he had the sharp case-knife we used for slicing bacon; and he was industriously and realistically trying to take Bill's scalp, according to the sentence that had been pronounced upon him the evening before.

I got the knife away from the kid and made him lie down again. But, from that moment, Bill's spirit was broken. He laid down on his side of the bed, but he never closed an eye again in sleep as long as that boy was with us. I dozed off for a while, but along toward sun-up I remembered that Red Chief had said I was to be burned at the stake at the rising of the sun. I wasn't nervous or afraid; but I sat up and lit my pipe and leaned against a rock.

"What you getting up so soon for, Sam?" asked Bill.

"Me?" says I. "Oh, I got a kind of a pain in my shoulder. I thought sitting up would rest it."

"You're a liar!" says Bill. "You're afraid. You was to be burned at sunrise, and you was afraid he'd do it. And he would, too, if he could find a match. Ain't it awful, Sam? Do you think anybody will pay out money to get a little imp like that back home?"

"Sure," said I. "A rowdy kid like that is just the kind that parents dote on. Now, you and the Chief get up and cook breakfast, while I go up on the top of this mountain and reconnoitre."

I went up on the peak of the little mountain and ran my eye over the contiguous vicinity. Over towards Summit I expected to see the sturdy yeomanry of the village armed with scythes and pitchforks beating the countryside for the dastardly kidnappers. But what I saw was a peaceful landscape dotted with one man ploughing with a dun mule. Nobody was dragging the creek; no couriers dashed hither and yon, bringing tidings of no news to the distracted parents. There was a sylvan attitude of somnolent sleepiness pervading that section of the external outward surface of Alabama that lay exposed to my view. "Perhaps," says I to myself, "it has not yet been discovered that the wolves have borne away the tender lambkin from the fold. Heaven help the wolves!" says I, and I went down the mountain to breakfast.

When I got to the cave I found Bill backed up against the side of it, breathing hard, and the boy threatening to smash him with a rock half as big as a cocoanut.

"He put a red-hot boiled potato down my back," explained Bill, "and then mashed it with his foot; and I boxed his ears. Have you got a gun about you, Sam?"

I took the rock away from the boy and kind of patched up the argument. "I'll fix you," says the kid to Bill. "No man ever yet struck the Red Chief but he got paid for it. You better beware!"

After breakfast the kid takes a piece of leather with strings wrapped around it out of his pocket and goes outside the cave unwinding it.

"What's he up to now?" says Bill, anxiously. "You don't think he'll run away, do you, Sam?"

"No fear of it," says I. "He don't seem to be much of a home body. But we've got to fix up some plan about the ransom. There don't seem to be much excitement around Summit on account of his disappearance; but maybe they haven't realized yet that he's gone. His folks may think he's spending the night with Aunt Jane or one of the neighbors. Anyhow, he'll be missed to-day. To-night we must get a message to his father demanding the two thousand dollars for his return."

Just then we heard a kind of war-whoop, such as David might have emitted when he knocked out the champion Goliath. It was a sling that Red Chief had pulled out of his pocket, and he was whirling it around his head.

I dodged, and heard a heavy thud and a kind of a sigh from Bill, like a horse gives out when you take his saddle off. A niggerhead rock the size of an egg had caught Bill just behind his left ear. He loosened himself all over and fell in the fire across the frying pan of hot water for washing the dishes. I dragged him out and poured cold water on his head for half an hour.

By and by, Bill sits up and feels behind his ear and says: "Sam, do you know who my favorite Biblical character is?"

"Take it easy," says I. "You'll come to your senses presently."

"King Herod," says he. "You won't go away and leave me here alone, will you, Sam?"

I went out and caught that boy and shook him until his freckles rattled.

"If you don't behave," says I, "I'll take you straight home. Now, are you going to be good, or not?"

"I was only funning," says he sullenly. "I didn't mean to hurt Old Hank. But what did he hit me for? I'll behave, Snake-eye, if you won't send me home, and if you'll let me play the Black Scout to-day."

"I don't know the game," says I. "That's for you and Mr. Bill to decide. He's your playmate for the day. I'm going away for a while, on business. Now, you come in and make friends with him and say you are sorry for hurting him, or home you go, at once."

I made him and Bill shake hands, and then I took Bill aside and told him I was going to Poplar Grove, a little village three miles from the cave, and find out what I could about how the kidnapping had been regarded in Summit. Also, I thought it best to send a peremptory letter to old man Dorset that day, demanding the ransom and dictating how it should be paid.

"You know, Sam," says Bill, "I've stood by you without batting an eye in earthquakes, fire and flood—in poker games, dynamite outrages, police raids, train robberies, and cyclones. I never lost my nerve yet till we kidnapped that two-legged skyrocket of a kid. He's got me going. You won't leave me long with him, will you, Sam?"

"I'll be back some time this afternoon," says I. "You must keep the boy amused and quiet till I return. And now we'll write the letter to old Dorset."

Bill and I got paper and pencil and worked on the letter while Red Chief, with a blanket wrapped around him, strutted up and down, guarding the mouth of the cave. Bill begged me tearfully to make the ransom fifteen hundred dollars instead of two thousand. "I ain't attempting," says he, "to decry the celebrated moral aspect of parental affection, but we're dealing with humans, and it ain't human for anybody to give up two thousand dollars for that forty-pound chunk of freckled wildcat. I'm willing to take a chance at fifteen hundred dollars. You can charge the difference up to me."

So, to relieve Bill, I acceded, and we collaborated a letter that ran this way:

Ebenezer Dorset, Esq.:

We have your boy concealed in a place far from Summit. It is useless for you or the most skilful detectives to attempt to find him. Absolutely, the only terms on which you can have him restored to you are these: We demand fifteen hundred dollars in large bills for his return; the money to be left at midnight to-night at the same spot and in the same box as your reply—as hereinafter described. If you agree to these terms, send your answer in writing by a solitary messenger to-night at half-past eight o'clock. After crossing Owl Creek on the road to Poplar Grove the fence of the wheat field on the right-hand side. At the bottom of the fence-post, opposite the third tree, will be found a small pasteboard box.

The messenger will place the answer in this box and return immediately to Summit.

If you attempt any treachery or fail to comply with our demand as stated, you will never see your boy again.

If you pay the money as demanded, he will be returned to you safe and well within three hours. These terms are final, and if you do not accede to them no further communication will be attempted.

Two Desperate Men

I addressed this letter to Dorset, and put it in my pocket. As I was about to start, the kid comes up to me and says:

"Aw, Snake-eye, you said I could play the Black Scout while you was gone."

"Play it, of course," says I. "Mr. Bill will play with you. What kind of a game is it?"

"I'm the Black Scout," says Red Chief, "and I have to ride to the stockade to warn the settlers that the Indians are coming. I'm tired of playing Indian myself. I want to be the Black Scout."

"All right," says I. "It sounds harmless to me. I guess Mr. Bill will help you foil the pesky savages."

"What am I to do?" asks Bill, looking at the kid suspiciously.

"You are the hoss," says Black Scout. "Get down on your hands and knees. How can I ride to the stockade without a hoss?"

"You'd better keep him interested," said I, "till we get the scheme going. Loosen up."

Bill gets down on his all fours, and a look comes in his eye like a rabbit's when you catch it in a trap.

"How far is it to the stockade, kid?" he asks, in a husky manner of voice.

"Ninety miles," says the Black Scout. "And you have to hump yourself to get there on time. Whoa, now!"

The Black Scout jumps on Bill's back and digs his heels in his side.

"For Heaven's sake," says Bill, "hurry back, Sam, as soon as you can. I wish we hadn't made the ransom more than a thousand. Say, you quit kicking me or I'll get up and warm you good."

I walked over to Poplar Grove and sat around the post-office and store, talking with the chaw-bacons that came in to trade. One whiskerando says that he hears Summit is all upset on account of Elder Ebenezer Dorset's boy having been lost or stolen. That was all I wanted to know. I bought some smoking tobacco, referred casually to the price of black-eyed peas, posted my letter surreptitiously, and came away. The post-master said the mail-carrier would come by in an hour to take the mail to Summit.

When I got back to the cave Bill and the boy were not to be found. I explored the vicinity of the cave, and risked a yodel or two, but there was no response.

So I lighted my pipe and sat down on a mossy bank to await developments.

In about half an hour I heard the bushes rustle, and Bill wabbled out into the little glade in front of the cave. Behind him was the kid, stepping softly like a scout, with a broad grin on his face. Bill stopped, took off his hat, and wiped his face with a red handkerchief. The kid stopped about eight feet behind him.

"Sam," says Bill, "I suppose you'll think I'm a renegade, but I couldn't help it. I'm a grown person with masculine proclivities and habits of self-defense, but there is a time when all systems of egotism and predominance fail. The boy is gone. I have sent him home. All is off. There was martyrs in old times," goes on Bill, "that suffered death rather than give up the particular graft they enjoyed. None of 'em ever was subjugated to such supernatural tortures as I have been. I tried to be faithful to our articles of depredation; but there came a limit."

"What's the trouble, Bill?" I asks him.

"I was rode," says Bill, "the ninety miles to the stockade, not barring an inch. Then, when the settlers was rescued, I was given oats. Sand ain't a palatable substitute. And then, for an hour I had to try to explain to him why there was nothin' in holes, how a road can run both ways, and what makes the grass green. I tell you, Sam, a human can only stand so much. I takes him by the neck of his clothes and drags him down the mountain. On the way he kicks my legs black and blue from the knees down; and I've got to have two or three bites on my thumb and hand cauterized.

"But he's gone"—continues Bill—"gone home. I showed him the road to Summit and kicked him about eight feet nearer there at one kick. I'm sorry we lose the ransom; but it was either that or Bill Driscoll to the madhouse."

Bill is puffing and blowing, but there is a look of ineffable peace and growing content on his rose-pink features.

"Bill," says I, "there isn't any heart disease in your family, is there?"

"No," says Bill, "nothing chronic except malaria and accidents. Why?"

"Then you might turn around," says I, "and have a look behind you."

Bill turns and sees the boy, and loses his complexion and sits down plump on the ground and begins to pluck aimlessly at grass and little sticks. For an hour I was afraid of his mind. And then I told him that my scheme was to put the whole job through immediately and that we would get the ransom and be off with it by midnight if old Dorset fell in with our proposition. So Bill braced up enough to give the kid a weak sort of a smile and a promise to play the Russian in a Japanese war with him as soon as he felt a little better.

I had a scheme for collecting that ransom without danger of being caught by counterplots that ought to commend itself to professional kidnappers. The tree under which the answer was to be left—and the money later on—was close to the road fence with big, bare fields on all sides. If a gang of constables should be watching for any one to come for the note, they could see him a long way off crossing the fields or in the road. But no, sirree! At half-past eight I was up in that tree as well hidden as a tree toad, waiting for the messenger to arrive.

Exactly on time, a half-grown boy rides up the road on a bicycle, locates the pasteboard box at the foot of the fence-post, slips a folded piece of paper into it, and pedals away again back toward Summit.

I waited an hour and then concluded the thing was square. I slid down the tree, got the note, slipped along the fence till I struck the woods, and was back at the cave in another half an hour. I opened the note, got near the lantern, and read it to Bill. It was written with a pen in a crabbed hand, and the sum and substance of it was this:

Two Desperate Men:

Gentlemen: I received your letter to-day by post, in regard to the ransom you ask for the return of my son. I think you are a little high in your demands, and I hereby make you a counter-proposition, which I am inclined to believe you will accept. You bring Johnny home and pay me two hundred and fifty dollars in cash, and I agree to take him off your hands. You had better come at night, for the neighbors believe he is lost, and I couldn't be responsible for what they would do to anybody they saw bringing him back.

Very respectfully,
Ebenezer Dorset

"Great pirates of Penzance," says I; "of all the impudent—"

But I glanced at Bill, and hesitated. He had the most appealing look in his eyes I ever saw on the face of a dumb or a talking brute.

"Sam," says he, "what's two hundred and fifty dollars, after all? We've got the money. One more night of this kid will send me to a bed in Bedlam. Besides being a thorough gentleman, I think Mr. Dorset is a spendthrift for making us such a liberal offer. You ain't going to let the chance go, are you?"

"Tell you the truth, Bill," says I, "this little he ewe lamb has somewhat got on my nerves too. We'll take him home, pay the ransom, and make our getaway."

We took him home that night. We got him to go by telling him that his father had bought a silver-mounted rifle and a pair of moccasins for him, and we were going to hunt bears the next day.

It was just twelve o'clock when we knocked at Ebenezer's front door. Just at the moment when I should have been abstracting the fifteen hundred dollars from the box under the tree, according to the original proposition, Bill was counting out two hundred and fifty dollars into Dorset's hand.

When the kid found out we were going to leave him at home he started up a howl like a calliope and fastened himself as tight as a leech to Bill's leg. His father peeled him away gradually, like a porous plaster.

"How long can you hold him?" asks Bill.

"I'm not as strong as I used to be," says old Dorset, "but I think I can promise you ten minutes."

"Enough," says Bill. "In ten minutes I shall cross the Central, Southern and Middle Western States, and be legging it trippingly for the Canadian border."

And, as dark as it was, and as fat as Bill was, and as good a runner as I am, he was a good mile and a half out of Summit before I could catch up with him.

SOURCE: O. Henry. *Whirligigs*. New York: Doubleday, Page and Company, 1910.

EMMA GOLDMAN

In the first two decades of the twentieth century, Emma Goldman (1869–1940), born in Russia, was one of the most famous and controversial speakers on socialism and women's rights. As a teenager, she was educated in Germany before she moved to the United States, where she became an anarchist and free-speech advocate. Immediately after this speech in the spring in San Francisco, an American war veteran complimented (or, as he would claim, simply greeted) her, and was consequently arrested for treason and sentenced to five years in prison. Goldman herself would serve two years in prison for encouraging resistance to the draft for World War I and was thereafter deported from the United States.

What Is Patriotism? (1908)

Men and Women:

What is patriotism? Is it love of one's birthplace, the place of childhood's recollections and hopes, dreams and aspirations? Is it the place where, in childlike naiveté, we would watch the passing clouds, and wonder why we, too, could not float so swiftly? The place where we would count the milliard glittering stars, terror-stricken lest each one "an eye should be," piercing the very depths of our little souls? Is it the place where we would listen to the music of the birds and long to have wings to fly, even as they, to distant lands? Or is it the place where we would sit on Mother's knee, enraptured by tales of great deeds and conquests? In short, is it love for the spot, every inch representing dear and precious recollections of a happy, joyous and playful childhood?

If that were patriotism, few American men of today would be called upon to be patriotic, since the place of play has been turned into factory, mill, and mine, while deepening sounds of machinery have replaced the music of the birds. No longer can we hear the tales of great deeds, for the stories our mothers tell today are but those of sorrow, tears and grief.

What, then, is patriotism? "Patriotism, sir, is the last resort of scoundrels," said Dr. Samuel Johnson. Leo Tolstoy, the greatest anti-patriot of our time, defines patriotism as the principle that will justify the training of wholesale murderers; a trade that requires better equipment in the exercise of man-killing than the making of such necessities as shoes, clothing, and houses; a trade that guarantees better returns and greater glory than that of the honest workingman.

Indeed, conceit, arrogance and egotism are the essentials of patriotism. Let me illustrate. Patriotism assumes that our globe is divided into little spots, each one surrounded by an iron gate. Those who have had the fortune of being born on some particular spot consider themselves nobler, better, grander, more intelligent than those living beings inhabiting any other spot. It is, therefore, the duty of everyone living on that chosen spot to fight, kill and die in the attempt to impose his superiority upon all the others.

The inhabitants of the other spots reason in like manner, of course, with the result that from early infancy the mind of the child is provided with blood-curdling stories about the Germans, the French, the Italians, Russians, etc. When the child has reached manhood he is thoroughly saturated with the belief that he is chosen by the Lord himself to defend his country against the attack or invasion of any foreigner. It is for that purpose that we are clamoring for a greater army and navy, more battleships and ammunition.

An army and navy represent the people's toys. To make them more attractive and acceptable, hundreds and thousands of dollars are being spent for the display of toys. That was the purpose of the American government in equipping a fleet and sending it along the Pacific coast, that every American citizen should be made to feel the pride and glory of the United States.

The city of San Francisco spent one hundred thousand dollars for the entertainment of the fleet; Los Angeles, sixty thousand; Seattle and Tacoma, about one hundred thousand. Yes, two hundred and sixty thousand dollars were spent on fireworks, theater parties, and revelries, at a time when men, women, and children through the breadth and length of the country were starving in the streets; when thousands of unemployed were ready to sell their labor at any price.

What could not have been accomplished with such an enormous sum? But instead of bread and shelter, the children of those cities were taken to see the fleet, that it may remain, as one newspaper said, "a lasting memory for the child." A wonderful thing to remember, is it not? The implements of civilized slaughter. If the mind of the child is poisoned with such memories, what hope is there for a true realization of human brotherhood?

We Americans claim to be a peace-loving people. We hate bloodshed; we are opposed to violence. Yet we go into spasms of joy over the possibility of projecting dynamite bombs from flying machines upon helpless citizens. We are ready to hang, electrocute, or lynch anyone, who, from economic necessity, will risk his own life in the attempt upon that of some industrial magnate. Yet our hearts swell with pride at the thought that America is becoming the most powerful nation on earth, and that she will eventually plant her iron foot on the necks of all other nations.

Such is the logic of patriotism.

Thinking men and women the world over are beginning to realize that patriotism is too narrow and limited a conception to meet the necessities of our time. The centralization of power has brought into being an international feeling of solidarity among the oppressed nations of the world; a solidarity which represents a greater harmony of interests between the workingman of America and his brothers abroad than between the American miner and his exploiting compatriot; a solidarity which fears not foreign invasion, because it is bringing all the workers to the point when they will say to their masters, "Go and do your own killing. We have done it long enough for you." The proletariat of Europe has realized the great force of that solidarity and has, as a result, inaugurated a war against patriotism and its bloody specter, militarism. Thousands of men fill the prisons of France, Germany, Russia and the Scandinavian countries because they dared to defy the ancient superstition.

America will have to follow suit. The spirit of militarism has already permeated all walks of life. Indeed, I am convinced that militarism is a greater danger here than anywhere else, because of the many bribes capitalism holds out to those whom it wishes to destroy.

The beginning has already been made in the schools. Children are trained in military tactics, the glory of military achievements extolled in the curriculum, and the youthful mind perverted to suit the government. Further, the youth of the country is appealed to in glaring posters to join the Army and the Navy. "A fine chance to see the world!" cries the governmental huckster. Thus innocent boys are morally shanghaied into patriotism, and the military Moloch strides conquering through the nation.

When we have undermined the patriotic lie, we shall have cleared the path for the great structure where all shall be united into a universal brotherhood—a truly free society.

SOURCE: *Great Speeches of the Twentieth Century*. Mineola, New York: Dover Publications, 2011.

EZRA POUND

For the first half of the twentieth century, the poet, translator and critic Ezra Pound (1885–1972) was America and England's most important guide and promoter of literature; he advocated for the support of and interest in great writing, no matter its origins or era. Unfortunately, by the 1930s he took up economic theory and became an anti-Semite and fascist. He served a dozen years in a prison-hospital in Washington, D.C., for treason before exiling himself to Italy.

Translations from Heine (1911)

From *Die Heimkehr*

1.

Is your hate, then, of such measure?
Do you, truly, so detest me?
Through all the world will I complain
Of *how* you have addressed me.

O ye lips that are ungrateful,
Hath it never once distressed you,
That you can say such *awful* things
Of *any* one who ever kissed you?

4.

I dreamt that I was God Himself
Whom heavenly joy immerses,
And all the angels sat about
And praised my verses.

8. Night Song

And have you thoroughly kissed my lips.
There was no particular haste,
And are you not ready when evening's come?
There's no *particular* haste.

You've got the whole night before you,
Heart's-all-beloved-my-own;
In an uninterrupted night one can
Get a good deal of kissing done.

SOURCE: Ezra Pound. *Canzoni.* London: Elkin Mathews. 1911.

The Seafarer (1912)

(FROM THE EARLY ANGLO-SAXON TEXT)

May I for my own self song's truth reckon,
Journey's jargon, how I in harsh days
Hardship endured oft.
Bitter breast-cares have I abided,
Known on my keel many a care's hold,
And dire sea-surge, and there I oft spent
Narrow nightwatch nigh the ship's head
While she tossed close to cliffs. Coldly afflicted,
My feet were by frost benumbed.
Chill its chains are; chafing sighs
Hew my heart round and hunger begot
Mere-weary mood. Lest man know not
That he on dry land loveliest liveth,
List how I, care-wretched, on ice-cold sea,
Weathered the winter, wretched outcast
Deprived of my kinsmen;
Hung with hard ice-flakes, where hail-scur flew,
There I heard naught save the harsh sea
And ice-cold wave, at whiles the swan cries,
Did for my games the gannet's clamour,
Sea-fowls' loudness was for me laughter,
The mews' singing all my mead-drink.
Storms, on the stone-cliffs beaten, fell on the stern

In icy feathers; full oft the eagle screamed
With spray on his pinion.
Not any protector
May make merry man faring needy.
This he little believes, who aye in winsome life
Abides 'mid burghers some heavy business,
Wealthy and wine-flushed, how I weary oft
Must bide above brine.
Neareth nightshade, snoweth from north,
Frost froze the land, hail fell on earth then
Corn of the coldest. Nathless there knocketh now
The heart's thought that I on high streams
The salt-wavy tumult traverse alone.
Moaneth alway my mind's lust
That I fare forth, that I afar hence
Seek out a foreign fastness.
For this there's no mood-lofty man over earth's midst,
Not though he be given his good, but will have in his youth greed;
Nor his deed to the daring, nor his king to the faithful
But shall have his sorrow for sea-fare
Whatever his lord will.
He hath not heart for harping, nor in ring-having
Nor winsomeness to wife, nor world's delight
Nor any whit else save the wave's slash,
Yet longing comes upon him to fare forth on the water.
Bosque taketh blossom, cometh beauty of berries,
Fields to fairness, land fares brisker,
All this admonisheth man eager of mood,
The heart turns to travel so that he then thinks
On flood-ways to be far departing.
Cuckoo calleth with gloomy crying,
He singeth summerward, bodeth sorrow,
The bitter heart's blood. Burgher knows not—
He the prosperous man—what some perform
Where wandering them widest draweth.
So that but now my heart burst from my breast-lock,
My mood 'mid the mere-flood,
Over the whale's acre, would wander wide.
On earth's shelter cometh oft to me,
Eager and ready, the crying lone-flyer,
Whets for the whale-path the heart irresistibly,

O'er tracks of ocean; seeing that anyhow
My lord deems to me this dead life
On loan and on land, I believe not
That any earth-weal eternal standeth
Save there be somewhat calamitous
That, ere a man's tide go, turn it to twain.
Disease or oldness or sword-hate
Beats out the breath from doom-gripped body.
And for this, every earl whatever, for those speaking after—
Laud of the living, boasteth some last word,
That he will work ere he pass onward,
Frame on the fair earth 'gainst foes his malice,
Daring ado, . . .
So that all men shall honour him after
And his laud beyond them remain 'mid the English,
Aye, for ever, a lasting life's-blast,
Delight mid the doughty.
Days little durable,
And all arrogance of earthen riches,
There come now no kings nor Cæsars
Nor gold-giving lords like those gone.
Howe'er in mirth most magnified,
Whoe'er lived in life most lordliest,
Drear all this excellence, delights undurable!
Waneth the watch, but the world holdeth.
Tomb hideth trouble. The blade is layed low.
Earthly glory ageth and seareth.
No man at all going the earth's gait,
But age fares against him, his face paleth,
Grey-haired he groaneth, knows gone companions,
Lordly men are to earth o'ergiven,
Nor may he then the flesh-cover, whose life ceaseth,
Nor eat the sweet nor feel the sorry,
Nor stir hand nor think in mid heart,
And though he strew the grave with gold,
His born brothers, their buried bodies
Be an unlikely treasure hoard.

SOURCE: Ezra Pound. *Ripostes of Ezra Pound*. London: S. Swift, 1912.

The Garden (1916)

En robe de parade.
Samain.

Like a skein of loose silk blown against a wall
She walks by the railing of a path in Kensington Gardens,
And she is dying piece-meal
  of a sort of emotional anæmia.

And round about there is a rabble
Of the filthy, sturdy, unkillable infants of the very poor.
They shall inherit the earth.

In her is the end of breeding.
Her boredom is exquisite and excessive.
She would like someone to speak to her,
And is almost afraid that I
  will commit that indiscretion.

SOURCE: Ezra Pound. *Lustra of Ezra Pound with Earlier Poems.* London: Elkin Mathews, 1916.

Meditatio (1916)

When I carefully consider the curious habits of dogs
I am compelled to conclude
That man is the superior animal.

When I consider the curious habits of man
I confess, my friend, I am puzzled.

SOURCE: Ezra Pound. *Lustra of Ezra Pound with Earlier Poems.* London: Elkin Mathews, 1916.

In a Station of the Metro (1916)

The apparition of these faces in the crowd;
Petals on a wet, black bough.

SOURCE: Ezra Pound. *Lustra of Ezra Pound with Earlier Poems.* London: Elkin Mathews. 1916.

Alba (1916)

As cool as the pale wet leaves
    of lily-of-the-valley
She lay beside me in the dawn.

SOURCE: Ezra Pound. *Lustra of Ezra Pound with Earlier Poems.* London: Elkin Mathews, 1916.

The Lake Isle (1917)

O God, O Venus, O Mercury, patron of thieves,
Give me in due time, I beseech you, a little tobacco-shop,
With the little bright boxes
            piled up neatly upon the shelves
And the loose fragrant cavendish
            and the shag,
And the bright Virginia
            loose under the bright glass cases,
And a pair of scales
            not too greasy,
And the *volailles* dropping in for a word or two in passing,
For a flip word, and to tidy their hair a bit.

O God, O Venus, O Mercury, patron of thieves,
Lend me a little tobacco-shop,
            or install me in any profession
Save this damn'd profession of writing,
            where one needs one's brains all the time.

SOURCE: Ezra Pound. *Lustra of Ezra Pound with Earlier Poems.* New York: Alfred A. Knopf, 1917.

Song of the Bowmen of Shu (1917)

Here we are, picking the first fern-shoots
And saying: When shall we get back to our country?
Here we are because we have the Ken-nin for our foemen,
We have no comfort because of these Mongols.
We grub the soft fern-shoots,
When anyone says "Return," the others are full of sorrow.
Sorrowful minds, sorrow is strong, we are hungry and thirsty.
Our defence is not yet made sure, no one can let his friend
 return.
We grub the old fern-stalks.
We say: Will we be let to go back in October?
There is no ease in royal affairs, we have no comfort.
Our sorrow is bitter, but we would not return to our country.
What flower has come into blossom?
Whose chariot? The General's.
Horses, his horses even, are tired. They were strong.
We have no rest, three battles a month.
By heaven, his horses are tired.
The generals are on them, the soldiers are by them.
The horses are well trained, the generals have ivory arrows and
 quivers ornamented with fish-skin.
The enemy is swift, we must be careful.
When we set out, the willows were drooping with spring,
We come back in the snow,
We go slowly, we are hungry and thirsty,
Our mind is full of sorrow, who will know of our grief?

By Bunno.
Reputedly 1100 B.C.

SOURCE: Ezra Pound. *Lustra of Ezra Pound with Earlier Poems*. New York: Alfred A. Knopf, 1917.

The River-Merchant's Wife: A Letter (1917)

While my hair was still cut straight across my forehead
I played about the front gate, pulling flowers
You came by on bamboo stilts, playing horse,

You walked about my seat, playing with blue plums.
And we went on living in the village of Chokan:
Two small people, without dislike or suspicion.

At fourteen I married My Lord you.
I never laughed, being bashful.
Lowering my head, I looked at the wall.
Called to, a thousand times, I never looked back.

At fifteen I stopped scowling,
I desired my dust to be mingled with yours
Forever and forever, and forever.
Why should I climb the look out?

At sixteen you departed,
You went into far Ku-to-Yen, by the river of swirling eddies,
And you have been gone five months.
The monkeys make sorrowful noise overhead.
You dragged your feet when you went out.
By the gate now, the moss is grown, the different mosses,
Too deep to clear them away!
The leaves fall early this autumn, in wind.
The paired butterflies are already yellow with August
Over the grass in the West garden,
They hurt me.
I grow older,
If you are coming down through the narrows of the river Kiang,
Please let me know beforehand,
And I will come out to meet you,
As far as Cho-fu-Sa.

By Rihaku.

SOURCE: Ezra Pound. *Lustra of Ezra Pound with Earlier Poems.* New York: Alfred A. Knopf, 1917.

The Jewel Stairs' Grievance (1917)

The jewelled steps are already quite white with dew,
It is so late that the dew soaks my gauze stockings,
And I let down the crystal curtain
And watch the moon through the clear autumn.

By Rihaku.

[Pound's] Note: Jewel stairs, therefore a palace. Grievance, therefore there is something to complain of. Gauze stockings, therefore a court lady, not a servant who complains. Clear autumn, therefore he has no excuse on account of weather. Also she has come early, for the dew has not merely whitened the stairs, but has soaked her stockings. The poem is especially prized because she utters no direct reproach.

SOURCE: Ezra Pound. *Lustra of Ezra Pound with Earlier Poems*. New York: Alfred A. Knopf, 1917.

Lament of the Frontier Guard (1917)

By the North Gate, the wind blows full of sand,
Lonely from the beginning of time until now!
Trees fall, the grass goes yellow with autumn.
I climb the towers and towers
  to watch out the barbarous land:
Desolate castle, the sky, the wide desert.
There is no wall left to this village.
Bones white with a thousand frosts,
High heaps, covered with trees and grass;
Who brought this to pass?
Who has brought the flaming imperial anger?
Who has brought the army with drums and with kettle-drums?
Barbarous kings.
A gracious spring, turned to blood-ravenous autumn,
A turmoil of wars-men, spread over the middle kingdom,
Three hundred and sixty thousand,
And sorrow, sorrow like rain.
Sorrow to go, and sorrow, sorrow returning,
Desolate, desolate fields,
And no children of warfare upon them,

No longer the men for offence and defence.
Ah, how shall you know the dreary sorrow at the North Gate,
With Rihoku's name forgotten,
And we guardsmen fed to the tigers.

By Rihaku.

SOURCE: Ezra Pound. *Lustra of Ezra Pound with Earlier Poems.* New York: Alfred A. Knopf, 1917.

Exile's Letter (1917)

To So-Kin of Rakuyo, ancient friend, Chancellor of Gen.
Now I remember that you built me a special tavern
By the south side of the bridge at Ten-Shin.
With yellow gold and white jewels, we paid for songs and laughter
And we were drunk for month on month, forgetting the kings and princes.
Intelligent men came drifting in from the sea and from the west border,
And with them, and with you especially
There was nothing at cross purpose,
And they made nothing of sea-crossing or of mountain crossing,
If only they could be of that fellowship,
And we all spoke out our hearts and minds, and without regret.

And then I was sent off to South Wei,
smothered in laurel groves,
And you to the north of Raku-hoku,
Till we had nothing but thoughts and memories in common.
And then, when separation had come to its worst,
We met, and travelled into Sen-Go,
Through all the thirty-six folds of the turning and twisting waters,
Into a valley of the thousand bright flowers,
That was the first valley;
And into ten thousand valleys full of voices and pine-winds.
And with silver harness and reins of gold,
Out came the East of Kan foreman and his company.

And there came also the "True man" of Shi-yo to meet me,
Playing on a jewelled mouth-organ.
In the storied houses of San-Ko they gave us more Sennin music,
Many instruments, like the sound of young phoenix broods.
The foreman of Kan Chu, drunk, danced
because his long sleeves wouldn't keep still
With that music playing.
And I, wrapped in brocade, went to sleep with my head on his lap,
And my spirit so high it was all over the heavens,
And before the end of the day we were scattered like stars, or rain.
I had to be off to So, far away over the waters,
You back to your river-bridge.

And your father, who was brave as a leopard,
Was governor in Hei Shu, and put down the barbarian rabble.
And one May he had you send for me,
despite the long distance.
And what with broken wheels and so on, I won't say it wasn't hard going,
Over roads twisted like sheep's guts.
And I was still going, late in the year,
in the cutting wind from the North,
And thinking how little you cared for the cost,
and you caring enough to pay it.
And what a reception:
Red jade cups, food well set on a blue jewelled table,
And I was drunk, and had no thought of returning.
And you would walk out with me to the western corner of the castle,
To the dynastic temple, with water about it clear as blue jade,
With boats floating, and the sound of mouth-organs and drums,
With ripples like dragon-scales, going grass green on the water,
Pleasure lasting, with courtezans, going and coming without hindrance,
With the willow flakes falling like snow,
And the vermilioned girls getting drunk about sunset,
And the water a hundred feet deep reflecting green eyebrows
—Eyebrows painted green are a fine sight in young moonlight,
Gracefully painted—

And the girls singing back at each other,
Dancing in transparent brocade,
And the wind lifting the song, and interrupting it,
Tossing it up under the clouds.
    And all this comes to an end.
    And is not again to be met with.
I went up to the court for examination,
Tried Layu's luck, offered the Choyo song,
And got no promotion,
    and went back to the East Mountains
        white-headed.
And once again, later, we met at the South bridge-head.
And then the crowd broke up, you went north to San palace,
And if you ask how I regret that parting:
    It is like the flowers falling at Spring's end
        Confused, whirled in a tangle.
What is the use of talking, and there is no end of talking,
There is no end of things in the heart.
I call in the boy,
Have him sit on his knees here
        To seal this,
And send it a thousand miles, thinking.

By Rihaku.

SOURCE: Ezra Pound. *Lustra of Ezra Pound with Earlier Poems.* New York: Alfred A. Knopf, 1917.

Separation on the River Kiang (1917)

Ko-jin goes west from Ko-kaku-ro,
The smoke-flowers are blurred over the river.
His lone sail blots the far sky.
And now I see only the river,
    The long Kiang, reaching heaven.

By Rihaku.

SOURCE: Ezra Pound. *Lustra of Ezra Pound with Earlier Poems.* New York: Alfred A. Knopf, 1917.

Homage to Sextus Propertius (Sections VII, IX)
(1921)

VII.

Me happy, night, night full of brightness;
Oh couch made happy by my long delectations;
How many words talked out with abundant candles;
Struggles when the lights were taken away;
Now with bared breasts she wrestled against me,
        Tunic spread in delay;
And she then opening my eyelids fallen in sleep,
Her lips upon them; and it was her mouth saying:
  Sluggard!

In how many varied embraces, our changing arms,
Her kisses, how many, lingering on my lips.
"Turn not Venus into a blinded motion,
      Eyes are the guides of love,
Paris took Helen naked coming from the bed of Menelaus,
Endymion's naked body, bright bait for Diana,"
      —such at least is the story.

While our fates twine together, sate we our eyes with love;
For long night comes upon you
        and a day when no day returns.
Let the gods lay chains upon us
        so that no day shall unbind them.

Fool who would set a term to love's madness,
For the sun shall drive with black horses,
        earth shall bring wheat from barley,
The flood shall move toward the fountain
      Ere love know moderations,
      The fish shall swim in dry streams.
No, now while it may be, let not the fruit of life cease.

      Dry wreaths drop their petals,
        their stalks are woven in baskets,
      To-day we take the great breath of lovers,
        to-morrow fate shuts us in.

Though you give all your kisses
you give but a few.

Nor can I shift my pains to other,
Hers will I be dead,
If she confers such nights upon me,
long is my life, long in years,
If she give me many,
God am I for the time.

IX.

1

The twisted rhombs ceased their clamour of accompaniment;
The scorched laurel lay in the fire-dust;
The moon still declined to descend out of heaven,

But the black ominous owl hoot was audible.

And one raft bears our fates
on the veiled lake toward Avernus
Sails spread on Cerulean waters, I would shed tears for two;
I shall live, if she continue in life,
If she dies, I shall go with her.
Great Zeus, save the woman,
or she will sit before your feet in a veil,
and tell out the long list of her troubles.

2

Persephone and Dis, Dis, have mercy upon her,
There are enough women in hell,
quite enough beautiful women,
Iope, and Tyro, and Pasiphae, and the formal girls of Achaia,
And out of Troad, and from the Campania,
Death has its tooth in the lot,
Avernus lusts for the lot of them,
Beauty is not eternal, no man has perennial fortune,
Slow foot, or swift foot, death delays but for a season.

3

My light, light of my eyes,
you are escaped from great peril,
Go back to Great Dian's dances bearing suitable gifts,
Pay up your vow of night watches
to Dian goddess of virgins,
And unto me also pay debt:
the ten nights of your company you have promised me.

SOURCE: Ezra Pound. *Poems 1918–21, Including Three Portraits and Four Cantos*. New York: Boni and Liveright, 1921.

EDITH WHARTON

Edith Wharton (1862–1937) hit her stride as a novelist in her early forties. This grimly romantic novel opens with a long introduction telling of the male narrator's interest in the mystery of the hard life of Ethan Frome and concludes with his reflections and discoveries; the middle, the bulk of the story, is told in the third person. "The qualities that make Wharton a great writer," observes her excellent biographer Hermione Lee, "her mixture of harshly detached, meticulously perceptive, disabused realism, with a language of poignant feeling and deep passion, and her setting of the most confined of private lives in a thick, complex network of social forces—were the product of years of observation, reading, practice and refinement."[1]

Ethan Frome (1911)

I HAD THE story, bit by bit, from various people, and, as generally happens in such cases, each time it was a different story.

If you know Starkfield, Massachusetts, you know the post-office. If you know the post-office you must have seen Ethan Frome drive up to it, drop the reins on his hollow-backed bay and drag himself across the brick pavement to the white colonnade; and you must have asked who he was.

It was there that, several years ago, I saw him for the first time; and the sight pulled me up sharp. Even then he was the most striking figure in Starkfield, though he was but the ruin of a man. It was not so much his great height that marked him, for the "natives" were easily singled out by their lank longitude from the stockier foreign breed: it was the careless powerful look he had, in spite of a lameness checking each step like the jerk of a chain. There was something bleak and unapproachable in his face, and he

1. Hermione Lee. *Edith Wharton: A Biography*. New York: Knopf, 2007.

was so stiffened and grizzled that I took him for an old man and was surprised to hear that he was not more than fifty-two. I had this from Harmon Gow, who had driven the stage from Bettsbridge to Starkfield in pre-trolley days and knew the chronicle of all the families on his line.

"He's looked that way ever since he had his smash-up; and that's twenty-four years ago come next February," Harmon threw out between reminiscent pauses.

The "smash-up" it was—I gathered from the same informant—which, besides drawing the red gash across Ethan Frome's forehead, had so shortened and warped his right side that it cost him a visible effort to take the few steps from his buggy to the post-office window. He used to drive in from his farm every day at about noon, and as that was my own hour for fetching my mail I often passed him in the porch or stood beside him while we waited on the motions of the distributing hand behind the grating. I noticed that, though he came so punctually, he seldom received anything but a copy of the *Bettsbridge Eagle,* which he put without a glance into his sagging pocket. At intervals, however, the post-master would hand him an envelope addressed to Mrs. Zenobia—or Mrs. Zeena—Frome, and usually bearing conspicuously in the upper left-hand corner the address of some manufacturer of patent medicine and the name of his specific. These documents my neighbour would also pocket without a glance, as if too much used to them to wonder at their number and variety, and would then turn away with a silent nod to the post-master.

Every one in Starkfield knew him and gave him a greeting tempered to his own grave mien; but his taciturnity was respected and it was only on rare occasions that one of the older men of the place detained him for a word. When this happened he would listen quietly, his blue eyes on the speaker's face, and answer in so low a tone that his words never reached me; then he would climb stiffly into his buggy, gather up the reins in his left hand and drive slowly away in the direction of his farm.

"It was a pretty bad smash-up?" I questioned Harmon, looking after Frome's retreating figure, and thinking how gallantly his lean brown head, with its shock of light hair, must have sat on his strong shoulders before they were bent out of shape.

"Wust kind," my informant assented. "More'n enough to kill most men. But the Fromes are tough. Ethan'll likely touch a hundred."

"Good God!" I exclaimed. At the moment Ethan Frome, after climbing to his seat, had leaned over to assure himself of the security of a wooden box—also with a druggist's label on it—which he had placed in the back of the buggy, and I saw his face as it probably looked when he thought himself alone. *"That* man touch a hundred? He looks as if he was dead and in hell now!"

Harmon drew a slab of tobacco from his pocket, cut off a wedge and pressed it into the leather pouch of his cheek. "Guess he's been in Starkfield too many winters. Most of the smart ones get away."

"Why didn't *he?"*

"Somebody had to stay and care for the folks. There warn't ever anybody but Ethan. Fust his father—then his mother—then his wife."

"And then the smash-up?"

Harmon chuckled sardonically. "That's so. He *had* to stay then."

"I see. And since then they've had to care for him?"

Harmon thoughtfully passed his tobacco to the other cheek. "Oh, as to that: I guess it's always Ethan done the caring."

Though Harmon Gow developed the tale as far as his mental and moral reach permitted there were perceptible gaps between his facts, and I had the sense that the deeper meaning of the story was in the gaps. But one phrase stuck in my memory and served as the nucleus about which I grouped my subsequent inferences: "Guess he's been in Starkfield too many winters."

Before my own time there was up I had learned to know what that meant. Yet I had come in the degenerate day of trolley, bicycle and rural delivery, when communication was easy between the scattered mountain villages, and the bigger towns in the valleys, such as Bettsbridge and Shadd's Falls, had libraries, theatres and Y.M.C.A. halls to which the youth of the hills could descend for recreation. But when winter shut down on Starkfield, and the village lay under a sheet of snow perpetually renewed from the pale skies, I began to see what life there—or rather its negation—must have been in Ethan Frome's young manhood.

I had been sent up by my employers on a job connected with the big power-house at Corbury Junction, and a long-drawn carpenters' strike had so delayed the work that I found myself anchored at Starkfield—the nearest habitable spot—for the best part of the winter. I chafed at first, and then, under the hypnotising effect of routine, gradually began to find a grim satisfaction in the life. During the early part of my stay I had been struck by the contrast between the vitality of the climate and the deadness of the community. Day by day, after the December snows were over, a blazing blue sky poured down torrents of light and air on the white landscape, which gave them back in an intenser glitter. One would have supposed that such an atmosphere must quicken the emotions as well as the blood; but it seemed to produce no change except that of retarding still more the sluggish pulse of Starkfield. When I had been there a little longer, and had seen this phase of crystal clearness followed by long stretches of sunless cold; when the storms of February had pitched their white tents about the devoted village and the wild cavalry of March winds had charged down to their support; I began to understand why Starkfield emerged from its six months' siege like a starved garrison capitulating without quarter. Twenty years earlier the means of resistance must have been far fewer, and the enemy in command of almost all the lines of access between the beleaguered villages; and, considering these things, I felt the sinister force of Harmon's phrase: "Most of the smart ones get away." But if that were the case, how could any combination of obstacles have hindered the flight of a man like Ethan Frome?

During my stay at Starkfield I lodged with a middle-aged widow colloquially known as Mrs. Ned Hale. Mrs. Hale's father had been the village lawyer of the previous generation, and "lawyer Varnum's house," where my landlady still lived with her mother, was the most considerable mansion in the village. It stood at one end of the main street, its classic portico and small-paned windows looking down a flagged path between Norway spruces to the slim white steeple of the Congregational church. It was clear that the Varnum fortunes were at the ebb, but the two women did what they could to preserve a decent dignity; and Mrs. Hale, in particular, had a certain wan refinement not out of keeping with her pale old-fashioned house.

In the "best parlour," with its black horse-hair and mahogany weakly illuminated by a gurgling Carcel lamp, I listened every evening to another and more delicately shaded version of the Starkfield chronicle. It was not that Mrs. Ned Hale felt, or affected, any social superiority to the people about her; it was only that the accident of a finer sensibility and a little more education had put just enough distance between herself and her neighbours to enable her to judge them with detachment. She was not unwilling to exercise this faculty, and I had great hopes of getting from her the missing facts of Ethan Frome's story, or rather such a key to his character as should co-ordinate the facts I knew. Her mind was a store-house of innocuous anecdote and any question about her acquaintances brought forth a volume of detail; but on the subject of Ethan Frome I found her unexpectedly reticent. There was no hint of disapproval in her reserve; I merely felt in her an insurmountable reluctance to speak of him or his affairs, a low "Yes, I knew them both . . . it was awful . . ." seeming to be the utmost concession that her distress could make to my curiosity.

So marked was the change in her manner, such depths of sad initiation did it imply, that, with some doubts as to my delicacy, I put the case anew to my village oracle, Harmon Gow; but got for my pains only an uncomprehending grunt.

"Ruth Varnum was always as nervous as a rat; and, come to think of it, she was the first one to see 'em after they was picked up. It happened right below lawyer Varnum's, down at the bend of the Corbury road, just round about the time that Ruth got engaged to Ned Hale. The young folks was all friends, and I guess she just can't bear to talk about it. She's had troubles enough of her own."

All the dwellers in Starkfield, as in more notable communities, had had troubles enough of their own to make them comparatively indifferent to those of their neighbours; and though all conceded that Ethan Frome's had been beyond the common measure, no one gave me an explanation of the look in his face which, as I persisted in thinking, neither poverty nor physical suffering could have put there. Nevertheless, I might have contented myself with the story pieced together from these hints had it not been for the provocation of Mrs. Hale's silence, and—a little later—for the accident of personal contact with the man.

On my arrival at Starkfield, Denis Eady, the rich Irish grocer, who was the proprietor of Starkfield's nearest approach to a livery stable, had entered into an agreement to send me over daily to Corbury Flats, where I had to pick up my train for the Junction. But about the middle of the winter Eady's horses fell ill of a local epidemic. The illness spread to the other Starkfield stables and for a day or two I was put to it to find a means of transport. Then Harmon Gow suggested that Ethan Frome's bay was still on his legs and that his owner might be glad to drive me over.

I stared at the suggestion. "Ethan Frome? But I've never even spoken to him. Why on earth should he put himself out for me?"

Harmon's answer surprised me still more. "I don't know as he would; but I know he wouldn't be sorry to earn a dollar."

I had been told that Frome was poor, and that the sawmill and the arid acres of his farm yielded scarcely enough to keep his household through the winter; but I had not supposed him to be in such want as Harmon's words implied, and I expressed my wonder.

"Well, matters ain't gone any too well with him," Harmon said. "When a man's been setting round like a hulk for twenty years or more, seeing things that want doing, it eats inter him, and he loses his grit. That Frome farm was always 'bout as bare's a milkpan when the cat's been round; and you know what one of them old water-mills is wuth nowadays. When Ethan could sweat over 'em both from sun-up to dark he kinder choked a living out of 'em; but his folks ate up most everything, even then, and I don't see how he makes out now. Fust his father got a kick, out haying, and went soft in the brain, and gave away money like Bible texts afore he died. Then his mother got queer and dragged along for years as weak as a baby; and his wife Zeena, she's always been the greatest hand at doctoring in the county. Sickness and trouble: that's what Ethan's had his plate full up with, ever since the very first helping."

The next morning, when I looked out, I saw the hollow-backed bay between the Varnum spruces, and Ethan Frome, throwing back his worn bearskin, made room for me in the sleigh at his side. After that, for a week, he drove me over every morning to Corbury Flats, and on my return in the afternoon met me again and carried me back through the icy night to Starkfield. The distance each way was barely three miles, but the old bay's pace was slow, and even with firm snow under the runners we were nearly an hour on the way. Ethan Frome drove in silence, the reins loosely held in his left hand, his brown seamed profile, under the helmet-like peak of the cap, relieved against the banks of snow like the bronze image of a hero. He never turned his face to mine, or answered, except in monosyllables, the questions I put, or such slight pleasantries as I ventured. He seemed a part of the mute melancholy landscape, an incarnation of its frozen woe, with all that was warm and sentient in him fast bound below the surface; but there was nothing unfriendly in his silence. I simply felt that he lived in a depth of moral isolation too remote for casual access, and I had the sense that his loneliness was not merely the result of his personal plight, tragic as I guessed that to be, but had in it, as

Harmon Gow had hinted, the profound accumulated cold of many Starkfield winters.

Only once or twice was the distance between us bridged for a moment; and the glimpses thus gained confirmed my desire to know more. Once I happened to speak of an engineering job I had been on the previous year in Florida, and of the contrast between the winter landscape about us and that in which I had found myself the year before; and to my surprise Frome said suddenly: "Yes: I was down there once, and for a good while afterward I could call up the sight of it in winter. But now it's all snowed under."

He said no more, and I had to guess the rest from the inflection of his voice and his sharp relapse into silence.

Another day, on getting into my train at the Flats, I missed a volume of popular science—I think it was on some recent discoveries in biochemistry—which I had carried with me to read on the way. I thought no more about it till I got into the sleigh again that evening, and saw the book in Frome's hand.

"I found it after you were gone," he said.

I put the volume into my pocket and we dropped back into our usual silence; but as we began to crawl up the long hill from Corbury Flats to the Starkfield ridge I became aware in the dusk that he had turned his face to mine.

"There are things in that book that I didn't know the first word about," he said.

I wondered less at his words than at the queer note of resentment in his voice. He was evidently surprised and slightly aggrieved at his own ignorance.

"Does that sort of thing interest you?" I asked.

"It used to."

"There are one or two rather new things in the book: there have been some big strides lately in that particular line of research." I waited a moment for an answer that did not come; then I said: "If you'd like to look the book through I'd be glad to leave it with you."

He hesitated, and I had the impression that he felt himself about to yield to a stealing tide of inertia; then, "Thank you—I'll take it," he answered shortly.

I hoped that this incident might set up some more direct communication between us. Frome was so simple and straightforward that I was sure his curiosity about the book was based on a genuine interest in its subject. Such tastes and acquirements in a man of his condition made the contrast more poignant between his outer situation and his inner needs, and I hoped that the chance of giving expression to the latter might at least unseal his lips. But something in his past history, or in his present way of living, had apparently driven him too deeply into himself for any casual impulse to draw him back to his kind. At our next meeting he made no allusion to the book, and our intercourse seemed fated to remain as negative and one-sided as if there had been no break in his reserve.

Frome had been driving me over to the Flats for about a week when one morning I looked out of my window into a thick snowfall. The height of the white waves massed against the garden-fence and along the wall of the church showed that the storm must have been going on all night, and that the drifts were likely to be heavy in the open. I thought it probable that my train would be delayed; but I had to be at the power-house for an hour or two that afternoon, and I decided, if Frome turned up, to push through to the Flats and wait there till my train came in. I don't know why I put it in the conditional, however, for I never doubted that Frome would appear. He was not the kind of man to be turned from his business by any commotion of the elements; and at the appointed hour his sleigh glided up through the snow like a stage-apparition behind thickening veils of gauze.

I was getting to know him too well to express either wonder or gratitude at his keeping his appointment; but I exclaimed in surprise as I saw him turn his horse in a direction opposite to that of the Corbury road.

"The railroad's blocked by a freight-train that got stuck in a drift below the Flats," he explained, as we jogged off into the stinging whiteness.

"But look here—where are you taking me, then?"

"Straight to the Junction, by the shortest way," he answered, pointing up School House Hill with his whip.

"To the Junction—in this storm? Why, it's a good ten miles!"

"The bay'll do it if you give him time. You said you had some business there this afternoon. I'll see you get there."

He said it so quietly that I could only answer: "You're doing me the biggest kind of a favour."

"That's all right," he rejoined.

Abreast of the schoolhouse the road forked, and we dipped down a lane to the left, between hemlock boughs bent inward to their trunks by the weight of the snow. I had often walked that way on Sundays, and knew that the solitary roof showing through bare branches near the bottom of the hill was that of Frome's saw-mill. It looked exanimate enough, with its idle wheel looming above the black stream dashed with yellow-white spume, and its cluster of sheds sagging under their white load. Frome did not even turn his head as we drove by, and still in silence we began to mount the next slope. About a mile farther, on a road I had never travelled, we came to an orchard of starved apple-trees writhing over a hillside among outcroppings of slate that nuzzled up through the snow like animals pushing out their noses to breathe. Beyond the orchard lay a field or two, their boundaries lost under drifts; and above the fields, huddled against the white immensities of land and sky, one of those lonely New England farm-houses that make the landscape lonelier.

"That's my place," said Frome, with a sideway jerk of his lame elbow; and in the distress and oppression of the scene I did not know what to answer. The snow had ceased, and a flash of watery sunlight exposed the house on the slope above us in all its plaintive ugliness. The black wraith of a deciduous creeper flapped from the porch, and the thin wooden walls, under their worn coat of paint, seemed to shiver in the wind that had risen with the ceasing of the snow.

"The house was bigger in my father's time: I had to take down the 'L,' a while back," Frome continued, checking with a twitch of the left rein the bay's evident intention of turning in through the broken-down gate.

I saw then that the unusually forlorn and stunted look of the house was partly due to the loss of what is known in New England as the "L": that long deep-roofed adjunct usually built at right angles to the main house, and connecting it, by way of store-rooms and tool-house, with the wood-shed and cow-barn. Whether because of its symbolic sense, the image it presents of a life linked with the soil, and enclosing in itself the chief sources of warmth and nourishment, or whether merely because of the consolatory thought that it enables the dwellers in that harsh climate to get to their morning's work without facing the weather, it is certain that the "L" rather than the house itself seems to be the centre, the actual hearth-stone of the New England farm. Perhaps this connection of ideas, which had often occurred to me in my rambles about Starkfield, caused me to hear a wistful note in Frome's words, and to see in the diminished dwelling the image of his own shrunken body.

"We're kinder side-tracked here now," he added, "but there was considerable passing before the railroad was carried through to the Flats." He roused the lagging bay with another twitch; then, as if the mere sight of the house had let me too deeply into his confidence for any farther pretence of reserve, he went on slowly: "I've always set down the worst of mother's trouble to that. When she got the rheumatism so bad she couldn't move around she used to sit up there and watch the road by the hour; and one year, when they was six months mending the Bettsbridge pike after the floods, and Harmon Gow had to bring his stage round this way, she picked up so that she used to get down to the gate most days to see him. But after the trains begun running nobody ever come by here to speak of, and mother never could get it through her head what had happened, and it preyed on her right along till she died."

As we turned into the Corbury road the snow began to fall again, cutting off our last glimpse of the house; and Frome's silence fell with it, letting down between us the old veil of reticence. This time the wind did not cease with the return of the snow. Instead, it sprang up to a gale which now and then, from a tattered sky, flung pale sweeps of sunlight over a landscape chaotically tossed. But the bay was as good as Frome's word, and we pushed on to the Junction through the wild white scene.

In the afternoon the storm held off, and the clearness in the west seemed to my inexperienced eye the pledge of a fair evening. I finished my business as quickly as possible, and we set out for Starkfield with a good chance of getting there for supper. But at sunset the clouds gathered again, bringing an earlier night, and the snow began to fall straight and steadily from a sky without wind, in a soft universal diffusion more confusing than the gusts and eddies of the morning. It seemed to be a part of the thickening darkness, to be the winter night itself descending on us layer by layer.

The small ray of Frome's lantern was soon lost in this smothering medium, in which even his sense of direction, and the bay's homing instinct, finally ceased to serve us. Two or three times some ghostly landmark sprang up to warn us that we were astray, and then was sucked back into the mist; and when we finally regained our road the old horse began to show signs of exhaustion. I felt myself to blame for having accepted Frome's offer, and after a short discussion I persuaded him to let me get out of the sleigh and walk along through the snow at the bay's side. In this way we struggled on for another mile or two, and at last reached a point where Frome, peering into what seemed to me formless night, said: "That's my gate down yonder."

The last stretch had been the hardest part of the way. The bitter cold and the heavy going had nearly knocked the wind out of me, and I could feel the horse's side ticking like a clock under my hand.

"Look here, Frome," I began, "there's no earthly use in your going any farther—" but he interrupted me: "Nor you neither. There's been about enough of this for anybody."

I understood that he was offering me a night's shelter at the farm, and without answering I turned into the gate at his side, and followed him to the barn, where I helped him to unharness and bed down the tired horse. When this was done he unhooked the lantern from the sleigh, stepped out again into the night, and called to me over his shoulder: "This way."

Far off above us a square of light trembled through the screen of snow. Staggering along in Frome's wake I floundered toward it, and in the darkness almost fell into one of the deep drifts against the front of the house. Frome scrambled up the slippery steps of the porch, digging a way through the snow with his heavily booted foot. Then he lifted his lantern, found the latch, and led the way into the house. I went after him into a low unlit passage, at the back of which a ladder-like staircase rose into obscurity. On our right a line of light marked the door of the room which had sent its ray across the night; and behind the door I heard a woman's voice droning querulously.

Frome stamped on the worn oil-cloth to shake the snow from his boots, and set down his lantern on a kitchen chair which was the only piece of furniture in the hall. Then he opened the door.

"Come in," he said; and as he spoke the droning voice grew still . . .

It was that night that I found the clue to Ethan Frome, and began to put together this vision of his story.

★ ★ ★

1.

The village lay under two feet of snow, with drifts at the windy corners. In a sky of iron the points of the Dipper hung like icicles and Orion flashed his cold fires. The moon had set, but the night was so transparent that the white house-fronts between the elms looked gray against the snow, clumps of bushes made black stains on it, and the basement windows of the church sent shafts of yellow light far across the endless undulations.

Young Ethan Frome walked at a quick pace along the deserted street, past the bank and Michael Eady's new brick store and Lawyer Varnum's house with the two black Norway spruces at the gate. Opposite the Varnum gate, where the road fell away toward the Corbury valley, the church reared its slim white steeple and narrow peristyle. As the young man walked toward it the upper windows drew a black arcade along the side wall of the building, but from the lower openings, on the side where the ground sloped steeply down to the Corbury road, the light shot its long bars, illuminating many fresh furrows in the track leading to the basement door, and showing, under an adjoining shed, a line of sleighs with heavily blanketed horses.

The night was perfectly still, and the air so dry and pure that it gave little sensation of cold. The effect produced on Frome was rather of a complete absence of atmosphere, as though nothing less tenuous than ether intervened between the white earth under his feet and the metallic dome overhead. "It's like being in an exhausted receiver," he thought. Four or five years earlier he had taken a year's course at a technological college at Worcester, and dabbled in the laboratory with a friendly professor of physics; and the images supplied by that experience still cropped up, at unexpected moments, through the totally different associations of thought in which he had since been living. His father's death, and the misfortunes following it, had put a premature end to Ethan's studies; but though they had not gone far enough to be of much practical use they had fed his fancy and made him aware of huge cloudy meanings behind the daily face of things.

As he strode along through the snow the sense of such meanings glowed in his brain and mingled with the bodily flush produced by his sharp tramp. At the end of the village he paused before the darkened front of the church. He stood there a moment, breathing quickly, and looking up and down the street, in which not another figure moved. The pitch of the Corbury road, below Lawyer Varnum's spruces, was the favourite coasting-ground of Starkfield, and on clear evenings the church corner rang till late with the shouts of the coasters; but to-night not a sled darkened the whiteness of the long declivity. The hush of midnight lay on the village, and all its waking life was gathered behind the church windows, from which strains of dance-music flowed with the broad bands of yellow light.

The young man, skirting the side of the building, went down the slope toward the basement door. To keep out of range of the revealing rays from within he made a circuit through the untrodden snow and gradually approached the farther angle of the basement wall. Thence, still hugging the shadow, he edged his way cautiously forward to the nearest window, holding back his straight spare body and craning his neck till he got a glimpse of the room.

Seen thus, from the pure and frosty darkness in which he stood, it seemed to be seething in a mist of heat. The metal reflectors of the gas-jets sent crude waves of light against the whitewashed walls, and the iron flanks of the stove at the end of the hall looked as though they were heaving with volcanic fires. The floor was thronged with girls and young men. Down the side wall facing the window stood a row of kitchen chairs from which the older women had just risen. By this time the music had stopped, and the musicians—a fiddler, and the young lady who played the harmonium on Sundays—were hastily refreshing themselves at one corner of the supper-table which aligned its devastated pie-dishes and ice-cream saucers on the platform at the end of the hall. The guests were preparing to leave, and the tide had already set toward the passage where coats and wraps were hung, when a young man with a sprightly foot and a shock of black hair shot into the middle of the floor and clapped his hands. The signal took instant effect. The musicians hurried to their instruments, the dancers—some already half-muffled for departure—fell into line down each side of the room, the older spectators slipped back to their chairs, and the lively young man, after diving about here and there in the throng, drew forth a girl who had already wound a cherry-coloured "fascinator" about her head, and, leading her up to the end of the floor, whirled her down its length to the bounding tune of a Virginia reel.

Frome's heart was beating fast. He had been straining for a glimpse of the dark head under the cherry-coloured scarf and it vexed him that another eye should have been quicker than his. The leader of the reel, who looked as if he had Irish blood in his veins, danced well, and his partner caught his fire. As she passed down the line, her light figure swinging from hand to hand in circles of increasing swiftness, the scarf flew off her head and stood out behind her shoulders, and Frome, at each turn, caught sight of her laughing panting lips, the cloud of dark hair about her forehead, and the dark eyes which seemed the only fixed points in a maze of flying lines.

The dancers were going faster and faster, and the musicians, to keep up with them, belaboured their instruments like jockeys lashing their mounts on the homestretch; yet it seemed to the young man at the window that the reel would never end. Now and then he turned his eyes from the girl's face to that of her partner, which, in the exhilaration of the dance, had taken on a look of almost impudent ownership. Denis Eady was the son of Michael Eady, the ambitious Irish grocer, whose suppleness and effrontery had given Starkfield its first notion of "smart" business methods, and whose new brick store testified to the success of the attempt. His son seemed likely to follow in his steps, and was meanwhile applying the same arts to the conquest of the Starkfield maidenhood. Hitherto Ethan Frome had been content to think him a mean fellow; but now he positively invited a horse-whipping. It was strange that the girl did not seem aware of it: that she could lift her rapt face to her dancer's, and drop her hands into his, without appearing to feel the offence of his look and touch.

Frome was in the habit of walking into Starkfield to fetch home his wife's cousin, Mattie Silver, on the rare evenings when some chance of amusement drew her to the village. It was his wife who had suggested, when the girl came to live with them, that such opportunities should be put in her way. Mattie Silver came from Stamford, and when she entered the Fromes' household to act as her cousin Zeena's aid it was thought best, as she came without pay, not to let her feel too sharp a contrast between the life she had left and the isolation of a Starkfield farm. But for this—as Frome sardonically reflected—it would hardly have occurred to Zeena to take any thought for the girl's amusement.

When his wife first proposed that they should give Mattie an occasional evening out he had inwardly demurred at having to do the extra two miles to the village and back after his hard day on the farm; but not long afterward he had reached the point of wishing that Starkfield might give all its nights to revelry.

Mattie Silver had lived under his roof for a year, and from early morning till they met at supper he had frequent chances of seeing her; but no moments in her company were comparable to those when, her arm in his, and her light step flying to keep time with his long stride, they walked back through the night to the farm. He had taken to the girl from the first day, when he had driven over to the Flats to meet her, and she had smiled and waved to him from the train, crying out, "You must be Ethan!" as she jumped down with her bundles, while he reflected, looking over her slight person: "She don't look much on housework, but she ain't a fretter, anyhow." But it was not only that the coming to his house of a bit of hopeful young life was like the lighting of a fire on a cold hearth. The girl was more than the bright serviceable creature he had thought her. She had an eye to see and an ear to hear: he could show her things and tell her things, and taste the bliss of feeling that all he imparted left long reverberations and echoes he could wake at will.

It was during their night walks back to the farm that he felt most intensely the sweetness of this communion. He had always been more sensitive than the people about him to the appeal of natural beauty. His unfinished studies had given form to this sensibility and even in his unhappiest moments field and sky spoke to him with a deep and powerful persuasion. But hitherto the emotion had remained in him as a silent ache, veiling with sadness the beauty that evoked it. He did not even know whether any one else in the world felt as he did, or whether he was the sole victim of this mournful privilege. Then he learned that one other spirit had trembled with the same touch of wonder: that at his side, living under his roof and eating his bread, was a creature to whom he could say: "That's Orion down yonder; the big fellow to the right is Aldebaran, and the bunch of little ones—like bees swarming—they're the Pleiades . . ." or whom he could hold entranced before a ledge of granite thrusting up through the fern while he unrolled the huge panorama of the ice age, and the long dim stretches of succeeding time. The fact that admiration for his learning mingled with Mattie's wonder at what he taught was not the least part of his pleasure. And there were other sensations, less definable but more exquisite, which drew them together with a shock of silent joy: the cold red of sunset behind winter hills, the flight of cloud-flocks over slopes of golden stubble, or the intensely blue shadows of hemlocks on sunlit snow. When she said to him once: "It looks just as if it was painted!" it seemed to Ethan that the art of definition could go no farther, and that words had at last been found to utter his secret soul. . . .

As he stood in the darkness outside the church these memories came back with the poignancy of vanished things. Watching Mattie whirl down the floor from hand to hand he wondered how he could ever have thought that his dull talk interested her. To him, who was never gay but in her presence, her gaiety seemed plain proof of indifference. The face she lifted to her dancers was the same which, when she saw him, always looked like a window that has caught the sunset. He even noticed two or three gestures which, in his fatuity, he had thought she kept for him: a way of throwing her head back when she was amused, as if to taste her laugh before she let it out, and a trick of sinking her lids slowly when anything charmed or moved her.

The sight made him unhappy, and his unhappiness roused his latent fears. His wife had never shown any jealousy of Mattie, but of late she had grumbled increasingly over the house-work and found oblique ways of attracting attention to the girl's inefficiency. Zeena had always been what Starkfield called "sickly," and Frome had to admit that, if she were as ailing as she believed, she needed the help of a stronger arm than the one which lay so lightly in his during the night walks to the farm. Mattie had no natural turn for housekeeping, and her training had done nothing to remedy the defect. She was quick to learn, but forgetful and dreamy, and not disposed to take the matter seriously. Ethan had an idea that if she were to marry a man she was fond of the dormant instinct would wake, and her pies and biscuits become the pride of the county; but domesticity in the abstract did not interest her. At first she was so awkward that he could not help laughing at her; but she laughed with him and that made them better friends. He did his best to supplement her unskilled efforts, getting up earlier than usual to light the kitchen fire, carrying in the wood overnight, and neglecting the mill for the farm that he might help her about the house during the day. He even crept down on Saturday nights to scrub the kitchen floor after the women had gone to bed; and Zeena, one day, had surprised him at the churn and had turned away silently, with one of her queer looks.

Of late there had been other signs of her disfavour, as intangible but more disquieting. One cold winter morning, as he dressed in the dark, his candle flickering in the draught of the ill-fitting window, he had heard her speak from the bed behind him.

"The doctor don't want I should be left without anybody to do for me," she said in her flat whine.

He had supposed her to be asleep, and the sound of her voice had startled him, though she was given to abrupt explosions of speech after long intervals of secretive silence.

He turned and looked at her where she lay indistinctly outlined under the dark calico quilt, her high-boned face taking a grayish tinge from the whiteness of the pillow.

"Nobody to do for you?" he repeated.

"If you say you can't afford a hired girl when Mattie goes."

Frome turned away again, and taking up his razor stooped to catch the reflection of his stretched cheek in the blotched looking-glass above the wash-stand.

"Why on earth should Mattie go?"

"Well, when she gets married, I mean," his wife's drawl came from behind him.

"Oh, she'd never leave us as long as you needed her," he returned, scraping hard at his chin.

"I wouldn't ever have it said that I stood in the way of a poor girl like Mattie marrying a smart fellow like Denis Eady," Zeena answered in a tone of plaintive self-effacement.

Ethan, glaring at his face in the glass, threw his head back to draw the razor from ear to chin. His hand was steady, but the attitude was an excuse for not making an immediate reply.

"And the doctor don't want I should be left without anybody," Zeena continued. "He wanted I should speak to you about a girl he's heard about, that might come—"

Ethan laid down the razor and straightened himself with a laugh.

"Denis Eady! If that's all, I guess there's no such hurry to look round for a girl."

"Well, I'd like to talk to you about it," said Zeena obstinately.

He was getting into his clothes in fumbling haste. "All right. But I haven't got the time now; I'm late as it is," he returned, holding his old silver turnip-watch to the candle.

Zeena, apparently accepting this as final, lay watching him in silence while he pulled his suspenders over his shoulders and jerked his arms into his coat; but as he went toward the door she said, suddenly and incisively: "I guess you're always late, now you shave every morning."

That thrust had frightened him more than any vague insinuations about Denis Eady. It was a fact that since Mattie Silver's coming he had taken to shaving every day; but his wife always seemed to be asleep when he left her side in the winter darkness, and he had stupidly assumed that she would not notice any change in his appearance. Once or twice in the past he had been faintly disquieted by Zenobia's way of letting things happen without seeming to remark them, and then, weeks afterward, in a casual phrase, revealing that she had all along taken her notes and drawn her inferences. Of late, however, there had been no room in his thoughts for such vague apprehensions. Zeena herself, from an oppressive reality, had faded into an insubstantial shade. All his life was lived in the sight and sound of Mattie Silver, and he could no longer conceive of its being otherwise. But now, as he stood outside the church, and saw Mattie spinning down the floor with Denis Eady, a throng of disregarded hints and menaces wove their cloud about his brain . . .

2.

As the dancers poured out of the hall Frome, drawing back behind the projecting storm-door, watched the segregation of the grotesquely muffled groups, in which a moving lantern ray now and then lit up a face flushed with food and dancing. The villagers, being afoot, were the first to climb the slope to the main street, while the country neighbours packed themselves more slowly into the sleighs under the shed.

"Ain't you riding, Mattie?" a woman's voice called back from the throng about the shed, and Ethan's heart gave a jump. From where he stood he could not see the persons coming out of the hall till they had advanced a few steps beyond the wooden sides of the storm-door; but through its cracks he heard a clear voice answer: "Mercy no! Not on such a night."

She was there, then, close to him, only a thin board between. In another moment she would step forth into the night, and his eyes, accustomed to the obscurity, would discern her as clearly as though she stood in daylight. A wave of shyness pulled him back into the dark angle of the wall, and he stood there in silence instead of making his presence known to her. It had been one of the wonders of their intercourse that from the first, she, the quicker, finer, more expressive, instead of crushing him by the contrast, had given him something of her own ease and freedom; but now he felt as heavy and loutish as in his student days, when he had tried to "jolly" the Worcester girls at a picnic.

He hung back, and she came out alone and paused within a few yards of him. She was almost the last to leave the hall, and she stood looking uncertainly about her as if wondering why he did not show himself. Then a man's figure approached, coming so close to her that under their formless wrappings they seemed merged in one dim outline.

"Gentleman friend gone back on you? Say, Matt, that's tough! No, I wouldn't be mean enough to tell the other girls. I ain't as low-down as that." (How Frome hated his cheap banter!) "But look a here, ain't it lucky I got the old man's cutter down there waiting for us?"

Frome heard the girl's voice, gaily incredulous: "What on earth's your father's cutter doin' down there?"

"Why, waiting for me to take a ride. I got the roan colt too. I kinder knew I'd want to take a ride tonight." Eady, in his triumph, tried to put a sentimental note into his bragging voice.

The girl seemed to waver, and Frome saw her twirl the end of her scarf irresolutely about her fingers. Not for the world would he have made a sign to her, though it seemed to him that his life hung on her next gesture.

"Hold on a minute while I unhitch the colt," Denis called to her, springing toward the shed.

She stood perfectly still, looking after him, in an attitude of tranquil expectancy torturing to the hidden watcher. Frome noticed that she no longer turned her head from side to side, as though peering through the night for another figure. She let Denis Eady lead out the horse, climb into the cutter and fling back the bearskin to make room for her at his side; then, with a swift motion of flight, she turned about and darted up the slope toward the front of the church.

"Good-bye! Hope you'll have a lovely ride!" she called back to him over her shoulder.

Denis laughed, and gave the horse a cut that brought him quickly abreast of her retreating figure.

"Come along! Get in quick! It's as slippery as thunder on this turn," he cried, leaning over to reach out a hand to her.

She laughed back at him: "Good-night! I'm not getting in."

By this time they had passed beyond Frome's earshot and he could only follow the shadowy pantomime of their silhouettes as they continued to move along the crest of the slope above him. He saw Eady, after a moment, jump from the cutter and go toward the girl with the reins over one arm. The other he tried to slip through hers; but she eluded him nimbly, and Frome's heart, which had swung out over a black void, trembled back to safety. A moment later he heard the jingle of departing sleigh bells and discerned a figure advancing alone toward the empty expanse of snow before the church.

In the black shade of the Varnum spruces he caught up with her and she turned with a quick "Oh!"

"Think I'd forgotten you, Matt?" he asked with sheepish glee.

She answered seriously: "I thought maybe you couldn't come back for me."

"Couldn't? What on earth could stop me?"

"I knew Zeena wasn't feeling any too good to-day."

"Oh, she's in bed long ago." He paused, a question struggling in him. "Then you meant to walk home all alone?"

"Oh, I ain't afraid!" she laughed.

They stood together in the gloom of the spruces, an empty world glimmering about them wide and grey under the stars. He brought his question out.

"If you thought I hadn't come, why didn't you ride back with Denis Eady?"

"Why, where *were* you? How did you know? I never saw you!"

Her wonder and his laughter ran together like spring rills in a thaw. Ethan had the sense of having done something arch and ingenious. To prolong the effect he groped for a dazzling phrase, and brought out, in a growl of rapture: "Come along."

He slipped an arm through hers, as Eady had done, and fancied it was faintly pressed against her side; but neither of them moved. It was so dark under the spruces that he could barely see the shape of her head beside his shoulder. He longed to stoop his cheek and rub it against her scarf. He would have liked to stand there with her all night in the blackness. She moved forward a step or two and then paused again above the dip of the Corbury road. Its icy slope, scored by innumerable runners, looked like a mirror scratched by travellers at an inn.

"There was a whole lot of them coasting before the moon set," she said.

"Would you like to come in and coast with them some night?" he asked.

"Oh, *would* you, Ethan? It would be lovely!"

"We'll come to-morrow if there's a moon."

She lingered, pressing closer to his side. "Ned Hale and Ruth Varnum came just as *near* running into the big elm at the bottom.

We were all sure they were killed." Her shiver ran down his arm. "Wouldn't it have been too awful? They're so happy!"

"Oh, Ned ain't much at steering. I guess I can take you down all right!" he said disdainfully.

He was aware that he was "talking big," like Denis Eady; but his reaction of joy had unsteadied him, and the inflection with which she had said of the engaged couple "They're so happy!" made the words sound as if she had been thinking of herself and him.

"The elm *is* dangerous, though. It ought to be cut down," she insisted.

"Would you be afraid of it, with me?"

"I told you I ain't the kind to be afraid," she tossed back, almost indifferently; and suddenly she began to walk on with a rapid step.

These alterations of mood were the despair and joy of Ethan Frome. The motions of her mind were as incalculable as the flit of a bird in the branches. The fact that he had no right to show his feelings, and thus provoke the expression of hers, made him attach a fantastic importance to every change in her look and tone. Now he thought she understood him, and feared; now he was sure she did not, and despaired. To-night the pressure of accumulated misgivings sent the scale drooping toward despair, and her indifference was the more chilling after the flush of joy into which she had plunged him by dismissing Denis Eady. He mounted School House Hill at her side and walked on in silence till they reached the lane leading to the saw-mill; then the need of some definite assurance grew too strong for him.

"You'd have found me right off if you hadn't gone back to have that last reel with Denis," he brought out awkwardly. He could not pronounce the name without a stiffening of the muscles of his throat.

"Why, Ethan, how could I tell you were there?"

"I suppose what folks say is true," he jerked out at her, instead of answering.

She stopped short, and he felt, in the darkness, that her face was lifted quickly to his. "Why, what do folks say?"

"It's natural enough you should be leaving us," he floundered on, following his thought.

"Is that what they say?" she mocked back at him; then with a sudden drop of her sweet treble: "You mean that Zeena—ain't suited with me any more?" she faltered.

Their arms had slipped apart and they stood motionless, each seeking to distinguish the other's face.

"I know I ain't anything like as smart as I ought to be," she went on, while he vainly struggled for expression. "There's lots of things a hired girl could do that come awkward to me still—and I haven't got much strength in my arms. But if she'd only tell me I'd try. You know she hardly ever says anything, and sometimes I can see she ain't suited, and yet I don't know why." She turned on him with a sudden flash of indignation. "You'd ought to tell me, Ethan Frome—you'd ought to! Unless *you* want me to go too—"

Unless he wanted her to go too! The cry was balm to his raw wound. The iron heavens seemed to melt and rain down sweetness. Again he struggled for the all-expressive word, and again, his arm in hers, found only a deep "Come along."

They walked on in silence through the blackness of the hemlock-shaded lane, where Ethan's saw-mill gloomed through the night, and out again into the comparative clearness of the fields. On the farther side of the hemlock belt the open country rolled away before them grey and lonely under the stars. Sometimes their way led them under the shade of an overhanging bank or through the thin obscurity of a clump of leafless trees. Here and there a farm-house stood far back among the fields, mute and cold as a grave-stone. The night was so still that they heard the frozen snow crackle under their feet. The crash of a loaded branch falling far off in the woods reverberated like a musket-shot, and once a fox barked, and Mattie shrank closer to Ethan, and quickened her steps.

At length they sighted the group of larches at Ethan's gate, and as they drew near it the sense that the walk was over brought back his words.

"Then you don't want to leave us, Matt?"

He had to stoop his head to catch her stifled whisper: "Where'd I go, if I did?"

The answer sent a pang through him but the tone suffused him with joy. He forgot what else he had meant to say and pressed her against him so closely that he seemed to feel her warmth in his veins.

"You ain't crying are you, Matt?"

"No, of course I'm not," she quavered.

They turned in at the gate and passed under the shaded knoll where, enclosed in a low fence, the Frome gravestones slanted at crazy angles through the snow. Ethan looked at them curiously.

For years that quiet company had mocked his restlessness, his desire for change and freedom. "We never got away—how should you?" seemed to be written on every headstone; and whenever he went in or out of his gate he thought with a shiver: "I shall just go on living here till I join them." But now all desire for change had vanished, and the sight of the little enclosure gave him a warm sense of continuance and stability.

"I guess we'll never let you go, Matt," he whispered, as though even the dead, lovers once, must conspire with him to keep her; and brushing by the graves, he thought: "We'll always go on living here together, and some day she'll lie there beside me."

He let the vision possess him as they climbed the hill to the house. He was never so happy with her as when he abandoned himself to these dreams. Halfway up the slope Mattie stumbled against some unseen obstruction and clutched his sleeve to steady herself. The wave of warmth that went through him was like the prolongation of his vision. For the first time he stole his arm about her, and she did not resist. They walked on as if they were floating on a summer stream.

Zeena always went to bed as soon as she had had her supper, and the shutterless windows of the house were dark. A dead cucumber-vine dangled from the porch like the crape streamer tied to the door for a death, and the thought flashed through Ethan's brain: "If it was there for Zeena—" Then he had a distinct sight of his wife lying in their bedroom asleep, her mouth slightly open, her false teeth in a tumbler by the bed . . .

They walked around to the back of the house, between the rigid gooseberry bushes. It was Zeena's habit, when they came back late from the village, to leave the key of the kitchen door under the mat. Ethan stood before the door, his head heavy with dreams, his arms still about Mattie. "Matt—" he began, not knowing what he meant to say.

She slipped out of his hold without speaking, and he stooped down and felt for the key.

"It's not there!" he said, straightening himself with a start.

They strained their eyes at each other through the icy darkness. Such a thing had never happened before.

"Maybe she's forgotten it," Mattie said in a tremulous whisper; but both of them knew that it was not like Zeena to forget.

"It might have fallen off into the snow," Mattie continued, after a pause during which they had stood intently listening.

"It must have been pushed off, then," he rejoined in the same tone. Another wild thought tore through him. What if tramps had been there—what if . . .

Again he listened, fancying he heard a distant sound in the house; then he felt in his pocket for a match, and kneeling down, passed its light slowly over the rough edges of snow about the doorstep.

He was still kneeling when his eyes, on a level with the lower panel of the door, caught a faint ray beneath it. Who could be stirring in that silent house? He heard a step on the stairs, and again for an instant the thought of tramps tore through him. Then the door opened and he saw his wife.

Against the dark background of the kitchen she stood up tall and angular, one hand drawing a quilted counterpane to her flat breast, while the other held a lamp. The light, on a level with her chin, drew out of the darkness her puckered throat and the projecting wrist of the hand that clutched the quilt, and deepened fantastically the hollows and prominences of her high-boned face under its ring of crimping-pins. To Ethan, still in the rosy haze of his hour with Mattie, the sight came with the intense precision of the last dream before waking. He felt as if he had never before known what his wife looked like.

She drew aside without speaking, and Mattie and Ethan passed into the kitchen, which had the deadly chill of a vault after the dry cold of the night.

"Guess you forgot about us, Zeena," Ethan joked, stamping the snow from his boots.

"No, I just felt so mean I couldn't sleep."

Mattie came forward, unwinding her wraps, the colour of the cherry scarf in her fresh lips and cheeks. "I'm so sorry, Zeena! Isn't there anything I can do?"

"No; there's nothing." Zeena turned away from her. "You might a' shook off that snow outside," she said to her husband.

She walked out of the kitchen ahead of them and pausing in the hall raised the lamp at arm's-length, as if to light them up the stairs.

Ethan paused also, affecting to fumble for the peg on which he hung his coat and cap. The doors of the two bedrooms faced each other across the narrow upper landing, and to-night it was peculiarly repugnant to him that Mattie should see him follow Zeena.

"I guess I won't come up yet awhile," he said, turning as if to go back to the kitchen.

Zeena stopped short and looked at him. "For the land's sake—what you going to do down here?"

"I've got the mill accounts to go over."

She continued to stare at him, the flame of the unshaded lamp bringing out with microscopic cruelty the fretful lines of her face.

"At this time o' night? You'll ketch your death. The fire's out long ago."

Without answering he moved away toward the kitchen. As he did so his glance crossed Mattie's and he fancied that a fugitive warning gleamed through her lashes. The next moment they sank to her flushed cheeks and she began to mount the stairs ahead of Zeena.

"That's so. It *is* powerful cold down here," Ethan assented; and with lowered head he went up in his wife's wake, and followed her across the threshold of their room.

3.

There was some hauling to be done at the lower end of the wood-lot, and Ethan was out early the next day.

The winter morning was as clear as crystal. The sunrise burned red in a pure sky, the shadows on the rim of the wood-lot were darkly blue, and beyond the white and scintillating fields patches of far-off forest hung like smoke.

It was in the early morning stillness, when his muscles were swinging to their familiar task and his lungs expanding with long draughts of mountain air, that Ethan did his clearest thinking. He and Zeena had not exchanged a word after the door of their room had closed on them. She had measured out some drops from a medicine-bottle on a chair by the bed and, after swallowing them, and wrapping her head in a piece of yellow flannel, had lain down with her face turned away. Ethan undressed hurriedly and blew out the light so that he should not see her when he took his place at her side. As he lay there he could hear Mattie moving about in her room, and her candle, sending its small ray across the landing, drew a scarcely perceptible line of light under his door. He kept his eyes fixed on the light till it vanished. Then the room grew perfectly black, and not a sound was audible but Zeena's asthmatic breathing. Ethan felt confusedly that there were many things he ought to think about, but through his tingling veins and tired brain only one sensation throbbed: the warmth of Mattie's shoulder against his. Why had he not kissed her when he held her there? A few hours earlier he would not have asked himself the question. Even a few minutes earlier, when they had stood alone outside the house, he would not have dared to think of kissing her. But since he had seen her lips in the lamplight he felt that they were his.

Now, in the bright morning air, her face was still before him. It was part of the sun's red and of the pure glitter on the snow. How the girl had changed since she had come to Starkfield! He remembered what a colourless slip of a thing she had looked the day he had met her at the station. And all the first winter, how she had shivered with cold when the northerly gales shook the thin clapboards and the snow beat like hail against the loose-hung windows!

He had been afraid that she would hate the hard life, the cold and loneliness; but not a sign of discontent escaped her. Zeena took the view that Mattie was bound to make the best of Starkfield since she hadn't any other place to go to; but this did not strike Ethan as conclusive. Zeena, at any rate, did not apply the principle in her own case.

He felt all the more sorry for the girl because misfortune had, in a sense, indentured her to them. Mattie Silver was the daughter of a cousin of Zenobia Frome's, who had inflamed his clan with mingled sentiments of envy and admiration by descending from the hills to Connecticut, where he had married a Stamford girl and succeeded to her father's thriving "drug" business. Unhappily Orin Silver, a man of far-reaching aims, had died too soon to prove that the end justifies the means. His accounts revealed merely what the means had been; and these were such that it was fortunate for his wife and daughter that his books were examined only after his impressive funeral. His wife died of the disclosure, and Mattie, at twenty, was left alone to make her way on the fifty dollars obtained from the sale of her piano. For this purpose her equipment, though varied, was inadequate. She could trim a hat, make molasses candy, recite "Curfew shall not ring to-night," and play "The Lost Chord" and a pot-pourri from "Carmen." When she tried to extend the field of her activities in the direction of stenography and book-keeping her health broke down, and six months on her feet behind the counter of a department store did not tend to restore it. Her nearest relations had been induced to place their savings in her father's hands, and though, after his death, they ungrudgingly acquitted themselves of the Christian duty of returning good for evil by giving his daughter all the advice at their disposal, they could hardly be expected to supplement it by material aid. But when Zenobia's doctor recommended her looking about for some one to help her with the house-work the clan instantly saw the chance of exacting a compensation from Mattie. Zenobia, though doubtful of the girl's efficiency, was tempted by the freedom to find fault without much risk of losing her; and so Mattie came to Starkfield.

Zenobia's fault-finding was of the silent kind, but not the less penetrating for that. During the first months Ethan alternately burned with the desire to see Mattie defy her and trembled with fear of the result. Then the situation grew less strained. The pure air, and the long summer hours in the open, gave back life and elasticity to Mattie, and Zeena, with more leisure to devote to her complex ailments, grew less watchful of the girl's omissions; so that Ethan, struggling on under the burden of his barren farm and failing saw-mill, could at least imagine that peace reigned in his house.

There was really, even now, no tangible evidence to the contrary; but since the previous night a vague dread had hung on his sky-line. It was formed of Zeena's obstinate silence, of Mattie's sudden look of warning, of the memory of just such fleeting imperceptible signs as those which told him, on certain stainless mornings, that before night there would be rain.

His dread was so strong that, man-like, he sought to postpone certainty. The hauling was not over till mid-day, and as the lumber was to be delivered to Andrew Hale, the Starkfield builder, it was really easier for Ethan to send Jotham Powell, the hired man, back to the farm on foot, and drive the load down to the village himself. He had scrambled up on the logs, and was sitting astride of them, close over his shaggy grays, when, coming between him and their steaming necks, he had a vision of the warning look that Mattie had given him the night before.

"If there's going to be any trouble I want to be there," was his vague reflection, as he threw to Jotham the unexpected order to unhitch the team and lead them back to the barn.

It was a slow trudge home through the heavy fields, and when the two men entered the kitchen Mattie was lifting the coffee from the stove and Zeena was already at the table. Her husband stopped short at sight of her. Instead of her usual calico wrapper and knitted shawl she wore her best dress of brown merino, and above her thin strands of hair, which still preserved the tight undulations of the crimping-pins, rose a hard perpendicular bonnet, as to which Ethan's clearest notion was that he had to pay five dollars for it at the Bettsbridge Emporium. On the floor beside her stood his old valise and a bandbox wrapped in newspapers.

"Why, where are you going, Zeena?" he exclaimed.

"I've got my shooting pains so bad that I'm going over to Bettsbridge to spend the night with Aunt Martha Pierce and see that new doctor," she answered in a matter-of-fact tone, as if she had said she was going into the store-room to take a look at the preserves, or up to the attic to go over the blankets.

In spite of her sedentary habits such abrupt decisions were not without precedent in Zeena's history. Twice or thrice before she had suddenly packed Ethan's valise and started off to Bettsbridge, or even Springfield, to seek the advice of some new doctor, and her husband had grown to dread these expeditions because of their cost. Zeena always came back laden with expensive remedies, and her last visit to Springfield had been commemorated by her paying twenty dollars for an electric battery of which she had never been able to learn the use. But for the moment his sense of relief was so great as to preclude all other feelings. He had now no doubt that Zeena had spoken the truth in saying, the night before, that she had sat up because she felt "too mean" to sleep: her abrupt resolve to seek medical advice showed that, as usual, she was wholly absorbed in her health.

As if expecting a protest, she continued plaintively; "If you're too busy with the hauling I presume you can let Jotham Powell drive me over with the sorrel in time to ketch the train at the Flats."

Her husband hardly heard what she was saying. During the winter months there was no stage between Starkfield and Bettsbridge, and the trains which stopped at Corbury Flats were slow and infrequent. A rapid calculation showed Ethan that Zeena could not be back at the farm before the following evening. . . .

"If I'd supposed you'd 'a' made any objection to Jotham Powell's driving me over—" she began again, as though his silence had implied refusal. On the brink of departure she was always seized with a flux of words. "All I know is," she continued, "I can't go on the way I am much longer. The pains are clear away down to my ankles now, or I'd 'a' walked in to Starkfield on my own feet, sooner'n put you out, and asked Michael Eady to let me ride over on his wagon to the Flats, when he sends to meet the train that brings his groceries. I'd 'a' had two hours to wait in the station, but I'd sooner 'a' done it, even with this cold, than to have you say—"

"Of course Jotham'll drive you over," Ethan roused himself to answer. He became suddenly conscious that he was looking at Mattie while Zeena talked to him, and with an effort he turned his eyes to his wife. She sat opposite the window, and the pale light reflected from the banks of snow made her face look more than usually drawn and bloodless, sharpened the three parallel creases between ear and cheek, and drew querulous lines from her thin nose to the corners of her mouth. Though she was but seven years her husband's senior, and he was only twenty-eight, she was already an old woman.

Ethan tried to say something befitting the occasion, but there was only one thought in his mind: the fact that, for the first time since Mattie had come to live with them, Zeena was to be away for a night. He wondered if the girl were thinking of it too. . . .

He knew that Zeena must be wondering why he did not offer to drive her to the Flats and let Jotham Powell take the lumber to Starkfield, and at first he could not think of a pretext for not doing so; then he said: "I'd take you over myself, only I've got to collect the cash for the lumber."

As soon as the words were spoken he regretted them, not only because they were untrue—there being no prospect of his receiving cash payment from Hale—but also because he knew from experience the imprudence of letting Zeena think he was in funds on the eve of one of her therapeutic excursions. At the moment, however, his one desire was to avoid the long drive with her behind the ancient sorrel who never went out of a walk.

Zeena made no reply: she did not seem to hear what he had said. She had already pushed her plate aside, and was measuring out a draught from a large bottle at her elbow.

"It ain't done me a speck of good, but I guess I might as well use it up," she remarked; adding, as she pushed the empty bottle toward Mattie: "If you can get the taste out it'll do for pickles."

4.

As soon as his wife had driven off Ethan took his coat and cap from the peg. Mattie was washing up the dishes, humming one of the dance tunes of the night before. He said "So long, Matt," and she answered gaily "So long, Ethan"; and that was all.

It was warm and bright in the kitchen. The sun slanted through the south window on the girl's moving figure, on the cat dozing in a chair, and on the geraniums brought in from the door-way, where Ethan had planted them in the summer to "make a garden" for Mattie. He would have liked to linger on, watching her tidy up and then settle down to her sewing; but he wanted still more to get the hauling done and be back at the farm before night.

All the way down to the village he continued to think of his return to Mattie. The kitchen was a poor place, not "spruce" and shining as his mother had kept it in his boyhood; but it was surprising what a home-like look the mere fact of Zeena's absence gave it. And he pictured what it would be like that evening, when he and Mattie were there after supper. For the first time they would be alone together indoors, and they would sit there, one on each side of the stove, like a married couple, he in his stocking feet and smoking his pipe, she laughing and talking in that funny way she had, which was always as new to him as if he had never heard her before.

The sweetness of the picture, and the relief of knowing that his fears of "trouble" with Zeena were unfounded, sent up his spirits with a rush, and he, who was usually so silent, whistled and sang aloud as he drove through the snowy fields. There was in him a slumbering spark of sociability which the long Starkfield winters had not yet extinguished. By nature grave and inarticulate, he admired recklessness and gaiety in others and was warmed to the marrow by friendly human intercourse. At Worcester, though he had the name of keeping to himself and not being much of a hand at a good time, he had secretly gloried in being clapped on the back and hailed as "Old Ethe" or "Old Stiff"; and the cessation of such familiarities had increased the chill of his return to Starkfield.

There the silence had deepened about him year by year. Left alone, after his father's accident, to carry the burden of farm and mill, he had had no time for convivial loiterings in the village; and when his mother fell ill the loneliness of the house grew more oppressive than that of the fields. His mother had been a talker in her day, but after her "trouble" the sound of her voice was seldom heard, though she had not lost the power of speech. Sometimes, in the long winter evenings, when in desperation her son asked her why she didn't "say something," she would lift a finger and answer: "Because I'm listening"; and on stormy nights, when the loud wind was about the house, she would complain, if he spoke to her: "They're talking so out there that I can't hear you."

It was only when she drew toward her last illness, and his cousin Zenobia Pierce came over from the next valley to help him nurse her, that human speech was heard again in the house. After the mortal silence of his long imprisonment Zeena's volubility was music in his ears. He felt that he might have "gone like his mother" if the sound of a new voice had not come to steady him. Zeena seemed to understand his case at a glance. She laughed at him for not knowing the simplest sick-bed duties and told him to "go right along out" and leave her to see to things. The mere fact of obeying her orders, of feeling free to go about his business again and talk with other men, restored his shaken balance and magnified his sense of what he owed her. Her efficiency shamed and dazzled him. She seemed to possess by instinct all the household wisdom that his long apprenticeship had not instilled in him. When the end came it was she who had to tell him to hitch up and go for the undertaker, and she thought it "funny" that he had not settled beforehand who was to have his mother's clothes and the sewing-machine. After the funeral, when he saw her preparing to go away, he was seized with an unreasoning dread of being left alone on the farm; and before he knew what he was doing he had asked her to stay there with him. He had often thought since that it would not have happened if his mother had died in spring instead of winter . . .

When they married it was agreed that, as soon as he could straighten out the difficulties resulting from Mrs. Frome's long illness, they would sell the farm and saw-mill and try their luck in a large town. Ethan's love of nature did not take the form of a taste for agriculture. He had always wanted to be an engineer, and to live in towns, where there were lectures and big libraries and "fellows doing things." A slight engineering job in Florida, put in his way during his period of study at Worcester, increased his faith in his ability as well as his eagerness to see the world; and he felt sure that, with a "smart" wife like Zeena, it would not be long before he had made himself a place in it.

Zeena's native village was slightly larger and nearer to the railway than Starkfield, and she had let her husband see from the first that life on an isolated farm was not what she had expected when she married. But purchasers were slow in coming, and while he waited for them Ethan learned the impossibility of transplanting her. She chose to look down on Starkfield, but she could not have lived in a place which looked down on her. Even Bettsbridge or Shadd's Falls would not have been sufficiently aware of her, and in the greater cities which attracted Ethan she would have suffered a complete loss of identity. And within a year of their marriage she developed the "sickliness" which had since made her notable even in a community rich in pathological instances. When she came to take care of his mother she had seemed to Ethan like the very genius of health, but he soon saw that her skill as a nurse had been acquired by the absorbed observation of her own symptoms.

Then she too fell silent. Perhaps it was the inevitable effect of life on the farm, or perhaps, as she sometimes said, it was because Ethan "never listened." The charge was not wholly unfounded. When she spoke it was only to complain, and to complain of things not in his power to remedy; and to check a tendency to impatient retort he had first formed the habit of not answering her, and finally of thinking of other things while she talked. Of late, however, since he had had reasons for observing her more closely, her silence had begun to trouble him. He recalled his mother's growing taciturnity, and wondered if Zeena were also turning "queer." Women did, he knew. Zeena, who had at her fingers' ends the pathological chart of the whole region, had cited many cases of the kind while she was nursing his mother; and he himself knew of certain lonely farm-houses in the neighbourhood where stricken creatures pined, and of others where sudden tragedy had come of their presence. At times, looking at Zeena's shut face, he felt the chill of such forebodings. At other times her silence seemed deliberately assumed to conceal far-reaching intentions, mysterious conclusions drawn from suspicions and resentments impossible to guess. That supposition was even more disturbing than the other; and it was the one which had come to him the night before, when he had seen her standing in the kitchen door.

Now her departure for Bettsbridge had once more eased his mind, and all his thoughts were on the prospect of his evening with Mattie. Only one thing weighed on him, and that was his having told Zeena that he was to receive cash for the lumber. He foresaw so clearly the consequences of this imprudence that with considerable reluctance he decided to ask Andrew Hale for a small advance on his load.

When Ethan drove into Hale's yard the builder was just getting out of his sleigh.

"Hello, Ethe!" he said. "This comes handy."

Andrew Hale was a ruddy man with a big gray moustache and a stubby double-chin unconstrained by a collar; but his scrupulously clean shirt was always fastened by a small diamond stud. This display of opulence was misleading, for though he did a fairly good business it was known that his easygoing habits and the demands of his large family frequently kept him what Starkfield called "behind." He was an old friend of Ethan's family, and his house one of the few to which Zeena occasionally went, drawn there by the fact that Mrs. Hale, in her youth, had done more "doctoring" than any other woman in Starkfield, and was still a recognised authority on symptoms and treatment.

Hale went up to the grays and patted their sweating flanks.

"Well, sir," he said, "you keep them two as if they was pets."

Ethan set about unloading the logs and when he had finished his job he pushed open the glazed door of the shed which the builder used as his office. Hale sat with his feet up on the stove, his back propped against a battered desk strewn with papers: the place, like the man, was warm, genial and untidy.

"Sit right down and thaw out," he greeted Ethan.

The latter did not know how to begin, but at length he managed to bring out his request for an advance of fifty dollars. The blood rushed to his thin skin under the sting of Hale's astonishment. It was the builder's custom to pay at the end of three months, and there was no precedent between the two men for a cash settlement.

Ethan felt that if he had pleaded an urgent need Hale might have made shift to pay him; but pride, and an instinctive prudence, kept him from resorting to this argument. After his father's death it had taken time to get his head above water, and he did not want Andrew Hale, or any one else in Starkfield, to think he was going under again. Besides, he hated lying; if he wanted the money he wanted it, and it was nobody's business to ask why. He therefore made his demand with the awkwardness of a proud man who will not admit to himself that he is stooping; and he was not much surprised at Hale's refusal.

The builder refused genially, as he did everything else: he treated the matter as something in the nature of a practical joke, and wanted to know if Ethan meditated buying a grand piano or adding a "cupolo" to his house; offering, in the latter case, to give his services free of cost.

Ethan's arts were soon exhausted, and after an embarrassed pause he wished Hale good day and opened the door of the office. As he passed out the builder suddenly called after him: "See here—you ain't in a tight place, are you?"

"Not a bit," Ethan's pride retorted before his reason had time to intervene.

"Well, that's good! Because I *am,* a shade. Fact is, I was going to ask you to give me a little extra time on that payment. Business is pretty slack, to begin with, and then I'm fixing up a little house for Ned and Ruth when they're married. I'm glad to do it for 'em, but it costs." His look appealed to Ethan for sympathy. "The young people like things nice. You know how it is yourself: it's not so long ago since you fixed up your own place for Zeena."

Ethan left the grays in Hale's stable and went about some other business in the village. As he walked away the builder's last phrase lingered in his ears, and he reflected grimly that his seven years with Zeena seemed to Starkfield "not so long."

The afternoon was drawing to an end, and here and there a lighted pane spangled the cold gray dusk and made the snow look whiter. The bitter weather had driven every one indoors and Ethan had the long rural street to himself. Suddenly he heard the brisk play of sleigh-bells and a cutter passed him, drawn by a free-going horse. Ethan recognised Michael Eady's roan colt, and young Denis Eady, in a handsome new fur cap, leaned forward and waved a greeting. "Hello, Ethe!" he shouted and spun on.

The cutter was going in the direction of the Frome farm, and Ethan's heart contracted as he listened to the dwindling bells. What more likely than that Denis Eady had heard of Zeena's departure for Bettsbridge, and was profiting by the opportunity to spend an hour with Mattie? Ethan was ashamed of the storm of jealousy in his breast. It seemed unworthy of the girl that his thoughts of her should be so violent.

He walked on to the church corner and entered the shade of the Varnum spruces, where he had stood with her the night before. As he passed into their gloom he saw an indistinct outline just ahead of him. At his approach it melted for an instant into two separate shapes and then conjoined again, and he heard a kiss, and a half-laughing "Oh!" provoked by the discovery of his presence. Again the outline hastily disunited and the Varnum gate slammed on one half while the other hurried on ahead of him. Ethan smiled at the discomfiture he had caused. What did it matter to Ned Hale and Ruth Varnum if they were caught kissing each other? Everybody in Starkfield knew they were engaged. It pleased Ethan to have surprised a pair of lovers on the spot where he and Mattie had stood with such a thirst for each other in their hearts; but he felt a pang at the thought that these two need not hide their happiness.

He fetched the grays from Hale's stable and started on his long climb back to the farm. The cold was less sharp than earlier in the day and a thick fleecy sky threatened snow for the morrow. Here and there a star pricked through, showing behind it a deep well of blue. In an hour or two the moon would push up over the ridge behind the farm, burn a gold-edged rent in the clouds, and then be swallowed by them. A mournful peace hung on the fields, as though they felt the relaxing grasp of the cold and stretched themselves in their long winter sleep.

Ethan's ears were alert for the jingle of sleigh-bells, but not a sound broke the silence of the lonely road. As he drew near the farm he saw, through the thin screen of larches at the gate, a light twinkling in the house above him. "She's up in her room," he said to himself, "fixing herself up for supper"; and he remembered Zeena's sarcastic stare when Mattie, on the evening of her arrival, had come down to supper with smoothed hair and a ribbon at her neck.

He passed by the graves on the knoll and turned his head to glance at one of the older headstones, which had interested him deeply as a boy because it bore his name.

SACRED TO THE MEMORY OF
ETHAN FROME AND ENDURANCE HIS WIFE,
WHO DWELLED TOGETHER IN PEACE
FOR FIFTY YEARS.

He used to think that fifty years sounded like a long time to live together, but now it seemed to him that they might pass in a flash. Then, with a sudden dart of irony, he wondered if, when their turn came, the same epitaph would be written over him and Zeena.

He opened the barn-door and craned his head into the obscurity, half-fearing to discover Denis Eady's roan colt in the stall beside the sorrel. But the old horse was there alone, mumbling his crib with toothless jaws, and Ethan whistled cheerfully while he bedded down the grays and shook an extra measure of oats into their mangers. His was not a tuneful throat, but harsh melodies burst from it as he locked the barn and sprang up the hill to the house. He reached the kitchen-porch and turned the door-handle; but the door did not yield to his touch.

Startled at finding it locked he rattled the handle violently; then he reflected that Mattie was alone and that it was natural she should barricade herself at nightfall. He stood in the darkness expecting to hear her step. It did not come, and after vainly straining his ears he called out in a voice that shook with joy: "Hello, Matt!"

Silence answered; but in a minute or two he caught a sound on the stairs and saw a line of light about the door-frame, as he had seen it the night before. So strange was the precision with which the incidents of the previous evening were repeating themselves that he half expected, when he heard the key turn, to see his wife before him on the threshold; but the door opened, and Mattie faced him.

She stood just as Zeena had stood, a lifted lamp in her hand, against the black background of the kitchen. She held the light at the same level, and it drew out with the same distinctness her slim young throat and the brown wrist no bigger than a child's. Then, striking upward, it threw a lustrous fleck on her lips, edged her eyes with velvet shade, and laid a milky whiteness above the black curve of her brows.

She wore her usual dress of darkish stuff, and there was no bow at her neck; but through her hair she had run a streak of crimson ribbon. This tribute to the unusual transformed and glorified her. She seemed to Ethan taller, fuller, more womanly in shape and motion. She stood aside, smiling silently, while he entered, and then moved away from him with something soft and flowing in her gait. She set the lamp on the table, and he saw that it was carefully laid for supper, with fresh doughnuts, stewed blueberries and his favourite pickles in a dish of gay red glass. A bright fire glowed in the stove and the cat lay stretched before it, watching the table with a drowsy eye.

Ethan was suffocated with the sense of well-being. He went out into the passage to hang up his coat and pull off his wet boots. When he came back Mattie had set the teapot on the table and the cat was rubbing itself persuasively against her ankles.

"Why, Puss! I nearly tripped over you," she cried, the laughter sparkling through her lashes.

Again Ethan felt a sudden twinge of jealousy. Could it be his coming that gave her such a kindled face?

"Well, Matt, any visitors?" he threw off, stooping down carelessly to examine the fastening of the stove.

She nodded and laughed "Yes, one," and he felt a blackness settling on his brows.

"Who was that?" he questioned, raising himself up to slant a glance at her beneath his scowl.

Her eyes danced with malice. "Why, Jotham Powell. He came in after he got back, and asked for a drop of coffee before he went down home."

The blackness lifted and light flooded Ethan's brain. "That all? Well, I hope you made out to let him have it." And after a pause he felt it right to add: "I suppose he got Zeena over to the Flats all right?"

"Oh, yes; in plenty of time."

The name threw a chill between them, and they stood a moment looking sideways at each other before Mattie said with a shy laugh: "I guess it's about time for supper."

They drew their seats up to the table, and the cat, unbidden, jumped between them into Zeena's empty chair. "Oh, Puss!" said Mattie, and they laughed again.

Ethan, a moment earlier, had felt himself on the brink of eloquence; but the mention of Zeena had paralysed him. Mattie seemed to feel the contagion of his embarrassment, and sat with downcast lids, sipping her tea, while he feigned an insatiable appetite for doughnuts and sweet pickles. At last, after casting about for an effective opening, he took a long gulp of tea, cleared his throat, and said: "Looks as if there'd be more snow."

She feigned great interest. "Is that so? Do you suppose it'll interfere with Zeena's getting back?" She flushed red as the question escaped her, and hastily set down the cup she was lifting.

Ethan reached over for another helping of pickles. "You never can tell, this time of year, it drifts so bad on the Flats." The name had benumbed him again, and once more he felt as if Zeena were in the room between them.

"Oh, Puss, you're too greedy!" Mattie cried.

The cat, unnoticed, had crept up on muffled paws from Zeena's seat to the table, and was stealthily elongating its body in the direction of the milk-jug, which stood between Ethan and Mattie. The two leaned forward at the same moment and their hands met on the handle of the jug. Mattie's hand was underneath, and Ethan kept his clasped on it a moment longer than was necessary. The cat, profiting by this unusual demonstration, tried to effect an unnoticed retreat, and in doing so backed into the pickle-dish, which fell to the floor with a crash.

Mattie, in an instant, had sprung from her chair and was down on her knees by the fragments.

"Oh, Ethan, Ethan—it's all to pieces! What will Zeena say?"

But this time his courage was up. "Well, she'll have to say it to the cat, any way!" he rejoined with a laugh, kneeling down at Mattie's side to scrape up the swimming pickles.

She lifted stricken eyes to him. "Yes, but, you see, she never meant it should be used, not even when there was company; and I had to get up on the step-ladder to reach it down from the top shelf of the china-closet, where she keeps it with all her best things, and of course she'll want to know why I did it—"

The case was so serious that it called forth all of Ethan's latent resolution.

"She needn't know anything about it if you keep quiet. I'll get another just like it to-morrow. Where did it come from? I'll go to Shadd's Falls for it if I have to!"

"Oh, you'll never get another even there! It was a wedding present—don't you remember? It came all the way from Philadelphia, from Zeena's aunt that married the minister. That's why she wouldn't ever use it. Oh, Ethan, Ethan, what in the world shall I do?"

She began to cry, and he felt as if every one of her tears were pouring over him like burning lead. "Don't, Matt, don't—oh, *don't!*" he implored her.

She struggled to her feet, and he rose and followed her helplessly while she spread out the pieces of glass on the kitchen dresser. It seemed to him as if the shattered fragments of their evening lay there.

"Here, give them to me," he said in a voice of sudden authority.

She drew aside, instinctively obeying his tone. "Oh, Ethan, what are you going to do?"

Without replying he gathered the pieces of glass into his broad palm and walked out of the kitchen to the passage. There he lit a candle-end, opened the china-closet, and, reaching his long arm up to the highest shelf, laid the pieces together with such accuracy of touch that a close inspection convinced him of the impossibility of detecting from below that the dish was broken. If he glued it together the next morning months might elapse before his wife noticed what had happened, and meanwhile he might after all be able to match the dish at Shadd's Falls or Bettsbridge. Having satisfied himself that there was no risk of immediate discovery he went back to the kitchen with a lighter step, and found Mattie disconsolately removing the last scraps of pickle from the floor.

"It's all right, Matt. Come back and finish supper," he commanded her.

Completely reassured, she shone on him through tear-hung lashes, and his soul swelled with pride as he saw how his tone subdued her. She did not even ask what he had done. Except when he was steering a big log down the mountain to his mill he had never known such a thrilling sense of mastery.

5.

They finished supper, and while Mattie cleared the table Ethan went to look at the cows and then took a last turn about the house. The earth lay dark under a muffled sky and the air was so still that now and then he heard a lump of snow come thumping down from a tree far off on the edge of the wood-lot.

When he returned to the kitchen Mattie had pushed up his chair to the stove and seated herself near the lamp with a bit of sewing. The scene was just as he had dreamed of it that morning. He sat down, drew his pipe from his pocket and stretched his feet to the glow. His hard day's work in the keen air made him feel at once lazy and light of mood, and he had a confused sense of being in another world, where all was warmth and harmony and time could bring no change. The only drawback to his complete well-being was the fact that he could not see Mattie from where he sat; but he was too indolent to move and after a moment he said: "Come over here and sit by the stove."

Zeena's empty rocking-chair stood facing him. Mattie rose obediently, and seated herself in it. As her young brown head detached itself against the patch-work cushion that habitually framed his wife's gaunt countenance, Ethan had a momentary shock. It was almost as if the other face, the face of the superseded woman, had obliterated that of the intruder. After a moment Mattie seemed to be affected by the same sense of constraint. She changed her position, leaning forward to bend her head above her work, so that he saw only the foreshortened tip of her nose and the streak of red in her hair; then she slipped to her feet, saying "I can't see to sew," and went back to her chair by the lamp.

Ethan made a pretext of getting up to replenish the stove, and when he returned to his seat he pushed it sideways that he might get a view of her profile and of the lamplight falling on her hands. The cat, who had been a puzzled observer of these unusual movements, jumped up into Zeena's chair, rolled itself into a ball, and lay watching them with narrowed eyes.

Deep quiet sank on the room. The clock ticked above the dresser, a piece of charred wood fell now and then in the stove, and the faint sharp scent of the geraniums mingled with the odour of Ethan's smoke, which began to throw a blue haze about the lamp and to hang its greyish cobwebs in the shadowy corners of the room.

All constraint had vanished between the two, and they began to talk easily and simply. They spoke of every-day things, of the prospect of snow, of the next church sociable, of the loves and quarrels of Starkfield. The commonplace nature of what they said produced in Ethan an illusion of long-established intimacy which no outburst of emotion could have given, and he set his imagination adrift on the fiction that they had always spent their evenings thus and would always go on doing so . . .

"This is the night we were to have gone coasting, Matt," he said at length, with the rich sense, as he spoke, that they could go on any other night they chose, since they had all time before them.

She smiled back at him. "I guess you forgot!"

"No, I didn't forget; but it's as dark as Egypt outdoors. We might go to-morrow if there's a moon."

She laughed with pleasure, her head tilted back, the lamplight sparkling on her lips and teeth. "That would be lovely, Ethan!"

He kept his eyes fixed on her, marvelling at the way her face changed with each turn of their talk, like a wheat-field under a summer breeze. It was intoxicating to find such magic in his clumsy words, and he longed to try new ways of using it.

"Would you be scared to go down the Corbury road with me on a night like this?" he asked.

Her cheeks burned redder. "I ain't any more scared than you are!"

"Well, *I'd* be scared, then; I wouldn't do it. That's an ugly corner down by the big elm. If a fellow didn't keep his eyes open he'd go plumb into it." He luxuriated in the sense of protection and authority which his words conveyed. To prolong and intensify the feeling he added: "I guess we're well enough here."

She let her lids sink slowly, in the way he loved. "Yes, we're well enough here," she sighed.

Her tone was so sweet that he took the pipe from his mouth and drew his chair up to the table. Leaning forward, he touched the farther end of the strip of brown stuff that she was hemming. "Say, Matt," he began with a smile, "what do you think I saw under the Varnum spruces, coming along home just now? I saw a friend of yours getting kissed."

The words had been on his tongue all the evening, but now that he had spoken them they struck him as inexpressibly vulgar and out of place.

Mattie blushed to the roots of her hair and pulled her needle rapidly twice or thrice through her work, insensibly drawing the end of it away from him. "I suppose it was Ruth and Ned," she said in a low voice, as though he had suddenly touched on something grave.

Ethan had imagined that his allusion might open the way to the accepted pleasantries, and these perhaps in turn to a harmless caress, if only a mere touch on her hand. But now he felt as if her blush had set a flaming guard about her. He supposed it was his natural awkwardness that made him feel so. He knew that most young men made nothing at all of giving a pretty girl a kiss, and he remembered that the night before, when he had put his arm about Mattie, she had not resisted. But that had been out-of-doors, under the open irresponsible night. Now, in the warm lamplit room, with all its ancient implications of conformity and order, she seemed infinitely farther away from him and more unapproachable.

To ease his constraint he said: "I suppose they'll be setting a date before long."

"Yes. I shouldn't wonder if they got married some time along in the summer." She pronounced the word *married* as if her voice caressed it. It seemed a rustling covert leading to enchanted glades. A pang shot through Ethan, and he said, twisting away from her in his chair: "It'll be your turn next, I wouldn't wonder."

She laughed a little uncertainly. "Why do you keep on saying that?"

He echoed her laugh. "I guess I do it to get used to the idea."

He drew up to the table again and she sewed on in silence, with dropped lashes, while he sat in fascinated contemplation of the way in which her hands went up and down above the strip of stuff, just as he had seen a pair of birds make short perpendicular flights over a nest they were building. At length, without turning her head or lifting her lids, she said in a low tone: "It's not because you think Zeena's got anything against me, is it?"

His former dread started up full-armed at the suggestion. "Why, what do you mean?" he stammered.

She raised distressed eyes to his, her work dropping on the table between them. "I don't know. I thought last night she seemed to have."

"I'd like to know what," he growled.

"Nobody can tell with Zeena." It was the first time they had ever spoken so openly of her attitude toward Mattie, and the repetition of the name seemed to carry it to the farther corners of the room and send it back to them in long repercussions of sound. Mattie waited, as if to give the echo time to drop, and then went on: "She hasn't said anything to *you?*"

He shook his head. "No, not a word."

She tossed her hair back from her forehead with a laugh. "I guess I'm just nervous, then. I'm not going to think about it any more."

"Oh, no—don't let's think about it, Matt!"

The sudden heat of his tone made her colour mount again, not with a rush, but gradually, delicately, like the reflection of a thought stealing slowly across her heart. She sat silent, her hands clasped on her work, and it seemed to him that a warm current flowed toward him along the strip of stuff that still lay unrolled between them. Cautiously he slid his hand palm-downward along the table till his finger-tips touched the end of the stuff. A faint vibration of her lashes seemed to show that she was aware of his gesture, and that it had sent a counter-current back to her; and she let her hands lie motionless on the other end of the strip.

As they sat thus he heard a sound behind him and turned his head. The cat had jumped from Zeena's chair to dart at a mouse in the wainscot, and as a result of the sudden movement the empty chair had set up a spectral rocking.

"She'll be rocking in it herself this time to-morrow," Ethan thought. "I've been in a dream, and this is the only evening we'll ever have together." The return to reality was as painful as the return to consciousness after taking an anæsthetic. His body and brain ached with indescribable weariness, and he could think of nothing to say or to do that should arrest the mad flight of the moments.

His alteration of mood seemed to have communicated itself to Mattie. She looked up at him languidly, as though her lids were weighted with sleep and it cost her an effort to raise them. Her glance fell on his hand, which now completely covered the end of her work and grasped it as if it were a part of herself. He saw a scarcely perceptible tremor cross her face, and without knowing what he did he stooped his head and kissed the bit of stuff in his hold. As his lips rested on it he felt it glide slowly from beneath them, and saw that Mattie had risen and was silently rolling up her work. She fastened it with a pin, and then, finding her thimble and scissors, put them with the roll of stuff into the box covered with fancy paper which he had once brought to her from Bettsbridge.

He stood up also, looking vaguely about the room. The clock above the dresser struck eleven.

"Is the fire all right?" she asked in a low voice.

He opened the door of the stove and poked aimlessly at the embers. When he raised himself again he saw that she was dragging toward the stove the old soap-box lined with carpet in which the cat made its bed. Then she recrossed the floor and lifted two of the geranium pots in her arms, moving them away from the cold window. He followed her and brought the other geraniums, the hyacinth bulbs in a cracked custard bowl and the German ivy trained over an old croquet hoop.

When these nightly duties were performed there was nothing left to do but to bring in the tin candlestick from the passage, light the candle and blow out the lamp. Ethan put the candlestick in Mattie's hand and she went out of the kitchen ahead of him, the light that she carried before her making her dark hair look like a drift of mist on the moon.

"Good night, Matt," he said as she put her foot on the first step of the stairs.

She turned and looked at him a moment. "Good night, Ethan," she answered, and went up.

When the door of her room had closed on her he remembered that he had not even touched her hand.

6.

The next morning at breakfast Jotham Powell was between them, and Ethan tried to hide his joy under an air of exaggerated indifference, lounging back in his chair to throw scraps to the cat, growling at the weather, and not so much as offering to help Mattie when she rose to clear away the dishes.

He did not know why he was so irrationally happy, for nothing was changed in his life or hers. He had not even touched the tip of her fingers or looked her full in the eyes. But their evening together had given him a vision of what life at her side might be, and he was glad now that he had done nothing to trouble the sweetness of the picture. He had a fancy that she knew what had restrained him . . .

There was a last load of lumber to be hauled to the village, and Jotham Powell—who did not work regularly for Ethan in winter—had "come round" to help with the job. But a wet snow, melting to sleet, had fallen in the night and turned the roads to glass. There was more wet in the air and it seemed likely to both men that the weather would "milden" toward afternoon and make the going safer. Ethan therefore proposed to his assistant that they should load the sledge at the wood-lot, as they had done on the previous morning, and put off the "teaming" to Starkfield till later in the day. This plan had the advantage of enabling him to send Jotham to the Flats after dinner to meet Zenobia, while he himself took the lumber down to the village.

He told Jotham to go out and harness up the greys, and for a moment he and Mattie had the kitchen to themselves. She had plunged the breakfast dishes into a tin dish-pan and was bending above it with her slim arms bared to the elbow, the steam from the hot water beading her forehead and tightening her rough hair into little brown rings like the tendrils on the traveller's joy.

Ethan stood looking at her, his heart in his throat. He wanted to say: "We shall never be alone again like this." Instead, he reached down his tobacco-pouch from a shelf of the dresser, put it into his pocket and said: "I guess I can make out to be home for dinner."

She answered "All right, Ethan," and he heard her singing over the dishes as he went.

As soon as the sledge was loaded he meant to send Jotham back to the farm and hurry on foot into the village to buy glue for the pickle-dish. With ordinary luck he should have had time to carry out this plan; but everything went wrong from the start. On the way over to the wood-lot one of the greys slipped on a glare of ice and cut his knee; and when they got him up again Jotham had to go back to the barn for a strip of rag to bind the cut. Then, when the loading finally began, a sleety rain was coming down once more, and the tree trunks were so slippery that it took twice as long as usual to lift them and get them in place on the sledge. It was what Jotham called a sour morning for work, and the horses, shivering and stamping under their wet blankets, seemed to like it as little as the men. It was long past the dinner-hour when the job was done, and Ethan had to give up going to the village because he wanted to lead the injured horse home and wash the cut himself.

He thought that by starting out again with the lumber as soon as he had finished his dinner he might get back to the farm with the glue before Jotham and the old sorrel had had time to fetch Zenobia from the Flats; but he knew the chance was a slight one. It turned on the state of the roads and on the possible lateness of the Bettsbridge train. He remembered afterward, with a grim flash of self-derision, what importance he had attached to the weighing of these probabilities . . .

As soon as dinner was over he set out again for the wood-lot, not daring to linger till Jotham Powell left. The hired man was still drying his wet feet at the stove, and Ethan could only give Mattie a quick look as he said beneath his breath: "I'll be back early."

He fancied that she nodded her comprehension; and with that scant solace he had to trudge off through the rain.

He had driven his load half-way to the village when Jotham Powell overtook him, urging the reluctant sorrel toward the Flats. "I'll have to hurry up to do it," Ethan mused, as the sleigh dropped down ahead of him over the dip of the school-house hill. He worked like ten at the unloading, and when it was over hastened on to Michael Eady's for the glue. Eady and his assistant were both "down street," and young Denis, who seldom deigned to take their place, was lounging by the stove with a knot of the golden youth of Starkfield. They hailed Ethan with ironic compliment and offers of conviviality; but no one knew where to find the glue. Ethan, consumed with the longing for a last moment alone with Mattie, hung about impatiently while Denis made an ineffectual search in the obscurer corners of the store.

"Looks as if we were all sold out. But if you'll wait around till the old man comes along maybe he can put his hand on it."

"I'm obliged to you, but I'll try if I can get it down at Mrs. Homan's," Ethan answered, burning to be gone.

Denis's commercial instinct compelled him to aver on oath that what Eady's store could not produce would never be found at the widow Homan's; but Ethan, heedless of this boast, had already climbed to the sledge and was driving on to the rival establishment. Here, after considerable search, and sympathetic questions as to what he wanted it for, and whether ordinary flour paste wouldn't do as well if she couldn't find it, the widow Homan finally hunted down her solitary bottle of glue to its hiding-place in a medley of cough-lozenges and corset-laces.

"I hope Zeena ain't broken anything she sets store by," she called after him as he turned the greys toward home.

The fitful bursts of sleet had changed into a steady rain and the horses had heavy work even without a load behind them. Once or twice, hearing sleigh-bells, Ethan turned his head, fancying that Zeena and Jotham might overtake him; but the old sorrel was not in sight, and he set his face against the rain and urged on his ponderous pair.

The barn was empty when the horses turned into it and, after giving them the most perfunctory ministrations they had ever received from him, he strode up to the house and pushed open the kitchen door.

Mattie was there alone, as he had pictured her. She was bending over a pan on the stove; but at the sound of his step she turned with a start and sprang to him.

"See, here, Matt, I've got some stuff to mend the dish with! Let me get at it quick," he cried, waving the bottle in one hand while he put her lightly aside; but she did not seem to hear him.

"Oh, Ethan—Zeena's come," she said in a whisper, clutching his sleeve.

They stood and stared at each other, pale as culprits.

"But the sorrel's not in the barn!" Ethan stammered.

"Jotham Powell brought some goods over from the Flats for his wife, and he drove right on home with them," she explained.

He gazed blankly about the kitchen, which looked cold and squalid in the rainy winter twilight.

"How is she?" he asked, dropping his voice to Mattie's whisper.

She looked away from him uncertainly. "I don't know. She went right up to her room."

"She didn't say anything?"

"No."

Ethan let out his doubts in a low whistle and thrust the bottle back into his pocket. "Don't fret; I'll come down and mend it in the night," he said. He pulled on his wet coat again and went back to the barn to feed the greys.

While he was there Jotham Powell drove up with the sleigh, and when the horses had been attended to Ethan said to him: "You might as well come back up for a bite." He was not sorry to assure himself of Jotham's neutralising presence at the supper table, for Zeena was always "nervous" after a journey. But the hired man, though seldom loth to accept a meal not included in his wages, opened his stiff jaws to answer slowly: "I'm obliged to you, but I guess I'll go along back."

Ethan looked at him in surprise. "Better come up and dry off. Looks as if there'd be something hot for supper."

Jotham's facial muscles were unmoved by this appeal and, his vocabulary being limited, he merely repeated: "I guess I'll go along back."

To Ethan there was something vaguely ominous in this stolid rejection of free food and warmth, and he wondered what had happened on the drive to nerve Jotham to such stoicism. Perhaps Zeena had failed to see the new doctor or had not liked his counsels: Ethan knew that in such cases the first person she met was likely to be held responsible for her grievance.

When he re-entered the kitchen the lamp lit up the same scene of shining comfort as on the previous evening. The table had been as carefully laid, a clear fire glowed in the stove, the cat dozed in its warmth, and Mattie came forward carrying a plate of doughnuts.

She and Ethan looked at each other in silence; then she said, as she had said the night before: "I guess it's about time for supper."

7.

Ethan went out into the passage to hang up his wet garments. He listened for Zeena's step and, not hearing it, called her name up the stairs. She did not answer, and after a moment's hesitation he went up and opened her door. The room was almost dark, but in the obscurity he saw her sitting by the window, bolt upright, and knew by the rigidity of the outline projected against the pane that she had not taken off her travelling dress.

"Well, Zeena," he ventured from the threshold.

She did not move, and he continued: "Supper's about ready. Ain't you coming?"

She replied: "I don't feel as if I could touch a morsel."

It was the consecrated formula, and he expected it to be followed, as usual, by her rising and going down to supper. But she remained seated, and he could think of nothing more felicitous than: "I presume you're tired after the long ride."

Turning her head at this, she answered solemnly: "I'm a great deal sicker than you think."

Her words fell on his ear with a strange shock of wonder. He had often heard her pronounce them before—what if at last they were true?

He advanced a step or two into the dim room. "I hope that's not so, Zeena," he said.

She continued to gaze at him through the twilight with a mien of wan authority, as of one consciously singled out for a great fate. "I've got complications," she said.

Ethan knew the word for one of exceptional import. Almost everybody in the neighbourhood had "troubles," frankly localized and specified; but only the chosen had "complications." To have them was in itself a distinction, though it was also, in most cases, a death-warrant. People struggled on for years with "troubles," but they almost always succumbed to "complications."

Ethan's heart was jerking to and fro between two extremities of feeling, but for the moment compassion prevailed. His wife looked so hard and lonely, sitting there in the darkness with such thoughts.

"Is that what the new doctor told you?" he asked, instinctively lowering his voice.

"Yes. He says any regular doctor would want me to have an operation."

Ethan was aware that, in regard to the important question of surgical intervention, the female opinion of the neighbourhood was divided, some glorying in the prestige conferred by operations while others shunned them as indelicate. Ethan, from motives of economy, had always been glad that Zeena was of the latter faction.

In the agitation caused by the gravity of her announcement he sought a consolatory short cut. "What do you know about this doctor anyway? Nobody ever told you that before."

He saw his blunder before she could take it up: she wanted sympathy, not consolation.

"I didn't need to have anybody tell me I was losing ground every day. Everybody but you could see it. And everybody in Bettsbridge knows about Dr. Buck. He has his office in Worcester, and comes over once a fortnight to Shadd's Falls and Bettsbridge for consultations. Eliza Spears was wasting away with kidney trouble before she went to him, and now she's up and around, and singing in the choir."

"Well, I'm glad of that. You must do just what he tells you," Ethan answered sympathetically.

She was still looking at him. "I mean to," she said. He was struck by a new note in her voice. It was neither whining nor reproachful, but drily resolute.

"What does he want you should do?" he asked, with a mounting vision of fresh expenses.

"He wants I should have a hired girl. He says I oughtn't to have to do a single thing around the house."

"A hired girl?" Ethan stood transfixed.

"Yes. And Aunt Martha found me one right off. Everybody said I was lucky to get a girl to come away out here, and I agreed to give her a dollar extry to make sure. She'll be over to-morrow afternoon."

Wrath and dismay contended in Ethan. He had foreseen an immediate demand for money, but not a permanent drain on his scant resources. He no longer believed what Zeena had told him of the supposed seriousness of her state: he saw in her expedition to Bettsbridge only a plot hatched between herself and her Pierce relations to foist on him the cost of a servant; and for the moment wrath predominated.

"If you meant to engage a girl you ought to have told me before you started," he said.

"How could I tell you before I started? How did I know what Dr. Buck would say?"

"Oh, Dr. Buck—" Ethan's incredulity escaped in a short laugh. "Did Dr. Buck tell you how I was to pay her wages?"

Her voice rose furiously with his. "No, he didn't. For I'd 'a' been ashamed to tell *him* that you grudged me the money to get back my health, when I lost it nursing your own mother!"

"*You* lost your health nursing mother?"

"Yes; and my folks all told me at the time you couldn't do no less than marry me after—"

"Zeena!"

Through the obscurity which hid their faces their thoughts seemed to dart at each other like serpents shooting venom. Ethan was seized with horror of the scene and shame at his own share in it. It was as senseless and savage as a physical fight between two enemies in the darkness.

He turned to the shelf above the chimney, groped for matches and lit the one candle in the room. At first its weak flame made no impression on the shadows; then Zeena's face stood grimly out against the uncurtained pane, which had turned from grey to black.

It was the first scene of open anger between the couple in their sad seven years together, and Ethan felt as if he had lost an irretrievable advantage in descending to the level of recrimination. But the practical problem was there and had to be dealt with.

"You know I haven't got the money to pay for a girl, Zeena. You'll have to send her back: I can't do it."

"The doctor says it'll be my death if I go on slaving the way I've had to. He doesn't understand how I've stood it as long as I have."

"Slaving!—" He checked himself again. "You sha'n't lift a hand, if he says so. I'll do everything round the house myself—"

She broke in: "You're neglecting the farm enough already," and this being true, he found no answer, and left her time to add ironically: "Better send me over to the almshouse and done with it . . . I guess there's been Fromes there afore now."

The taunt burned into him, but he let it pass. "I haven't got the money. That settles it."

There was a moment's pause in the struggle, as though the combatants were testing their weapons. Then Zeena said in a level voice: "I thought you were to get fifty dollars from Andrew Hale for that lumber."

"Andrew Hale never pays under three months." He had already spoken when he remembered the excuse he had made for not accompanying his wife to the station the day before; and the blood rose to his frowning brows.

"Why, you told me yesterday you'd fixed it up with him to pay cash down. You said that was why you couldn't drive me over to the Flats."

Ethan had no suppleness in deceiving. He had never before been convicted of a lie, and all the resources of evasion failed him. "I guess that was a misunderstanding," he stammered.

"You ain't got the money?"

"No."

"And you ain't going to get it?"

"No."

"Well, I couldn't know that when I engaged the girl, could I?"

"No." He paused to control his voice. "But you know it now. I'm sorry, but it can't be helped. You're a poor man's wife, Zeena; but I'll do the best I can for you."

For a while she sat motionless, as if reflecting, her arms stretched along the arms of her chair, her eyes fixed on vacancy. "Oh, I guess we'll make out," she said mildly.

The change in her tone reassured him. "Of course we will! There's a whole lot more I can do for you, and Mattie—"

Zeena, while he spoke, seemed to be following out some elaborate mental calculation. She emerged from it to say: "There'll be Mattie's board less, anyhow—"

Ethan, supposing the discussion to be over, had turned to go down to supper. He stopped short, not grasping what he heard. "Mattie's board less—?" he began.

Zeena laughed. It was an odd unfamiliar sound—he did not remember ever having heard her laugh before. "You didn't suppose I was going to keep two girls, did you? No wonder you were scared at the expense!"

He still had but a confused sense of what she was saying. From the beginning of the discussion he had instinctively avoided the mention of Mattie's name, fearing he hardly knew what: criticism, complaints, or vague allusions to the imminent probability of her marrying. But the thought of a definite rupture had never come to him, and even now could not lodge itself in his mind.

"I don't know what you mean," he said. "Mattie Silver's not a hired girl. She's your relation."

"She's a pauper that's hung onto us all after her father'd done his best to ruin us. I've kep' her here a whole year: it's somebody else's turn now."

As the shrill words shot out Ethan heard a tap on the door, which he had drawn shut when he turned back from the threshold.

"Ethan—Zeena!" Mattie's voice sounded gaily from the landing, "do you know what time it is? Supper's been ready half an hour."

Inside the room there was a moment's silence; then Zeena called out from her seat: "I'm not coming down to supper."

"Oh, I'm sorry! Aren't you well? Sha'n't I bring you up a bite of something?"

Ethan roused himself with an effort and opened the door. "Go along down, Matt. Zeena's just a little tired. I'm coming."

He heard her "All right!" and her quick step on the stairs; then he shut the door and turned back into the room. His wife's attitude was unchanged, her face inexorable, and he was seized with the despairing sense of his helplessness.

"You ain't going to do it, Zeena?"

"Do what?" she emitted between flattened lips.

"Send Mattie away—like this?"

"I never bargained to take her for life!"

He continued with rising vehemence: "You can't put her out of the house like a thief—a poor girl without friends or money. She's done her best for you and she's got no place to go to. You may forget she's your kin but everybody else'll remember it. If you do a thing like that what do you suppose folks'll say of you?"

Zeena waited a moment, as if giving him time to feel the full force of the contrast between his own excitement and her composure. Then she replied in the same smooth voice: "I know well enough what they say of my having kep' her here as long as I have."

Ethan's hand dropped from the door-knob, which he had held clenched since he had drawn the door shut on Mattie. His wife's retort was like a knife-cut across the sinews and he felt suddenly weak and powerless. He had meant to humble himself, to argue that Mattie's keep didn't cost much, after all, that he could make out to buy a stove and fix up a place in the attic for the hired girl—but Zeena's words revealed the peril of such pleadings.

"You mean to tell her she's got to go—at once?" he faltered out, in terror of letting his wife complete her sentence.

As if trying to make him see reason she replied impartially: "The girl will be over from Bettsbridge to-morrow, and I presume she's got to have somewheres to sleep."

Ethan looked at her with loathing. She was no longer the listless creature who had lived at his side in a state of sullen self-absorption, but a mysterious alien presence, an evil energy secreted from the long years of silent brooding. It was the sense of his helplessness that sharpened his antipathy. There had never been anything in her that one could appeal to; but as long as he could ignore and command he had remained indifferent. Now she had mastered him and he abhorred her. Mattie was her relation, not his: there were no means by which he could compel her to keep the girl under her roof. All the long misery of his baffled past, of his youth of failure, hardship and vain effort, rose up in his soul in bitterness and seemed to take shape before him in the woman who at every turn had barred his way. She had taken everything else from him; and now she meant to take the one thing that made up for all the others. For a moment such a flame of hate rose in him that it ran down his arm and clenched his fist against her. He took a wild step forward and then stopped.

"You're—you're not coming down?" he said in a bewildered voice.

"No. I guess I'll lay down on the bed a little while," she answered mildly; and he turned and walked out of the room.

In the kitchen Mattie was sitting by the stove, the cat curled up on her knees. She sprang to her feet as Ethan entered and carried the covered dish of meat-pie to the table.

"I hope Zeena isn't sick?" she asked.

"No."

She shone at him across the table. "Well, sit right down then. You must be starving." She uncovered the pie and pushed it over to him. So they were to have one more evening together, her happy eyes seemed to say!

He helped himself mechanically and began to eat; then disgust took him by the throat and he laid down his fork.

Mattie's tender gaze was on him and she marked the gesture.

"Why, Ethan, what's the matter? Don't it taste right?"

"Yes—it's first-rate. Only I—" He pushed his plate away, rose from his chair, and walked around the table to her side. She started up with frightened eyes.

"Ethan, there's something wrong! I *knew* there was!"

She seemed to melt against him in her terror, and he caught her in his arms, held her fast there, felt her lashes beat his cheek like netted butterflies.

"What is it—what is it?" she stammered; but he had found her lips at last and was drinking unconsciousness of everything but the joy they gave him.

She lingered a moment, caught in the same strong current; then she slipped from him and drew back a step or two, pale and troubled. Her look smote him with compunction, and he cried out, as if he saw her drowning in a dream: "You can't go, Matt! I'll never let you!"

"Go—go?" she stammered. "Must I go?"

The words went on sounding between them as though a torch of warning flew from hand to hand through a black landscape.

Ethan was overcome with shame at his lack of self-control in flinging the news at her so brutally. His head reeled and he had to support himself against the table. All the while he felt as if he were still kissing her, and yet dying of thirst for her lips.

"Ethan, what has happened? Is Zeena mad with me?"

Her cry steadied him, though it deepened his wrath and pity. "No, no," he assured her, "it's not that. But this new doctor has scared her about herself. You know she believes all they say the first time she sees them. And this one's told her she won't get well unless she lays up and don't do a thing about the house—not for months—"

He paused, his eyes wandering from her miserably. She stood silent a moment, drooping before him like a broken branch. She was so small and weak-looking that it wrung his heart; but suddenly she lifted her head and looked straight at him. "And she wants somebody handier in my place? Is that it?"

"That's what she says to-night."

"If she says it to-night she'll say it to-morrow."

Both bowed to the inexorable truth: they knew that Zeena never changed her mind, and that in her case a resolve once taken was equivalent to an act performed.

There was a long silence between them; then Mattie said in a low voice: "Don't be too sorry, Ethan."

"Oh, God—oh, God," he groaned. The glow of passion he had felt for her had melted to an aching tenderness. He saw her quick lids beating back the tears, and longed to take her in his arms and soothe her.

"You're letting your supper get cold," she admonished him with a pale gleam of gaiety.

"Oh, Matt—Matt—where'll you go to?"

Her lids sank and a tremor crossed her face. He saw that for the first time the thought of the future came to her distinctly. "I might get something to do over at Stamford," she faltered, as if knowing that he knew she had no hope.

He dropped back into his seat and hid his face in his hands. Despair seized him at the thought of her setting out alone to renew the weary quest for work. In the only place where she was known she was surrounded by indifference or animosity; and what chance had she, inexperienced and untrained, among the million bread-seekers of the cities? There came back to him miserable tales he had heard at Worcester, and the faces of girls whose lives had begun as hopefully as Mattie's. . . . It was not possible to think of such things without a revolt of his whole being. He sprang up suddenly.

"You can't go, Matt! I won't let you! She's always had her way, but I mean to have mine now—"

Mattie lifted her hand with a quick gesture, and he heard his wife's step behind him.

Zeena came into the room with her dragging down-at-the-heel step, and quietly took her accustomed seat between them.

"I felt a little mite better, and Dr. Buck says I ought to eat all I can to keep my strength up, even if I ain't got any appetite," she said in her flat whine, reaching across Mattie for the teapot. Her "good" dress had been replaced by the black calico and brown knitted shawl which formed her daily wear, and with them she had put on her usual face and manner. She poured out her tea, added a great deal of milk to it, helped herself largely to pie and pickles, and made the familiar gesture of adjusting her false teeth before she began to eat. The cat rubbed itself ingratiatingly against her, and she said "Good Pussy," stooped to stroke it and gave it a scrap of meat from her plate.

Ethan sat speechless, not pretending to eat, but Mattie nibbled valiantly at her food and asked Zeena one or two questions about her visit to Bettsbridge. Zeena answered in her every-day tone and, warming to the theme, regaled them with several vivid descriptions of intestinal disturbances among her friends and relatives. She looked straight at Mattie as she spoke, a faint smile deepening the vertical lines between her nose and chin.

When supper was over she rose from her seat and pressed her hand to the flat surface over the region of her heart. "That pie of yours always sets a mite heavy, Matt," she said, not ill-naturedly.

She seldom abbreviated the girl's name, and when she did so it was always a sign of affability.

"I've a good mind to go and hunt up those stomach powders I got last year over in Springfield," she continued. "I ain't tried them for quite a while, and maybe they'll help the heartburn."

Mattie lifted her eyes. "Can't I get them for you, Zeena?" she ventured.

"No. They're in a place you don't know about," Zeena answered darkly, with one of her secret looks.

She went out of the kitchen and Mattie, rising, began to clear the dishes from the table. As she passed Ethan's chair their eyes met and clung together desolately. The warm still kitchen looked as peaceful as the night before. The cat had sprung to Zeena's rocking-chair, and the heat of the fire was beginning to draw out the faint sharp scent of the geraniums. Ethan dragged himself wearily to his feet.

"I'll go out and take a look around," he said, going toward the passage to get his lantern.

As he reached the door he met Zeena coming back into the room, her lips twitching with anger, a flush of excitement on her sallow face. The shawl had slipped from her shoulders and was dragging at her down-trodden heels, and in her hands she carried the fragments of the red glass pickle-dish.

"I'd like to know who done this," she said, looking sternly from Ethan to Mattie.

There was no answer, and she continued in a trembling voice: "I went to get those powders I'd put away in father's old spectacle-case, top of the china-closet, where I keep the things I set store by, so's folks sha'n't meddle with them—" Her voice broke, and two small tears hung on her lashless lids and ran slowly down her cheeks. "It takes the step-ladder to get at the top shelf, and I put Aunt Philura Maple's pickle-dish up there o' purpose when we was married, and it's never been down since, 'cept for the spring cleaning, and then I always lifted it with my own hands, so's 't shouldn't get broke." She laid the fragments reverently on the table. "I want to know who done this," she quavered.

At the challenge Ethan turned back into the room and faced her. "I can tell you, then. The cat done it."

"The *cat?*"

"That's what I said."

She looked at him hard, and then turned her eyes to Mattie, who was carrying the dish-pan to the table.

"I'd like to know how the cat got into my china-closet," she said.

"Chasin' mice, I guess," Ethan rejoined. "There was a mouse round the kitchen all last evening."

Zeena continued to look from one to the other; then she emitted her small strange laugh. "I knew the cat was a smart cat," she said in a high voice, "but I didn't know he was smart enough to pick up the pieces of my pickle-dish and lay 'em edge to edge on the very shelf he knocked 'em off of."

Mattie suddenly drew her arms out of the steaming water. "It wasn't Ethan's fault, Zeena! The cat *did* break the dish; but I got it down from the china-closet, and I'm the one to blame for its getting broken."

Zeena stood beside the ruin of her treasure, stiffening into a stony image of resentment. "*You* got down my pickle-dish—what for?"

A bright flush flew to Mattie's cheeks. "I wanted to make the supper-table pretty," she said.

"You wanted to make the supper-table pretty; and you waited till my back was turned, and took the thing I set most store by of everything I've got, and wouldn't never use it, not even when the minister come to dinner, or Aunt Martha Pierce come over from Bettsbridge—" Zeena paused with a gasp, as if terrified by her own evocation of the sacrilege. "You're a bad girl, Mattie Silver, and I always known it. It's the way your father begun, and I was warned of it when I took you, and I tried to keep my things where you couldn't get at 'em—and now you've took from me the one I cared for most of all—" She broke off in a short spasm of sobs that passed and left her more than ever like a shape of stone.

"If I'd 'a' listened to folks, you'd 'a' gone before now, and this wouldn't 'a' happened," she said; and gathering up the bits of broken glass she went out of the room as if she carried a dead body . . .

8.

When Ethan was called back to the farm by his father's illness his mother gave him, for his own use, a small room behind the untenanted "best parlour." Here he had nailed up shelves for his books, built himself a box-sofa out of boards and a mattress, laid out his papers on a kitchen-table, hung on the rough plaster wall an engraving of Abraham Lincoln and a calendar with "Thoughts from the Poets," and tried, with these meagre properties, to produce some likeness to the study of a "minister" who had been kind to him and lent him books when he was at Worcester. He still took refuge there in summer, but when Mattie came to live at the farm he had had to give her his stove, and consequently the room was uninhabitable for several months of the year.

To this retreat he descended as soon as the house was quiet, and Zeena's steady breathing from the bed had assured him that there was to be no sequel to the scene in the kitchen. After Zeena's departure he and Mattie had stood speechless, neither seeking to approach the other. Then the girl had returned to her task of clearing up the kitchen for the night and he had taken his lantern and gone on his usual round outside the house. The kitchen was empty when he came back to it; but his tobacco-pouch and pipe had been laid on the table, and under them was a scrap of paper torn from the back of a seedsman's catalogue, on which three words were written: "Don't trouble, Ethan."

Going into his cold dark "study" he placed the lantern on the table and, stooping to its light, read the message again and again. It was the first time that Mattie had ever written to him, and the possession of the paper gave him a strange new sense of her nearness; yet it deepened his anguish by reminding him that henceforth they would have no other way of communicating with each other. For the life of her smile, the warmth of her voice, only cold paper and dead words!

Confused motions of rebellion stormed in him. He was too young, too strong, too full of the sap of living, to submit so easily to the destruction of his hopes. Must he wear out all his years at the side of a bitter querulous woman? Other possibilities had been in him, possibilities sacrificed, one by one, to Zeena's narrow-mindedness and ignorance. And what good had come of it? She was a hundred times bitterer and more discontented than when he had married her: the one pleasure left her was to inflict pain on him. All the healthy instincts of self-defense rose up in him against such waste . . .

He bundled himself into his old coon-skin coat and lay down on the box-sofa to think. Under his cheek he felt a hard object with strange protuberances. It was a cushion which Zeena had made for him when they were engaged—the only piece of needlework he had ever seen her do. He flung it across the floor and propped his head against the wall . . .

He knew a case of a man over the mountain—a young fellow of about his own age—who had escaped from just such a life of misery by going West with the girl he cared for. His wife had divorced him, and he had married the girl and prospered. Ethan had seen the couple the summer before at Shadd's Falls, where they had come to visit relatives. They had a little girl with fair curls, who wore a gold locket and was dressed like a princess. The deserted wife had not done badly either. Her husband had given her the farm and she had managed to sell it, and with that and the alimony she had started a lunch-room at Bettsbridge and bloomed into activity and importance. Ethan was fired by the thought. Why should he not leave with Mattie the next day, instead of letting her go alone? He would hide his valise under the seat of the sleigh, and Zeena would suspect nothing till she went upstairs for her afternoon nap and found a letter on the bed . . .

His impulses were still near the surface, and he sprang up, re-lit the lantern, and sat down at the table. He rummaged in the drawer for a sheet of paper, found one, and began to write.

"Zeena, I've done all I could for you, and I don't see as it's been any use. I don't blame you, nor I don't blame myself. Maybe both of us will do better separate. I'm going to try my luck West, and you can sell the farm and mill, and keep the money—"

His pen paused on the word, which brought home to him the relentless conditions of his lot. If he gave the farm and mill to Zeena what would be left him to start his own life with? Once in the West he was sure of picking up work—he would not have feared to try his chance alone. But with Mattie depending on him the case was different. And what of Zeena's fate? Farm and mill were mortgaged to the limit of their value, and even if she found a purchaser—in itself an unlikely chance—it was doubtful if she could clear a thousand dollars on the sale. Meanwhile, how could she keep the farm going? It was only by incessant labour and personal supervision that Ethan drew a meagre living from his land, and his wife, even if she were in better health than she imagined, could never carry such a burden alone.

Well, she could go back to her people, then, and see what they would do for her. It was the fate she was forcing on Mattie—why not let her try it herself? By the time she had discovered his whereabouts, and brought suit for divorce, he would probably—wherever he was—be earning enough to pay her a sufficient alimony. And the alternative was to let Mattie go forth alone, with far less hope of ultimate provision . . .

He had scattered the contents of the table-drawer in his search for a sheet of paper, and as he took up his pen his eye fell on an old copy of the *Bettsbridge Eagle.* The advertising sheet was folded uppermost, and he read the seductive words: "Trips to the West: Reduced Rates."

He drew the lantern nearer and eagerly scanned the fares; then the paper fell from his hand and he pushed aside his unfinished letter. A moment ago he had wondered what he and Mattie were to live on when they reached the West; now he saw that he had not even the money to take her there. Borrowing was out of the question: six months before he had given his only security to raise funds for necessary repairs to the mill, and he knew that without security no one at Starkfield would lend him ten dollars. The inexorable facts closed in on him like prison-warders handcuffing a convict. There was no way out—none. He was a prisoner for life, and now his one ray of light was to be extinguished.

He crept back heavily to the sofa, stretching himself out with limbs so leaden that he felt as if they would never move again. Tears rose in his throat and slowly burned their way to his lids.

As he lay there, the window-pane that faced him, growing gradually lighter, inlaid upon the darkness a square of moon-suffused sky. A crooked tree-branch crossed it, a branch of the apple-tree under which, on summer evenings, he had sometimes found Mattie sitting when he came up from the mill. Slowly the rim of the rainy vapours caught fire and burnt away, and a pure moon swung into the blue. Ethan, rising on his elbow, watched the landscape whiten and shape itself under the sculpture of the moon. This was the night on which he was to have taken Mattie coasting, and there hung the lamp to light them! He looked out at the slopes bathed in lustre, the silver-edged darkness of the woods, the spectral purple of the hills against the sky, and it seemed as though all the beauty of the night had been poured out to mock his wretchedness . . .

He fell asleep, and when he woke the chill of the winter dawn was in the room. He felt cold and stiff and hungry, and ashamed of being hungry. He rubbed his eyes and went to the window. A red sun stood over the grey rim of the fields, behind trees that looked black and brittle. He said to himself: "This is Matt's last day," and tried to think what the place would be without her.

As he stood there he heard a step behind him and she entered.

"Oh, Ethan—were you here all night?"

She looked so small and pinched, in her poor dress, with the red scarf wound about her, and the cold light turning her paleness sallow, that Ethan stood before her without speaking.

"You must be frozen," she went on, fixing lustreless eyes on him.

He drew a step nearer. "How did you know I was here?"

"Because I heard you go down stairs again after I went to bed, and I listened all night, and you didn't come up."

All his tenderness rushed to his lips. He looked at her and said: "I'll come right along and make up the kitchen fire."

They went back to the kitchen, and he fetched the coal and kindlings and cleared out the stove for her, while she brought in the milk and the cold remains of the meat-pie. When warmth began to radiate from the stove, and the first ray of sunlight lay on the kitchen floor, Ethan's dark thoughts melted in the mellower air. The sight of Mattie going about her work as he had seen her on so many mornings made it seem impossible that she should ever cease to be a part of the scene. He said to himself that he had doubtless exaggerated the significance of Zeena's threats, and that she too, with the return of daylight, would come to a saner mood.

He went up to Mattie as she bent above the stove, and laid his hand on her arm. "I don't want you should trouble either," he said, looking down into her eyes with a smile.

She flushed up warmly and whispered back: "No, Ethan, I ain't going to trouble."

"I guess things'll straighten out," he added.

There was no answer but a quick throb of her lids, and he went on: "She ain't said anything this morning?"

"No. I haven't seen her yet."

"Don't you take any notice when you do."

With this injunction he left her and went out to the cow-barn. He saw Jotham Powell walking up the hill through the morning mist, and the familiar sight added to his growing conviction of security.

As the two men were clearing out the stalls Jotham rested on his pitch-fork to say: "Dan'l Byrne's goin' over to the Flats to-day noon, an' he c'd take Mattie's trunk along, and make it easier ridin' when I take her over in the sleigh."

Ethan looked at him blankly, and he continued: "Mis' Frome said the new girl'd be at the Flats at five, and I was to take Mattie then, so's 't she could ketch the six o'clock train for Stamford."

Ethan felt the blood drumming in his temples. He had to wait a moment before he could find voice to say: "Oh, it ain't so sure about Mattie's going—"

"That so?" said Jotham indifferently; and they went on with their work.

When they returned to the kitchen the two women were already at breakfast. Zeena had an air of unusual alertness and activity. She drank two cups of coffee and fed the cat with the scraps left in the pie-dish; then she rose from her seat and, walking over to the window, snipped two or three yellow leaves from the geraniums. "Aunt Martha's ain't got a faded leaf on 'em; but they pine away when they ain't cared for," she said reflectively. Then she turned to Jotham and asked: "What time'd you say Dan'l Byrne'd be along?"

The hired man threw a hesitating glance at Ethan. "Round about noon," he said.

Zeena turned to Mattie. "That trunk of yours is too heavy for the sleigh, and Dan'l Byrne'll be round to take it over to the Flats," she said.

"I'm much obliged to you, Zeena," said Mattie.

"I'd like to go over things with you first," Zeena continued in an unperturbed voice. "I know there's a huckabuck towel missing; and I can't make out what you done with that match-safe 't used to stand behind the stuffed owl in the parlour."

She went out, followed by Mattie, and when the men were alone Jotham said to his employer: "I guess I better let Dan'l come round, then."

Ethan finished his usual morning tasks about the house and barn; then he said to Jotham: "I'm going down to Starkfield. Tell them not to wait dinner."

The passion of rebellion had broken out in him again. That which had seemed incredible in the sober light of day had really come to pass, and he was to assist as a helpless spectator at Mattie's banishment. His manhood was humbled by the part he was compelled to play and by the thought of what Mattie must think of him. Confused impulses struggled in him as he strode along to the village. He had made up his mind to do something, but he did not know what it would be.

The early mist had vanished and the fields lay like a silver shield under the sun. It was one of the days when the glitter of winter shines through a pale haze of spring. Every yard of the road was alive with Mattie's presence, and there was hardly a branch against the sky or a tangle of brambles on the bank in which some bright shred of memory was not caught. Once, in the stillness, the call of a bird in a mountain ash was so like her laughter that his heart tightened and then grew large; and all these things made him see that something must be done at once.

Suddenly it occurred to him that Andrew Hale, who was a kind-hearted man, might be induced to reconsider his refusal and advance a small sum on the lumber if he were told that Zeena's ill-health made it necessary to hire a servant. Hale, after all, knew enough of Ethan's situation to make it possible for the latter to renew his appeal without too much loss of pride; and, moreover, how much did pride count in the ebullition of passions in his breast?

The more he considered his plan the more hopeful it seemed. If he could get Mrs. Hale's ear he felt certain of success, and with fifty dollars in his pocket nothing could keep him from Mattie . . .

His first object was to reach Starkfield before Hale had started for his work; he knew the carpenter had a job down the Corbury road and was likely to leave his house early. Ethan's long strides grew more rapid with the accelerated beat of his thoughts, and as he reached the foot of School House Hill he caught sight of Hale's sleigh in the distance. He hurried forward to meet it, but as it drew nearer he saw that it was driven by the carpenter's youngest boy and that the figure at his side, looking like a large upright cocoon in spectacles, was that of Mrs. Hale. Ethan signed to them to stop, and Mrs. Hale leaned forward, her pink wrinkles twinkling with benevolence.

"Mr. Hale? Why, yes, you'll find him down home now. He ain't going to his work this forenoon. He woke up with a touch o' lumbago, and I just made him put on one of old Dr. Kidder's plasters and set right up into the fire."

Beaming maternally on Ethan, she bent over to add: "I on'y just heard from Mr. Hale 'bout Zeena's going over to Bettsbridge to see that new doctor. I'm real sorry she's feeling so bad again! I hope he thinks he can do something for her? I don't know anybody round here's had more sickness than Zeena. I always tell Mr. Hale I don't know what she'd 'a' done if she hadn't 'a' had you to look after her; and I used to say the same thing 'bout your mother. You've had an awful mean time, Ethan Frome."

She gave him a last nod of sympathy while her son chirped to the horse; and Ethan, as she drove off, stood in the middle of the road and stared after the retreating sleigh.

It was a long time since any one had spoken to him as kindly as Mrs. Hale. Most people were either indifferent to his troubles, or disposed to think it natural that a young fellow of his age should have carried without repining the burden of three crippled lives. But Mrs. Hale had said, "You've had an awful mean time, Ethan Frome," and he felt less alone with his misery. If the Hales were sorry for him they would surely respond to his appeal . . .

He started down the road toward their house, but at the end of a few yards he pulled up sharply, the blood in his face. For the first time, in the light of the words he had just heard, he saw what he was about to do. He was planning to take advantage of the Hales' sympathy to obtain money from them on false pretences. That was a plain statement of the cloudy purpose which had driven him in headlong to Starkfield.

With the sudden perception of the point to which his madness had carried him, the madness fell and he saw his life before him as it was. He was a poor man, the husband of a sickly woman, whom his desertion would leave alone and destitute; and even if he had had the heart to desert her he could have done so only by deceiving two kindly people who had pitied him.

He turned and walked slowly back to the farm.

9.

At the kitchen door Daniel Byrne sat in his sleigh behind a big-boned grey who pawed the snow and swung his long head restlessly from side to side.

Ethan went into the kitchen and found his wife by the stove. Her head was wrapped in her shawl, and she was reading a book called "Kidney Troubles and Their Cure" on which he had had to pay extra postage only a few days before.

Zeena did not move or look up when he entered, and after a moment he asked: "Where's Mattie?"

Without lifting her eyes from the page she replied: "I presume she's getting down her trunk."

The blood rushed to his face. "Getting down her trunk—alone?"

"Jotham Powell's down in the wood-lot, and Dan'l Byrne says he darsn't leave that horse," she returned.

Her husband, without stopping to hear the end of the phrase, had left the kitchen and sprung up the stairs. The door of Mattie's room was shut, and he wavered a moment on the landing. "Matt," he said in a low voice; but there was no answer, and he put his hand on the door-knob.

He had never been in her room except once, in the early summer, when he had gone there to plaster up a leak in the eaves, but he remembered exactly how everything had looked: the red-and-white quilt on her narrow bed, the pretty pin-cushion on the chest of drawers, and over it the enlarged photograph of her mother, in an oxydized frame, with a bunch of dyed grasses at the back. Now these and all other tokens of her presence had vanished and the room looked as bare and comfortless as when Zeena had shown her into it on the day of her arrival. In the middle of the floor stood her trunk, and on the trunk she sat in her Sunday dress, her back turned to the door and her face in her hands. She had not heard Ethan's call because she was sobbing and she did not hear his step till he stood close behind her and laid his hands on her shoulders.

"Matt—oh, don't—oh, *Matt!*"

She started up, lifting her wet face to his. "Ethan—I thought I wasn't ever going to see you again!"

He took her in his arms, pressing her close, and with a trembling hand smoothed away the hair from her forehead.

"Not see me again? What do you mean?"

She sobbed out: "Jotham said you told him we wasn't to wait dinner for you, and I thought—"

"You thought I meant to cut it?" he finished for her grimly.

She clung to him without answering, and he laid his lips on her hair, which was soft yet springy, like certain mosses on warm slopes, and had the faint woody fragrance of fresh sawdust in the sun.

Through the door they heard Zeena's voice calling out from below: "Dan'l Byrne says you better hurry up if you want him to take that trunk."

They drew apart with stricken faces. Words of resistance rushed to Ethan's lips and died there. Mattie found her handkerchief and dried her eyes; then, bending down, she took hold of a handle of the trunk.

Ethan put her aside. "You let go, Matt," he ordered her.

She answered: "It takes two to coax it round the corner"; and submitting to this argument he grasped the other handle, and together they manœuvred the heavy trunk out to the landing.

"Now let go," he repeated; then he shouldered the trunk and carried it down the stairs and across the passage to the kitchen. Zeena, who had gone back to her seat by the stove, did not lift her head from her book as he passed. Mattie followed him out of the door and helped him to lift the trunk into the back of the sleigh. When it was in place they stood side by side on the door-step, watching Daniel Byrne plunge off behind his fidgety horse.

It seemed to Ethan that his heart was bound with cords which an unseen hand was tightening with every tick of the clock. Twice he opened his lips to speak to Mattie and found no breath. At length, as she turned to re-enter the house, he laid a detaining hand on her.

"I'm going to drive you over, Matt," he whispered.

She murmured back: "I think Zeena wants I should go with Jotham."

"I'm going to drive you over," he repeated; and she went into the kitchen without answering.

At dinner Ethan could not eat. If he lifted his eyes they rested on Zeena's pinched face, and the corners of her straight lips seemed to quiver away into a smile. She ate well, declaring that the mild weather made her feel better, and pressed a second helping of beans on Jotham Powell, whose wants she generally ignored.

Mattie, when the meal was over, went about her usual task of clearing the table and washing up the dishes. Zeena, after feeding the cat, had returned to her rocking-chair by the stove, and Jotham Powell, who always lingered last, reluctantly pushed back his chair and moved toward the door.

On the threshold he turned back to say to Ethan: "What time'll I come round for Mattie?"

Ethan was standing near the window, mechanically filling his pipe while he watched Mattie move to and fro. He answered: "You needn't come round; I'm going to drive her over myself."

He saw the rise of the colour in Mattie's averted cheek, and the quick lifting of Zeena's head.

"I want you should stay here this afternoon, Ethan," his wife said. "Jotham can drive Mattie over."

Mattie flung an imploring glance at him, but he repeated curtly: "I'm going to drive her over myself."

Zeena continued in the same even tone: "I wanted you should stay and fix up that stove in Mattie's room afore the girl gets here. It ain't been drawing right for nigh on a month now."

Ethan's voice rose indignantly. "If it was good enough for Mattie I guess it's good enough for a hired girl."

"That girl that's coming told me she was used to a house where they had a furnace," Zeena persisted with the same monotonous mildness.

"She'd better ha' stayed there then," he flung back at her; and turning to Mattie he added in a hard voice: "You be ready by three, Matt; I've got business at Corbury."

Jotham Powell had started for the barn, and Ethan strode down after him aflame with anger. The pulses in his temples throbbed and a fog was in his eyes. He went about his task without knowing what force directed him, or whose hands and feet were fulfilling its orders. It was not till he led out the sorrel and backed him between the shafts of the sleigh that he once more became conscious of what he was doing. As he passed the bridle over the horse's head, and wound the traces around the shafts, he remembered the day when he had made the same preparations in order to drive over and meet his wife's cousin at the Flats. It was little more than a year ago, on just such a soft afternoon, with a "feel" of spring in the air. The sorrel, turning the same big ringed eye on him, nuzzled the palm of his hand in the same way; and one by one all the days between rose up and stood before him . . .

He flung the bearskin into the sleigh, climbed to the seat, and drove up to the house. When he entered the kitchen it was empty, but Mattie's bag and shawl lay ready by the door. He went to the foot of the stairs and listened. No sound reached him from above, but presently he thought he heard some one moving about in his deserted study, and pushing open the door he saw Mattie, in her hat and jacket, standing with her back to him near the table.

She started at his approach and turning quickly, said: "Is it time?"

"What are you doing here, Matt?" he asked her.

She looked at him timidly. "I was just taking a look round—that's all," she answered, with a wavering smile.

They went back into the kitchen without speaking, and Ethan picked up her bag and shawl.

"Where's Zeena?" he asked.

"She went upstairs right after dinner. She said she had those shooting pains again, and didn't want to be disturbed."

"Didn't she say good-bye to you?"

"No. That was all she said."

Ethan, looking slowly about the kitchen, said to himself with a shudder that in a few hours he would be returning to it alone. Then the sense of unreality overcame him once more, and he could not bring himself to believe that Mattie stood there for the last time before him.

"Come on," he said almost gaily, opening the door and putting her bag into the sleigh. He sprang to his seat and bent over to tuck the rug about her as she slipped into the place at his side. "Now then, go 'long," he said, with a shake of the reins that sent the sorrel placidly jogging down the hill.

"We got lots of time for a good ride, Matt!" he cried, seeking her hand beneath the fur and pressing it in his. His face tingled and he felt dizzy, as if he had stopped in at the Starkfield saloon on a zero day for a drink.

At the gate, instead of making for Starkfield, he turned the sorrel to the right, up the Bettsbridge road. Mattie sat silent, giving no sign of surprise; but after a moment she said: "Are you going round by Shadow Pond?"

He laughed and answered: "I knew you'd know!"

She drew closer under the bearskin, so that, looking sideways around his coat-sleeve, he could just catch the tip of her nose and a blown brown wave of hair. They drove slowly up the road between fields glistening under the pale sun, and then bent to the right down a lane edged with spruce and larch. Ahead of them, a long way off, a range of hills stained by mottlings of black forest flowed away in round white curves against the sky. The lane passed into a pine-wood with boles reddening in the afternoon sun and delicate blue shadows on the snow. As they entered it the breeze fell and a warm stillness seemed to drop from the branches with the dropping needles. Here the snow was so pure that the tiny tracks of wood-animals had left on it intricate lace-like patterns, and the bluish cones caught in its surface stood out like ornaments of bronze.

Ethan drove on in silence till they reached a part of the wood where the pines were more widely spaced, then he drew up and helped Mattie to get out of the sleigh. They passed between the aromatic trunks, the snow breaking crisply under their feet, till they came to a small sheet of water with steep wooded sides. Across its frozen surface, from the farther bank, a single hill rising against the western sun threw the long conical shadow which gave the lake its name. It was a shy secret spot, full of the same dumb melancholy that Ethan felt in his heart.

He looked up and down the little pebbly beach till his eye lit on a fallen tree-trunk half submerged in snow.

"There's where we sat at the picnic," he reminded her.

The entertainment of which he spoke was one of the few that they had taken part in together: a "church picnic" which, on a long afternoon of the preceding summer, had filled the retired place with merry-making. Mattie had begged him to go with her but he had refused. Then, toward sunset, coming down from the mountain where he had been felling timber, he had been caught by some stray revellers and drawn into the group by the lake, where Mattie, encircled by facetious youths, and bright as a blackberry under her spreading hat, was brewing coffee over a gipsy fire. He remembered the shyness he had felt at approaching her in his uncouth clothes, and then the lighting up of her face, and the way she had broken through the group to come to him with a cup in her hand. They had sat for a few minutes on the fallen log by the pond, and she had missed her gold locket, and set the young men searching for it; and it was Ethan who had spied it in the moss. . . . That was all; but all their intercourse had been made up of just such inarticulate flashes, when they seemed to come suddenly upon happiness as if they had surprised a butterfly in the winter woods . . .

"It was right there I found your locket," he said, pushing his foot into a dense tuft of blueberry bushes.

"I never saw anybody with such sharp eyes!" she answered.

She sat down on the tree-trunk in the sun and he sat down beside her.

"You were as pretty as a picture in that pink hat," he said.

She laughed with pleasure. "Oh, I guess it was the hat!" she rejoined.

They had never before avowed their inclination so openly, and Ethan, for a moment, had the illusion that he was a free man, wooing the girl he meant to marry. He looked at her hair and longed to touch it again, and to tell her that it smelt of the woods; but he had never learned to say such things.

Suddenly she rose to her feet and said: "We mustn't stay here any longer."

He continued to gaze at her vaguely, only half-roused from his dream. "There's plenty of time," he answered.

They stood looking at each other as if the eyes of each were straining to absorb and hold fast the other's image. There were things he had to say to her before they parted, but he could not say them in that place of summer memories, and he turned and followed her in silence to the sleigh. As they drove away the sun sank behind the hill and the pine-boles turned from red to gray.

By a devious track between the fields they wound back to the Starkfield road. Under the open sky the light was still clear, with a reflection of cold red on the eastern hills. The clumps of trees in the snow seemed to draw together in ruffled lumps, like birds with their heads under their wings; and the sky, as it paled, rose higher, leaving the earth more alone.

As they turned into the Starkfield road Ethan said: "Matt, what do you mean to do?"

She did not answer at once, but at length she said: "I'll try to get a place in a store."

"You know you can't do it. The bad air and the standing all day nearly killed you before."

"I'm a lot stronger than I was before I came to Starkfield."

"And now you're going to throw away all the good it's done you!"

There seemed to be no answer to this, and again they drove on for a while without speaking. With every yard of the way some spot where they had stood, and laughed together or been silent, clutched at Ethan and dragged him back.

"Isn't there any of your father's folks could help you?"

"There isn't any of 'em I'd ask."

He lowered his voice to say: "You know there's nothing I wouldn't do for you if I could."

"I know there isn't."

"But I can't—"

She was silent, but he felt a slight tremor in the shoulder against his.

"Oh, Matt," he broke out, "if I could ha' gone with you now I'd ha' done it—"

She turned to him, pulling a scrap of paper from her breast. "Ethan—I found this," she stammered. Even in the failing light he saw it was the letter to his wife that he had begun the night before and forgotten to destroy. Through his astonishment there ran a fierce thrill of joy. "Matt—" he cried; "if I could ha' done it, would you?"

"Oh, Ethan, Ethan—what's the use?" With a sudden movement she tore the letter in shreds and sent them fluttering off into the snow.

"Tell me, Matt! Tell me!" he adjured her.

She was silent for a moment; then she said, in such a low tone that he had to stoop his head to hear her: "I used to think of it sometimes, summer nights, when the moon was so bright I couldn't sleep."

His heart reeled with the sweetness of it. "As long ago as that?"

She answered, as if the date had long been fixed for her: "The first time was at Shadow Pond."

"Was that why you gave me my coffee before the others?"

"I don't know. Did I? I was dreadfully put out when you wouldn't go to the picnic with me; and then, when I saw you coming down the road, I thought maybe you'd gone home that way o' purpose; and that made me glad."

They were silent again. They had reached the point where the road dipped to the hollow by Ethan's mill and as they descended the darkness descended with them, dropping down like a black veil from the heavy hemlock boughs.

"I'm tied hand and foot, Matt. There isn't a thing I can do," he began again.

"You must write to me sometimes, Ethan."

"Oh, what good'll writing do? I want to put my hand out and touch you. I want to do for you and care for you. I want to be there when you're sick and when you're lonesome."

"You mustn't think but what I'll do all right."

"You won't need me, you mean? I suppose you'll marry!"

"Oh, Ethan!" she cried.

"I don't know how it is you make me feel, Matt. I'd a'most rather have you dead than that!"

"Oh, I wish I was, I wish I was!" she sobbed.

The sound of her weeping shook him out of his dark anger, and he felt ashamed.

"Don't let's talk that way," he whispered.

"Why shouldn't we, when it's true? I've been wishing it every minute of the day."

"Matt! You be quiet! Don't you say it."

"There's never anybody been good to me but you."

"Don't say that either, when I can't lift a hand for you!"

"Yes; but it's true just the same."

They had reached the top of School House Hill and Starkfield lay below them in the twilight. A cutter, mounting the road from the village, passed them by in a joyous flutter of bells, and they straightened themselves and looked ahead with rigid faces. Along the main street lights had begun to shine from the house-fronts and stray figures were turning in here and there at the gates. Ethan, with a touch of his whip, roused the sorrel to a languid trot.

As they drew near the end of the village the cries of children reached them, and they saw a knot of boys, with sleds behind them, scattering across the open space before the church.

"I guess this'll be their last coast for a day or two," Ethan said, looking up at the mild sky.

Mattie was silent, and he added: "We were to have gone down last night."

Still she did not speak and, prompted by an obscure desire to help himself and her through their miserable last hour, he went on discursively: "Ain't it funny we haven't been down together but just that once last winter?"

She answered: "It wasn't often I got down to the village."

"That's so," he said.

They had reached the crest of the Corbury road, and between the indistinct white glimmer of the church and the black curtain of the Varnum spruces the slope stretched away below them without a sled on its length. Some erratic impulse prompted Ethan to say: "How'd you like me to take you down now?"

She forced a laugh. "Why, there isn't time!"

"There's all the time we want. Come along!" His one desire now was to postpone the moment of turning the sorrel toward the Flats.

"But the girl," she faltered. "The girl'll be waiting at the station."

"Well, let her wait. You'd have to if she didn't. Come!"

The note of authority in his voice seemed to subdue her, and when he had jumped from the sleigh she let him help her out, saying only, with a vague feint of reluctance: "But there isn't a sled round anywheres."

"Yes, there is! Right over there under the spruces."

He threw the bearskin over the sorrel, who stood passively by the roadside, hanging a meditative head. Then he caught Mattie's hand and drew her after him toward the sled.

She seated herself obediently and he took his place behind her, so close that her hair brushed his face. "All right, Matt?" he called out, as if the width of the road had been between them.

She turned her head to say: "It's dreadfully dark. Are you sure you can see?"

He laughed contemptuously: "I could go down this coast with my eyes tied!" and she laughed with him, as if she liked his audacity. Nevertheless he sat still a moment, straining his eyes down the long hill, for it was the most confusing hour of the evening, the hour when the last clearness from the upper sky is merged with the rising night in a blur that disguises landmarks and falsifies distances.

"Now!" he cried.

The sled started with a bound, and they flew on through the dusk, gathering smoothness and speed as they went, with the hollow night opening out below them and the air singing by like an organ. Mattie sat perfectly still, but as they reached the bend at the foot of the hill, where the big elm thrust out a deadly elbow, he fancied that she shrank a little closer.

"Don't be scared, Matt!" he cried exultantly, as they spun safely past it and flew down the second slope; and when they reached the level ground beyond, and the speed of the sled began to slacken, he heard her give a little laugh of glee.

They sprang off and started to walk back up the hill. Ethan dragged the sled with one hand and passed the other through Mattie's arm.

"Were you scared I'd run you into the elm?" he asked with a boyish laugh.

"I told you I was never scared with you," she answered.

The strange exaltation of his mood had brought on one of his rare fits of boastfulness. "It *is* a tricky place, though. The least swerve, and we'd never ha' come up again. But I can measure distances to a hair's-breadth—always could."

She murmured: "I always say you've got the surest eye . . ."

Deep silence had fallen with the starless dusk, and they leaned on each other without speaking; but at every step of their climb Ethan said to himself: "It's the last time we'll ever walk together."

They mounted slowly to the top of the hill. When they were abreast of the church he stooped his head to her to ask: "Are you tired?" and she answered, breathing quickly: "It was splendid!"

With a pressure of his arm he guided her toward the Norway spruces. "I guess this sled must be Ned Hale's. Anyhow I'll leave it where I found it." He drew the sled up to the Varnum gate and rested it against the fence. As he raised himself he suddenly felt Mattie close to him among the shadows.

"Is this where Ned and Ruth kissed each other?" she whispered breathlessly, and flung her arms about him. Her lips, groping for his, swept over his face, and he held her fast in a rapture of surprise.

"Good-bye—good-bye," she stammered, and kissed him again.

"Oh, Matt, I can't let you go!" broke from him in the same old cry.

She freed herself from his hold and he heard her sobbing. "Oh, I can't go either!" she wailed.

"Matt! What'll we do? What'll we do?"

They clung to each other's hands like children, and her body shook with desperate sobs.

Through the stillness they heard the church clock striking five.

"Oh, Ethan, it's time!" she cried.

He drew her back to him. "Time for what? You don't suppose I'm going to leave you now?"

"If I missed my train where'd I go?"

"Where are you going if you catch it?"

She stood silent, her hands lying cold and relaxed in his.

"What's the good of either of us going anywheres without the other one now?" he said.

She remained motionless, as if she had not heard him. Then she snatched her hands from his, threw her arms about his neck, and pressed a sudden drenched cheek against his face. "Ethan! Ethan! I want you to take me down again!"

"Down where?"

"The coast. Right off," she panted. "So 't we'll never come up any more."

"Matt! What on earth do you mean?"

She put her lips close against his ear to say: "Right into the big elm. You said you could. So 't we'd never have to leave each other any more."

"Why, what are you talking of? You're crazy!"

"I'm not crazy; but I will be if I leave you."

"Oh, Matt, Matt—" he groaned.

She tightened her fierce hold about his neck. Her face lay close to his face.

"Ethan, where'll I go if I leave you? I don't know how to get along alone. You said so yourself just now. Nobody but you was ever good to me. And there'll be that strange girl in the house . . . and she'll sleep in my bed, where I used to lay nights and listen to hear you come up the stairs . . ."

The words were like fragments torn from his heart. With them came the hated vision of the house he was going back to—of the stairs he would have to go up every night, of the woman who would wait for him there. And the sweetness of Mattie's avowal, the wild wonder of knowing at last that all that had happened to him had happened to her too, made the other vision more abhorrent, the other life more intolerable to return to . . .

Her pleadings still came to him between short sobs, but he no longer heard what she was saying. Her hat had slipped back and he was stroking her hair. He wanted to get the feeling of it into his hand, so that it would sleep there like a seed in winter. Once he found her mouth again, and they seemed to be by the pond together in the burning August sun. But his cheek touched hers, and it was cold and full of weeping, and he saw the road to the Flats under the night and heard the whistle of the train up the line.

The spruces swathed them in blackness and silence. They might have been in their coffins underground. He said to himself: "Perhaps it'll feel like this . . ." and then again: "After this I sha'n't feel anything . . ."

Suddenly he heard the old sorrel whinny across the road, and thought: "He's wondering why he doesn't get his supper . . ."

"Come," Mattie whispered, tugging at his hand.

Her sombre violence constrained him: she seemed the embodied instrument of fate. He pulled the sled out, blinking like a night-bird as he passed from the shade of the spruces into the transparent dusk of the open. The slope below them was deserted. All Starkfield was at supper, and not a figure crossed the open space before the church. The sky, swollen with the clouds that announce a thaw, hung as low as before a summer storm. He strained his eyes through the dimness, and they seemed less keen, less capable than usual.

He took his seat on the sled and Mattie instantly placed herself in front of him. Her hat had fallen into the snow and his lips were in her hair. He stretched out his legs, drove his heels into the road to keep the sled from slipping forward, and bent her head back between his hands. Then suddenly he sprang up again.

"Get up," he ordered her.

It was the tone she always heeded, but she cowered down in her seat, repeating vehemently: "No, no, no!"

"Get up!"

"Why?"

"I want to sit in front."

"No, no! How can you steer in front?"

"I don't have to. We'll follow the track."

They spoke in smothered whispers, as though the night were listening.

"Get up! Get up!" he urged her; but she kept on repeating: "Why do you want to sit in front?"

"Because I—because I want to feel you holding me," he stammered, and dragged her to her feet.

The answer seemed to satisfy her, or else she yielded to the power of his voice. He bent down, feeling in the obscurity for the glassy slide worn by preceding coasters, and placed the runners carefully between its edges. She waited while he seated himself with crossed legs in the front of the sled; then she crouched quickly down at his back and clasped her arms about him. Her breath in his neck set him shuddering again, and he almost sprang from his seat. But in a flash he remembered the alternative. She was right: this was better than parting. He leaned back and drew her mouth to his . . .

Just as they started he heard the sorrel's whinny again, and the familiar wistful call, and all the confused images it brought with it, went with him down the first reach of the road. Half-way down there was a sudden drop, then a rise, and after that another long delirious descent. As they took wing for this it seemed to him that they were flying indeed, flying far up into the cloudy night, with Starkfield immeasurably below them falling away like a speck in space . . . Then the big elm shot up ahead, lying in wait for them at the bend of the road, and he said between his teeth: "We can fetch it; I know we can fetch it—"

As they flew toward the tree Mattie pressed her arms tighter, and her blood seemed to be in his veins. Once or twice the sled swerved a little under them. He slanted his body to keep it headed for the elm, repeating to himself again and again: "I know we can fetch it"; and little phrases she had spoken ran through his head and danced before him on the air. The big tree loomed bigger and closer, and as they bore down on it he thought: "It's waiting for us: it seems to know." But suddenly his wife's face, with twisted monstrous lineaments, thrust itself between him and his goal, and he made an instinctive movement to brush it aside. The sled swerved in response, but he righted it again, kept it straight, and drove down on the black projecting mass. There was a last instant when the air shot past him like millions of fiery wires; and then the elm . . .

The sky was still thick, but looking straight up he saw a single star, and tried vaguely to reckon whether it was Sirius, or—or—The effort tired him too much, and he closed his heavy lids and thought that he would sleep . . . The stillness was so profound that he heard a little animal twittering somewhere near by under the snow. It made a small frightened *cheep* like a field mouse, and he wondered languidly if it were hurt. Then he understood that it must be in pain: pain so excruciating that he seemed, mysteriously, to feel it shooting through his own body. He tried in vain to roll over in the direction of the sound, and stretched his left arm out across the snow. And now it was as though he felt rather than heard the twittering; it seemed to be under his palm, which rested on something soft and springy. The thought of the animal's suffering was intolerable to him and he struggled to raise himself, and could not because a rock, or some huge mass, seemed to be lying on him. But he continued to finger about cautiously with his left hand, thinking he might get hold of the little creature and help it; and all at once he knew that the soft thing he had touched was Mattie's hair and that his hand was on her face.

He dragged himself to his knees, the monstrous load on him moving with him as he moved, and his hand went over and over her face, and he felt that the twittering came from her lips . . .

He got his face down close to hers, with his ear to her mouth, and in the darkness he saw her eyes open and heard her say his name.

"Oh, Matt, I thought we'd fetched it," he moaned; and far off, up the hill, he heard the sorrel whinny, and thought: "I ought to be getting him his feed . . ."

The querulous drone ceased as I entered Frome's kitchen, and of the two women sitting there I could not tell which had been the speaker.

One of them, on my appearing, raised her tall bony figure from her seat, not as if to welcome me—for she threw me no more than a brief glance of surprise—but simply to set about preparing the meal which Frome's absence had delayed. A slatternly calico wrapper hung from her shoulders and the wisps of her thin grey hair were drawn away from a high forehead and fastened at the back by a broken comb. She had pale opaque eyes which revealed nothing and reflected nothing, and her narrow lips were of the same sallow colour as her face.

The other woman was much smaller and slighter. She sat huddled in an arm-chair near the stove, and when I came in she turned her head quickly toward me, without the least corresponding movement of her body. Her hair was as grey as her companion's, her face as bloodless and shrivelled, but amber-tinted, with swarthy shadows sharpening the nose and hollowing the temples. Under her shapeless dress her body kept its limp immobility, and her dark eyes had the bright witch-like stare that disease of the spine sometimes gives.

Even for that part of the country the kitchen was a poor-looking place. With the exception of the dark-eyed woman's chair, which looked like a soiled relic of luxury bought at a country auction, the furniture was of the roughest kind. Three coarse china plates and a broken-nosed milk-jug had been set on a greasy table scored with knife-cuts, and a couple of straw-bottomed chairs and a kitchen dresser of unpainted pine stood meagrely against the plaster walls.

"My, it's cold here! The fire must be 'most out," Frome said, glancing about him apologetically as he followed me in.

The tall woman, who had moved away from us toward the dresser, took no notice; but the other, from her cushioned niche, answered complainingly, in a high thin voice: "It's on'y just been made up this very minute. Zeena fell asleep and slep' ever so long, and I thought I'd be frozen stiff before I could wake her up and get her to 'tend to it."

I knew then that it was she who had been speaking when we entered.

Her companion, who was just coming back to the table with the remains of a cold mince-pie in a battered pie-dish, set down her unappetising burden without appearing to hear the accusation brought against her.

Frome stood hesitatingly before her as she advanced; then he looked at me and said: "This is my wife, Mis' Frome." After another interval he added, turning toward the figure in the arm-chair: "And this is Miss Mattie Silver . . ."

Mrs. Hale, tender soul, had pictured me as lost in the Flats and buried under a snow-drift; and so lively was her satisfaction on seeing me safely restored to her the next morning that I felt my peril had caused me to advance several degrees in her favour.

Great was her amazement, and that of old Mrs. Varnum, on learning that Ethan Frome's old horse had carried me to and from Corbury Junction through the worst blizzard of the winter; greater still their surprise when they heard that his master had taken me in for the night.

Beneath their wondering exclamations I felt a secret curiosity to know what impressions I had received from my night in the Frome household, and divined that the best way of breaking down their reserve was to let them try to penetrate mine. I therefore confined myself to saying, in a matter-of-fact tone, that I had been received with great kindness, and that Frome had made a bed for me in a room on the ground floor which seemed in happier days to have been fitted up as a kind of writing-room or study.

"Well," Mrs. Hale mused, "in such a storm I suppose he felt he couldn't do less than take you in—but I guess it went hard with Ethan. I don't believe but what you're the only stranger has set foot in that house for over twenty years. He's that proud he don't even like his oldest friends to go there; and I don't know as any do, any more, except myself and the doctor . . ."

"You still go there, Mrs. Hale?" I ventured.

"I used to go a good deal after the accident, when I was first married; but after awhile I got to think it made 'em feel worse to see us. And then one thing and another came, and my own troubles . . . But I generally make out to drive over there round about New Year's, and once in the summer. Only I always try to pick a day when Ethan's off somewheres. It's bad enough to see the two women sitting there—but *his* face, when he looks round that bare place, just kills me . . . You see, I can look back and call it up in his mother's day, before their troubles."

Old Mrs. Varnum, by this time, had gone up to bed, and her daughter and I were sitting alone, after supper, in the austere seclusion of the horse-hair parlour. Mrs. Hale glanced at me tentatively, as though trying to see how much footing my conjectures gave her; and I guessed that if she had kept silence till now it was because she had been waiting, through all the years, for some one who should see what she alone had seen.

I waited to let her trust in me gather strength before I said: "Yes, it's pretty bad, seeing all three of them there together."

She drew her mild brows into a frown of pain. "It was just awful from the beginning. I was here in the house when they were carried up—they laid Mattie Silver in the room you're in. She and I were great friends, and she was to have been my bridesmaid in the spring . . . When she came to I went up to her and stayed all night. They gave her things to quiet her, and she didn't know much till to'rd morning, and then all of a sudden she woke up just like herself, and looked straight at me out of her big eyes, and said . . . Oh, I don't know why I'm telling you all this," Mrs. Hale broke off, crying.

She took off her spectacles, wiped the moisture from them, and put them on again with an unsteady hand. "It got about the next day," she went on, "that Zeena Frome had sent Mattie off in a hurry because she had a hired girl coming, and the folks here could never rightly tell what she and Ethan were doing that night coasting, when they'd ought to have been on their way to the Flats to ketch the train . . . I never knew myself what Zeena thought—I don't to this day. Nobody knows Zeena's thoughts. Anyhow, when she heard o' the accident she came right in and stayed with Ethan over to the minister's, where they'd carried him. And as soon as the doctors said that Mattie could be moved, Zeena sent for her and took her back to the farm."

"And there she's been ever since?"

Mrs. Hale answered simply: "There was nowhere else for her to go"; and my heart tightened at the thought of the hard compulsions of the poor.

"Yes, there she's been," Mrs. Hale continued, "and Zeena's done for her, and done for Ethan, as good as she could. It was a miracle, considering how sick she was—but she seemed to be raised right up just when the call came to her. Not as she's ever given up doctoring, and she's had sick spells right along; but she's had the strength given her to care for those two for over twenty years, and before the accident came she thought she couldn't even care for herself."

Mrs. Hale paused a moment, and I remained silent, plunged in the vision of what her words evoked. "It's horrible for them all," I murmured.

"Yes: it's pretty bad. And they ain't any of 'em easy people either. Mattie *was,* before the accident; I never knew a sweeter nature. But she's suffered too much—that's what I always say when folks tell me how she's soured. And Zeena, she was always cranky. Not but what she bears with Mattie wonderful—I've seen that myself. But sometimes the two of them get going at each other, and then Ethan's face'd break your heart . . . When I see that, I think it's *him* that suffers most . . . anyhow it ain't Zeena, because she ain't got the time . . . It's a pity, though," Mrs. Hale ended, sighing, "that they're all shut up there'n that one kitchen. In the summertime, on pleasant days, they move Mattie into the parlour, or out in the door-yard, and that makes it easier . . . but winters there's the fires to be thought of; and there ain't a dime to spare up at the Fromes'."

Mrs. Hale drew a deep breath, as though her memory were eased of its long burden, and she had no more to say; but suddenly an impulse of complete avowal seized her.

She took off her spectacles again, leaned toward me across the bead-work table-cover, and went on with lowered voice: "There was one day, about a week after the accident, when they all thought Mattie couldn't live. Well, I say it's a pity she *did.* I said it right out to our minister once, and he was shocked at me. Only he wasn't with me that morning when she first came to . . . And I say, if she'd ha' died, Ethan might ha' lived; and the way they are now, I don't see's there's much difference between the Fromes up at the farm and the Fromes down in the graveyard; 'cept that down there they're all quiet, and the women have got to hold their tongues."

SOURCE: Edith Wharton. *Ethan Frome*. New York: Charles Scribner's Sons, 1911.

CARL SANDBURG

In the mode of Walt Whitman, the popular poet Carl Sandburg (1878–1967) celebrated Chicago and American places.

Chicago (1914)

Hog Butcher for the World,
Tool Maker, Stacker of Wheat,
Player with Railroads and the Nation's Freight Handler;
Stormy, husky, brawling,
City of the Big Shoulders:

They tell me you are wicked and I believe them, for I have seen
your painted women under the gas lamps luring the farm boys.
And they tell me you are crooked and I answer: Yes, it is true I
have seen the gunman kill and go free to kill again.
And they tell me you are brutal and my reply is: On the faces of
women and children I have seen the marks of wanton hunger.
And having answered so I turn once more to those who sneer at
this my city, and I give them back the sneer and say to them:
Come and show me another city with lifted head singing so
proud to be alive and coarse and strong and cunning.
Flinging magnetic curses amid the toil of piling job on job, here
is a tall bold slugger set vivid against the little soft cities;
Fierce as a dog with tongue lapping for action, cunning as a
savage pitted against the wilderness,
Bareheaded,
Shoveling,
Wrecking,

Planning,
Building, breaking, rebuilding,
Under the smoke, dust all over his mouth, laughing with white teeth,
Under the terrible burden of destiny laughing as a young man laughs,
Laughing even as an ignorant fighter laughs who has never lost a battle,
Bragging and laughing that under his wrist is the pulse, and under his ribs the heart of the people,
Laughing!
Laughing the stormy, husky, brawling laughter of Youth, half-naked, sweating, proud to be Hog Butcher, Tool Maker, Stacker of Wheat, Player with Railroads and Freight Handler to the Nation.

SOURCE: *Poetry* (March 1914).

Fog (1916)

The fog comes
on little cat feet.

It sits looking
over harbor and city
on silent haunches
and then moves on.

SOURCE: Carl Sandburg. *Chicago Poems.* New York: Henry Holt and Company, 1916.

Window (1916)

Night from a railroad car window
Is a great, dark, soft thing
Broken across with slashes of light.

SOURCE: Carl Sandburg. *Chicago Poems.* New York: Henry Holt and Company, 1916.

H.D. (HILDA DOOLITTLE)

Under the pen-name H.D., Hilda Doolittle (1886–1961) wrote these Imagistic and classical Greek-inspired poems. Born in Pennsylvania, she spent most of her adult life in Europe.

The Garden (1915)

I.

You are clear,
O rose, cut in rock,
hard as the descent of hail.

I could scrape the colour
from the petal,
like spilt dye from a rock.

If I could break you
I could break a tree.

If I could stir
I could break a tree,
I could break you.

II.

O wind,
rend open the heat,
cut apart the heat,
rend it sideways.

Fruit can not drop
through this thick air:
fruit can not fall into heat
that presses up and blunts
the points of pears
and rounds the grapes.

Cut the heat,
plough through it,
turning it on either side
of your path.

SOURCE: *Poetry* (March 1915).

The Pool (1915)

Are you alive?
I touch you.
You quiver like a sea-fish.
I cover you with my net.
What are you—banded one?

SOURCE: *Poetry* (March 1915).

Fragment XXXVI (1921)

I know not what to do:
My mind is divided.
—SAPPHO

I know not what to do—
My mind is reft.
Is song's gift best?
Is love's gift loveliest?
I know not what to do,
Now sleep has pressed
Weight on your eyelids.

Shall I break your rest,
Devouring, eager?
Is love's gift best?—

Nay, song's the loveliest.
Yet, were you lost,
What rapture could I take from song?—
What song were left?

I know not what to do:
To turn and slake
The rage that burns,
With my breath burn
And trouble your cool breath—
So shall I turn and take
Snow in my arms,
(Is love's gift best?)
Yet flake on flake
Of snow were comfortless,
Did you lie wondering,
Wakened yet unawake.

Shall I turn and take
Comfortless snow within my arms,
Press lips to lips that answer not,
Press lips to flesh
That shudders not nor breaks?

Is love's gift best?—
Shall I turn and slake
All the wild longing?
Oh, I am eager for you!
As the Pleiads shake
White light in whiter water,
So shall I take you?

My mind is quite divided;
My mind hesitates,
So perfect matched
I know not what to do.
Each strives with each:
As two white wrestlers,
Standing for a match,
Ready to turn and clutch,
Yet never shake
Muscle or nerve or tendon;

So my mind waits
To grapple with my mind—
Yet I am quiet,
I would seem at rest.

I know not what to do.
Strain upon strain,
Sound surging upon sound,
Makes my brain blind;
As a wave line may wait to fall,
Yet waiting for its falling
Still the wind may take,
From off its crest,
White flake on flake of foam,
That rises
Seeming to dart and pulse
And rend the light,
So my mind hesitates
Above the passion
Quivering yet to break,
So my mind hesitates above my mind
Listening to song's delight.

I know not what to do.
Will the sound break,
Rending the night
With rift on rift of rose
And scattered light?
Will the sound break at last
As the wave hesitant,
Or will the whole night pass
And I lie listening awake?

SOURCE: *Poetry* (October 1921).

Song (1921)

You are as gold
As the half-ripe grain
That merges to gold again,

As white as the white rain
That beats through
The half-opened flowers
Of the great flower tufts
Thick on the black limbs
Of an Illyrian apple bough.

Can honey distil such fragrance
As your bright hair?—
For your face is as fair as rain,
Yet as rain that lies clear
On white honey-comb
Lends radiance to the white wax,
So your hair on your brow
Casts light for a shadow.

SOURCE: *Poetry* (October 1921).

At Baia (1921)

I should have thought
In a dream you would have brought
Some lovely perilous thing:
Orchids piled in a great sheath,
As who would say, in a dream,
"I send you this,
Who left the blue veins
Of your throat unkissed."

Why was it that your hands,
That never took mine—
Your hands that I could see
Drift over the orchid heads
So carefully;
Your hands, so fragile, sure to lift
So gently, the fragile flower stuff—
Ah, ah, how was it

You never sent, in a dream,
The very form, the very scent,
Not heavy, not sensuous,

But perilous—perilous!—
Of orchids, piled in a great sheath,
And folded underneath on a bright scroll,
Some word:

Flower sent to flower;
For white hands the lesser white,
Less lovely, of flower leaf.

Or,

Lover to lover—no kiss,
No touch, but forever and ever this!

SOURCE: *Poetry* (October 1921).

T. S. ELIOT

The poet Thomas Stearns Eliot (1888–1965) was born in St. Louis and graduated from Harvard. A dozen years after he began working in London, first as a bank clerk, then, more fittingly, as an editor, he became a British citizen. His friend and mentor (for a time), Ezra Pound, helped him edit and shape the most famous American poem of the twentieth century, "The Waste Land."

The Love Song of J. Alfred Prufrock (1915)

S'io credesse che mia risposta fosse
A persona che mai tornasse al mondo,
Questa fiamma staria senza piu scosse.
Ma perciocche giammai di questo fondo
Non torno vivo alcun, s'i'odo il vero,
Senza tema d'infamia ti rispondo.[1]

Let us go then, you and I,
When the evening is spread out against the sky
Like a patient etherised upon a table;
Let us go, through certain half-deserted streets,
The muttering retreats

---

1. "If I did think my answer were to one
Who ever could return unto the world,
This flame should rest unshaken. But since ne'er,
If true be told me, any from his depth
Has found his upward way, I answer thee,
Nor fear lest infamy record the words."

—*The Divine Comedy of Dante Alighieri: Hell, Purgatory, Paradise. [Hell,* Canto 27. Lines 61-66.] Translated by Henry F. Cary. New York: P. F. Collier and Son, 1909.

Of restless nights in one-night cheap hotels
And sawdust restaurants with oyster-shells:
Streets that follow like a tedious argument
Of insidious intent
To lead you to an overwhelming question . . .
Oh, do not ask, "What is it?"
Let us go and make our visit.

In the room the women come and go
Talking of Michelangelo.

The yellow fog that rubs its back upon the window-panes,
The yellow smoke that rubs its muzzle on the window-panes,
Licked its tongue into the corners of the evening,
Lingered upon the pools that stand in drains,
Let fall upon its back the soot that falls from chimneys,
Slipped by the terrace, made a sudden leap,
And seeing that it was a soft October night,
Curled once about the house, and fell asleep.

And indeed there will be time
For the yellow smoke that slides along the street,
Rubbing its back upon the window-panes;
There will be time, there will be time
To prepare a face to meet the faces that you meet;
There will be time to murder and create,
And time for all the works and days of hands
That lift and drop a question on your plate;
Time for you and time for me,
And time yet for a hundred indecisions,
And for a hundred visions and revisions,
Before the taking of a toast and tea.

In the room the women come and go
Talking of Michelangelo.

And indeed there will be time
To wonder, "Do I dare?" and, "Do I dare?"
Time to turn back and descend the stair,
With a bald spot in the middle of my hair—
(They will say: "How his hair is growing thin!")

My morning coat, my collar mounting firmly to the chin,
My necktie rich and modest, but asserted by a simple pin—
(They will say: "But how his arms and legs are thin!")
Do I dare
Disturb the universe?
In a minute there is time
For decisions and revisions which a minute will reverse.

For I have known them all already, known them all:
Have known the evenings, mornings, afternoons,
I have measured out my life with coffee spoons;
I know the voices dying with a dying fall
Beneath the music from a farther room.
So how should I presume?

And I have known the eyes already, known them all—
The eyes that fix you in a formulated phrase,
And when I am formulated, sprawling on a pin,
When I am pinned and wriggling on the wall,
Then how should I begin
To spit out all the butt-ends of my days and ways?
And how should I presume?

And I have known the arms already, known them all—
Arms that are braceleted and white and bare
(But in the lamplight, downed with light brown hair!)
Is it perfume from a dress
That makes me so digress?
Arms that lie along a table, or wrap about a shawl.
And should I then presume?
And how should I begin?

* * * * *

Shall I say, I have gone at dusk through narrow streets
And watched the smoke that rises from the pipes
Of lonely men in shirt-sleeves, leaning out of windows? . . .

I should have been a pair of ragged claws
Scuttling across the floors of silent seas.

* * * * *

And the afternoon, the evening, sleeps so peacefully!
Smoothed by long fingers,
Asleep . . . tired . . . or it malingers,
Stretched on the floor, here beside you and me.
Should I, after tea and cakes and ices,
Have the strength to force the moment to its crisis?
But though I have wept and fasted, wept and prayed,
Though I have seen my head (grown slightly bald) brought in upon a platter,
I am no prophet—and here's no great matter;
I have seen the moment of my greatness flicker,
And I have seen the eternal Footman hold my coat, and snicker,
And in short, I was afraid.

And would it have been worth it, after all,
After the cups, the marmalade, the tea,
Among the porcelain, among some talk of you and me,
Would it have been worth while,
To have bitten off the matter with a smile,
To have squeezed the universe into a ball
To roll it toward some overwhelming question,
To say: "I am Lazarus, come from the dead,
Come back to tell you all, I shall tell you all"—
If one, settling a pillow by her head,
Should say: "That is not what I meant at all;
That is not it, at all."

And would it have been worth it, after all,
Would it have been worth while,
After the sunsets and the dooryards and the sprinkled streets,
After the novels, after the teacups, after the skirts that trail along the floor—
And this, and so much more?—
It is impossible to say just what I mean!
But as if a magic lantern threw the nerves in patterns on a screen:
Would it have been worth while
If one, settling a pillow or throwing off a shawl,
And turning toward the window, should say:

"That is not it at all,
That is not what I meant, at all."

★ ★ ★ ★ ★

No! I am not Prince Hamlet, nor was meant to be;
Am an attendant lord, one that will do
To swell a progress, start a scene or two,
Advise the prince; no doubt, an easy tool,
Deferential, glad to be of use,
Politic, cautious, and meticulous;
Full of high sentence, but a bit obtuse;
At times, indeed, almost ridiculous—
Almost, at times, the Fool.

I grow old . . . I grow old . . .
I shall wear the bottoms of my trousers rolled.

Shall I part my hair behind? Do I dare to eat a peach?
I shall wear white flannel trousers, and walk upon the beach.
I have heard the mermaids singing, each to each.

I do not think that they will sing to me.

I have seen them riding seaward on the waves
Combing the white hair of the waves blown back
When the wind blows the water white and black.

We have lingered in the chambers of the sea
By sea-girls wreathed with seaweed red and brown
Till human voices wake us, and we drown.

SOURCE: T. S. Eliot. *Prufrock and Other Observations*. London: The Egoist Ltd., 1917. [First published: *Poetry*, June 1915.]

The Waste Land (1922)

"Nam Sibyllam quidem Cumis ego ipse oculis meis vidi in ampulla pendere, et cum illi pueri dicerent: Σίβυλλα τί θέλεις; respondebat illa: ἀποθανειν θέλω."

For Ezra Pound
il miglior fabbro

I. The Burial of the Dead

April is the cruellest month, breeding
Lilacs out of the dead land, mixing
Memory and desire, stirring
Dull roots with spring rain.
Winter kept us warm, covering
Earth in forgetful snow, feeding
A little life with dried tubers.
Summer surprised us, coming over the Starnbergersee
With a shower of rain; we stopped in the colonnade,
And went on in sunlight, into the Hofgarten,
And drank coffee, and talked for an hour.
Bin gar keine Russin, stamm' aus Litauen, echt deutsch.
And when we were children, staying at the archduke's,
My cousin's, he took me out on a sled,
And I was frightened. He said, Marie,
Marie, hold on tight. And down we went.
In the mountains, there you feel free.
I read, much of the night, and go south in the winter.

What are the roots that clutch, what branches grow
Out of this stony rubbish? Son of man,
You cannot say, or guess, for you know only
A heap of broken images, where the sun beats,
And the dead tree gives no shelter, the cricket no relief,
And the dry stone no sound of water. Only
There is shadow under this red rock,
(Come in under the shadow of this red rock),
And I will show you something different from either
Your shadow at morning striding behind you
Or your shadow at evening rising to meet you;
I will show you fear in a handful of dust.

Frisch weht der Wind
Der Heimat zu
Mein Irisch Kind,
Wo weilest du?
"You gave me hyacinths first a year ago;
"They called me the hyacinth girl."
—Yet when we came back, late, from the Hyacinth garden,
Your arms full, and your hair wet, I could not
Speak, and my eyes failed, I was neither
Living nor dead, and I knew nothing,
Looking into the heart of light, the silence.
Oed' und leer das Meer.

Madame Sosostris, famous clairvoyante,
Had a bad cold, nevertheless
Is known to be the wisest woman in Europe,
With a wicked pack of cards. Here, said she,
Is your card, the drowned Phoenician Sailor,
(Those are pearls that were his eyes. Look!)
Here is Belladonna, the Lady of the Rocks,
The lady of situations.
Here is the man with three staves, and here the Wheel,
And here is the one-eyed merchant, and this card,
Which is blank, is something he carries on his back,
Which I am forbidden to see. I do not find
The Hanged Man. Fear death by water.
I see crowds of people, walking round in a ring.
Thank you. If you see dear Mrs. Equitone,
Tell her I bring the horoscope myself:
One must be so careful these days.

Unreal City,
Under the brown fog of a winter dawn,
A crowd flowed over London Bridge, so many,
I had not thought death had undone so many.
Sighs, short and infrequent, were exhaled,
And each man fixed his eyes before his feet.
Flowed up the hill and down King William Street,
To where Saint Mary Woolnoth kept the hours
With a dead sound on the final stroke of nine.
There I saw one I knew, and stopped him, crying: "Stetson!

"You who were with me in the ships at Mylae!
"That corpse you planted last year in your garden,
"Has it begun to sprout? Will it bloom this year?
"Or has the sudden frost disturbed its bed?
"Oh keep the Dog far hence, that's friend to men,
"Or with his nails he'll dig it up again!
"You! hypocrite lecteur!—mon semblable,—mon frère!"

II. A Game of Chess

The Chair she sat in, like a burnished throne,
Glowed on the marble, where the glass
Held up by standards wrought with fruited vines
From which a golden Cupidon peeped out
(Another hid his eyes behind his wing)
Doubled the flames of sevenbranched candelabra
Reflecting light upon the table as
The glitter of her jewels rose to meet it,
From satin cases poured in rich profusion;
In vials of ivory and coloured glass
Unstoppered, lurked her strange synthetic perfumes,
Unguent, powdered, or liquid—troubled, confused
And drowned the sense in odours; stirred by the air
That freshened from the window, these ascended
In fattening the prolonged candle-flames,
Flung their smoke into the laquearia,
Stirring the pattern on the coffered ceiling.
Huge sea-wood fed with copper
Burned green and orange, framed by the coloured stone,
In which sad light a carvèd dolphin swam.
Above the antique mantel was displayed
As though a window gave upon the sylvan scene
The change of Philomel, by the barbarous king
So rudely forced; yet there the nightingale
Filled all the desert with inviolable voice
And still she cried, and still the world pursues,
"Jug Jug" to dirty ears.
And other withered stumps of time
Were told upon the walls; staring forms
Leaned out, leaning, hushing the room enclosed.
Footsteps shuffled on the stair.

Under the firelight, under the brush, her hair
Spread out in fiery points
Glowed into words, then would be savagely still.

"My nerves are bad to-night. Yes, bad. Stay with me.
"Speak to me. Why do you never speak. Speak.
"What are you thinking of? What thinking? What?
"I never know what you are thinking. Think."

I think we are in rats' alley
Where the dead men lost their bones.

"What is that noise?"
The wind under the door.
"What is that noise now? What is the wind doing?"
Nothing again nothing.
"Do
"You know nothing? Do you see nothing? Do you remember
"Nothing?"

I remember
Those are pearls that were his eyes.
"Are you alive, or not? Is there nothing in your head?"
But
O O O O that Shakespeherian Rag—
It's so elegant
So intelligent
"What shall I do now? What shall I do?"
"I shall rush out as I am, and walk the street
"With my hair down, so. What shall we do to-morrow?
"What shall we ever do?"
The hot water at ten.
And if it rains, a closed car at four.
And we shall play a game of chess,
Pressing lidless eyes and waiting for a knock upon the door.

When Lil's husband got demobbed, I said—
I didn't mince my words, I said to her myself,
HURRY UP PLEASE ITS TIME
Now Albert's coming back, make yourself a bit smart.
He'll want to know what you done with that money he gave you

To get yourself some teeth. He did, I was there.
You have them all out, Lil, and get a nice set,
He said, I swear, I can't bear to look at you.
And no more can't I, I said, and think of poor Albert,
He's been in the army four years, he wants a good time,
And if you don't give it him, there's others will, I said.
Oh is there, she said. Something o' that, I said.
Then I'll know who to thank, she said, and give me a straight look.
Hurry up please its time
If you don't like it you can get on with it, I said,
Others can pick and choose if you can't.
But if Albert makes off, it won't be for lack of telling.
You ought to be ashamed, I said, to look so antique.
(And her only thirty-one.)
I can't help it, she said, pulling a long face,
It's them pills I took, to bring it off, she said.
(She's had five already, and nearly died of young George.)
The chemist said it would be alright, but I've never been the same.
You are a proper fool, I said.
Well, if Albert won't leave you alone, there it is, I said,
What you get married for if you don't want children?
Hurry up please its time
Well, that Sunday Albert was home, they had a hot gammon,
And they asked me in to dinner, to get the beauty of it hot—
Hurry up please its time
Hurry up please its time
Goonight Bill. Goonight Lou. Goonight May. Goonight.
Ta ta. Goonight. Goonight.
Good night, ladies, good night, sweet ladies, good night, good night.

III. The Fire Sermon

The river's tent is broken: the last fingers of leaf
Clutch and sink into the wet bank. The wind
Crosses the brown land, unheard. The nymphs are departed.
Sweet Thames, run softly, till I end my song.
The river bears no empty bottles, sandwich papers,
Silk handkerchiefs, cardboard boxes, cigarette ends
Or other testimony of summer nights. The nymphs are departed.

And their friends, the loitering heirs of city directors;
Departed, have left no addresses.
By the waters of Leman I sat down and wept . . .
Sweet Thames, run softly till I end my song,
Sweet Thames, run softly, for I speak not loud or long.
But at my back in a cold blast I hear
The rattle of the bones, and chuckle spread from ear to ear.
A rat crept softly through the vegetation
Dragging its slimy belly on the bank
While I was fishing in the dull canal
On a winter evening round behind the gashouse
Musing upon the king my brother's wreck
And on the king my father's death before him.
White bodies naked on the low damp ground
And bones cast in a little low dry garret,
Rattled by the rat's foot only, year to year.
But at my back from time to time I hear
The sound of horns and motors, which shall bring
Sweeney to Mrs. Porter in the spring.
O the moon shone bright on Mrs. Porter
And on her daughter
They wash their feet in soda water
Et O ces voix d'enfants, chantant dans la coupole!

Twit twit twit
Jug jug jug jug jug jug
So rudely forc'd.
Tereu

Unreal City
Under the brown fog of a winter noon
Mr. Eugenides, the Smyrna merchant
Unshaven, with a pocket full of currants
C.i.f. London: documents at sight,
Asked me in demotic French
To luncheon at the Cannon Street Hotel
Followed by a weekend at the Metropole.

At the violet hour, when the eyes and back
Turn upward from the desk, when the human engine waits
Like a taxi throbbing waiting,

I Tiresias, though blind, throbbing between two lives,
Old man with wrinkled female breasts, can see
At the violet hour, the evening hour that strives
Homeward, and brings the sailor home from sea,
The typist home at teatime, clears her breakfast, lights
Her stove, and lays out food in tins.
Out of the window perilously spread
Her drying combinations touched by the sun's last rays,
On the divan are piled (at night her bed)
Stockings, slippers, camisoles, and stays.
I Tiresias, old man with wrinkled dugs
Perceived the scene, and foretold the rest—
I too awaited the expected guest.
He, the young man carbuncular, arrives,
A small house agent's clerk, with one bold stare,
One of the low on whom assurance sits
As a silk hat on a Bradford millionaire.
The time is now propitious, as he guesses,
The meal is ended, she is bored and tired,
Endeavours to engage her in caresses
Which still are unreproved, if undesired.
Flushed and decided, he assaults at once;
Exploring hands encounter no defence;
His vanity requires no response,
And makes a welcome of indifference.
(And I Tiresias have foresuffered all
Enacted on this same divan or bed;
I who have sat by Thebes below the wall
And walked among the lowest of the dead.)
Bestows one final patronising kiss,
And gropes his way, finding the stairs unlit . . .

She turns and looks a moment in the glass,
Hardly aware of her departed lover;
Her brain allows one half-formed thought to pass:
"Well now that's done: and I'm glad it's over."
When lovely woman stoops to folly and
Paces about her room again, alone,
She smoothes her hair with automatic hand,
And puts a record on the gramophone.

"This music crept by me upon the waters"
And along the Strand, up Queen Victoria Street.
O City city, I can sometimes hear
Beside a public bar in Lower Thames Street,
The pleasant whining of a mandoline
And a clatter and a chatter from within
Where fishmen lounge at noon: where the walls
Of Magnus Martyr hold
Inexplicable splendour of Ionian white and gold.

The river sweats
Oil and tar
The barges drift
With the turning tide
Red sails
Wide
To leeward, swing on the heavy spar.
The barges wash
Drifting logs
Down Greenwich reach
Past the Isle of Dogs.
Weialala leia
Wallala leialala

Elizabeth and Leicester
Beating oars
The stern was formed
A gilded shell
Red and gold
The brisk swell
Rippled both shores
Southwest wind
Carried down stream
The peal of bells
White towers
Weialala leia
Wallala leialala

"Trams and dusty trees.
Highbury bore me. Richmond and Kew

Undid me. By Richmond I raised my knees
Supine on the floor of a narrow canoe."

"My feet are at Moorgate, and my heart
Under my feet. After the event
He wept. He promised a 'new start.'
I made no comment. What should I resent?"

"On Margate Sands.
I can connect
Nothing with nothing.
The broken fingernails of dirty hands.
My people humble people who expect
Nothing."
la la

To Carthage then I came

Burning burning burning burning
O Lord Thou pluckest me out
O Lord Thou pluckest

burning

IV. Death by Water

Phlebas the Phoenician, a fortnight dead,
Forgot the cry of gulls, and the deep sea swell
And the profit and loss.
A current under sea
Picked his bones in whispers. As he rose and fell
He passed the stages of his age and youth
Entering the whirlpool.
Gentile or Jew
O you who turn the wheel and look to windward,
Consider Phlebas, who was once handsome and tall as you.

V. What the Thunder Said

After the torchlight red on sweaty faces
After the frosty silence in the gardens

After the agony in stony places
The shouting and the crying
Prison and palace and reverberation
Of thunder of spring over distant mountains
He who was living is now dead
We who were living are now dying
With a little patience

Here is no water but only rock
Rock and no water and the sandy road
The road winding above among the mountains
Which are mountains of rock without water
If there were water we should stop and drink
Amongst the rock one cannot stop or think
Sweat is dry and feet are in the sand
If there were only water amongst the rock
Dead mountain mouth of carious teeth that cannot spit
Here one can neither stand nor lie nor sit
There is not even silence in the mountains
But dry sterile thunder without rain
There is not even solitude in the mountains
But red sullen faces sneer and snarl
From doors of mudcracked houses
If there were water
And no rock
If there were rock
And also water
And water
A spring
A pool among the rock
If there were the sound of water only
Not the cicada
And dry grass singing
But sound of water over a rock
Where the hermit-thrush sings in the pine trees
Drip drop drip drop drop drop drop
But there is no water

Who is the third who walks always beside you?
When I count, there are only you and I together
But when I look ahead up the white road

There is always another one walking beside you
Gliding wrapt in a brown mantle, hooded
I do not know whether a man or a woman
—But who is that on the other side of you?

What is that sound high in the air
Murmur of maternal lamentation
Who are those hooded hordes swarming
Over endless plains, stumbling in cracked earth
Ringed by the flat horizon only
What is the city over the mountains
Cracks and reforms and bursts in the violet air
Falling towers
Jerusalem Athens Alexandria
Vienna London
Unreal

A woman drew her long black hair out tight
And fiddled whisper music on those strings
And bats with baby faces in the violet light
Whistled, and beat their wings
And crawled head downward down a blackened wall
And upside down in air were towers
Tolling reminiscent bells, that kept the hours
And voices singing out of empty cisterns and exhausted wells.

In this decayed hole among the mountains
In the faint moonlight, the grass is singing
Over the tumbled graves, about the chapel
There is the empty chapel, only the wind's home.
It has no windows, and the door swings,
Dry bones can harm no one.
Only a cock stood on the rooftree
Co co rico co co rico
In a flash of lightning. Then a damp gust
Bringing rain

Ganga was sunken, and the limp leaves
Waited for rain, while the black clouds
Gathered far distant, over Himavant.
The jungle crouched, humped in silence.

Then spoke the thunder
DA
Datta: what have we given?
My friend, blood shaking my heart
The awful daring of a moment's surrender
Which an age of prudence can never retract
By this, and this only, we have existed
Which is not to be found in our obituaries
Or in memories draped by the beneficent spider
Or under seals broken by the lean solicitor
In our empty rooms
DA
Dayadhvam: I have heard the key
Turn in the door once and turn once only
We think of the key, each in his prison
Thinking of the key, each confirms a prison
Only at nightfall, aethereal rumours
Revive for a moment a broken Coriolanus
DA
Damyata: The boat responded
Gaily, to the hand expert with sail and oar
The sea was calm, your heart would have responded
Gaily, when invited, beating obedient
To controlling hands

I sat upon the shore
Fishing, with the arid plain behind me
Shall I at least set my lands in order?
London Bridge is falling down falling down falling down
Poi s'ascose nel foco che gli affina
Quando fiam uti chelidon—O swallow swallow
Le Prince d'Aquitaine à la tour abolie
These fragments I have shored against my ruins
Why then Ile fit you. Hieronymo's mad againe.
Datta. Dayadhvam. Damyata.
Shantih shantih shantih

SOURCE: T. S. Eliot. *The Waste Land.* New York: Horace Liveright, 1922.

WALLACE STEVENS

The insurance executive Wallace Stevens (1879–1955) was one of the century's most original and influential poets. In 1914, at the age of thirty-five, Stevens made his deliberate entry onto the literary scene. As his poems appeared in avant-garde magazines, he gained his reputation as a writer of dazzling language and intellectual badinage. His first book, Harmonium *(1923), contained the poems in this selection.*

Peter Quince at the Clavier (1915)

I

Just as my fingers on these keys
Make music, so the self-same sounds
On my spirit make a music, too.

Music is feeling, then, not sound;
And thus it is that what I feel,
Here in this room, desiring you,

Thinking of your blue-shadowed silk,
Is music. It is like the strain
Waked in the elders by Susanna:

Of a green evening, clear and warm,
She bathed in her still garden, while
The red-eyed elders, watching, felt

The basses of their beings throb
In witching chords, and their thin blood
Pulse pizzicati of Hosanna.

II

In the green water, clear and warm,
Susanna lay.
She searched
The touch of springs,
And found
Concealed imaginings.
She sighed,
For so much melody.

Upon the bank, she stood
In the cool
Of spent emotions.
She felt, among the leaves,
The dew
Of old devotions.

She walked upon the grass,
Still quavering.
The winds were like her maids,
On timid feet,
Fetching her woven scarves,
Yet wavering.

A breath upon her hand
Muted the night.
She turned—
A cymbal crashed,
Amid roaring horns.

III

Soon, with a noise like tambourines,
Came her attendant Byzantines.

They wondered why Susanna cried
Against the elders by her side;

And as they whispered, the refrain
Was like a willow swept by rain.

Anon, their lamps' uplifted flame
Revealed Susanna and her shame.

And then, the simpering Byzantines,
Fled, with a noise like tambourines.

IV

Beauty is momentary in the mind—
The fitful tracing of a portal;
But in the flesh it is immortal.

The body dies; the body's beauty lives.
So evenings die, in their green going,
A wave, interminably flowing.
So gardens die, their meek breath scenting
The cowl of Winter, done repenting.
So maidens die, to the auroral
Celebration of a maiden's choral.

Susanna's music touched the bawdy strings
Of those white elders; but, escaping,
Left only Death's ironic scraping.
Now, in its immortality, it plays
On the clear viol of her memory,
And makes a constant sacrament of praise.

SOURCE: *Others: A Magazine of the New Verse* (August 1915).

Sunday Morning[1] (1915)

I

Complacencies of the peignoir, and late
Coffee and oranges in a sunny chair,
And the green freedom of a cockatoo
Upon a rug, mingle to dissipate
The holy hush of ancient sacrifice.
She dreams a little, and she feels the dark
Encroachment of that old catastrophe,
As a calm darkens among water-lights.
The pungent oranges and bright, green wings
Seem things in some procession of the dead,
Winding across wide water, without sound.
The day is like wide water, without sound,
Stilled for the passing of her dreaming feet
Over the seas, to silent Palestine,
Dominion of the blood and sepulcher.

II

She hears, upon that water without sound,
A voice that cries, "The tomb in Palestine
Is not the porch of spirits lingering;
It is the grave of Jesus, where he lay."
We live in an old chaos of the sun,
Or old dependency of day and night,
Or island solitude, unsponsored, free,
Of that wide water, inescapable.
Deer walk upon our mountains, and the quail
Whistle about us their spontaneous cries;
Sweet berries ripen in the wilderness;
And, in the isolation of the sky,
At evening, casual flocks of pigeons make

1. The following version is the "Sunday Morning" as it was first published—cropped and rearranged by the editor of *Poetry Magazine*, Harriet Monroe. Stevens restored the poem in 1923 in *Harmonium*.

Ambiguous undulations as they sink,
Downward to darkness, on extended wings.

III

She says, "I am content when wakened birds,
Before they fly, test the reality
Of misty fields, by their sweet questionings;
But when the birds are gone, and their warm fields
Return no more, where, then, is paradise?"
There is not any haunt of prophecy,
Nor any old chimera of the grave,
Neither the golden underground, nor isle
Melodious, where spirits gat them home,
Nor visionary South, nor cloudy palm
Remote on heaven's hill, that has endured
As April's green endures; or will endure
Like her remembrance of awakened birds,
Or her desire for June and evening, tipped
By the consummation of the swallow's wings.

IV

She says, "But in contentment I still feel
The need of some imperishable bliss."
Death is the mother of beauty; hence from her,
Alone, shall come fulfilment to our dreams
And our desires. Although she strews the leaves
Of sure obliteration on our paths—
The path sick sorrow took, the many paths
Where triumph rang its brassy phrase, or love
Whispered a little out of tenderness—
She makes the willow shiver in the sun
For maidens who were wont to sit and gaze
Upon the grass, relinquished to their feet.
She causes boys to bring sweet-smelling pears
And plums in ponderous piles. The maidens taste
And stray impassioned in the littering leaves.

V

Supple and turbulent, a ring of men
Shall chant in orgy on a summer morn
Their boisterous devotion to the sun—
Not as a god, but as a god might be,
Naked among them, like a savage source.
Their chant shall be a chant of paradise,
Out of their blood, returning to the sky;
And in their chant shall enter, voice by voice,
The windy lake wherein their lord delights,
The trees, like seraphim, and echoing hills,
That choir among themselves long afterward.
They shall know well the heavenly fellowship
Of men that perish and of summer morn—
And whence they came and whither they shall go,
The dew upon their feet shall manifest.

SOURCE: *Poetry* (November 1915).

The Worms at Heaven's Gate (1916)

Out of the tomb, we bring Badroulbadour,
Within our bellies, we her chariot,
Here is an eye. And here are, one by one,
The lashes of that eye and its white lid.
Here is the cheek on which that lid declined,
And, finger after finger, here, the hand,
The genius of that cheek. Here are the lips,
The bundle of the body and the feet.

* * * *

Out of the tomb we bring Badroulbadour.

Source: *Others: A Magazine of the New Verse* (July 1916).

Thirteen Ways of Looking at a Blackbird (1917)

I

Among twenty snowy mountains,
The only moving thing
Was the eye of the blackbird.

II

I was of three minds,
Like a tree
In which there are three blackbirds.

III

The blackbird whirled in the autumn winds,
It was a small part of the pantomime.

IV

A man and a woman
Are one.
A man and a woman and a blackbird
Are one.

V

I do not know which to prefer—
The beauty of inflections
Or the beauty of innuendoes,
The blackbird whistling
Or just after.

VI

Icicles filled the long window
With barbaric glass.
The shadow of the blackbird

Crossed it, to and fro.
The mood
Traced in the shadow
An indecipherable cause.

VII

O thin men of Haddam,
Why do you imagine golden birds?
Do you not see how the blackbird
Walks around the feet
Of the women about you?

VIII

I know noble accents
And lucid, inescapable rhythms;
But I know, too,
That the blackbird is involved
In what I know.

IX

When the blackbird flew out of sight,
It marked the edge
Of one of many circles.

X

At the sight of blackbirds
Flying in a green light,
Even the bawds of euphony
Would cry out sharply.

XI

He rode over Connecticut
In a glass coach.
Once, a fear pierced him,
In that he mistook

The shadow of his equipage
For blackbirds.

XII

The river is moving.
The blackbird must be flying.

XIII

It was evening all afternoon.
It was snowing
And it was going to snow.
The blackbird sat
In the cedar-limbs.

SOURCE: *Others: A Magazine of the New Verse* (October 1917).

The Wind Shifts (1917)

This is how the wind shifts:
Like the thoughts of an old human,
Who still thinks eagerly
And despairingly.
The wind shifts like this:
Like a human without illusions,
Who still feels irrational things within her.
The wind shifts like this:
Like humans approaching proudly,
Like humans approaching angrily.
This is how the wind shifts:
Like a human, heavy and heavy,
Who does not care.

SOURCE: *Others: A Magazine of the New Verse* (October 1917).

Le Monocle de Mon Oncle (1918)

I

"Mother of heaven, regina of the clouds,
O sceptre of the sun, crown of the moon,
There is not nothing, no, no, never nothing,
Like the clashed edges of two words that kill."
And so I mocked her in magnificent measure.
Or was it that I mocked myself alone?
I wish that I might be a thinking stone.
The sea of spuming thought foists up again
The radiant bubble that she was. And then
A deep up-pouring from some saltier well
Within me, bursts its watery syllable.

II

A red bird flies across the golden floor.
It is a red bird that seeks out his choir
Among the choirs of wind and wet and wing.
A torrent will fall from him when he finds.
Shall I uncrumple this much-crumpled thing?
I am a man of fortune greeting heirs;
For it has come that thus I greet the spring.
These choirs of welcome choir for me farewell.
No spring can follow past meridian.
Yet you persist with anecdotal bliss
To make believe a starry *connaissance*.

III

Is it for nothing, then, that old Chinese
Sat tittivating by their mountain pools
Or in the Yangtse studied out their beards?
I shall not play the flat historic scale.
You know how Utamaro's beauties sought
The end of love in their all-speaking braids.
You know the mountainous coiffures of Bath.
Alas! Have all the barbers lived in vain
That not one curl in nature has survived?

Why, without pity on these studious ghosts,
Do you come dripping in your hair from sleep?

IV

This luscious and impeccable fruit of life
Falls, it appears, of its own weight to earth.
When you were Eve, its acrid juice was sweet,
Untasted, in its heavenly, orchard air—
An apple serves as well as any skull
To be the book in which to read a round,
And is as excellent, in that it is composed
Of what, like skulls, comes rotting back to ground.
But it excels in this that as the fruit
Of love, it is a book too mad to read
Before one merely reads to pass the time.

V

In the high West there burns a furious star.
It is for fiery boys that star was set
And for sweet-smelling virgins close to them.
The measure of the intensity of love
Is measure, also, of the verve of earth.
For me, the firefly's quick, electric stroke
Ticks tediously the time of one more year.
And you? Remember how the crickets came
Out of their mother grass, like little kin
In the pale nights, when your first imagery
Found inklings of your bond to all that dust.

VI

If men at forty will be painting lakes
The ephemeral blues must merge for them in one,
The basic slate, the universal hue.
There is a substance in us that prevails.
But in our amours amorists discern
Such fluctuations that their scrivening
Is breathless to attend each quirky turn.

When amorists grow bald, then amours shrink
Into the compass and curriculum
Of introspective exiles, lecturing.
It is a theme for Hyacinth alone.

VII

The mules that angels ride come slowly down
The blazing passes, from beyond the sun.
Descensions of their tinkling bells arrive.
These muleteers are dainty of their way.
Meantime, centurions guffaw and beat
Their shrilling tankards on the table-boards.
This parable, in sense, amounts to this:
The honey of heaven may or may not come,
But that of earth both comes and goes at once.
Suppose these couriers brought amid their train
A damsel heightened by eternal bloom.

VIII

Like a dull scholar, I behold, in love,
An ancient aspect touching a new mind.
It comes, it blooms, it bears its fruit and dies.
This trivial trope reveals a way of truth.
Our bloom is gone. We are the fruit thereof.
Two golden gourds distended on our vines,
We hang like warty squashes, streaked and rayed,
Into the autumn weather, splashed with frost,
Distorted by hale fatness, turned grotesque.
The laughing sky will see the two of us
Washed into rinds by rotting winter rains.

IX

In verses wild with motion, full of din,
Loudened by cries, by clashes, quick and sure
As the deadly thought of men accomplishing
Their curious fates in war, come, celebrate
The faith of forty, ward of Cupido.
Most venerable heart, the lustiest conceit

Is not too lusty for your broadening.
I quiz all sounds, all thoughts, all everything
For the music and manner of the paladins
To make oblation fit. Where shall I find
Bravura adequate to this great hymn?

X

The fops of fancy in their poems leave
Memorabilia of the mystic spouts,
Spontaneously watering their gritty soils.
I am a yeoman, as such fellows go.
I know no magic trees, no balmy boughs,
No silver-ruddy, gold-vermilion fruits.
But, after all, I know a tree that bears
A semblance to the thing I have in mind.
It stands gigantic, with a certain tip
To which all birds come sometime in their time.
But when they go that tip still tips the tree.

XI

If sex were all, then every trembling hand
Could make us squeak, like dolls, the wished-for words.
But note the unconscionable treachery of fate,
That makes us weep, laugh, grunt and groan, and shout
Doleful heroics, pinching gestures forth
From madness or delight, without regard
To that first, foremost law. Anguishing hour!
Last night, we sat beside a pool of pink,
Clippered with lilies, scudding the bright chromes,
Keen to the point of starlight, while a frog
Boomed from his very belly, odious chords.

XII

A blue pigeon it is, that circles the blue sky,
On side-long wing, around and round and round.
A white pigeon it is, that flutters to the ground,
Grown tired of flight. Like a dark rabbi, I
Observed, when young, the nature of mankind,

In lordly study. Every day, I found
Man proved a gobbet in my mincing world.
Like a rose rabbi, later, I pursued,
And still pursue, the origin and course
Of love, but until now I never knew
That fluttering things have so distinct a shade.

SOURCE: *Others: A Magazine of the New Verse.* (December 1918).

Earthy Anecdote (1919)

Every time the bucks went clattering
Over Oklahoma,
A firecat bristled in the way.

Wherever they went,
They went clattering,
Until they swerved,
In a swift, circular line,
To the right,
Because of the firecat.

Or until they swerved,
In a swift, circular line,
To the left,
Because of the firecat.

The bucks clattered.
The firecat went leaping,
To the right, to the left,
And
Bristled in the way.

Later, the firecat closed his bright eyes
And slept.

SOURCE: *Others: A Magazine of the New Verse* (July 1919).

Anecdote of the Jar (1919)

I placed a jar in Tennessee,
And round it was, upon a hill.
It made the slovenly wilderness
Surround that hill.

The wilderness rose up to it,
And sprawled around, no longer wild.
The jar was round upon the ground
And tall and of a port in air.

It took dominion everywhere.
The jar was gray and bare.
It did not give of bird or bush,
Like nothing else in Tennessee.

SOURCE: *Poetry* (October 1919).

The Man Whose Pharynx Was Bad (1921)

The time of year has grown indifferent.
Mildew of summer and the deepening snow
Are both alike in the routine I know.
I am too dumbly in my being pent.

The wind attendant on the solstices
Blows on the shutters of the metropoles,
Stirring no poet in his sleep, and tolls
The grand ideas of the villages.

The malady of the quotidian . . .
Perhaps, if summer ever came to rest
And lengthened, deepened, comforted, caressed
Through days like oceans in obsidian

Horizons full of night's midsummer blaze;
Perhaps, if winter once could penetrate

Through all its purples to the final slate,
Persisting bleakly in an icy haze;

One might in turn become less diffident—
Out of such mildew plucking neater mould
And spouting new orations of the cold.
One might. One might. But time will not relent.

SOURCE: *The New Republic* (September 14, 1921).

The Snow Man (1921)

One must have a mind of winter
To regard the frost and the boughs
Of the pine-trees crusted with snow;

And have been cold a long time
To behold the junipers shagged with ice,
The spruces rough in the distant glitter

Of the January sun; and not to think
Of any misery in the sound of the wind,
In the sound of a few leaves,

Which is the sound of the land
Full of the same wind
That is blowing in the same bare place

For the listener, who listens in the snow,
And, nothing himself, beholds
Nothing that is not there and the nothing that is.

SOURCE: *Poetry* (October 1921).

Of Heaven Considered as a Tomb (1921)

What word have you, interpreters, of men
Who in the tomb of heaven walk by night,
The darkened ghosts of our old comedy?
Do they believe they range the gusty cold,
With lanterns borne aloft to light the way,
Freemen of death, about and still about
To find whatever it is they seek? Or does
That burial, pillared up each day as porte
And spiritous passage into nothingness,
Foretell each night the one abysmal night,
When the host shall no more wander, nor the light
Of the steadfast lanterns creep across the dark?
Make hue among the dark comedians,
Halloo them in the topmost distances
For answer from their icy Elysée.

SOURCE: *Poetry* (October 1921).

The Bird with the Coppery, Keen Claws (1921)

Above the forest of the parakeets,
A parakeet of parakeets prevails,
A pip of life amid a mort of tails.

(The rudiments of tropics are around,
Aloe of ivory, pear of rusty rind).
His lids are white because his eyes are blind.

He is not paradise of parakeets,
Of his gold ether, golden alguazil,
Except because he broods there and is still.

Panache upon panache, his tails deploy
Upward and outward, in green-vented forms,
His tip a drop of water full of storms.

But though the turbulent tinges undulate
As his pure intellect applies its laws,
He moves not on his coppery, keen claws.

He munches a dry shell while he exerts
His will, yet never ceases, perfect cock,
To flare, in the sun-pallor of his rock.

SOURCE: *Broom: An International Magazine of the Arts* (December 1921).

Bantams in Pine-Woods (1922)

Chieftain Iffucan of Azcan in caftan
Of tan with henna hackles, halt!

Damned universal cock, as if the sun
Was blackamoor to bear your blazing tail.

Fat! Fat! Fat! Fat! I am the personal.
Your world is you. I am my world.

You ten-foot poet among inchlings. Fat!
Begone! An inchling bristles in these pines,

Bristles, and points their Appalachian tangs,
And fears not portly Azcan nor his hoos.

SOURCE: *The Dial* (July 1922).

The Emperor of Ice-Cream (1922)

Call the roller of big cigars,
The muscular one, and bid him whip
In kitchen cups concupiscent curds.
Let the wenches dawdle in such dress
As they are used to wear, and let the boys
Bring flowers in last month's newspapers.
Let be be finale of seem.
The only emperor is the emperor of ice-cream.

Take from the dresser of deal,
Lacking the three glass knobs, that sheet
On which she embroidered fantails once
And spread it so as to cover her face.
If her horny feet protrude, they come
To show how cold she is, and dumb.
Let the lamp affix its beam.
The only emperor is the emperor of ice-cream.

Source: *The Dial* (July 1922).

WILLIAM CARLOS WILLIAMS

William Carlos Williams (1883–1963) was probably the most influential American poet of the twentieth century; his work, so vivid and clear, conveyed image and thought in lightning strokes. For most of his life, Williams was a doctor in Rutherford, New Jersey, and wrote poetry, fiction, and essays in the moments and periods that he wasn't seeing patients.

The Young Housewife (1916)

At ten A.M. the young housewife
moves about in négligé behind
the wooden walls of her husband's house.
I pass solitary in my car.

Then again she comes to the curb
to call the ice-man, fish-man, and stands
shy, uncorseted, tucking in
stray ends of hair, and I compare her
to a fallen leaf.

The noiseless wheels of my car
rush with a crackling sound over
dried leaves as I bow and pass smiling.

SOURCE: *Others: A Magazine of the New Verse.* December 1916.

Pastoral ("When I was younger") (1917)

When I was younger
it was plain to me
I must make something of myself.
Older now
I walk back streets
admiring the houses
of the very poor:
roof out of line with sides
the yards cluttered
with old chicken wire, ashes,
furniture gone wrong;
the fences and outhouses
built of barrel-staves
and parts of boxes, all,
if I am fortunate,
smeared a bluish green
that properly weathered
pleases me best
of all colors.

No one
will believe this
of vast import to the nation.

Source: William Carlos Williams. *Al Que Quiere!* Boston: The Four Seas Company, 1917.

Apology (1917)

Why do I write today?

The beauty of
the terrible faces
of our nonentities
stirs me to it:

colored women
day workers—
old and experienced—
returning home at dusk
in cast off clothing
faces like
old Florentine oak.

Also

the set pieces
of your faces stir me—
leading citizens—
but not
in the same way.

SOURCE: William Carlos Williams. *Al Que Quiere!* Boston: The Four Seas Company, 1917.

Danse Russe (1917)

If I when my wife is sleeping
and the baby and Kathleen
are sleeping
and the sun is a flame-white disc
in silken mists
above shining trees,—
if I in my north room
danse naked, grotesquely
before my mirror
waving my shirt round my head
and singing softly to myself:
"I am lonely, lonely.
I was born to be lonely,
I am best so!"
If I admire my arms, my face
my shoulders, flanks, buttocks
against the yellow drawn shades,—

who shall say I am not
the happy genius of my household?

SOURCE: William Carlos Williams. *Al Que Quiere!* Boston: The Four Seas Company, 1917.

Smell! (1917)

Oh strong ridged and deeply hollowed
nose of mine! what will you not be smelling?
What tactless asses we are, you and I, boney nose,
always indiscriminate, always unashamed,
and now it is the souring flowers of the bedraggled
poplars: a festering pulp on the wet earth
beneath them. With what deep thirst
we quicken our desires
to that rank odor of a passing springtime!
Can you not be decent? Can you not reserve your ardors
for something less unlovely? What girl will care
for us, do you think, if we continue in these ways?
Must you taste everything? Must you know everything?
Must you have a part in everything?

SOURCE: William Carlos Williams. *Al Que Quiere!* Boston: The Four Seas Company, 1917.

Spring Strains (1917)

In a tissue-thin monotone of blue-grey buds
crowded erect with desire against
the sky—
                    tense blue-grey twigs
slenderly anchoring them down, drawing
them in—
                    two blue-grey birds chasing
a third struggle in circles, angles,
swift convergings to a point that bursts
instantly!

Vibrant bowing limbs
pull downward, sucking in the sky
that bulges from behind, plastering itself
against them in packed rifts, rock blue
and dirty orange!
But—
(Hold hard, rigid jointed trees!)
the blinding and red-edged sun-blur—
creeping energy, concentrated
counterforce—welds sky, buds, trees,
rivets them in one puckering hold!
Sticks through! Pulls the whole
counter-pulling mass upward, to the right,
locks even the opaque, not yet defined
ground in a terrific drag that is
loosening the very tap-roots!

On a tissue-thin monotone of blue-grey buds
two blue-grey birds, chasing a third,
at full cry! Now they are
flung outward and up—disappearing suddenly!

SOURCE: William Carlos Williams. *Al Que Quiere!* Boston: The Four Seas Company, 1917.

To a Solitary Disciple (1917)

Rather notice, mon cher,
that the moon is
tilted above
the point of the steeple
than that its color
is shell-pink.

Rather observe
that it is early morning
than that the sky
is smooth
as a turquoise.

Rather grasp
how the dark
converging lines
of the steeple
meet at the pinnacle—
perceive how
its little ornament
tries to stop them—

See how it fails!
See how the converging lines
of the hexagonal spire
escape upward—
receding, dividing!
—sepals
that guard and contain
the flower!

Observe
how motionless
the eaten moon
lies in the protecting lines.

It is true:
in the light colors
of morning
brown-stone and slate
shine orange and dark blue.

But observe
the oppressive weight
of the squat edifice!
Observe
the jasmine lightness
of the moon.

Source: William Carlos Williams. *Al Que Quiere!* Boston: The Four Seas Company, 1917.

Dedication for a Plot of Ground (1917)

This plot of ground
facing the waters of this inlet
is dedicated to the living presence of
Emily Richardson Wellcome
who was born in England; married;
lost her husband and with
her five year old son
sailed for New York in a two-master;
was driven to the Azores;
ran adrift on Fire Island shoal,
met her second husband
in a Brooklyn boarding house,
went with him to Puerto Rico
bore three more children, lost
her second husband, lived hard
for eight years in St. Thomas,
Puerto Rico, San Domingo, followed
the oldest son to New York,
lost her daughter, lost her "baby,"
seized the two boys of
the oldest son by the second marriage
mothered them—they being
motherless—fought for them
against the other grandmother
and the aunts, brought them here
summer after summer, defended
herself here against thieves,
storms, sun, fire,
against flies, against girls
that came smelling about, against
drought, against weeds, storm-tides,
neighbors, weasles that stole her chickens,
against the weakness of her own hands,
against the growing strength of
the boys, against wind, against
the stones, against trespassers,
against rents, against her own mind.

She grubbed this earth with her own hands,
domineered over this grass plot,
blackguarded her oldest son
into buying it, lived here fifteen years,
attained a final loneliness and—

If you can bring nothing to this place
but your carcass, keep out.

Source: William Carlos Williams. *Al Que Quiere!* Boston: The Four Seas Company, 1917.

Le Médicin Malgré Lui (1918)

Oh I suppose I should
Wash the walls of my office,
Polish the rust from
My instruments and keep them
Definitely in order;
Build shelves in
The little laboratory;
Empty out the old stains,
Clean the bottles
And refill them; buy
Another lens; put
My journals on edge instead of
Letting them lie flat
In heaps—then begin
Ten years back and
Gradually
Read them to date,
Cataloguing important
Articles for ready reference.
I suppose I should
Read the new books.
If to this I added
A bill at the tailor's
And the cleaner's
And grew a decent beard

And cultivated a look
Of importance—
Who can tell? I might be
A credit to my Lady Happiness
And never think anything
But a white thought!

SOURCE: *Poetry: A Magazine of Verse*. July 1918.

To Mark Anthony in Heaven (1920)

This quiet morning light
reflected, how many times!
from grass and trees and clouds
enters my north room
touching the walls with
grass and clouds and trees,
Anthony,
trees and grass and clouds.
Why did you follow
that beloved body
with your ships at Actium?
I hope it was because
you knew her inch by inch
from slanting feet upward
to the roots of her hair
and down again and that
you saw her
above the battle's fury
reflecting—
clouds and trees and grass
for then
you are listening in heaven.

SOURCE: *The Little Review*. January 1920.

To Waken an Old Lady (1921)

Old age is
a flight of small
cheeping birds
skimming
bare trees
above a snow glaze.
Gaining and failing
they are buffetted
by a dark wind—
But what?
On harsh weedstalks
the flock has rested,
the snow
is covered with broken
seedhusks
and the wind tempered
by a shrill
piping of plenty.

SOURCE: William Carlos Williams. *Sour Grapes*. Boston: The Four Seas Company, 1921.

Complaint (1921)

They call me and I go
It is a frozen road
past midnight, a dust
of snow caught
in the rigid wheeltracks.
The door opens.
I smile, enter and
shake off the cold.
Here is a great woman
on her side in the bed.
She is sick,
perhaps vomiting,
perhaps laboring
to give birth to

a tenth child. Joy! Joy!
Night is a room
darkened for lovers,
through the jalousies the sun
has sent one gold needle!
I pick the hair from her eyes
and watch her misery
with compassion.

SOURCE: William Carlos Williams. *Sour Grapes*. Boston: The Four Seas Company, 1921.

Complete Destruction (1921)

It was an icy day.
We buried the cat,
then took her box
and set fire to it
in the back yard.
Those fleas that escaped
earth and fire
died by the cold.

SOURCE: William Carlos Williams. *Sour Grapes*. Boston: The Four Seas Company, 1921.

The Widow's Lament in Springtime (1921)

Sorrow is my own yard
where the new grass
flames as it has flamed
often before but not
with the cold fire
that closes round me this year.
Thirtyfive years
I lived with my husband.
The plumtree is white today
with masses of flowers.
Masses of flowers

load the cherry branches
and color some bushes
yellow and some red
but the grief in my heart
is stronger than they
for though they were my joy
formerly, today I notice them
and turn away forgetting.
Today my son told me
that in the meadows,
at the edge of the heavy woods
in the distance, he saw
trees of white flowers.
I feel that I would like
to go there
and fall into those flowers
and sink into the marsh near them.

SOURCE: William Carlos Williams. *Sour Grapes*. Boston: The Four Seas Company, 1921.

The Lonely Street (1921)

School is over. It is too hot
to walk at ease. At ease
in light frocks they walk the streets
to while the time away.
They have grown tall. They hold
pink flames in their right hands.
In white from head to foot,
with sidelong, idle look—
in yellow, floating stuff,
black sash and stockings—
touching their avid mouths
with pink sugar on a stick—
like a carnation each holds in her hand—
they mount the lonely street.

SOURCE: William Carlos Williams. *Sour Grapes*. Boston: The Four Seas Company, 1921.

The Great Figure (1921)

Among the rain
and lights
I saw the figure 5
in gold
on a red
firetruck
moving
with weight and urgency
tense
unheeded
to gong clangs
siren howls
and wheels rumbling
through the dark city.

SOURCE: William Carlos Williams. *Sour Grapes*. Boston: The Four Seas Company, 1921.

THEODORE DREISER

In this story, Theodore Dreiser (1871–1945), famous for his naturalistic novels Sister Carrie *and* An American Tragedy, *describes the touching, pathetic hallucinations of a widower.*

The Lost Phœbe (1916)

THEY LIVED TOGETHER in a part of the country which was not so prosperous as it had once been, about three miles from one of those small towns that, instead of increasing in population, is steadily decreasing. The territory was not very thickly settled; perhaps a house every other mile or so, with large areas of corn- and wheat-land and fallow fields that at odd seasons had been sown to timothy and clover. Their particular house was part log and part frame, the log portion being the old original home of Henry's grandfather. The new portion, of now rain-beaten, time-worn slabs, through which the wind squeaked in the chinks at times, and which several overshadowing elms and a butternut-tree made picturesque and reminiscently pathetic, but a little damp, was erected by Henry when he was twenty-one and just married.

That was forty-eight years before. The furniture inside, like the house outside, was old and mildewy and reminiscent of an earlier day. You have seen the what-not of cherry wood, perhaps, with spiral legs and fluted top. It was there. The old-fashioned four poster bed, with its ball-like protuberances and deep curving incisions, was there also, a sadly alienated descendant of an early Jacobean ancestor. The bureau of cherry was also high and wide and solidly built, but faded-looking, and with a musty odor. The rag carpet that underlay all these sturdy examples of enduring furniture was a weak, faded, lead-and-pink-colored affair woven by

Phœbe Ann's own hands, when she was fifteen years younger than she was when she died. The creaky wooden loom on which it had been done now stood like a dusty, bony skeleton, along with a broken rocking-chair, a worm-eaten clothes-press—Heaven knows how old—a lime-stained bench that had once been used to keep flowers on outside the door, and other decrepit factors of household utility, in an east room that was a lean-to against this so-called main portion. All sorts of other broken-down furniture were about this place; an antiquated clothes-horse, cracked in two of its ribs; a broken mirror in an old cherry frame, which had fallen from a nail and cracked itself three days before their youngest son, Jerry, died; an extension hat-rack, which once had had porcelain knobs on the ends of its pegs; and a sewing-machine, long since outdone in its clumsy mechanism by rivals of a newer generation.

The orchard to the east of the house was full of gnarled old apple-trees, worm-eaten as to trunks and branches, and fully ornamented with green and white lichens, so that it had a sad, greenish-white, silvery effect in moonlight. The low outhouses, which had once housed chickens, a horse or two, a cow, and several pigs, were covered with patches of moss as to their roof, and the sides had been free of paint for so long that they were blackish gray as to color, and a little spongy. The picket-fence in front, with its gate squeaky and askew, and the side fences of the stake-and-rider type were in an equally run-down condition. As a matter of fact, they had aged synchronously with the persons who lived here, old Henry Reifsneider and his wife Phœbe Ann.

They had lived here, these two, ever since their marriage, forty-eight years before, and Henry had lived here before that from his childhood up. His father and mother, well along in years when he was a boy, had invited him to bring his wife here when he had first fallen in love and decided to marry; and he had done so. His father and mother were the companions of himself and his wife for ten years after they were married, when both died; and then Henry and Phœbe were left with their five children growing lustily apace. But all sorts of things had happened since then. Of the seven children, all told, that had been born to them, three had died; one girl had gone to Kansas; one boy had gone to Sioux Falls, never even to be heard of after; another boy had gone to Washington; and the last girl lived five counties away in the same State, but was so burdened with cares of her own that she rarely gave them a thought. Time and a commonplace home life that had never been attractive had weaned them thoroughly, so that, wherever they were, they gave little thought as to how it might be with their father and mother.

Old Henry Reifsneider and his wife Phœbe were a loving couple. You perhaps know how it is with simple natures that fasten themselves like lichens on the stones of circumstance and weather their days to a crumbling conclusion. The great world sounds widely, but it has no call for them. They have no soaring intellect. The orchard, the meadow, the corn-field, the pig-pen, and the chicken-lot measure the range of their human activities. When the wheat is headed it is reaped and threshed; when the corn is browned and frosted it is cut and shocked; when the timothy is in full head it is cut, and the hay-cock erected. After that comes winter, with the hauling of grain to market, the sawing and splitting of wood, the simple chores of fire-building, meal-getting, occasional repairing, and visiting. Beyond these and the changes of weather—the snows, the rains, and the fair days—there are no immediate, significant things. All the rest of life is a far-off, clamorous phantasmagoria, flickering like Northern lights in the night, and sounding as faintly as cow-bells tinkling in the distance.

Old Henry and his wife Phœbe were as fond of each other as it is possible for two old people to be who have nothing else in this life to be fond of. He was a thin old man, seventy when she died, a queer, crotchety person with coarse gray-black hair and beard, quite straggly and unkempt. He looked at you out of dull, fishy, watery eyes that had deep-brown crow's-feet at the sides. His clothes, like the clothes of many farmers, were aged and angular and baggy, standing out at the pockets, not fitting about the neck, protuberant and worn at elbow and knee. Phœbe Ann was thin and shapeless, a very umbrella of a woman, clad in shabby black, and with a black bonnet for her best wear. As time had passed, and they had only themselves to look after, their movements had become slower and slower, their activities fewer and fewer. The annual keep of pigs had been reduced from five to one grunting porker, and the single horse which Henry now retained was a sleepy animal, not over-nourished and not very clean. The chickens, of which formerly there was a large flock, had almost disappeared, owing to ferrets, foxes, and the lack of proper care, which produces disease. The former healthy garden was now a straggling memory of itself, and the vines and flower-beds that formerly ornamented the windows and dooryard had now become choking thickets. A will had been made which divided the small tax-eaten property equally among the remaining four, so that it was really of no interest to any of them. Yet these two lived together in peace and sympathy, only that now and then old Henry would become unduly cranky, complaining almost invariably that something had been neglected or mislaid which was of no importance at all.

"Phœbe, where's my corn-knife? You ain't never minded to let my things alone no more."

"Now you hush, Henry," his wife would caution him in a cracked and squeaky voice. "If you don't, I'll leave yuh. I'll git up and walk out of here some day, and then where would y' be? Y' ain't got anybody but me to look after yuh, so yuh just behave yourself. Your corn-knife's on the mantel where it's allus been unless you've gone an' put it summers else."

Old Henry, who knew his wife would never leave him in any circumstances, used to speculate at times as to what he would do if she were to die. That was the one leaving that he really feared. As he climbed on the chair at night to wind the old, long-pendulumed, double-weighted clock, or went finally to the front and the back door to see that they were safely shut in, it was a comfort to know that Phœbe was there, properly ensconced on her side of the bed, and that if he stirred restlessly in the night, she would be there to ask what he wanted.

"Now, Henry, do lie still! You're as restless as a chicken."

"Well, I can't sleep, Phœbe."

"Well, yuh needn't roll so, anyhow. Yuh kin let me sleep."

This usually reduced him to a state of somnolent ease. If she wanted a pail of water, it was a grumbling pleasure for him to get it; and if she did rise first to build the fires, he saw that the wood was cut and placed within easy reach. They divided this simple world nicely between them.

As the years had gone on, however, fewer and fewer people had called. They were well-known for a distance of as much as ten square miles as old Mr. and Mrs. Reifsneider, honest, moderately Christian, but too old to be really interesting any longer. The writing of letters had become an almost impossible burden too difficult to continue or even negotiate via others, although an occasional letter still did arrive from the daughter in Pemberton County. Now and then some old friend stopped with a pie or cake or a roasted chicken or duck, or merely to see that they were well; but even these kindly minded visits were no longer frequent.

One day in the early spring of her sixty-fourth year Mrs. Reifsneider took sick, and from a low fever passed into some indefinable ailment which, because of her age, was no longer curable. Old Henry drove to Swinnerton, the neighboring town, and procured a doctor. Some friends called, and the immediate care of her was taken off his hands. Then one chill spring night she died, and old Henry, in a fog of sorrow and uncertainty, followed her body to the nearest graveyard, an unattractive space with a few pines growing in it. Although he might have gone to the daughter in Pemberton or sent for her, it was really too much trouble and he was too weary and fixed. It was suggested to him at once by one friend and another that he come to stay with them awhile, but he did not see fit. He was so old and so fixed in his notions and so accustomed to the exact surroundings he had known all his days, that he could not think of leaving. He wanted to remain near where they had put his Phœbe; and the fact that he would have to live alone did not trouble him in the least. The living children were notified and the care of him offered if he would leave, but he would not.

"I kin make a shift for myself," he continually announced to old Dr. Morrow, who had attended his wife in this case. "I kin cook a little, and, besides, it don't take much more'n coffee an' bread in the mornin's to satisfy me. I'll get along now well enough. Yuh just let me be." And after many pleadings and proffers of advice, with supplies of coffee and bacon and baked bread duly offered and accepted, he was left to himself. For a while he sat idly outside his door brooding in the spring sun. He tried to revive his interest in farming, and to keep himself busy and free from thought by looking after the fields, which of late had been much neglected. It was a gloomy thing to come in of an evening, however, or in the afternoon and find no shadow of Phœbe where everything suggested her. By degrees he put a few of her things away. At night he sat beside his lamp and read in the papers that were left him occasionally or in a Bible that he had neglected for years, but he could get little solace from these things. Mostly he held his hand over his mouth and looked at the floor as he sat and thought of what had become of her, and how soon he himself would die. He made a great business of making his coffee in the morning and frying himself a little bacon at night; but his appetite was gone. The shell in which he had been housed so long seemed vacant, and its shadows were suggestive of immedicable griefs. So he lived quite dolefully for five long months, and then a change began.

It was one night, after he had looked after the front and the back door, wound the clock, blown out the light, and gone through all the selfsame motions that he had indulged in for years, that he went to bed not so much to sleep as to think. It was a moonlight night. The green-lichen-covered orchard just outside and to be seen from his bed where he now lay was a silvery affair, sweetly spectral. The moon shone through the east windows, throwing the pattern of the panes on the wooden floor, and making the old furniture, to which he was accustomed, stand out dimly in the room. As usual he had been thinking of Phœbe and the years when they had been young together, and of the children who had gone, and the poor shift he was making of his present days. The house was coming to be in a very bad state indeed. The bed-clothes were in disorder and not clean, for he made a wretched shift of washing. It was a terror to him. The roof leaked, causing things, some of them, to remain damp for weeks at a time, but he was getting into that brooding state where he would accept anything rather than exert himself. He preferred to pace slowly to and fro or to sit and think.

By twelve o'clock of this particular night he was asleep, however, and by two had waked again. The moon by this time had shifted to a position on the western side of the house, and it now shone in through the windows of the living-room and those of the kitchen beyond. A certain combination of furniture—a chair near a table, with his coat on it, the half-open kitchen door casting a shadow, and the position of a lamp near a paper—gave him an exact representation of Phœbe leaning over the table as he had often seen her do in life. It gave him a great start. Could it be she—or her ghost? He had scarcely ever believed in spirits; and still—He looked her fixedly in the feeble half-light, his old hair tingling oddly at the roots, and then sat up. The figure did not move. He put this thin legs out of the bed and sat looking at her, wondering if this could really be Phœbe. They had talked of ghosts often in their lifetime, of apparitions and omens; but they had never agreed that such things could be. It had never been a part of his wife's creed that she could have a spirit that could return to walk the earth. Her after-world was quite a different affair, a vague heaven, no less, from which the righteous did not trouble to return. Yet here she was now, bending over the table in her black skirt and gray shawl, her pale profile outlined against the moonlight.

"Phœbe," he called, thrilling from head to toe and putting out one bony hand, "have yuh come back?"

The figure did not stir, and he arose and walked uncertainly to the door, looking at it fixedly the while. As he drew near, however, the apparition resolved itself into its primal content—his old coat over the high-backed chair, the lamp by the paper, the half-open door.

"Well," he said to himself, his mouth open, "I thought shore I saw her." And he ran his hand strangely and vaguely through his hair, the while his nervous tension relaxed. Vanished as it had, it gave him the idea that she might return.

Another night, because of this first illusion, and because his mind was now constantly on her and he was old, he looked out of the window that was nearest his bed and commanded a hen-coop and pig-pen and a part of the wagon-shed, and there, a faint mist exuding from the damp of the ground, he thought he saw her again. It was one of those little wisps of mist, one of those faint exhalations of the earth that rise in a cool night after a warm day, and flicker like small white cypresses of fog before they disappear. In life it had been a custom of hers to cross this lot from her kitchen door to the pig-pen to throw in any scrap that was left from her cooking, and here she was again. He sat up and watched it strangely, doubtfully, because of his previous experience, but inclined, because of the nervous titillation that passed over his body, to believe that spirits really were, and that Phœbe, who would be concerned because of his lonely state, must be thinking about him, and hence returning. What other way would she have? How otherwise could she express herself? It would be within the province of her charity so to do, and like her loving interest in him. He quivered and watched it eagerly; but, a faint breath of air stirring, it wound away toward the fence and disappeared.

A third night, as he was actually dreaming, some ten days later, she came to his bedside and put her hand on his head.

"Poor Henry!" she said. "It's too bad."

He roused out of his sleep, actually to see her, he thought, moving from his bed-room into the one living-room, her figure a shadowy mass of black. The weak straining of his eyes caused little points of light to flicker about the outlines of her form. He arose, greatly astonished, walked the floor in the cool room, convinced that Phœbe was coming back to him. If he only thought sufficiently, if he made it perfectly clear by his feeling that he needed her greatly, she would come back, this kindly wife, and tell him what to do. She would perhaps be with him much of the time, in the night, anyhow; and that would make him less lonely, this state more endurable.

In age and with the feeble it is not such a far cry from the subtleties of illusion to actual hallucination, and in due time this transition was made for Henry. Night after night he waited, expecting her return. Once in his weird mood he thought he saw a pale light moving about the room, and another time he thought he saw her walking in the orchard after dark. It was one morning when the details of his lonely state were virtually unendurable that he woke with the thought that she was not dead. How he had arrived at this conclusion it is hard to say. His mind had gone. In its place was a fixed illusion. He and Phœbe had had a senseless quarrel. He had reproached her for not leaving his pipe where he was accustomed to find it, and she had left. It was an aberrated fulfillment of her old jesting threat that if he did not behave himself she would leave him.

"I guess I could find yuh ag'in," he had always said. But her cackling threat had always been:

"Yuh'll not find me if I ever leave yuh. I guess I kin git some place where yuh can't find me."

This morning when he arose he did not think to build the fire in the customary way or to grind his coffee and cut his bread, as was his wont, but solely to meditate as to where he should search for her and how he should induce her to come back. Recently the one horse had been dispensed with because he found it cumbersome and beyond his needs. He took down his soft crush hat after he had dressed himself, a new glint of interest and determination in his eye, and taking his black crook cane from behind the door, where he had always placed it, started out briskly to look for her among the nearest neighbors. His old shoes clumped soundly in the dust as he walked, and his gray-black locks, now grown rather long, straggled out in a dramatic fringe or halo from under his hat. His short coat stirred busily as he walked, and his hands and face were peaked and pale.

"Why, hello, Henry! Where're yuh goin' this mornin'?" inquired Farmer Dodge, who, hauling a load of wheat to market, encountered him on the public road. He had not seen the aged farmer in months, not since his wife's death, and he wondered now, seeing him looking so spry.

"Yuh ain't seen Phœbe, have yuh?" inquired the old man, looking up quizzically.

"Phœbe who?" inquired Farmer Dodge, not for the moment connecting the name with Henry's dead wife.

"Why, my wife Phœbe, o' course. Who do yuh s'pose I mean?" He stared up with a pathetic sharpness of glance from under his shaggy, gray eyebrows.

"Wall, I'll swan, Henry, yuh ain't jokin', are yuh?" said the solid Dodge, a pursy man, with a smooth, hard, red face. "It can't be your wife yuh're talkin' about. She's dead."

"Dead! Shucks!" retorted the demented Reifsneider. "She left me early this mornin', while I was sleepin'. She allus got up to build the fire, but she's gone now. We had a little spat last night, an' I guess that's the reason. But I guess I kin find her. She's gone over to Matilda Race's; that's where she's gone."

He started briskly up the road, leaving the amazed Dodge to stare in wonder after him.

"Well, I'll be switched!" he said aloud to himself. "He's clean out'n his head. That poor old feller's been livin' down there till he's gone outen his mind. I'll have to notify the authorities." And he flicked his whip with great enthusiasm. "Geddap!" he said, and was off.

Reifsneider met no one else in this poorly populated region until he reached the whitewashed fence of Matilda Race and her husband three miles away. He had passed several other houses en route, but these not being within the range of his illusion were not considered. His wife, who had known Matilda well, must be here. He opened the picket-gate which guarded the walk, and stamped briskly up to the door.

"Why, Mr. Reifsneider," exclaimed old Matilda herself, a stout woman, looking out of the door in answer to his knock, "what brings yuh here this mornin'?"

"Is Phœbe here?" he demanded eagerly.

"Phœbe who? What Phœbe?" replied Mrs. Race, curious as to this sudden development of energy on his part.

"Why, my Phœbe, o' course. My wife Phœbe. Who do yuh s'pose? Ain't she here now?"

"Lawsy me!" exclaimed Mrs. Race, opening her mouth. "Yuh pore man! So you're clean out'n your mind now. Yuh come right in and sit down. I'll git yuh a cup o' coffee. O' course your wife ain't here; but yuh come in an' sit down. I'll find her fer yuh after a while. I know where she is."

The old farmer's eyes softened, and he entered. He was so thin and pale a specimen, pantalooned and patriarchal, that he aroused Mrs. Race's extremest sympathy as he took off his hat and laid it on his knees quite softly and mildly.

"We had a quarrel last night, an' she left me," he volunteered.

"Laws! laws!" sighed Mrs. Race, there being no one present with whom to share her astonishment as she went to her kitchen. "The pore man! Now somebody's just got to look after him. He can't be allowed to run around the country this way lookin' for his dead wife. It's turrible."

She boiled him a pot of coffee and brought in some of her new-baked bread and fresh butter. She set out some of her best jam and put a couple of eggs to boil, lying whole-heartedly the while.

"Now yuh stay right there, Uncle Henry, till Jake comes in, an' I'll send him to look for Phœbe. I think it's more'n likely she's over to Swinnerton with some o' her friends. Anyhow, we'll find out. Now yuh just drink this coffee an' eat this bread. Yuh must be tired. Yuh've had a long walk this mornin'." Her idea was to take counsel with Jake, "her man," and perhaps have him notify the authorities.

She bustled about, meditating on the uncertainties of life, while old Reifsneider thrummed on the rim of his hat with his pale fingers and later ate abstractedly of what she offered. His mind was on his wife, however, and since she was not here, or did not appear, it wandered vaguely away to a family by the name of Murray, miles away in another direction. He decided after a time that he would not wait for Jake Race to hunt his wife but would seek her for himself. He must be on, and urge her to come back.

"Well, I'll be goin'," he said, getting up and looking strangely about him. "I guess she didn't come here after all. She went over to the Murrays', I guess. I'll not wait any longer, Mis' Race. There's a lot to do over to the house to-day." And out he marched in the face of her protests taking to the dusty road again in the warm spring sun, his cane striking the earth as he went.

It was two hours later that this pale figure of a man appeared in the Murrays' doorway, dusty, perspiring, eager. He had tramped all of five miles, and it was noon. An amazed husband and wife of sixty heard his strange query, and realized also that he was mad.

They begged him to stay to dinner, intending to notify the authorities later and see what could be done; but though he stayed to partake of a little something, he did not stay long, and was off again to another distant farmhouse, his idea of many things to do and his need of Phœbe impelling him. So it went for that day and the next and the next, the circle of his inquiry ever widening.

The process by which a character assumes the significance of being peculiar, his antics weird, yet harmless, in such a community is often involute and pathetic. This day, as has been said, saw Reifsneider at other doors, eagerly asking his unnatural question, and leaving a trail of amazement, sympathy, and pity in his wake. Although the authorities were informed—the county sheriff, no less—it was not deemed advisable to take him into custody; for when those who knew old Henry, and had for so long, reflected on the condition of the county insane asylum, a place which, because of the poverty of the district, was of staggering aberration and sickening environment, it was decided to let him remain at large; for, strange to relate, it was found on investigation that at night he returned peaceably enough to his lonesome domicile there to discover whether his wife had returned, and to brood in loneliness until the morning. Who would lock up a thin, eager, seeking old man with iron-gray hair and an attitude of kindly, innocent inquiry, particularly when he was well known for a past of only kindly servitude and reliability? Those who had known him best rather agreed that he should be allowed to roam at large. He could do no harm. There were many who were willing to help him as to food, old clothes, the odds and ends of his daily life—at least at first. His figure after a time became not so much a common-place as an accepted curiosity, and the replies, "Why, no, Henry; I ain't see her," or "No, Henry; she ain't been here to-day," more customary.

For several years thereafter then he was an odd figure in the sun and rain, on dusty roads and muddy ones, encountered occasionally in strange and unexpected places, pursuing his endless search. Undernourishment, after a time, although the neighbors and those who knew his history gladly contributed from their store, affected his body; for he walked much and ate little. The longer he roamed the public highway in this manner, the deeper became his strange hallucination; and finding it harder and harder to return from his more and more distant pilgrimages, he finally began taking a few utensils with him from his home, making a small package of them, in order that he might not be compelled to return. In an old tin coffee-pot of large size he placed a small tin cup, a knife, fork, and spoon, some salt and pepper, and to the outside of it, by a string forced through a pierced hole, he fastened a plate, which could be released, and which was his woodland table. It was no trouble for him to secure the little food that he needed, and with a strange, almost religious dignity, he had no hesitation in asking for that much. By degrees his hair became longer and longer, his once black hat became an earthen brown, and his clothes threadbare and dusty.

For all of three years he walked, and none knew how wide were his perambulations, nor how he survived the storms and cold. They could not see him, with homely rural understanding and forethought, sheltering himself in hay-cocks, or by the sides of cattle, whose warm bodies protected him from the cold, and whose dull understandings were not opposed to his harmless presence. Overhanging rocks and trees kept him at times from the rain, and a friendly hay-loft or corn-crib was not above his humble consideration.

The involute progression of hallucination is strange. From asking at doors and being constantly rebuffed or denied, he finally came to the conclusion that although his Phœbe might not be in any of the houses at the doors of which he inquired, she might nevertheless be within the sound of his voice. And so, from patient inquiry, he began to call sad, occasional cries, that ever and anon waked the quiet landscapes and ragged hill regions, and set to echoing his thin "O-o-o Phœbe! O-o-o Phœbe!" It had a pathetic, albeit insane, ring, and many a farmer or plowboy came to know it even from afar and say, "There goes old Reifsneider."

Another thing that puzzled him greatly after a time and after many hundreds of inquiries was, when he no longer had any particular dooryard in view and no special inquiry to make, which way to go. These cross-roads, which occasionally led in four or even six directions, came after a time to puzzle him. But to solve this knotty problem, which became more and more of a puzzle, there came to his aid another hallucination. Phœbe's spirit or some power of the air or wind or nature would tell him. If he stood at the center of the parting of the ways, closed his eyes, turned thrice about, and called "O-o-o Phœbe!" twice, and then threw his cane straight before him, that would surely indicate which way to go for Phœbe, or one of these mystic powers would surely govern its direction and fall! In whichever direction it went, even though, as was not infrequently the case, it took him back along the path he had already come, or across fields, he was not so far gone in his mind but that he gave himself ample time to search before he called again. Also the hallucination seemed to persist that at some time he would surely find her. There were hours when his feet were sore, and his limbs weary, when he would stop in the heat to wipe his seamed brow, or in the cold to beat his arms. Sometimes, after throwing away his cane, and finding it indicating the direction from which he had just come, he would shake his head wearily and philosophically, as if contemplating the unbelievable or an untoward fate, and then start briskly off. His strange figure came finally to be known in the farthest reaches of three or four counties. Old Reifsneider was a pathetic character. His fame was wide.

Near a little town called Watersville, in Green County, perhaps four miles from that minor center of human activity, there was a place or precipice locally known as the Red Cliff, a sheer wall of red sandstone, perhaps a hundred feet high, which raised its sharp face for half a mile or more above the fruitful corn-fields and orchards that lay beneath, and which was surmounted by a thick grove of trees. The slope that slowly led up to it from the opposite side was covered by a rank growth of beech, hickory, and ash, through which threaded a number of wagon-tracks crossing at various angles. In fair weather it had become old Reifsneider's habit, so inured was he by now to the open, to make his bed in some such patch of trees as this to fry his bacon or boil his eggs at the foot of some tree before laying himself down for the night. Occasionally, so light and inconsequential was his sleep, he would walk at night. More often, the moonlight or some sudden wind stirring in the trees or a reconnoitering animal arousing him, he would sit up and think, or pursue his quest in the moonlight or the dark, a strange, unnatural, half wild, half savage-looking but utterly harmless creature, calling at lonely road crossings, staring at dark and shuttered houses, and wondering where, where Phœbe could really be.

That particular lull that comes in the systole-diastole of this earthly ball at two o'clock in the morning invariably aroused him, and though he might not go any farther he would sit up and contemplate the darkness or the stars, wondering. Sometimes in the strange processes of his mind he would fancy that he saw moving among the trees the figure of his lost wife, and then he would get up to follow, taking his utensils, always on a string, and his cane. If she seemed to evade him too easily he would run, or plead, or, suddenly losing track of the fancied figure, stand awed or disappointed, grieving for the moment over the almost insurmountable difficulties of his search.

It was in the seventh year of these hopeless peregrinations, in the dawn of a similar springtime to that in which his wife had died, that he came at last one night to the vicinity of this self-same patch that crowned the rise to the Red Cliff. His far-flung cane, used as a divining-rod at the last cross-roads, had brought him hither. He had walked many, many miles. It was after ten o'clock at night, and he was very weary. Long wandering and little eating had left him but a shadow of his former self. It was a question now not so much of physical strength but of spiritual endurance which kept him up. He had scarcely eaten this day, and now exhausted he set himself down in the dark to rest and possibly to sleep.

Curiously on this occasion a strange suggestion of the presence of his wife surrounded him. It would not be long now, he counseled with himself, although the long months had brought him nothing, until he should see her, talk to her. He fell asleep after a time, his head on his knees. At midnight the moon began to rise, and at two in the morning, his wakeful hour, was a large silver disk shining through the trees to the east. He opened his eyes when the radiance became strong, making a silver pattern at his feet and lighting the woods with strange lusters and silvery, shadowy forms. As usual, his old notion that his wife must be near occurred to him on this occasion, and he looked about him with a speculative, anticipatory eye. What was it that moved in the distant shadows along the path by which he had entered—a pale, flickering will-o'-the-wisp that bobbed gracefully among the trees and riveted his expectant gaze? Moonlight and shadows combined to give it a strange form and a stranger reality, this fluttering of bog-fire or dancing of wandering fire-flies. Was it truly his lost Phœbe? By a circuitous route it passed about him, and in his fevered state he fancied that he could see the very eyes of her, not as she was when he last saw her in the black dress and shawl but now a strangely younger Phœbe, gayer, sweeter, the one whom he had known years before as a girl. Old Reifsneider got up. He had been expecting and dreaming of this hour all these years, and now as he saw the feeble light dancing lightly before him he peered at it questioningly, one thin hand in his gray hair.

Of a sudden there came to him now for the first time in many years the full charm of her girlish figure as he had known it in boyhood, the pleasing, sympathetic smile, the brown hair, the blue sash she had once worn about her waist at a picnic, her gay, graceful movements. He walked around the base of the tree, straining with his eyes, forgetting for once his cane and utensils, and following eagerly after. On she moved before him, a will-o'-the-wisp of the spring, a little flame above her head, and it seemed as though among the small saplings of ash and beech and the thick trunks of hickory and elm that she signaled with a young, a lightsome hand.

"O Phœbe! Phœbe!" he called. "Have yuh really come? Have yuh really answered me?" And hurrying faster, he fell once, scrambling lamely to his feet, only to see the light in the distance dancing illusively on. On and on he hurried until he was fairly running, brushing his ragged arms against the trees, striking his hands and face against impeding twigs. His hat was gone, his lungs were breathless, his reason quite astray, when coming to the edge of the cliff he saw her below among a silvery bed of apple-trees now blooming in the spring.

"O Phœbe!" he called. "O Phœbe! Oh, no, don't leave me!" And feeling the lure of a world where love was young and Phœbe as this vision presented her, a delightful epitome of their quondam youth, he gave a gay cry of "Oh, wait, Phœbe!" and leaped.

Some farmer-boys, reconnoitering this region of bounty and prospect some few days afterward, found first the tin utensils tied together under the tree where he had left them, and then later at the foot of the cliff, pale, broken, but elate, a molded smile of peace and delight upon his lips, his body. His old hat was discovered lying under some low-growing saplings the twigs of which had held it back. No one of all the simple population knew how eagerly and joyously he had found his lost mate.

SOURCE: *The Century Magazine* (April 1916).

ROBERT FROST

Born in San Francisco in 1874, Frost moved east with his family at age eleven, and, through his poetry and persona, became associated with New England. Certainly the most popular and famous American poet of the twentieth century, Frost wrote in measured forms but with a spare, fresh colloquial voice. He died in 1963.

The Road Not Taken (1916)

Two roads diverged in a yellow wood,
And sorry I could not travel both
And be one traveler, long I stood
And looked down one as far as I could
To where it bent in the undergrowth;

Then took the other, as just as fair,
And having perhaps the better claim,
Because it was grassy and wanted wear;
Though as for that the passing there
Had worn them really about the same,

And both that morning equally lay
In leaves no step had trodden black.
Oh, I kept the first for another day!
Yet knowing how way leads on to way,
I doubted if I should ever come back.

I shall be telling this with a sigh
Somewhere ages and ages hence:
Two roads diverged in a wood, and I—

I took the one less traveled by,
And that has made all the difference.

SOURCE: Robert Frost. *Mountain Interval.* New York: Henry Holt and Company, 1916.

Meeting and Passing (1916)

As I went down the hill along the wall
There was a gate I had leaned at for the view
And had just turned from when I first saw you
As you came up the hill. We met. But all
We did that day was mingle great and small
Footprints in summer dust as if we drew
The figure of our being less than two
But more than one as yet. Your parasol

Pointed the decimal off with one deep thrust.
And all the time we talked you seemed to see
Something down there to smile at in the dust.
(Oh, it was without prejudice to me!)
Afterward I went past what you had passed
Before we met and you what I had passed.

SOURCE: Robert Frost. *Mountain Interval.* New York: Henry Holt and Company, 1916.

Birches (1916)

When I see birches bend to left and right
Across the lines of straighter darker trees,
I like to think some boy's been swinging them.
But swinging doesn't bend them down to stay.
Ice-storms do that. Often you must have seen them
Loaded with ice a sunny winter morning
After a rain. They click upon themselves
As the breeze rises, and turn many-colored
As the stir cracks and crazes their enamel.
Soon the sun's warmth makes them shed crystal shells
Shattering and avalanching on the snow-crust—

Such heaps of broken glass to sweep away
You'd think the inner dome of heaven had fallen.
They are dragged to the withered bracken by the load,
And they seem not to break; though once they are bowed
So low for long, they never right themselves:
You may see their trunks arching in the woods
Years afterwards, trailing their leaves on the ground
Like girls on hands and knees that throw their hair
Before them over their heads to dry in the sun.
But I was going to say when Truth broke in
With all her matter-of-fact about the ice-storm
(Now am I free to be poetical?)
I should prefer to have some boy bend them
As he went out and in to fetch the cows—
Some boy too far from town to learn baseball,
Whose only play was what he found himself,
Summer or winter, and could play alone.
One by one he subdued his father's trees
By riding them down over and over again
Until he took the stiffness out of them,
And not one but hung limp, not one was left
For him to conquer. He learned all there was
To learn about not launching out too soon
And so not carrying the tree away
Clear to the ground. He always kept his poise
To the top branches, climbing carefully
With the same pains you use to fill a cup
Up to the brim, and even above the brim.
Then he flung outward, feet first, with a swish,
Kicking his way down through the air to the ground.
So was I once myself a swinger of birches.
And so I dream of going back to be.
It's when I'm weary of considerations,
And life is too much like a pathless wood
Where your face burns and tickles with cobwebs
Broken across it, and one eye is weeping
From a twig's having lashed across it open.
I'd like to get away from the earth awhile
And then come back to it and begin over.
May no fate willfully misunderstand me
And half grant what I wish and snatch me away

Not to return. Earth's the right place for love:
I don't know where it's likely to go better.
I'd like to go by climbing a birch tree,
And climb black branches up a snow-white trunk
Toward heaven, till the tree could bear no more,
But dipped its top and set me down again.
That would be good both going and coming back.
One could do worse than be a swinger of birches.

SOURCE: Robert Frost. *Mountain Interval.* New York: Henry Holt and Company, 1916.

A Time to Talk (1916)

When a friend calls to me from the road
And slows his horse to a meaning walk,
I don't stand still and look around
On all the hills I haven't hoed,
And shout from where I am, What is it?
No, not as there is a time to talk.
I thrust my hoe in the mellow ground,
Blade-end up and five feet tall,
And plod: I go up to the stone wall
For a friendly visit.

SOURCE: Robert Frost. *Mountain Interval.* New York: Henry Holt and Company, 1916.

The Line-Gang (1916)

Here come the line-gang pioneering by.
They throw a forest down less cut than broken.
They plant dead trees for living, and the dead
They string together with a living thread.
They string an instrument against the sky
Wherein words whether beaten out or spoken
Will run as hushed as when they were a thought.
But in no hush they string it: they go past
With shouts afar to pull the cable taut,
To hold it hard until they make it fast,

To ease away—they have it. With a laugh,
An oath of towns that set the wild at naught
They bring the telephone and telegraph.

SOURCE: Robert Frost. *Mountain Interval.* New York: Henry Holt and Company, 1916.

The Sound of the Trees (1916)

I wonder about the trees.
Why do we wish to bear
Forever the noise of these
More than another noise
So close to our dwelling place?
We suffer them by the day
Till we lose all measure of pace,
And fixity in our joys,
And acquire a listening air.
They are that that talks of going
But never gets away;
And that talks no less for knowing,
As it grows wiser and older,
That now it means to stay.
My feet tug at the floor
And my head sways to my shoulder
Sometimes when I watch trees sway,
From the window or the door.
I shall set forth for somewhere,
I shall make the reckless choice
Some day when they are in voice
And tossing so as to scare
The white clouds over them on.
I shall have less to say,
But I shall be gone.

SOURCE: Robert Frost. *Mountain Interval.* New York: Henry Holt and Company, 1916.

Fragmentary Blue (1920)

Why make so much of fragmentary blue
In here and there a bird, or butterfly,
Or flower, or wearing-stone, or open eye,
When heaven presents in sheets the solid hue?

Since earth is earth, perhaps, not heaven (as yet)—
Though some savants make earth include the sky;
And blue so far above us comes so high,
It only gives our wish for blue a whet.

SOURCE: *Harper's Magazine.* July 1920.

Place for a Third (1920)

Nothing to say to all those marriages!
She had made three herself to three of his.
The score was even for them, three to three.
But come to die she found she cared so much:
She thought of children in a burial row;
Three children in a burial row were sad.
One man's three women in a burial row
Somehow made her impatient with the man.
And so she said to Laban, "You have done
A good deal right; don't do the last thing wrong.
Don't make me lie with those two other women."

Laban said, No, he would not make her lie
With anyone but that she had a mind to,
If that was how she felt, of course, he said.
She went her way. But Laban having caught
This glimpse of lingering person in Eliza,
And anxious to make all he could of it
With something he remembered in himself,
Tried to think how he could exceed his promise,
And give good measure to the dead, though thankless.
If that was how she felt, he kept repeating.
His first thought under pressure was a grave
In a new boughten grave plot by herself,

Under he didn't care how great a stone:
He'd sell a yoke of steers to pay for it.
And weren't there special cemetery flowers,
That, once grief sets to growing, grief may rest;
The flowers will go on with grief awhile,
And no one seem neglecting or neglected?
A prudent grief will not despise such aids.
He thought of evergreen and everlasting.
And then he had a thought worth many of these.
Somewhere must be the grave of the young boy
Who married her for playmate more than helpmate,
And sometimes laughed at what it was between them.
How would she like to sleep her last with him?
Where was his grave? Did Laban know his name?

He found the grave a town or two away,
The headstone cut with *John, Beloved Husband,*
Beside it room reserved; the say a sister's;
A never-married sister's of that husband,
Whether Eliza would be welcome there.
The dead was bound to silence: ask the sister.
So Laban saw the sister, and, saying nothing
Of where Eliza wanted *not* to lie,
And who had thought to lay her with her first love,
Begged simply for the grave. The sister's face
Fell all in wrinkles of responsibility.
She wanted to do right. She'd have to think.
Laban was old and poor, yet seemed to care;
And she was old and poor—but she cared, too.
They sat. She cast one dull, old look at him,
Then turned him out to go on other errands
She said he might attend to in the village,
While she made up her mind how much she cared—
And how much Laban cared—and why he cared,
(She made shrewd eyes to see where he came in.)

She'd looked Eliza up her second time,
A widow at her second husband's grave,
And offered her a home to rest awhile
Before she went the poor man's widow's way,
Housekeeping for the next man out of wedlock.

She and Eliza had been friends through all.
Who was she to judge marriage in a world
Whose Bible's so confused up in marriage counsel?
The sister had not come across this Laban;
A decent product of life's ironing-out;
She must not keep him waiting. Time would press
Between the death day and the funeral day.
So when she saw him coming in the street
She hurried her decision to be ready
To meet him with his answer at the door.
Laban had known about what it would be
From the way she had set her poor old mouth,
To do, as she had put it, what was right.

She gave it through the screen door closed between them:
"No, not with John. There wouldn't be no sense.
Eliza's had too many other men."

Laban was forced to fall back on his plan
To buy Eliza a plot to lie alone in:
Which gives him for himself a choice of lots
When his time comes to die and settle down.

SOURCE: *Harper's Magazine.* July 1920.

Fire and Ice (1920)

Some say the world will end in fire
Some say in ice.
From what I've tasted of desire
I hold with those who favor fire.
But if it had to perish twice,
I think I know enough of hate
To know that for destruction ice
Is also great
And would suffice.

SOURCE: *Harper's Magazine.* December 1920.

ROSE COHEN

In these extraordinarily touching episodes from her memoir, Rose Cohen (1880–1925) narrates not her arrival in America but her family's preparations for leaving Russia and her imaginings of what she has in store. Cohen wrote her book when she was thirty-eight, at the encouragement of her night-school teacher in Manhattan.

From *Out of the Shadow: A Russian Jewish Girlhood on the Lower East Side* (1918)

FATHER HAD BEEN in America but a short time when grandmother realised that his emigration had lessened Aunt Masha's prospects of marriage. When she came to this conclusion her peace was gone. She wept night and day. "Poor Masha," she moaned, "what is to become of her? Her chances had been small enough without a dowry. And now, burdened with an aged father and a blind helpless mother, the best she can expect is a middle-aged widower with half a dozen children!"

Mother tried to comfort her by telling her that she would remain in Russia as long as grandmother lived, so that she would not have to live with Masha. But this only irritated her. "You talk like a child," she wept. "You stay here and wait for my death, while my son, at the other end of the world, will be leading a life of loneliness. And as for me, would I have any peace, knowing that I was the cause?"

Mother, seeing that she could do nothing to comfort her, silently awaited results.

One night I woke hearing a muffled sound of crying. I felt for grandmother, with whom I slept. But she was not beside me. Frightened, I sat up and peered into the darkness. The crying came from the foot of the bed. And soon I discerned grandmother sitting there. With her hands clasped about her knees and her face buried in her lap she sat rocking gently and weeping.

I called to her in a whisper to come and lie down, but she did not answer. For a while I sat trembling with cold and fear. Then I slipped far back under the warm comforter and tried to sleep. But the picture of grandmother sitting alone in the dark and cold haunted me. And so again I arose.

Creeping over to her quickly I curled up close to her and put my arms around her cold, trembling form. At first she did not take any notice of me. But after a few minutes she lifted her head and unclasping her hands, she drew me under her shawl, saying as she laid her wet face against mine, "Oh, you little mouse, how you do creep up to one! But you had better go back to your place or you will catch cold."

When I went back and as grandmother tucked me in, I asked her why she cried so. "Never mind, you little busybody," she said, "go to sleep." But I teased her to tell me. And finally she said with a sigh and speaking more to herself than to me, "It is about Masha. Go to sleep now, you will hear all about it to-morrow."

She sat down on the edge of the bed gently patting my shoulder, as she had often done when I was a little child. Soon I fell asleep.

The next day the rings under her eyes were darker, and her eyelids were more red and swollen than usual. But otherwise she seemed more calm than she had been for a long time.

After dinner she said to mother, hesitating at every word as she spoke, "You know, I decided last night, that when you go to America Masha should go with you." This startled mother so that she almost dropped the baby whom she was swinging on her foot.

"What are you saying? Masha go to America and you left here alone?"

"Yes, alone," she sighed, "as if I never had any children. But so it must be. True, I have not had a happy life. But happy or not I have lived it. And now, it is almost at an end. But Masha has just begun to live, and in America she will have a better chance, for there are fewer women there, they say. As for me, I shall not be without comfort in my last days. When I am lonely, I shall think of her happily married and surrounded by dear little children like yours. And now listen to this plan. Of course I can not be left here alone, though my needs are few. And so before you start for America you will take me to my niece in the city. She is a very pious woman and so I am sure she will give me a little space in some corner of her house. Of course you will pay her for a year of my board. And after that perhaps you will send her money. But I hope it won't be necessary. Indeed, I feel that I won't trouble this world much longer."

Mother tried to dissuade her from this plan but she turned a deaf ear and insisted that we write to father at once. And we did.

About a month passed before we received an answer. The letter was heavier than usual. And when we opened it, two yellow tickets fell out from among the two closely-written sheets.

"What is this?" we all asked at once. "Not money. And this writing must be English."

We handed the tickets to grandmother who held out her hand for them. Suddenly her hand began to tremble and she said, "Perhaps these are steamer tickets. Quickly read the letter."

After the usual greetings father wrote, "Since Masha is to come to America she might as well start as soon as she can get ready. And Rahel had better come with her. I am sure she can earn at least three dollars a week. With her help I'll be able to bring the rest of the family over much sooner, perhaps in a year or so. And besides, now she can still travel on half a ticket, which I am enclosing with the one for Masha."

Quite bewildered, I looked at mother. Her lips were opening and closing without making a sound. Suddenly she caught me into her arms and burst into tears.

IX.

For many days mother could not look at the steamer tickets without tears in her eyes. And even then though she tried to speak cheerfully about my going to America, I noticed that the anxious look which came into her eyes while the letter was being read, never left them. Also I felt her eyes following me about on every step. But once only, she gave way to her feelings openly.

One morning while she was fastening the back of my dress I caught a few disconnected words, which she uttered low as though she were speaking to herself.

"Good Heavens! child twelve years old—care—herself." Then came those inward tearless sobs and I felt her hands tremble on my back.

But grandmother took the news in a manner that astonished us all. When I looked at her over my mother's shoulder, after the letter was read, I saw her sitting at the table in her usual position. Her head was bent low and a little to one side, and her hands were folded in her lap. Very quietly she sat, not a word, not a tear came from her.

Even grandfather, who never took any notice of her except to scold, looked at her in surprise.

"Well, Baila!" he said. "Have you wept yourself dry? Or perhaps you have come to your senses at last and realise how useless tears are. Remember, that you are sending your child away yourself. I can always take care of my needs but you will die in the poorhouse."

Grandfather and grandmother were always quarrelling. Grandfather claimed that she wept her eyes out. And grandmother said that all her troubles came because of his impiety. But when I grew older I learned that there was a deeper reason for their quarrels.

As a rule when grandfather scolded, grandmother would retort with great spirit. But this time it was as if she did not hear him.

She called me and dictated a letter to Aunt Masha, to come home at once. Then she went to her trunk and took out the ball of fine linen thread which she had been saving for years. And while starting a pair of stockings for Aunt Masha I heard her figuring quietly, what we would need for the journey, how long it would take us to get ready, and what day we would start.

As for me, I became suddenly a very important person. At home I was looked upon as a guest. Now mother never pressed me to do any work. On the contrary, as soon as I would start to do something, she would say,

"Run out and play, you will work hard enough pretty soon." Neither did I find it necessary to feign illness as I had often done before that I might be fondled and caressed. No, indeed; now mother would often put baby down to take me on her lap.

And the young women of the village, who never took any notice of me before, would stop to speak to me.

One day, at sundown, I sat on our gate munching a bit of carrot, and watching the red sun disappearing gradually behind the treetops, when I became aware of some one standing in back of me. I turned around and saw Miriam. She was a pretty, gypsy-like young woman whose dark eyes always looked moist and a little red as though she had just been crying.

"So you are going to America," she said, looking at me wistfully, "you are very fortunate. Of course you are too young to realise it now but you will, later, when you grow older and think of this." She pointed to Siomka's half-tumbled hut, and the little pig who stood at the door and squealed to be let in.

"No," she continued, almost in a whisper, "your life won't be wasted like—." Here Siomka's little pig squealed louder than ever and Miriam turned suddenly and went away. I sat for a long while wondering what the last word might have been. Then I jumped down from the gate and ran into the house to look at the steamer tickets, perhaps for the tenth time that day.

I do not know whether I considered myself fortunate in going to America or not. But I do remember that when I convinced myself, by looking at the tickets often, that it was not a dream like many others I had had, that I would really start for America in a month or six weeks, I felt a great joy. Of course I was a little ashamed of this joy. I saw that mother was unhappy. And grandmother's sorrow, very awful, in its calmness, was double now. For I felt that I was almost as dear to her as Aunt Masha.

When a week passed we cleaned the house as thoroughly as if it were for Easter, in honour of Aunt Masha's coming.

During the five years that she had been away she visited us twice. The last time had been three years before. And so we were all excited and eager to see her.

As the days passed and the time drew near for her coming, grandmother became so impatient and nervous that she would jump at the least outdoor sound, asking excitedly,

"What is that? I think I hear the rumbling of wheels. Isn't that some one coming?" Then we would all rush to the door and windows and find that it was only a cart passing on the road, or a pig scratching his back against the sharp corner of the house.

One day we really heard a cart drive up to the door. When we ran out we saw a small, plump, pretty young woman in a brown dress jump lightly to the ground.

"Oh, grandmother, quickly come, it is Aunt Masha."

In a moment grandmother tumbled out of bed, but before she could reach the door she was in Aunt Masha's arms. And for a while there was sobbing in every corner of the room.

X.

We children scarcely knew Aunt Masha. All I remembered of her two visits, was that both times she had come to stay a month, but went away at the end of a week, and that we felt depressed afterwards, and grandmother cried for days and days.

And so it was only now that we began to know her. When she had been home a short time we found that she was affectionate, but also severe, and hot-tempered. If we did not obey her promptly she scolded severely, or worse still, stopped speaking to us. Aunt Masha was also a painfully clean person and spent a great deal of time in washing us. Brother, whose skin was dark, often appeared, after she was through with him, with his neck red and tears in his eyes.

But the greatest trouble was caused by Aunt Masha's personal belongings. Nothing of hers must be touched. And as we were very curious about things that came from the city there was a world of trouble.

One morning I arose earlier than usual. All were asleep except mother and grandfather, who were out. As I passed Aunt Masha's bed I was attracted by her little shoes which stood close together on the floor beside her bed, looking like two soldiers keeping watch. They were the smallest things with high tops, pointed toes and elastic sides. Often I had longed to try them on. And once I even asked Aunt Masha if I might. But she said, "No, you would burst them." Now as I stood looking at them and at my own clumsy lace shoes, made by our village shoemaker, I thought, "Yes, they would fit. Oh, how I should like to try them on, just for a moment."

I glanced at Aunt Masha's face. The wrinkle between her eyebrows was there even now, and it was saying to me, "No!" But the lips which were partly open showing the white strong teeth, seemed to smile, "Yes."

Very quietly I tiptoed over to the bed, took the shoes and hastened to the bench near the oven. My fingers trembled so, that I could not open my laces. They became knotted and it took me a long time to break them open. But at last my shoes were off.

I remember how rapidly my heart beat when I began to draw one of hers on. I thought, "If it does not go on easily, I won't force it." But it did, and felt comfortable. And the elastic fitted snugly around the ankles. With a feeling of pleasure I stepped down on the floor to see how much taller I looked with high heels. As I stood up I glanced anxiously toward Aunt Masha's bed. What I saw sent the blood rushing to my face.

She was sitting up in bed looking as though she saw a ghost.

"I suppose you have burst them. I told you not to put them on," she said and frowned. This frown brought back my earliest recollections of her. I remembered how I feared it. Now as I stood looking at her it deepened and deepened until it seemed to darken her whole face, and reminded me of an angry cloud.

Quickly I took off her shoes, put them near her bed and ran from her as from an approaching storm.

Outside I met mother, who saw that something had happened, the minute she looked at me. When I told her she scolded.

"You should not have tried on the shoes when you were told not to do it. Now I think you had better go and apologise."

I had never apologised in my life. In the days when I was given the choice between apologising and a spanking, I always chose the spanking. Now when I knew that no spanking was coming I certainly refused to do it. But mother coaxed and begged, and reasoned,

"You are going out into the wide world alone, among strangers. Don't harden your heart against your only friend. Oh, how I wish you had more sense!" She turned away and cried like a little child.

I was miserable. The very thought of apologising made my face burn. But here stood mother crying.

"I won't have many more chances of pleasing her," I thought.

"Mother, I'll apologise, but—not now," I begged. She turned to me. "That is a dear child," she said, looking brighter, "but if you do it at all, do it now."

"What shall I say?" I asked.

"Oh, just say you are sorry you disobeyed."

We went into the house. Aunt Masha was dressed and stood at the window, combing out her beautiful brown hair. It fell all about her, covering almost half of her small body. When she heard the door close she parted her hair in front, as if it were a curtain, and looked. She dropped it quickly when she saw me and went on combing carefully. Slowly I went over to her. "Aunt Masha," I said. My voice sounded strange to me. Again she parted her hair and looked at me. I thought I saw an expression of triumph in her steel grey eyes. This hurt me. And almost before I could think I blurted out, angrily,

"Aunt Masha, I'll never, never, touch anything of yours again, as if it were—swine!"

Aunt Masha fairly gasped. And mother looked horrified. Indeed, I was horrified myself at what I had done. I turned to mother and tried to explain. But I could not make her understand me. I was not good at explanations when I myself was concerned. Quite miserable, I ran out of the house and wandered about in the fields for the rest of the morning.

Aunt Masha did not speak to me for three days. During that time when our eyes happened to meet, I tried to tell her, in a dumb way, that I was sorry. But she always turned her face away quickly. Once when we met near the door, our shoulders almost touching, I saw a smile come quivering to her lips. And so I waited, hoping she would speak to me. But the next moment she frowned it down and passed on as if she did not know me. On the fourth day, at twilight, I came up on her so suddenly, while she was outside, that she gave a little scream of fright. I, too, was frightened, and caught hold of her hand. And she let it stay in mine.

XI.

All through the Spring, while mother, grandmother and Aunt Masha were sewing and knitting stockings for Aunt Masha and me to take along to America, I wandered about in the fields, restless and unable to play at anything.

Early, while the flowers were still heavy with the morning dew, I would take baby, who was a little over a year old, on my back, tie him on to me with a shawl, so that I could rest my arms when they grew tired, and start out followed by the rest of the children. For hours we would wander about like gypsies.

More often than anywhere we went to the lake, where it was very lively at that time of the year, as the peasant women were bleaching their linens. There, sister and brother would go off digging for flagroot. And I would put the two little ones on the flat rock near the edge and climbing up beside them, we would all sit quietly for the longest while, watching, listening.

It was a pleasant spot. The clear blue water lay quietly rippling and sparkling in the sun. On the edge were the women with red kerchiefs on their heads and beads of many colours around their necks, swinging their wooden mallets in unison. And the neighborhood rang with the echoes which seemed to come from the dense, mysterious looking forest across the lake. While through the air floated the sweet odour of new wet linen.

But the time I loved this spot best was late in the afternoon, when the light grew soft and the women went away to their homes. Then came a peculiar hush, and yet there seemed to be a thousand voices in the air whispering softly. They came from everywhere, from the tall stately forest trees across the lake, the hazelnut bushes, the flags as the wind passed over them. And the lake, a deeper blue now in the soft light, rippled gently as if with laughter. Sometimes these fairy-like voices would be lost for a moment in the louder sound of a dry twig breaking and falling to the ground, the cuckoo of a bird or the splash of a fish.

I do not know what effect this had on the children. It made me unspeakably happy and sad at the same time. I remember that I used to want to laugh and cry and sing and dance, and very often I did. To dance I would clasp hands with the children, and we would spin around, and around, until we fell down breathless and dizzy.

At twilight we would start for home, walking very slowly and feeling very sad at the thought of bed time.

So the Spring passed.

As the second of June, the day for our departure to America, drew near, I stayed more in the house and followed mother about more closely. Gradually I became conscious of two things. One was the fear of going out into the world. Just what I feared I did not know. And the other was regret. I had not realised how dear to me were my people and home until I was about to leave them. But the one whom I regretted to leave most was grandmother.

Grandfather was not fond of me and so he cared little about my going away. And mother and the children I should see again. But that grandmother cared I knew. And I also knew and she knew that her I should never see again.

One day grandmother and I were alone in the house, at least, I think we were alone. For as I look back now I can see no one but the two of us. I am standing at the window, and she is walking across the room, with her slow, hesitating step, and her hands stretched in front of her for protection. Coming upon a bench in the middle of the room she sat down heavily, saying, with a sigh,

"It is strange, but the room seems to have grown larger."

"What is that shadow at the window, Rahel? Come, child, let me lean on you. There, your shoulder just fits under my arm. Do you remember when you first began to lead me about? That was when you still called yourself by name."

When we reached the window she raised her hand, shaded her eyes from the strong light and stood quietly for a while, looking out. Then she said,

"This must be a beautiful day. For my eyelids are not as heavy when it is clear."

"Oh, grandmother, it is glorious! There is not a cloud in the sky. And, that thing waving in front of the window, can you make out what it is?"

"I see a black, shapeless mass. What is it?"

"It is the wild apple tree, white with blossoms."

"H-m-m—yes," she said, meditatively, "it was a day just like this."

"When, grandmother?"

She did not answer for a long while and when she spoke at last her voice was low and passionate.

"When God took my sight from me. My eyes had never been strong. One day in the Spring, it was beautiful like to-day, I was digging in the garden, but a little while it seemed to me, when I was startled by a crash of thunder so that the very earth under my feet seemed to tremble. I looked up. The sun was gone and a black angry cloud hung over our house. Quickly I gathered up the tools and hastened toward home. I was but a few steps away when a wind-storm came. It rocked the trees, blew the loosened shingles from the roof, and swept the dry sand in a whirl before me. At the same moment I felt a stinging pain in my eyes so that I could not see the door. In darkness I groped about for a long time, till I found it. For twenty-four hours I was beside myself with pain. At the end of that time it went away as suddenly as it came. When your father, who was a little boy then, untied the kerchief from my eyes I asked him if it were night.

"'Why, mother,' I heard his frightened voice, 'it is daylight. Don't you see the sun across your bed?' Then I knew."

She stood silent and motionless for a while. Then she said more calmly,

"But I must not sin. For if God has taken my sight, He has given me dear little grandchildren who have been everything I wanted. Ah, if I had only been worthy enough to keep them with me!" Here she turned to me suddenly and taking my face between her cold soft hands she said entreatingly,

"Rahel, promise me that you won't cry when you are starting. You hear? It is bad luck to cry when one is starting on a journey. And—I want you to write me whether there are any synagogues in America."

"I promise!"

Still holding my face between her hands she bent over it and looked at it intently. I saw a strained expression come into her face and the eyes move about restlessly under the heavy red lids, as though she were trying to see. Then came a pitiful moan, and tears rolled down her cheeks and fell on mine.

What happened after this I do not remember until the very minute of starting on the second of June. And even then, as I look back I can see nothing at first, but a thick grey mist. But the sounds I recall very distinctly.

There was Aunt Masha's voice crying, a crack of a whip, horses' hoofs striking against stones. Then there was a sudden jolt and I felt myself falling backwards. And now I remember what I saw, too.

When I rose I found myself sitting in a straw-lined wagon, with my back to the horse. Besides me were mother and the baby, who were coming to the city with us, and Aunt Masha who was lying with her face hidden in the straw, crying aloud.

I remembered grandmother's warning, "Nothing but bad luck could come to one who is crying while starting on a journey," and felt sorry for Aunt Masha. But as we were pulling out through the gate and I saw grandmother looking so lonely and forsaken, as she stood leaning against the house, and when I saw grandfather and the children who stood at the gate, looking after us and crying, I could not keep my own tears back, though I opened my eyes wide and blinked hard.

We were still but a short distance from the house when I saw grandmother go in through the open door, and close it behind her with unusual quickness. As she was passing the window I caught a last glimpse of her white kerchief tied about her head.

When we turned the corner I could not see grandfather's and the children's faces any more but I still heard their voices carried over by the wind.

One by one we passed the dear familiar places. Each one brought back sad and happy recollections. As I looked at my favourite bush while we were passing it, I saw my little make-believe companions spring up in it one after another. And among them I saw the swarthy face of my imaginary brother Ephraim. I waved my hand to him, and then hid my face on mother's shoulder.

When I looked up again the road was unknown to me.

SOURCE: Rose Cohen. *Out of the Shadow: A Russian Jewish Girlhood on the Lower East Side*. New York: George H. Doran Company, 1918.

WILLA CATHER

Willa Cather (1873–1947) has come to be regarded as one of the major fiction writers of American literature. This story about a difficult high school student was originally published in a slightly bowdlerized version, in McClure's Magazine *in 1905, as "Paul's Case: A Study in Temperament." We have used Cather's book version instead. Paul, it is fair to say, is the* Catcher in the Rye *character Holden Caulfield's literary grandfather.*

Paul's Case (1920)

It was Paul's afternoon to appear before the faculty of the Pittsburgh High School to account for his various misdemeanours. He had been suspended a week ago, and his father had called at the Principal's office and confessed his perplexity about his son. Paul entered the faculty room suave and smiling. His clothes were a trifle out-grown, and the tan velvet on the collar of his open overcoat was frayed and worn; but for all that there was something of the dandy about him, and he wore an opal pin in his neatly knotted black four-in-hand, and a red carnation in his button-hole. This latter adornment the faculty somehow felt was not properly significant of the contrite spirit befitting a boy under the ban of suspension.

Paul was tall for his age and very thin, with high, cramped shoulders and a narrow chest. His eyes were remarkable for a certain hysterical brilliancy, and he continually used them in a conscious, theatrical sort of way, peculiarly offensive in a boy. The pupils were abnormally large, as though he were addicted to belladonna, but there was a glassy glitter about them which that drug does not produce.

When questioned by the Principal as to why he was there, Paul stated, politely enough, that he wanted to come back to school. This was a lie, but Paul was quite accustomed to lying; found it, indeed, indispensable for overcoming friction. His teachers were asked to state their respective charges against him, which they did with such a rancour and aggrievedness as evinced that this was not a usual case. Disorder and impertinence were among the offences named, yet each of his instructors felt that it was scarcely possible to put into words the real cause of the trouble, which lay in a sort of hysterically defiant manner of the boy's; in the contempt which they all knew he felt for them, and which he seemingly made not the least effort to conceal. Once, when he had been making a synopsis of a paragraph at the blackboard, his English teacher had stepped to his side and attempted to guide his hand. Paul had started back with a shudder and thrust his hands violently behind him. The astonished woman could scarcely have been more hurt and embarrassed had he struck at her. The insult was so involuntary and definitely personal as to be unforgettable. In one way and another, he had made all his teachers, men and women alike, conscious of the same feeling of physical aversion. In one class he habitually sat with his hand shading his eyes; in another he always looked out of the window during the recitation; in another he made a running commentary on the lecture, with humorous intent.

His teachers felt this afternoon that his whole attitude was symbolized by his shrug and his flippantly red carnation flower, and they fell upon him without mercy, his English teacher leading the pack. He stood through it smiling, his pale lips parted over his white teeth. (His lips were continually twitching, and he had a habit of raising his eyebrows that was contemptuous and irritating to the last degree.) Older boys than Paul had broken down and shed tears under that ordeal, but his set smile did not once desert him, and his only sign of discomfort was the nervous trembling of the fingers that toyed with the buttons of his overcoat, and an occasional jerking of the other hand which held his hat. Paul was always smiling, always glancing about him, seeming to feel that people might be watching him and trying to detect something. This conscious expression, since it was as far as possible from boyish mirthfulness, was usually attributed to insolence or "smartness."

As the inquisition proceeded, one of his instructors repeated an impertinent remark of the boy's, and the Principal asked him whether he thought that a courteous speech to make to a woman. Paul shrugged his shoulders slightly and his eyebrows twitched.

"I don't know," he replied. "I didn't mean to be polite or impolite, either. I guess it's a sort of way I have, of saying things regardless."

The Principal asked him whether he didn't think that a way it would be well to get rid of. Paul grinned and said he guessed so. When he was told that he could go, he bowed gracefully and went out. His bow was like a repetition of the scandalous red carnation.

His teachers were in despair, and his drawing master voiced the feeling of them all when he declared there was something about the boy which none of them understood. He added: "I don't really believe that smile of his comes altogether from insolence; there's something sort of haunted about it. The boy is not strong, for one thing. There is something wrong about the fellow."

The drawing master had come to realize that, in looking at Paul, one saw only his white teeth and the forced animation of his eyes. One warm afternoon the boy had gone to sleep at his drawing-board, and his master had noted with amazement what a white, blue-veined face it was; drawn and wrinkled like an old man's about the eyes, the lips twitching even in his sleep.

His teachers left the building dissatisfied and unhappy; humiliated to have felt so vindictive toward a mere boy, to have uttered this feeling in cutting terms, and to have set each other on, as it were, in the grewsome game of intemperate reproach. One of them remembered having seen a miserable street cat set at bay by a ring of tormentors.

As for Paul, he ran down the hill whistling the Soldiers' Chorus from *Faust,* looking wildly behind him now and then to see whether some of his teachers were not there to witness his light-heartedness. As it was now late in the afternoon and Paul was on duty that evening as usher at Carnegie Hall, he decided that he would not go home to supper.

When he reached the concert hall the doors were not yet open. It was chilly outside, and he decided to go up into the picture gallery—always deserted at this hour—where there were some of Raffelli's gay studies of Paris streets and an airy blue Venetian scene or two that always exhilarated him. He was delighted to find no one in the gallery but the old guard, who sat in the corner, a newspaper on his knee, a black patch over one eye and the other closed. Paul possessed himself of the place and walked confidently up and down, whistling under his breath. After a while he sat down before a blue Rico and lost himself. When he bethought him to look at his watch, it was after seven o'clock, and he rose with a start and ran downstairs, making a face at Augustus Cæsar, peering out from the cast-room, and an evil gesture at the Venus of Milo as he passed her on the stairway.

When Paul reached the ushers' dressing-room half-a-dozen boys were there already, and he began excitedly to tumble into his uniform. It was one of the few that at all approached fitting, and Paul thought it very becoming—though he knew the tight, straight coat accentuated his narrow chest, about which he was exceedingly sensitive. He was always excited while he dressed, twanging all over to the tuning of the strings and the preliminary flourishes of the horns in the music-room; but tonight he seemed quite beside himself, and he teased and plagued the boys until, telling him that he was crazy, they put him down on the floor and sat on him.

Somewhat calmed by his suppression, Paul dashed out to the front of the house to seat the early comers. He was a model usher. Gracious and smiling he ran up and down the aisles. Nothing was too much trouble for him; he carried messages and brought programs as though it were his greatest pleasure in life, and all the people in his section thought him a charming boy, feeling that he remembered and admired them. As the house filled, he grew more and more vivacious and animated, and the colour came to his cheeks and lips. It was very much as though this were a great reception and Paul were the host. Just as the musicians came out to take their places, his English teacher arrived with checks for the seats which a prominent manufacturer had taken for the season. She betrayed some embarrassment when she handed Paul the tickets, and a *hauteur* which subsequently made her feel very foolish. Paul was startled for a moment, and had the feeling of wanting to put her out; what business had she here among all these fine people and gay colours? He looked her over and decided that she was not appropriately dressed and must be a fool to sit downstairs in such togs. The tickets had probably been sent her out of kindness, he reflected, as he put down a seat for her, and she had about as much right to sit there as he had.

When the symphony began Paul sank into one of the rear seats with a long sigh of relief, and lost himself as he had done before the Rico. It was not that symphonies, as such, meant anything in particular to Paul, but the first sigh of the instruments seemed to free some hilarious spirit within him; something that struggled there like the Genius in the bottle found by the Arab fisherman. He felt a sudden zest of life; the lights danced before his eyes and the concert hall blazed into unimaginable splendour. When the soprano soloist came on, Paul forgot even the nastiness of his teacher's being there, and gave himself up to the peculiar intoxication such personages always had for him. The soloist chanced to be a German woman, by no means in her first youth, and the mother of many children; but she wore a satin gown and a tiara, and she had that indefinable air of achievement, that world-shine upon her, which always blinded Paul to any possible defects.

After a concert was over, Paul was often irritable and wretched until he got to sleep,—and tonight he was even more than usually restless. He had the feeling of not being able to let down; of its being impossible to give up this delicious excitement which was the only thing that could be called living at all. During the last number he withdrew and, after hastily changing his clothes in the dressing-room, slipped out to the side door where the singer's carriage stood. Here he began pacing rapidly up and down the walk, waiting to see her come out.

Over yonder the Schenley, in its vacant stretch, loomed big and square through the fine rain, the windows of its twelve stories glowing like those of a lighted card-board house under a Christmas tree. All the actors and singers of any importance stayed there when they were in the city, and a number of the big manufacturers of the place lived there in the winter. Paul had often hung about the hotel, watching the people go in and out, longing to enter and leave school-masters and dull care behind him for ever.

At last the singer came out, accompanied by the conductor, who helped her into her carriage and closed the door with a cordial *auf wiedersehen,*—which set Paul to wondering whether she were not an old sweetheart of his. Paul followed the carriage over to the hotel, walking so rapidly as not to be far from the entrance when the singer alighted and disappeared behind the swinging glass doors which were opened by a negro in a tall hat and a long coat. In the moment that the door was ajar, it seemed to Paul that he, too, entered. He seemed to feel himself go after her up the steps, into the warm, lighted building, into an exotic, a tropical world of shiny, glistening surfaces and basking ease. He reflected upon the mysterious dishes that were brought into the dining-room, the green bottles in buckets of ice, as he had seen them in the supper party pictures of the Sunday supplement. A quick gust of wind brought the rain down with sudden vehemence, and Paul was startled to find that he was still outside in the slush of the gravel driveway; that his boots were letting in the water and his scanty overcoat was clinging wet about him; that the lights in front of the concert hall were out, and that the rain was driving in sheets between him and the orange glow of the windows above him. There it was, what he wanted—tangibly before him, like the fairy world of a Christmas pantomime; as the rain beat in his face, Paul wondered whether he were destined always to shiver in the black night outside, looking up at it.

He turned and walked reluctantly toward the car tracks. The end had to come sometime; his father in his night-clothes at the top of the stairs, explanations that did not explain, hastily improvised fictions that were forever tripping him up, his upstairs room and its horrible yellow wall-paper, the creaking bureau with the greasy plush collar-box, and over his painted wooden bed the pictures of George Washington and John Calvin, and the framed motto, "Feed my Lambs," which had been worked in red worsted by his mother, whom Paul could not remember.

Half an hour later, Paul alighted from the Negley Avenue car and went slowly down one of the side streets off the main thoroughfare. It was a highly respectable street, where all the houses were exactly alike, and where business men of moderate means begot and reared large families of children, all of whom went to Sabbath-school and learned the shorter catechism, and were interested in arithmetic; all of whom were as exactly alike as their homes, and of a piece with the monotony in which they lived. Paul never went up Cordelia Street without a shudder of loathing. His home was next the house of the Cumberland minister. He approached it tonight with the nerveless sense of defeat, the hopeless feeling of sinking back forever into ugliness and commonness that he had always had when he came home. The moment he turned into Cordelia Street he felt the waters close above his head. After each of these orgies of living, he experienced all the physical depression which follows a debauch; the loathing of respectable beds, of common food, of a house permeated by kitchen odours; a shuddering repulsion for the flavourless, colourless mass of everyday existence; a morbid desire for cool things and soft lights and fresh flowers.

The nearer he approached the house, the more absolutely unequal Paul felt to the sight of it all; his ugly sleeping chamber; the cold bath-room with the grimy zinc tub, the cracked mirror, the dripping spiggots; his father, at the top of the stairs, his hairy legs sticking out from his nightshirt, his feet thrust into carpet slippers. He was so much later than usual that there would certainly be inquiries and reproaches. Paul stopped short before the door. He felt that he could not be accosted by his father tonight; that he could not toss again on that miserable bed. He would not go in. He would tell his father that he had no car fare, and it was raining so hard he had gone home with one of the boys and stayed all night.

Meanwhile, he was wet and cold. He went around to the back of the house and tried one of the basement windows, found it open, raised it cautiously, and scrambled down the cellar wall to the floor. There he stood, holding his breath, terrified by the noise he had made; but the floor above him was silent, and there was no creak on the stairs. He found a soap-box, and carried it over to the soft ring of light that streamed from the furnace door, and sat down. He was horribly afraid of rats, so he did not try to sleep, but sat looking distrustfully at the dark, still terrified lest he might have awakened his father. In such reactions, after one of the experiences which made days and nights out of the dreary blanks of the calendar, when his senses were deadened, Paul's head was always singularly clear. Suppose his father had heard him getting in at the window and had come down and shot him for a burglar? Then, again, suppose his father had come down, pistol in hand, and he had cried out in time to save himself, and his father had been horrified to think how nearly he had killed him? Then, again, suppose a day should come when his father would remember that night, and wish there had been no warning cry to stay his hand? With this last supposition Paul entertained himself until daybreak.

The following Sunday was fine; the sodden November chill was broken by the last flash of autumnal summer. In the morning Paul had to go to church and Sabbath-school, as always. On seasonable Sunday afternoons the burghers of Cordelia Street usually sat out on their front "stoops," and talked to their neighbours on the next stoop, or called to those across the street in neighbourly fashion. The men sat placidly on gay cushions placed upon the steps that led down to the sidewalk, while the women, in their Sunday "waists," sat in rockers on the cramped porches, pretending to be greatly at their ease. The children played in the streets; there were so many of them that the place resembled the recreation grounds of a kindergarten. The men on the steps—all in their shirt sleeves, their vests unbuttoned—sat with their legs well apart, their stomachs comfortably protruding, and talked of the prices of things, or told anecdotes of the sagacity of their various chiefs and overlords. They occasionally looked over the multitude of squabbling children, listened affectionately to their high-pitched, nasal voices, smiling to see their own proclivities reproduced in their offspring, and interspersed their legends of the iron kings with remarks about their sons' progress at school, their grades in arithmetic, and the amounts they had saved in their toy banks.

On this last Sunday of November, Paul sat all the afternoon on the lowest step of his "stoop," staring into the street, while his sisters, in their rockers, were talking to the minister's daughters next door about how many shirt-waists they had made in the last week, and how many waffles some one had eaten at the last church supper. When the weather was warm, and his father was in a particularly jovial frame of mind, the girls made lemonade, which was always brought out in a red-glass pitcher, ornamented with forget-me-nots in blue enamel. This the girls thought very fine, and the neighbours joked about the suspicious colour of the pitcher.

Today Paul's father, on the top step, was talking to a young man who shifted a restless baby from knee to knee. He happened to be the young man who was daily held up to Paul as a model, and after whom it was his father's dearest hope that he would pattern. This young man was of a ruddy complexion, with a compressed, red mouth, and faded, near-sighted eyes, over which he wore thick spectacles, with gold bows that curved about his ears. He was clerk to one of the magnates of a great steel corporation, and was looked upon in Cordelia Street as a young man with a future. There was a story that, some five years ago—he was now barely twenty-six—he had been a trifle "dissipated," but in order to curb his appetites and save the loss of time and strength that a sowing of wild oats might have entailed, he had taken his chief's advice, oft reiterated to his employés, and at twenty-one had married the first woman whom he could persuade to share his fortunes. She happened to be an angular school-mistress, much older than he, who also wore thick glasses, and who had now borne him four children, all near-sighted, like herself.

The young man was relating how his chief, now cruising in the Mediterranean, kept in touch with all the details of the business, arranging his office hours on his yacht just as though he were at home, and "knocking off work enough to keep two stenographers busy." His father told, in turn, the plan his corporation was considering, of putting in an electric railway plant at Cairo. Paul snapped his teeth; he had an awful apprehension that they might spoil it all before he got there. Yet he rather liked to hear these legends of the iron kings, that were told and retold on Sundays and holidays; these stories of palaces in Venice, yachts on the Mediterranean, and high play at Monte Carlo appealed to his fancy, and he was interested in the triumphs of cash boys who had become famous, though he had no mind for the cash-boy stage.

After supper was over, and he had helped to dry the dishes, Paul nervously asked his father whether he could go to George's to get some help in his geometry, and still more nervously asked for car-fare. This latter request he had to repeat, as his father, on principle, did not like to hear requests for money, whether much or little. He asked Paul whether he could not go to some boy who lived nearer, and told him that he ought not to leave his school work until Sunday; but he gave him the dime. He was not a poor man, but he had a worthy ambition to come up in the world. His only reason for allowing Paul to usher was that he thought a boy ought to be earning a little.

Paul bounded upstairs, scrubbed the greasy odour of the dish-water from his hands with the ill-smelling soap he hated, and then shook over his fingers a few drops of violet water from the bottle he kept hidden in his drawer. He left the house with his geometry conspicuously under his arm, and the moment he got out of Cordelia Street and boarded a downtown car, he shook off the lethargy of two deadening days, and began to live again.

The leading juvenile of the permanent stock company which played at one of the downtown theatres was an acquaintance of Paul's, and the boy had been invited to drop in at the Sunday-night rehearsals whenever he could. For more than a year Paul had spent every available moment loitering about Charley Edwards's dressing-room. He had won a place among Edwards's following not only because the young actor, who could not afford to employ a dresser, often found him useful, but because he recognized in Paul something akin to what churchmen term "vocation."

It was at the theatre and at Carnegie Hall that Paul really lived; the rest was but a sleep and a forgetting. This was Paul's fairy tale, and it had for him all the allurement of a secret love. The moment he inhaled the gassy, painty, dusty odour behind the scenes, he breathed like a prisoner set free, and felt within him the possibility of doing or saying splendid, brilliant things. The moment the cracked orchestra beat out the overture from *Martha,* or jerked at the serenade from *Rigoletto,* all stupid and ugly things slid from him, and his senses were deliciously, yet delicately fired.

Perhaps it was because, in Paul's world, the natural nearly always wore the guise of ugliness, that a certain element of artificiality seemed to him necessary in beauty. Perhaps it was because his experience of life elsewhere was so full of Sabbath-school picnics, petty economies, wholesome advice as to how to succeed in life, and the unescapable odours of cooking, that he found this existence so alluring, these smartly-clad men and women so attractive, that he was so moved by these starry apple orchards that bloomed perennially under the lime-light.

It would be difficult to put it strongly enough how convincingly the stage entrance of that theatre was for Paul the actual portal of Romance. Certainly none of the company ever suspected it, least of all Charley Edwards. It was very like the old stories that used to float about London of fabulously rich Jews, who had subterranean halls, with palms, and fountains, and soft lamps and richly apparelled women who never saw the disenchanting light of London day. So, in the midst of that smoke-palled city, enamoured of figures and grimy toil, Paul had his secret temple, his wishing-carpet, his bit of blue-and-white Mediterranean shore bathed in perpetual sunshine.

Several of Paul's teachers had a theory that his imagination had been perverted by garish fiction; but the truth was, he scarcely ever read at all. The books at home were not such as would either tempt or corrupt a youthful mind, and as for reading the novels that some of his friends urged upon him—well, he got what he wanted much more quickly from music; any sort of music, from an orchestra to a barrel organ. He needed only the spark, the indescribable thrill that made his imagination master of his senses, and he could make plots and pictures enough of his own. It was equally true that he was not stage-struck—not, at any rate, in the usual acceptation of that expression. He had no desire to become an actor, any more than he had to become a musician. He felt no necessity to do any of these things; what he wanted was to see, to be in the atmosphere, float on the wave of it, to be carried out, blue league after blue league, away from everything.

After a night behind the scenes, Paul found the school-room more than ever repulsive; the bare floors and naked walls; the prosy men who never wore frock coats, or violets in their button-holes; the women with their dull gowns, shrill voices, and pitiful seriousness about prepositions that govern the dative. He could not bear to have the other pupils think, for a moment, that he took these people seriously; he must convey to them that he considered it all trivial, and was there only by way of a joke, anyway. He had autograph pictures of all the members of the stock company which he showed his classmates, telling them the most incredible stories of his familiarity with these people, of his acquaintance with the soloists who came to Carnegie Hall, his suppers with them and the flowers he sent them. When these stories lost their effect, and his audience grew listless, he would bid all the boys good-bye, announcing that he was going to travel for awhile; going to Naples, to California, to Egypt. Then, next Monday, he would slip back, conscious and nervously smiling; his sister was ill, and he would have to defer his voyage until spring.

Matters went steadily worse with Paul at school. In the itch to let his instructors know how heartily he despised them, and how thoroughly he was appreciated elsewhere, he mentioned once or twice that he had no time to fool with theorems; adding—with a twitch of the eyebrows and a touch of that nervous bravado which so perplexed them—that he was helping the people down at the stock company; they were old friends of his.

The upshot of the matter was, that the Principal went to Paul's father, and Paul was taken out of school and put to work. The manager at Carnegie Hall was told to get another usher in his stead; the doorkeeper at the theatre was warned not to admit him to the house; and Charley Edwards remorsefully promised the boy's father not to see him again.

The members of the stock company were vastly amused when some of Paul's stories reached them—especially the women. They were hard-working women, most of them supporting indolent husbands or brothers, and they laughed rather bitterly at having stirred the boy to such fervid and florid inventions. They agreed with the faculty and with his father, that Paul's was a bad case.

★ ★ ★

The east-bound train was ploughing through a January snowstorm; the dull dawn was beginning to show grey when the engine whistled a mile out of Newark. Paul started up from the seat where he had lain curled in uneasy slumber, rubbed the breath-misted window glass with his hand, and peered out. The snow was whirling in curling eddies above the white bottom lands, and the drifts lay already deep in the fields and along the fences, while here and there the long dead grass and dried weed stalks protruded black above it. Lights shone from the scattered houses, and a gang of labourers who stood beside the track waved their lanterns.

Paul had slept very little, and he felt grimy and uncomfortable. He had made the all-night journey in a day coach because he was afraid if he took a Pullman he might be seen by some Pittsburgh business man who had noticed him in Denny & Carson's office. When the whistle woke him, he clutched quickly at his breast pocket, glancing about him with an uncertain smile. But the little, clay-bespattered Italians were still sleeping, the slatternly women across the aisle were in open-mouthed oblivion, and even the crumby, crying babies were for the nonce stilled. Paul settled back to struggle with his impatience as best he could.

When he arrived at the Jersey City station, he hurried through his breakfast, manifestly ill at ease and keeping a sharp eye about him. After he reached the Twenty-third Street station, he consulted a cabman, and had himself driven to a men's furnishing establishment which was just opening for the day. He spent upward of two hours there, buying with endless reconsidering and great care. His new street suit he put on in the fitting-room; the frock coat and dress clothes he had bundled into the cab with his new shirts. Then he drove to a hatter's and a shoe house. His next errand was at Tiffany's, where he selected silver mounted brushes and a scarf-pin. He would not wait to have his silver marked, he said. Lastly, he stopped at a trunk shop on Broadway, and had his purchases packed into various travelling bags.

It was a little after one o'clock when he drove up to the Waldorf, and, after settling with the cabman, went into the office. He registered from Washington; said his mother and father had been abroad, and that he had come down to await the arrival of their steamer. He told his story plausibly and had no trouble, since he offered to pay for them in advance, in engaging his rooms; a sleeping-room, sitting-room and bath.

Not once, but a hundred times Paul had planned this entry into New York. He had gone over every detail of it with Charley Edwards, and in his scrap book at home there were pages of description about New York hotels, cut from the Sunday papers.

When he was shown to his sitting-room on the eighth floor, he saw at a glance that everything was as it should be; there was but one detail in his mental picture that the place did not realize, so he rang for the bell boy and sent him down for flowers. He moved about nervously until the boy returned, putting away his new linen and fingering it delightedly as he did so. When the flowers came, he put them hastily into water, and then tumbled into a hot bath. Presently he came out of his white bath-room, resplendent in his new silk underwear, and playing with the tassels of his red robe. The snow was whirling so fiercely outside his windows that he could scarcely see across the street; but within, the air was deliciously soft and fragrant. He put the violets and jonquils on the tabouret beside the couch, and threw himself down with a long sigh, covering himself with a Roman blanket. He was thoroughly tired; he had been in such haste, he had stood up to such a strain, covered so much ground in the last twenty-four hours, that he wanted to think how it had all come about. Lulled by the sound of the wind, the warm air, and the cool fragrance of the flowers, he sank into deep, drowsy retrospection.

It had been wonderfully simple; when they had shut him out of the theatre and concert hall, when they had taken away his bone, the whole thing was virtually determined. The rest was a mere matter of opportunity. The only thing that at all surprised him was his own courage—for he realized well enough that he had always been tormented by fear, a sort of apprehensive dread that, of late years, as the meshes of the lies he had told closed about him, had been pulling the muscles of his body tighter and tighter. Until now, he could not remember a time when he had not been dreading something. Even when he was a little boy, it was always there—behind him, or before, or on either side. There had always been the shadowed corner, the dark place into which he dared not look, but from which something seemed always to be watching him—and Paul had done things that were not pretty to watch, he knew.

But now he had a curious sense of relief, as though he had at last thrown down the gauntlet to the thing in the corner.

Yet it was but a day since he had been sulking in the traces; but yesterday afternoon that he had been sent to the bank with Denny & Carson's deposit, as usual—but this time he was instructed to leave the book to be balanced. There was above two thousand dollars in checks, and nearly a thousand in the bank notes which he had taken from the book and quietly transferred to his pocket. At the bank he had made out a new deposit slip. His nerves had been steady enough to permit of his returning to the office, where he had finished his work and asked for a full day's holiday tomorrow, Saturday, giving a perfectly reasonable pretext. The bank book, he knew, would not be returned before Monday or Tuesday, and his father would be out of town for the next week. From the time he slipped the bank notes into his pocket until he boarded the night train for New York, he had not known a moment's hesitation.

How astonishingly easy it had all been; here he was, the thing done; and this time there would be no awakening, no figure at the top of the stairs. He watched the snow flakes whirling by his window until he fell asleep.

When he awoke, it was four o'clock in the afternoon. He bounded up with a start; one of his precious days gone already! He spent nearly an hour in dressing, watching every stage of his toilet carefully in the mirror. Everything was quite perfect; he was exactly the kind of boy he had always wanted to be.

When he went downstairs, Paul took a carriage and drove up Fifth avenue toward the Park. The snow had somewhat abated; carriages and tradesmen's wagons were hurrying soundlessly to and fro in the winter twilight; boys in woollen mufflers were shovelling off the doorsteps; the avenue stages made fine spots of colour against the white street. Here and there on the corners whole flower gardens blooming behind glass windows, against which the snow flakes stuck and melted; violets, roses, carnations, lilies of the valley—somehow vastly more lovely and alluring that they blossomed thus unnaturally in the snow. The Park itself was a wonderful stage winter-piece.

When he returned, the pause of the twilight had ceased, and the tune of the streets had changed. The snow was falling faster, lights streamed from the hotels that reared their many stories fearlessly up into the storm, defying the raging Atlantic winds. A long, black stream of carriages poured down the avenue, intersected here and there by other streams, tending horizontally. There were a score of cabs about the entrance of his hotel, and his driver had to wait. Boys in livery were running in and out of the awning stretched across the sidewalk, up and down the red velvet carpet laid from the door to the street. Above, about, within it all, was the rumble and roar, the hurry and toss of thousands of human beings as hot for pleasure as himself, and on every side of him towered the glaring affirmation of the omnipotence of wealth.

The boy set his teeth and drew his shoulders together in a spasm of realization; the plot of all dramas, the text of all romances, the nerve-stuff of all sensations was whirling about him like the snow flakes. He burnt like a faggot in a tempest.

When Paul came down to dinner, the music of the orchestra floated up the elevator shaft to greet him. As he stepped into the thronged corridor, he sank back into one of the chairs against the wall to get his breath. The lights, the chatter, the perfumes, the bewildering medley of colour—he had, for a moment, the feeling of not being able to stand it. But only for a moment; these were his own people, he told himself. He went slowly about the corridors, through the writing-rooms, smoking-rooms, reception-rooms, as though he were exploring the chambers of an enchanted palace, built and peopled for him alone.

When he reached the dining-room he sat down at a table near a window. The flowers, the white linen, the many-coloured wine glasses, the gay toilettes of the women, the low popping of corks, the undulating repetitions of the *Blue Danube* from the orchestra, all flooded Paul's dream with bewildering radiance. When the roseate tinge of his champagne was added—that cold, precious, bubbling stuff that creamed and foamed in his glass—Paul wondered that there were honest men in the world at all. This was what all the world was fighting for, he reflected; this was what all the struggle was about. He doubted the reality of his past. Had he ever known a place called Cordelia Street, a place where fagged looking business men boarded the early car? Mere rivets in a machine they seemed to Paul,—sickening men, with combings of children's hair always hanging to their coats, and the smell of cooking in their clothes. Cordelia Street—Ah, that belonged to another time and country! Had he not always been thus, had he not sat here night after night, from as far back as he could remember, looking pensively over just such shimmering textures, and slowly twirling the stem of a glass like this one between his thumb and middle finger? He rather thought he had.

He was not in the least abashed or lonely. He had no especial desire to meet or to know any of these people; all he demanded was the right to look on and conjecture, to watch the pageant. The mere stage properties were all he contended for. Nor was he lonely later in the evening, in his loge at the Opera. He was entirely rid of his nervous misgivings, of his forced aggressiveness, of the imperative desire to show himself different from his surroundings. He felt now that his surroundings explained him. Nobody questioned the purple; he had only to wear it passively. He had only to glance down at his dress coat to reassure himself that here it would be impossible for anyone to humiliate him.

He found it hard to leave his beautiful sitting-room to go to bed that night, and sat long watching the raging storm from his turret window. When he went to sleep, it was with the lights turned on in his bedroom; partly because of his old timidity, and partly so that, if he should wake in the night, there would be no wretched moment of doubt, no horrible suspicion of yellow wall-paper, or of Washington and Calvin above his bed.

On Sunday morning the city was practically snow-bound. Paul breakfasted late, and in the afternoon he fell in with a wild San Francisco boy, a freshman at Yale, who said he had run down for a "little flyer" over Sunday. The young man offered to show Paul the night side of the town, and the two boys went off together after dinner, not returning to the hotel until seven o'clock the next morning. They had started out in the confiding warmth of a champagne friendship, but their parting in the elevator was singularly cool. The freshman pulled himself together to make his train, and Paul went to bed. He awoke at two o'clock in the afternoon, very thirsty and dizzy, and rang for ice-water, coffee, and the Pittsburgh papers.

On the part of the hotel management, Paul excited no suspicion. There was this to be said for him, that he wore his spoils with dignity and in no way made himself conspicuous. His chief greediness lay in his ears and eyes, and his excesses were not offensive ones. His dearest pleasures were the grey winter twilights in his sitting-room; his quiet enjoyment of his flowers, his clothes, his wide divan, his cigarette and his sense of power. He could not remember a time when he had felt so at peace with himself. The mere release from the necessity of petty lying, lying every day and every day, restored his self-respect. He had never lied for pleasure, even at school; but to make himself noticed and admired, to assert his difference from other Cordelia Street boys; and he felt a good deal more manly, more honest, even, now that he had no need for boastful pretensions, now that he could, as his actor friends used to say, "dress the part." It was characteristic that remorse did not occur to him. His golden days went by without a shadow, and he made each as perfect as he could.

On the eighth day after his arrival in New York, he found the whole affair exploited in the Pittsburgh papers, exploited with a wealth of detail which indicated that local news of a sensational nature was at a low ebb. The firm of Denny & Carson announced that the boy's father had refunded the full amount of his theft, and that they had no intention of prosecuting. The Cumberland minister had been interviewed, and expressed his hope of yet reclaiming the motherless lad, and Paul's Sabbath-school teacher declared that she would spare no effort to that end. The rumour had reached Pittsburgh that the boy had been seen in a New York hotel, and his father had gone East to find him and bring him home.

Paul had just come in to dress for dinner; he sank into a chair, weak in the knees, and clasped his head in his hands. It was to be worse than jail, even; the tepid waters of Cordelia Street were to close over him finally and forever. The grey monotony stretched before him in hopeless, unrelieved years; Sabbath-school, Young People's Meeting, the yellow-papered room, the damp dish-towels; it all rushed back upon him with sickening vividness. He had the old feeling that the orchestra had suddenly stopped, the sinking sensation that the play was over. The sweat broke out on his face, and he sprang to his feet, looked about him with his white, conscious smile, and winked at himself in the mirror. With something of the childish belief in miracles with which he had so often gone to class, all his lessons unlearned, Paul dressed and dashed whistling down the corridor to the elevator.

He had no sooner entered the dining-room and caught the measure of the music, than his remembrance was lightened by his old elastic power of claiming the moment, mounting with it, and finding it all sufficient. The glare and glitter about him, the mere scenic accessories had again, and for the last time, their old potency. He would show himself that he was game, he would finish the thing splendidly. He doubted, more than ever, the existence of Cordelia Street, and for the first time he drank his wine recklessly. Was he not, after all, one of these fortunate beings? Was he not still himself, and in his own place? He drummed a nervous accompaniment to the music and looked about him, telling himself over and over that it had paid.

He reflected drowsily, to the swell of the violin and the chill sweetness of his wine, that he might have done it more wisely. He might have caught an outbound steamer and been well out of their clutches before now. But the other side of the world had seemed too far away and too uncertain then; he could not have waited for it; his need had been too sharp. If he had to choose over again, he would do the same thing tomorrow. He looked affectionately about the dining-room, now gilded with a soft mist. Ah, it had paid indeed!

Paul was awakened next morning by a painful throbbing in his head and feet. He had thrown himself across the bed without undressing, and had slept with his shoes on. His limbs and hands were lead heavy, and his tongue and throat were parched. There came upon him one of those fateful attacks of clear-headedness that never occurred except when he was physically exhausted and his nerves hung loose. He lay still and closed his eyes and let the tide of realities wash over him.

His father was in New York; "stopping at some joint or other," he told himself. The memory of successive summers on the front stoop fell upon him like a weight of black water. He had not a hundred dollars left; and he knew now, more than ever, that money was everything, the wall that stood between all he loathed and all he wanted. The thing was winding itself up; he had thought of that on his first glorious day in New York, and had even provided a way to snap the thread. It lay on his dressing-table now; he had got it out last night when he came blindly up from dinner,—but the shiny metal hurt his eyes, and he disliked the look of it, anyway.

He rose and moved about with a painful effort, succumbing now and again to attacks of nausea. It was the old depression exaggerated; all the world had become Cordelia Street. Yet somehow he was not afraid of anything, was absolutely calm; perhaps because he had looked into the dark corner at last, and knew. It was bad enough, what he saw there; but somehow not so bad as his long fear of it had been. He saw everything clearly now. He had a feeling that he had made the best of it, that he had lived the sort of life he was meant to live, and for half an hour he sat staring at the revolver. But he told himself that was not the way, so he went downstairs and took a cab to the ferry.

When Paul arrived at Newark, he got off the train and took another cab, directing the driver to follow the Pennsylvania tracks out of the town. The snow lay heavy on the roadways and had drifted deep in the open fields. Only here and there the dead grass or dried weed stalks projected, singularly black, above it. Once well into the country, Paul dismissed the carriage and walked, floundering along the tracks, his mind a medley of irrelevant things. He seemed to hold in his brain an actual picture of everything he had seen that morning. He remembered every feature of both his drivers, the toothless old woman from whom he had bought the red flowers in his coat, the agent from whom he had got his ticket, and all of his fellow-passengers on the ferry. His mind, unable to cope with vital matters near at hand, worked feverishly and deftly at sorting and grouping these images. They made for him a part of the ugliness of the world, of the ache in his head, and the bitter burning on his tongue. He stooped and put a handful of snow into his mouth as he walked, but that, too, seemed hot. When he reached a little hillside, where the tracks ran through a cut some twenty feet below him, he stopped and sat down.

The carnations in his coat were drooping with the cold, he noticed; all their red glory over. It occurred to him that all the flowers he had seen in the show windows that first night must have gone the same way, long before this. It was only one splendid breath they had, in spite of their brave mockery at the winter outside the glass. It was a losing game in the end, it seemed, this revolt against the homilies by which the world is run. Paul took one of the blossoms carefully from his coat and scooped a little hole in the snow, where he covered it up. Then he dozed a while, from his weak condition, seeming insensible to the cold.

The sound of an approaching train woke him, and he started to his feet, remembering only his resolution, and afraid lest he should be too late. He stood watching the approaching locomotive, his teeth chattering, his lips drawn away from them in a frightened smile; once or twice he glanced nervously sidewise, as though he were being watched. When the right moment came, he jumped. As he fell, the folly of his haste occurred to him with merciless clearness, the vastness of what he had left undone. There flashed through his brain, clearer than ever before, the blue of Adriatic water, the yellow of Algerian sands.

He felt something strike his chest,—his body was being thrown swiftly through the air, on and on, immeasurably far and fast, while his limbs gently relaxed. Then, because the picture making mechanism was crushed, the disturbing visions flashed into black, and Paul dropped back into the immense design of things.

SOURCE: Willa Cather. *Youth and the Bright Medusa.* New York: Alfred A. Knopf, 1920.

SHERWOOD ANDERSON

Sherwood Anderson (1876–1941) was, for a time, seen as the master of American short fiction, which the following two stories justify. As the editor Joslyn Pine notes in the Dover edition of The Egg and Other Stories, *Anderson "significantly influenced the style and concerns of a whole generation of American writers . . . most notably William Faulkner and Ernest Hemingway."*

The Egg (1921)

MY FATHER WAS, I am sure, intended by nature to be a cheerful, kindly man. Until he was thirty-four years old he worked as a farm-hand for a man named Thomas Butterworth whose place lay near the town of Bidwell, Ohio. He had then a horse of his own and on Saturday evenings drove into town to spend a few hours in social intercourse with other farm-hands. In town he drank several glasses of beer and stood about in Ben Head's saloon—crowded on Saturday evenings with visiting farm-hands. Songs were sung and glasses thumped on the bar. At ten o'clock father drove home along a lonely country road, made his horse comfortable for the night and himself went to bed, quite happy in his position in life. He had at that time no notion of trying to rise in the world.

It was in the spring of his thirty-fifth year that father married my mother, then a country school-teacher, and in the following spring I came wriggling and crying into the world. Something happened to the two people. They became ambitious. The American passion for getting up in the world took possession of them.

It may have been that mother was responsible. Being a school-teacher she had no doubt read books and magazines. She had, I presume, read of how Garfield, Lincoln, and other Americans rose from poverty to fame and greatness and as I lay beside her—in the days of her lying-in—she may have dreamed that I would some day rule men and cities. At any rate she induced father to give up his place as a farm-hand, sell his horse and embark on an independent enterprise of his own. She was a tall silent woman with a long nose and troubled grey eyes. For herself she wanted nothing. For father and myself she was incurably ambitious.

The first venture into which the two people went turned out badly. They rented ten acres of poor stony land on Griggs's Road, eight miles from Bidwell, and launched into chicken raising. I grew into boyhood on the place and got my first impressions of life there. From the beginning they were impressions of disaster and if, in my turn, I am a gloomy man inclined to see the darker side of life, I attribute it to the fact that what should have been for me the happy joyous days of childhood were spent on a chicken farm.

One unversed in such matters can have no notion of the many and tragic things that can happen to a chicken. It is born out of an egg, lives for a few weeks as a tiny fluffy thing such as you will see pictured on Easter cards, then becomes hideously naked, eats quantities of corn and meal bought by the sweat of your father's brow, gets diseases called pip, cholera, and other names, stands looking with stupid eyes at the sun, becomes sick and dies. A few hens and now and then a rooster, intended to serve God's mysterious ends, struggle through to maturity. The hens lay eggs out of which come other chickens and the dreadful cycle is thus made complete. It is all unbelievably complex. Most philosophers must have been raised on chicken farms. One hopes for so much from a chicken and is so dreadfully disillusioned. Small chickens, just setting out on the journey of life, look so bright and alert and they are in fact so dreadfully stupid. They are so much like people they mix one up in one's judgments of life. If disease does not kill them they wait until your expectations are thoroughly aroused and then walk under the wheels of a wagon—to go squashed and dead back to their maker. Vermin infest their youth, and fortunes must be spent for curative powders. In later life I have seen how a literature has been built up on the subject of fortunes to be made out of the raising of chickens. It is intended to be read by the gods who have just eaten of the tree of the knowledge of good and evil. It is a hopeful literature and declares that much may be done by simple ambitious people who own a few hens. Do not be led astray by it. It was not written for you. Go hunt for gold on the frozen hills of Alaska, put your faith in the honesty of a politician, believe if you will that the world is daily growing better and that good will triumph over evil, but do not read and believe the literature that is written concerning the hen. It was not written for you.

I, however, digress. My tale does not primarily concern itself with the hen. If correctly told it will centre on the egg. For ten years my father and mother struggled to make our chicken farm pay and then they gave up that struggle and began another. They moved into the town of Bidwell, Ohio, and embarked in the restaurant business. After ten years of worry with incubators that did not hatch, and with tiny—and in their own way lovely—balls of fluff that passed on into semi-naked pullethood and from that into dead henhood, we threw all aside and packing our belongings on a wagon drove down Griggs's Road toward Bidwell, a tiny caravan of hope looking for a new place from which to start on our upward journey through life.

We must have been a sad looking lot, not, I fancy, unlike refugees fleeing from a battlefield. Mother and I walked in the road. The wagon that contained our goods had been borrowed for the day from Mr. Albert Griggs, a neighbor. Out of its sides stuck the legs of cheap chairs and at the back of the pile of beds, tables, and boxes filled with kitchen utensils was a crate of live chickens, and on top of that the baby carriage in which I had been wheeled about in my infancy. Why we stuck to the baby carriage I don't know. It was unlikely other children would be born and the wheels were broken. People who have few possessions cling tightly to those they have. That is one of the facts that make life so discouraging.

Father rode on top of the wagon. He was then a bald-headed man of forty-five, a little fat and from long association with mother and the chickens he had become habitually silent and discouraged. All during our ten years on the chicken farm he had worked as a laborer on neighboring farms and most of the money he had earned had been spent for remedies to cure chicken diseases, on Wilmer's White Wonder Cholera Cure or Professor Bidlow's Egg Producer or some other preparations that mother found advertised in the poultry papers. There were two little patches of hair on father's head just above his ears. I remember that as a child I used to sit looking at him when he had gone to sleep in a chair before the stove on Sunday afternoons in the winter. I had at that time already begun to read books and have notions of my own and the bald path that led over the top of his head was, I fancied, something like a broad road, such a road as Caesar might have made on which to lead his legions out of Rome and into the wonders of an unknown world. The tufts of hair that grew above father's ears were, I thought, like forests. I fell into a half-sleeping, half-waking state and dreamed I was a tiny thing going along the road into a far beautiful place where there were no chicken farms and where life was a happy eggless affair.

One might write a book concerning our flight from the chicken farm into town. Mother and I walked the entire eight miles—she to be sure that nothing fell from the wagon and I to see the wonders of the world. On the seat of the wagon beside father was his greatest treasure. I will tell you of that.

On a chicken farm where hundreds and even thousands of chickens come out of eggs surprising things sometimes happen. Grotesques are born out of eggs as out of people. The accident does not often occur—perhaps once in a thousand births. A chicken is, you see, born that has four legs, two pairs of wings, two heads or what not. The things do not live. They go quickly back to the hand of their maker that has for a moment trembled. The fact that the poor little things could not live was one of the tragedies of life to father. He had some sort of notion that if he could but bring into henhood or roosterhood a five-legged hen or a two-headed rooster his fortune would be made. He dreamed of taking the wonder about to county fairs and of growing rich by exhibiting it to other farm-hands.

At any rate he saved all the little monstrous things that had been born on our chicken farm. They were preserved in alcohol and put each in its own glass bottle. These he had carefully put into a box and on our journey into town it was carried on the wagon seat beside him. He drove the horses with one hand and with the other clung to the box. When we got to our destination the box was taken down at once and the bottles removed. All during our days as keepers of a restaurant in the town of Bidwell, Ohio, the grotesques in their little glass bottles sat on a shelf back of the counter. Mother sometimes protested but father was a rock on the subject of his treasure. The grotesques were, he declared, valuable. People, he said, liked to look at strange and wonderful things.

Did I say that we embarked in the restaurant business in the town of Bidwell, Ohio? I exaggerated a little. The town itself lay at the foot of a low hill and on the shore of a small river. The railroad did not run through the town and the station was a mile away to the north at a place called Pickleville. There had been a cider mill and pickle factory at the station, but before the time of our coming they had both gone out of business. In the morning and in the evening busses came down to the station along a road called Turner's Pike from the hotel on the main street of Bidwell. Our going to the out of the way place to embark in the restaurant business was mother's idea. She talked of it for a year and then one day went off and rented an empty store building opposite the railroad station. It was her idea that the restaurant would be profitable. Travelling men, she said, would be always waiting around to take trains out of town and town people would come to the station to await incoming trains. They would come to the restaurant to buy pieces of pie and drink coffee. Now that I am older I know that she had another motive in going. She was ambitious for me. She wanted me to rise in the world, to get into a town school and become a man of the towns.

At Pickleville father and mother worked hard as they always had done. At first there was the necessity of putting our place into shape to be a restaurant. That took a month. Father built a shelf on which he put tins of vegetables. He painted a sign on which he put his name in large letters. Below his name was the sharp command—"EAT HERE" that was so seldom obeyed. A show case was bought and filled with cigars and tobacco. Mother scrubbed the floor and the walls of the room. I went to school in the town and was glad to be away from the farm and from the presence of the discouraged, sad-looking chickens. Still I was not very joyous. In the evening I walked home from school along Turner's Pike and remembered the children I had seen playing in the town school yard. A troop of little girls had gone hopping about and singing. I tried that. Down along the frozen road I went hopping solemnly on one leg. "Hippity Hop To The Barber Shop," I sang shrilly. Then I stopped and looked doubtfully about. I was afraid of being seen in my gay mood. It must have seemed to me that I was doing a thing that should not be done by one who, like myself, had been raised on a chicken farm where death was a daily visitor.

Mother decided that our restaurant should remain open at night. At ten in the evening a passenger train went north past our door followed by a local freight. The freight crew had switching to do in Pickleville and when the work was done they came to our restaurant for hot coffee and food. Sometimes one of them ordered a fried egg. In the morning at four they returned north-bound and again visited us. A little trade began to grow up. Mother slept at night and during the day tended the restaurant and fed our boarders while father slept. He slept in the same bed mother had occupied during the night and I went off to the town of Bidwell and to school. During the long nights, while mother and I slept, father cooked meats that were to go into sandwiches for the lunch baskets of our boarders. Then an idea in regard to getting up in the world came into his head. The American spirit took hold of him. He also became ambitious.

In the long nights when there was little to do father had time to think. That was his undoing. He decided that he had in the past been an unsuccessful man because he had not been cheerful enough and that in the future he would adopt a cheerful outlook on life. In the early morning he came upstairs and got into bed with mother. She woke and the two talked. From my bed in the corner I listened.

It was father's idea that both he and mother should try to entertain the people who came to eat at our restaurant. I cannot now remember his words, but he gave the impression of one about to become in some obscure way a kind of public entertainer. When people, particularly young people from the town of Bidwell, came into our place, as on very rare occasions they did, bright entertaining conversation was to be made. From father's words I gathered that something of the jolly innkeeper effect was to be sought. Mother must have been doubtful from the first, but she said nothing discouraging. It was father's notion that a passion for the company of himself and mother would spring up in the breasts of the younger people of the town of Bidwell. In the evening bright happy groups would come singing down Turner's Pike. They would troop shouting with joy and laughter into our place. There would be song and festivity. I do not mean to give the impression that father spoke so elaborately of the matter. He was as I have said an uncommunicative man. "They want some place to go. I tell you they want some place to go," he said over and over. That was as far as he got. My own imagination has filled in the blanks.

For two or three weeks this notion of father's invaded our house. We did not talk much, but in our daily lives tried earnestly to make smiles take the place of glum looks. Mother smiled at the boarders and I, catching the infection, smiled at our cat. Father became a little feverish in his anxiety to please. There was no doubt, lurking somewhere in him, a touch of the spirit of the showman. He did not waste much of his ammunition on the railroad men he served at night but seemed to be waiting for a young man or woman from Bidwell to come in to show what he could do. On the counter in the restaurant there was a wire basket kept always filled with eggs, and it must have been before his eyes when the idea of being entertaining was born in his brain. There was something pre-natal about the way eggs kept themselves connected with the development of his idea. At any rate an egg ruined his new impulse in life. Late one night I was awakened by a roar of anger coming from father's throat. Both mother and I sat upright in our beds. With trembling hands she lighted a lamp that stood on a table by her head. Downstairs the front door of our restaurant went shut with a bang and in a few minutes father tramped up the stairs. He held an egg in his hand and his hand trembled as though he were having a chill. There was a half insane light in his eyes. As he stood glaring at us I was sure he intended throwing the egg at either mother or me. Then he laid it gently on the table beside the lamp and dropped on his knees beside mother's bed. He began to cry like a boy and I, carried away by his grief, cried with him. The two of us filled the little upstairs room with our wailing voices. It is ridiculous, but of the picture we made I can remember only the fact that mother's hand continually stroked the bald path that ran across the top of his head. I have forgotten what mother said to him and how she induced him to tell her of what had happened downstairs. His explanation also has gone out of my mind. I remember only my own grief and fright and the shiny path over father's head glowing in the lamp light as he knelt by the bed.

As to what happened downstairs. For some unexplainable reason I know the story as well as though I had been a witness to my father's discomfiture. One in time gets to know many unexplainable things. On that evening young Joe Kane, son of a merchant of Bidwell, came to Pickleville to meet his father, who was expected on the ten o'clock evening train from the South. The train was three hours late and Joe came into our place to loaf about and to wait for its arrival. The local freight train came in and the freight crew were fed. Joe was left alone in the restaurant with father.

From the moment he came into our place the Bidwell young man must have been puzzled by my father's actions. It was his notion that father was angry at him for hanging around. He noticed that the restaurant keeper was apparently disturbed by his presence and he thought of going out. However, it began to rain and he did not fancy the long walk to town and back. He bought a five-cent cigar and ordered a cup of coffee. He had a newspaper in his pocket and took it out and began to read. "I'm waiting for the evening train. It's late," he said apologetically.

For a long time father, whom Joe Kane had never seen before, remained silently gazing at his visitor. He was no doubt suffering from an attack of stage fright. As so often happens in life he had thought so much and so often of the situation that now confronted him that he was somewhat nervous in its presence.

For one thing, he did not know what to do with his hands. He thrust one of them nervously over the counter and shook hands with Joe Kane. "How-de-do," he said. Joe Kane put his newspaper down and stared at him. Father's eye lighted on the basket of eggs that sat on the counter and he began to talk. "Well," he began hesitatingly, "well, you have heard of Christopher Columbus, eh?" He seemed to be angry. "That Christopher Columbus was a cheat," he declared emphatically. "He talked of making an egg stand on its end. He talked, he did, and then he went and broke the end of the egg."

My father seemed to his visitor to be beside himself at the duplicity of Christopher Columbus. He muttered and swore. He declared it was wrong to teach children that Christopher Columbus was a great man when, after all, he cheated at the critical moment. He had declared he would make an egg stand on end and then when his bluff had been called he had done a trick. Still grumbling at Columbus, father took an egg from the basket on the counter and began to walk up and down. He rolled the egg between the palms of his hands. He smiled genially. He began to mumble words regarding the effect to be produced on an egg by the electricity that comes out of the human body. He declared that without breaking its shell and by virtue of rolling it back and forth in his hands he could stand the egg on its end. He explained that the warmth of his hands and the gentle rolling movement he gave the egg created a new centre of gravity, and Joe Kane was mildly interested. "I have handled thousands of eggs," father said. "No one knows more about eggs than I do."

He stood the egg on the counter and it fell on its side. He tried the trick again and again, each time rolling the egg between the palms of his hands and saying the words regarding the wonders of electricity and the laws of gravity. When after a half hour's effort he did succeed in making the egg stand for a moment he looked up to find that his visitor was no longer watching. By the time he had succeeded in calling Joe Kane's attention to the success of his effort the egg had again rolled over and lay on its side.

Afire with the showman's passion and at the same time a good deal disconcerted by the failure of his first effort, father now took the bottles containing the poultry monstrosities down from their place on the shelf and began to show them to his visitor. "How would you like to have seven legs and two heads like this fellow?" he asked, exhibiting the most remarkable of his treasures. A cheerful smile played over his face. He reached over the counter and tried to slap Joe Kane on the shoulder as he had seen men do in Ben Head's saloon when he was a young farm-hand and drove to town on Saturday evenings. His visitor was made a little ill by the sight of the body of the terribly deformed bird floating in the alcohol in the bottle and got up to go. Coming from behind the counter father took hold of the young man's arm and led him back to his seat. He grew a little angry and for a moment had to turn his face away and force himself to smile. Then he put the bottles back on the shelf. In an outburst of generosity he fairly compelled Joe Kane to have a fresh cup of coffee and another cigar at his expense. Then he took a pan and filling it with vinegar, taken from a jug that sat beneath the counter, he declared himself about to do a new trick. "I will heat this egg in this pan of vinegar," he said. "Then I will put it through the neck of a bottle without breaking the shell. When the egg is inside the bottle it will resume its normal shape and the shell will become hard again. Then I will give the bottle with the egg in it to you. You can take it about with you wherever you go. People will want to know how you got the egg in the bottle. Don't tell them. Keep them guessing. That is the way to have fun with this trick."

Father grinned and winked at his visitor. Joe Kane decided that the man who confronted him was mildly insane but harmless. He drank the cup of coffee that had been given him and began to read his paper again. When the egg had been heated in vinegar father carried it on a spoon to the counter and going into a back room got an empty bottle. He was angry because his visitor did not watch him as he began to do his trick, but nevertheless went cheerfully to work. For a long time he struggled, trying to get the egg to go through the neck of the bottle. He put the pan of vinegar back on the stove, intending to reheat the egg, then picked it up and burned his fingers. After a second bath in the hot vinegar the shell of the egg had been softened a little but not enough for his purpose. He worked and worked and a spirit of desperate determination took possession of him. When he thought that at last the trick was about to be consummated the delayed train came in at the station and Joe Kane started to go nonchalantly out at the door. Father made a last desperate effort to conquer the egg and make it do the thing that would establish his reputation as one who knew how to entertain guests who came into his restaurant. He worried the egg. He attempted to be somewhat rough with it. He swore and the sweat stood out on his forehead. The egg broke under his hand. When the contents spurted over his clothes, Joe Kane, who had stopped at the door, turned and laughed.

A roar of anger rose from my father's throat. He danced and shouted a string of inarticulate words. Grabbing another egg from the basket on the counter, he threw it, just missing the head of the young man as he dodged through the door and escaped.

Father came upstairs to mother and me with an egg in his hand. I do not know what he intended to do. I imagine he had some idea of destroying it, of destroying all eggs, and that he intended to let mother and me see him begin. When, however, he got into the presence of mother something happened to him. He laid the egg gently on the table and dropped on his knees by the bed as I have already explained. He later decided to close the restaurant for the night and to come upstairs and get into bed. When he did so he blew out the light and after much muttered conversation both he and mother went to sleep. I suppose I went to sleep also, but my sleep was troubled. I awoke at dawn and for a long time looked at the egg that lay on the table. I wondered why eggs had to be and why from the egg came the hen who again laid the egg. The question got into my blood. It has stayed there, I imagine, because I am the son of my father. At any rate, the problem remains unsolved in my mind. And that, I conclude, is but another evidence of the complete and final triumph of the egg—at least as far as my family is concerned.

SOURCE: Sherwood Anderson. *The Triumph of the Egg: A Book of Impressions from American Life in Tales and Poems*. New York: B. W. Huebsch, Inc., 1921.

The Other Woman (1921)

"I AM IN love with my wife," he said—a superflous remark, as I had not questioned his attachment to the woman he had married. We walked for ten minutes and then he said it again. I turned to look at him. He began to talk and told me the tale I am now about to set down.

The thing he had on his mind happened during what must have been the most eventful week of his life. He was to be married on Friday afternoon. On Friday of the week before he got a telegram announcing his appointment to a government position. Something else happened that made him very proud and glad. In secret he was in the habit of writing verses and during the year before several of them had been printed in poetry magazines. One of the societies that give prizes for what they think the best poems published during the year put his name at the head of its list. The story of his triumph was printed in the newspapers of his home city and one of them also printed his picture.

As might have been expected he was excited and in a rather highly strung nervous state all during that week. Almost every evening he went to call on his fiancée, the daughter of a judge. When he got there the house was filled with people and many letters, telegrams and packages were being received. He stood a little to one side and men and women kept coming up to speak to him. They congratulated him upon his success in getting the government position and on his achievement as a poet. Everyone seemed to be praising him and when he went home and to bed he could not sleep. On Wednesday evening he went to the theatre and it seemed to him that people all over the house recognized him. Everyone nodded and smiled. After the first act five or six men and two women left their seats to gather about him. A little group was formed. Strangers sitting along the same row of seats stretched their necks and looked. He had never received so much attention before, and now a fever of expectancy took possession of him.

As he explained when he told me of his experience, it was for him an altogether abnormal time. He felt like one floating in air. When he got into bed after seeing so many people and hearing so many words of praise his head whirled round and round. When he closed his eyes a crowd of people invaded his room. It seemed as though the minds of all the people of his city were centered on himself. The most absurd fancies took possession of him. He imagined himself riding in a carriage through the streets of a city. Windows were thrown open and people ran out at the doors of houses. "There he is. That's him," they shouted, and at the words a glad cry arose. The carriage drove into a street blocked with people. A hundred thousand pairs of eyes looked up at him. "There you are! What a fellow you have managed to make of yourself!" the eyes seemed to be saying.

My friend could not explain whether the excitement of the people was due to the fact that he had written a new poem or whether, in his new government position, he had performed some notable act. The apartment where he lived at that time was on a street perched along the top of a cliff far out at the edge of his city, and from his bedroom window he could look down over trees and factory roofs to a river. As he could not sleep and as the fancies that kept crowding in upon him only made him more excited, he got out of bed and tried to think.

As would be natural under such circumstances, he tried to control his thoughts, but when he sat by the window and was wide awake a most unexpected and humiliating thing happened. The night was clear and fine. There was a moon. He wanted to dream of the woman who was to be his wife, to think out lines for noble poems or make plans that would affect his career. Much to his surprise his mind refused to do anything of the sort.

At a corner of the street where he lived there was a small cigar store and newspaper stand run by a fat man of forty and his wife, a small active woman with bright grey eyes. In the morning he stopped there to buy a paper before going down to the city. Sometimes he saw only the fat man, but often the man had disappeared and the woman waited on him. She was, as he assured me at least twenty times in telling me his tale, a very ordinary person with nothing special or notable about her, but for some reason he could not explain, being in her presence stirred him profoundly. During that week in the midst of his distraction she was the only person he knew who stood out clear and distinct in his mind. When he wanted so much to think noble thoughts he could think only of her. Before he knew what was happening his imagination had taken hold of the notion of having a love affair with the woman.

"I could not understand myself," he declared, in telling me the story. "At night, when the city was quiet and when I should have been asleep, I thought about her all the time. After two or three days of that sort of thing the consciousness of her got into my daytime thoughts. I was terribly muddled. When I went to see the woman who is now my wife I found that my love for her was in no way affected by my vagrant thoughts. There was but one woman in the world I wanted to live with and to be my comrade in undertaking to improve my own character and my position in the world, but for the moment, you see, I wanted this other woman to be in my arms. She had worked her way into my being. On all sides people were saying I was a big man who would do big things, and there I was. That evening when I went to the theatre I walked home because I knew I would be unable to sleep, and to satisfy the annoying impulse in myself I went and stood on the sidewalk before the tobacco shop. It was a two story building, and I knew the woman lived upstairs with her husband. For a long time I stood in the darkness with my body pressed against the wall of the building, and then I thought of the two of them up there and no doubt in bed together. That made me furious.

"Then I grew more furious with myself. I went home and got into bed, shaken with anger. There are certain books of verse and some prose writings that have always moved me deeply, and so I put several books on a table by my bed.

"The voices in the books were like the voices of the dead. I did not hear them. The printed words would not penetrate into my consciousness. I tried to think of the woman I loved, but her figure had also become something far away, something with which I for the moment seemed to have nothing to do. I rolled and tumbled about in the bed. It was a miserable experience.

"On Thursday morning I went into the store. There stood the woman alone. I think she knew how I felt. Perhaps she had been thinking of me as I had been thinking of her. A doubtful hesitating smile played about the corners of her mouth. She had on a dress made of cheap cloth and there was a tear on the shoulder. She must have been ten years older than myself. When I tried to put my pennies on the glass counter, behind which she stood, my hand trembled so that the pennies made a sharp rattling noise. When I spoke the voice that came out of my throat did not sound like anything that had ever belonged to me. It barely arose above a thick whisper. 'I want you,' I said. 'I want you very much. Can't you run away from your husband? Come to me at my apartment at seven tonight.'

"The woman did come to my apartment at seven. That morning she didn't say anything at all. For a minute perhaps we stood looking at each other. I had forgotten everything in the world but just her. Then she nodded her head and I went away. Now that I think of it I cannot remember a word I ever heard her say. She came to my apartment at seven and it was dark. You must understand this was in the month of October. I had not lighted a light and I had sent my servant away.

"During that day I was no good at all. Several men came to see me at my office, but I got all muddled up in trying to talk with them. They attributed my rattle-headedness to my approaching marriage and went away laughing.

"It was on that morning, just the day before my marriage, that I got a long and very beautiful letter from my fiancée. During the night before she also had been unable to sleep and had got out of bed to write the letter. Everything she said in it was very sharp and real, but she herself, as a living thing, seemed to have receded into the distance. It seemed to me that she was like a bird, flying far away in distant skies, and that I was like a perplexed bare-footed boy standing in the dusty road before a farm house and looking at her receding figure. I wonder if you will understand what I mean?

"In regard to the letter. In it she, the awakening woman, poured out her heart. She of course knew nothing of life, but she was a woman. She lay, I suppose, in her bed feeling nervous and wrought up as I had been doing. She realized that a great change was about to take place in her life and was glad and afraid too. There she lay thinking of it all. Then she got out of bed and began talking to me on the bit of paper. She told me how afraid she was and how glad too. Like most young women she had heard things whispered. In the letter she was very sweet and fine. 'For a long time, after we are married, we will forget we are a man and woman,' she wrote. 'We will be human beings. You must remember that I am ignorant and often I will be very stupid. You must love me and be very patient and kind. When I know more, when after a long time you have taught me the way of life, I will try to repay you. I will love you tenderly and passionately. The possibility of that is in me or I would not want to marry at all. I am afraid but I am also happy. O, I am so glad our marriage time is near at hand!'

"Now you see clearly enough what a mess I was in. In my office, after I had read my fiancée's letter, I became at once very resolute and strong. I remember that I got out of my chair and walked about, proud of the fact that I was to be the husband of so noble a woman. Right away I felt concerning her as I had been feeling about myself before I found out what a weak thing I was. To be sure I took a strong resolution that I would not be weak. At nine that evening I had planned to run in to see my fiancée. 'I'm all right now,' I said to myself. 'The beauty of her character has saved me from myself. I will go home now and send the other woman away.' In the morning I had telephoned to my servant and told him that I did not want him to be at the apartment that evening and I now picked up the telephone to tell him to stay at home.

"Then a thought came to me. 'I will not want him there in any event,' I told myself. 'What will he think when he sees a woman coming in my place on the evening before the day I am to be married?' I put the telephone down and prepared to go home. 'If I want my servant out of the apartment it is because I do not want him to hear me talk with the woman. I cannot be rude to her. I will have to make some kind of an explanation,' I said to myself.

"The woman came at seven o'clock, and, as you may have guessed, I let her in and forgot the resolution I had made. It is likely I never had any intention of doing anything else. There was a bell on my door, but she did not ring, but knocked very softly. It seems to me that everything she did that evening was soft and quiet, but very determined and quick. Do I make myself clear? When she came I was standing just within the door where I had been standing and waiting for a half hour. My hands were trembling as they had trembled in the morning when her eyes looked at me and when I tried to put the pennies on the counter in the store. When I opened the door she stepped quickly in and I took her into my arms. We stood together in the darkness. My hands no longer trembled. I felt very happy and strong.

"Although I have tried to make everything clear I have not told you what the woman I married is like. I have emphasized, you see, the other woman. I make the blind statement that I love my wife, and to a man of your shrewdness that means nothing at all. To tell the truth, had I not started to speak of this matter I would feel more comfortable. It is inevitable that I give you the impression that I am in love with the tobacconist's wife. That's not true. To be sure I was very conscious of her all during the week before my marriage, but after she had come to me at my apartment she went entirely out of my mind.

"Am I telling the truth? I am trying very hard to tell what happened to me. I am saying that I have not since that evening thought of the woman who came to my apartment. Now, to tell the facts of the case, that is not true. On that evening I went to my fiancée at nine, as she had asked me to do in her letter. In a kind of way I cannot explain the other woman went with me. This is what I mean—you see I had been thinking that if anything happened between me and the tobacconist's wife I would not be able to go through with my marriage. 'It is one thing or the other with me,' I had said to myself.

"As a matter of fact I went to see my beloved on that evening filled with a new faith in the outcome of our life together. I am afraid I muddle this matter in trying to tell it. A moment ago I said the other woman, the tobacconist's wife, went with me. I do not mean she went in fact. What I am trying to say is that something of her faith in her own desires and her courage in seeing things through went with me. Is that clear to you? When I got to my fiancée's house there was a crowd of people standing about. Some were relatives from distant places I had not seen before. She looked up quickly when I came into the room. My face must have been radiant. I never saw her so moved. She thought her letter had affected me deeply, and of course it had. Up she jumped and ran to meet me. She was like a glad child. Right before the people who turned and looked inquiringly at us, she said the thing that was in her mind. 'O, I am so happy,' she cried. 'You have understood. We will be two human beings. We will not have to be husband and wife.'

"As you may suppose everyone laughed, but I did not laugh. The tears came into my eyes. I was so happy I wanted to shout. Perhaps you understand what I mean. In the office that day when I read the letter my fiancée had written I had said to myself, 'I will take care of the dear little woman.' There was something smug, you see, about that. In her house when she cried out in that way, and when everyone laughed, what I said to myself was something like this: 'We will take care of ourselves.' I whispered something of the sort into her ears. To tell you the truth I had come down off my perch. The spirit of the other woman did that to me. Before all the people gathered about I held my fiancée close and we kissed. They thought it very sweet of us to be so affected at the sight of each other. What they would have thought had they known the truth about me God only knows!

"Twice now I have said that after that evening I never thought of the other woman at all. That is partially true but, sometimes in the evening when I am walking alone in the street or in the park as we are walking now, and when evening comes softly and quickly as it has come to-night, the feeling of her comes sharply into my body and mind. After that one meeting I never saw her again. On the next day I was married and I have never gone back into her street. Often however as I am walking along as I am doing now, a quick sharp earthy feeling takes possession of me. It is as though I were a seed in the ground and the warm rains of the spring had come. It is as though I were not a man but a tree.

"And now you see I am married and everything is all right. My marriage is to me a very beautiful fact. If you were to say that my marriage is not a happy one I could call you a liar and be speaking the absolute truth. I have tried to tell you about this other woman. There is a kind of relief in speaking of her. I have never done it before. I wonder why I was so silly as to be afraid that I would give you the impression I am not in love with my wife. If I did not instinctively trust your understanding I would not have spoken. As the matter stands I have a little stirred myself up. To-night I shall think of the other woman. That sometimes occurs. It will happen after I have gone to bed. My wife sleeps in the next room to mine and the door is always left open. There will be a moon to-night, and when there is a moon long streaks of light fall on her bed. I shall awake at midnight to-night. She will be lying asleep with one arm thrown over her head.

"What is it that I am now talking about? A man does not speak of his wife lying in bed. What I am trying to say is that, because of this talk, I shall think of the other woman to-night. My thoughts will not take the form they did during the week before I was married. I still wonder what has become of the woman. For a moment I will again feel myself holding her close. I will think that for an hour I was closer to her than I have ever been to anyone else. Then I will think of the time when I will be as close as that to my wife. She is still, you see, an awakening woman. For a moment I will close my eyes and the quick, shrewd, determined eyes of that other woman will look into mine. My head will swim and then I will quickly open my eyes and see again the dear woman with whom I have undertaken to live out my life. Then I will sleep and when I awake in the morning it will be as it was that evening when I walked out of my dark apartment after having had the most notable experience of my life. What I mean to say, you understand is that, for me, when I awake, the other woman will be utterly gone."

SOURCE: Sherwood Anderson. *The Triumph of the Egg: A Book of Impressions from American Life in Tales and Poems*. New York: B. W. Huebsch, Inc., 1921.

EDNA ST. VINCENT MILLAY

The poetry of Edna St. Vincent Millay (1892–1950) remains attractive and engaging for its clarity, range of topics and passionate voice.

Thursday (1921)

And if I loved you Wednesday,
  Well, what is that to you?
I do not love you Thursday—
  So much is true.

And why you come complaining
  Is more than I can see.
I loved you Wednesday,—yes—but what
  Is that to me?

SOURCE: Edna St. Vincent Millay. *A Few Figs from Thistles: Poems and Sonnets*. New York: Frank Shay, 1921.

To the Not Impossible Him (1921)

How shall I know, unless I go
  To Cairo and Cathay,
Whether or not this blessed spot
  Is blest in every way?

Now it may be, the flower for me
Is this beneath my nose;
How shall I tell, unless I smell
The Carthaginian rose?

The fabric of my faithful love
No power shall dim or ravel
Whilst I stay here,—but oh, my dear,
If I should ever travel!

SOURCE: Edna St. Vincent Millay. *A Few Figs from Thistles: Poems and Sonnets.* New York: Frank Shay, 1921.

Exiled (1921)

Searching my heart for its true sorrow,
This is the thing I find to be:
That I am weary of words and people,
Sick of the city, wanting the sea;

Wanting the sticky, salty sweetness
Of the strong wind and shattered spray;
Wanting the loud sound and the soft sound
Of the big surf that breaks all day.

Always before about my dooryard,
Marking the reach of the winter sea,
Rooted in sand and dragging drift-wood,
Straggled the purple wild sweet-pea;

Always I climbed the wave at morning,
Shook the sand from my shoes at night,
That now am caught beneath great buildings,
Stricken with noise, confused with light.

If I could hear the green piles groaning
Under the windy wooden piers,
See once again the bobbing barrels,
And the black sticks that fence the weirs,

If I could see the weedy mussels
Crusting the wrecked and rotting hulls,

Hear once again the hungry crying
Overhead, of the wheeling gulls,

Feel once again the shanty straining
Under the turning of the tide,
Fear once again the rising freshet,
Dread the bell in the fog outside,—

I should be happy,—that was happy
All day long on the coast of Maine!
I have a need to hold and handle
Shells and anchors and ships again!

I should be happy, that am happy
Never at all since I came here.
I am too long away from water.
I have a need of water near.

SOURCE: Edna St. Vincent Millay. *Second April.* New York: Harper and Brothers Publishers, 1921.

Travel (1921)

The railroad track is miles away,
And the day is loud with voices speaking,
Yet there isn't a train goes by all day
But I hear its whistle shrieking.

All night there isn't a train goes by,
Though the night is still for sleep and dreaming
But I see its cinders red on the sky,
And hear its engine steaming.

My heart is warm with the friends I make,
And better friends I'll not be knowing,
Yet there isn't a train I wouldn't take,
No matter where it's going.

SOURCE: Edna St. Vincent Millay. *Second April.* New York: Harper and Brothers Publishers, 1921.

LANGSTON HUGHES

Langston Hughes (1902–1967), whose writing career spanned the Harlem Renaissance and continued its persistent path until his death, was a colloquial poet who often wrote in the voice of his subjects; throughout his life, he was a determined advocate for black Americans and writers. This was his first famous published poem.

The Negro Speaks of Rivers (1921)

I've known rivers:
I've known rivers ancient as the world and older than the flow of
  human blood in human veins.

My soul has grown deep like the rivers.

I bathed in the Euphrates when dawns were young.
I built my hut near the Congo and it lulled me to sleep.
I looked upon the Nile and raised the pyramids above it.
I heard the singing of the Mississippi when Abe Lincoln
  went down to New Orleans, and I've seen its muddy
  bosom turn all golden in the sunset

I've known rivers:
Ancient, dusky rivers.

My soul has grown deep like the rivers.

SOURCE: *The Crisis: A Record of the Darker Races* (June 1921).

GERTRUDE STEIN

One of the greatest of experimenters in sound and sense, Gertrude Stein (1874–1946) grew up in Oakland, California, but lived most of her life in Paris, where she mentored and befriended numerous international writers and artists.

Every Afternoon: A Dialogue (1922)

I get up.
So do you get up.
We are pleased with each other.
Why are you.
Because we are hopeful.
Have you any reason to be.
We have reason to be.
What is it.
I am not prepared to say.
Is there any change.
Naturally.
I know what you mean.
I consider that it is not necessary for me to teach languages.
It would be foolish of you to.
It would here.
It would anywhere.
I do not care about Peru.
I hope you do.

Do I begin this.
Yes you began this.
Of course we did.
Yes indeed we did.

When will we speak of another.
Not today I assure you.
Yes certainly you mentioned it.
We mentioned everything.
To another.
I do not wish reasons.
You mean you are taught early.
That is exactly what I mean.
And I feel the same.
You feel it to be the same.
Don't tempt him.
Do not tempt him.
This evening there was no question of temptation he was not the least interested.
Neither was she.
Of course she wasn't.
It's really not necessary to ask her.
I found it necessary.
You did
Certainly.
And when have you leisure.
Reading and knitting.
Reading or knitting.
Reading or knitting.
Yes reading or knitting.
In the evening.
Actively first.
He was very settled.
Where was he settled.
In Marseilles.
I cannot understand words.
Cannot you.
You are so easily deceived you don't ask what do they decide what are they to decide.
There is no reason.
No there is no reason.
Between meals.
Do you really sew.
He was so necessary to me.
We are equally pleased.
Come and stay.

Do so.
Do you mean to be rude.
Did he.
I ask you why.
Tomorrow.
Yes tomorrow.
Every afternoon.
A dialogue.
What did you do with your dog.
We sent him into the country.
Was he a trouble.
Not at all but we thought he would be better off there.
Yes it isn't right to keep a large dog in the city.
Yes I agree with you.
Yes
Coming.
Yes certainly.
Do be quick.
Not in breathing.
No you know you don't mind.
We said yes.
Come ahead.
That sounded like an animal.
Were you expecting something.
I don't know.
Don't you know about it at all.
You know I don't believe it.
She did.
Well they are different
I am not very careful.
Mention that again.
Here.
Not here.
Don't receive wood.
Don't receive wood.
Well we went and found it.
Tomorrow.
Come tomorrow.
Come tomorrow.
Yes we said yes. Come tomorrow.

Coming very well. Don't be irritable. Don't say you haven't been told. You know I want a telegram. Why.
Because emperors didn't.
I don't remember that.
I don't care for a long time.
For a long time to pass away.
Why not.
Because I like him.
That's what she said.
We said.
We will gladly come Saturday.
She will go.
Oh yes she will.
What is a conversation.
We can all sing.
A great many people come in.
A great many people come in.
Why do the days pass so quickly.
Because we are very happy.
Yes that's so.
That's it.
That is it.
Who cares for daisies.
Do you hear me.
Yes I can hear you.
Very well then explain.
That I care for daisies.
That we care for daisies.
Come in come in.
Yes and I will not cry.
No indeed.
We will picnic.
Oh yes.
We are very happy.
Very happy.
And content.
And content.
We will go and hear Tito Ruffo.
Here.
Yes here.
Oh yes I remember about that. He is to be here.

To begin with what did we buy.
Scolding.
If you remember you will remember other things that frighten you.
Will I.
Yes and there is no necessity the explanation is not in your walking first of walking last of walking beside me the only reason that there is plenty of room is that I choose it.
Then we will say that it will rain.
The other day there was bright moonlight.
Not here.
No not here but on the whole there is more moonlight than in Brittany.
Come again.
Come in again.
Coming again.
Coming in again.
Come again.
I say I do understand calling.
Calling him.
Yes Polybe.
Come.
Come.
Come again and bring a book.
We meet him so often.
We meant to see about it. You mean the light.
I am proud of her. You have every reason to be and she takes it so naturally.
It is better that it is her hands.
Yes of course.
Nothing can pay for that.
Republics are so ungrateful.
Do you desire to appear here.
Why of course in that sense.
I do not know those words.
It is really wretched.
You do see it.
I don't see it that way.
No you wouldn't you would prefer the words well and tall.
Say it to me.
You know I never wished to be blamed.

An effort to eat quickly.
Did you promise him.
Did I promise him the woods.
The woods.
Not now.
You mean not now.

SOURCE: Gertrude Stein. *Geography and Plays*. Boston: The Four Seas Company, 1922.

F. SCOTT FITZGERALD

F. Scott Fitzgerald, born in 1896, was the rising star in American fiction at the beginning of the 1920s. He wrote gorgeously phrased, engaging stories for big magazines, many of them about attractive, young, rich men and women. His most famous work today, the novel The Great Gatsby, *appeared in 1925. Though he was enormously talented, alcoholism took a toll on him; after moving to Hollywood in the late 1930s, he died in 1940. "The Curious Case of Benjamin Button" prompted Fitzgerald's amused and amusing note in the Table of Contents of* Tales of the Jazz Age*: "This story was inspired by a remark of Mark Twain's to the effect that it was a pity that the best part of life came at the beginning and the worst part at the end. By trying the experiment upon only one man in a perfectly normal world I have scarcely given his idea a fair trial. Several weeks after completing it, I discovered an almost identical plot in Samuel Butler's Note-books. The story was published in* Collier's *last summer and provoked this startling letter from an anonymous admirer in Cincinnati: 'Sir—I have read the story Benjamin Button in* Colliers *and I wish to say that as a short story writer you would make a good lunatic I have seen many peices of cheese in my life but of all the peices of cheese I have ever seen you are the biggest peice. I hate to waste a peice of stationary on you but I will.'"*

The Curious Case of Benjamin Button (1922)

Chapter 1

As long ago as 1860 it was the proper thing to be born at home. At present, so I am told, the high gods of medicine have decreed that the first cries of the young shall be uttered upon the anesthetic air of a hospital, preferably a fashionable one. So young Mr. and Mrs. Roger Button were fifty years ahead of style when they decided, one day in the summer of 1860, that their first baby should be born in a hospital. Whether this anachronism had any bearing upon the astonishing history I am about to set down will never be known.

I shall tell you what occurred, and let you judge for yourself.

The Roger Buttons held an enviable position, both social and financial, in ante-bellum Baltimore. They were related to the This Family and the That Family, which, as every Southerner knew, entitled them to membership in that enormous peerage which largely populated the Confederacy. This was their first experience with the charming old custom of having babies—Mr. Button was naturally nervous. He hoped it would be a boy so that he could be sent to Yale College in Connecticut, at which institution Mr. Button himself had been known for four years by the somewhat obvious nickname of "Cuff."

On the September morning consecrated to the enormous event he arose nervously at six o'clock, dressed himself, adjusted an impeccable stock, and hurried forth through the streets of Baltimore to the hospital, to determine whether the darkness of the night had borne in new life upon its bosom.

When he was approximately a hundred yards from the Maryland Private Hospital for Ladies and Gentlemen he saw Doctor Keene, the family physician, descending the front steps, rubbing his hands together with a washing movement—as all doctors are required to do by the unwritten ethics of their profession.

Mr. Roger Button, the president of Roger Button & Co., Wholesale Hardware, began to run toward Doctor Keene with much less dignity than was expected from a Southern gentleman of that picturesque period. "Doctor Keene!" he called. "Oh, Doctor Keene!"

The doctor heard him, faced around, and stood waiting, a curious expression settling on his harsh, medicinal face as Mr. Button drew near.

"What happened?" demanded Mr. Button, as he came up in a gasping rush. "What was it? How is she? A boy? Who is it? What—"

"Talk sense!" said Doctor Keene sharply. He appeared somewhat irritated.

"Is the child born?" begged Mr. Button.

Doctor Keene frowned. "Why, yes, I suppose so—after a fashion." Again he threw a curious glance at Mr. Button.

"Is my wife all right?"

"Yes."

"Is it a boy or a girl?"

"Here now!" cried Doctor Keene in a perfect passion of irritation, "I'll ask you to go and see for yourself. Outrageous!" He snapped the last word out in almost one syllable, then he turned away muttering: "Do you imagine a case like this will help my professional reputation? One more would ruin me—ruin anybody."

"What's the matter?" demanded Mr. Button, appalled. "Triplets?"

"No, not triplets!" answered the doctor cuttingly. "What's more, you can go and see for yourself. And get another doctor. I brought you into the world, young man, and I've been physician to your family for forty years, but I'm through with you! I don't want to see you or any of your relatives ever again! Good-by!"

Then he turned sharply, and without another word climbed into his phaeton, which was waiting at the curbstone, and drove severely away.

Mr. Button stood there upon the sidewalk, stupefied and trembling from head to foot. What horrible mishap had occurred? He had suddenly lost all desire to go into the Maryland Private Hospital for Ladies and Gentlemen—it was with the greatest difficulty that, a moment later, he forced himself to mount the steps and enter the front door.

A nurse was sitting behind a desk in the opaque gloom of the hall. Swallowing his shame, Mr. Button approached her.

"Good-morning," she remarked, looking up at him pleasantly.

"Good-morning. I—I am Mr. Button."

At this a look of utter terror spread itself over the girl's face. She rose to her feet and seemed about to fly from the hall, restraining herself only with the most apparent difficulty.

"I want to see my child," said Mr. Button.

The nurse gave a little scream. "Oh—of course!" she cried hysterically. "Up-stairs. Right up-stairs. Go—*up!*"

She pointed the direction, and Mr. Button, bathed in a cool perspiration, turned falteringly, and began to mount to the second floor. In the upper hall he addressed another nurse who approached him, basin in hand. "I'm Mr. Button," he managed to articulate. "I want to see my—"

Clank! The basin clattered to the floor and rolled in the direction of the stairs. Clank! Clank! It began a methodical descent as if sharing in the general terror which this gentleman provoked.

"I want to see my child!" Mr. Button almost shrieked. He was on the verge of collapse.

Clank! The basin had reached the first floor. The nurse regained control of herself, and threw Mr. Button a look of hearty contempt.

"All *right*, Mr. Button," she agreed in a hushed voice. "Very *well!* But if you *knew* what state it's put us all in this morning! It's perfectly outrageous! The hospital will never have the ghost of a reputation after—"

"Hurry!" he cried hoarsely. "I can't stand this!"

"Come this way, then, Mr. Button."

He dragged himself after her. At the end of a long hall they reached a room from which proceeded a variety of howls—indeed, a room which, in later parlance, would have been known as the "crying-room." They entered. Ranged around the walls were half a dozen white-enameled rolling cribs, each with a tag tied at the head.

"Well," gasped Mr. Button, "which is mine?"

"There!" said the nurse.

Mr. Button's eyes followed her pointing finger, and this is what he saw. Wrapped in a voluminous white blanket, and partially crammed into one of the cribs, there sat an old man apparently about seventy years of age. His sparse hair was almost white, and from his chin dripped a long smoke-colored beard, which waved absurdly back and forth, fanned by the breeze coming in at the window. He looked up at Mr. Button with dim, faded eyes in which lurked a puzzled question.

"Am I mad?" thundered Mr. Button, his terror resolving into rage. "Is this some ghastly hospital joke?"

"It doesn't seem like a joke to us," replied the nurse severely. "And I don't know whether you're mad or not—but that is most certainly your child."

The cool perspiration redoubled on Mr. Button's forehead. He closed his eyes, and then, opening them, looked again. There was no mistake—he was gazing at a man of threescore and ten—a *baby* of threescore and ten, a baby whose feet hung over the sides of the crib in which it was reposing.

The old man looked placidly from one to the other for a moment, and then suddenly spoke in a cracked and ancient voice. "Are you my father?" he demanded.

Mr. Button and the nurse started violently.

"Because if you are," went on the old man querulously, "I wish you'd get me out of this place—or, at least, get them to put a comfortable rocker in here,"

"Where in God's name did you come from? Who are you?" burst out Mr. Button frantically.

"I can't tell you *exactly* who I am," replied the querulous whine, "because I've only been born a few hours—but my last name is certainly Button."

"You lie! You're an impostor!"

The old man turned wearily to the nurse. "Nice way to welcome a new-born child," he complained in a weak voice. "Tell him he's wrong, why don't you?"

"You're wrong. Mr. Button," said the nurse severely. "This is your child, and you'll have to make the best of it. We're going to ask you to take him home with you as soon as possible—some time to-day."

"Home?" repeated Mr. Button incredulously.

"Yes, we can't have him here. We really can't, you know?"

"I'm right glad of it," whined the old man. "This is a fine place to keep a youngster of quiet tastes. With all this yelling and howling, I haven't been able to get a wink of sleep. I asked for something to eat"—here his voice rose to a shrill note of protest—"and they brought me a bottle of milk!"

Mr. Button sank down upon a chair near his son and concealed his face in his hands. "My heavens!" he murmured, in an ecstasy of horror. "What will people say? What must I do?"

"You'll have to take him home," insisted the nurse—"immediately!"

A grotesque picture formed itself with dreadful clarity before the eyes of the tortured man—a picture of himself walking through the crowded streets of the city with this appalling apparition stalking by his side. "I can't. I can't," he moaned.

People would stop to speak to him, and what was he going to say? He would have to introduce this—this septuagenarian: "This is my son, born early this morning." And then the old man would gather his blanket around him and they would plod on, past the bustling stores, the slave market—for a dark instant Mr. Button wished passionately that his son was black—past the luxurious houses of the residential district, past the home for the aged. . . .

"Come! Pull yourself together," commanded the nurse.

"See here," the old man announced suddenly, "if you think I'm going to walk home in this blanket, you're entirely mistaken."

"Babies always have blankets."

With a malicious crackle the old man held up a small white swaddling garment. "Look!" he quavered. "*This* is what they had ready for me."

"Babies always wear those," said the nurse primly.

"Well," said the old man, "this baby's not going to wear anything in about two minutes. This blanket itches. They might at least have given me a sheet."

"Keep it on! Keep it on!" said Mr. Button hurriedly. He turned to the nurse. "What'll I do?"

"Go down town and buy your son some clothes."

Mr. Button's son's voice followed him down into the hall: "And a cane, father. I want to have a cane."

Mr. Button banged the outer door savagely. . . .

Chapter 2

"Good-morning," Mr. Button said, nervously, to the clerk in the Chesapeake Dry Goods Company. "I want to buy some clothes for my child."

"How old is your child, sir?"

"About six hours," answered Mr. Button, without due consideration.

"Babies' supply department in the rear."

"Why, I don't think—I'm not sure that's what I want. It's—he's an unusually large-size child. Exceptionally—ah—large."

"They have the largest child's sizes."

"Where is the boys' department?" inquired Mr. Button, shifting his ground desperately. He felt that the clerk must surely scent his shameful secret.

"Right here."

"Well—" He hesitated. The notion of dressing his son in men's clothes was repugnant to him. If, say, he could only find a *very* large boy's suit, he might cut off that long and awful beard, dye the white hair brown, and thus manage to conceal the worst, and to retain something of his own self-respect—not to mention his position in Baltimore society.

But a frantic inspection of the boys' department revealed no suits to fit the new-born Button. He blamed the store, of course—in such cases it is the thing to blame the store.

"How old did you say that boy of yours was?" demanded the clerk curiously.

"He's—sixteen."

"Oh, I beg your pardon. I thought you said six *hours*. You'll find the youths' department in the next aisle."

Mr. Button turned miserably away. Then he stopped, brightened, and pointed his finger toward a dressed dummy in the window display. "There!" he exclaimed. "I'll take that suit, out there on the dummy."

The clerk stared. "Why," he protested, "that's not a child's suit. At least it *is*, but it's for fancy dress. You could wear it yourself!"

"Wrap it up," insisted his customer nervously. "That's what I want."

The astonished clerk obeyed.

Back at the hospital Mr. Button entered the nursery and almost threw the package at his son. "Here's your clothes," he snapped out.

The old man untied the package and viewed the contents with a quizzical eye.

"They look sort of funny to me," he complained, "I don't want to be made a monkey of—"

"You've made a monkey of me!" retorted Mr. Button fiercely. "Never you mind how funny you look. Put them on—or I'll—or I'll *spank* you." He swallowed uneasily at the penultimate word, feeling nevertheless that it was the proper thing to say.

"All right, father"—this with a grotesque simulation of filial respect—"you've lived longer; you know best. Just as you say."

As before, the sound of the word "father" caused Mr. Button to start violently.

"And hurry."

"I'm hurrying, father."

When his son was dressed Mr. Button regarded him with depression. The costume consisted of dotted socks, pink pants, and a belted blouse with a wide white collar. Over the latter waved the long whitish beard, drooping almost to the waist. The effect was not good.

"Wait!"

Mr. Button seized a hospital shears and with three quick snaps amputated a large section of the beard. But even with this improvement the ensemble fell far short of perfection. The remaining brush of scraggly hair, the watery eyes, the ancient teeth, seemed oddly out of tone with the gayety of the costume. Mr. Button, however, was obdurate—he held out his hand. "Come along!" he said sternly.

His son took the hand trustingly. "What are you going to call me, dad?" he quavered as they walked from the nursery—"just 'baby' for a while? till you think of a better name?"

Mr. Button grunted. "I don't know," he answered harshly. "I think we'll call you Methuselah."

Chapter 3

Even after the new addition to the Button family had had his hair cut short and then dyed to a sparse unnatural black, had had his face shaved so close that it glistened, and had been attired in small-boy clothes made to order by a flabbergasted tailor, it was impossible for Mr. Button to ignore the fact that his son was a poor excuse for a first family baby. Despite his aged stoop, Benjamin Button—for it was by this name they called him instead of by the appropriate but invidious Methuselah—was five feet eight inches tall. His clothes did not conceal this, nor did the clipping and dyeing of his eyebrows disguise the fact that the eyes underneath were faded and watery and tired. In fact, the baby-nurse who had been engaged in advance left the house after one look, in a state of considerable indignation.

But Mr. Button persisted in his unwavering purpose. Benjamin was a baby, and a baby he should remain. At first he declared that if Benjamin didn't like warm milk he could go without food altogether, but he was finally prevailed upon to allow his son bread and butter, and even oatmeal by way of a compromise. One day he brought home a rattle and, giving it to Benjamin, insisted in no uncertain terms that he should "play with it," whereupon the old man took it with a weary expression and could be heard jingling it obediently at intervals throughout the day.

There can be no doubt, though, that the rattle bored him, and that he found other and more soothing amusements when he was left alone. For instance, Mr. Button discovered one day that during the preceding week he had smoked more cigars than ever before—a phenomenon which was explained a few days later when, entering the nursery unexpectedly, he found the room full of faint blue haze and Benjamin, with a guilty expression on his face, trying to conceal the butt of a dark Havana. This, of course, called for a severe spanking, but Mr. Button found that he could not bring himself to administer it. He merely warned his son that he would "stunt his growth."

Nevertheless he persisted in his attitude. He brought home lead soldiers, he brought toy trains, he brought large pleasant animals made of cotton, and, to perfect the illusion which he was creating—for himself at least—he passionately demanded of the clerk in the toy-store whether "the paint would come off the pink duck if the baby put it in his mouth." But, despite all his father's efforts, Benjamin refused to be interested. He would steal down the back stairs and return to the nursery with a volume of the *Encyclopædia Britannica*, over which he would pore through an afternoon, while his cotton cows and his Noah's ark were left neglected on the floor. Against such a stubbornness Mr. Button's efforts were of little avail.

The sensation created in Baltimore was, at first, prodigious. What the mishap would have cost the Buttons and their kinsfolk socially cannot be determined, for the outbreak of the Civil War drew the city's attention to other things. A few people who were unfailingly polite racked their brains for compliments to give to the parents—and finally hit upon the ingenious device of declaring that the baby resembled his grandfather, a fact which, due to the standard state of decay common to all men of seventy, could not be denied. Mr. and Mrs. Roger Button were not pleased, and Benjamin's grandfather was furiously insulted.

Benjamin, once he left the hospital, took life as he found it. Several small boys were brought to see him, and he spent a stiff-jointed afternoon trying to work up an interest in tops and marbles—he even managed, quite accidentally, to break a kitchen window with a stone from a sling shot, a feat which secretly delighted his father.

Thereafter Benjamin contrived to break something every day, but he did these things only because they were expected of him, and because he was by nature obliging.

When his grandfather's initial antagonism wore off, Benjamin and that gentleman took enormous pleasure in one another's company. They would sit for hours, these two so far apart in age and experience, and, like old cronies, discuss with tireless monotony the slow events of the day. Benjamin felt more at ease in his grandfather's presence than in his parents'—they seemed always somewhat in awe of him and, despite the dictatorial authority they exercised over him, frequently addressed him as "Mr."

He was as puzzled as any one else at the apparently advanced age of his mind and body at birth. He read up on it in the medical journal, but found that no such case had been previously recorded. At his father's urging he made an honest attempt to play with other boys, and frequently he joined in the milder games—football shook him up too much, and he feared that in case of a fracture his ancient bones would refuse to knit.

When he was five he was sent to kindergarten, where he was initiated into the art of pasting green paper on orange paper, of weaving colored maps and manufacturing eternal cardboard necklaces. He was inclined to drowse off to sleep in the middle of these tasks, a habit which both irritated and frightened his young teacher. To his relief she complained to his parents, and he was removed from the school. The Roger Buttons told their friends that they felt he was too young.

By the time he was twelve years old his parents had grown used to him. Indeed, so strong is the force of custom that they no longer felt that he was different from any other child—except when some curious anomaly reminded them of the fact. But one day a few weeks after his twelfth birthday, while looking in the mirror, Benjamin made, or thought he made, an astonishing discovery. Did his eyes deceive him, or had his hair turned in the dozen years of his life from white to iron-gray under its concealing dye? Was the network of wrinkles on his face becoming less pronounced? Was his skin healthier and firmer, with even a touch of ruddy winter color? He could not tell. He knew that he no longer stooped and that his physical condition had improved since the early days of his life.

"Can it be—?" he thought to himself, or, rather, scarcely dared to think.

He went to his father. "I am grown," he announced determinedly. "I want to put on long trousers."

His father hesitated. "Well," he said finally, "I don't know. Fourteen is the age for putting on long trousers—and you are only twelve."

"But you'll have to admit," protested Benjamin, "that I'm big for my age."

His father looked at him with illusory speculation. "Oh, I'm not so sure of that," he said. "I was as big as you when I was twelve."

This was not true—it was all part of Roger Button's silent agreement with himself to believe in his son's normality.

Finally a compromise was reached. Benjamin was to continue to dye his hair. He was to make a better attempt to play with boys of his own age. He was not to wear his spectacles or carry a cane in the street. In return for these concessions he was allowed his first suit of long trousers. . . .

Chapter 4

Of the life of Benjamin Button between his twelfth and twenty-first year I intend to say little. Suffice to record that they were years of normal ungrowth. When Benjamin was eighteen he was erect as a man of fifty; he had more hair and it was of a dark gray; his step was firm, his voice had lost its cracked quaver and descended to a healthy baritone. So his father sent him up to Connecticut to take examinations for entrance to Yale College. Benjamin passed his examination and became a member of the freshman class.

On the third day following his matriculation he received a notification from Mr. Hart, the college registrar, to call at his office and arrange his schedule. Benjamin, glancing in the mirror, decided that his hair needed a new application of its brown dye, but an anxious inspection of his bureau drawer disclosed that the dye bottle was not there. Then he remembered—he had emptied it the day before and thrown it away.

He was in a dilemma. He was due at the registrar's in five minutes. There seemed to be no help for it—he must go as he was. He did.

"Good-morning," said the registrar politely. "You've come to inquire about your son."

"Why, as a matter of fact, my name's Button—" began Benjamin, but Mr. Hart cut him off.

"I'm very glad to meet you, Mr. Button. I'm expecting your son here any minute."

"That's me!" burst out Benjamin. "I'm a freshman."

"What!"

"I'm a freshman."

"Surely you're joking."

"Not at all."

The registrar frowned and glanced at a card before him. "Why, I have Mr. Benjamin Button's age down here as eighteen."

"That's my age," asserted Benjamin, flushing slightly.

The registrar eyed him wearily. "Now surely, Mr. Button, you don't expect me to believe that."

Benjamin smiled wearily. "I am eighteen," he repeated.

The registrar pointed sternly to the door. "Get out," he said. "Get out of college and get out of town. You are a dangerous lunatic."

"I am eighteen."

Mr. Hart opened the door. "The idea!" he shouted. "A man of your age trying to enter here as a freshman. Eighteen years old, are you? Well, I'll give you eighteen minutes to get out of town."

Benjamin Button walked with dignity from the room, and half a dozen undergraduates, who were waiting in the hall, followed him curiously with their eyes. When he had gone a little way he turned around, faced the infuriated registrar, who was still standing in the doorway, and repeated in a firm voice: "I am eighteen years old."

To a chorus of titters which went up from the group of undergraduates, Benjamin walked away.

But he was not fated to escape so easily. On his melancholy walk to the railroad station he found that he was being followed by a group, then by a swarm, and finally by a dense mass of undergraduates. The word had gone around that a lunatic had passed the entrance examinations for Yale and attempted to palm himself off as a youth of eighteen. A fever of excitement permeated the college. Men ran hatless out of classes, the football team abandoned its practice and joined the mob, professors' wives with bonnets awry and bustles out of position, ran shouting after the procession, from which proceeded a continual succession of remarks aimed at the tender sensibilities of Benjamin Button.

"He must be the Wandering Jew!"

"He ought to go to prep school at his age!"

"Look at the infant prodigy!"

"He thought this was the old men's home."

"Go up to Harvard!"

Benjamin increased his gait, and soon he was running. He would show them! He *would* go to Harvard, and then they would regret these ill-considered taunts!

Safely on board the train for Baltimore, he put his head from the window. "You'll regret this!" he shouted.

"Ha-ha!" the undergraduates laughed. "Ha-ha-ha!" It was the biggest mistake that Yale College had ever made. . . .

Chapter 5

In 1880 Benjamin Button was twenty years old, and he signalized his birthday by going to work for his father in Roger Button & Co., Wholesale Hardware. It was in that same year that he began "going out socially"—that is, his father insisted on taking him to several fashionable dances. Roger Button was now fifty, and he and his son were more and more companionable—in fact, since Benjamin had ceased to dye his hair (which was still grayish) they appeared about the same age, and could have passed for brothers.

One night in August they got into the phaeton attired in their full-dress suits and drove out to a dance at the Shevlins' country house, situated just outside of Baltimore. It was a gorgeous evening. A full moon drenched the road to the lustreless color of platinum, and late-blooming harvest flowers breathed into the motionless air aromas that were like low, half-heard laughter. The open country, carpeted for rods around with bright wheat, was translucent as in the day. It was almost impossible not to be affected by the sheer beauty of the sky—almost.

"There's a great future in the dry-goods business," Roger Button was saying. He was not a spiritual man—his esthetic sense was rudimentary.

"Old fellows like me can't learn new tricks," he observed profoundly. "It's you youngsters with energy and vitality that have the great future before you."

Far up the road the lights of the Shevlins' country house drifted into view, and presently there was a sighing sound that crept persistently toward them—it might have been the fine plaint of violins or the rustle of the silver wheat under the moon.

They pulled up behind a handsome brougham whose passengers were disembarking at the door. A lady got out, then an elderly gentleman, then another young lady, beautiful as sin. Benjamin started; an almost chemical change seemed to dissolve and recompose the very elements of his body. A rigor passed over him, blood rose into his cheeks, his forehead, and there was a steady thumping in his ears. It was first love.

The girl was slender and frail, with hair that was ashen under the moon and honey-colored under the sputtering gas-lamps of the porch. Over her shoulders was thrown a Spanish mantilla of softest yellow, butterflied in black; her feet were glittering buttons at the hem of her bustled dress.

Roger Button leaned over to his son. "That," he said, "is young Hildegarde Moncrief, the daughter of General Moncrief."

Benjamin nodded coldly. "Pretty little thing," he said indifferently. But when the negro boy had led the buggy away, he added: "Dad, you might introduce me to her."

They approached a group of which Miss Moncrief was the centre. Reared in the old tradition, she courtesied low before Benjamin. Yes, he might have a dance. He thanked her and walked away—staggered away.

The interval until the time for his turn should arrive dragged itself out interminably. He stood close to the wall, silent, inscrutable, watching with murderous eyes the young bloods of Baltimore as they eddied around Hildegarde Moncrief, passionate admiration in their faces. How obnoxious they seemed to Benjamin; how intolerably rosy! Their curling brown whiskers aroused in him a feeling equivalent to indigestion.

But when his own time came, and he drifted with her out upon the changing floor to the music of the latest waltz from Paris, his jealousies and anxieties melted from him like a mantle of snow. Blind with enchantment, he felt that life was just beginning.

"You and your brother got here just as we did, didn't you?" asked Hildegarde, looking up at him with eyes that were like bright blue enamel.

Benjamin hesitated. If she took him for his father's brother, would it be best to enlighten her? He remembered his experience at Yale, so he decided against it. It would be rude to contradict a lady; it would be criminal to mar this exquisite occasion with the grotesque story of his origin. Later, perhaps. So he nodded, smiled, listened, was happy.

"I like men of your age," Hildegarde told him. "Young boys are so idiotic. They tell me how much champagne they drink at college, and how much money they lose playing cards. Men of your age know how to appreciate women."

Benjamin felt himself on the verge of a proposal—with an effort he choked back the impulse.

"You're just the romantic age," she continued—"fifty. Twenty-five is too worldly-wise; thirty is apt to be pale from overwork; forty is the age of long stories that take a whole cigar to tell; sixty is—oh, sixty is too near seventy; but fifty is the mellow age. I love fifty."

Fifty seemed to Benjamin a glorious age. He longed passionately to be fifty.

"I've always said," went on Hildegarde, "that I'd rather marry a man of fifty and be taken care of than marry a man of thirty and take care of *him*."

For Benjamin the rest of the evening was bathed in a honey-colored mist. Hildegarde gave him two more dances, and they discovered that they were marvellously in accord on all the questions of the day. She was to go driving with him on the following Sunday, and then they would discuss all these questions further.

Going home in the phaeton just before the crack of dawn, when the first bees were humming and the fading moon glimmered in the cool dew, Benjamin knew vaguely that his father was discussing wholesale hardware.

". . . . And what do you think should merit our biggest attention after hammers and nails?" the elder Button was saying.

"Love," replied Benjamin absent-mindedly.

"Lugs?" exclaimed Roger Button, "Why, I've just covered the question of lugs."

Benjamin regarded him with dazed eyes just as the eastern sky was suddenly cracked with light, and an oriole yawned piercingly in the quickening trees. . . .

Chapter 6

When, six months later, the engagement of Miss Hildegarde Moncrief to Mr. Benjamin Button was made known (I say "made known," for General Moncrief declared he would rather fall upon his sword than announce it), the excitement in Baltimore society reached a feverish pitch. The almost forgotten story of Benjamin's birth was remembered and sent out upon the winds of scandal in picaresque and incredible forms. It was said that Benjamin was really the father of Roger Button, that he was his brother who had been in prison for forty years, that he was John Wilkes Booth in disguise—and, finally, that he had two small conical horns sprouting from his head.

The Sunday supplements of the New York papers played up the case with fascinating sketches which showed the head of Benjamin Button attached to a fish, to a snake, and, finally, to a body of solid brass. He became known, journalistically, as the Mystery Man of Maryland. But the true story, as is usually the case, had a very small circulation.

However, every one agreed with General Moncrief that it was "criminal" for a lovely girl who could have married any beau in Baltimore to throw herself into the arms of a man who was assuredly fifty. In vain Mr. Roger Button published his son's birth certificate in large type in the Baltimore *Blaze*. No one believed it. You had only to look at Benjamin and see.

On the part of the two people most concerned there was no wavering. So many of the stories about her fiancé were false that Hildegarde refused stubbornly to believe even the true one. In vain General Moncrief pointed out to her the high mortality among men of fifty—or, at least, among men who looked fifty; in vain he told her of the instability of the wholesale hardware business. Hildegarde had chosen to marry for mellowness, and marry she did. . . .

Chapter 7

In one particular, at least, the friends of Hildegarde Moncrief were mistaken. The wholesale hardware business prospered amazingly. In the fifteen years between Benjamin Button's marriage in 1880 and his father's retirement in 1895, the family fortune was doubled—and this was due largely to the younger member of the firm.

Needless to say, Baltimore eventually received the couple to its bosom. Even old General Moncrief became reconciled to his son-in-law when Benjamin gave him the money to bring out his *History of the Civil War* in twenty volumes, which had been refused by nine prominent publishers.

In Benjamin himself fifteen years had wrought many changes. It seemed to him that the blood flowed with new vigor through his veins. It began to be a pleasure to rise in the morning, to walk with an active step along the busy, sunny street, to work untiringly with his shipments of hammers and his cargoes of nails. It was in 1890 that he executed his famous business coup: he brought up the suggestion that *all nails used in nailing up the boxes in which nails are shipped are the property of the shippee*, a proposal which became a statute, was approved by Chief Justice Fossile, and saved Roger Button and Company, Wholesale Hardware, more than *six hundred nails every year.*

In addition, Benjamin discovered that he was becoming more and more attracted by the gay side of life. It was typical of his growing enthusiasm for pleasure that he was the first man in the city of Baltimore to own and run an automobile. Meeting him on the street, his contemporaries would stare enviously at the picture he made of health and vitality.

"He seems to grow younger every year," they would remark. And if old Roger Button, now sixty-five years old, had failed at first to give a proper welcome to his son he atoned at last by bestowing on him what amounted to adulation.

And here we come to an unpleasant subject which it will be well to pass over as quickly as possible. There was only one thing that worried Benjamin Button; his wife had ceased to attract him.

At that time Hildegarde was a woman of thirty-five, with a son, Roscoe, fourteen years old. In the early days of their marriage Benjamin had worshipped her. But, as the years passed, her honey-colored hair became an unexciting brown, the blue enamel of her eyes assumed the aspect of cheap crockery—moreover, and, most of all, she had become too settled in her ways, too placid, too content, too anemic in her excitements, and too sober in her taste. As a bride it been she who had "dragged" Benjamin to dances and dinners—now conditions were reversed. She went out socially with him, but without enthusiasm, devoured already by that eternal inertia which comes to live with each of us one day and stays with us to the end.

Benjamin's discontent waxed stronger. At the outbreak of the Spanish-American War in 1898 his home had for him so little charm that he decided to join the army. With his business influence he obtained a commission as captain, and proved so adaptable to the work that he was made a major, and finally a lieutenant-colonel just in time to participate in the celebrated charge up San Juan Hill. He was slightly wounded, and received a medal.

Benjamin had become so attached to the activity and excitement of army life that he regretted to give it up, but his business required attention, so he resigned his commission and came home. He was met at the station by a brass band and escorted to his house.

Chapter 8

Hildegarde, waving a large silk flag, greeted him on the porch, and even as he kissed her he felt with a sinking of the heart that these three years had taken their toll. She was a woman of forty now, with a faint skirmish line of gray hairs in her head. The sight depressed him.

Up in his room he saw his reflection in the familiar mirror—he went closer and examined his own face with anxiety, comparing it after a moment with a photograph of himself in uniform taken just before the war.

"Good Lord!" he said aloud. The process was continuing. There was no doubt of it—he looked now like a man of thirty. Instead of being delighted, he was uneasy—he was growing younger. He had hitherto hoped that once he reached a bodily age equivalent to his age in years, the grotesque phenomenon which had marked his birth would cease to function. He shuddered. His destiny seemed to him awful, incredible.

When he came down-stairs Hildegarde was waiting for him. She appeared annoyed, and he wondered if she had at last discovered that there was something amiss. It was with an effort to relieve the tension between them that he broached the matter at dinner in what he considered a delicate way.

"Well," he remarked lightly, "everybody says I look younger than ever."

Hildegarde regarded him with scorn. She sniffed. "Do you think it's anything to boast about?"

"I'm not boasting," he asserted uncomfortably.

She sniffed again. "The idea," she said, and after a moment: "I should think you'd have enough pride to stop it."

"How can I?" he demanded.

"I'm not going to argue with you," she retorted. "But there's a right way of doing things and a wrong way. If you've made up your mind to be different from everybody else, I don't suppose I can stop you, but I really don't think it's very considerate."

"But, Hildegarde, I can't help it."

"You can too. You're simply stubborn. You think you don't want to be like any one else. You always have been that way, and you always will be. But just think how it would be if every one else looked at things as you do—what would the world be like?"

As this was an inane and unanswerable argument Benjamin made no reply, and from that time on a chasm began to widen between them. He wondered what possible fascination she had ever exercised over him.

To add to the breach, he found, as the new century gathered headway, that his thirst for gayety grew stronger. Never a party of any kind in the city of Baltimore but he was there, dancing with the prettiest of the young married women, chatting with the most popular of the débutantes, and finding their company charming, while his wife, a dowager of evil omen, sat among the chaperons, now in haughty disapproval, and now following him with solemn, puzzled, and reproachful eyes.

"Look!" people would remark. "What a pity! A young fellow that age tied to a woman of forty-five. He must be twenty years younger than his wife." They had forgotten—as people inevitably forget—that back in 1880 their mammas and papas had also remarked about this same ill-matched pair.

Benjamin's growing unhappiness at home was compensated for by his many new interests. He took up golf and made a great success of it. He went in for dancing: in 1906 he was an expert at "The Boston," and in 1908 he was considered proficient at the "Maxixe," while in 1909 his "Castle Walk" was the envy of every young man in town.

His social activities, of course, interfered to some extent with his business, but then he had worked hard at wholesale hardware for twenty-five years and felt that he could soon hand it on to his son, Roscoe, who had recently graduated from Harvard.

He and his son were, in fact, often mistaken for each other. This pleased Benjamin—he soon forgot the insidious fear which had come over him on his return from the Spanish-American War, and grew to take a naïve pleasure in his appearance. There was only one fly in the delicious ointment—he hated to appear in public with his wife. Hildegarde was almost fifty, and the sight of her made him feel absurd. . . .

Chapter 9

One September day in 1910—a few years after Roger Button & Co., Wholesale Hardware, had been handed over to young Roscoe Button—a man, apparently about twenty years old, entered himself as a freshman at Harvard University in Cambridge. He did not make the mistake of announcing that he would never see fifty again, nor did he mention the fact that his son had been graduated from the same institution ten years before.

He was admitted, and almost immediately attained a prominent position in the class, partly because he seemed a little older than the other freshmen, whose average age was about eighteen.

But his success was largely due to the fact that in the football game with Yale he played so brilliantly, with so much dash and with such a cold, remorseless anger that he scored seven touchdowns and fourteen field goals for Harvard, and caused one entire eleven of Yale men to be carried singly from the field, unconscious. He was the most celebrated man in college.

Strange to say, in his third or junior year he was scarcely able to "make" the team. The coaches said that he had lost weight, and it seemed to the more observant among them that he was not quite as tall as before. He made no touchdowns—indeed, he was retained on the team chiefly in hope that his enormous reputation would bring terror and disorganization to the Yale team.

In his senior year he did not make the team at all. He had grown so slight and frail that one day he was taken by some sophomores for a freshman, an incident which humiliated him terribly. He became known as something of a prodigy—a senior who was surely no more than sixteen—and he was often shocked at the worldliness of some of his classmates. His studies seemed harder to him—he felt that they were too advanced. He had heard his classmates speak of St. Midas', the famous preparatory school, at which so many of them had prepared for college, and he determined after his graduation to enter himself at St. Midas', where the sheltered life among boys his own size would be more congenial to him.

Upon his graduation in 1914 he went home to Baltimore with his Harvard diploma in his pocket. Hildegarde was now residing in Italy, so Benjamin went to live with his son, Roscoe. But though he was welcomed in a general way, there was obviously no heartiness in Roscoe's feeling toward him—there was even perceptible a tendency on his son's part to think that Benjamin, as he moped about the house in adolescent mooniness, was somewhat in the way. Roscoe was married now and prominent in Baltimore life, and he wanted no scandal to creep out in connection with his family.

Benjamin, no longer persona grata with the débutantes and younger college set, found himself left much alone, except for the companionship of three or four fifteen-year-old boys in the neighborhood. His idea of going to St. Midas' school recurred to him.

"Say," he said to Roscoe one day, "I've told you over and over that I want to go to prep school."

"Well, go, then," replied Roscoe shortly. The matter was distasteful to him, and he wished to avoid a discussion.

"I can't go alone," said Benjamin helplessly. "You'll have to enter me and take me up there."

"I haven't got time," declared Roscoe abruptly. His eyes narrowed and he looked uneasily at his father. "As a matter of fact," he added, "you'd better not go on with this business much longer. You better pull up short. You better—you better"—he paused and his face crimsoned as he sought for words—"you better turn right around and start back the other way. This has gone too far to be a joke. It isn't funny any longer. You—you behave yourself!"

Benjamin looked at him, on the verge of tears.

"And another thing," continued Roscoe, "when visitors are in the house I want you to call me 'Uncle'—not 'Roscoe,' but 'Uncle,' do you understand? It looks absurd for a boy of fifteen to call me by my first name. Perhaps you'd better call me 'Uncle' *all* the time, so you'll get used to it."

With a harsh look at his father, Roscoe turned away. . . .

Chapter 10

At the termination of this interview, Benjamin wandered dismally up-stairs and stared at himself in the mirror. He had not shaved for three months, but he could find nothing on his face but a faint white down with which it seemed unnecessary to meddle. When he had first come home from Harvard, Roscoe had approached him with the proposition that he should wear eye-glasses and imitation whiskers glued to his cheeks, and it had seemed for a moment that the farce of his early years was to be repeated. But whiskers had itched and made him ashamed. He wept and Roscoe had reluctantly relented.

Benjamin opened a book of boys' stories, "The Boy Scouts in Bimini Bay," and began to read. But he found himself thinking persistently about the war. America had joined the Allied cause during the preceding month, and Benjamin wanted to enlist, but, alas, sixteen was the minimum age, and he did not look that old. His true age, which was fifty-seven, would have disqualified him, anyway.

There was a knock at his door, and the butler appeared with a letter bearing a large official legend in the corner and addressed to

Mr. Benjamin Button. Benjamin tore it open eagerly, and read the enclosure with delight. It informed him that many reserve officers who had served in the Spanish-American War were being called back into service with a higher rank, and it enclosed his commission as brigadier-general in the United States army with orders to report immediately.

Benjamin jumped to his feet fairly quivering with enthusiasm. This was what he had wanted. He seized his cap and ten minutes later he had entered a large tailoring establishment on Charles Street, and asked in his uncertain treble to be measured for a uniform.

"Want to play soldier, sonny?" demanded a clerk, casually.

Benjamin flushed. "Say! Never mind what I want!" he retorted angrily. "My name's Button and I live on Mt. Vernon Place, so you know I'm good for it."

"Well," admitted the clerk, hesitantly, "if you're not, I guess your daddy is, all right."

Benjamin was measured, and a week later his uniform was completed. He had difficulty in obtaining the proper general's insignia because the dealer kept insisting to Benjamin that a nice Y.W.C.A. badge would look just as well and be much more fun to play with.

Saying nothing to Roscoe, he left the house one night and proceeded by train to Camp Mosby, in South Carolina, where he was to command an infantry brigade. On a sultry April day he approached the entrance to the camp, paid off the taxicab which had brought him from the station, and turned to the sentry on guard.

"Get some one to handle my luggage!" he said briskly.

The sentry eyed him reproachfully. "Say," he remarked, "where you goin' with the general's duds, sonny?"

Benjamin, veteran of the Spanish-American War, whirled upon him with fire in his eye, but with, alas, a changing treble voice.

"Come to attention!" he tried to thunder; he paused for breath—then suddenly he saw the sentry snap his heels together and bring his rifle to the present. Benjamin concealed a smile of gratification, but when he glanced around his smile faded. It was not he who had inspired obedience, but an imposing artillery colonel who was approaching on horseback.

"Colonel!" called Benjamin shrilly.

The colonel came up, drew rein, and looked coolly down at him with a twinkle in his eyes. "Whose little boy are you?" he demanded kindly.

"I'll soon darn well show you whose little boy I am!" retorted Benjamin in a ferocious voice. "Get down off that horse!"

The colonel roared with laughter.

"You want him, eh, general?"

"Here!" cried Benjamin desperately. "Read this." And he thrust his commission toward the colonel.

The colonel read it, his eyes popping from their sockets.

"Where'd you get this?" he demanded, slipping the document into his own pocket.

"I got it from the Government, as you'll soon find out!"

"You come along with me," said the colonel with a peculiar look. "We'll go up to headquarters and talk this over. Come along."

The colonel turned and began walking his horse in the direction of headquarters. There was nothing for Benjamin to do but follow with as much dignity as possible—meanwhile promising himself a stern revenge.

But this revenge did not materialize. Two days later, however, his son Roscoe materialized from Baltimore, hot and cross from a hasty trip, and escorted the weeping general, *sans* uniform, back to his home.

Chapter 11

In 1920 Roscoe Button's first child was born. During the attendant festivities, however, no one thought it "the thing" to mention that the little grubby boy, apparently about ten years of age who played around the house with lead soldiers and a miniature circus, was the new baby's own grandfather.

No one disliked the little boy whose fresh, cheerful face was crossed with just a hint of sadness, but to Roscoe Button his presence was a source of torment. In the idiom of his generation Roscoe did not consider the matter "efficient." It seemed to him that his father, in refusing to look sixty, had not behaved like a "red-blooded he-man"—this was Roscoe's favorite expression—but in a curious and perverse manner. Indeed, to think about the matter for as much as half an hour drove him to the edge of insanity. Roscoe believed that "live wires" should keep young, but carrying it out on such a scale was—was—was inefficient. And there Roscoe rested.

Five years later Roscoe's little boy had grown old enough to play childish games with little Benjamin under the supervision of the same nurse. Roscoe took them both to kindergarten on the same day, and Benjamin found that playing with little strips of colored paper, making mats and chains and curious and beautiful designs, was the most fascinating game in the world. Once he was bad and had to stand in the corner—then he cried—but for the most part there were gay hours in the cheerful room, with the sunlight coming in the windows and Miss Bailey's kind hand resting for a moment now and then in his tousled hair.

Roscoe's son moved up into the first grade after a year, but Benjamin stayed on in the kindergarten. He was very happy. Sometimes when other tots talked about what they would do when they grew up a shadow would cross his little face as if in a dim, childish way he realized that those were things in which he was never to share.

The days flowed on in monotonous content. He went back a third year to the kindergarten, but he was too little now to understand what the bright shining strips of paper were for. He cried because the other boys were bigger than he and he was afraid of them. The teacher talked to him, but though he tried to understand he could not understand at all.

He was taken from the kindergarten. His nurse, Nana, in her starched gingham dress, became the centre of his tiny world. On bright days they walked in the park; Nana would point at a great gray monster and say "elephant," and Benjamin would say it after her, and when he was being undressed for bed that night he would say it over and over aloud to her: "Elyphant, elyphant, elyphant." Sometimes Nana let him jump on the bed, which was fun, because if you sat down exactly right it would bounce you up on your feet again, and if you said "Ah" for a long time while you jumped you got a very pleasing broken vocal effect.

He loved to take a big cane from the hat-rack and go around hitting chairs and tables with it and saying: "Fight, fight, fight." When there were people there the old ladies would cluck at him, which interested him, and the young ladies would try to kiss him, which he submitted to with mild boredom. And when the long day was done at five o'clock he would go up-stairs with Nana and be fed oatmeal and nice soft mushy foods with a spoon.

There were no troublesome memories in his childish sleep; no token came to him of his brave days at college, of the glittering years when he flustered the hearts of many girls. There were only the white, safe walls of his crib and Nana and a man who came to see him sometimes, and a great big orange ball that Nana pointed at just before his twilight bed hour and called "sun." When the sun went his eyes were sleepy—there were no dreams, no dreams to haunt him.

The past—the wild charge at the head of his men up San Juan Hill; the first years of his marriage when he worked late into the summer dusk down in the busy city for young Hildegarde whom he loved; the days before that when he sat smoking far into the night in the gloomy old Button house on Monroe Street with his grandfather—all these had faded like unsubstantial dreams from his mind as though they had never been.

He did not remember. He did not remember clearly whether the milk was warm or cool at his last feeding or how the days passed—there was only his crib and Nana's familiar presence. And then he remembered nothing. When he was hungry he cried—that was all. Through the noons and nights he breathed and over him there were soft mumblings and murmurings that he scarcely heard, and faintly differentiated smells, and light and darkness.

Then it was all dark, and his white crib and the dim faces that moved above him, and the warm sweet aroma of the milk, faded out altogether from his mind.

SOURCE: F. Scott Fitzgerald. *Tales of the Jazz Age*. New York: Charles Scribner's Sons, 1922.

INDEX OF AUTHORS